The Copper Sign

Forthcoming from Katia Fox:

The Silver Falcon
The Golden Throne

The Copper Sign

Katia Fox

TRANSLATED BY LEE CHADEAYNE

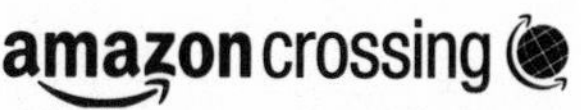

The Copper Sign by Katia Fox was first published in 2006 by Bastei Lübbe in Köln, Germany, as Das kupferne Zeichen.

Translated from the German by Lee Chadeayne.
First published in English in 2012 by AmazonCrossing.

Published by AmazonCrossing
P.O. Box 400818
Las Vegas, NV 89140

ISBN-13: 9781611090345
ISBN-10: 1611090342
Library of Congress Control Number: 2011908778

For my children

Frédéric, Lisanne, and Céline

Dear Readers,

I invite you to follow me on a trip through England and France during the Middle Ages and meet both the fictional characters of the book as well as the Norman knights who actually lived at the time: Baudoin de Béthune, Thomas de Coulonces, and Adam d'Yqueboeuf, for example, but above all Guillaume (pronounced *giyome*) le Maréshal, known in the English-speaking world as William Marshal, Earl of Pembroke. He is regarded still today as the best, the greatest knight of all times, and has captured my heart from the very first moment I met him in a history book.

With warmest wishes,
Katia Fox

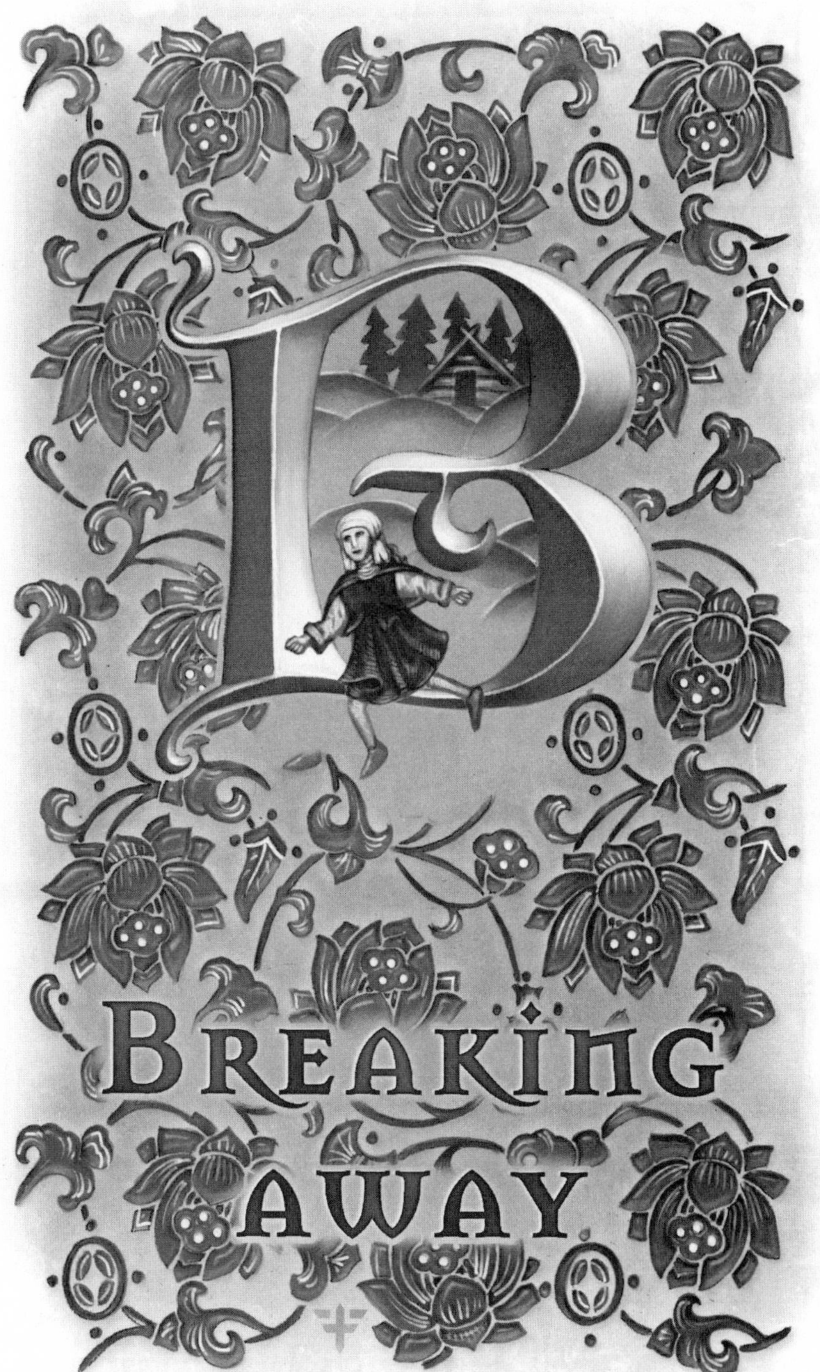
Breaking
Away

BOOK ONE

BREAKING AWAY

Orford in England, July 1161

"Good Lord, Ellenweore, if only you were a boy!" Despite his harsh words, Osmond looked at his daughter proudly, wiping the anvil with his hand in order to remove the tinder. "What an awful shame—I have a son who sneaks off as soon as I turn my back, while my little girl is a born blacksmith." He gave her a gentle pat on the shoulder. Osmond did not often speak so approvingly of her.

Ellen felt a happy sense of warmth, and blood rushed to her cheeks. "Aedith!" she said, with a quiet sigh, when her sister flung the heavy wooden door open and stood at the threshold to the workshop.

As always, Aedith refused to enter the smithy, afraid of soiling her fine clothing. Kenny, her little brother and Osmond's youngest child, kept tugging at her arm, but the more he persisted, the harder she dug her fingers into his little wrist. Suddenly she grabbed him by the ear and pulled him up. Kenny stretched as far as he could and stopped squirming.

"Mother told me to bring him out here to you," Aedith said with contempt in her voice, pushing her little brother into the smithy. She motioned with her chin toward her older sister. "And Mother wants Ellen to go and fetch water and gather wood." Aedith stood at the door, shifting impatiently from one foot to the other. "Come on, Ellen," she scolded, "hurry up! You don't think I have all day, do you?"

Osmond was clearly finding it hard to remain silent. The striker who helped him with the bigger jobs had been sick for a week, and he needed Ellen for the next step. Kenny was still too young and not of any real help yet, but Ellen knew very well that Osmond wouldn't contradict his wife. He had never done that, and he wouldn't do it this time either. With a deep sigh, she put down the tongs, slowly took off her beloved apron, and stooped over to tie it around her little brother. The leather apron reached down to his ankles, and the belt was so long that Ellen had to wrap it twice around his thin little waist.

Osmond watched her in silence. Not until she looked up at him did he nod, a bit peeved.

"Did you want to say something?" her sister sneered.

Ellen shook her head and followed Aedith to the house. Shoving the heavy iron bolt aside, she pushed the door open and entered.

"Haven't I told you a thousand times to stop pestering your father in the shop?" Leofrun scolded.

"Yes, Mother, but…"

"Don't always contradict me, you impertinent thing," her mother interrupted harshly. "You know Kenny's supposed to be helping Osmond in the smithy. You are the eldest and your job is to take care of the house, whether you like to or not. Now get to work!"

A resounding slap caught Ellen by surprise. She raised her head and turned away with a burning cheek. But not for anything in the world would she have let her mother see how much it hurt. She wouldn't allow either her mother or Aedith to savor such a triumph. Early in life she had gotten used to bearing the pain of beatings. This was exactly what she did best—defying her mother by neither crying nor giving in. But it wasn't so easy to swallow the bitter and angry feelings. Did she have to do all these boring things just because she was a girl? Any idiot could go and get water, gather wood, clean the house, do the wash—even Aedith, she thought with condescension. She knelt down at the fireplace, swept the ashes into a little pile, and when she closed her eyes, it almost smelled like being in the smithy again.

Kenny would be a smith someday, but she couldn't, although as far back as she could remember, she had spent most of her time in the smithy with Osmond. That was a place where she felt safe and secure, maybe because Leofrun never once set foot in there. As soon as she was on her own little feet, Ellen had started sorting the coal by size for Osmond to use. When she was five or six she cleaned the hearth for the first time. For the last three winters she had been allowed to use the bellows and hold the iron in the tongs while her father hammered it. And last spring, when she got to use a hammer for the first time herself, she could feel the power metal had in it.

Hammering a hot iron made a dull sound, as the metal drew strength from your arm and took shape. On a cold anvil though, the sound of metal rang clear, and the hammer sprang back all on its own. This rhythm—three or four blows on the iron, then one on the anvil—saved strength and sounded like music. Ellen took a deep breath. It just wasn't fair! But there was no point in arguing with her mother. Leofrun hated her more than anything, that was sure, and never missed a chance to let her know. Ellen picked up the two leather buckets, poured all the water left in them into the kettle beside the hearth, and quickly left. Outside, next to the house, her youngest sister Mildred was kneeling in the vegetable garden, patiently picking hungry caterpillars off the cabbage.

"Keep a few for me to put in Aedith's bed," whispered Ellen to her, grinning.

Mildred looked up, surprised, and smiled bashfully. She was the quietest and best behaved of Leofrun's children. Ellen walked listlessly down the stony path to the brook that wound its way through the meadows behind the smithy. She took off her shoes, gathered up her skirt, and waded into the cool, sparkling water where it was easier to fill the buckets. Suddenly a form emerged sputtering from the water and squirted a mouthful of water at her.

"I don't have any time, I've got to fetch water," she snapped at her friend Simon before he could say a word.

"Oh, come on, first take a swim. It's so hot today."

Ellen filled her bucket and worked her way back to shore. "Besides, I don't want to," she lied sullenly, and sat down on a rough, grey rock. In reality, she envied Simon, and except for working in the smithy, there was hardly anything she liked more than to go swimming with him. Even so, she had turned him down with one excuse after the other this year. When Simon ducked underwater again, she folded her arms across her chest. Last summer she could still go swimming without her chemise, but all that had changed within the last few months. She felt with embarrassment the little bumps that had begun to grow under her smock. They were firm and sometimes a bit tender. "It's stupid being a girl," she grumbled. Had she come to the world as a boy it would have been a lot better—that's exactly what Osmond thought, too!

Simon waded ashore. "Do you know what I'd like now more than anything?"

Ellen shook her head. "No, but since you have a bottomless pit for a stomach, I expect it has something to do with eating."

Simon grinned, nodded vigorously, and licked his lips. "Blackberries!"

"What about the water?" said Ellen, pointing at the two buckets she had filled. "And I still have to go and get wood."

"We'll do that later."

"If I'm gone too long, Mother will hit me again. I don't know if I can take that again today and not fight back."

"If we do it together we'll be finished faster, and she won't even notice we took a little time for fun." The drops of water on his shoulders sparkled in the sun. He shook himself like a dog, and the water flew off in all directions. Then he pulled on his dirty grey shirt. "The biggest, juiciest blackberries are out by the old cottage at the edge of the forest, and they taste soooo good!" He rolled his eyes in anticipation. "Come on, let's go!"

"Are you crazy?" Ellen tapped her forehead. "Old Jacoba was a witch, and goblins live in her house!" Ellen felt the hair standing up on her arms and all down her back.

"Oh, that's nonsense. Goblins live in the forest, not in cabins," Simon replied with a boastful swagger. "Besides, I was in the house, and I didn't see any goblins there, really." He tilted his head to the side and looked at Ellen out of the corner of his eye. "So tell me, since when have you been such a scaredy cat?"

"But I'm not!" Ellen replied angrily. There was no way she could let that criticism stand, so she followed Simon across the meadow that lay between the river and the forest. Most of the dry grass had been stripped bare by the sheep. The only spot the sheep hadn't chewed up yet was the dry grass on the hill on the west side of the field. The grass here was almost chest high, hiding dense patches of prickly thistles that scratched their legs and stinging nettles that raised smarting, red welts on bare skin. Ellen wanted to turn back, but then Simon would have said again that she was a coward. Arriving at the top of the hill, she looked along the forest's edge, blinking in the bright sunlight. There, behind a few birches, stood the ramshackle cottage. On the left, only a stone's throw away, a sturdy horse with a gleaming reddish-brown coat was peacefully grazing in the shadows. Ellen ducked behind the foliage.

Instinctively, Simon did the same. "What's the matter?" he whispered, surprised.

"What's that horse doing here?" she said, pointing at it. "It's Sir Miles who rides that sorrel."

Shortly after being named Lord Chancellor by King Henry II, Thomas Becket was granted an income from the County of Eye, to which Orford belonged. Sir Miles was a member of Becket's household, but he acted as if Orford belonged to him. Everyone knew how unscrupulous he was in filling his own pockets, and they feared his bad temper. The only ones who openly admired him were her mother and Aedith—they found him elegant and stately. They cackled like geese whenever Sir Miles came to the smithy, where he treated Osmond like dirt.

"Oh, him," Simon said with contempt as he stood up.

Simon won't simmer down until his belly is full, Ellen thought to herself, and followed him cautiously. She looked around, but there was nobody to be seen. All was calm and peaceful—yet the forest seemed to have eyes. The summer sun was hot. Honeybees and bumblebees took advantage of the fair weather to collect nectar, and the air was humming with their busy comings and goings. Ellen was just about to go over to Simon when out of the corner of her eye she saw a figure moving silently out from the other side of the forest, heading toward the cottage.

Her heart missed a beat. Was this place haunted by goblins after all? She squinted and looked carefully again. The figure was too large for a goblin. She breathed a deep sigh of relief. It was just a woman in a simple blue linen dress. Ellen couldn't see who she was because of the brown scarf wrapped around her head. After looking anxiously in the direction she had come from, the woman slipped into the cottage.

Now with hesitant steps, Ellen went over to Simon. She didn't know what troubled her more: the goblins that might be hiding in the underbrush and watching her, or the presence of Sir Miles and the strange woman. She kept looking over at the cabin, but nothing was stirring there.

"Mmm, don't they taste great?" Simon said, smacking his lips. "Try some." He reached out his hand to give her a blackberry. His wide grin revealed a row of dark blue teeth, and the juice from the berries was dribbling down the side of his mouth onto his chin.

"I'll be right back." Ellen could no longer restrain her curiosity and left Simon to himself.

Without paying any further attention to her, he turned around and continued to feast on the sweet berries, while she sneaked over to the cabin.

There was a crack way up high in one of the weathered boards. With trembling knees, Ellen stood on her tiptoes to look through, turning her head to the side and pressing one eye against the moldy wood. She couldn't see Sir Miles or the woman, and all she could hear was the sound of her own heart beating. Then she heard a rustling sound like a mouse scurrying through straw. And again it was silent. She wondered if anyone was actually still in the cabin. She had to stretch so much that her ankles ached. She was turning away in disappointment when suddenly she heard a loud thud. Startled, she strained once more to look through the crack in the wall. It took a moment for her eyes to grow accustomed to the dark again. Something was moving in the room and coming closer! Suddenly she saw the hairy back of Sir Miles. *He looks like a mangy dog,* Ellen thought with disgust, but she couldn't figure out why he was bare to the waist. He was standing so close now that she could smell his sweat through the crack in the boards. Her heart pounded.

"Take your clothes off," she heard him say in a rough voice.

Ellen could hardly breathe, but then she caught sight of the woman slinking toward him. Ellen moved down a little but still couldn't see her face. With slow, graceful movements, the mysterious woman removed her clothes and let her dress and linen chemise slip to the floor. Sir Miles reached out to grasp her and caress the fine, almost transparent skin of her breasts. For a brief moment, Ellen closed her eyes and everything seemed to be spinning around. When she opened them again, Sir Miles had sunk to his knees. He took the pink nipples in his mouth and sucked on them like a child until the woman's chest rose and fell again faster and faster. Suddenly he stood up and slammed her against the wall. The whole cabin was shaking. The pain in Ellen's ankles was unbearable by now and her knees were giving out, but she didn't move. She had to see what would happen next. Naturally, she knew that men and women mated. They did it just like cows, goats, and dogs in order to make babies. Ellen had overheard her mother telling Aedith that this was one of the duties the wife had to take on, whether she liked it or not. And sometimes she had watched when Osmond would lie down on her mother. It didn't take long, and a peculiar, fishy odor would spread through the room. Osmond would be panting, but Leofrun would lie under him as stiff as a board and never utter a sound.

With this mysterious woman it was different. She passed her hands longingly through the hair on Sir Miles's chest and gave it a tug here and there to tease him. Then she began to run her hands up and down his back as if she didn't want to overlook an inch of his body. Breathing faster and louder, she grabbed his buttocks with both hands and rubbed her intimate parts against his leg.

Ellen felt a dull pounding in her belly. She was seized with an odd feeling of both repugnance and bliss that terrified her, and for a moment she thought of returning to Simon. Until now she had been sure—this physical union was a torment for all women and could only be pleasurable to men. But—was she mistaken? As if under a spell she stood there looking through the crack in the wall. Sir Miles thrust his rough hand between the woman's gleaming white thighs and rubbed her until she began to make soft, groaning sounds. Then he went over to a pile of hay, lay down, and motioned to her. The woman straddled him, settling down eagerly over his stiff phallus.

Ellen started to breathe faster.

The woman moved up and down on top of him as if riding a horse. Suddenly her murmurs grew louder; she seemed to shudder with ecstasy and threw back her head. Ellen saw a torrent of blond hair the color of wheat fall over the woman's slender, bony back, and then she could see the face transfigured with desire. And now Ellen could see who she was. It shot through her like a bolt of lightning—Leofrun! A hot flash and a strange, hitherto unknown feeling of revulsion came over her, and she burst into tears.

"You whore!" she shrieked, turning away from the crack in the wall and sobbing.

Simon turned around in astonishment and ran toward her. "Have you lost your mind? What do you care who he's messing around with in there?" He didn't even seem to be surprised that Sir Miles had used the cottage as a trysting place. "Do you have any idea how dangerous that is for us?" he snapped at her and began pulling her away.

Ellen was as pale as a ghost.

"What are you making such a fuss about? Grown men and women do things like that," he said, trying to calm her down.

Ellen pounded his shoulder with her fist and pushed him away, furious. "But that woman in there is my mother!"

Simon's face turned red with shame. "Ah…I didn't know."

Suddenly, the door to the cottage swung open.

"Let's get out of here! God help us if he catches us!" Simon said, grabbing Ellen by the arm and pulling her along with him.

Sir Miles appeared half naked in front of the cabin and raised his fist. "I'll get you, just wait, you little brat," he called after them. "I'll rip your prying eyes out and cut off your saucy tongue!" Ellen was running as fast as she could.

Simon turned around a few times. "He's not following us, at least not yet," he gasped, and kept on running.

They ran without stopping all the way to the tannery. Tanners needed lots of water for their work, and for this reason Simon's family had settled on the banks of the Ore many generations ago. Simon lived there with his parents, grandmother, and four younger brothers in a little cottage of wattle and clay with a straw-thatched roof. Strong fumes from the tanning pit rose in a heavy haze that hung in the air and made their eyes sting. Completely out of breath, Ellen sat down on a tree stump far from the tanning pit and scraped her feet nervously in the dust.

"Goblins! Don't make me laugh! She just wanted us to stay away from the cottage." Ellen's eyes flashed angrily.

"Well, if I had caught my mother like that…then I would have…" Simon couldn't finish his sentence. "What a bitch!" he said with contempt, and spat on the ground.

"It was so…ugly," Ellen mumbled, staring at a line of busy ants dragging a bee along the ground. "The Lord will punish them for that, both of them," she growled defiantly.

"In any case, though, you can't go home now just as if nothing happened. If she'd whip you till you're black and blue for nothing, who's to say what she'll do with you now?" Ellen could see by his frown that Simon was worried about her.

"But what shall I do?"

The tanner's son shrugged. "Why did you have to be so nosy?" he chided her. "You should have come and eaten the berries like me." Then he threw a handful of dirt at the ants, which by now had come closer to where he was standing.

The busy little ants paid no attention to the cloud of dust and kept pulling the bee along.

"I'm not the one who wanted to go to the cottage! All you can ever think of is eating—that's why we had to go there," Ellen huffed.

"I'm scared," Simon whispered, feeling guilty.

"Me too." Ellen rubbed her temple with one finger. Worry showed in her eyes, and their color seemed to change from bright green to a mossy dark hue, though her red hair was still gleaming in the sunlight.

In the distance they could hear a jay calling. The wind was sighing through the trees, and the mighty Ore burbled along peacefully. Close by, dirty white bubbles drifted along the surface of the tanning pit, then gathered at shallower places in the stream and were quickly carried off again. The river became somewhat narrower at the tannery, though it was still wide enough to allow two merchant ships to sail past one another.

"But what shall I do now?" Ellen stooped down to pick up a flat stone and flung it far out into the river. It skipped once across the water with a splash and then sank with a dull plop. Simon was much better at that—his stones jumped across the water like grasshoppers.

"In any case, you can't stay here. Go to see the good woman, Aelfgiva; she'll surely know what to do." Simon wiped his runny nose on his shirtsleeve.

"Simon," they heard his mother calling. "Simon, come and help your father rinse out the hides." Her warm and friendly voice didn't seem to be in keeping with her gaunt appearance. Her linen dress was the color of sand—coarse and dirty—and it hung on her like a sack. Her face was pale. Ellen felt repelled by her calloused, gnarled hands and fingernails stained yellow from working in the tannic acid. Worst of all was the odor of urine and oak bark she gave off.

"Brrr, you're all wet, boy." The tanner's wife ran her hands lovingly through Simon's hair.

Ellen couldn't bear to look at his mother. She was so different from Leofrun. She loved her children and would no doubt have let herself be drawn and quartered for each of them. Nevertheless, a bath now and then wouldn't do her any harm, Ellen thought. Leofrun washed daily and put a drop of lavender oil behind each ear, just like the wives and daughters of the rich merchants of Ipswich. But inside she stank worse than the tanner's wife, Ellen thought angrily to herself. Never could she wash this sin from her soul.

"Come now, Simon, and help your father. You two can see each other again tomorrow."

Ellen stared at the ground, her eyes welling up with tears. *Who knows what tomorrow will bring*, she thought dejectedly.

"Good luck," Simon whispered, giving her a quick peck on the cheek. Then he got up and followed his mother into the house, his head hanging. He turned around just once and waved sadly.

Ellen was startled by a rustling in the underbrush and turned around, but nobody was there. Simon was right, Sir Miles and Leofrun must never find her; she had to go to Aelfgiva. If anyone knew what to do, she would. Suddenly Ellen realized she had to hurry. She ran through the forest so fast her feet barely touched the ground, and she didn't feel the sharp stones poking through her thin leather soles. She hardly even noticed those pale yellow flowers she loved so much that covered the ground around her. She couldn't expect any mercy from Leofrun. Aelfgiva just had to help her! Before long she reached the midwife's cottage in the little clearing and stopped, all out of breath.

Little dust particles danced like specks of gold in the sunlight that penetrated the thick foliage surrounding the clearing.

Aelfgiva was in her herb garden, bending down to gather up the yellow and orange calendula blossoms that she used to make salves and tinctures. Her snow-white hair, which she always wore tied in a bun, shone just like snow among the flowers. Aelfgiva placed her hand against her back and stood up slowly as Ellen came running toward her. "Ellenweore!" she cried out, delighted. Her face wrinkled up when she laughed, and her kindly, wise eyes glistened.

Ellen stopped in front of her, choking back tears.

"Come, come now, child, what's wrong? You look like you have seen a ghost." Aelfgiva spread her arms out and embraced the crying girl compassionately. "Let's go inside. I have some cabbage soup left over that I can warm up while you sit yourself down and tell me all about it." Aelfgiva picked up her basket and led Ellen by the hand back to the cottage.

"She rolled around in the straw with Sir Miles, that disgusting show-off!" Ellen said, her voice full of hatred and despair. "I saw it myself." As she told all that had happened, she grimaced with disgust, sobbing at first and then becoming more and more indignant.

After she had finished, Aelfgiva arose, walked to the hearth, and stirred the ashes nervously. Then she sat down again, fumbled around at her décolletage, and pinched herself in the folds of her neck. "Your mother must have been about as old as you are now. Oh Lord, forgive me, I know I have promised never to tell anyone." Aelfgiva turned her eyes up and crossed herself.

Ellen looked at her, wondering.

"She was promised to a very well-to-do soap merchant, but then she met a young Norman and fell in love with him." Aelfgiva took a deep breath, as if it were difficult to go on. "Your poor mother knew nothing about the consequences of love, and soon she was carrying a child. Your grandfather was furious when he found out. The young Norman was of noble birth, which made a marriage impossible, but her betrothal to the soap merchant had to be broken off as well. That man was so angry, he even threatened to have Leofrun thrown into the stocks if she didn't leave town at once."

Aelfgiva took Ellen by both hands and looked at her intently. "A harsh fate awaits a woman who has a child out of wedlock. They shear her hair and whip her. Some do not survive the pain and disgrace and die in the pillory. But even those who survive can no longer lead an honorable life. Many a poor lass like that later commits the gravest of all sins and puts an end to her own wretched existence. Your grandfather had to save his reputation and the life of his only child. So he forced her into marriage against her will, sending her away from Ipswich before anyone noticed the scandal."

Aelfgiva's worried face turned soft as she continued. "Osmond fell in love with your beautiful mother at once. She was lucky then that he took her—otherwise she might have been dead by now.

"She had to pay dearly for her innocence of mind, having to marry a simple craftsman rather than a rich merchant with whom she could enjoy a life of ease. She hates the dirt and poverty of the life she was forced to lead, and that's why she's so full of anger," the old woman tried to explain.

"And what became of the child?" Ellen asked curiously.

Aelfgiva stroked her curly locks. "Ah, my dear, that's you. Why do you think she treats you that way? To her, you alone are the reason for her misfortune."

Ellen stared at Aelfgiva in astonishment. "But then I am not his…and Osmond is not my…" she stammered, and hardly dared to think where this was all leading. No, that just couldn't be true!

"Osmond is my father, he raised me, and everything I know and love about being a blacksmith I learned from him." Ellen stamped the ground with her foot.

"Even if he isn't your father, you were his one and all from the very first moment." Aelfgiva looked at Ellen wistfully. "Your head was so tiny in his big, strong hand." The memory made her smile. Then she sat up straight. "In any case, you can't go back home. Sir Miles has no doubt already sent his men out to get you. You must leave here as quickly as possible."

"But I don't want to go!"

Aelfgiva took her in her arms and rocked her like a little child. “Alas, I will lose you as well,” she murmured, shaking her head. Then she got up and went straight to two large trunks standing one on top of the other in the farthest corner of the room. She started to rummage about in the top one. But she finally found what she was looking for in the one underneath. “Ah, here it is!” Aelfgiva held up a carefully tied bundle and put it on the table. There she loosened the knots and unfolded it. The linen shirt and loose trousers inside were slightly yellow. The tunic of dark-brown wool and the pair of earth-colored hose looked almost new. “He hardly wore these things. I had just finished making them for him when he…” Aelfgiva stopped suddenly.

“Are those Adam’s?”

Aelfgiva nodded. “I knew they would come in handy someday. He was just thirteen at the time.” Aelfgiva turned around quickly.

Ellen suspected she was trying to hide her tears. The year before Ellen was born, many people in Orford had suffered from high fever and diarrhea, and some had died. Almost every family suffered some loss, and even Aelfgiva with all her knowledge of healing herbs had lost her husband and her only child. “Do you know what? I have an idea.” Aelfgiva brought out a pair of scissors. “Haven’t you always said boys have it better?”

Ellen nodded hesitantly.

“So there—you’ll be one now!”

The thought had something appealing about it, but…Ellen looked at the old woman in disbelief. “How can I possibly do that?”

“Well, of course we can’t make a real boy out of you, but if we shorten your hair and dress you in Adam’s clothes, everyone will think you are one.”

That sounded plausible.

Aelfgiva cut off Ellen's long ponytail and cut her hair back almost as far as her ears. "And as far as color goes..." She thought about it for a moment and then brought out a sharp-smelling dark liquid. She had made it from walnut shells and used it for dyeing cloth. The tincture also turned her hair dark brown, but it stung Ellen's scalp and left spots on her smock that looked like blood.

"Change your clothes now," Aelfgiva urged. "Something tells me you don't have much time to waste."

Ellen felt strange putting on Adam's clothing. It seemed as if she were crawling inside someone else's skin. The things were all a little too big, but that had the advantage that they would still fit her for a long time.

Aelfgiva picked up Ellen's smock and smiled. "I think I've just had a good idea. Tonight I'll put your clothes down by the swamp. I'll rip them up and sprinkle blood on them from a bird or a little marten. Let's see what I can catch. When Sir Miles's men find the clothing, they'll think you were eaten by swamp spirits and they'll stop looking for you."

Ellen shuddered and turned pale at the thought of all the stories she had heard about those monsters.

Aelfgiva patted her cheeks to reassure her. "Don't be afraid, everything will work out." The old woman looked her over. Then she went over to the hearth, took some ashes from one side, and rubbed them on Ellen's forehead and cheeks. "Now it's much better. I'll put a little bit more dirt from outside in your hair, and I'll bet no one will recognize you. But don't let anyone see you around the smithy." She took Ellen by the shoulders, turned her around, and nodded with satisfaction.

"Do you really think he will send someone to get me?"

"The lord chancellor is a man of the church and would certainly never allow any of his men to chase after married women. Sir Miles will do everything he can to see that his master never hears of it." Aelfgiva looked up and underscored her explanation with a sharp movement of her thumb, running her nail over her throat. "In any case, you must make sure that nobody recognizes you, do you hear?" Aelfgiva put together a few useful things and tied them up in her best piece of cloth. Then pressing the bundle into Ellen's hand and pushing her toward the door, she added, "And now, it's best you go. You are not safe here with me."

—

Ellen ran through the forest toward the main road, as Aelfgiva had told her to do, and was soon farther away from Orford than she had ever been before. The sun began to set, bathing the forest in a soft, orange glow. Ellen relieved herself behind a large bush and washed her hands, face, and neck in a little brook, taking care only to scoop up clear water. Dark water in the shadows, Aelfgiva had warned her, could be possessed by demons and be very dangerous. She opened the bundle the old woman had given her. Aelfgiva had really thought of everything—there was a piece of goat cheese she had made herself, a little bacon, three onions, an apple, and half a loaf of bread, all tied together in the woolen cloth. Ellen closed her eyes and stuck her nose in the soft material. It smelled of smoke and herbs, like Aelfgiva herself. Ellen swallowed hard. When would she see Aelfgiva again?

Lost in thought, she slowly ate her precious supper. If she was very frugal she would have enough food for two days. After that, everything was in God's hands. Until now, though, He hadn't once answered her prayers, and His saints hadn't shown themselves to be too reliable either. When Leofrun and Aedith had gone to her grandfather's house in Ipswich last year, she had prayed to Saint Christopher, the patron saint of travelers, imploring him to put better people under his protective wing than these two. But it had done no good, and they came back unscathed. Was God watching over her also? Ellen knelt down and prayed, but it brought her no comfort. She was facing her first night alone in the forest and would have to find some sort of shelter.

When the sun set, the butterflies and bees disappeared as well. Only the gnats remained, and even grew in numbers and persistence. As it got darker, the trees seemed to grow larger, looking somber and strange. The sky filled with dark clouds. Ellen looked around anxiously for a place to hide and finally discovered a protruding ledge nearby where she could take safe shelter. Thieves and outlaws as well as goblins and elves prowled the forests at night and robbed or killed travelers in their sleep. One also had to contend with bears and wild boar.

Ellen felt small and helpless. With tears in her eyes, she rolled up under the ledge, placed her bundle under her head, and listened. Every noise she heard in the dark forest terrified her. The air was heavy and oppressive, with a thunderstorm brewing. A bright bolt of lightning flashed through the dark night, and for a brief moment everything looked as bright as day. Then came a loud roll of thunder. It started to rain and became a bit cooler. The forest floor began to smell of herbs and wet earth. Ellen pressed against the comforting rock wall, closed her eyes, and listened to the sound of the rain until she fell asleep.

In the middle of the night she suddenly heard voices and opened her eyes. It was pitch black. First she only heard a soft whisper; then it sounded like laughter. Lying there motionless, Ellen hardly dared to breathe.

"She's worthless. Kill her. All my misfortune is her fault," a voice whispered. It sounded like Leofrun.

"Besides that, she's so ugly and stupid," said a second voice.

Ellen was numb with fear.

"We'll cut her into pieces and feed her to the wild boars. Nobody will miss her."

"Pull her out of there!" said the first voice.

Ellen lashed out in all directions; her hand banged against the rock and the pain woke her up. All around it was dark and quiet. The only thing she could hear was the call of an owl. "Is anyone there?" she called out in a trembling voice. "Mother? Aedith?" There was no answer, and it took a while before Ellen calmed down enough to realize it was only a bad dream.

—

As she was walking along the next morning, she met a group of friendly looking people. Their leader, a strong man with a tangled blond beard, was accompanied by two young men, his wife, and three children. Ellen asked politely if she could join them part of the way, and the heavy woman nodded she could. Despite the cool morning, beads of perspiration had already appeared on her round face.

It was only after they had walked several miles together and there had been a number of clear hints that Ellen finally understood. The woman was expecting a child. Ellen blushed with embarrassment that she had been so slow at realizing it.

The men shook with laughter.

"Don't be embarrassed, young fellow. It's just that you haven't had any experience with women," said the husband, grinning and with a wink of his eye. "That will come by and by, and when she's as round as *that* it's far too late to be careful." He patted Ellen on the shoulder and laughed loudly.

He'd said "young fellow"! Ellen had completely forgotten that she was disguised as a boy.

The men were carpenters on the way to Framlingham, where the local lord was building a new stone castle.

"Do you think they could use him as a helper in the smithy?" asked one of the carpenters.

"Sure, why not? Do you know anything about it?" The carpenter looked at Ellen curiously.

"My father…ah, yes, I've worked in a smithy before."

"What's your name, anyway?" the carpenter asked.

"Ellen," she replied without thinking, and at the next moment was shocked at what she had said. She had forgotten again that she was a boy now. She stood there as if rooted to the spot and thought she would sink into the ground. She hadn't even begun to think about a suitable name!

The carpenter's wife was walking directly behind her and bumped into her. "Hey, boy, watch out. You can't just stop like that," she scolded her angrily.

The carpenter turned around, walked over to Ellen, and stretched out his hand. "Glad to know you, Alan. These are my younger brothers, Oswin and Albert. I'm Curt, and the tubby bird who just scolded you is my dear wife Bertha." He burst out laughing.

Bertha mumbled some unintelligible oath but then managed to smile.

Ellen felt a weight fall from her shoulders. The carpenter thought she had said "Alan"!

“What do you think, Bertha my dear, shall we take the lad with us?”

Bertha looked Ellen up and down carefully. “I don’t know, maybe he’s a criminal, a robber, or even a killer.”

Her eyes wide with fear, Ellen shook her head vehemently.

“Leave him be, Bertha darling. This boy wouldn’t hurt a fly, believe me, I can see that. If you wish, you can come to Framlingham with us, Alan. I’ll ask the master builder for work for ourselves, and maybe there will be something for you to do as well.

“Thank you, Master Curt,” Ellen answered politely. “And you also, mistress,” she said, nodding to Bertha in hope of appeasing the woman. With a silent prayer, Ellen thanked God that she wouldn’t have to spend another night alone.

—

Framlingham was teeming with people. Stonemasons, scaffolders, and apprentices scurried about, while women, children, poultry, and pigs all ran around amid the wagons and building sites. Ellen was astonished at the deafening noise made by the hewing of the stones and all the other work.

While Curt went to see the master builder, the others sat down in a meadow and rested a while.

“They said they’d be glad to have good carpenters like us,” Curt called to them as he came back. “My brothers get four pennies a day, I’ll get six, and there’s a hot meal at noon. By the way, the master builder is a friend of Albert of Colchester, and when he heard we had worked for him he showed me a stable on the east side of the building site where we can set up house. It’s just like everywhere else, work from sunrise to sunset, and that every day except for Sundays and holidays. If the master builder is happy with us, we'll have work for at least three years, and maybe longer."

Bertha was elated. "Three years? You are the best man any woman could ask for. Come here and let me kiss you!" Beaming with delight, she ran her hand over her round belly.

"Well then, let's have a kiss," Curt laughed, pulling his wife over and giving her a long kiss on the lips.

Ellen thought of what she had seen in the cottage, and blushed.

Curt's brothers noticed her embarrassment and nudged one another with their elbows, grinning.

"Oh yes, Alan," said Curt, rubbing his hand over his blond beard as if trying to wipe away Bertha's kiss. "I also spoke with the smith, and you can go to him right away. He wants to see if he can use you."

"Oh, thank you, Curt!" Ellen was happy she could stop sitting around doing nothing. She jumped up and dashed off.

"You'll find him by the castle wall, just beyond the archway on the right," he called after her.

Ellen's heart sank when she saw the smith, a grumpy-looking man with hands the size of barrelheads. She was sure he'd laugh at the sight of her skinny frame and almost wanted to turn around and run away. But he had caught sight of her already and motioned for her to come over.

"You're the boy that the carpenter told me about, are you?" His dirty blond hair stuck out from his head, and as he scratched his chin Ellen noticed that the tip of his left middle finger was missing.

"Have you ever worked in a smithy?"

"Yes, master." She didn't dare to be more precise.

"Did you work as a striker?"

"No, master, I only held the piece. I'm not yet strong enough to swing the sledgehammer." Ellen was sure she had ruined any chance for work, being so honest. But the smith just nodded.

He took an iron bar and put it in the hearth. "I can see all right that you're not very strong, but a little practice will change that. You still have some growing to do. How old are you?"

"Twelve, I think," Ellen answered meekly.

"That's a good age for learning," the smith said. "Let's see what you can do. When the iron is hot enough, take it out and pound it into a square." He pointed toward the hearth. "My name's Llewyn, by the way; they also call me the Irishman." Sweat was dripping down his cheeks, and he wiped his brow on his sleeve.

"My name's Alan." After a moment of silence, she added, "I thought the Irish were all redheads like me."

Llewyn broke out into a wide grin, and Ellen thought he actually seemed very nice when he didn't have such a grumpy look on his face.

"I'm not used to working in the daylight," Ellen mumbled apologetically when she saw the sparks coming from the hearth, indicating that the iron was too hot. She put the rod down on the anvil. It used to drive Osmond crazy when her point was bent to one side or the other, and so she had practiced that until she was good at it. To forge a good square point you had to roll the bar a quarter turn in one direction between strokes, then exactly a quarter turn back again. It was most important to work evenly. When the iron had cooled, she put it back in the forge.

"I can see you've done that before," the smith said with satisfaction. "I expect hard work from you—there's more to it than just polishing the tools and pumping the bellows, but you'll learn. For that I can pay you one and a half pennies a day, but you'll have to find your own sleeping quarters."

Ellen was delighted, and accepted at once. Later, she spoke with Bertha and arranged for supper and a place to sleep in return for half a penny a day and some help in the household. How easy it was to work things out as a boy! Wistfully, Ellen thought of Osmond and how proud he would have been of her.

—

During the first few weeks, Ellen had the worst muscle pains in her life. Sometimes her shoulders hurt so much she could barely lift the hammer. She tried hard not to let it show and bravely stuck it out. Llewyn seemed to look at her as a weak young lad who only needed to work hard enough to become strong, so he did not make it easy for her. In the first few months, Ellen's hands were covered with blisters that constantly broke open and bled from rubbing on the wooden handle. Sometimes it hurt so much that her eyes filled with tears, but Llewyn pretended not to notice. At night she staggered out of the smithy dead tired, with a feeling of discouragement and despair and a constant fear that she wouldn't make it through the next day.

Often she was so exhausted that she couldn't eat a bite. She just crawled onto her straw sack, crying, and sank into a deep, dreamless sleep.

When October arrived, sweeping the bright leaves from the trees with its strong winds, Bertha gave birth to a son. Ellen found him much too skinny and ugly.

Bertha and Curt, though, were happy to have a second boy. "Sons are the wealth of the plain folk," Curt liked to say. Ellen agreed, and envied the child for his safe birth. She herself was and remained a girl. Her voice would never get deeper and her face would never sprout a beard, so she took special care not to arouse suspicion through girlish behavior. She took advantage of every moment she spent with the carpenters, studying and trying to emulate the men's gestures and expressions. And until one Sunday in November, when her game was almost discovered, she quite enjoyed it.

Thomas, the son of the master builder, and his friends had picked up a few big brown spiders in the autumn leaves that they let run down their arms and even over their faces to show how brave they were. They enjoyed watching the girls—how they kept looking at them, fascinated by their courage, but then turned away shrieking because they were so repelled by the hairy creatures.

"Here's one for you," Thomas said patronizingly, placing one of the eight-legged monsters in Ellen's hand.

Disgusted, she threw the spider down, but the boys started laughing and making fun of her, and she quickly realized she had to come up with something. She puckered her nose, snorted, and spat at the spider. She had practiced doing that for a long time and was good enough at it to make a direct hit. "Got him!" Beaming, she thrust her right fist into the air and was duly admired for her good aim. "Damn thing," she added scornfully, because curses were part of the way men were supposed to act. After just managing to escape detection, she was now especially careful to behave like a boy: She swore a lot, ate with her mouth open, and belched especially loudly when drinking beer. She ran around with her legs far apart and tried to walk like a man. Only when the boys had peeing contests did she back off, though she really would have loved to take part in that. Why hadn't the Lord let her come into the world as a boy?

—

A wet, stormy autumn was followed by an icy, early winter that brought an end to most of the building work. The smiths, however, continued to work outdoors because costs already had gone far beyond early estimates and the stone workshops that had been promised were not finished. The smiths had sheltered the sides of their workshops with wooden planks in order not to freeze, but the wind still came through the open front. Ellen had to water down the walls every day so that sparks would not set fire to the wood. The water froze into beautiful floral patterns but made her hands red and rough. She trembled with cold as she worked, and even Llewyn, who seemed less bothered by the weather than she was, kept stamping his feet. The forge provided warmth only to the body and face of the person standing right in front of it, but their feet were still cold and soon became so numb they could scarcely feel their toes. If they didn't keep moving, their toes could freeze. Only when the cold became too great did they stop, put out the fire, and go back to the Red Buck, the only tavern in Framlingham that served decent beer and good food at reasonable prices. Sometimes they sat there together all afternoon without saying a word, and Ellen kept thinking of home. She missed Osmond, Mildred, and Kenny, and of course Simon and Aelfgiva more and more every day. She even stopped being so angry at Leofrun and almost felt a longing for Aedith. There wouldn't have been much point in talking with Llewyn about her homesickness. He had neither a wife nor children and in any case wasn't a man of many words. He only spoke to her when they were working, and in her opinion he had too much to say then with his constant, repetitive explanations of every step that nearly drove her to distraction. Ellen needed only to watch how to do something once in order to remember it and do it herself in the future, no matter how many steps were involved or how complicated each step was. There was a reason for everything, and she picked it up easily. What she needed were not explanations but practice and personal experience!

When the first May flowers emerged in the springtime and started reaching toward the sun, everyone bustled about in the warm, pleasant days, but Ellen suddenly realized she was a half-shilling short in her clay money jar. She was very careful in saving her money and was pleased to see the growing number of coins. But now her heart pounded. Maybe she had counted wrong? She counted again, with the same result—seven and a half pennies were missing. The only possibility she could think of was that the money had been stolen by someone in the carpenter's family. Bertha was careful that someone was always in the stable to guard against theft. Tearfully and with great disappointment, Ellen placed the remaining coins back in the pot and hid it under her bed's straw mattress.

A few days passed without anything happening, and Ellen was almost ready to forget the matter when she saw someone poking around her bed. It was Curt's oldest daughter Jane.

Ellen lunged at her. "You miserable thief!"

The girl began to scream like a stuck pig, and Bertha, who was cleaning vegetables outside the door, came rushing in.

"It was Alan who took your coins, that's what I thought right away," Jane shouted, holding Ellen's clay pot in her hand. "Just look and see how many coins he has. Do you think he saved that many?" Jane's voice almost broke. "You took him in like a son and he thanks you by stealing from you!" Jane looked at Ellen with tear-filled eyes and took a number of pennies from the pot. She scampered down the ladder to the room below and reached out her hand to her mother. "Here, Mother, your money!"

"You'll pay for that, lad!" Bertha said threateningly, tucking the money under her apron. "Curt will decide this evening what to do about you. If it were up to me, we'd take you to court. The word is that Lord Bigod has something against thieves and sees to it that they are punished harshly." Bertha turned away, seething with rage, and went back to work. Jane grinned at Ellen triumphantly and followed her mother out of the room.

Ellen stood there, stunned. Jane must have stolen not just from her, but even from her own parents! "What a bitch!" she exclaimed, angrily kicking at a bale of hay; then she broke out in a sweat and tears ran down her cheeks. If they threw her into prison it would only be a matter of time before they discovered she was not a boy—and she didn't even dare to think what would happen to her then. She had made up her mind what to do, and ran as fast as she could to the blacksmith shop.

Finding herself face to face with Llewyn she announced breathlessly, "I'm leaving Framlingham."

The blacksmith was visibly disappointed but replied, "I understand your desire to move on—there is really not much more you have to learn from me, anyway."

Ellen looked at him in dismay. She hadn't meant to hurt him. "It is not about you or my work here, but…" Ellen hesitated, then looked down at her feet.

"That's all right," Llewyn replied without looking at her. "You needn't explain anything, you're a free man. Do you know where you want to go?"

"Ipswich, I think." Actually, she had no idea where she wanted to go, but she didn't want to admit that.

"Ipswich." Llewyn nodded approvingly. "That's good. What do you want to do there?"

"Work as a blacksmith, what else? I don't know anything else."

"It's what you do best. I know only one man who has such an unfailing sense about iron as you do. You could still learn a lot from him. When you get to Ipswich, ask for Master Donovan. He is the best swordsmith in East Anglia. With him, you'll be a complete beginner once again!" Llewyn stood motionless for a moment, thinking. "He was a friend of my father. Tell him I send you to him with my highest recommendation." Then he added softly, "I was not good enough, but you are." And speaking more loudly, "Don't be put off by him, do you hear? Donovan is a cranky old fellow, but you must do everything you can to get him to take you. Promise me!"

"Yes, master," Ellen replied in a husky voice.

As they parted, Llewyn gave her his hammer, adding, "My master gave it to me. Cherish it." Then he cleared his throat and gave her an encouraging pat on the shoulder. "Good luck, lad."

"Thank you, Llewyn," Ellen whispered in a choked voice, unable to say anything more. She sneaked back to the stable, fetched her money, and left Framlingham like a thief.

Ipswich, Early May 1162

Ellen entered Ipswich through the north gate. For a moment she hesitated, unsure where to turn. The warm spring sunshine of the last few days was fading and giving way to thick rain clouds. A few drops fell on the tip of her nose, and anxiously she looked up at the sky. Only a small patch of blue was still showing, and no doubt she would be standing in the rain soon. In contrast to her, most travelers coming through the north gate as she had seemed to know exactly where to go, hurrying forward without looking around. Ellen wandered slowly toward the south. Nobody was waiting for her, so she had all the time in the world to explore the town. She stopped at the first crossing and looked about. Farther south she could see ships' masts, so this had to be where the harbor was. To her left and to her right were winding streets lined with many houses close together. Ellen rubbed her temples, looking both ways, but couldn't decide which way to go, so she sat down on a stone wall, her legs dangling, and took a final gulp of water from her flask. *I've got to refill it*, she was thinking, when she heard an excited cackling of young girls behind her. Curious, she turned around.

The girls were standing nearby, talking and giggling with such excitement that everyone passing by turned to look. A buxom maid ran her hand through her dark hair, laughing loudly and apparently seeking attention. Ellen could see how much she enjoyed the obvious admiration of the men and the envy of her friends, who were now laughing even more loudly and shrilly so someone would pay attention to them as well.

"Come on, what are you waiting for?" a skinny girl with red hands asked impatiently, grabbing one of her friends by the arm and pulling her in the direction of the market square. "Let's stop dallying and get going!"

"You can hardly wait to get to the fair, can you," sneered the dark-haired girl, winking at one of the other girls. "She's got her eye on the tooth puller," she explained, nudging the girl next to her.

The skinny girl blushed and looked down at the ground in embarrassment.

It was market day in Ipswich, and Ellen's heart leaped for joy. Aedith had told her all about it once and was almost breathless with excitement about everything there was to see there. A fair was really something special. Only big, important cities could afford them since they could be held only with the permission of the king, who demanded a heavy tribute for granting this privilege. Many merchants came from distant places in order to sell their spices, costly fabrics, and remarkable gadgets. Fairs were announced far in advance and attracted preachers, jugglers, clowns, and musicians, all of whom made a living entertaining people.

As the girls headed off, giggling, Ellen slid down from the wall excitedly and followed them. The farther they went, the more crowded the streets became, and Ellen noticed people streaming in from all directions seemingly headed to the same place. The streets got narrower, and the houses stood closer together. In the meanwhile, the clouds had swallowed up the last bit of blue, and the grey clouds seemed to merge with the grey roofs of the townhouses. Though it was just after noon, it looked as if was already beginning to get dark. Ellen hadn't gotten very far before the rain started to fall in big drops, turning the dusty street in a few moments into a muddy quagmire. Everyone, including Ellen, crowded in close to the houses trying to stay out of the rain. But as fast as the rain had come, it now quickly passed. The earth rapidly absorbed the water, and after a short time the only reminders of the brief cloudburst were a few puddles here and there. A few rays of sunlight even fell on the narrow lane, and the pigs that had run off during the rain appeared again, pushing their way through the crowd and rooting in the mud for something to eat. Ellen's shoes were still dry for the most part, and to make sure they stayed that way she took care not to let herself be pushed into the puddles as the crowd pressed forward.

On the steps of the church in Cornhill, where the different markets were located, Ellen caught sight of a beggar. His clothes looked as if they had seen better days even though they were now soiled and torn. He sat there, slumped down and motionless and with a gaping wound full of maggots in his right leg that must have been very painful. He kept his face covered, perhaps out of shame over his wretched condition, and Ellen wondered what he might have done for God to punish him so severely. Quite unmoved by this sight and no doubt accustomed to scenes of poverty and filth, a few children played with sticks and stones in the mud just a few feet away. Three older girls, presumably their older sisters who were supposed to be keeping an eye on them, stood whispering in a corner. They were so involved in their conversation that they did not even notice the rat that was boldly running up to bite one of the children. Two boys about ten years of age began fighting and pushing one another. Ellen was surprised they looked so much alike. She had heard about identical twins but had never seen them. She stopped for a moment and watched, wondering what it would be like to have a twin sister. The thought was somewhat consoling, although twins clearly did not always agree on everything—the two boys were arguing more loudly now and finally came to blows.

Ellen was carried along by the crowd toward the marketplace and lost sight of the children. The closer she got, the more crowded the streets became, and she had difficulty moving forward. On the other side of the street just slightly ahead of her Ellen was watching as a man sneaked up to a well-dressed traveler and surreptitiously cut a money purse from his belt. Ellen gasped for air. Before the victim realized what had happened, the thief made off, running straight toward her. As he pushed past, she could see he was no man but a boy hardly older than herself and just a bit taller. His straggly, dirty hair was clinging to his pimply forehead, and his cold gaze looked her over from head to foot. A shudder ran through her—she was outraged at what he had done, but at the same time was afraid he could make off with her own purse as well as he ran past. She quickly put her hand on her chest, but there was nothing to worry about: the purse was hanging right there where it belonged under her shirt. She turned around, but the boy had disappeared.

"Freshly baked fish pasties!" a girl was shouting. She had large eyes with dark circles under them, and her voice carried astonishingly far over the crowd considering her delicate, almost scrawny body clothed in a worn, dark grey linen dress. Ellen could smell the aroma of dill and clove seasoning used in the pasties and made her way through the crowd to where the girl stood.

"How much?" she asked, pointing to one of the delicious-looking little pasties in the basked the girl was carrying in her arm.

"Three farthings."

A farthing was a quarter pence, and three farthings for such a pasty was a steep price. Nevertheless, Ellen decided to buy one of the splendidly fragrant pasties, as she had not eaten and was as hungry as a bear. She could hardly introduce herself to a smith with a growling stomach. Reaching under her shirt, she took the coins from her purse. The girl looked down bashfully as Ellen approached her, then looked up, smiled, and blushed, revealing two cute little dimples in her cheeks. She chose a very large, golden pasty out of her basket and handed it to Ellen with a smile.

"It really looks good," said Ellen, thanking her politely.

The girl blushed again deeply.

Ellen chuckled to herself, seeing that she was clearly perceived as an attractive young lad. "Mm." She rolled her eyes to show how much she enjoyed the pasty. "It tastes wonderful." She licked her lips, and the girl gave her a warm smile.

"I buy the fish the first thing in the morning and bake them fresh every day," she said, beaming at Ellen.

"Do you perhaps know where I can find Donovan, the blacksmith?" Ellen asked, still chewing on her pasty.

The girl shook her head regretfully.

Ellen shrugged. "It doesn't matter, I'll find him." Just as she was turning away she noticed a small band of armed men coming toward the fish-cake vendor.

"Hey, girly, what are you asking for the basket of pastries?" one of them shouted loudly.

The girl cringed and hardly dared to look toward her questioner.

An enormous older knight with a deep scar on his left cheek approached her. He was wearing a stitched doublet that looked almost new, and spurs on his boots that jingled at his every step. From his accent, Ellen thought he must be a Norman. His companions stood a distance away and waited for him, eyeing the streetwalkers standing on the next corner and beckoning to them.

The pastry vendor looked pleadingly at Ellen and then into her basket.

It seemed she was trying to count how many pastries were left and figure out what the knight would owe her. It took a long time, and Ellen was afraid the Norman might be getting impatient. "Hurry up," she said hissing through her teeth, nudging the girl with her elbow. Didn't she know how quickly such a knight could become dangerous when he got angry?

The knight noticed the vendor's dilemma and handed her a shiny silver coin. "I think this should be more than you need."

Ellen squinted and looked at the coin as the knight reached out his hand. There was a head stamped on it, and though Ellen didn't know its value, she nudged the vendor again and said, "Give him the basket, let's go!"

A broad grin passed over the knight's face, and he added with some amusement and feigned sorrow: "This is the first time I've paid a pretty lass who has given me a cold shoulder! So please be so good as to relieve my distress." Then he laughed loudly.

As fast as if the handle of her basket had caught fire in her hands, she reached out to him. "I hope you enjoy them, my lord," she said with a trembling voice.

"I hope so, too, and if they're not fresh and good, I'll get my money back and rip off your head." He suddenly had a fearsome look in his eyes as he gazed at her. He was no longer laughing.

The girl looked up anxiously, and Ellen saw the fear in her eyes.

"I just had one myself. They're still warm, fresh, and nicely seasoned, I'll assure you, my lord," Ellen said, amazed at herself and how outspoken she was.

"Now, young man, then I hope your tongue is not only insolent but discriminating."

The knight raised his eyebrows derisively, then burst out laughing and gave Ellen a friendly but forceful slap on the back that nearly took her breath away for a moment. Still laughing loudly and shaking his head, he returned to his companions, handed them the basket, and said something to them in a foreign tongue. The men looked at him and roared with laughter.

When they finally left, Ellen breathed a sigh of relief.

The little fish-cake vendor looked stunned. "I'll have to buy myself a new basket," she stammered. "Otherwise, how can I sell my pasties tomorrow?" She didn't look happy at all, as one would expect after such a good sale. "A basket like that is not cheap. I hope I have enough money left to buy one. If my mother thinks I haven't come home with enough, she'll have her seven-tailed cat jumping on my back."

Ellen saw the tears in the girl's eyes and was sorry for her, though she didn't know what a seven-tailed cat was. In any case, it sounded frightful to her. She wondered whether it could be worse than being whipped with Leofrun's leather strap. "His coin is surely worth much more than the basket with the fish cakes," she ventured, trying to cheer her up. "Your mother will surely be happy with you."

"It was really brave of you to say that the fish cakes are good," said the girl, looking her directly in the eyes, "and very courageous, too." Then she looked up proudly. "If you're here again tomorrow, I'll have a free one for you, as a thank-you." She smiled and left with a kiss to Ellen's cheek before she hurried off.

This time it was Ellen who blushed. She wandered slowly along until she reached the market square, where she watched a juggler and a magician who made the bashful girls blush and caused the rest of the crowd to laugh at the girls' discomfort.

Again and again he bowed with a grin and thanked the crowd for their applause and the coins they tossed at him.

Not far from him stood a fire-eater and sword-swallower, a stout fellow with a hairy, naked chest and bald head who put a long sword through his mouth and thrust it deep into his throat to the astonishment of the onlookers. Ellen turned to watch a group of jugglers when suddenly a piercing cry diverted her attention to a cluster of people.

She pushed her way through the crowd. The tooth puller that the girl had spoken of and a barber were standing atop a big wooden platform at the far corner of the market square.

As one could tell from the greyish, weathered color of the platform, it stood outside there all year long at this spot. Perhaps trials were held up there, adulteresses whipped, crooks pilloried, or thieves had their hands cut off. Maybe even executions took place up there where you could see dark splotches on the wood. But now there were two large chairs to accommodate the patients.

The tooth puller had a little table where his tools were displayed: clamps and tongs in various sizes as well as herbs and tinctures to promote faster healing. Ellen thought of the girl with the red hands and wondered if she actually had fallen in love with the morose-looking old man who was just spreading out the instruments. Only when a handsome young man in a maroon robe appeared on the platform did Ellen understand that the old man was just the tooth puller's assistant.

On the other side of the crowd, close to the stairway, Ellen saw the maid, completely absorbed at the sight of the young man. Ellen hoped the girl would think of something other than having her tooth pulled in order to get his attention.

The barber-surgeon needed more equipment and a larger table. On one side there were his herbs, medicines, and cloths for making plaster and bandages, and on the other the saws for amputations as well as pairs of tweezers, scalpels, and needles of various sizes. A brazier and a branding iron stood nearby, too. Both the barber-surgeon and the tooth puller used broad leather straps to tie down their patients securely so they couldn't jump up in fright or pain and run away.

Sweat poured down the faces of even the bravest of them when a tooth had to be pulled or a wound sewed up. Patients were standing all around the platform, and in their faces one could see their fear of the pain as well as their hope for a cure.

Curious bystanders also besieged the podium in hopes of witnessing an amputation or other horrible thing. The crowd carefully watched every move the men made, commenting on their gestures with disgust or astonishment and shouting taunts at the patients. Apparently the spectacle was a welcome diversion for many of them.

Ellen couldn't bear to watch any longer. The repulsive odor of pus and rot, blood and burned flesh was just too much for her stomach. And it was only with difficulty and a strong will that she managed not to throw up her fish pasty.

On the other side of the square, the booths were huddled close together. Their roofs were of colored cloth or leather used to collect rainwater, and the merchants poked at them from below with sticks so the rain would run off. Farmers, monks, and all kinds of merchants had brought their goods to Ipswich. Whatever anyone could want could be found at this market: iron or copper pots in all sizes and shapes, all sorts of clay vessels and baskets, toys and household goods, leather and leather goods, cloth, straps, decorations, and anything useful made of horn, bone, wood, or metal.

In one corner, two monks in threadbare cowls were selling beer that they ladled from large, bulging kegs. Though they both appeared to be impoverished, their brew was no doubt very good, as a long line of customers holding one or more large tankards had formed alongside their wagon.

Farther along, live poultry was for sale along with eggs, flour, herbs, salted and smoked meat, fruit, vegetables, and other condiments for the kitchen.

Most unusual, though, and always surrounded by curious onlookers were the stalls with exotic fruits and spices such as dates, pomegranates, pepper, ginger, anise, cinnamon, and mustard. Ellen took a deep whiff of the tantalizing aromas. When she closed her eyes, it almost seemed to her that she was in another world.

All the merchants were shouting and extolling the quality of their goods. At the costume jewelry booth there were crowds of women and girls of all ages pushing and shoving in order to see the pretty goods and perhaps be able to touch them as well. Even though it had become second nature in recent months for Ellen to act like a boy, she stood there, like all the girls, with mouth and eyes wide open, marveling at the colorful hair ribbons and other attractive finery. The beautiful, bright colors, the exotic odors in the marketplace, and the huge variety of goods offered there was as intoxicating as a tankard of strong beer.

"Move along, lad," a pale-looking merchant barked at him, "you're blocking the view for the ladies!"

The next moment he was smiling and extolling his cords, braids, and ribbons while at the same time trying to chase Ellen away with an angry look—and suddenly all the wonderful, blissful feeling vanished. *What is more important to you, you silly goose,* Ellen thought to herself—*to be a blacksmith or to dress up with colorful ribbons in your hair?* She was angry that she had been so taken in by these pretty, worthless things. She turned her back resolutely on the knickknack stall. *I've got to make sure,* she thought, reaching for her moneybag, *that I find this blacksmith Llewyn was telling me about instead of standing around with my mouth open.* As long as she had no work, all she had left were her savings.

Suddenly she broke out in a cold sweat. She looked under her shirt—there was nothing there! Then she reached for the leather cord around her neck. It was still there, but the purse with the money was gone, cut off. Her heart began to pound, and she felt a humming in her ears. Frantically she reflected on how and when the theft could have taken place. Had she forgotten, after buying the fish pasty, to slip the purse back down again under her shirt? She looked around helplessly. Who could have stolen it? Was it perhaps the nice little pasty vendor? She felt as if an enormous hole had opened up in front of her and was about to devour her. Her eyes filled with tears.

At that moment she caught sight of the purse thief that she had seen before. He was pushing his way through the crowd, moving farther and farther away from her.

He was the one who had robbed her! She tried desperately to fight her way through the crowd as well, but she just couldn't catch up with the boy and eventually lost sight of him. He must have turned into one of the narrow alleys.

In despair Ellen leaned against the wall of a house. She stared blankly into space with tears in her eyes, unable to think about what to do next. She had nothing left but the clothes on her back. The tears were running down her cheeks—she had worked so hard for her money, and now what could she do now? She wiped her eyes and looked around helplessly.

A tall, older man caught her attention. She was so struck by his appearance that for a moment she forgot her grief and stared at him in disbelief. His elegant, long clothes were of the finest dark blue cloth and trimmed with brown fur. He had a walking stick with a silver knob on it that he leaned on as he strode along. The stick, his fine clothing, and his glistening grey hair lent him an aura of elegance. But it was his piercing blue eyes and the pinched look around his mouth that intrigued her so much, as it reminded her of her mother. Instinctively, she followed him up to a large house where he stopped, took a heavy iron key from his belt, and prepared to open the elaborately carved oaken door. Before he could place the key in the lock, however, the door opened by itself as if by magic.

A young girl appeared in the entrance.

Ellen moved closer to the two in order to get a better view.

The girl's sky blue dress was made of shiny material and was embroidered with silver threads at the neckline. It looked precious, elegant, and unpretentious at the same time. Ellen had never seen anything more beautiful! But when she looked into the face of the angelic figure, she gasped. It was Aedith! She had grown since Ellen had last seen her.

The old man, who looked so much like Leofrun, had to be her grandfather!

Ellen suddenly felt a huge lump in her throat, and a wave of homesickness came over her. For a moment she thought about going to the two and embracing them. She was bursting with curiosity about her grandfather, and suddenly her anger at her sister seemed to have disappeared.

Aedith must have come to Ipswich in order to marry the silk merchant to whom she was given in marriage by Leofrun more than a year ago. Ellen wondered whether Mildred and Kenny were also there.

As Aedith closed the door behind the grandfather, she briefly glanced at Ellen, clearly thinking her sister was just another simple street urchin not worthy of attention.

She hasn't changed, Ellen thought bitterly, disappointed that Aedith had not recognized her.

As Ellen walked away, despondent, she suddenly caught sight of the young thief again, who seemed to have already found a new victim. Her anger at his shameless behavior and the hope of getting her purse back lent her new courage. After all, she was a boy now and knew how to handle such fellows!

She carefully approached him from behind and took the rest of the leather thong between her hands, grabbing it tightly. The boy was a little bigger than she, but slender. Ellen carefully crept up to him, wrapped the lace around his neck, and with a strong tug pulled him into an alley. The boy staggered backward and tried to pull off the lace that was cutting into his neck.

"Where is the purse that was attached to this cord until just a while ago?" Ellen hissed, pulling the defenseless youth farther back into the narrow, dark alleyway.

The boy gasped in vain for air. "I don't have it anymore," he wheezed.

"Then let's go and get it. Right now!" Ellen snarled. She loosened the thong so he could get a bit more air but was ready to tighten the noose again if she had to in order to keep him under control.

"I can't do it."

"Why not?"

"He would kill me, and you too."

"Who?"

"One-Eyed Gilbert."

"Now just who might that be?" Ellen grumbled.

"He has a brothel over on Tart Lane. If I don't bring back enough money from my forays, he will whip me almost to death."

Ellen spat on the ground in disgust. "Do you think that's a reason to steal other people's hard-earned money?" she snorted. "Leave him, go out, and get yourself a decent job. You are still young," she said, giving gave him an angry punch in the stomach.

"I can't. He has my little sister, and as long as I steal for him he will spare her. If I run away or if I don't bring back enough money, he'll hand her over to his customers."

For a moment, Ellen was sorry for the boy—but he was probably lying. She could sense he was calming down.

"I can't give you back your purse, but I could rob someone else for you, if you want." His voice rose expectantly, and Ellen saw that his face had brightened.

She thought about his suggestion and frowned. He probably would go on stealing in any case, so why shouldn't he steal for her? Ellen thought of the woman he had been watching. She had been holding a small boy by the hand and certainly needed the money to buy food and other essentials for her family. Should she pay for his debts, and if she didn't, who would? The next victim? Didn't everyone need money?

"Please let me go, my neck hurts so much," the boy pleaded.

"Get out of my sight, go on, leave!" Ellen shouted at him and pushed him away.

The boy fell on his knees, pulled himself together again, and ran off.

Ellen tore at her hair. She didn't have a penny left, and if she didn't find work right away she would be lost. She gripped the hammer on her belt. She had to find Master Donovan, as she had promised Llewyn she would. That was her last chance. She looked around—apparently she was on the Cloth Merchants Street—and decided to ask at one of the booths where to find the blacksmiths.

An older woman who had just bought a large piece of linen smiled at her. "I'll show you the way, if you want to come along with me for a bit," she suggested, piling the cloth on top of her basketful of other things.

Ellen offered politely to carry her purchases, and the woman accepted gratefully.

"Then come along. My name is Glenna, by the way, and my husband Donovan is the blacksmith, too."

"Oh!" Ellen beamed at hearing the unexpected good news.

"You have already heard of him?" Glenna's question sounded more like a statement.

"Yes, I have." Ellen nodded and followed her, frantically trying to figure out what to do next. If she first told the master's wife what she wanted, then he might think Ellen was trying to do something behind his back and would be annoyed at her. On the other hand, it was impolite not to tell her anything at all. As the master's wife she was in charge of everyone living in the house, including apprentices and helpers. Ellen considered the pros and cons but came to no decision.

"You are too young to be a journeyman, but I see a hammer on your belt that has seen a lot of use," the woman noted.

Ellen decided to seize this favorable moment to bring up her concern. "You are right, I am not yet a journeyman," she answered politely. "I was not even a real apprentice but just a helper in the blacksmith shop and got the hammer as a gift from my master, Llewyn. In Framlingham they call him the Irishman, and I think your husband knows him."

"Llewyn!" the woman exclaimed, beaming. She added with a laugh, "You certainly can say he knows him. He raised him as a child!"

Ellen lifted her eyebrows and stared at Glenna in amazement. "All he told me was that his father knew Master Donovan well."

"Llewyn's father was Donovan's best and possibly only friend. What a stubborn Irishman! Only someone like that could get along with Don." Glenna nodded emphatically and brushed a strand of grey hair out of her face. "Llewyn's mother was a delicate girl from Wales and did not survive her son's birth. A few years later his father died too, and the poor lad was all alone in the world. We took him in when he was no more than four years old, just after Donovan and I had married." She stopped for a moment and put her hand on Ellen's arm. "How is my Llewyn?"

Ellen thought of Llewyn and how their parting was harder for her than she had expected. His calm, even temper had given her a feeling of confidence and security. "He is well, very well," she said reassuringly. Ellen liked the woman at once, perhaps because she had such a sparkle in her eye when she spoke of Llewyn.

"Is he married? Does he have children?"

"No." Ellen shook her head.

Glenna looked a bit disappointed.

"How many children do you have?" Ellen asked.

"We have no children of our own—this is not a blessing the Lord has given to us. That's why He gave us Llewyn." This time the woman sounded sad.

Ellen hadn't meant to make her feel miserable and looked down in embarrassment.

"If Llewyn gave you this hammer, he must think a lot of you." Glenna stopped again. "May I?" she asked, reaching for the tool and examining it. "I thought so. He got the hammer from Donovan after he had finished his apprenticeship. Do you see the marking there on the head of the hammer? That's Donovan's sign, I'm quite sure of that."

Ellen was moved, realizing for the first time how much this hammer must have meant to Llewyn. She remembered the nostalgic expression in his eyes when he spoke of Donovan and wondered why he had not also become a swordsmith. She couldn't imagine that he was not good enough. Despite her curiosity, she decided not to ask Glenna about it. If she should get hired by Donovan, she would find out soon enough.

"So here we are. This is our house, and there is the forge," Glenna said, pointing to the workshop nearby.

A cat was lying in the sun in the courtyard of the smithy, a few chickens were pecking contentedly in the dirt, and on a small patch of land next to the house a goat was tied to a stake. A smithy made of stone was nothing unusual, but the house was, too, and that was a sign of wealth. Donovan must indeed be a famous swordsmith to afford that.

Ellen had grown up in a simpler house made of oak beams, clay, and straw, like most of the houses in Orford. Only the church and Orford Manor, the estate house, were built of stone.

Glenna opened the door. "Come on in. You must be thirsty, and perhaps hungry as well. Sit down at the table and put the basket there on the chair." She beckoned for Ellen to enter and presented her with a pitcher of cider, a smoked chicken leg, and a slice of bread.

"Smoked chicken?" Ellen inquired in astonishment and immediately got her appetite back again. "It tastes very good!" she said. "Back in Orford we have smoked cheese, which is also very good." She chattered away but then got angry at herself for being so careless and telling where she had come from.

Fortunately, Glenna was lost in thought at the moment and hadn't been listening. One could see in her face that she had been thinking of Llewyn.

"Excuse me, please, what did you say?" she asked.

"Really good, the cider, too," Ellen said quickly, and reminded herself to be more careful in the future.

"I assume you want to ask Donovan for work?"

Ellen thought she detected a look of sympathy in her face.

"I promised Llewyn I would." Ellen tried hard not to make it sound like an apology.

"Then you should go over and talk to him right away. It won't be easy, I'll tell you that. He's a stubborn man who has made up his mind not to take on any new apprentice." Glenna patted Ellen on the shoulder. "Nevertheless, you should ask for a trial period, no matter how much he curses or berates you." She nodded encouragingly. "Now off you go…but wait, what's your name?"

"Alan."

"So, Alan, go then, and good luck!"

"Thank you!"

"And don't let him put you off—remember what I told you," Glenna called to Ellen as she left.

—

When Ellen entered the smithy, it was as if she were coming home. The arrangement of things inside the stone building was very similar to that in Osmond's workshop. Donovan looked quite different than what she had imagined. She had expected a large, powerful man like Llewyn, but Donovan was small, almost dainty looking, and more like a goldsmith than a famous swordsmith.

"Close the door!" he thundered with an astonishingly deep bass voice.

Ellen quickly did so. Osmond had hated it, too, when the door to his workshop was left open. But since Llewyn had continued working outdoors in the springtime despite the promises of the builder, Ellen was no longer accustomed to closing the door to the workshop after entering.

"Greetings, Master Donovan," she said, hoping he hadn't noticed the trembling in her voice.

"What do you want?" he asked gruffly, looking at her from head to toe with a wrinkled brow.

Ellen had never felt so worthless as she did under his withering gaze. "I'd like to work for you and learn your trade, master."

"And why should I share what I know with you? How will you pay me?" he asked coldly, without even taking the trouble to look at her.

Ellen was horrified. How could any self-respecting master ask a question like that? Was he only interested in money? Would he sell his knowledge like a commodity to whoever paid him the most rather than to the worthiest person?

"No, master, I can't pay," she said sheepishly.

"Aha! That's what I thought," he grumbled.

"But I can work hard in return for your knowledge." Ellen noticed how flippant she had sounded and regretted her lack of control. *I sound like an old fishwife, not a smith's apprentice.*

"I don't need a helper. I already have a good one."

"I can do more than just assist you. Try me out!"

"I have a lot to do and no time to waste. Go to the devil, you snotty little brat."

Even though the smith sounded angry and dismissive, Ellen thought she saw something akin to helplessness in his eyes. At first glance she didn't really care for Donovan, but if Llewyn held him in such high esteem, there had to be a reason. Ellen decided to listen to Glenna and just ignore the rude insult. "Well, if you have so much to do, wouldn't it be a good idea for me to help?" The trembling in her voice had given way to cool detachment. She set her ragged bundle down in a corner and looked around the workshop.

Order was essential in a forge. The various tongs, hammers, and other tools had to always be in the same place so they would be quickly available when needed. Donovan's workshop was organized almost exactly like Llewyn's, and it would not be hard for her to find her way around.

"Just who do you think I am? Do you think you can just walk in here and tell me what to do?" Donovan seemed both angry and surprised.

"My name is Alan, I have worked in a blacksmith shop for quite a while, and if I may say so never heard the name of Donovan the swordsmith until a few days ago." Ellen was astonished herself at just how impudent she could sound, but she kept on talking. "I don't know you even if you are the best swordsmith in East Anglia. And who gets to decide that anyway? I came to you because a blacksmith I highly respect recommended you. He thought you could teach me more than he did."

"Well, now, tell me who that might be?" Donovan didn't seem to care too much about the opinions of other blacksmiths.

"My master's name is Llewyn, and I think you know him well."

When he heard the name Llewyn, Donovan's eyes narrowed to little slits. He was clearly angered. Ellen even worried he might attack her, but he just snorted with contempt. "Llewyn couldn't do it."

"He thought he wasn't good enough for you."

Donovan flared up. "But he thinks you are, is that right?"

"Yes, master," Ellen replied calmly.

Donovan was silent for a long time, his face not disclosing his thoughts.

"If you want me to test you, come back tomorrow before noon," he said finally, and turned away.

"I'll be here!" she replied proudly, picked up her bundle, and closed the door behind her without another word.

—

When Glenna and Donovan were sitting silently alone at supper, his wife was the first to break the silence. "You must at least give the boy the chance to show what he can do or you will always wonder whether Llewyn was right."

"Llewyn wasn't good enough," Donovan replied roughly. "How could he judge whether…?"

"Nonsense. Not good enough? Don't make me laugh. He wasn't able to stand up to you. You surely know he could have done it! But you were too strict with him, never praised him, never told him you believed in him. I know how much you miss him. Don't reject him again. This lad is his present to you, a sign that Llewyn has forgiven you." With a gesture of determination, Glenna swept a few crumbs from the table.

"Forgiven me? I did nothing wrong—I always treated him like a son. What is there to forgive?" Donovan jumped up from the table.

"Even a son would have eventually fled from a father like you. He could have been your equal, but you never gave him time enough—you were too impatient. You learn quickly and remember everything, but you can't expect that of everyone. You have a very special talent, something not everyone has. He had to work hard for the things that came to you so easily. Please listen to me. Give the boy a chance…for your sake as well!"

"But what good will that do? I have tried for years to find an apprentice and never had one that did not break down and quit after just a short time. Maybe I ask too much from them, but I can't work any slower, and I can't always repeat everything. It's just not possible." Donovan's fury had given way to despair. "I lost Llewyn because I cannot be patient enough, but why should I take in a boy who is a complete stranger?"

"What do you have to lose? If he's no good, send him away." Glenna looked at him, pleading.

"Every time I send a boy away, it's like losing a battle. I don't want any more defeats." Donovan was dejected and holding his head in his hands.

"Don, please think about how it was when Art came here. You didn't want to take him because he was such a big man. 'He's dumb and strong,' you said, and you believed he could never keep up with you. Nevertheless, you got accustomed to working together, you got to know each other's strengths and weaknesses. Would you be able to get along without him today?"

"No, of course not," he grumbled. "But Art is no apprentice!" he protested.

"Please, Donovan, I know Alan is the right apprentice for you. I can feel it!"

For a while, the smith said nothing, and then he continued. "I told him he can come tomorrow if he wants to take the test. We'll see if he dares. In any case, I won't make it easier for him just because Llewyn has sent him."

Glenna seemed happy with this reply. She was sure the lad would make the grade. If Donovan took him on as an apprentice he would be particularly demanding with him, precisely because Llewyn had sent him. But if he was good, Donovan would see it, and it would make him happy.

—

Ellen had left the workshop without stopping to see Glenna again. Even though she would have liked to speak with her again, she didn't want Donovan to see her and think she needed to go to anyone to seek sympathy. Donovan's stubbornness and prejudice were deeply offensive to her. Even if he was in fact one of the best swordsmiths in England, did that give him the right to treat other people like that?

Of course, she knew that masters had very special rights while apprentices had only obligations. Time would tell if she ever would be able to make it to the rank of apprentice. First she would have to pass the test. When she thought about what would happen the next morning she felt a tingling in the pit of her stomach—a mixture of hope and fear. Ellen tried to tell herself she was good enough to pass the test. If not, would Llewyn have made her promise to take it? Seeking some assurance, she decided to go to a church. It certainly wouldn't hurt to ask the Lord for His help.

Ellen spent the night in a corner of St. Clement's Church and in the morning set out on her way to see Donovan. As she entered the workshop, the smith greeted her very cordially, and Ellen wondered what might have caused his change of heart.

Donovan had a simple way to decide whether a boy would be any good. He took out fragments of bloom iron and showed them to Ellen. "I assume that up to now you have worked only with wrought iron in bars or rods?"

Ellen nodded.

"This is bloom iron—raw iron just as it comes from the bloomery, which has not yet been wrought. When you examine the spongy texture of each piece, you will see the edges all look different. It is that texture that tells me how to work the iron later and above all whether it is suited for the softer but ductile core of the blade or the harder and more rigid jacket wrapped around it. All you must do is to sort the pieces according to whether they are suited for the jacket or for the core. A grainy, shiny texture indicates the iron is hard while an even, finely grained quality shows it is soft. In addition, you can detect impurities like slag by differences in color." Donovan handed her one piece of each, nodded, and pointed to the pile of bloom iron in front of them. He seemed almost jubilant. He probably used the same test for all the young men who wanted to serve an apprenticeship with him, and they probably all failed.

Blacksmiths who made only simple tools, fittings, and frames of black iron worked with wrought iron that they could work with right off—that's why Ellen had never heard of bloom. But she had listened carefully to Donovan's explanations and remembered every single word.

Sitting down cross-legged on the hard clay floor of the shop, she picked up the pieces he had shown her, examined them carefully once more, and then tried to determine their characteristics. Donovan acted as if he were busy with something else but was watching her surreptitiously. Calmly, she took the first two pieces, weighed them in her hand, then eyed them closely, turning them, smelling them, and touching them all over. After a while, she placed them on the ground in front of her: one on the right and one on the left. Then she took the next piece, examined it in the same way, then put it down on one side or the other.

The longer she looked at the bloom iron pieces the more she understood what to do. She was sure even Donovan needed time to sort them out. Even though she knew practically nothing about making swords, she was certain the quality of such a weapon depended to a large degree on the material it was made of. She decided to make two additional piles alongside the two large piles. When she was finished, she stood up and went over to Master Donovan.

The expression on his face was impossible to fathom.

"Master, I am finished."

Donovan walked over to the piles with her.

"Here is the material for the jacket, there's the material for the core of the blade, and alongside them I have placed the pieces that seem to me especially impure."

Donovan looked at her skeptically but with interest, then turned to the two larger piles. He examined each piece individually, as Ellen had done, and nodded only after he had examined them all.

Ellen could see he was pleased with her work, but when he turned to look at her, his face was dark again. What in the world had Llewyn had in mind when he sent her to him?

Ellen considered Donovan arrogant and rude. Nevertheless, something special had clicked in her while he was explaining the job to her—something she could not put into words but brought them together despite their differences. They both seemed to attack a project in the same way. Donovan's explanations were terse, to the point, and precise, and not at all like the instructions from Llewyn or Osmond.

"I'll think about whether I can take you on. Come back in the afternoon when I have made my decision," he said, looking at her darkly, as before.

This old curmudgeon just can't stand me, she thought. *But I don't care much for him either.* As she left the forge, she met Glenna, who was hanging up clothes on the line.

"Hello, Alan!" she called out cheerfully, waving to Ellen like an old friend.

"Greetings, mistress," Ellen replied politely, but it was impossible not to hear the disappointment in her voice.

"Well?"

"I did what he asked of me."

"Were you able to sort out the bloom iron?"

"Yes, I did it correctly. He looked at every piece, one at a time, and put each one down again where I had placed it."

"Well, then I must congratulate you. But why do you look so sad?" Glenna took a large sheet and hung it over the clothesline.

"The master has not yet decided. He wants me to come back later. I don't think he likes me."

"He is a bitter old grumbler and needs a little time. It's not you he can't stand, but himself. Also, he is still angry at Llewyn, but things will work out, believe me!" She gave Ellen a look of encouragement.

While Donovan made Ellen feel rebellious and uncomfortable, Glenna gave her a feeling of security and motherly affection.

"I'll be back, then," Ellen said halfheartedly, and decided to go back again to the market square.

—

When Ellen arrived at the place she had seen the fish-pasty vendor the day before, she couldn't find her. It was noontime, and her stomach was growling. She looked around carefully in the crowd—after all, the vendor still owed her a pasty. Just as she was about to leave, the girl approached, waving cheerfully.

"That silver piece yesterday was worth much more than my pasties and the basket. The knight could have had three baskets full of them and still they would have been overpriced. And my basket was not even full!" She picked out two nice pasties and handed them to Ellen. "Here, these are for you!"

"But you gave me two!"

"Oh, that doesn't matter," she replied, her cheeks aglow.

"Thanks! These are the best I ever had!" Ellen bit into the first one. "By the way, I found the smith I asked you about yesterday, and I'll learn this afternoon if he will take me on."

"Oh, I hope it works out," the girl said with a seductive wink. "Then you can come and see me more often."

She is actually thinking of me as a boyfriend, Ellen thought with dismay, nodding to her briefly before plunging back into the crowd and sauntering across the market square.

Through the crowd she caught sight of a stately gentleman. Ellen's heart skipped a beat, and she was so anxious she felt rooted to the spot. Sir Miles! But when the man turned to the side and she could see his face straight on, she realized she had been mistaken. With a sigh of relief, she continued on until she heard two women squabbling.

Curious onlookers had already gathered around them, and Ellen joined them. A burly market woman with dirty brown hair was hawking all kinds of ribbons and braids, simple ones made of cotton, costly ones of smooth silk or brocade, plain ones, and others woven in many colors, some elaborately embroidered, others long, short, thick, or thin.

An angry customer was shouting so loudly her voice nearly broke: "I paid you for thirteen ribbons, each an ell in length, and now you want more money, you shameless swindler!"

"You paid me for thirteen plain ribbons, but five of the ribbons you picked out are of silk, and embroidered, and they cost more, and so do the four woven ones you took. So you still owe me half a shilling."

"Go and get the market inspector!" suggested the woman at the next booth. "These rich young women are either dumb or trying to cheat honest people. You should not let her get away with that."

The customer no doubt suspected she was wrong. When faced with having her complaint referred to the market inspector, she mumbled a few curses, took out the money the merchant had demanded, and paid. Only after she had turned around did Ellen see who the customer was. She hadn't even recognized Aedith's voice.

"Get out of my way!" the woman shouted impatiently to the amused crowd standing around her.

Ellen knew that Aedith hated nothing more than to be ridiculed. The merchants would be watching out for her in the future.

With a haughty expression, Aedith elbowed her way past Ellen shouting, "Why are you staring at me like that, you silly brat?" Ellen seethed with rage and without thinking stuck out her foot to trip her sister, just as she used to do. Aedith stumbled, and the people laughed even harder at her. Surprised and angered, she looked around. For a brief moment Ellen looked into her eyes, saw how she was crying, and suddenly felt sympathy for her.

"Ellenweore?"

Ellen was startled. Aedith put out her hand, but before she could get hold of her, Ellen had spun around and disappeared in the crowd as if chased by the devil. Her heart was pounding. Breathless, she hid behind a cart and from a safe distance watched Aedith struggling to get through the crowd.

Defiant as always but with a little less haughty expression, she disappeared in the Cloth Merchants Street.

Ellen struck her forehead with her fist, furious at herself for what she had done. *Can't I ever control myself? Why did I have to trip her up? Couldn't I have just let her go by?* Now, even if Donovan took her on, she would always run the risk of being discovered and betrayed by Aedith. She felt a wave of despair come over her. Would she always be running away? How far could she go, and where could she go without money? For what seemed like an eternity, Ellen just sat and stared into space. *Aedith is my sister—I shouldn't fear her*, she thought, trying to console herself, but she couldn't really bring herself to believe it.

After she had commiserated with herself a while, she got up, stretched her shoulders, and jutted her chin out defiantly. First she would go to Donovan to learn of his decision. When she arrived at the forge, she saw a half dozen horses standing in front of Donovan's workshop. One was without a rider, and the others seemed to be waiting for him. Ellen paid no attention to them but considered leaving again. Perhaps it was good that Donovan obviously was busy. Now she could go over to the house and explain to Glenna that she had offended the daughter of a merchant and had better leave town. Glenna would certainly understand, and Donovan wouldn't care if she never came back.

Just as she was about to knock, the door swung open and out stepped the Norman who had purchased the fish pasties.

He almost ran into her and grabbed her by the shoulders, laughing. "Well, well, if this isn't our young pasty taster."

"My lord," Ellen replied, lowering her eyes.

"You didn't tell me you also have an apprentice, Master Donovan," he said. As he was looking toward the house, Donovan appeared in the doorway.

"How fortunate that he seems to be such a courageous fellow. A coward wouldn't be of much use to you on a trip like that."

"But I..." Ellen was trying to explain that she was not an apprentice, but the Norman paid no attention to her and spoke only to Donovan.

"We're shipping out on the day after Pentecost. You're not to take too much luggage with you, and no animals: just your tools. They'll give you everything else you'll need in Tancarville. Come down to the harbor first thing in the morning and don't keep us waiting. The harbormaster knows our ships and will show you the way. Between now and then, learn some French," he said, laughing boisterously.

Donovan grumbled something unintelligible.

Perhaps Ellen should have said something in order to avoid a misunderstanding, but she remained silent. What did it matter? The Norman took her for what she absolutely wanted to be! But only now that the chance had passed did she realize how much she wanted to be Donovan's apprentice. What could this trip be that the knight spoke of?

Even after the men had left, Donovan simply ignored her.

Ellen stood there as if rooted to the spot and couldn't figure out what to do. Visibly distraught, Glenna came rushing out of the house.

"Tell me, Don, I just can't understand. Why is the king angry at you, and why is he sending you away?"

Donovan patted his wife's cheek tenderly and replied, "The king isn't angry with me at all, dear, that's the strange part. William of Tancarville is a close confidant of the king. He has sent FitzHamlin to get me and bring me to Normandy to be his swordsmith, an honor only a really important smith would receive."

"And so you really mean to go?" Glenna said.

"We *must* go! It would be an offense to the king if I turned down this invitation. I was able to set down a few conditions, but couldn't do more." Donovan had first spoken with FitzHamlin alone and only later with Glenna.

"And what are those conditions?" she asked suspiciously.

"I said we needed a comfortable house, of course, and that someone would have to look after our home here in Ipswich until we came back. And I asked that we not be required to stay more than ten years."

"Ten years?" Glenna shouted, and her face turned white. "Who knows if we will even live that long?"

"It might be only three or four years," Donovan ventured, trying to calm her down, but it didn't even sound as if he believed it himself.

"Can we at least take Art along, and the boy?" Glenna asked, gasping.

Donovan nodded without hesitation.

Ellen had no idea what to think of it, but she would have to leave Ipswich in any case. Why not then go to Normandy?

Her heart leaped at the thought of such an adventurous journey. On the other hand, once more an important decision regarding her future was being made by someone else. No one had even asked for her opinion.

Ellen watched as Donovan left for the workshop and wanted to follow him.

But Glenna tugged gently at her sleeve. "Give him a little time. Tomorrow is another day!" Glenna sighed and pushed Ellen into the house. "Come, I'll show you where you will sleep. It will be a hard time, but I'm sure you can make it."

It seemed to Ellen that Glenna was trying more to boost her own spirits than to convince her, but she nodded.

—

Ellen would have loved to tell the pasty vendor about the adventure awaiting her but didn't dare return to the market in Ipswich for fear of meeting Aedith. Nevertheless, the days until her departure were the most exciting she had ever known. On the first day she rose before dawn in order to be in the forge before Donovan arrived. She got dressed quickly and left for the workshop without even having breakfast. She carefully memorized where every tool belonged so she could hand them to Donovan quickly and then put them back where they belonged after the work was done. She filled the water trough and cleaned off the forge, as she would every morning from now on, and was ready then to work with the master.

From the very first morning, Donovan acted as if she had always been his apprentice. He gave her a few instructions for the day's work and then turned to his task in order to complete all his orders before they left. It was wonderful watching him!

Some days he was so absorbed in his work that he forgot to eat. Each of his motions was so carefully executed that no moment was wasted.

Ellen thought she understood now why Llewyn had said he had not been good enough for Donovan. Llewyn was a good blacksmith, but for him forging was a trade; for Donovan, however, it was a calling.

He seldom commented on his work, but Ellen understood each step; she felt, she sensed how and why he did things. She wasn't even disturbed at having only to watch, for the time being, and not do things. She observed very closely how Donovan worked, and learned more each day than she could have learned anywhere else in weeks. At night her eyes hurt and she fell into bed as tired as if she had been doing hard physical labor all day even though she had not even swung a hammer. Donovan hardly spoke to her, but every day he seemed a bit friendlier.

On the morning of their departure, Ellen got up even earlier than usual. She was so excited that she had hardly slept in any case. Glenna had given her some undergarments, two linen shirts, and a smock that probably once had belonged to Llewyn. Ellen packed them along with the few other belongings she had in the cloth that Aelfgiva had given her. Although it no longer had the old scent on it, it brought tears to Ellen's eyes whenever she bundled her things in it.

Glenna, too, had risen before dawn. She had been sleeping badly for days and was thus in a bad mood, tormented with questions of what to take along on the trip and what to leave at home. She would have liked to take everything but had to limit herself to things she was especially attached to. The furniture and larger household goods had to be left behind. She kept changing her mind, packing and unpacking the two large trunks they would take along. Finally, everything was stowed away—clothing, sheets, candleholders, blankets, some household goods, and most importantly the document that one of FitzHamlin's knights had brought to them.

As dawn broke, Donovan and Art arose and sat down quietly for breakfast. Later, neighbors and friends arrived to give their farewells accompanied by good wishes and friendly slaps on the back. Since Ellen barely knew any of them, she retreated behind the forge for a moment, took out the little wooden chaplet that the priest of St. Clement's had given her after the last Sunday mass, and knelt down, caressing the wooden rosary beads and praying for the people she loved, not knowing if she would ever see them again. Then she was ready for the trip.

"And take care of the goat. You mustn't slaughter her even if she stops giving milk, do you hear?" Glenna told the neighbors who would be taking care of their house, with tears in her eyes. Her nerves had finally given out.

"Just forget that," Donovan grumbled, even angrier than usual. "The goat is not important."

"We'll forge many fine swords for young knights!" Art said cheerfully. His sunny mood was the only thing one could depend on recently.

Donovan gave him an angry poke in the ribs. "Come now, Art, we've got to leave!" Glenna started to sob as they set out, and she kept looking around at the house until they turned a corner and it was no longer visible.

Ellen was all the more excited, as she had never been down by the docks. Even though Orford was an important harbor and Ellen had been aboard a simple fishing boat, she had never before been on a real ship. With great interest, she looked all around the harbor. Barrels, cases, bales, and sacks were piled everywhere.

Close by there was a simple wooden shed that looked as if it might collapse at any moment, and outside it a crowd of hungry-looking men standing around in shabby clothing. They were day laborers hoping to find work with the harbormaster. It was miserable, hard work loading and unloading the huge cases, barrels, and bales. The pay was bad, and the work was dangerous. Sometimes men were killed by falling cargo or drowned when they fell into the water and could not be saved in time.

Oxcarts that were used to bring or take away goods were standing on the wharves. The wagoners complained loudly and made a dreadful racket as they maneuvered for position on the docks.

The harbor was swarming with travelers. In one corner pilgrims had gathered and were excitedly discussing the most comfortable and safest ways to travel. Merchants were buzzing around the travelers, trying to sell them various things that might or might not be of any use to them. In front of a beautiful, brightly colored ship some members of the clergy were waiting—papal envoys perhaps, Ellen thought, judging by the sight of their luxurious crimson and purple robes. The monks and priests around them looked like poor little field mice in their simple woolen cowls. Scholars, doctors, and young noblemen were also present and were observing the members of the clergy with great interest.

Merchants were there also, and adventurers—often they were one and the same person—and they lined up to board their ship in Ipswich. People were standing or sitting around on walls, bales of straw, trunks, or cases, waiting. They all wanted to stay on shore as long as possible until the ship was just about to cast off. None of them wanted to spend more time than absolutely necessary on the tossing ship.

After a long search, Donovan and the others finally found the harbormaster in the swirling crowd. He was rude and unfriendly and stank of alcohol and rotten fish but directed them to a rather imposing two-master, the largest vessel in the harbor.

Dockworkers hauled large barrels of food, drinking water, and other goods up a wooden ramp and stowed them inside the ship. Some of the workers were almost invisible beneath the huge bales they carried on their backs.

An older Norman officer seemed to know every corner of the ship and gave exact instructions on where things were to go. The cargo was to be tied down with thick ropes so as not to shift and become dangerous projectiles in a heavy sea. The knights' horses were also led aboard, along with some sheep and baskets of chicken. The confusion on deck seemed to grow, but the officer was watching everything carefully and remained calm. "Hey, you over there, take the lances below decks! There is still room in the back on the far right. Put them points up and tie them together, is that clear?"

The squire nodded and made haste to do what he was told.

"The cases with the chain mail shirts and those with the shields go over there—hurry up!"

Ellen looked around. Off to one side a few ordinary people were standing—people who, like Donovan and his wife, were neither knights nor foot soldiers. They, too, were watching as the ship's cargo was taken aboard.

She nudged Glenna and pointed with her chin at the small group. "I wonder whether these are tradesmen, too, traveling to Tancarville?"

"Oh, indeed they are," Glenna replied, turning to her husband. "Look, that's Edsel, the goldsmith," she whispered, "with his wife and their two children!" Cheerfully she went over to the small group, tugging at Ellen's sleeve to bring her along.

The Normans had gathered many Englishmen of all sorts: Fletcher, the arrow smith, and Ives, the bow maker, were huddled together. They were brothers and had never gone separate ways, Glenna whispered to Ellen, as Edsel came over to her. He held a young boy by the hand who reminded Ellen of Kenny. She smiled and sighed wistfully, but when the boy stuck his tongue out at her, she gasped for air and was furious.

"Over there are the Websters, a couple of weavers from Norwich; they are coming along, too," Edsel explained. He said nothing about the two prostitutes who were conspicuous with their gaudy yellow scarves and garish makeup on their lips and cheeks.

"And who is the young girl over there?" Glenna asked.

"I have no idea. I think she bakes fish pasties," he replied condescendingly, and shrugged.

Now Ellen, too, spotted the girl. In amazement she rushed over to her. "What in the world are you doing here?" she asked.

"The knight—well you know who I mean—said my fish cakes were the best he had ever eaten. His master is a great lover of seafood, he said, and he offered me good pay and full-time employment. I would never have dared to dream I would be going so far from home."

"What did your mother say about that? Did she approve?" Ellen asked incredulously.

"She knows nothing about it. I just left as I do every morning. When she notices, I'll already be long gone on the high seas and free! And how about you? Didn't you want to work for a smith? Didn't it work out?"

"It did, and that's why I'm here! It's a long story." Ellen grinned. She was happy to know someone on the ship in addition to the smith, Glenna, and Art.

"By the way, my name is Rose." The girl wiped her hand on her apron and held it out to Ellen.

"Alan," she answered, proffering a manly handshake while trying not to crush the other girl's hand.

Rose looked at her with undisguised admiration and winked at her seductively.

Ellen felt uneasy and dismayed. *She really thinks I am coming on to her*, she thought.

They talked until the ship's hold was full, and finally the passengers were asked to come aboard. The captain told everyone to hurry. There was little space in the cargo area, and everyone had to stow their crates and bundles and try to get settled as best they could in the tight quarters. As the ship put out to sea, Ellen was sitting with her back against a barrel that was tied down securely and smelled of oak and wine.

"I hope there are no rats on board!" Glenna whined, looking around warily before taking a seat.

"I'd be surprised if there weren't, as there's no such thing as a ship without rats. And it's probably good to have a few of them on board, as they say rats leave a sinking ship. When they jump overboard, we know at least that the ship is going down," Donovan said, smirking.

Glenna looked at him in shock. "If you're trying to be witty or funny, you have failed," she snorted and turned her back on her husband.

Donovan shrugged and went to join the other English craftsmen who were standing on the deck and talking.

As soon as the ship put to sea, the knights settled down for a game of dice.

Only one man in elegant clothing and shoulder-length, slightly matted hair stood at the railing. They learned from one of the prostitutes that his name was Walter Map and that he was a servant of the king. He was in England on his last trip when he fell ill and was not able to travel back to Normandy. Therefore, FitzHamlin had agreed to take care of him and return him to his master when he recovered. Walter Map had been raised in Paris, could read and write—a service he performed for the king—and knew Latin and grammar. But he was not only learned, he was also kind to everyone. He treated all the women on board like ladies and tried to amuse and entertain the anxious travelers with little jokes.

When the seas got heavier and a strong wind kicked up, he hung over the railing like almost everyone else, trembling and green, and emptied his rebellious stomach into the sea. Except for the sailors, Ellen and Rose appeared to be the only ones who were not sick, but the stench of vomit became harder and harder for them to bear. When Ellen stood up to check on Walter, who had been leaning over the railing, the back of her shirt slipped up, and Rose noticed a reddish-brown spot on her trousers. She grabbed her by the arm. "Look, you must have hurt yourself. You have blood on your braies." Even a simple scratch on a rusty nail could be fatal. Rose examined the boards that Ellen had been sitting on but couldn't find anything. "There's nothing here that would have caused that scratch. Maybe it happened some time ago."

Ellen could not figure out where the blood might have come from. She hadn't felt anything except for some terrible stomach cramps that had been bothering her for a while and which she thought were the first signs of seasickness. She retreated to a quiet corner where no one could see her, pulled her braies down, and saw that the blood was coming from her most intimate part. She was seized with fear, remembering vaguely that her mother had bled—"unclean," she had called it—but why she bled and how long it lasted and what she should do about it she didn't know. She felt completely helpless. What would happen if Glenna saw it? She would know immediately that Ellen wasn't a boy, and she would tell Donovan. Then the trip would be over practically before it began. Ellen's eyes filled with tears. Perhaps she would even be punished for it or imprisoned or simply abandoned in Normandy. Hot flashes alternated with the cramps in her stomach.

Suddenly Rose appeared again. She looked down at Ellen's still uncovered private parts. Something was missing. In the place where men had their male organ she had only a little pubic hair covering her.

"You're not a boy at all," Rose said. "Is this the first time you have bled?"

Ellen nodded silently and was so ashamed she couldn't bear to look Rose in the eye.

"I'll go and talk to Hazel. Whores know all about such things."

"Please, you mustn't do that, don't give me away!" Ellen whispered and looked at her imploringly.

"I won't—you must have reasons to pass yourself off as a boy. Don't worry, I'll just say I am bleeding." Rose seemed to know more about this than Ellen did. "Does it hurt?"

"My stomach does." Ellen remained crouched in a corner and pulled up her braies.

When Rose returned she had learned enough to make Ellen feel better.

"Hazel gave me a few pieces of linen and showed me how to tie them together. Women are careful not to sit on their dresses so they don't get any spots on them, but you are wearing braies and chausses so you have to be careful that your undergarments always cover them but that you are not sitting on them. You also have to wash and change the linens regularly so they don't smell." Rose handed Ellen the cloths. "And here is some mugwort. Put a few leaves of it under your tongue and it will help the cramps. Do you have another pair of braies?"

Ellen nodded. "In my pack." She wasn't able to do anything and was so grateful Rose was there to take care of everything for her.

"Here, put them on and give me the ones with the stain. I'll wash them out along with the cloths, too, and nobody will notice," Rose said after she had fetched the bundle and taken out the braies.

"I'm really indebted to you for all this. Thank you," Ellen whispered, placing a folded cloth between her legs. To make sure it didn't slip, Rose tied a larger one around her hips just as Hazel had shown her, and Ellen pulled the fresh braies over it. *If Llewyn knew about this*, she thought. She had trouble suppressing a hysterical giggle that suddenly came over her.

Rose fit right in with her role as Ellen's protectress and guardian, and Ellen was more than thankful for such a friend.

"Are you feeling better?" Hazel asked Rose sometime later, and at first Rose didn't know what she meant.

"Oh, me? Yes! I never felt better."

"Mugwort always works well for me, but it doesn't do anything for Tyra," she said, pointing over to her friend. "It's different for everyone."

Only now did Rose catch on, and she managed to lie without blushing. "I'm really very grateful to you. The cramps were terrible, but I am feeling much better now."

"If it gets bad again, come to me. I have plenty of it."

"Thank you," Rose whispered.

"I'll leave you now before the men get any foolish ideas," the prostitute said in a conspiratorial whisper. "Whenever they walk past Tyra or me, they whistle, lick their lips, and make lewd remarks. You are a decent girl and shouldn't be treated like that."

"Then why do you do it?" Rose asked.

"I don't know how to do anything else." Hazel shrugged indifferently. "My mother and my grandmother were whores, I was born in a brothel, and I don't know any other life. I had no choice, you know."

"Are all men like that?"

"Almost all," Hazel said, looking over the railing. "There are some who don't leer at us—Walter Map and young Alan. They are nice, and I think the boy likes you!"

"We are friends, nothing more, really."

"Come now, don't give up right away, just wait and see," said Hazel, who thought she heard a trace of disappointment in Rose's voice and patted her on the shoulder with a grin.

—

On the fourth day of their journey, shortly after sunrise, Ellen was standing with Walter along the railing. She liked his fine sense of humor and his reserved manner.

"Have you noticed how Rose looks at you?" He took Ellen by the shoulder and looked her closely in the eyes.

"What do you mean?" Ellen didn't understand what he was trying to say.

"She runs after you like the devil runs after a poor soul, my dear Alan," he whispered in her ear. "She jealously watches every step you make. She is standing back there again and watching you."

Ellen laughed. Rose was her only friend. They had stayed up all night again, talking softly. "Oh, Map, you have a vivid imagination."

Walter raised his eyebrows. "If you would like my well-intentioned advice, be careful if you don't have feelings for her. Love scorned often turns to the most dangerous hatred. Believe me, and don't forget my words."

"It's not what you think, really. We are just friends," Ellen answered confidently.

"As you wish." Walter stared out across the sea, seeming somewhat offended. But then he started pointing excitedly at something in the distance.

"Look there! That's the coast of Normandy. Do you see the mouth of the river? That's where the Seine empties into the ocean. We'll sail up the river to Tancarville," he explained.

Ellen put her hand to her forehead and looked off to the east. They had a favorable wind, but the entry into the estuary took longer than Ellen had expected. She kept looking out at the coast, which was getting closer and closer. An old, unshaven Norman sailor tanned by the sun and sea came running over from the other side of the ship and leaned out over the railing.

Ellen raised her eyebrows in surprise, looked at Walter questioningly, and said, "Can you believe he's seasick?" He was the only Englishman who also knew French and thus was a party to everything happening on board the ship.

Map shook his head and laughed.

At that very moment, the unshaven sailor cupped his hands to his mouth and cried out something to the helmsman she didn't understand. Then he ran to the other side of the ship and leaned over the railing there as well.

"What in heaven's name is he doing?"

Walter grinned and replied: "Sailors say that the Seine has more shoals than there are oysters in Honfleur. If he gets distracted just for a moment, our trip could be over even before we arrive in Tancarville." Map could see from Ellen's expression that this answer did not suffice. "He is leaning so far over the railing in order to have a better look. A man like him must have many years of experience so the ship doesn't run aground. Do you see the young sailor back there?"

"Sure, I have eyes in the back of my head," Ellen said, and was surprised she sounded so annoyed.

"The old sailor probably started out just like him and learned from looking over the shoulder of an experienced sailor. The sailors go to the bars in the seaports not just to get drunk but to exchange experiences. That's no doubt the way he learned from other sailors and on earlier voyages about the shoals in the river. He can tell where they must be by looking at the landscape as well as by how cliffs jut out into the river and even the color of the water. That's why he watches everything so closely."

"How do you know all that?" Ellen asked, impressed.

Map smiled mischievously. "Not everyone is so secretive as you are. Except for you, almost everyone tells me what's on their mind."

Ellen fell silent and quietly viewed the strange countryside on both sides of the Seine. The earth was fertile and dark brown, and a seemingly endless number of colorful spring flowers were growing in the bright green, lush grass on the meadow. The sight awakened in Ellen the strong wish to feel solid ground under her feet once again.

"Good Lord, how I hate this lurching around!" she moaned.

Walter looked at her in astonishment. "Don't tell me that now, so close to the end of our voyage, you're going to get sick, too. The sea isn't rough at all here!"

"Oh, nonsense, I'm just fine. I only want to be able to walk straight ahead again as before," she answered gruffly.

On the shore, well-fed brown and white cows stared blankly at the passing ship. "And look behind them—sheep! And lambs," Ellen cried out in surprise, pointing to another meadow.

"Alan, I'm beginning to worry seriously about your state of mind. Sheep have grazed over half of England until it is almost bare, so why for heaven's sake are you so excited at seeing those bleating four-legged creatures?"

"We took sheep along with us," Ellen said excitedly, "so I thought there weren't any in Normandy."

"Oh, I see," said Walter, nodding and grinning at the same time.

Ellen was annoyed that she knew so little about Normandy.

"English sheep give more and better wool than any other animals, so the Normans take our sheep and are trying to resettle them in their country. Nevertheless, for some reason the animals in England are still better. I think that comes from what they get to eat." Map seemed lost in thought for a moment. "Or maybe it's due to the English weather…" He hadn't quite finished thinking about it when they were joined by Webster, the cloth merchant.

"It's because of how they are shorn," he said. "That's something the English farmers know how to do better. Moreover, they pray regularly to their patron saints, and I do think it's not too bad to have the Lord on your side." Webster spoke as if he were the expert.

Walter nodded pensively, and Ellen was happy he no longer seemed to be regarding her so facetiously. She looked up into the grey afternoon sky and then viewed the flat, broad expanse of land ahead of them. Extensive deciduous and pine forests alternated with meadows and fields, and in between were thousands of apple trees in bloom. The faded pink petals were wafted away by the warm spring winds and carried off like a sea of snowflakes. *This will be a good place to live*, Ellen thought.

"Look, up ahead! Tancarville!" someone shouted.

Ellen peered out curiously.

In the distance a magnificent castle sat enthroned on a steep triangular spur that jutted far out into the river. Water surrounded the fortress on two sides, giving it protection from attackers. The bright, smoothly hewn stones of the castle had a silvery glow in the light of the setting sun. Countless little hovels huddled up against the hill as if trying to storm the castle, yet there was something peaceful emanating from this site. Two large merchant ships and many fishing vessels bobbed up and down in a small cove beneath the castle. The Seine here was lined with dense forests teeming with game and therefore a favorite hunting ground for the Lord of Tancarville and his men.

By now, all the travelers had come onto deck, curious to see and admire their new homeland. Each of them had brought along hopes and fears, but now they saw only the beauty of Tancarville and fell under its spell.

In the west, the setting sun cast a soft light, and pink clouds drifted like painted sheep through the grey-blue sky. Soon it would set in a sea of color. Only in the north did the sky look dark grey and threatening as if a storm were brewing.

Tancarville, 1162

While Donovan was busy handling the building of the forge, Ellen was often free to stroll through the castle courtyard and the village. She enjoyed the pleasant summer days and her freedom, which would end as soon as the workshop was finished. Whenever the order came from FitzHamlin for the village priest to come and teach the English tradesmen some French, Ellen ran off. She hated to pass herself off as a boy to the priest. After all, he was a man of God, and you couldn't play God for a fool. In any case, the haggard man of God with melancholy brown eyes seemed to regard the classes as nothing more than an onerous task. He made no secret of his horror at what these foreigners did with his beautiful language when they vainly tried to emulate what he had just told them in his elegant, nasal accent.

Although Donovan scolded her each time, Ellen preferred to take the time off to watch the Norman tradesmen in their work. In this way she learned much more, in any case, than she could have from the priest. Sometimes she also lingered around the fountain listening to the maids and trying to understand their silly chatter.

Her favorite place to sit, however, was atop a huge bale of hay where she could look down on the drill ground where the pages and squires were being trained in the use of weapons. She could sit there forever with a straw in her mouth, dangling her feet over the side. When the young men took their places in little groups nearby to practice sword fighting, she listened closely and concentrated on the foreign language. She quickly learned more French that way than all the other newcomers put together and soon mastered the pronunciation better than her countrymen, especially Art, who had great difficulty articulating the soft-sounding foreign words with his thick tongue.

Rose, on the other hand, who worked at the bakery, managed quite well and could make herself understood with few words using her hands and feet. At noontime Ellen often stopped to pick her up. They would sit down in a corner of the courtyard to enjoy the warm summer sun and to chatter, laugh, and eat. At the bakery, the other employees teased Rose with suggestive gestures, thinking that the young blacksmith was coming on to her. Rose had also noticed that the Norman servants looked away in disappointment when Ellen arrived. They surely believed that as an Englishman he had better chances with her than they did. Rose found that all very amusing. She fanned the rumor by sometimes blowing a kiss to Ellen when she left. Rose felt at home in Tancarville just as fast as Ellen did, perhaps because they were both young and looked ahead instead of backward.

Even Glenna, who had at first been so fearful of being sent to a foreign land, began to feel much happier. The Lord of Tancarville had a fine house built for them and provided workers and material to furnish it. In the spacious living room there was a large fireplace, a long oaken table with two benches, and close by in a corner a heavy wooden shelf stocked with cooking pots, soup bowls, and earthenware. Glenna's greatest pride in her new home, however, were two magnificent armchairs with high backs and carved armrests such as were otherwise seen only in the homes of lords and ladies. There were two small bedrooms under the roof that could be reached by way of a steep wooden stairway. The smith and his wife slept in one of them, and the other was for the helpers.

Donovan was absorbed in overseeing the building of the workshop. With two large forges—each at least twice as big as the ones he had had in England—three anvils, and two massive stone troughs for the quenching of long blades, the new workshop was large enough for the master, two or three journeymen, and three or four helpers. The Lord of Tancarville had insisted that Donovan's workshop be roomy enough to accommodate additional men to learn the trade. Even though Donovan found it hard to imagine how he could train smiths who were only moderately gifted, he had to resign himself to it and soon selected two young men.

Arnaud, the elder of the two, had worked for three years in the village with a blacksmith and had at least some basic knowledge that Donovan could build on. Arnaud would have to completely relearn some things but seemed at least to understand what a privilege it was to be allowed to work for Donovan. He obviously did everything he could to curry favor with the master. Donovan had not even asked him to take the test of sorting the bloom iron pieces, however, and that displeased Ellen very much. Arnaud was a decent fellow with hazel-colored eyes and arched eyebrows. He was quite aware of the impression he made on the fair sex and loved to talk about it, something Ellen didn't appreciate too much.

Vincent was a bit younger than Arnaud and was meant to be trained as a blacksmith's helper in order to relieve Art of some of his work. He was as strong as an ox and had deep-set eyes and a nose that was much too wide. He was full of admiration for Arnaud and followed him around like a little puppy with an almost childlike devotion.

Arnaud despised him but graciously allowed him to worship him nonetheless.

Ellen didn't trust Arnaud and avoided contact with him outside the forge. In any case, the presence of the two helpers had the advantage that now Donovan could give additional time to Ellen.

The more she learned about the smith and his work, the more she appreciated the master. She had long ago forgiven the gruff way he had treated her at first and was greatly impressed with what he could do with iron. Whereas most blacksmiths pounded it with long and heavy blows into the desired shape, Donovan seemed to be giving it light, almost tender love pats like the ones mothers sometimes give their children to make them laugh. Ellen was intrigued by the way he worked and was convinced that iron could be perfectly wrought only in this very special way and with a deep understanding of the material.

Although Ellen loved every moment in the forge, she especially enjoyed Sundays when they all went to church. After the mass they stood around conversing with the other Anglo-Saxon tradesmen. When the weather was good, they often sat down in the grass and ate together. Ellen would then be seated with Rose, and the two chatted and laughed, but Ellen always needed to be on guard not to be exposed as a girl.

Since they had left Orford, the two sensitive little buds on her chest had turned into chubby protuberances. She leaned forward with her shoulders to hide it but often had the feeling that everyone was looking at her. One Sunday when she was alone in her room, she pulled her shirt down tightly and could see how her breasts bulged out. "Somehow I have to do something about it," she mumbled to herself, frowning.

Suddenly she heard a commotion out in the stairwell, and Art came rushing into the room. Ellen turned around quickly and pretended to be making her bed. She breathed a big sigh of relief when Art dropped onto the bed without noticing anything and immediately fell asleep. As always when he had had too much cider to drink, he snored loudly. Ellen lay down, too, but she tossed and turned restlessly and found it hard to get to sleep.

In the middle of the night she awakened with a start. She had been dreaming, and in her dream she had enormous breasts that she carried in front of her like trophies. She looked around. It was still dark except for the moonlight falling through the cracks in the little wooden shutters. After making sure that Art was still asleep, she sat up in bed, pulled her shirt over her head, and felt her breasts. Of course they weren't as large as in the dream. Then she drew her shoulders back and passed her hand back and forth over her chest, almost proudly. But then a wave of despair came over her again—she wouldn't be able to conceal her womanly shape much longer. What could she do? Just recently she had bought a large piece of linen cloth to make padding for her monthly bleeding, but she hadn't started doing that yet. Maybe she could tie a piece of it around her breasts like a bandage. She pulled the cloth out from under her straw mattress and unfolded it. Then she measured a strip over two feet wide and ripped it off lengthwise. She was startled when Art began making loud snoring sounds and cursed herself for not having kept her shirt on. She took the strip of cloth and wrapped it as tightly as possible around her chest. Then she raised her right arm as if she were going to strike something with a hammer, lowered it again, and shook her head. It would be impossible to work like that. She loosened the cloth just enough so that she could raise her arm and still get enough air to breathe. That's how she would have to do it.

The next morning she wrapped up her chest again. At first her movements were stiff, but in the course of the day she began to feel comfortable with it. In the afternoon, however, she noticed that the cloth had slipped down and was on her hips. She mumbled a few words of apology and hurried out of the smithy.

In the following days she practiced wrapping the cloth around her midsection so it could not slip down, and finally succeeded, and she never again dreamed of the giant breasts.

Arnaud sneered and complained that Alan was worse than a girl with his constant running to the latrine, and she feared he might already suspect something.

She cursed and spat more frequently now and during her unclean days scratched her crotch as men often do, checking the cloth in her braies. Nevertheless, she was in constant fear of being found out.

—

With November came foggy days. At times the heavy, wet blanket hung over Tancarville from morning to night, melancholy and impenetrable. Sometimes it seemed as if the fog wanted to lift, bringing with it a hope for brighter, friendlier days; but then once again it would rise from the Seine, reaching out with its cold, clammy fingers to clutch the hearts of men. On other days, the fog in the morning seemed as heavy as lead but dissipated before noon like a silken cloth raised up into the heavens by a gentle wind. On such a day, Ellen returned to the castle for the first time in weeks.

Directly behind the open door a boy stood on a tree stump that was not even wide enough to accommodate both feet at the same time. He was tall and strong, perhaps two or three years older than she was, and stood at attention, without moving, looking straight ahead. His hands were folded behind his back, and in them he was holding a little bag full of sand. Ellen paid no further heed to him. Presumably he had been standing there like that since midnight and was almost done. Ellen knew from overhearing conversations between the squires that this was only one of the many tests every page had to take before he could become a squire. When his turn came, he would be wakened rudely and without warning in the middle of the night and ordered to stand on the tree stump. Dead tired, suffering from the cold and dampness and with the weight of the sandbag on their backs, most of them had a hard time making it to the pealing of the first bell at noon. Some gave up sooner and were denounced and disgraced. As for the others—those who held out until noon—their arms trembled from the exertion and their legs were numb and paralyzed as well. The worst of it was the painful pressure on their bladder. Some wet themselves and got so cold they had to step down. Others broke out in tears before jumping down and running behind the nearest shed to relieve themselves, accompanied by the malicious laughter of the onlookers.

When Ellen walked past the boy again in the afternoon, she was astonished to find him still standing on the tree stump. His tousled brown hair hung down his forehead to eyes that were so blue they seemed to be a reflection of the sky above. Only now did she notice how proud he appeared. His gaze was clear, and his arms, still holding the sandbag behind his back, did not tremble even a bit. He stood there calmly, gazing with a straight face into the distance.

Pages and squires had gathered around him to see when he would finally give up.

"William is damned stubborn—he intends to hold out until sundown," said one thickset, dark-haired squire admiringly. "Just the same, I bet he doesn't make it. After all, it's November and the nights are cold. But when I see him standing there like that," he said with a smile and rubbing his index finger and thumb together, "I probably won't get my money anytime soon."

"Aw, he's just a show-off anyway," another boy said haughtily.

"You be quiet, you're just jealous," the first one replied glibly. "I can remember how you didn't even make it to the tolling of the noon bell!"

"Gosh, he must have a bladder as big as a cow's udder," said a young, red-cheeked squire whose own test had taken place not so long ago.

The others nodded and laughed with relief because they didn't have to stand up there.

Ellen was thinking about the point of such a test and what could lead the young page to hold out for so long—he had passed the test and no one could have criticized him if he got down now. What on earth drove him to go on?

"When William has decided to do something, then he will do it, come what may. If he said he would stay there until sunset, then that's exactly what he'll do," said one of the young pages to the others. He seemed to have chosen William, who was a few years older than himself, as his own personal hero.

Ellen shook her head. *Such heroic deeds are just wastes of time and energy*, she thought as she headed off to her meeting—and something she couldn't possibly appreciate.

Rose was waiting impatiently for her at the agreed spot. "Here you are finally! Just look at the shadows under your eyes. Did you have more bad dreams?" Rose certainly didn't waste any time getting right to the heart of things.

"Yes, I dreamed, but bad dreams? No."

Rose raised her eyebrows and looked at her curiously. "Then you dreamed of a lover! It's no wonder you look like you haven't had any sleep," she added with a mischievous wink.

"A lover? What nonsense. In my dream I was working," Ellen replied gruffly.

"Well, excuse me!" said Rose, looking off to the side so Ellen didn't notice she was rolling her eyes.

"For several nights now I have had the same dream," Ellen began. "Sometimes I'm so happy I don't even want to wake up. In my dream I'm a famous blade smith! Even Donovan is proud of me because knights come from far away to buy my swords. And then trumpets sound! It's the king! And he's coming to order a sword from me! And just at that moment, when I am happiest, I wake up. For a moment I want to believe everything is true, just as in my dream, but then I begin to realize who I am, stand up, and secretly put the wrap around my chest."

Rose didn't know how to console her friend. "You can't always pretend to be a man—sooner or later you'll have to stop." She patted Ellen's cheek in an almost maternal way. "Wait, I have an idea!" Her face brightened. "As a woman you can't be a smith, is that right?"

"I'm afraid so."

"Well then, you can just marry a smith. You can work with him as his wife!" Rose looked at her friend expectantly, but Ellen just shook her head.

"Don't you think I've thought of that? But it's not the solution. I want to be a smith in my own workshop and make my own decisions, not just be a smith's assistant. If I wanted to do that, I wouldn't have to slave away working for Donovan. I've long ago mastered everything a simple assistant needs to know. Do you think a man would permit his wife to be something better than he is?"

Rose shook her head. "I don't think so."

"But you see, that's just what I want—to be better than the others. I know I can become a great smith someday, I can feel it!" Ellen sounded determined and a bit defiant.

“I’ll not make it so hard on myself. I’ll marry a miller, and from his flour I’ll make the best cakes and pastries.” Rose laughed, shaking her head from side to side, and pulled Ellen away with her. “Come on, we’ll go to the drill grounds, then you’ll feel better.”

“Since when have you been interested in war games?” said Ellen, incredulous.

“Not in war games, but in squires!” Rose laughed and blushed a little.

“It will be dark soon, and then they’ll stop because they can’t see well enough. And neither can you!” Ellen joked, already in a better mood.

On their way to the drill grounds they passed through the castle gate once more.

“He’s still there,” Ellen whispered admiringly when she saw how William was still standing proudly on the block of wood.

“That’s not my taste, too rough. I prefer the elegant boys, like that one over there.” Rose pointed to a handsome lad who was about her age, and blushed.

“I think his name is Thibault,” Ellen said in a conspiratorial whisper.

“I’ll remember the name,” Rose said, smiling.

Tancarville, Summer of 1163

It was too cool for that time of year. The sky had been grey for days, and it was drizzling constantly. The dreary, sunless month of June made Ellen depressed, and on top of that Rose was busy with work because company was expected at the castle. Ellen was bored, and she wandered wearily down to the drill grounds, but since it was Sunday the squires were not there. As she turned around and was about to go back to the forge, she overheard the conversation of two squires walking by. One of the sword masters was looking for a farm boy who would serve as an opponent and do battle with them using a long stick. The squires laughed and joked at how they would take great pleasure in beating the stuffing out of such a farm kid. Ellen wasn't listening anymore, but ran off. She had been working for Donovan for over a year now and realized that he was not unreasonable. He would have to let her try! Ellen had never fought with a stick, and it wasn't so much a matter of wanting to fight or of the penny that would be paid for doing it. She just wanted to gain access to the drill field in order to observe sword-fighting technique from close up. Secretly she hoped that if she could show her skill she would be allowed to learn sword fighting with the squires. This would certainly enable her to produce better weapons later on.

Ellen pleaded with Donovan and assured him it was completely safe to compete against the squires because the boys practiced only with wooden swords. The smith did not seem especially enthused at her idea and only reluctantly gave his permission. The very next day Ellen went to the drill grounds.

The training instructor for Sir Ansgar's squires was named Ours, that is, *bear* in French. Ellen wondered whether his parents had given him the name because they knew how strong he would become or whether Ours became strong in order to live up to his name. It did not even occur to her that it might be just a nickname. Ours was big and strong like all sword masters, but he seemed a bit clumsier, and it was for that reason perhaps that he was easily underestimated. Ours was sly, cruel, and contrary to all expectations could be amazingly fast. He enjoyed driving the young squires until they were totally exhausted, and he reveled in their fear of him. He was a cold and calculating soldier and an astonishingly good tactician. Since the squires were deathly afraid of him, they listened carefully and did everything they could to please him. In this way they made quick progress. Ellen, too, was afraid of Ours: after all, this was her first time fighting with the squires, and she had no experience at all with the stick.

"You're poking that thing around as if you were trying to herd pigs. You've got to keep an eye out all around you," Ours fumed, attacking her from the side. His sword was not made of wood, and with a few blows he hacked her stick into little pieces.

The squires enjoyed it immensely because this time they were not the targets of his attacks.

"This isn't a ladies' club. We're not here to do our embroidery!" Ours thundered.

Ellen winced. Had she betrayed herself? For a moment, she was seized with panic.

Ours tore the rest of the stick from her hand so violently she started to tremble. "You have to try harder and stop standing around dreaming, or give it up. For a penny I can also find a better fellow."

Ellen put on her fiercest face. "Yes, sire, I'll try harder," she replied confidently.

Ours ordered the boys, one after the other, to do battle with Ellen, and that was too much for her. Tears of anger and pain welled up in her eyes as she fell to the ground again. Her last opponent was the only one to politely reach out to her and help her up at the end. It was Thibault, the boy Rose liked so much. He had brown eyes and golden freckles, and his sand-colored hair was cut off above the ears in the Norman fashion. He looked at her in a kindly way and must have noticed the telltale gleam of tears in her eyes, because he whispered, "Ours made us all cry. Chin up! Don't give him the pleasure of seeing you break down."

Ellen nodded gratefully and tried hard to control herself, but she couldn't help blinking. A tear rolled down her cheek, and she quickly wiped it off on her sleeve so no one would see it.

After she had gotten up, Thibault let go of her hand and looked at her, somewhat annoyed. Then he turned and left.

When on the next day Ellen was beaten again, Thibault's voice could be clearly heard over the taunts of the others.

"Why are you laughing at me even louder than the rest? I thought we could be friends," she whispered as again she faced him as an opponent.

"Friends?" Thibault spat the words out like a rotten cherry. "We can't be friends. You don't belong here. It would be best for you to leave." He started beating her with his wooden sword even before they were separated at the prescribed distance. That was a violation of the rules, of course, and Ours should have called his pupil to order, but he didn't. Thibault thrashed at her so furiously that she had to step back, and fell. Thibault pounced, and their faces came close together. His eyes were wide open and his pupils huge and black. Then he jumped away and ran off, leaving her lying in the dirt. Ellen got up, gave Ours a furious glance for not disciplining Thibault, and left the drill field without a word.

—

Thibault, too, stomped away angrily, marching with great strides through the gate and across the adjacent hayfield. The sky was filled with dark grey clouds, and the air was hot and heavy. Surely a thunderstorm was brewing. Thibault's pace slackened considerably—he started wandering about aimlessly to and fro, but finally took a seat on a tree stump. His heart was still pounding, and his feelings alternated between fury and fear. There was something remarkable about this Alan. He was so…terribly attractive! Thibault couldn't believe it. His blood had been seething as he lay on top of Alan and smelled his sweet, honey-scented breath!

"How stupid! I'm not in love!" he exclaimed, and shuddered at the harsh sound of his own voice. *Alan is a boy, just like me*, he told himself, trying to calm down a bit. *But men are attracted to women, that's the way nature intended it.* Thibault could feel sweat pouring down his temples. Of course he had heard of such aberrations, but…why couldn't this simpleton have remained in England?

Thibault caught sight of two black bugs with yellow stripes running around in circles and copulating in the dust by his feet, their backsides linked together. He watched them for a while, then mercilessly crushed them with his foot.

"This is against nature, good Lord, against nature!" he cursed under his breath, and he was not thinking of the two bugs.

All this is such nonsense, he thought, greatly troubled. After all, he knew everything about girls and had already made love to two of them. They had blushed and giggled when he smiled at them and turned around to watch him when he walked by. One was a little older than he and easy to have. With the second he had to make more of an effort, but he got an even bigger thrill and feeling of power when he succeeded in robbing her of her virginity. Of course, it had meant less to him, but that was only natural—he was a man! And as such, he had the reins of power in his hand.

But why was his heart beating like this? Thibault tried to think if any girl had ever awakened such feelings in him, but aside from the physical satisfaction, he had never really cared for girls. With reluctance, but with determination, he examined himself, going over in his mind all the pages and squires in the castle to see whether thinking of any of them aroused abnormal feelings in him. He was relieved to learn that was not so. But then he thought of Alan and how he had lain on the ground, his green—oh, so green!—eyes sparkling with tears. And again his heart started pounding wildly. His mouth turned dry, and his stomach felt like it was filled with butterflies, all beating their wings. "A crying boy!" he spluttered disapprovingly. "You'll pay for this, Alan," he swore, clenching his fists. "I'll fight you, humiliate, and harass you until I drive you away!"

From that day forward Thibault sneaked out of the large bedroom he shared with the other squires almost every night to thrash himself with a freshly cut willow switch in order to drive away the abnormal thoughts. Sometimes his mind dwelled on Alan's innocent smile and then he whipped himself even harder and longer. When he thought of Alan, his male organ became stiff and twitched ecstatically. Only after he had bloodied his back with the switch did he surrender to exhaustion and pain and go back to bed, but his guilty conscience concerning the lustful thoughts still plagued him. His lacerated back became a constant reminder, both terrible and titillating. Sometimes he feared his longing for Alan would drive him mad, and for that reason he hated him even more.

—

When Ellen did not show up for dinner that evening, Donovan went out to search for her. She was standing in the courtyard and with dogged determination was practicing combat with the stick. Donovan stepped closer.

“What’s wrong? Why are you so full of anger, Alan?”

She beat the ground with her stick. “One of the squires who was friendly at first is now especially mean to me. Practically overnight he became my worst enemy. He incites the others against me and fights so unfairly.” Ellen had to get hold of herself in order not to break down and cry.

“A stick is the weapon of common people. The squires compete with you so that someday as knights they will be able to defeat people like us. Think about whether you really want to do that. The better you fight against them now, the more they will learn. They are soon to be barons and knights, and you are a smith. Don’t forget that.”

Ellen shivered with happiness. Donovan had referred to her as a smith, not as a smith’s apprentice. She knew that he valued her work, but until now she had waited in vain for a word of praise. This single word, possibly spoken in error, was worth more than anything else he could have said.

“You will never be their equal, even if they need our work to win their battles, because if *we* don’t make the best swords, others will. Everyone is replaceable—everyone, including the squire who is tormenting you so much. Just forget him and steer clear of him.” Donovan took the stick out of her hand and put it down.

"Come, let's eat now. You need your strength for tomorrow. We have much work to do."

Ellen obeyed Donovan. She mulled over what he had said and followed him into the workshop after dinner.

"You're right, master, I won't let myself be humiliated again and won't let them use me. It was silly of me to think I could learn sword fighting that way."

Ellen didn't miss Thibault and his friends. The only one she truly admired, though she had never spoken a word to him, was William. At his test the past year he actually remained standing on the tree stump until sunset, something that didn't make him especially popular with the other squires. Moreover, most of them envied him for being an excellent swordsman, determined, concentrated, and always fair.

When Ellen arrived at the drill grounds to tell Sir Ansgar that she did not intend to fight anymore, William was at that moment reprimanding Thibault for having behaved dishonorably toward another boy. Ours didn't stop him, and since William was older, Thibault had to take it, though with great reluctance.

Serves him right, Ellen thought, gloating, and walked over to Ours.

"Well, did you hear that? The smith is afraid of us and doesn't want to fight anymore!" Thibault jeered, his eyes flashing, and the squires around him hooted noisily.

Ellen ignored him and left the drill grounds, holding her head high. Was she imagining it, or did William nod briefly at her?

—

Only one day later, Thibault met Rose. Her beautiful long black hair shimmered in the sunshine like a raven's feathers. He had seen her a few times before together with Alan, but today she was alone. Certainly she had the day off, for it was Sunday, the Lord's day. What a stroke of fate that was! Alan seemed to have had an eye on her for some time now, and perhaps they were even a couple. At the thought of that, Thibault felt a twinge of jealousy. Wouldn't it be sweet revenge if he could take the girl from him? Thibault's hunting instincts were aroused. He greeted the English girl politely and smiled engagingly. Rose blushed, curtsied shyly, and smiled in return. Thibault felt jubilant. Judging from the way she looked at him, he would have an easy time with her.

"I'll be taking a little walk in the forest. Would you like to come along?" He proffered his arm gallantly as if she were a young lady from a good family.

Rose blushed again, nodded, then placing her hand on his forearm walked proudly along beside him. She gazed into his face eagerly, her eyes sparkling.

Thibault had regular features, a fine straight nose, and was smoothly shaven.

He enjoyed her admiring gaze and was pleased to see how she turned away in embarrassment when he looked at her. The path down from the castle was stony and steep, and with her wooden shoes Rose stumbled. Thibault grabbed her around the waist and held her firmly in his arms. "Now you can't slip," he told her and pulled her even closer to him.

They sat down in the parched grass of a meadow. Thibault watched her for a while out of the corner of his eye as she picked the last wildflowers of the summer. She kept looking at him wonderingly with her large, doe-like eyes.

That rotten little Englishman has good taste, Thibault thought bitterly, but deep down he was glad Rose was not an ugly girl. His revenge on Alan would be much sweeter with this delightful creature. "You're beautiful, do you know that?"

Thibault took a blade of grass and stroked her neck.

Rose giggled and lay down in the grass.

"I don't even know your name yet!"

"Rose," she whispered with a trembling voice.

"Rose! That suits you perfectly." Thibault looked deep into her eyes, then bent over and kissed her tenderly on the neck just at the place where he could see the pounding of her heart. Rose closed her eyes. She was trembling all over, and her eyelids started to flutter. Thibault passed his finger over her forehead, down along her delightful, heavenly nose, and then around her lips. She opened her mouth, and he slipped the tip of his finger inside, then down her chin and neck and warily to her breast. She was breathing hard, and Thibault was more aroused than he had ever been. All his lust was focused on this girl. Gently he stroked her firm breasts that stood out clearly from under her linen dress. His hand moved farther down below her waist, and she groaned softly as he touched her there. She didn't stop him, so he ran his hand down her legs to her ankles and then under her skirt and gently up her legs. He stroked the inside of her thigh until he was certain she wanted nothing more than for him to continue. He kissed her tenderly and impetuously at the same time, plunging his hungry tongue into her mouth. His hand moved farther down to her lap, and he could feel that it was wet, wonderfully wet. His lust grew even greater. Was that not proof enough that his abnormal feeling were just an error? When he lay down on her, he wanted only Rose. Violently and almost desperately and brutally he penetrated her.

As they lay there exhausted, side by side, Rose gazed at him earnestly. "I want you, Thibault. I want you again and again."

Her openness surprised him but flattered him as well. Thibault was content with himself. Hadn't he just proven the stuff he was made of? Rose was the best medicine for his unchaste feelings for Alan.

"We'll meet again often, little Rose, I promise," he said tenderly.

After they had separated, Thibault went directly to his comrades, proud and full of confidence, and boasted of his conquest. From this time on he met frequently with the beautiful English girl. He needed her as an antidote to his feelings for Alan. Her body, which evoked such passion in him, also gave him the comforting feeling that everything was in order. Ever since he had met her, he rarely whipped himself anymore. Only when he saw Alan, whose eyes seemed to gaze into his innermost being, did he feel weak again. When he was with Rose he felt invincible. Sometimes he almost believed he loved her. In any case, he desired her even if she did not stir his soul—only Alan was able to do that. Thibault hated this unworthy feeling of helplessness, and he hated Alan for it. He would stop at nothing to prove his strength. His desire for revenge for his suffering dominated his feelings more and more. At night he was tormented by nightmares in which Rose and Alan had sex. He thrashed around in bed and was consumed by jealousy. To see Rose with someone else made his whole body tingle—after all, he could have her whenever he wanted. But to see Alan in someone's arms other than his own was hell.

March 1164

Only a few days after Ellen had given up stick fighting in the previous year, Donovan had come to her and given her a sword. He wouldn't be able to sell it, as the blade had cracked in the hardening process. Donovan had finished the sword just the same, but the thought of his master and his master's constant admonition to remain humble had kept him from selling it. That was fortunate, because it could have cost him his reputation and perhaps even his life. Ever since, he had kept the sword as a warning against excessive vanity.

"I'll lend it to you. Watch the squires and notice everything they do, then go secretly into the forest and practice. Even if the sword is worthless for real combat because the blade is brittle and could break if too much stress is put on it," he told Ellen, "it is nevertheless well balanced and has the proper weight. I wish I'd had such an opportunity in the past."

A small clearing well hidden in the forest became her drill ground. The trees here stood close together so that Ellen couldn't be seen from a distance, and the danger of being discovered was slight. Before winter came she had practiced here regularly, but after the first snow it became too dangerous, as her tracks were visible.

Since the winter, the squires had learned a new technique of attack that Ellen couldn't help thinking about. She squinted in the bright sunshine of March and decided to begin practicing again. To prevent the sword from rusting, she had polished it and rubbed it regularly with oil. Now she took it out of the trunk where Donovan kept it and hurried off to the forest.

She took her place, as the squires did, bowed to two imaginary opponents, and prepared to attack. She was completely absorbed in the mock battle when she heard a snapping sound in the brush. She turned around, startled.

William stepped slowly out of the shadow of the trees.

Ellen was breaking enough rules and laws to incur the ire of a nobleman and feared the worst. Numb with fright, she wasn't able to speak a word.

"Alan." William nodded a short greeting and then walked behind her and took the hand in which she was holding the sword. "Don't turn your wrist so much, hold your arm a bit higher, and lower your shoulder. Now try the attack once more." He stepped back a pace and waited.

Ellen's stomach contracted. Did he mean to have his fun with her before he hauled her off to the castle to have her punished? She struggled against the anger that was growing inside her and did what he said.

William examined her stance and movements but didn't say a word about the sword or the rules she was violating. Every time he came over and stood close to her in order to correct her, she felt a tingling in her stomach.

"You didn't take part in the training very long on the drill field," William asserted.

"I had no interest, and no more time either."

"That doesn't surprise me. It's no fun with men like Thibault."

"He hates me, and I have no idea why. At first he was very nice, and then..." Ellen bit her tongue because William was not a friend of hers. She thought she had better be careful who she confided in.

"He has lots to learn if ever he wants to be a nobleman like his father," William said disdainfully.

"Do you know his father?" she asked curiously.

“I know his reputation, and it’s much better than Thibault deserves.”

“I can understand that he sent his son away because he is impossible,” said Ellen. “But how about you? Why didn’t you stay and learn from your father? What did you all do that made your families send you away to learn so far from home?”

William nearly choked with laughter. “What did we do? That’s the funniest thing I’ve ever heard. Are you really that dumb, or are you just pretending?”

Ellen looked at William, seething. “What’s so dumb about that?” she sputtered. “A farmer teachers his son how to work the fields and care for the livestock. A shoemaker, tailor, smith, or any sort of tradesman teaches his son what he knows so the son can take over the business someday. Why shouldn’t a knight teach his own son what courage and honor are?”

William stopped laughing and looked at Ellen earnestly. “Basically, you are right—to be honest, I have never thought about it before. With pages and squires it’s just different. My older brothers left home long before I did, and then it was my turn.” William paused.

Ellen, too, turned silent and scuffed her heels back and forth on the damp forest floor.

“I am an Englishman just as you are.” William suddenly started speaking in English. “Did you know that?”

Ellen shook her head without answering.

“I grew up in Marlborough Castle. My father lost it and about a year later sent me here. I can hardly remember him anymore, for I rarely saw him. Only the faces of my mother and my nurse are burned into my memory. Were you ever in Oxford? That’s not far from Marlborough.”

No, she had never heard of Oxford even though it sounded so much like Orford.

"Where do you come from?" William asked in a friendly voice.

"East Anglia," Ellen answered, trying to stifle the trembling in her voice.

William nodded knowingly. "You were lucky you could come here with your father."

"Do you mean Donovan, the smith? He's not my father."

William looked at her in amazement.

"But you just told me that you learn from your fathers."

"It didn't work out that way for me," she answered curtly.

"Did you get into trouble?" He grinned and shook his finger at her in jest.

Ellen ignored the question.

William sat down on a rock. "My forefathers were Normans, you know, but I am an Englishman and will always remain one. Do you ever dream of going back?"

"No, if I ever want to return, I'll just do it. For now, I'm happy here." Ellen smiled. She was a little less tense, as he hadn't said a word about her sword. "I must go home now," she said, noticing that the sun was already on the horizon in the west, but she forgot to disguise her voice. Fortunately, William didn't seem to notice.

"If you like, we can practice here again next Sunday," he suggested, "if only I don't have to go away with the soldiers!" The way he spoke it almost sounded as if it were normal for a squire to make a date with a young smith boy for drill practice.

Ellen simply nodded, fearing that the next time her voice trembled it wouldn't sound like that of a young man whose voice was breaking.

"I'll take another way back," William said. "It's best we aren't seen together."

Ellen raised her hand to wave, and left. *Just don't look around,* she told herself, *or he'll figure out right away that you're a girl.* She didn't look back once during the entire walk home to the smithy.

—

The very next day she told Rose about the meeting with William. "I was never so afraid! I can't imagine what would happen if he reported me..." Ellen spoke so fast that Rose immediately understood her predicament.

"Not everyone has such a high opinion of him as you do. They call him Gasteviande—Glutton. And they say when he isn't eating, he's sleeping."

"They're just jealous! If you had ever seen him fight..." Ellen gushed.

"That wouldn't have done any good because I can't tell how well anyone fights. You should hurry up and learn some more curses and dumb jokes or he'll notice for sure the next time that you are a girl and have fallen in love with him!"

"Rose!" Ellen looked at her in dismay. "What are you saying?"

"I see what I see. If you blush as much when you're with him as you do now in talking about him..." Rose clicked her tongue.

"Oh, you old shrew!" Ellen cried out, rushing at her in feigned anger and tugging gently at her hair.

"Enough, enough, my child," Rose said somewhat patronizingly, trying to calm her down.

Ellen was annoyed at her behavior and couldn't help noticing how much Rose had changed recently. Ellen had suspected for some time that Rose had a boyfriend, and it hurt her that Rose hadn't told her anything about it.

For the rest of the week Ellen was distracted, and her work suffered for it. She made the kinds of errors she never had before.

Donovan was exasperated when she had another accident on Saturday. "If you don't care for this work anymore, you might want to look around for something else!" he shouted.

"Everything always has to be done your way," she replied defiantly. "Why can't I ever try anything new?" Ellen knew how foolish it was to criticize his stubbornness especially at that moment. Her accident had nothing to do with it. Her attack on him was just stupid and impertinent, and it offended Donovan much more than she suspected.

"Get out of here, get out of my workshop!" he yelled.

Ellen left the hammer on the anvil, rushed out of the workshop, and slammed the door behind her. She marched into the house, climbed the stairs two at a time, and lay down on her bed. The room was so small that her mattress and Art's were only a few feet apart. His snoring never disturbed her, but she was disgusted with whatever else he was doing in the dark. At first she had no idea what it was, but then she saw how he rubbed his male organ until he was relieved and collected the semen in a dirty rag. The fact that he almost never washed it was especially disgusting to her. That day, however, Art was still in the forge with Donovan, and she was alone in the room. She wrapped herself up in her wool blanket and, thinking of William, fell asleep.

—

It was already light when she awoke the next morning. For once Art had gotten up before she did, and neither Glenna nor Donovan were in the house. Ellen took a piece of bread and drank a few sips of cider. The sweet, sparkling drink was consumed everywhere in Normandy and at all times of day. Beer was less common. Sometimes on holidays Glenna would make ale, and then the English tradesmen would come over and drink with them until everyone was in a jolly mood. Ellen was happy she hadn't seen the master that morning and started out on her way to church.

She stood far back in the crowd, and all she could think of during the mass was William. Would he really show up at the clearing? Why didn't he report her? When she thought of him she felt a tingling through her whole body as if cider instead of blood were flowing through her veins. Suddenly she felt someone staring at her and turned around to look.

Glenna was standing in front off to one side. Her look was both reproachful and questioning. Donovan must have told her about Ellen's insolent behavior.

Of course she had been wrong, it was her mistake, but she couldn't bring herself to lower her eyes. It was the wrong moment to complain, but she still felt she had done the right thing. She straightened her shoulders, but when she noticed the sad expression in Glenna's eyes, she turned her head away. *If I really were a man, then*...Ellen didn't think it through to the end. She looked at Glenna again, but now her head was bowed in prayer. Ellen imagined how disappointed Glenna must be in her and suddenly felt small and vulnerable. Donovan could simply throw her out, and William could betray her at any time. Thibault hated her, and Ours would have gladly thrown her to the dogs. Recently, even Rose didn't seem to care too much for her company.

Ellen wondered why she had looked forward so much to Sunday. Why had her work in the forge, once the most important thing in the world to her, suddenly become only of secondary importance in recent days? Maybe it would be better for her not to go to the forest, but if William was really waiting for her there, wouldn't it look as if she were a coward? *I'll go*, she decided, even though she was quite certain he wouldn't come. Right after church she fetched the sword from the workshop, being careful to avoid Donovan or Glenna, and ran into the forest.

When she got to the clearing she saw that William was already waiting. Her heart pounded, and she had butterflies in her stomach.

"Here," he said, "I brought two wooden swords along for us. There are so many in the armory that no one will notice if one is missing. In any case, I'll bring them back."

Ellen stared wide-eyed at William and nodded. *There's no understanding men*, she thought.

"May I have your sword for a moment?" he asked politely, and Ellen handed it to him. It was wrapped in a cloth, which he carefully unwound.

"It didn't survive the quenching. The blade is too brittle for a real battle," she explained.

William looked at it and frowned. "It looks perfectly all right to me."

"To harden the blade, you heat it and then chill it in water. That's a very difficult step, and sometimes a blade becomes brittle in the process and is unusable. But you have to quench the blade, and no matter how good the smith is, sooner or later something like that will happen. I'll use this sword only for practice and can never use it in a real fight. That would be much too dangerous, do you see?"

"Hm, I think so."

They practiced enthusiastically all morning, and Ellen's fear of William gave way to genuine esteem for his abilities and simple way of teaching her the essentials.

"Why are you doing this, anyway? You'll never be allowed to carry a sword," he said, out of breath when they stopped for a break.

"Do you think a shoemaker who always runs around barefoot can make good shoes?"

Ellen's answer surprised William, and he broke out laughing. "You are no doubt right. And considering how good you are in wielding a sword, you will certainly someday be a damned good swordsmith." William patted her cordially on the shoulder.

"You may be right. That's my plan, in any case. Someday I will forge a sword for the king!" Ellen was surprised at how confidently she spoke, but she knew that was exactly what she wanted to do. And that was probably the reason she dreamed about it all the time.

"I'm impressed," said William, bowing somewhat teasingly. "But I have set my goals just as high as you have—I wish to be a knight in the king's household. It's true I am only the fourth son of the Marshal and as such have no claim to a high position, land, or money, in fact not even a chance of marrying well, but I am sure the Lord will show me the right way and someday I will receive what I dream of: fame, honor, and the favor of my king!" William's eyes sparkled; then he suddenly grinned impishly. "But now let's eat. I'm dying of hunger, and that would be too bad because nothing would come of my plans."

They sat down alongside a spring they had discovered in the forest and hungrily pounced upon the food William had brought along.

—

Ellen had completely forgotten her impudent behavior toward Donovan and headed home in a cheerful mood. She only thought about it again when Glenna met her at the door with a reproachful expression. Ashamed of herself, she lowered her gaze. It was inexcusable that she hadn't gone to Donovan right after church to ask his forgiveness.

Ellen sensed that someone was looking at her and turned around. "Is something wrong?" she growled at Arnaud.

"It seems you had a problem with the old man." His mouth was twisted in a triumphant smirk. "Today for once I wouldn't want to be in your shoes."

In his first year at the smithy Arnaud had tried, first secretly and then more and more openly, to get her in trouble with the master. Only after Donovan had strongly reprimanded him and threatened to throw him out of the forge had he become a little more prudent. Now he seemed to be in a better position.

"Ah, yes, and before I forget it, the master wishes to see you in the workshop at once!" he told her, pointing over his shoulder with a broad sneer.

Ellen tried to squeeze past Arnaud and jostled him when he didn't get out of the way. Her pride melted quickly as she approached the workshop. She entered the forge with hunched shoulders and bowed head. "You wish to speak with me, master?" she asked sheepishly.

Donovan stood with his back to her and did not turn around. "I should never have taken you on as an apprentice," he said bitterly. "I knew from the start that it wouldn't work out. On the first day you showed me you wouldn't accept a subordinate role. You have no respect. Glenna wouldn't listen to me and said I absolutely had to take you. Now she knows better, too."

Ellen swallowed deeply. If she had lost Glenna's affection as well, she was really in trouble. She stared at the ground quietly as Donovan continued.

Only now did he turn around to look at her, furiously cleaning a knife blade that was already highly polished. "You always think you have to have it your own way and try things that won't work."

"But…" Ellen wanted to answer, but his furious expression deterred her.

"You won't respect the experience of an older person, and that is the most important requirement for an apprentice."

"You're wrong!" Ellen protested. There was no one she admired more than Donovan. She respected him for his knowledge and his skill even if she was not able to express those feelings in words.

"Now you are contradicting me again!" he growled at her.

"Please excuse me, I didn't mean it that way," she replied, contritely.

"I should just throw you out—after all, I never promised you anything. You know yourself that you were able to weasel your way into my forge through a misunderstanding."

Ellen looked at him, deeply disappointed. After all, she had taken the test. Donovan walked around to the other side of the anvil and looked her directly in the eye.

His gaze was so cold it made Ellen shiver.

"You're neither particularly strong nor persevering. The only thing you have is your talent," he scolded her. "You understand iron better than anyone else I know. At your age I only knew half as much as you do, and I didn't have a quarter as much intuition. You have what it takes to do something special, Alan, and that is the only reason I am not throwing you out." Donovan was so angry he had to stop and catch his breath. "If you work hard, you can be one of the best someday. And if anyone asks you then who your master was, you will have to say it was Donovan from Ipswich. And I will be proud of you." Donovan stared at her, took a few steps forward, and reached for her shirt. "This is your last chance, do you understand? Don't throw it away."

Ellen nodded, relieved.

"I don't know why you have been so distracted in the last few weeks. Glenna thinks it may be because of the English girl you are going with. I was young at one time, too, and know what love can do to us men. Therefore, this one time, I'll excuse you, but there will be no second chance."

Tancarville, 1166

Two years had passed since their big confrontation, and there were no further incidents. Ellen worked even harder and Donovan demanded even more of her, but their talk had led to a new closeness.

Glenna thought it was almost as if Donovan had a son again. She found her husband happier, and that also made her happy.

Donovan now always included Ellen in his plans when he had an order for a new sword. He discussed the design and materials with her as well as the cost and time required and left more and more important details in her hands. The confidence he placed in her relieved her of the feeling that she had to always prove herself to him and gave her more confidence in her own ability.

Although the smith often made her work longer than Arnaud and gave her the hardest jobs, which he monitored very closely, Ellen was surprised when one day he asked her to make a sword all by herself, and to begin at once.

Donovan gave her a pile of bloom iron and offered to assist her if she needed his help, though he didn't expect she would. He looked a bit more sullen than usual when he said that, but nonetheless amiable. He had prepared Ellen well for this great assignment.

She knew she could do it but nevertheless was so excited she got stomach cramps.

"Why Alan and not me?" Arnaud asked angrily. He was older and had two more years of experience than she, but Donovan figured he needed more time and put him off until later. Arnaud was too error prone to be able to make a sword on his own. He was an extremely proud young man and quite skillful but didn't have the same talent as Ellen.

"Thickheaded Norman kid," Donovan grumbled in English when he saw how offended Arnaud looked.

Ellen and Art grinned while Arnaud and Vincent just scowled vacantly. From the very start they had refused to learn even a word of English, though Donovan had urged them to do so.

"Why are you grinning like that?" Arnaud snapped at Art.

"Yes, that's just the question," Vincent said, agreeing as always with Arnaud.

Ellen refrained from any further comments. Arnaud was devious and quite able to harm her if he ever got the opportunity. He was jealous enough already, and there was no need to pour oil on the fire.

Making a sword without Donovan's help was a real challenge that Ellen was glad to take on. By now she had learned a number of fighting moves and knew exactly what was required of a weapon. A sword had to be comfortable to hold, sharp, and flexible at the same time, well balanced, and easy to use. All day she thought about the sword she was supposed to make, and the same evening she asked Donovan whom it was for. It was not a trivial question—was it for a younger man or an experienced knight, would the owner be left-handed or right-handed? She herself could work equally well with both hands. If her right arm became tired, she could change hands and swing her hammer with the other arm, and thus could often work on a piece longer than if she was using just one hand. Of course, she had tried using her left arm while practicing with William and learned there were different ways of holding the weapon, especially if the opponent was fighting with his right arm because then both swords would be on the same side.

"Just make a sword, that's all," Donovan told her gruffly.

Ellen complied, disappointed. It was much harder to make a really good sword for a stranger than for a person you knew. Some knights preferred a special shape for the pommel, and others didn't care. In addition, the length of the blade should ideally take into consideration the size of the owner. Ellen considered many options until she really didn't know what she wanted anymore. Her ideas applied to hundreds of types of swords, and so it was all the harder to decide on any specific design. She went into the forest—the same one where she had practiced with William—to think it over. It was more than two years ago that she had first met him there and had fallen in love with him. Rose was still the only person who knew Ellen's secret and what she suffered. William had no idea: to him she was just his friend Alan, the young smith. They still met on Sundays to practice when he was in Tancarville, but as he was now a squire he often had to be away with his master for weeks. This time, too, he had been gone for a long time. Ellen could hardly wait to see him again—she wanted so much to tell him about the sword and get his advice. William was so different from the farm boys or the tradesmen, no doubt because he had been trained as a knight. But it wasn't just that. He was the stubbornest person Ellen had ever met. No one could force him to do anything or keep him from carrying out his plans. In fact, his master had almost sent him back to his father because he had obstinately refused to learn to read and write. But William was firmly convinced that using a pen would soften and weaken his fighting hand. Sometimes Ellen had to laugh at his stubbornness, but on the other hand, it was just this quality that made him predictable.

Rose had very little time for Ellen anymore, and the lonely Sundays without William and his stories of knightly life, as Ellen called them, were terribly monotonous. William always had stories to tell. His excellent memory for details made them so vivid that Ellen often had the impression of being there in person. Spellbound, she hung on his every word, and in the course of time the traditions and values so important to pages, squires, and knights became more comprehensible to her and a little more meaningful and less brutal than they had seemed to be before. The more she learned about the life William led, however, the clearer it became to her that being a nobleman and thinking and acting like a knight was something you had to be born into. Ellen sat down at the side of the little brook where they had always taken a rest and imagined William sitting alongside her. She began to talk, explaining her uncertainties to him and why she couldn't decide on one design or the other. She sketched swords in the sand and talked and talked, completely forgetting she was all alone.

"*You think too much about it. Just make a sword like the one you would want to have*," she could almost hear William saying.

"That's it!" she cried out, and jumped up. Of course! She just had to think of what was most important to her in a sword. It needed a proper balance, that is, the size and weight of the pommel relative to the length of the blade was decisive because that determined the center of gravity of the finished sword. If this was done correctly, the sword would sit firmly in the hand and be easy to wield. In addition the sword had to be sharp, very sharp, and for this the hardening was critical. The iron had to be free of impurities and not become brittle during the quenching process. Since the customer for the sword was not known, it seemed easiest for Ellen just to make it for someone her own size. And since she was rather tall for a woman, there would be enough prospective customers among the knights. On the way back she thought through all the other details and could envision the sword in her mind.

The polishing, too, was extremely important for the quality of the blade. Only rarely did Donovan have this work done by a sword sweeper or sword polisher. Most of them were quite skilled and experienced in their trade, quite capable of polishing used swords, but according to Donovan only the smith who had fashioned the blade was really able to polish it to perfection. For this reason, Ellen had also become an expert in polishing, too. She loved doing it because it helped to perfect the beauty and sharpness of a blade. It was the crowning finish of a well-made sword. The form and size of the cross guard, on the other hand, were only of secondary importance as they were more a matter of taste and aesthetics. Ellen decided to fashion a short, broad cross guard. Then, of course, a sword required a scabbard fitted exactly to the blade. This work was done by a sheather or scabbard maker who could only begin when the weapon was finished. The grip, a wooden shaft for the tang, was wrapped with twisted or braided wire, leather, or cord, and was done by another specialist. Ellen would have to discuss her ideas for decorations on the blade and perhaps also on the pommel with a silversmith or goldsmith. She knew it was advisable to meet soon with all the tradesmen involved and let them know when their help would be needed in order to deliver her work on time. Donovan had given her four months, but she couldn't work on her sword all day, as there was other work in the forge to do.

Ellen fashioned the sword step by step just as the master had taught her. When she had to prepare the cutting edge of the blade, she considered asking Donovan for advice but decided not to.

To ask Art for his opinion would have been a waste of time. He worked carefully but was not able to develop his own ideas or make suggestions on improvements to a process.

So Ellen relied on her own abilities and finally completed it by herself. She had the pommel gilded after discussing the cost with Donovan. The goldsmith decorated the finished blade, with silver wire inlays forming the words IN NOMINE DOMINI—in the name of the Lord—the saying preceded and followed by a little cross. Ellen could neither read nor write, though unlike William she had no objection to learning it. It was just that she hadn't had the opportunity, and so she had to rely on the goldsmith's advice for the choice of words. He couldn't read, either, but had templates with a number of sayings that a scholar had prepared for him. The goldsmith had learned their meanings by heart and then could recommend them to his customers. He well knew which sayings were in demand by the knights. When after almost exactly four months the grip and the wrapping as well as the sword belt together with the scabbard were finished, Ellen would be ready to hand over the completed sword.

Ellen trembled inwardly with pride because the sword had turned out so well. She had tested it more than once for flexibility, sharpness, and stability. Yet she was still very nervous.

"Bad use of the fire, substandard iron, or a bad weld are not the worst enemies a smith has, but his own vanity," Donovan had warned her again and again.

She tried to be humble and patient and waited all day for the right moment to ask Donovan to look at the sword. She was so eager to hear her master's judgment that the day seemed never to end. When evening came and Donovan sent Vincent and Arnaud home, she stayed behind in the forge. "Master!" she said with a pounding heart, bowing reverently and handing him her treasure.

Donovan took the sword in both hands and tested its weight. Then he seized it by the grip and weighed it in one hand.

Ellen scrutinized his face, trying to figure out whether he was happy. Nervously she bit her lower lip.

Donovan slowly pulled the sword out of the scabbard.

Ellen held her breath.

The smith held up the grip close to his eyes and studied it closely, the tip of the sword pointing toward his right foot. He scrutinized the blade to see if it was straight. Then he shook the pommel and the grip to see if they were fixed securely. If they were loose, the sword was worthless. He passed his thumb over the riveting in the pommel and nodded slightly. Ellen's work was well done, but she scarcely dared to breathe. Donovan took a rag in order not to soil the blade with the oil in his hands and bent it into a half circle. Ellen knew that it would easily withstand the bending but was glad just the same when he released it and the blade was straight again. Finally, the master took a piece of cloth, folded it once around the blade, and pressed the blade through the cloth. It was a clean cut, and not a fiber was torn. Donovan repeated the test with the other side of the blade, and the result was the same.

Ellen breathed a scarcely audible sigh of relief. She had spent much time sharpening the blades, and nothing would be worse than a mediocre result. But for all that she felt more and more anxious—every twitch in Donovan's face seemed to suggest disappointment, and when he cleared his throat she felt sure it meant he was displeased. How could she ever have believed that Donovan would be happy with her? He had been friendlier to her recently and had acknowledged her talent, but was that any reason to think he would approve of her sword? *Surely he thinks the pommel is too gaudy and the silver inlays are inappropriate*, she thought, and suddenly doubted that they would ever be able to sell the sword. She completely forgot the high words of praise from the sheather and the goldsmith. Their opinions were meaningless in comparison to what Donovan had to say. Although it wasn't especially warm in the workshop, Ellen could feel the sweat on her brow.

As Donovan put the sword back in its scabbard, Ellen thought she noticed a slight nod. She watched in disappointment as he turned around, laid the sword down, and without saying a word walked over to the large box in which they kept seldom-used tools and a few other things. On top of this box there was a long, ordinary-looking chest that he picked up with both hands. He turned around, walked toward her, and looked her straight in the eye. "Your work is excellent," he said. "The sword is sharp and easy to hold, the blade is flexible, and the shape is well balanced. Your work is good and I am proud of you, but..." Donovan paused for a long time.

What's coming now? Ellen wondered impatiently. Couldn't he ever praise her without reservation?

"...but I expected nothing less of you," he said, and a smile darted across his face. "From now on you can call yourself a smith. The sword was your journeyman's piece." He handed her the chest.

It was so heavy that Ellen had to set it down before opening it. "Master!" she gasped in astonishment when she saw what was in it. Awestruck, she took out the new leather apron and tied it around her waist. It was exactly the right size. She could see from the symbol that was punched along one edge that the leather was from the best tanner in Tancarville. In addition to the apron there was a cap for her in the chest, which looked just like the one the master wore, and furthermore two tongs and a sledgehammer. These were the first tools she'd ever owned, if you didn't count Llewyn's hammer. Ellen had made the tongs and the sledgehammer herself but didn't know they would someday be her own.

"There's still something in the chest," Donovan said, again in his usual grumpy voice.

Only now did Ellen see that there was indeed something else at the bottom of the wooden box. It was wrapped in a dark woolen cloth and was heavy and long. It looked like a tool, only narrower. Ellen gasped in amazement when she discovered what was wrapped in the cloth. "A file! Master, you must be out of your mind!"

That was not exactly what she intended to say, but Donovan did not respond with a reprimand, but with a broad smile.

A file was an unusually expensive gift for a young smith. It must have taken a lot to bring him to part with so much money, but he seemed pleased that she appreciated it. Ellen struggled with tears, and if Donovan noticed the glint in her eyes he didn't say so. After all, a smith didn't cry, not even when deeply moved.

"You are a good lad, Alan, and I would be happy if you remained here with me."

"I thank you, master, and I'll be very happy to do so," Ellen said with a firm voice.

"We'll put the sword up for sale, and I think you will get a good price for it. You can pay me the cost of the materials and keep the rest for yourself."

Donovan must really be in a good mood to make such a generous offer, Ellen thought with surprise. How she would have loved to run to William to tell him about the sword, but he was still not back. She knew from Rose, though, that the Lord of Tancarville and his knights would be coming back soon.

In fact, William returned the very next Sunday to their meeting place in the forest. The autumn sun bathed the practice ground in a warm, friendly light.

Ellen should have noticed there was something different about William, but her joy in seeing him again and her desire to show him the sword and tell him all about it made her blind to everything else. William listened patiently.

"To make a sword all by myself…I thought I couldn't do that. There were so many things to decide on, do you understand?" Without waiting for an answer, Ellen continued. "The scariest moment was when I put the blade in the water to quench it. You can't imagine what a feeling that is. It's the moment that decides whether all those weeks of work paid off or whether it was all in vain. I thought I'd die from fear! To tell you the truth, I was listening so hard to hear whether there was even the slightest crackling sound that my ears, even my whole head ached. But all I heard was the hissing of the water. Good heavens, I was so relieved. The blade is sharp and flexible, just as it should be," she related excitedly.

"Good Lord, Alan, what a blabbermouth you are!" William interrupted her rather harshly.

Ellen was taken aback and looked at him with embarrassment. With the exception of Donovan, William was the only one with whom she could discuss swords, and she had waited so long for him to return.

"Sorry, Alan, I didn't mean it that way. Can I stop by the workshop sometime and have a look?" William hadn't yet seen the bundle lying in the grass next to Ellen.

"I brought it along," she whispered before breaking out in a wide smile and carefully unwrapping it.

"Are you crazy?" William looked around.

"I just wanted to show it to you!" she said with a shrug. After all, she had carried the other sword around with her, although that was not allowed either.

"What will you do if you get caught with it? This sword here is certainly very sharp!"

"It certainly is!" Ellen said proudly.

The gleam in William's eye when he saw the weapon made up for his strange behavior and long absence. He looked at the sword admiringly and whistled through his teeth as a sign of his approval. "If I had enough money, I'd buy it from you at once."

Ellen shrugged regretfully and carefully packed it up again. "Once you become a famous knight, I will make a magnificent sword for you that even the king will envy," she consoled him.

"Now there you go exaggerating again, you little rascal!" William laughed, grabbed her in a headlock, and roughed up her hair with his left hand.

Since she was still holding the sword in her hand, she couldn't resist without the risk of harming him. She tried to ignore the wonderful fluttering in her stomach. At this very moment she dreamed of lying in William's arms and being his wife and lover.

After he let her go she almost decided this was the time to tell him her secret, but at the last moment made up her mind not to.

"As for the sword for the famous knight, you can start with that soon. You see, I'm already a knight!" William declared proudly and waited for his words to have their effect.

"What? I thought that was supposed to be next year...Didn't you say it was your older brother's turn first?"

"Ah, the ways of the Lord..." he said, raising his arms to the heavens.

"You must tell me all about it, William!" Suddenly Ellen realized what his knighthood meant for her, and she turned serious. "I'm sorry...Sir William. You must explain that to me."

"Well, as long as it's just the two of us together, William is fine, as always." He grinned and threw a stone into the brook.

He doesn't at all look like a knight, Ellen thought wistfully. "So go ahead, tell me!" she urged him.

William nodded and shifted around on the trunk of the tree a bit until he was comfortable. "I hope you have a little time."

My whole life, Ellen almost replied, but she just nodded.

"It all started when William Talvas, Count of Ponthieu, became angered at King Henry, claiming that the king had not given him lands Talvas thought he was entitled to. For this reason he established an alliance with the Counts of Flanders and Boulogne. They attacked and occupied Eu, as a messenger informed my lord, so he summoned his troops and the very next day we set out for Neufchâtel to reinforce the garrison there. The enemy troops had to be prevented from breaking through and possibly attacking Rouen..."

"And what does that have to do with your being knighted? You told me that was the most important moment in a knight's life and was followed by a great celebration. Why didn't you tell me that you were to be knighted?" Ellen's eyes flashed in anger.

"Oh, Alan, don't be so stubborn!"

"I'm not being stubborn. I just think you could have told me that Tancarville intended to make you a knight."

"But he didn't! And if you don't let me continue my story, you'll never learn what happened. You are really the only person more stubborn than I," William grumbled.

"I'm sorry!" Ellen grimaced helplessly.

William picked up a stick and scrawled something in the damp ground. "These dots stand for Neufchâtel, Eu, Rouen, and Tancarville, and the wavy line is the Seine. Rouen, the capital of Normandy, is considered well fortified but not impregnable. The Count of Eu, Mandeville, and Tancarville agreed they absolutely had to prevent the enemy from advancing. Spies had given them precise information about their opponents, who were superior to them in number and armed to the teeth," William said. "So that I could attack the enemy with him, he conferred knighthood on me!" William waved his hands around excitedly as he spoke, jumping up to reenact the dangerous battles he had been in—how he had been surrounded and almost vanquished by the enemy. As proof of his story, he pulled up his shirt and showed Ellen the freshly healed scar on his shoulder.

She winced and gasped audibly. "That must have been painful. Does it still hurt?"

William shook his head and tried to put on a brave face. "I survived, but they butchered my horse. It was my only possession. After we returned, my lord Tancarville gave me a pair of spurs and a beautiful, heavy cloak, but he didn't replace my horse."

"You were ready to give your life for him and the king, and as thanks he didn't even give you a horse?" Ellen looked at him, dumbfounded.

"That won't happen again, believe me. The next time I'll look out for myself, and I also intend to be one of the victors in the future."

William's story had been so exciting that at least for that day Ellen had lost her appetite for any further fighting with him. Certainly his wound was still very painful to him.

"Let's not fight anymore today," Ellen suggested and lay down in the grass.

Without saying a word, William stretched out alongside her, and they both stared into the blue, late summer sky. He had given everything he had, putting his life on the line in battle expecting nothing more from it than the appreciation of his lord, and he was so bitterly disappointed. Sometimes life was so unjust, Ellen thought. Again she wondered whether she should entrust her secret to him. Would he then perhaps be better able to understand her? Once, a year ago, she had been at the point of telling him. She had thoroughly planned what she was going to say but then couldn't bring herself to do it—and it was the same this time.

They had been staring into the sky silently for quite a while when William suddenly sat up. "I saw you again recently with this English cook maid—what's her name?" William made a wide, suggestive gesture over his upper body and raised his eyebrows.

"Ah, you mean Rose," Ellen answered crossly.

A lot of servants and even a few squires had been giving Rose the eye. William was no "child of sadness," as he said, insinuating that he knew how to enjoy himself, so his allusion to Rose's shape made Ellen furiously jealous, but she of course could not let that show.

"Yes, that's who I mean. She's pretty cute. Are you getting it on with her?"

Ellen hated to hear William boast about his womanizing, but when he tried to coax a few piquant details from her nonexistent love life, she found that equally dreadful.

"That's all in the past," she lied and waved her hand dismissively, hoping he would drop the matter.

"So then, you're not the father."

William seemed happy with this conclusion, but Ellen gasped in horror. "What are you saying?"

"She's with child. Our dear friend Thibault is bragging that he…and I thought perhaps you were the one…I can really pity the poor girl if it was him!" William shook his head incredulously.

Ellen didn't know what to say. Why hadn't Rose told her anything? And why did it have to be Thibault? How could she? "Have the two been getting it on together for very long?" she asked angrily.

"It seems so. I don't know exactly, of course. I wasn't there holding the candle for them, you know," he said, mightily amused at his own joke.

"It's getting late," Ellen mumbled, even though the sun was still high up in the sky. "I have to go."

"It seems to upset you, the thing with Rose. If I had known that she meant so much to you…" William seemed to be seriously sorry.

"She doesn't, really. She's from Ipswich, just like my family—that's the only thing we have in common," Ellen answered gruffly. "And as you know, I can't stand Thibault. Rose doesn't deserve to be saddled with having his bastard child. I wonder why she ever got involved with him."

William shrugged. "Ah, who can understand women? They think differently from us men, if they even think at all. It's a waste of time." He rolled his eyes in mock despair.

"In any case, I must leave now," Ellen said. She stood up, took the bundle with the sword, said good-bye to William without looking him in the eye, and hurried out to the road.

—

On the way through the forest Ellen was thinking about Rose and Thibault and didn't hear the hoofbeats of approaching horses. With no time to hide, she stayed on the road, trying not to look too conspicuous, and carried her bundle with the sword in it as casually as possible.

As the riders approached, one of them rushed ahead and called out to her gruffly: "Hey, lad, is this the road to Tancarville? Answer me!" The young squire who had addressed her looked down haughtily from his horse.

A handsome knight with strikingly green eyes, evidently his master, came over and scolded him. "You have no reason to be so unfriendly—go back and join the others!" he snapped at his squire.

Ellen looked at the knight inquisitively, and as their eyes met it seemed to her that she knew him. Still, she couldn't remember ever meeting him before.

"What's your name, lad?"

"Alan, sire."

"That sounds like an Anglo-Saxon name to me."

"Yes, sire."

"Do you know the way to Tancarville castle?"

"Yes, sire. You just stay on this road—it isn't very far on horseback. After the next sharp turn in the road you will come out of the forest and then you can see the castle."

"Thank you."

The knight looked Ellen over from head to foot. His magnificent horse pranced about nervously. "What is that you're carrying?" he asked, pointing at her long bundle.

Ellen had the feeling that the question wasn't intended hostile way, but she was nevertheless wary. "My journeyman's piece." She made no move to unwrap it, hoping he wouldn't ask to see it.

"What is your trade?"

The friendly knight's curiosity made Ellen feel uneasy, but she replied modestly, "I am a blacksmith, sire." She hoped this answer would satisfy him.

"May I look?"

Ellen hesitated briefly and then shook her head. "Not here, please! It would be better if you came to the shop," she pleaded. "Ask for Donovan, please!"

Surprisingly, the knight gave a friendly nod. "Yes, I will do that, Alan. I'll see you soon." He gave a sign to his companions to follow him, and they rode off.

Ellen took a deep breath. One of the men kept turning around toward her, exchanging animated words with his master. Although she liked the knight at first glance, there was something about him that disturbed her.

—

The very next day the stranger came to the workshop, this time without his retinue. "A good morning to you, Master Donovan." The knight smiled amiably.

"Upon my soul, Béranger…excuse me, sire, Sir Béranger!"

The knight laughed. "Nice to see you again, Donovan. Everywhere people talk about your swords! Tancarville is mightily proud of you."

"Thank you, Sir Béranger. You were still a squire when I last saw you. How long ago was that?" Donovan asked, shaking his hand warmly.

"An eternity! It was almost twenty years ago that I was in Ipswich, and those were my best years. I was a free man then, if you know what I mean." He winked at Donovan and laughed. Then he turned to Ellen: "Good morning, Alan, I am coming to have a look at your journeyman's piece."

Donovan, astonished, looked back and forth from Ellen to Sir Béranger. "Do you know Sir Béranger? Then go and get the sword, Alan. It would suit him very well."

After Béranger de Tournai had carefully examined the sword, he nodded his approval. "That's a very nice piece—perhaps it would be something for my son. His knighting ceremony is still two or three years away, but it would certainly be an incentive for him. Perhaps you know him—his name is Thibault."

"Oh, I don't have any contact with the squires, but Alan knows most of them." Donovan gave Ellen a questioning look.

At the mention of Thibault's name, Ellen's mouth dropped and the color drained from her face. There was no way Thibault would get this sword, she would see to that. Ellen's mind raced, trying to think of what she could do or say to prevent the sale, but even before she had come up with something, Donovan suggested to the knight that he stop by at the workshop with his son.

"You are right, master. I'll come by with Thibault in the next few days so he can try it out."

"A wise decision, Sir Béranger." At that moment he caught sight of the ironmonger's wagon outside. "I hope you will excuse me…an important delivery." He bowed, and Sir Béranger nodded.

Ellen stayed behind with him in the workshop. How could this friendly nobleman be the father of that devil Thibault?

"Are you also from Ipswich?" he inquired. Ellen nodded absentmindedly, though that wasn't the case; then she corrected herself. "My mother was."

Béranger de Tournai nodded as if she had only confirmed what he had long since known. Stroking his smooth-shaven chin, he asked, "I think I know her. Isn't her name Leofrun?"

Ellen felt a burning sensation in the pit of her stomach that quickly spread to her head. "How do you know that?" she asked, surprised. No one here knew the name of her mother, not even Rose.

"She had beautiful hair, long and blond like the wheat fields of Normandy, and her eyes were as blue as the sea," the knight rhapsodized without answering her question.

The description of Leofrun seemed far too flowery to Ellen, and she didn't respond.

"She was the most beautiful maiden I ever saw. We were in love and met secretly. But one day she did not come and I never saw her again. Then I heard she had married."

Ellen was unable to understand his words and could neither speak nor move.

"When I saw you in the forest, I was still unsure, but Paul, my oldest friend, also noticed how much you look like her."

"Like my mother?" Ellen's voice cracked with scorn.

"No, Alan, you don't understand, you look like my mother!"

Ellen gasped for air, and suddenly the earth seemed to be spinning beneath her. All she could do was to shake her head violently, then run from the workshop without having any idea where she was going.

—

Aelfgiva's explanation that she was the illegitimate child of a Norman knight had caused her great pain, but it seemed less a story about her than of someone else. Never could she have imagined that she would ever meet this Norman libertine. Wasn't this an impossible coincidence? Why did they meet here? Why did she have to find him so nice that she almost wished she was his child? And why, at the same time, did he have to be the father of Thibault? She sat down on a tree stump and cried. What would happen when the truth came out? Ellen thought she would suffocate. The thought flashed through her mind that it would be best for her never to return to the blacksmith shop. But the more she turned it over in her mind, the angrier she got. The shop, Donovan, and Glenna—they were all she had. Who gave this Béranger de Tournai the right to drive her away? She didn't want to flee again. *After all*, she thought, *it's not my fault.* She would go back to the smithy, but she would never allow Thibault to possess her sword. Ellen turned back and ran right into Sir Béranger again.

"If you think I am your son, you are wrong, I can assure you of that," Ellen said, puffing out her chest. Her confidence in confronting Sir Béranger seemed to give him doubt, after all.

"What makes you so sure, Alan?" He looked at her sadly, and with disappointment.

Ellen couldn't answer at first and looked down at her feet. "Many girls in East Anglia are blond, and Leofrun is a common name. You are mistaken, sire, believe me. My mother is a respectable woman," she whispered finally, half to herself. Ever since she had known William she knew what love could do to you. Béranger was still a good-looking man; he was certainly chivalrous and had turned Leofrun's head using all the tricks of seduction. But this one time Ellen had understanding for her mother. Hadn't Béranger as a man known how impossible the situation would be for her, or was he just as dumb as his son? Ellen was still terribly angry.

"I'll come back in a few days," Béranger said calmly, and smiled.

"If you come as a customer, I welcome you," Ellen told him coolly and nodded as he left.

—

Two days later Béranger de Tournai returned to the smithy with his son, but by then Ellen's anger had vanished. Sir Béranger was certainly not a bad man, she could sense that. And somehow it felt good to know who her father was.

Tournai greeted her warmly while Thibault ignored her completely.

His father had clearly not told him anything, and Ellen was relieved about that.

"I want a sword from Master Donovan, not a journeyman's piece from Alan that's not worth anything," Thibault grumbled. Ellen breathed a sigh of relief. Thibault would obviously do everything possible to change his father's mind.

"I'll be glad to show you two other swords that Master Donovan made just recently," Ellen suggested eagerly. "If one of those pleases you..."

Thibault examined the swords without dignifying Ellen with even a glance. "I like that one," he decided quickly.

Ellen was not surprised by his choice. The sword had been commissioned by a young, arrogant baron. Shortly before he was to pick it up, he died from a minor wound that led to blood poisoning. Ellen thought the sword was far too heavy and showy, and therefore suited Thibault perfectly.

Béranger tried again to direct his son's attention to Ellen's sword: "Don't you want to try this one again?" he asked.

"No," Thibault answered coldly, and his father understood there was no point in trying to change his mind.

"Well, then I'll take it. I really like it very much," Béranger de Tournai said, looking Ellen right in the eye.

She understood how proud he was of her, and suddenly she was overcome by a feeling of embarrassment and turned her eyes down.

"And how about me, Father?" Thibault sounded annoyed.

"Yes, yes, you'll get the other one, my son."

Ellen was glad to see that the two obviously did not have a very close relationship.

"You had better speak with Master Donovan about the price. I'll go and get him," she said, and left without saying good-bye.

"I don't like Alan—he has no manners," Thibault said to his father so loudly that Ellen still heard it as she was leaving.

When the father and son had left, Donovan grinned at Ellen with satisfaction. "Just like that, the little fellow sells two swords!"

Ellen knew that Donovan didn't mean this disparagingly, it was more a term of endearment, and it was a rare occurrence when Donovan was in such an exuberant mood.

"Did he pay a good price?" Ellen was curious what her sword had fetched.

"Sir Béranger was really excited about your journeyman's piece. He tried to grill me about you, how I know you, how long you have been here with me, and so on. I asked a high price for your sword and he paid, without grumbling. He talked me down on the sword for his son though. After all, it's an ugly piece, so I'm nevertheless quite happy about it. Nasty fellow, by the way, this Thibault."

"Isn't that the truth, master!"

"But Sir Béranger is such a nice fellow, an entirely different kind of person. The boy no doubt takes after his mother." Donovan scowled.

Ellen was surprised at her master, who was so seldom talkative. He was no doubt really happy with the price he had gotten for her sword. "So is there something left for me?"

"After deducting expenses, there are ten *solidi* left for you."

Ellen opened her mouth in astonishment. That was more money than she had been able to save in all those years.

—

Two days later Béranger de Tournai returned to the smithy. "Master Donovan, I would like very much to borrow your journeyman. Could you do without him for a while?"

Donovan looked questioningly at Ellen, but she only shrugged indifferently. "As you wish, Sir Béranger. Alan, you may leave with the sire wherever he wants to go."

Ellen didn't know what to think of it, but her curiosity about her father gained the upper hand for the present. Everything would be fine as long as he didn't tell Thibault. She followed him without saying a word.

"Is your mother well?" he asked when they were alone, and suddenly Ellen lost control.

"How couldn't everything be well with her? Her engagement with the soap merchant was annulled, thanks to you, because she was expecting a child. All she dreamed of and all she ever wanted to be was the wife of a simple blacksmith. Of course! What woman would ever want to lead a carefree life as wife of a merchant or a knight? Not my mother. You got to know her and must be aware how much she likes the simple life." Ellen was not ready to forgive him so easily.

"I understand that she hated me after everything..." Sir Béranger interjected sadly.

"Hated you?" Now Ellen was really worked up. "It was me she hated, not you. I had nothing to do with your affair, and yet she made me the scapegoat. But it never took away her inclination for something higher. She went and shacked up with another knight like a cat in heat."

"How can you speak so disrespectfully of your mother?" Sir Béranger shouted at her, enraged.

"I caught the two of them together and her lover threatened to kill me, so I had to leave home. I hate her, and I hate you." Ellen collapsed in tears. Béranger put his arm around her, then took her by the shoulder.

"The son of Béranger de Tournai does not cry. Pull yourself together."

"I am not your son!" Ellen looked at him defiantly.

"But you are—I can see it and feel it."

"You don't see anything, and you don't feel anything either," she said bitterly. Not even her own father noticed that she was a girl! Were they all blind? Could they all just see what they wanted to? She looked him directly in the face, her eyes flashing with disdain.

"I will acknowledge you as my child, and you will be able to become a page and later a knight, just like your brother Thibault."

"Thibault!" Ellen sounded so scornful that he looked at her in astonishment. "He is a two-faced braggart, without any sense of honor!"

Every word was like a stab in the heart to Béranger because it sounded as if she were talking about him as well. "I know it's not simple, but...his mother..." he started to explain.

"Naturally you now say he is his mother's son, but no, Sir Béranger, he is just like you! Where was your sense of honor when you impregnated my mother?"

Béranger looked crestfallen, and Ellen almost felt a bit of compassion for him. But she continued: "He is your son in every way—he just recently got a young Anglo-Saxon girl in trouble!"

Béranger jumped up. "That's enough! I won't hear any more of that." Then he marched off without even looking back.

"Just ask him! Her name is Rose," Ellen called after him, though she wasn't sure he could still hear her.

—

Not until two weeks later when she spoke with Rose did she learn that Sir Béranger had indeed heard and understood.

"Thibault, this stupid fellow, must have gone around bragging to everyone that he knocked me up and his father learned of it. 'Make sure you take care of it,' he told Thibault." Rose didn't attach much importance to the fact that she hadn't told Ellen anything about her flirtation with the young squire, and at first Ellen didn't want to mention it.

"What did he mean by that?"

Rose shrugged. "I have no idea, but Thibault says I have to get rid of it. There's a woman who knows something about how that's done. I think he's right. What kind of life would it be for me being saddled with a bastard child?"

"Couldn't he take you to his father's castle and care for you there?" Ellen knew that her idea was childish, but she was furious at how quickly Thibault and his father found a solution that was so easy on them.

Rose shook her head. "You know that's nonsense."

"How about getting married?"

"But who? Some day laborer? A widower with a lot of children who will only take me so he has someone to beat and to work hard for him?" Rose sighed. "No, I don't think so. I'd rather go to the herb woman. Please, Ellen, can't you come along?" Just a moment ago she had seemed so sure of herself, but now she looked pleadingly at Ellen.

"Surely, if you wish."

Rose nodded gratefully. "I don't have the courage to do it alone."

"Why didn't you tell me that the two of you…?" Ellen's voice sounded soft and not at all reproachful.

"Can't you imagine why?" Rose smiled wanly. "You are my only friend, and Thibault and you hate each other. You certainly would have tried to talk me out of it, but I love him—it's as simple as that."

"I'm happy that now there are no more secrets between us. Of course I will help you and go to the herb woman with you. It would be best for us not to wait but to go tomorrow."

In the Woods Near Tancarville

Rose and Ellen met in the front of the castle gate just after sunrise. The meadows were still enshrouded in damp and impenetrable fog. They had to grope their way along until the mist lifted, and before long they had reached the house of the herb woman.

The entire way Rose had been restless, nervously tugging on her cape and drawing it closer and closer around her shoulders.

Ellen placed her arm around her and held her close. "Everything will be all right, you'll make it," she said, trying to cheer her up.

When they arrived at the little cottage, Ellen knocked on the door. The herb woman listened to Rose's concern, looked at Ellen crossly, and asked, "Why don't you marry her?"

"Me? I'm not the father," Ellen stammered, blushing.

"Alan is just coming along with me. The father of the child is a squire from Tancarville," Rose said, endeavoring to smile.

The old woman looked at the two condescendingly. "Doesn't really concern me—it's your business," she grumbled. "We'll do it with parsley. You'll have to stay here a few days."

Rose looked at Ellen helplessly.

"That will be all right, Rose. I'll tell them you're sick. They value your work and will be happy when you're better."

"It will take around five days if I care for her. That won't be cheap."

Rose fetched out a few coins, and the old woman took the money.

"That won't be enough," she snapped, and named her price. Rose was visibly shaken. "The child's father will pay—he promised me that," she said under her breath.

"I can assure you that you will get the money," Ellen interrupted. "Please, dear woman," she begged, "take care of her and see that everything goes well."

"I can't promise anything, but I'll do my best, young man. Just don't forget to bring me my money tomorrow."

—

On the way back to Tancarville, Ellen thought about how she could manage to get the money from Thibault. She could send a maid to him, but maids were too curious and talked too much. Even if many women did it, getting rid of an unborn child was strictly forbidden by the Church and severely punished. And so, with a heavy heart, she decided to go to Thibault herself, after work.

"You?" Thibault snorted, with contempt in his voice when she stood in front of him.

"Rose sent me."

Thibault looked Ellen over from head to toe without saying a word.

"She is getting rid of it, just as you wanted, and I'll take her the money for the herb woman." Ellen tried to stay calm though she was trembling with rage. When Thibault heard how much it would cost, he laughed scornfully.

"And do you really think I'll entrust all that money to you, of all people?"

"Feel free to take it yourself to the herb woman. After all, you told everyone it was your child," Ellen snapped at him, but she regretted saying so even before she finished the sentence.

Thibault turned red with anger. "Who knows who else she has been fooling around with? You're always fawning on her;

perhaps you're the father. I won't pay a penny for that little trollop."

Ellen gasped for air. "Rose loves you!" she shouted. "God knows why. As for me, I haven't touched her."

"Is that so? I have heard otherwise." He stepped closer to Ellen and said, "See how you can get her out of this mess, but not at my expense. Why don't you marry her yourself?" Thibault raised his eyebrows provocatively.

"It's not my child, but yours. It doesn't surprise me that you deny any responsibility and try to shift the blame onto someone else. Men in your family are really masters at doing that. Ask your father sometime—that's just what he did."

Ellen turned and strode away. She didn't even need to turn around to know that Thibault was standing there as if rooted to the spot, trying to understand what she meant. When she was out of sight, she turned limp. How could she have said something stupid like that? Even if Béranger had already left town, Ellen could have kicked herself for her big mouth. It would be only a matter of time before Thibault would see his father again. But she tried to put aside those feelings for now and concentrated on Rose, who had given the herb woman all her savings. She was still fifteen shillings short. It didn't take Ellen long to decide she would pay the rest from her own savings, although none of this really involved her. She hadn't forgotten how Rose had discovered her secret on board the ship and had kept it right up to the present, without ever expecting anything in return.

After work Ellen went to Donovan and asked him to give her part of the proceeds he had been keeping for her from the sale of the sword. He was surprised at the request but gave her the money without inquiring why she needed it. Ellen hurried off to the herb woman, not noticing that Arnaud was following her at a distance.

The old woman was waiting impatiently in front of her house. "Here you are finally! Do you have the money?"

"The young nobleman refuses to pay. He accuses poor Rose of permitting other young men to have their way with her as well. She loves him just the same, the stupid thing," she whispered so that Rose couldn't hear them. "Don't tell her that I paid instead of him."

The old woman shook her head. "Are you the father after all?"

"No, certainly not. I've never..." Ellen paused and lowered her gaze.

The woman seemed to believe her, and smiled. "All right then, I'll come down a bit on my price. I can see you are just a simple tradesman, and it doesn't really matter who the father is. We'll just get rid of it."

Ellen paid the amount she asked, looked in on Rose for a moment, and then left. On her way through the forest she stopped and knelt down to pray. Suddenly she heard a crackling sound in the underbrush, a bush parted, and out came Arnaud, smiling broadly.

"I am surprised you would be such a fool."

"Excuse me?" Ellen looked at him in astonishment.

"I can't blame you for having your fun with the little English girl. If I could have gotten anywhere with her I certainly wouldn't have turned down the chance. But with me she never would have gotten into trouble."

"Is that so?" Ellen saw no reason to correct Arnaud's error regarding the paternity.

"Of course. I know how to have fun without getting the girl in trouble."

"My compliments," Ellen said curtly.

"I can see how eager you are to hear my advice, so I won't hold out on you." He bowed patronizingly to Ellen, smiled, and added, "I take them…from behind!"

Ellen looked at him aghast. "But that's unholy," she gasped.

"Nonsense, our priests just want to forbid everything because they can't do it themselves." It was clear that Arnaud was proud of himself and his precautions.

"I couldn't care less what you do, and it doesn't concern me either. Rose isn't expecting a child from me, she is sick, that's all." Ellen stood up and was about to leave.

"Of course she is."

Ellen was sure he was making fun of her.

"You can think what you want," she snorted angrily.

"Don't worry, Alan, your secret will remain with me. I'll not say a word to the master. Now that you are his journeyman, Donovan may have more time for me and you might even put in a good word in my behalf." Arnaud gave her an innocent look. "Only if it's not too much trouble for you, of course."

Ellen turned away from him and left. Arnaud really thought he could make things hard for her, and by God, he had every reason to do so! She'd have to pay closer attention now when she went to the cottage to visit her friend.

Rose remained with the herb woman for a few days, as expected, and since there were no complications was able to return home soon.

Thibault steered clear of her and even had her turned away from the door when she came to see him. Rose was in despair and cried bitter tears in front of Ellen.

"Maybe he just can't come at the moment. Surely he'll visit you soon," Ellen tried to console her, even though she knew he never would.

—

Less than a month later, Rose came running to the smithy to see Ellen. She was completely out of breath.

"Please, I must tell you something right away, it is terribly important!" she panted.

Except for Arnaud there was no one in the workshop. Donovan, Glenna, Art, and Vincent had been invited to a wedding in the village. Ellen didn't want to go because she didn't feel like celebrating, and Arnaud was at loggerheads with the bride's father because he had seduced the girl before the marriage. He had not gotten her pregnant, however, and everyone agreed to keep silent about it. In the future, Arnaud was to stay away from her and of course not appear at the wedding.

"All right, you lovebirds. I'll leave you alone. I wanted to go to town anyway for a tankard of cider," he said, grinning.

Ellen was angry because he was exploiting the situation. Donovan had forbidden him to go into town so he wouldn't disturb the wedding, and it was Ellen's job to make sure he obeyed these instructions. She thought about what she could do. If she didn't say anything now and if he drank too much and misbehaved, Donovan would be furious at her. Rose shifted restlessly from one foot to another.

"You know very well what the master said. If you go to town, I'll tell him you sneaked away."

"Oh, I'm sure the master will understand you didn't see me leave because you had a little tryst with Rose," Arnaud answered calmly.

Once again he was trying to blackmail her.

"Please, Ellen, it's important!" Rose whispered, not knowing what was going on between Arnaud and Ellen.

"Go and do what you think is right," Ellen snorted, "but leave us alone now!"

"You can hardly wait, can you?" Arnold sneered as he was leaving, but then he turned around again and added, "I'll bet you won't take my advice and will get the poor girl in trouble again." He burst out laughing and sauntered off.

"Ugh, what a disgusting fellow. How can a girl be taken in by someone like him? So now, Rose, have a seat and take a deep breath. That will calm you down." Ellen directed her to a chest and pulled up a stool alongside her.

Rose's whole body was trembling. "I didn't want this to happen! You've got to believe me. I would never do anything to hurt you, but he made me so mad! I felt so helpless, and then it slipped out. If I had known what might happen then—I never would have said a word about it." She was crying so hard she could scarcely speak.

Ellen frowned. "Now let's take one thing at a time. I haven't understood a word. What did you say to whom, and how could it hurt me?"

"Thibault!" Rose sobbed.

Suddenly a strange fear overcame Ellen.

"He came to see me and said he was not the father of the child, but you were. He acted like a man whose wife had been cheating on him. I laughed and told him I had always been his." Rose broke down completely. "He was so mean, he even told me he hadn't paid the herb woman. 'Who was it, then?' I asked him. 'Do you think I had all that money?' he said. You can't imagine how he looked at me—I've never seen him like that before. 'It was Alan,' he snarled, 'Alan, the father of your child. He did it because he didn't want to marry you.'" Tears were streaming down her face. "I told him again and again that you're not the father, but he didn't believe me. He called me a whore and cursed me because I had double-crossed him with you. Then it slipped out."

"What?" Ellen asked.

Rose stared at the floor. "I told him it couldn't have been you because you are a girl. He was always my only love, Ellen!"

"Rose, no! You didn't!" Ellen's eyes were wide open in horror. "Do you know what you have done?"

Rose nodded, but Ellen assumed she wasn't really aware of the consequences of her betrayal. Ellen covered her face with her hands. She felt as if a gaping hole had opened up in front of her, threatening to engulf her. Everything she had achieved up to now was suddenly slipping away from her. Thibault wouldn't keep this to himself for very long, and that would make her life here in Tancarville impossible. Even worse, she would be punished; they would break her on the wheel or slit open her stomach. Ellen shuddered.

"I am so sorry, Ellen, honestly! I don't know what I expected to gain from that. Perhaps that he would just be relieved and no longer in the grip of this foolish anger toward you. I just wanted to have him back." Rose rubbed her eyes with her sleeve. "'A girl?' he repeated slowly. His voice was as cold as ice, and his face twisted in an evil grimace. I was overcome with fear and came running to you at once. Ellen, what can we do now?"

"Oh, *you* have done enough!" Ellen herself was surprised at how hard her voice sounded.

"Please, I didn't want to do anything to hurt you!" Rose pleaded with her. Then, after some hesitation, she asked sheepishly, "Is it true that you paid the herb woman?"

"Excuse me, but that's of no importance now. I've got to leave here at once," she said in a soft undertone. "I won't even get to say good-bye to Donovan and Glenna."

"Please don't go," Rose pleaded, gripping Ellen's arm tightly.

"You have sent me to my doom! Earlier, on the ship, you stayed with me and helped me, and I was always grateful for that. That's why I paid the herb woman. But I no longer owe you anything. We were friends, and I thought I could depend on you!" Ellen felt like a hunted animal and looked around the workshop trying to figure out what to take along.

"But why can't you stay?" Rose persisted, not wanting to believe how devastating her betrayal was for Ellen.

"Are you really that dumb?" Ellen said angrily. "There is nothing else I can do but to leave here as soon as possible. You know yourself how much Thibault hates me, heaven knows why! But now because of your stupid babbling he finally has something in hand to use against me. And he will no doubt use it. When word gets out of who I am, I'll be cast in prison for my deceit or I'll wind up on the gallows, and Donovan's reputation will also be ruined. Glenna would not survive that, and neither would he." While she was talking, she packed up her tools, cap, and leather apron. Then she rushed over to the house to pick up her money and the few possessions she had.

Rose followed her like a puppy. "Please, Ellen, say you forgive me!" she begged.

"You destroyed my life, and you want me to forgive you?" Ellen shouted. "Don't you think that is asking a bit too much?" She avoided looking at Rose but could hear her sobbing. "Stop your moaning! You don't really care what happens to me—you are only thinking of yourself and your own peace of mind. I don't want to leave, I'm happy here, but I have to go because you didn't think before you opened your mouth." Ellen closed the door and hurried back again to the shop. On the way, she met Arnaud. She had forgotten about him because she thought he had left for the village long ago. He grinned as if he knew more than he should. Had he been eavesdropping? How much of their conversation might he have heard?

"I'm leaving Tancarville, and Donovan will have lots of time for you now. Use it well," she said gruffly.

"Thank you so much, I'll do that." His smile infuriated Ellen even more. "If he asks what you are up to I'll say I know nothing about it—that would only hurt me, you do understand, don't you?" Arnaud's spoke in a sweet, silky voice that was nonetheless that of a vicious predator.

"But of course, you sweet, innocent child." Ellen slammed the door behind her and closed her eyes for a moment. Then she turned to leave.

"I'm so sorry, please believe me," Rose sobbed, looking up at her. Ellen stopped.

"Quit running after me."

Rose looked at her, pleading, "Isn't there anything I can do?"

"Go to Donovan tomorrow and tell him I had to leave suddenly." Ellen reflected for a moment. "Tell him I had urgent news from home, or think of something yourself. He must be told that there were important reasons for my leaving so he doesn't have anyone go out to look for me. And pray that Thibault drops the matter after I am gone."

"Whatever you want," Rose implored, rubbing her eyes. Her face was streaked with tears.

Ellen left her standing there and turned her back on the workshop without looking around again. In a daze she headed for the same highway she had always taken for her Sunday meetings with William. He had left Tancarville months ago. His master had, in fact, never replaced the lost horse, and even told his ward that he no longer wanted him at his court. He hired him for one last tournament, and William was anything but confident thinking about how he would soon be entirely on his own. Before he left Ellen he was nonetheless in a rebellious mood, jutting out his chin and declaring, “Wait and see, soon the whole world will know my battle cry!”

Ellen sighed. At least he wouldn’t find out she had been lying to him for all those years. Thibault would have really enjoyed rubbing William’s nose in this news. She was overcome with sadness thinking of William. Would she ever see him again?

Leaving Tancarville

The trees were already beginning to lose their colorful foliage. Ellen quickened her pace. The ground was completely covered in withered leaves that rustled under her feet. The golden rays of the sun that fell through the thinning canopy of vegetation no longer had the same intensity as in the summer and offered little warmth. *How can such a wonderful day end in such misfortune?* Ellen thought as she glanced up at the cloudless, bright blue sky and hastened on. Perhaps she'd manage to get out of the forest before nightfall. *But I have no idea where I am headed*, she thought dejectedly. *Shall I go back to England?*

Ellen heard hoofbeats behind her, and as always she left the highway and retreated into the woods, but it was too late. The rider had spotted her from a distance and spurred his horse on. By the time Ellen recognized who it was, she could no longer escape. The rider pursued her into the forest, the hoofs of his horse crushing the little mushrooms and the moss on the wet ground. When he had caught up with her, he jumped from the saddle and blocked her way.

"You are the bride of Satan, admit it!" he shouted at her, coming up close and looking her directly in the eye.

"What do you mean, Thibault?" Ellen stepped back.

"For all these years you have been deceiving me and everyone else into thinking you were a man! It's too bad William isn't here anymore. I would like to see the stupid expression on his face!" Thibault had dropped the reins of his horse, and the stallion was chewing peacefully on some dry grass.

Ellen noticed how tense every fiber in Thibault's body was as he walked toward her. She wanted to avoid a confrontation with him and kept stepping back until she stood with her back against a huge oak tree.

"I whipped myself at night until the blood streamed down my back because, silly fool that I was, I thought I had an unnatural yearning for Alan, the blacksmith's helper. Every time you looked at me with your green eyes, every time I touched you, my heart began to pound. I did penance again and again for those times I lusted so much after you, and that was much, much too often. But you're not a boy at all, so I atoned for something that was not a sin at all, and now you will pay for it." Thibault's eyes looked very small and black.

Ellen suppressed an apprehensive laugh. Though she was exceptionally strong for a woman, she was now overcome by fear. Even before she knew what was happening, he punched her right in the face.

"I'll beat the man out of you, you daughter of the devil," he snarled at her with a demented gaze.

Ellen could feel how her upper lip was swelling after the blow and could feel warm blood running down her chin. The next blow followed immediately and just as unexpectedly. It left a gash in her eyebrow, and the blood running down clouded her vision. The next blow was to the pit of her stomach, and it made her feel like she was going to vomit. She was too surprised to defend herself, but in any case she didn't stand much of a chance against a trained squire. *If I let him beat me, perhaps he'll stop soon,* she thought, sinking to the ground. She remembered the beatings her mother used to give her with the leather strap. At first they hurt terribly, but with time she had learned to disengage her spirit from her body. Sometimes it seemed to her as if she were hovering overhead, near the ceiling, and could look down and see herself lying on the ground.

Thibault knelt over her and shook her.

She did not resist. It seemed to her like she was far away, and she didn't even understand what was happening as he pushed up her shirt and discovered the cloth wrapped around her chest.

He broke out into a hoarse laugh. All it took was a little cut with his hunting knife to undo the bandage. With sadistic pleasure he slid the knife around her little breasts and down her belly to her navel. Then he tossed the knife aside and ripped off her braies.

"I wanted you from the very first day, you witch, and now you finally are mine!" Thibault panted with ecstasy and anger. "Woman is meant to be subordinate to the man," he whispered in her ear, forcing her legs apart.

Not until now did Ellen understand what he meant to do, and she shouted at him angrily: "You can't do that!" *If he knew he was my brother, he would never dare to do that*, she thought, half dazed. *I must tell him.*

"We'll see if I can do that. You are not the first virgin I have had," he laughed maliciously.

He wouldn't believe her anyway and would probably not even listen to her, so all she could do was to plead with him: "Please, Thibault, don't!"

Thibault grinned fiendishly. "You're whining now just the way a dog does. Just keep it up, but it won't do you any good."

Ellen resisted with all her strength, but Thibault was gripped with a possessive fury and much too strong. He pressed his left arm against her throat and thrust his fingers brutally into her most intimate part. There was a whooshing in Ellen's ears that got louder and louder as Thibault continued to press on her throat. She gasped for air, and Thibault released the pressure a bit so that she could breathe.

"I don't want you to faint—I want you to know everything that's happening." He grinned, and then he penetrated her, groaning.

Ellen retched as the sharp pain confirmed the loss of her virginity.

But Thibault exulted. He moved faster and faster into her, panting.

In pain and humiliation, Ellen desperately sought a way out. She ran her hand along the forest floor alongside her and grabbed hold of Thibault's knife. With her last ounce of strength, she slashed at him.

Thibault saw the attack coming out of the corner of his eye and reacted fast enough to prevent her from plunging the knife into his back, but she did cut him on his upper arm. The wound bled profusely, and the pain made Thibault even more furious, seeming almost to drive him out of his mind. He beat Ellen again and again, and then he got up and started kicking her.

I will die, Ellen thought, strangely indifferent to her fate, and then she passed out.

—

When she regained consciousness it was pitch dark. *Am I dead?* she wondered, trying to move. Her head felt like an anvil being pounded by a giant sledgehammer. She couldn't see anything, so she put her hands up to her eyes. Her face was badly swollen and painful, but when she looked up she discovered some points of light in the sky. It was night, and only a few stars were shining—that was the explanation. Ellen ran her hands all over her body. Her shirt was still pushed up to her breasts, and her lower body ached like one huge wound. She searched the forest floor for her braies and managed to put them on again, then pulled her shirt down and put her belt on. She even found her purse nearby with all the money still in it. Her belly hurt around her navel, and she remembered he had kicked her in the stomach. *That damned swine*, she thought, and then she staggered a few steps through the darkness before losing consciousness again.

When she came to in the morning, she was face to face with a woman who was bending over her. After the first shock, Ellen tried to move but then groaned with pain.

"Easy, easy…nothing more is going to happen to you. Do you think you can stand up if I help you?"

Ellen nodded hesitantly and clenched her teeth as she struggled to her feet.

"Your face doesn't look good. What kind of brute did that to you?" The woman shook her head disapprovingly but didn't seem to expect an answer. She took Ellen's arm and laid it over her shoulder, then reached under the other shoulder to support her and in so doing touched her breast. Astonished, she looked at Ellen. "You are a woman," she said. "I took you at first for a boy. You were lucky then, I believe."

Ellen understood that the woman had no idea of what Thibault had done to her and was grateful she didn't notice the shameful thing that had happened. She tried to walk despite the severe pain.

"Jacques, my lad, come and lend a hand," the woman called out, and a boy about twelve years of age came hobbling over. "We'll put her on the pony," the woman said. "You can walk, and when you get too tired I'll change places with you."

Jacques looked at his mother questioningly.

"Don't just stand there, go and pick up her bundle—it's right over there, do you see it?" The woman pointed to the place where she had found Ellen.

The boy nodded and trudged over to it. When he picked it up, he made a reluctant face.

"What is the problem?" the woman asked. "Come on."

"The bundle is heavy. What's in it, stones?"

His mother looked at him sternly.

"I am Claire, by the way, and this is my son Jacques. Would you mind telling us your name?"

"Ellenweore," she answered with a hoarse voice.

"Oh, like the queen! Did you hear, Jacques?" She was clearly delighted.

Ellen managed a weak smile.

"Now we have exchanged enough pleasantries." Claire took her water skin and held it to Ellen's mouth. "You must be thirsty."

Not until then did Ellen notice the burning in her throat, and she nodded gratefully. She drank a few sips and coughed.

"Somehow we must get you up on the pony. Can you ride?"

Ellen shook her head. "Not as far as I know."

"That doesn't matter. Judging from the way you look, we'll not make very fast progress anyway. The main thing is for you to hold onto the horse tightly and not fall down." Claire smiled engagingly.

Jacques, like so many boys his age, was not especially talkative and not much help.

"Where are we going?" Ellen asked after they had been traveling for a while, relieved to see they were not going back to Tancarville.

"We're from Béthune, in Flanders."

"Is that very far?" Ellen asked warily.

"A full week, at least, perhaps even two," Claire replied.

"May I travel part of the way with you?"

"Surely, and if you think you can manage, you can come all the way to Béthune with us."

"I'd like to do that." Ellen nodded gratefully and was glad they were going so far away.

On the
road

BOOK TWO

ON THE ROAD

Saint Agatha Nunnery, November 1166

The first night they spent huddled together around a fire in the forest, but they could hardly sleep because of the cold. For this reason, early in the evening of the second day they sought out a small convent that lay in a secluded location deep in the forest. An old woman, a charcoal burner whom they had met earlier, recommended that they stop there and ask for a place to spend the night. The sun had almost set, and once again the air was becoming uncomfortably damp and cold so that their breath rose up in front of them in white clouds.

Claire told Ellenweore to dismount, and then she slid down from the horse as well, walked over to the heavy oaken door, and knocked.

The gatekeeper opened a little barred window, peered out, and asked what they wanted.

"We are freezing, dear sister, and looking for a place to spend the night. My name is Claire. I am a tradeswoman accompanied by my son Jacques. On our way back home to Béthune we found this unfortunate girl in the forest. She had been attacked and badly beaten—here, see for yourself." She pushed Ellen up to the door.

"She doesn't look like a girl," the gatekeeper mumbled.

"The clothing is deceptive. Hers was torn, and all I had to give here were a few old things belonging to my husband. I tried to sell them in the marketplace but had no takers," she explained, and Ellen wondered why Claire lied for her.

Ellen's head started spinning again, and she slumped down. Claire was just able to catch her before she fell to the ground.

"Sister Agnes is our nurse. Wait, I'll call her," the gatekeeper mumbled before shutting the little window and shuffling away.

Shortly after, a small creaking door none of the visitors had noticed until that moment opened on the left side of the stone wall. A small woman ducked through the opening and then straightened up and walked toward them.

"I am Sister Agnes. Our sister the gatekeeper thought perhaps you needed my help."

By now night had come, and the forest encircled the nunnery like a black wall. All that was visible in the gathering darkness now were a few isolated trees.

Sister Agnes nodded briefly at Claire and then turned anxiously to Ellen, raising her lantern in order to see better.

"Your face looks bad—does anything else give you pain?"

"My entire body hurts," Ellen moaned. She was barely able to stand anymore.

"She's dizzy—she almost fell down just now," Claire explained.

The nun passed her hands over Ellen's shirt and upper body. "Two ribs may be broken, but I'm not sure," she said softly after she had felt her rib cage.

Ellen had to control herself in order not to laugh, as it tickled.

The nun also fleetingly touched her breasts—apparently part of her job was to check and see that Ellen actually was a girl.

"Perhaps we should go in, what do you think?" The sister shone the light first on Ellen and then on Claire, and then she turned to Jacques.

"You look like you are still a growing boy. You must be hungry."

Jacques nodded vigorously.

"Well, then I'll tell the sister in the kitchen to give you a good-size portion of food."

Jacques grinned, overjoyed.

"Say thank you, lad," his mother whispered.

Though he was just as tall as Sister Agnes, she tousled his hair as if he were a little child.

"Open the gate, Sister Clementine," she called out loudly. "We have guests for the night."

The gatekeeper shoved aside the heavy iron bolt and carefully opened the gate.

Ellen noticed that she was larger and stronger than Sister Agnes, and presumably that was the reason she had been chosen to serve as gatekeeper. But in spite of her size, she also seemed more anxious than her delicate fellow sister.

"A girl in men's clothing," the gatekeeper mumbled to herself, shaking her head. "Never heard of anything like that."

Ellen and Claire exchanged brief glances and followed the two nuns along a narrow corridor as the flickering light from their lanterns cast fitful shadows along the walls.

"We will inform Mother Superior of your arrival. She'll certainly want to meet you later, but I suggest for now that you come along with me," said Sister Agnes, turning to Ellen as they came to a flight of stairs. Then she turned to Claire and Jacques, saying, "You go with Sister Clementine, who will give you something to eat and show you where you can sleep.

"Sister Clementine, would you please be so kind as to ask the sister in the kitchen to prepare an especially large portion for our young guest?" said Sister Agnes, winking at Jacques. "I promised him that."

"As you wish, dear sister." The gatekeeper lowered her eyes submissively. "Are you sure you'll be able to manage by yourself?"

Sister Agnes reassured her with a nod and opened the door to the cloister's sickroom.

Two torches were burning along the walls, giving the group enough light to find their way. The room was clean and smelled of herbs. Ellen's gaze fell on a table with a bowl and a pitcher standing on it and two chairs at the sides. Along the wall there was a shelf containing earthen pots of different sizes, two baskets, and underneath it two large drawers full of wickerwork baskets. Ellen's right eye was badly swollen and throbbing, but she kept looking around nonetheless. In front, along the wall, there were two low wooden beds with a curtain that could be drawn between them. Someone was lying in the bed farthest away, and Sister Agnes led Ellen over to it.

"Sister Berthe, don't be alarmed," she whispered. "We have guests tonight."

After a moment, the woman turned around, groaning. Ellen had never seen such a withered face. The old woman seemed weak and could scarcely speak, but her eyes radiated kindness and wisdom. She nodded with difficulty and held a trembling hand out to Ellen.

Ellen reached out timidly to take her gnarled fingers, patting them gently, and then placed the old woman's hand softly back on the sheet that was covering her.

Even now, she wore a veil, and not a single strand of her presumably white hair protruded.

"Sister Berthe is the oldest sister in our convent and hasn't been able to stand for years. We moved her from her cell to this sickroom so she does not have to be alone so much. I spend most of my time here, and while I am working I tell her about the homilies and prayers of Mother Superior, about the novitiates, and about the few pupils we have. I also explain to her the effects of herbal medicines, what I learn from my studies, and whatever other news there may be. We rarely have visitors here." Sister Agnes lovingly caressed the cheeks of Sister Berthe, but she had gone back to sleep again and was snoring softly. "But now tell me about yourself. What happened?"

"I was attacked," Ellen said, her speech unclear because of her swollen lip. She grimaced a bit more than necessary to emphasize that she wanted to speak as little as possible.

Sister Agnes nodded and took a closer look at Ellen's facial wounds. "Your nose may be broken," she said in an undertone and asked Ellen to remove her shirt carefully so she could examine her ribs again.

Ellen was more relaxed lying down, but it still tickled when the nun's cool fingers moved across her bones. Her belly around her navel was all black and blue.

Sister Agnes looked at the marks left by those violent blows. "The Lord has seen it and will demand penance at the Last Judgment," she added, shaking her head and crossing herself.

The thought that the Lord might have seen it all was very embarrassing, and Ellen turned her head aside in shame.

"Did you vomit blood after you were kicked?" Sister Agnes asked.

Ellen shook her head.

"Being kicked can lead to serious consequences. Sometimes it doesn't look so bad, but two days later the victim suddenly dies." Sister Agnes sighed, but then she added quickly, "Excuse me, I didn't want to scare you. Sometimes it would be best if I held my tongue." She stood up and walked over to the iron shelf.

Ellen wondered how she knew about the danger of being kicked, but the droning in her head was so loud that she couldn't follow that train of the thought to the end.

Everything was in perfect order in Sister Agnes's sickroom. She quickly found a little basket and took out a handful of dried leaves.

"Coltsfoot," she explained. "A brew made from this helps our dear Sister Berthe to breathe better. She drinks some every day. I'll make the brew for you as well, but you won't be drinking it. We'll cleanse your wounds with it, and then I'll make compresses soaked in St. John's wort oil." Sister Agnes pointed to a little clay flask with oily specks on it. "You have to store coltsfoot dry and use it quickly because it easily gets moldy. We always have some in our garden. Just recently I dried some more leaves because Sister Berthe was having so much trouble breathing." She continued talking as she took a three-legged pot and put it on the little fireplace. Then she threw a few herbs and a little dry wood on the flames. They were soon burning, filling the room with a wonderful fragrance.

Ellen could no longer keep her eyes open and dozed off. When she awoke again, the brew had already percolated and had cooled off a bit.

Sister Agnes had a cloth in her hand and swabbed Ellen's wounds with the brew. Carefully but calmly she removed the dried blood.

It stung, but Ellen clenched her teeth.

"I'll have a look at your nose. Watch out, this will probably hurt a bit," she warned Ellen as she started to examine the bridge of her nose. Then she shook her head. "It looks fine—it doesn't seem that anything is broken." Then she applied the St. John's wort extract to her face, ribs, and stomach. Though her touch was extremely gentle, it was still terribly painful. "For the next few days you need to protect your face from the sun, or the St. John's wort extract may leave some ugly marks. But you'll see, it's the best thing for your injury and will be good for the black and blue marks."

Ellen was just able to nod wearily before falling asleep again, and this time she didn't awake until the following morning.

—

For breakfast, Sister Agnes gave Ellen a fresh piece of soft bread, ordinarily baked just for Sister Berthe, who had lost her teeth. Then she attended to Ellen's wounds again.

"The swelling has gone down a bit, and it looks better, especially over your eye." Just as she was carefully applying the St. John's wort again, Claire entered.

"How are you, Ellenweore?" Claire took her hand and squeezed it tenderly.

"Betthher," Ellen said, with a lopsided grin, as she still couldn't speak clearly.

"Her jaw is badly bruised. She was very lucky," Sister Agnes declared.

"Lucky?" Ellen's heart raced. She couldn't quite think of herself as lucky.

"After hearing the report from Sister Agnes," Claire said, "Mother Superior offered to let us stay a few days until you are better, so we won't have to leave right away."

"Mutthent you get home?" Ellen asked, barely able to move her mouth.

"Sure we must," Claire said, "but what are a few days in an entire life?" She shrugged and smiled cheerfully and seemed to take it for granted that they would wait until Ellen was able to go with them.

"When we leave, we'll ask Sister Agnes to give us a few of her potions, what do you think?"

Ellen looked at Sister Agnes, questioningly.

"In a few days the worst of the wounds will heal," Sister Agnes replied with a smile. "Then she'll only need some ointment that I'll prepare for her and she'll soon be like her old self again."

"Only the thame, not bether?" Ellen said, feigning disappointment.

"Well, I can't promise you that," Sister Agnes answered with a laugh, "but I see you haven't lost your spirit, and that's good."

"We'll stay a while longer then, is that all right?" Claire asked, just to make sure, and Sister Agnes nodded.

Ellen looked back and forth at both women and softly said, "Thank you."

—

Ellen enjoyed the tranquility of the convent, the good care she received from Sister Agnes, and the hearty food. She slept most of the day, and in the evening Claire would stop by at her bed to tell her about the work she did for the nuns and how much Jacques liked being there. Even though he had to fetch water and gather wood from time to time, he always got a double portion of food.

Ellen got better from day to day and after less than a week felt strong enough to move on. Her face and stomach were still black and blue, but the open wounds on her lips and eyebrows had healed quite well.

Shortly before sunrise on the sixth day, the time had come. After a good, hearty breakfast, the three said farewell to Sister Agnes and the other nuns and continued on toward Béthune. The trees were white with a thick covering of hoarfrost—branches, leaves, and even blades of grass were enveloped in a crystalline layer of ice. As the sun rose over the horizon, it turned the frost into a soft shade of pink, and before noon the ice had started to melt.

"If we don't dally, we can be home in a week," Claire told her son, trying to cheer him up.

It was clear he didn't like walking when it was so cold outside just because they had to take Ellen along, and he grumbled softly to himself.

Ellen couldn't bring herself to have much sympathy for the boy. She herself had never ridden on a pony, and after all, people have legs so they can walk. She was annoyed at his spineless behavior. When she was his age, she wasn't such a sissy. He kept whining about not being able to ride, and finally she stopped, slid down from the horse with clenched teeth, and held the reins out to him. "I see you're annoyed because your mother gave me the pony," she said, endeavoring to sound as calm and cool as possible, "so I'll just walk."

Jacques turned pale.

Either he'll break out in tears any moment, Ellen thought with surprise, *or he'll throw a fit.*

But the boy just shook his head vigorously and started walking faster, as if being chased by the devil in person.

It seemed he really wanted to walk ahead, so Ellen decided to get back on the pony again. It was fortunate the pony was stoic enough to remain standing patiently while she struggled to lift herself back up again.

Jacques kept his feelings to himself after that and tried to be polite to Ellen. He was even a bit friendlier to his mother than before.

"I think he likes you," Claire said the next day without seeming to be surprised about it. "He's not like other boys."

Ellen agreed completely—she thought he was childish and impolite. *She probably spoils him rotten*, she thought irritably.

"He's a bit…well, how shall I put it? Simple-minded." Claire smiled a bit in embarrassment.

Ellen stared at her, astonished. She had never thought of Jacques as feeble-minded, but it seemed that actually was what Claire was trying to say.

"He just needs a little more discipline," Ellen mumbled, somewhat embarrassed.

"Maybe I'm not strict enough. His father, God rest his soul, died two years ago." Claire crossed herself. "It's not always easy being alone with the boy." She shrugged nervously. "Ever since my husband died, I've been running his shop even though everyone in town expected I would get another master craftsman for the business. It wouldn't be unusual for me to manage a shop if I were a silk weaver or yarn maker, but as a scabbard maker that's a different story," she declared.

Ellen had to catch her breath with excitement at this good news.

"Please let me assist you and in this way repay in small part my gratitude to you. I can learn quickly and am good at working with my hands. You'll certainly not regret it," she pleaded.

"Agreed!" Claire smiled and spent the whole rest of the trip cheerfully telling stories. She knew about all the residents of the village where she lived, and when they finally arrived in Béthune, Ellen had the feeling she was no longer a complete stranger there.

The village consisted of around three dozen small houses of earth and wood with thatched roofs. They were crowded together around the village square and along the little country road, and each had a small vegetable garden and a field. Two linden trees stood near the fountain in the square, and behind them a church made of stone that had just recently been built.

Claire was greeted warmly by her neighbors, who scrutinized Ellen with curiosity. The next day, when Claire went back to work, she insisted that Ellen still take time to rest up.

On the first day, Ellen slept a lot, but on the second she was bored and complained so much that Claire finally allowed her to go to the shop.

The scabbard maker worked at a long table piled with pieces of wood, cloth, leather, and fur. On the hearth a fire was burning cheerfully, because scabbards couldn't be made with freezing fingers and the rabbit-skin glue had to be kept warm. Ellen sat down and watched. She had learned more or less in Tancarville how such scabbards were made. They had to be crafted individually and fitted exactly to the shape of the sword blade. The interior of two thin wooden slats was covered with the skin of cows, goats, or deer, with the grain running in the direction of the sword point. If the sheath fit properly, the fur prevented the weapon from slipping out. After the two wooden slats had been covered with fur, Claire would bind them together and wrap them with a cloth soaked in glue, which she then covered with some precious material, or with leather. To protect the point of the blade the sheath was finally given a metal binder called a chape. Most chapes were crafted by the swordsmith himself and made of brass, but special swords were given chapes of valuable metals such as silver and gold. The sheath was then tied to a belt with thin leather straps and a special wrapping technique so that the sword could be buckled on.

The very next day Ellen took a seat with Claire at the table without asking, as if it were just a matter of course, and helped her. At first, Ellen barely spoke; she worked, ate three times a day with Claire and Jacques, and slept at night in the shop.

"It's market day today, and we've got to get material to make you something decent to wear," Claire announced one day, walking in a circle around Ellen and scrutinizing her from tip to toe.

"You can't possibly go to church looking like that, in men's clothing! And this Sunday you have to go—there's no getting around that. You've been here for three weeks, and if you don't come, people will start saying you have something to hide," Claire said, looking questioningly out of the corner of her eye.

Ellen avoided looking at her directly. Her wounds had healed quite well, and all that remained of the dark, bleeding lesions on her face were a few black and blue spots. Her pain was gone, but she did still suffer from stomach cramps. It was worse in the morning and at night. At first she thought about what Sister Agnes had said and believed she might still die as a result of being kicked so hard by Thibault. She survived, but the nausea persisted. To hide it from Claire, she got up in the morning earlier than the others and went out into the garden when she felt the nausea coming on.

"I'll get my purse, and then we'll go," she said to Claire; then in spite of the nausea she felt coming on, she smiled wanly.

They bought some blue woolen cloth from an elderly salesman that appeared suitable and didn't cost too much. Ellen had worn the same clothes for years, first growing into them, then out of them. She had received a worn smock from Donovan and a shirt that Glenna had sewn for her. The bloodstains from when she was assaulted had been washed out long ago, and Claire had stitched up the small tear in the shirt. Ellen thought her clothes were still quite adequate and the thought of having to exchange them for new ones caused her to break out in a sweat. These clothes had been part of her life, had given her stability and protection—she couldn't just throw them away, and thus she kept putting it off. "Right now I'm sweating so much," she tried to explain. "And also, I'll get lime on the new material. Let me put it aside for a while and wait until I am a little surer of what I am doing at work," she said.

Thus, on the following Sunday as well, she still didn't have a dress for church. As every morning, she was awakened by her nausea, got up before the others, and staggered outside into the yard. In the last few days, rain had softened the ground; she almost slipped in the mud, and finally vomited behind a bush. *God is punishing me for my sins—everyone will notice*, she thought anxiously, and wondered what excuse she might invent not to go to church. This time, Claire certainly wouldn't accept the dress as an excuse, but Ellen had no time to think up a better one. Claire had already discovered her in the garden and was walking toward her.

"I was looking for you everywhere. What are you doing behind the bush?" Claire shook her head, not understanding. "Come, we've got to hurry, mass is beginning soon. Good Lord, you're still running around in the old dress! We positively have to make your dress next week. Here, take your cloak at least for this week," she prattled, without noticing how pale Ellen looked.

She didn't resist as Claire put the cape over her shoulders. *If the priest points to me and tells everyone about my sin, I'll die on the spot. The earth will open up and hell will swallow me up*, she thought gloomily as she walked silently to church alongside Claire.

Almost all the inhabitants of the village had gathered already inside the Lord's house. By now, Ellen knew more than half of the churchgoers and looked them over carefully. They were chatting with each other and took no notice of her.

Up in front by the altar, a richly dressed man was engrossed in a conversation with the priest.

"Who's the knight over there?" she whispered to Claire, pointing cautiously at him.

"The Advocate of Béthune. He had this church built when his eldest son was born. And behind him is Adelise de St. Pol, his wife," Claire whispered in reply. "She is the Lady of Béthune."

Ellen nodded. She really wanted to look more closely at the Lady of Béthune, but it was impolite to stare at her, so instead she let her gaze wander around the crowded church—old women already engaged in prayer, fidgety children shuffling their feet on the ground, men and women chatting, and a young girl who seemed to be looking around for a secret glance from her lover.

When the priest started reading the mass, the murmuring of the crowd died down. Ellen had great difficulty concentrating on his words, fearing that at any moment a bolt of lightning might come crashing down on the church, or something else equally dreadful, as a punishment for her offense.

During the Lord's Prayer, which was recited in unison, she couldn't help thinking of William and how much she missed him. She was startled when the murmuring ceased and nothing terrible had happened. As she left church with Claire, a little girl came running up to them.

The richly dressed lady ran after her and caught the child before she had lost her balance. "Were you trying to run away again, my little angel?" she scolded the girl, shaking her head. Her voice sounded soft and melodic. She took the child up in her arms and smiled at Claire and Ellen.

"She is so sweet, *madame*," Claire said, reaching for the child's hand.

"How are you, Claire?" the noblewoman asked, then looked questioningly at Ellen.

"Oh, thank you, *madame*, I am doing well. May I introduce you to my new maid? Her name is Ellenweore, and she is helping me in my shop."

Ellen curtsied politely, just as she had practiced it with Claire, and apologized for the wounds still visible on her face, inflicted, she said, during an attack by outlaws.

The noblewoman looked at her sympathetically and was about to pat her cheek, when suddenly a young woman started to wave her arms around and shouted, "Look over there! A child has fallen into the river. Why isn't anyone helping?"

Adelise de Béthune turned around and looked. "Where is Baudouin? Hasn't anyone seen him?" she suddenly cried out in a panic.

The child's maid shook her head, aware of her serious error.

With a quick presence of mind, Ellen dashed off.

The river was higher than usual due to the recent rains, and the rushing water had stirred up mud and carried off some tree branches.

Ellen could not see the child, but she kept watching the surface of the water carefully until something appeared. Then she jumped in. She hadn't been swimming ever since leaving Orford, and for a moment the icy cold water took her breath away, but she swam with all her strength in order to get to the child as fast as possible. When she arrived at the place she had last seen him, there was nothing there, so she dove under the water. It was dark and stung her eyes. She had lost her sense of direction and was thrashing about, groping through the water in hopes of finding the child. She had almost run out of breath and was about to head back to the surface when suddenly something caught her and drew her down. She kicked her legs and thrashed about in panic and suddenly felt the boy's arm. Grabbing him tightly, she pushed off from the river bottom and pulled the child up with her. The little fellow in her arms appeared lifeless. With her last bit of strength and courage born of desperation, she fought against the current that threatened to carry them away.

A few men from the village had gone to get poles, which they reached out to her. She grabbed hold and managed to reach the shore with the boy. Helping hands pulled her and the child up the bank of the river.

The boy lay there pale and lifeless, and no one standing around said or did anything. "Wake up!" Ellen screamed in horror, rubbing her hands over his tiny chest and shaking him. "Please, God, let him live," she pleaded in a barely audible voice, and pressed down on his chest. Suddenly the boy coughed and spat out water.

The relieved villagers broke out into cheers of joy, whistling and hooting.

The strong five- or six-year-old boy looked around bewildered, as Ellen beamed happily.

The dripping wet, pale lad looked at her shyly and asked, "Are you an angel?"

Ellen shook her head, but the boy didn't seem to believe her.

"Baudouin!" his mother called out, running up to join the group. She hugged the child and then turned to Ellen with a look of relief. "Praise the Lord! You saved my son's life," she said gratefully and hugged her son once more.

He snuggled up against his mother and cried.

Only now did Ellen realize how amazingly beautiful the woman was. Her delicate, smooth face was framed by a thick head of chestnut-brown hair and glowed with happiness.

"I am deeply indebted to you and will forever be grateful. If there is ever anything I can do for you, just come to me anytime."

Ellen nodded, but she didn't believe in such promises. The nobility were only too quick to forget to whom they were indebted to, as Aelfgiva had so often told her.

A knight came up to them, saying, "We ought to be leaving, *madame*. It is cold, the boy is freezing, and you are also soaked."

"Gauthier, give…what is your name, my child?"

"Ellenweore, *madame*."

"Give Ellenweore a blanket so she doesn't freeze to death," she told the knight, "and wrap one around Baudouin as well." Then she turned to leave.

"I will pray that not only your body but also your soul heals," she said softly, and walked away.

Ellen stood there trembling, as if rooted to the spot, and pulled the blanket she had received from the knight even tighter around her shoulders. Was the lady clairvoyant?

Claire suddenly appeared beside her and said, "If the farmers here are worried, they go to her and ask for her help. She always knows what to do, and everyone here loves her. Every one of us here would give our lives for her. You brought great honor to our village today." It was obvious how proud Claire was of what Ellen had done.

"I'm cold!" said Ellen, her teeth chattering.

"My goodness, how stupid of me! Off you go, and when we get home you can lie down in my bed with a hot stone or you'll catch a cold!" Claire led Ellen through the crowd of villagers, who patted her on the shoulder or shook her hand.

—

Ellen spent the rest of the day in bed.

Claire hung up a clothing line in the shop, lit a fire in the fireplace, and put Ellen's clothing out to dry.

The afternoon in a warm bed ensured that Ellen did not catch cold, but the nausea got worse from day to day, and Ellen finally realized she had to be with child.

"May you burn in hell forever; may fertility forsake your loins. Never again shall you impregnate a woman, never!" Ellen kept repeating the curse softly to herself and secretly made up her mind.

The stalks of parsley in a woman's womb had to be exchanged for new ones after two days, that was about all she knew, but as she picked the herb, an uncomfortable feeling crept over her. What she was thinking of doing was a sin! It was something forbidden and wrong, but she couldn't keep the child. Thibault had violated her, and he was her brother. Siblings couldn't have children: that, too, was a sin. God alone would be their judge.

With a heavy heart, Ellen decided to do what she thought was the only right thing, and in one of the following nights woke up with stomach cramps. Not even Thibault's blows had hurt that much. In order not to waken Claire and the boy and to keep her dreadful act a secret, Ellen took her bundle, tiptoed out of the shop, and struggled laboriously into the forest of oak trees outside the village. The pale moonlight lit her way through the cold, dark night. At one point she sat down, panting with pain. Only the fear of being discovered kept her from screaming as the cramps in her abdomen became more and more severe. "Oh, Rose, how brave you were," she mumbled. The thought of her former friend and their common fate helped her to stay calm. Ellen took a few old but clean linen cloths out of her pack and spread them out on the ground between her legs. She groaned with pain as her body aborted the bloody mass, and she couldn't bear to see what she was holding in the cloth. Sobbing and murmuring a fervent prayer, she buried the cloth with its grisly contents as blood ran down her trembling thighs.

—

"Ellenweore, please wake up! What happened, for God's sake?" Claire shook her shoulders, and it was impossible not to hear the fear in her voice.

Ellen tried to move her head, but she wasn't able to. The pounding in her head was unbearable, and she tried to open her eyes.

"Where did the blood on your hand come from? Holy Mary, Mother of Jesus, please help her!" Claire prayed, full of anxiety. Her voice sounded far away and barely audible.

Ellen had to wonder if Mary, of all people, would intercede on her behalf, but instead of fear, a warm feeling of peace came over her. She felt as light as a feather floating through balmy spring breezes and being carried away to a far-off place that is wonderful and bright. *That can only be paradise*, Ellen thought happily. *The Lord has forgiven me and is not sending me to hell!* She could feel warm tears of joy and gratitude flowing down her cold cheeks.

"Ellen, please, stay with me." She could now clearly hear Claire again, pleading with her, and she could feel how someone was rubbing her hands and arms that were numb from the cold.

"I am in heaven," she whispered without opening her eyes.

"No, you're lying here in the forest half dead, and if I don't get you home at once this will surely be the end of you, so pull yourself together!"

Ellen heard the severity in Claire's voice and smiled wearily.

"It doesn't hurt, not anymore now," she whispered.

"You're feverish," Claire said, touching her burning forehead, "and we must get you home at once. Can you walk if I help you?"

Ellen was still numb. She tried to regain control of her body but could hardly move her legs. Finally she struggled to her feet.

Claire put her arm around Ellen's waist and Ellen's hand over her shoulder, and slowly they started moving. But they had to stop again and again.

"I can't go any farther. Let me lie down here and die in peace," she whispered, just as they were coming out of the forest.

"Nothing doing, we'll make it the rest of the way as well. I'll take you home and get you back on your feet, and then you will tell me the whole story—why you were attacked and why you always wear men's clothing and who was the father of the child.

I trusted you even though I knew nothing about your past, and now you will tell me the truth, and don't forget that."

"You won't like the truth," Ellen sighed weakly.

"Let me decide that for myself. But first we have to bring down the fever and nurse you back to health."

—

For the first two days Ellen felt as if she were enveloped in fog. She was too weak to eat but swallowed without complaining when Claire told her to drink, then fell back into a restless sleep in which she was tormented by dreadful nightmares. Her face changed color from ghostly white to burning red, the fever rose, and her whole body was wracked with cramps.

On the fourth night she suddenly sat bolt upright in bed—the grotesque, contorted face of Thibault had followed her! Ellen was still weak but not as numb as before. Claire had dozed off on the floor next to her and was fast asleep. It had to be night, because it was dark and quiet. The stump of a small tallow candle was still flickering on the table, casting shadows that danced across the walls.

Ellen lay back with relief on the soft down pillow that Claire used to sleep on. Her sweaty hair stuck to her head.

When she pulled the sheet up to her chin, she couldn't help noticing that she was almost naked except for a folded piece of linen between her legs. She struggled to remember what had happened. Terrifying images flashed before her eyes. When she began to realize what had happened, she wished the ground would simply open and swallow her up. Claire must have wrapped the linen cloth around her in order not to get bloodstains on the sheets. Feebly she fell back and finally nodded off again. This time her sleep was dreamless and refreshing because the fever was finally subsiding.

The next morning she was awakened by the sweet fragrance of oats cooked in milk. She tried to stretch, but even the slightest movement caused her to wince and groan.

"How are you?" Claire said with a cheerful smile.

"Have you broken me on the wheel, or why does everything hurt?" Ellen smiled weakly.

"You had cramps from the fever. At times we didn't think you would make it. It's no wonder everything hurts."

"We? Does Jacques know what happened?"

"No, don't worry, he has been at the castle since the day it happened. I didn't know what else to do and asked the Lady of Béthune to take him. Jacques thinks he is there to teach one of her sons how to carve figures. He can make wonderful things, did you know that? All he needs is a good knife, a whetstone for sharpening it, and a piece of dry wood. His father taught him how to do it." Claire rubbed her nose.

"What in God's name did you tell the lady?"

"Nothing, that was not necessary. She didn't ask, she would never ask—she only wanted to help. If there is something you want to tell her, she'll listen, but if you are doing something unlawful, she won't be easy on you. I imagine this is the reason she doesn't ask and would rather not know whether it was God's will or your own. But as for me, I'd like to hear it all frankly and honestly, with nothing left out, and from the very beginning, if you please." Claire smiled, but with a look of determination that made it clear to Ellen how serious she was.

Claire filled a clay bowl with hot oatmeal and added a good portion of honey. "She brought this for you, to help you regain your strength." Claire blew into the bowl and handed it to Ellen.

Ellen ate the oatmeal slowly and with obvious enjoyment. "I've never had anything better!" she raved.

Claire smiled contentedly. "Here, take this," she said. "You should drink five cups of her herbal brew every day. It wasn't easy getting it into you while you were unconscious."

After a few sips, Ellen felt pressure in her bladder and looked around. When she caught sight of the chamber pot, she carefully crept out from under the bed sheets, removed the linen cloths between her legs, and put on a shirt that was laid out for her at the foot of the bed. By the looks of it, it had once belonged to Claire's husband. Ellen staggered over to the pot. Everything was spinning in her head, it was hard for her to breathe, and it felt like there was a heavy stone pressing down on her chest. Carefully, she sat down on the chamber pot. The pressure on her bladder was so great that it hurt to relieve herself. When she was done, she placed the cover back on the pot, pushed it aside, and shuffled back to her bed. Ellen wondered if Claire had set her on the pot when she was unconscious, and couldn't remember. She closed her eyes again.

"I think the worst is over. The bleeding has stopped and the fever is gone, but you still have to rest."

Ellen could hear Claire's voice, but it sounded far away, as she fell back to sleep again.

—

When she woke up in the afternoon, she felt better.

"You'll get better, but it has been a rough time. You were delirious with fever, and I was worried about whether you were losing your mind, and even if you would survive. You had such terrible cramps it seemed like you were possessed by the devil," Claire told her.

"Possessed by the devil!" Ellen repeated, turning those words over in her mind. "Yes, I was possessed by the devil, and his name is Thibault, and he is my half brother."

"Ellen!" Claire cried out in horror. "What are you trying to say?"

"The man who attacked and violated me is my half brother, and just imagine this: he doesn't even know it!"

Claire sat down on the bed beside her and listened.

When Ellen had finished her story it was already dark. Claire lay down alongside her and gently stroked her forehead until she fell asleep.

—

The next day she didn't wake up until noon.

"A messenger from your patroness brought a chicken a short while ago and told me I should make some soup. Well, I did it right away!" Claire declared with a laugh.

"Mm, it smells wonderful!" As proof of the sincerity of her words, her stomach growled loudly.

"We'll put some meat on your bones." Claire placed two soup bowls on the table and carefully filled them with the steaming liquid. Then she cut off a chicken leg for each of them, added some carrots and onions, and cut two thick slices from a large loaf of bread. "It's so tender the meat falls right off the bones." Claire licked her lips. "Do you think you can get up?"

"Yes, I think I can," Ellen replied. "I already feel a lot better."

"Then come and sit with me here at the table and eat so you'll get your strength back soon."

They eagerly ladled out the hot soup and dunked pieces of the crusty bread in it to soften them up.

"It tastes wonderful," Ellen said.

"I've washed your things and put them there on the chair."

Ellen looked in the corner where the chair stood and stared at the clothes. They seemed odd to her, like something out of an earlier life.

"Couldn't you make me the dress instead?" she asked shyly.

Claire beamed and nodded. "But of course! I'll go and get the material, and we can start right after the meal." She jumped up from her stool and rushed out of the room.

"We? You said we. But I can't even sew," Ellen called after her anxiously.

"I know, my dearest, but I first have to take measurements, and you will have to try it on a few times or else it will hang on you like a sack." Claire stroked her cheek to cheer her up.

When she heard that, Ellen couldn't help but think of the tanner's wife. Her life in Orford, and Simon, were so far, far away. Ellen felt a twinge of homesickness and sighed.

After the meal Claire took the long strip of cloth and measured Ellen's height down to her ankles. She folded the material, cut the longer piece, checked the size of the smaller piece, and nodded. Then she cut a hole and a slit in the middle of the material.

"Put it on, see if your head will fit through."

After Ellen had pulled the dress over her head, Claire tugged on it to straighten it out. "Your shoulders are so broad. It's good I checked again or my measurements would have been off and your stitches would probably have burst later on!" Claire's easy laughter took the weight off their minds and put sunlight back into their lives. Claire put the material on the table and made a cut on the left and on the right. "The shoulder will be here… well, I must still make an armhole," Claire explained, "and we'll put a gore on each side of the body piece to give your dress a nicer, wider shape." She pointed at the top of the main panel of fabric and picked up the two pieces she had cut before. Claire worked fast and carefully while Ellen watched patiently. Before she finally stitched up the sides, she had Ellen try the dress on once again. "And we will cut this piece here in two, to make the sleeves." Claire pointed at the remnant fabric she had cut off first.

Ellen was delighted that the dress was taking shape so quickly.

After she stitched up the side, Claire took some colorful trimming from a basket. "My husband gave it to me," she said, delighted with how well the colors went with the blue in Ellen's dress. "I think I'll sew it on up here along the neckline," she said.

"But he gave it to *you*." Ellen looked at Claire in astonishment. "Why don't you sew it on a new dress for yourself?"

"When it's on the neckline of my dress I can't see it, but on yours I'll see it every day! I'm sure it will look very good on you. It's your first real dress—please allow me the pleasure of giving it to you." Claire furrowed her brow and began sewing on the trimming.

"You are so good to me. How can I ever repay your friendship?"

"You already have, Ellen, through your trust in me." Claire looked at her with a gentle, beautiful smile.

—

Late in the afternoon Adelise de Béthune came to visit.

The dress was almost finished, and after the last fitting Ellen had simply not taken it off again.

Claire crouched down in front of her and finished the long seam.

"Heavens, what a change. Your cheeks have their color back again, child," the lady said, delighted.

"Your chicken soup and the new dress have done wonders!" Claire laughed.

"Thank you so much for everything, *madame*. Without the help from you and Claire, I would have been lost." Ellen looked down at the ground. "Is your son well?" she asked shyly.

"Yes, my child, he is very well, and no day goes by when he doesn't inquire about you. He calls you his angel and wants to know if you can visit him soon. But first you have to regain your strength. We certainly don't want to be the cause of a new fainting spell." The Lady of Béthune smiled knowingly and gave Ellen an almost imperceptible wink.

—

After he had assaulted Ellen, Thibault felt better for a while, but the initial satisfaction after his act of vengeance soon left a bitter taste in his mouth. Ellen got no pleasure in sleeping with him, and that spoiled his feeling of triumph. Never would she yearn for him as he did for her. Thibault was impossible for days and took his bad mood out on the younger squires until one day he again happened to see Rose. He missed her, the tender caresses that soothed his famished body, the devotion, the way she threw herself at him, and the delight she showed in their love play. Thibault brushed the hair from his eyes and smiled at her.

Rose blushed.

She was still in love with him!

She quickly looked away and disappeared into the servants' house.

Thibault straightened his shoulders. He had to win Rose back, and then he would feel better. He wasn't worried—it would be an easy thing for him to cast his spell over her. Perhaps he could buy her a spicy ham, some honey cakes, or a pretty bronze ring. He knew exactly what girls liked! Why hadn't he tried to win over Ellen instead of violating her? Furiously he pounded the door, and with a loud crash it flew open.

"What in the world is eating you?" Adam d'Yqueboeuf asked with a sigh. "Trouble with women?"

"Oh, shut up. What do you know about it? When they see you they run away, but with me they can't get enough," Thibault snapped at him.

"All right, all right!" Adam grumbled and returned to his bed. "Let me know when you are in a better mood."

Thibault also fell down on his bed. He'd let a little time pass before he went back to see Rose. Certainly by then she would be waiting impatiently for him. He'd have to be careful not to say the wrong thing when they spoke of Ellen. She was surely worried that her friend had run away, and all because of him. At the thought of Ellen and her anxious, wide-open eyes, his excitement began to grow.

—

It was easy for Thibault to seduce Rose again. He feigned remorse and explained it by his jealousy of her. Rose clung affectionately to his every word as he tried to convince her of his fear that he would lose her to the blacksmith's assistant. He even managed to convince her that he no longer had any reason to be angry at Ellen and pretended to regret she had left. In truth, he was torn between relief because Ellen was gone and the torment of his longing for her. Not even Rose's caresses could help him get over his lust for Ellen, and almost every night he dreamed of the mixture of fear and hatred in her eyes as she pretended to be resigned to her fate, only to finally slash out at him with a knife. Though he knew he would probably never see her again, he couldn't stop thinking of her. Sometimes he flirted with other maids just to torment Rose, but her jealousy did not quiet for long his desire to see Ellen suffer.

Béthune, 1169

For two years now, Ellen had been in Beuvry, a small village belonging to Béthune, and more and more frequently her thoughts turned to moving on. She hesitated only out of concern for abandoning Claire. Easter came and went, and the spring sun drove out the dark memories of a cold, hard winter.

Then, one day, Guiot returned to Béthune. He was just a young lad when his father sent him away with a stranger almost fifteen years earlier. The old folk who still remembered him gossiped, but so did the young folk who didn't even know him and wondered what brought him back to the village.

When Claire and Ellen arrived at the fountain, this was all people were talking about there, as well.

"Have you seen him yet?" asked Adele, looking expectantly at the others. She was not yet twenty years old and already a widow. As her year of mourning was now over, she could start thinking of marrying again, so a new man in town was very welcome.

The twins Gwenn and Alma shook their heads simultaneously, just as they always did things together at the same time.

Morgane, however, blushed. "He looks very handsome," she said shyly.

"Oh, tell us more," they all shouted in unison.

"I saw him just yesterday. He's big and strong and is building a shop right next to his father's cottage," she said, now with a bit more confidence.

"And how do you know that? Maybe it's just a shed. Did he tell you that? Have you spoken with him?" Adele rolled her eyes up, and red spots appeared on her neck, as always when she was excited.

"Yes, do tell us!" Gwenn and Alma chimed in, but before she could say anything, Claire spoke up.

"He won't bring you any happiness!"

The young women looked at her in surprise.

"Guiot was always a good-for-nothing, and that certainly hasn't changed," she said dismissively. She didn't say anything about the day, many years ago, when he grabbed her and pushed her against the wall behind the village barn, swore he would love her forever, and kissed her on the mouth. She was only eleven then, and it meant nothing to her, so why should the women think she was another competitor in the marriage market? Guiot didn't interest her in the least, and the kiss was something he had forced on her.

"Do you know him?" Morgane looked at Claire ecstatically.

"I knew him, but I have no interest in getting reacquainted. He's all yours, dear ladies!" As Claire was turning around, Morgane tugged at her sleeve.

"My father has no money for a dowry. Do you think he would...nevertheless...maybe...I mean if he really likes me?"

"Oh, Morgane, don't go throwing yourself at him. There are plenty of men who—" Claire couldn't finish her sentence because Adele interrupted.

"Just in case you haven't noticed, my dear Claire, there are at least two young women of marriageable age in our town for every available man, including widowers. And if you leave out the paupers, who can't feed a family anyway, and the old people who have one foot in the grave, then there isn't much of a selection." Adele was furious. Her voice almost cracked, and she had red spots not just on her neck now but on her cheeks and forehead.

"Anyone here who can't find a decent man can ask the lady for help. Béthune owns lots of villages, and not all of them are as short on men as we are here in Beuvry. She'll certainly make sure you all find decent husbands," said Claire, trying to calm the agitated crowd. Full of empathy, she caressed Morgane's pitch-black hair. Morgane was only sixteen and already consumed with fear that she would die an old maid.

"But I think he's nice!" Morgane protested.

Claire merely shrugged unsympathetically. At the time she had not been able to choose Jacques' father. The marriage was arranged by her own father and the old Lady of Béthune, the mother-in-law of the present lady. They wanted to convince a scabbard maker to settle down in the village, since there were no such tradesmen in the area and the local blacksmiths needed the service. So they offered the scabbard maker a pretty bride and a little cottage in Beuvry as a dowry. It had been a good deal for Claire's father, as he was able to marry his youngest daughter off to a respectable tradesman at no cost. When Claire first met him, she was unable to see anything attractive in him, but he turned out to be a good husband. He was calm, even a bit reserved, but he never hit her and had taught her everything she knew. Claire didn't think much of marriages for any dubious sentimental reasons. All that counted was that a husband treated his wife and children well and could care for them.

Morgane's curiosity was still not satisfied, and she interrupted Claire's reflections. "The word is that his father sold him years ago, and I wonder if that's true?" The very idea made her tremble.

Claire was unmoved and merely shrugged. "No one knows. Guiot's father, Jean, brought a stranger to town, and that very day he left again with the boy. Jean never said a word about it or where he had sent him, and everyone in the village believed he had sold Guiot. They were angry with the old man for doing that and avoided him thereafter. He was just a simple day laborer, but he wasn't really so poor that he had to sell his only son."

"Guiot must not have had it too bad, since he did come back to his father!" said Morgane, who had evidently decided to stand up for the father and the son.

"That may be, but honestly I don't really care where he was. I just hope he's not going to cause trouble here. As far as I'm concerned, he can go straight back to where he came from," Claire added gruffly. She was not comfortable that Guiot was coming back, and the very thought of him made her insides tremble ominously.

To Claire's great annoyance, after he had repaired the thatched roof of his father's cottage, Guiot in fact built a workshop and let everyone know that he was a scabbard maker. He traveled around the region introducing himself to the blacksmiths and trying to solicit business from them.

"And he was brazen enough not even to stop by and tell me personally that he intended to set up shop here as a scabbard maker, although there was already a workshop here. But that's the least of it," Claire said, getting more and more agitated, without noticing that Guiot was standing in the doorway just behind her.

She failed to notice Ellen's warning glances, and in the meanwhile Guiot broke out in a broad smile, took off his hat, and bowed.

"You are completely right, good woman. I should have come earlier, but some time ago when I heard that your husband had died I thought there had to be a need for a scabbard maker in

Béthune. I took it as a sign from heaven telling me finally to come back home," he declared with a smile.

Claire wheeled around, shocked, and then she blushed deeply.

"You can surely imagine how terrible I feel that no one needs me here," Guiot said with a sad, hangdog look.

Claire nodded with satisfaction. It served him right.

"All the blacksmiths I visited viewed me and my work suspiciously. They didn't even seriously examine samples of my work that I brought along and told me right off they didn't need me or my work. I couldn't understand why they reacted with such hostility—my work is good, I am sure of that."

"Bah!" said Claire saucily.

But Guiot just went on talking. His dark eyes sparkled just as they used to under his tousled, curly head of hair. Naturally, he was now older—back then he had been just a lad—but the mischievousness and the sparkle in his eyes had remained.

"The fifth or sixth took pity on me and told me my work was no better than yours. People didn't know me and saw no reason to risk a change in business relationships that had always been satisfactory. On my honor, I swear, I had no idea that you were carrying on your husband's business." He looked at her pleadingly.

But Claire was not moved by his charm. *On his honor*, she thought with contempt. *What could that be worth?* "Well, now you know," she replied quarrelsomely. "You can pack your things and move on. There's no room here for you."

"My father is an old man and I must look after him. For a long time now, he hasn't been able to make a decent living from his work. He…"

"You're strong—you can work as a servant or day laborer," Claire interrupted him coldly.

"But I love what I do," Guiot answered sorrowfully. His sad look however had no effect on Claire.

"Well, that's very nice for you, but please tell me what that has to do with me?" Even though Claire admired his devotion to his calling, she had no desire to continue this conversation. His presence made her feel too uneasy.

"Maybe you could give me some work," he asked softly, and his face brightened for a moment, as if he had just thought of this possibility.

Ellen had been listening to this conversation with great curiosity and chuckled at his mischievousness, as it seemed apparent he had planned in advance to ask Claire for a job.

"We can get along just fine without you," she replied coolly, annoyed that Guiot had spoken with her as if they were strangers. *If he really doesn't remember me, then it serves him right twice over that he's at his wits' end*, she thought angrily.

"If you will allow me, I would like to stop by to see you again in a few days," he said, bowing.

"Do what you have to, but don't get your hopes up," Claire answered as she turned back to her work.

The rest of the day she was unusually cross, and Ellen decided to leave her to herself until she had calmed down. In the past two years she had gotten to know Claire well enough to suspect why she was so gruff. She was afraid! But of what?

"This Guiot doesn't seem to be such a bad fellow," Ellen said at supper, as casually as possible.

"Even when he was just a lad he was the heartthrob of all the girls. They all fell for his big brown eyes. No sooner is he back and he's starting all over again. Such men are like poison. The women will fall for him one after the other, and they'll all be disappointed. Adele, Morgane, and the others, too."

Ah yes, his brown eyes, Ellen thought with amusement, but she tried not to let her feelings show.

Claire chewed listlessly on her slice of bread and finally said, "But the worst thing is that he'll try to steal my customers."

"But didn't he say he had no idea..."

"Nonsense," Claire interrupted her brusquely, "that's just nonsense. I'm sure he knew exactly but was only thinking that a woman was not a serious competitor. Men like him think they can get away with anything."

"But didn't he say he wants to work for you? Why not let him?"

"Oh, there are lots of reasons why," Claire said, a bit too fast.

Ellen looked at her and waited for the explanation, but Claire continued eating silently. Finally Ellen returned to her question: "And what are these reasons?"

Claire swallowed what was in her mouth. "Well, there's the question of the cost. The smiths pay me less because I'm a woman. They'd have to pay him more, and that's the only reason they'd rather deal with me. Up until now, that is. You see, if I have to pay him, I'd have to raise my prices." She jutted her chin forward. "Anyway, I just don't want him here—he's dangerous!" The last words she almost shouted.

It seems to me he's more dangerous for your heart than for your business, Ellen almost replied, but she kept silent.

"I figured out long ago what he's up to—I'm not stupid. He didn't get anywhere with the smiths, and so he thought he'd work for me for a while. And when they get to know him they'll eventually prefer a man's work, and that's how his plan would work."

Ellen nodded thoughtfully. Claire's reasoning in fact made sense, and of course she knew Guiot better than Ellen did.

"Then it would be best for you not to make an enemy of him."

"In any case, I won't knuckle under to him. It would be best for him to leave and try his luck somewhere else."

There was little hope, Ellen thought, that Guiot would do her this favor, and that's probably also what Claire was thinking and why she was so angry. Guiot had put his savings into the workshop, and Béthune was his hometown. Ellen was thinking that in his place she wouldn't give up so easily, either.

"On the other hand, if he's not ready to leave the village, there's only one solution to your problem: you've got to marry him," she said facetiously.

Claire blanched.

"Never!" she declared, and looked at Ellen angrily.

—

Barely a week later, Guiot returned to the workshop.

"Morgane asked me about what happened back then. I don't know why I didn't remember right away when I heard your name. You were a pretty girl, but that you'd someday turn into such a beautiful, strong woman..." He shook his head in disbelief.

Ellen noticed the familiar way he addressed Claire and wondered how she would react.

But she said nothing at all. She didn't even look up from her work—it was almost as if he weren't there.

"Even though you were always a stubborn kid," he said, grinning, "and a real daredevil. When I think of how you grabbed me back then and pulled me behind the barn!"

At hearing that, Claire lost her composure, and that's probably exactly what he had hoped for. "I pulled you behind the barn? It was you who without asking gave me a disgusting, sticky kiss and swore eternal love to me—as if that's anything I would ask you for!"

"And then I didn't even recognize you again. I know, I'm an impossible fellow!" he asserted, remorsefully. "But the truth is I never did forget you! You have become such a beautiful woman." Guiot sighed and grinned again.

Claire was still furious.

"I don't care one whit whether you recognized me or not—your childish protestations don't mean anything to me, either. Get out, save your sweet talk and your blarney for Morgane—she's still young enough to fall for that sort of thing." Angrily, Claire turned her back on him.

"Morgane," he said, stretching the word out. "Pretty but boring. I think experienced women are much more interesting." He winked at Ellen, who sat at the table, grinning.

Claire noticed it and gave Ellen a severe look before turning back to Guiot. "Go now, you impudent fellow!" she fumed.

Guiot ducked, nodded good-bye to Ellen, and left.

She couldn't see anything underhanded about him, but Claire got even angrier.

"Why doesn't he just clear out, this good-for-nothing?" she scolded after he had left the workshop.

Guiot came more frequently now to ask for work or to try to make amends, and each time he infuriated Claire.

The next time he visited the workshop, Claire was away.

"Can I help you?" Ellen asked politely.

"Well, you could put in a good word for me." He cocked his head to the side like a begging dog.

Ellen laughed. "That probably wouldn't do any good. Anyway, I don't know why I should do that for you."

"Have a look at my work yourself." He handed Ellen the two scabbards he was carrying.

They were carefully done, nicely decorated, and technically perfect. Claire would appreciate his work if she only didn't like him so much, Ellen thought.

Suddenly Claire stood on the threshold. "Now is he running after you? I told you, he makes eyes at all the women." She regarded him angrily.

"God, isn't she beautiful when she's mad?" Guiot asked, turning to Ellen.

"Here are some samples of his work. He wanted to show them to you in order to perhaps change your mind, but you weren't here. So I took a look at them." Ellen made a point of staying calm as she handed the two scabbards to Claire.

Surprisingly, Claire examined the samples, possibly because it was the best way not to have to look Guiot in the eye. "Good work! I find nothing wrong with it, but I explained to you that I don't need any help."

Guiot's gaze wandered to the pile of slats already cut and trimmed to size. That looked like plenty of work.

Claire followed his gaze and blushed, because it made her look like a liar. "I can't pay you decent wages even if I have lots of orders," she said in embarrassment.

Guiot nodded and seemed to understand. "How about us getting married? Then we could work together. Wouldn't that be the solution to our problem?" His voice sounded unemotional, but his eyes sparkled.

Claire looked at him in disbelief. "The solution to our problem? I didn't have any problem until you came back. I have always provided for us, and we have managed to get along. Why now should I submit to a man like you?"

"Because you love me?" Guiot smiled innocently.

"Just get out now, and don't ever come back, do you hear! I'd rather marry a stinking old geezer than you, of all people!" she scoffed.

Guiot lowered his eyes. *He looks like a man who is deeply in love*, Ellen thought sympathetically.

Without replying, he left the shop

—

The other women in the village who had placed their hopes on getting him as a husband wondered what might have happened to make Guiot change so much. He never came to the fountain anymore to chat with them and no longer spent evenings with his father sitting in front of their cottage. If anyone caught sight of him anywhere, he was always sad and depressed.

Two weeks later Morgane saw him leaving town as his father stood at the fence, crying. The entire village gossiped about why he had gone away.

Ever since his offer of marriage he had not returned to Claire's workshop. At first, she didn't seem to care, but after a while it appeared to Ellen as if she kept looking toward the door more than she used to.

"You see, I said from the very start, men like that are just no good. He comes back here suddenly after all these years, can hardly wait to propose marriage to me, and then he leaves again. Can you image how dumb I would have looked," she sputtered one day, "if I'd said yes?"

"Claire, do you still not get it…that he left for your sake? You love him, don't you, so why didn't you want to marry him?"

It was obviously a stroke of fate, but Claire had not been open to it.

"How would that have changed anything? Didn't you see how the other women in the village looked at him? Heavens, good-looking women like Morgane!"

"But it's really you he loves."

"I think differently. Men are not capable of true love; what they want above all is what they can't have. He wanted me because I rejected him, but once we got married he'd want the other women instead. Marriage out of love doesn't last, that's the way of the world, and it only makes you unhappy."

Now Ellen understood: Claire was afraid of love!

"He's gone, and it's better this way, believe me," Claire added, and Ellen wondered who she was trying to convince.

Ever since Guiot had left, Claire worked like one possessed. She tried hard to look happy, but she couldn't hide her feelings. She didn't laugh and didn't enjoy eating anymore.

Things couldn't go on this way! Claire was as stubborn as a mule! It wouldn't be easy to change her opinion about love—it seemed too late for that anyway—but Ellen wanted to help Claire and Guiot. She had to find a way for them. Guiot would make Claire happy again, and Ellen would be able to move on without having a guilty conscience.

—

"Excuse me if I'm disturbing you, but do you have a moment to give me?" Ellen asked politely when old Jean opened the door to his cottage.

"Come in, my child," he answered amiably.

The room was surprisingly clean and comfortable. Straw mats lay on the hard dirt floor, and there were clean sheets on the wooden bed in the corner. There were a number of hooks along one wall to hang clothing, and three of them were unused. *This is probably where Guiot hung his things*, Ellen thought.

"Do have a seat." The old man pointed to two chairs next to a table near the fireplace. He licked his wrinkled lips and fetched two cups and a pitcher of stale beer. Then he poured a cup and passed it to Ellen, took a big gulp out of the other one, and sat down.

"I've come because of Guiot," Ellen said, and was immediately angry at the way she put it. She didn't want the old man to think she herself was interested in his son. "And because of Claire," she quickly added.

The old man stared into space. "His mother died early and I raised him myself. The boy was all I had, and nevertheless I sent him away so he could learn a trade and would have things easier later on. I had to be thrifty and work hard to be able to afford the apprentice's premium, but it was worth it to me." The old man's eyes filled with tears that he quietly tried to wipe away.

Ellen took his rough, wrinkled hand and squeezed it compassionately.

"When Claire's husband died, I traveled to Eu and begged Guiot to come back, but he didn't want to. 'Do you know how many men will be chasing after his widow?' he asked me. 'I'm doing fine right here,' he said, and then a few weeks ago he was standing at my door. You can't believe how happy that made me."

Ellen thought of Osmond. How much she would love to see him again!

The old man's Adam's apple bounced up and down as he took a few big gulps, and then he continued: "Ever since they were little children he cared for her more than anyone else, and then he didn't even recognize her. You should have seen them when they were youngsters: Claire was a real broomstick, not especially pretty but lively and a bit fresh. It was only when she became a young girl that she was a real beauty. Her marriage and the child did her a world of good and taught her common sense. On his very first day back, Guiot fell in love with her and when he realized who she was, he made up his mind. 'I'll marry her,' he told me, and he looked happier than I have ever seen him. I was glad for him, but every time he visited her he came back home depressed. He hoped she would think it over, but she turned him down every time. He became lovesick and said he could only forget her if he never saw her again." The old man sounded bitter. "He's no worse than her first husband. If only for the sake of the business he would have been the right person for her."

"He's the right person for her," Ellen said emphatically, "and Claire knows that, too. But she's afraid."

The old man looked at her, perplexed. "That's just nonsense! Guiot would never hurt a fly."

"No, no, she's not afraid of being beaten," Ellen said, trying to reassure him. "She's afraid of losing his love once she belongs to him."

"She rejects him because she's afraid of losing him?" The old man looked at her in disbelief.

"Claire thinks men are unfaithful and that she will suffer less by rejecting him than if she found him cheating on her someday." Ellen took a deep breath.

"Women always make things more complicated than they really are," the old man opined, shaking his head in disapproval.

"You're right there, but that's just why I came to see you. Somebody must force them to do the right thing. I owe Claire a lot and want to help her. She doesn't admit it, but she is terribly unhappy because Guiot left."

"Serves her right," the old man grumbled.

"She loves Guiot, and with a little coaxing we can get her to marry him," Ellen said with a knowing smile.

"It's too late for that," old Jean said, sounding hopeless.

"I don't think so, unless you don't know where he went."

"He was going to go back to Eu."

"Then let's hope he is still there. I have an idea how we can make this all work out." Ellen smiled and stood up. "Don't give up hope—with a little luck your son will soon be back. But..." Ellen put her finger to her lips and put on a serious face. "Don't forget, not a word to anyone, or my plan won't work."

The old man nodded politely but skeptically and showed Ellen to the door. *I've got to do it*, she thought, rubbing her hands together. She had an idea on how to bring the two lovers together, and brimming with excitement she hurried to the castle.

—

"Halt! What is your business?" the guard at the gate demanded, blocking Ellen's way. "I have never seen you here before."

"I'm from Beuvry and wish to see the advocate's wife."

"What does it concern?" the guard asked slowly, in no hurry to let Ellen pass.

"That's none of your business. The lady knows me—I'm the one who saved her son's life, and if you don't believe me go and ask her. My name is Ellenweore." She planted herself in front of him just as she had done long ago as a blacksmith's boy. Her imperious manner unnerved the young guard.

"Then pass, but you will have to announce yourself again at the residence tower," he said, trying to look unfazed as he let Ellen through.

The second guard was more cordial and pointed to a large meadow behind the tower. "*Madame* is back there with her children. You may go to her."

Ellen watched from a distance and couldn't help admiring the lady's grace and beauty. She was sitting in the grass playing with her youngest child and fondling him. Two nurses played ring-around-the-rosy with the older children, giggling and dancing merrily. Adelise de St. Pol had married the Advocate of Béthune while still very young and had given him several sons and daughters, whom she raised with great devotion. The eldest son had already left home.

"How are you, Ellen? You look well. And Jacques and Claire, are they also in good health?" The lady received them holding her youngest child in her arms and allowing the child to tug at her hair.

"I'm worried about Claire, *madame*, and would like to ask you for help, even though you have long ago repaid everything we are entitled to with your generosity."

"What is wrong with Claire? Is she ill?" Adelise de Béthune looked concerned.

"I'm afraid she soon will be if we don't find a solution."

"Come and have a seat with us here in the grass."

Even before Ellen could sit down, little Baudouin saw her and came running toward her.

"My angel, my angel!" he exclaimed, laughing, and Ellen had to catch the little fellow in her arms. As she bent down to him, he cuddled up to her and wrapped his arms around her neck.

"My, how you've grown!" Ellen exclaimed.

"When I grow up, I'm going to be a knight," he said proudly, looking at her with a serious expression. "Then you can ask me to do anything you want."

"Be careful of what you promise, or I might ask you to marry me when I'm an old hag," Ellen grinned.

"You wouldn't do that," he objected, but then he added with uncertainty in his voice, "Or would you?" His mother and the nurses broke out in laughter.

"Baudouin, will you go to the kitchen with Hawise?" the lady asked, looking at her son and nodding to one of the maids. "Bring back some cookies for us all, and some cider so we can eat here in the garden."

"Oh yes!" he cried, and ran off.

"So now we have a moment to ourselves. Tell me what is troubling Claire."

Ellen told her about everything that had happened and what she planned to do. Lady Béthune looked troubled at first, but her face brightened with every word Ellen spoke.

"That's a wonderful idea, Ellen—a bit devious, but brilliant. Of course I'll help you with it."

Baudouin provided her amply with cookies and cider, and finally Ellen had a little sticky spot on her dress because the boy hadn't wiped his mouth before hugging her to say good-bye. Although Ellen had no experience dealing with children, she couldn't resist the charm of young Baudouin and kissed him on his reddish-brown hair, thinking for a moment of the child she had lost.

"Claire won't be exactly thrilled that I have been gone for such a long time, but I'll have to live with that. It's for a good cause, after all," she said, smiling and turning to Adelise de Béthune. With an almost perfect curtsy, she bade farewell and set out for home.

As expected, Claire was in a bad mood because Ellen had been away so long.

"I went to see Baudouin. I stayed longer than I meant to, but he and his mother insisted I stay for a while, and what could I do?" Ellen said apologetically.

"Just look at you!" Claire grumbled. "The beautiful dress!" She didn't usually get excited about such minor things.

"Baudouin, cider, and cookies," Ellen said, and shrugged.

"Get right to work—there's still time before it's dark. The scabbards for Master George aren't finished yet, and he wants them by the end of the week."

"I'll work as fast as the wind," Ellen declared lightheartedly.

Claire, who used to be so happy anytime Ellen showed even a hint of a good mood, looked at her crossly. "Why all this fuss? Just get to work!"

Ellen didn't reply but did what Claire asked. She was quietly humming a happy tune, and Claire looked at her several times with a stern expression but didn't say anything else to her.

—

Two uneventful weeks passed. Claire was busy and had little to say, and Ellen tried hard to do everything the way she wanted, although recently that had become almost impossible.

Then, one early morning in September when the air already had a touch of fall in it, men on horseback came riding into the village and stopped in front of the workshop.

Claire and Ellen went running out.

It was Adelise de Béthune accompanied by some other men. A young knight hastily dismounted from his horse to help. She waited patiently while he lifted her down.

"*Madame*, what an honor! What brings you here?" Claire said politely, and curtsied.

Adelise de Béthune beckoned to one of her escorts, an older man with a pinched mouth and warts on his nose, who struggled to dismount and walked over to them. He exuded an unpleasant odor of sweat and foul-smelling hair.

"My dear Claire, this is Basile, a scabbard maker just like your late husband. I know I should have long ago taken it upon myself to search for a new husband for you. The burden of running this shop is surely much too great for your delicate shoulders, and you are too young to stay single."

Claire gasped as if she wanted to interrupt the lady but couldn't say a word, and Adelise de Béthune continued her happy chatter. "My husband would like to help him get established in Beuvry and marry you." The Lady of Béthune beamed innocently at Claire, who said nothing.

Ellen suspected what Claire must be feeling. Of course she could refuse, but then she would have to worry whether the advocate would marry him off to another young woman and set them up in her house and her workshop.

Claire looked at him in disgust.

Adelise de Béthune smiled. "I told Basile how long you have been managing the workshop by yourself. He is very happy that you are such a good worker."

"Until we have children you can help me," Basile said haughtily, "and later you can stay at home." His wide grin revealed a few decaying teeth.

Claire lowered her eyes.

Basile leaned against the doorpost to the workshop and examined it as casually as if he were already the owner.

"As you wish, *madame*," Claire mumbled obediently, and she didn't look up so that no one would see the tears in her eyes.

"Very well, Claire, then we'll have a wedding a week from Sunday. You know how much I care for you, and thus I've decided to give you and Ellen a new dress for your wedding. Come to see me tomorrow so we can measure you, and please bring Jacques along as I would like to give him something decent to wear, too." Adelise de Béthune smiled amiably and was helped back up onto her horse.

"Come, Basile, let us leave. It won't be too long before the workshop belongs to you," she called out, turning her horse.

—

"He's dreadful!" Ellen exclaimed after they had left. "Just how could she do that to you?"

Claire endeavored to look nonchalant. "She means only the best for me. Do you think my first husband was any better? Certainly this Basile has his good side, too." Claire's voice was trembling.

"But he's old and his eyes are, oh, I don't know…so…piercing," Ellen replied, though she knew the anguish this would cause Claire. But she had to do it if her plan was to succeed—there was just no other way.

"It's the advocate's right to pick out a husband for me. Neither the house nor the workshop belongs to me. If I don't marry Basile, I shall have to leave Beuvry. But this is my home, and Jacques' home, too. So I'll marry him even if I get sick when I think of having to raise his children and share a bed with him for the rest of my days. Perhaps God will be merciful to me and I'll die in childbirth," she gasped.

Just as Ellen was considering giving away her secret, Claire regained her composure.

"Oh, God, my first husband was also no prize, but I found a way to get along with him," she said with determination.

Claire looked more miserable from day to day, and finally, on the evening before the wedding she was crying uncontrollably.

Ellen took her in her arms to console her.

"I've done everything wrong," Claire lamented. "I was so stupid! Certainly this is just what I deserve, but I don't know if I'll be able to go through with it."

Ellen tried hard to look horrified so that Claire wouldn't figure things out. Claire's eyes were red from crying, and it really grieved Ellen deeply to see her friend so saddened. She was almost at the point of releasing the poor woman from her sorrow, but she had resolved to hold the course even if it wasn't easy.

"Maybe they wouldn't have approved of Guiot. If the Lord of Béthune had wanted to, he could have planned for me to marry Guiot…if only he hadn't disappeared so fast…" Claire broke out in loud sobs.

"But my dear, you said yourself that an arranged marriage is the best thing that can happen to a woman." Ellen was a bit ashamed of how cruel she was.

"Yes, I know I said something dumb like that, and now I have to pay for it." Claire sat up and wiped the tears from her eyes. "I'll marry this Basile fellow tomorrow, proudly and with my head up. But he shouldn't put too much hope in my working in the kitchen and caring for our brood of children," she declared defiantly.

Ellen nodded, in agony. Perhaps she had been wrong about Claire after all, and she was in fact as strong as she always pretended to be. Would she truly acquiesce and go along with this marriage?

—

On her wedding day, Claire got up as early as on any other day. Ellen saw her going into the workshop and looking around sadly. All the ongoing projects were completed, and everything was tidied up. There wasn't a stray thread lying around, not a tool that had not been neatly put away. Although Claire had already put on her wedding dress, she swept up one more time. Now it looked as if no work had been done in the shop for a long time. Claire squared her shoulders and walked out.

Ellen watched as she left. She would have to summon up all her strength to make it all the way to the church. Stone-faced, Claire walked out of the cottage to meet her fate, looking not like a bride but like a convicted person on the way to her execution.

Adelise de Béthune and her attendants were already waiting at the church.

With apparent indifference and her head high, Claire marched toward the church, but when she caught sight of her repulsive-looking husband-to-be, she finally lost her composure. "I can't do it," she whispered with a trembling voice.

Ellen acted as if she hadn't heard, and a moment later Adelise de Béthune walked toward the two of them, smiling and reaching out to the bride with both hands. She greeted them warmly.

"Soon you will once more be a married woman, my child."

Claire shook her head and pulled the lady off to one side.

"Please, *madame*, you must release me from my obligation. I love another man. I can't marry Basile."

"What sort of nonsense is that, my child? You love another man? That's not really any reason not to marry Basile. It's foolish to build a marriage based on love—believe me, I know what I am talking about."

"That's what I always believed, too, until Guiot came back. He wanted to marry me, and I, silly goose that I am, said no." Claire was at the end of her rope.

"Well, then, everything is settled, and we can now finally celebrate your wedding," said Adelise de Béthune, looking at Claire with unusual severity. "Come now!"

Claire gave up and followed her. She was staring straight down at her feet so they couldn't run away and didn't notice that Guiot in the meanwhile had taken Basile's place. Her eyes filled with tears.

The priest began his homily about marriage, its duties, and the will of God.

Claire seemed hardly to hear what he said.

"Will you, Claire, widow of the scabbard maker Jacques and mother of his son Jacques, take this man Guiot standing before you, also a scabbard maker by trade, as a husband? Will you love him and cherish him..."

Claire's eyes suddenly shot up, like those of a startled deer. Had he said Guiot? In disbelief she looked to her side where she'd assumed Basile was standing.

Guiot smiled bashfully.

"...be faithful to him until your life's end, bear his children, and raise them in the fear of God as the Mother Church demands, and all this of your own free will, then answer yes." The priest looked at her questioningly.

"This wasn't my idea," Guiot whispered apologetically as the priest waited for an answer.

The priest patiently repeated his question.

This time she hastened to answer, "Yes," loudly and clearly, though her voice was trembling.

After Guiot had also answered affirmatively and the priest had given them his blessing, all her fear melted away.

"Who is behind this?" Claire asked, looking around and smiling at Guiot and the two women.

Guiot simply raised his hands and looked toward the Lady of Béthune.

"Oh, no, it wasn't my idea. I was only an instrument," she said, laughing and pointing to Ellen. "Only she was capable of contriving something like that!"

"Ellen!" Claire was much too happy to be annoyed.

"I couldn't just look on as you threw away your happiness. It's my way of thanking you. I have been thinking for a while of moving on and didn't want to leave you alone with all the work. Then, because you didn't want to hire him, being the obstinate person you are, I thought the best solution would be for you to marry Guiot. That's really what you wanted, wasn't it?"

"Thank you," Claire said in a choked voice.

Ellen took a wreath of little white flowers that she was holding behind her back, untied the tight bun behind Claire's head so that her beautiful dark-blond hair fell down over her shoulders in soft waves, and then placed the wreath on top of her head. "You are a beautiful bride, Claire, and Guiot is one lucky fellow!"

"Well, Claire is also lucky, and she'll soon realize that," Guiot said jokingly, pulling his bride to him in order to finally give her the second kiss he had yearned to give her for so many years.

"Is it better than the first?" he whispered.

Claire blushed and nodded.

The whole town had gathered at the church and broke out in applause. A few men whistled between their fingers, and the miller took his little flute and played a merry tune. The women sang a satirical song about marriage, an old custom in the village. Even Morgane, Adele, and the other young women seemed not to begrudge Claire her happiness. Perhaps they were thinking that if something so wonderful and unexpected could happen to one of them, then all of them might expect to find the right man someday.

Old Jean stepped out of the crowd with trembling legs, embraced his son who had returned, and cried softly at his good fortune.

Early March 1170

"We are running short of glue," Claire observed as casually as possible.

Ellen frowned a bit, but Claire seemed not to notice it. Ever since her wedding she was at times in a muddle. Had she really forgotten that tomorrow Ellen would be leaving forever?

"We're also running short on linen." Ellen's voice sounded thick.

Claire nodded without looking at her. "I'll bring some along tomorrow morning," she replied, but then suddenly muttered an apology and raced out of the workshop, nearly knocking Jacques over.

"Mom can't stop crying, and it's your fault." Jacques looked at Ellen disapprovingly.

"My fault?" Ellen asked indignantly.

"She's sad because you want to leave—and so am I," he said, embracing her awkwardly. As he got older his simple-mindedness became more noticeable.

"I'm sorry, too, Jacques, but it's time for me to move on." Ellen surreptitiously wiped a tear from the corner of her eye.

"I saw it, you're crying!" he crowed.

Ellen laughed, and this time a tear really did roll down her cheek.

"You need not cry—you can stay here, you know," Jacques pleaded affectionately, hugging her again.

"No, I must go, believe me," Ellen said, her voice trembling.

"But you will come again soon, won't you? And then I'll marry you," he said, with a broad smile.

Ellen couldn't help but think of little Baudouin, and laughed.

"Nonsense, Jacques! You'll marry a pretty young girl someday, not an old hag like me."

"You're not old at all," Jacques objected and looked at her as if he were offended. "Then I'll wait until I'm old, too," he replied, and left.

On the last day, it was hard for everyone to act as if it were just a day like any other, and as night fell, Claire finally turned to Ellen.

"I am certain that God sent you to us. You have done so much for me!" She squeezed Ellen's hand.

"Oh, no, Claire, you are the one who helped me! Without you I never would have found my way here, and because of you I have learned to believe in and have confidence in myself even if I wear a gown instead of braies and a shirt. I will always be indebted to you." Ellen overcame her shyness and for the first time of her own accord took Claire in her arms.

"Not at all! You don't owe me anything." Claire took her by the shoulders and looked her in the eye. "I owe all of my happiness to you."

"I agree with that," Guiot interjected, though he had heard only the last part of the conversation. He grinned and passed a pitcher to them. "Wine!" he said proudly. "I bought it so you would have pleasant memories of us." He smiled broadly.

Ellen relaxed a bit. "I see, I see, and you think that if I wake up tomorrow morning with a hangover," she teased, "I'll have pleasant memories of this evening."

"Sit down, you two beautiful people, and eat and drink with me." Guiot laughed and poured the red wine into the clay mugs on the table. To celebrate the day, Jacques also got a swallow. Guiot raised his mug in order to drink a toast with them.

"To you, Ellenweore!" he said warmly.

"To your future together and the child!" Ellen replied, nodding toward Claire.

She blushed, and Guiot took her proudly in his arms. “To your ambitious plans, Ellen! May you succeed in everything you do in life, and may you also find love!” he proclaimed, and clinked mugs with her.

Claire started to sob, placed the mug back on the table so hastily that the wine spilled out, and then went running from the room.

“Just let her go.” Ellen started to follow Claire, but Guiot held her back and motioned for her to have a seat again. “She’ll get hold of herself in a moment. If you go and join her now, you’ll both start crying, and it will just be worse.”

Ellen nodded. Guiot was right—it didn’t take long before Claire returned. Her eyes were red, but she sat down with them at the table and tried to smile.

To celebrate the day, they had roasted chicken with salsify roots and some heavy bread along with generous portions of wine, and for the rest of the evening they indulged in their reminiscences. When they finally went to bed, giggling and in high spirits, the wineskin was empty right down to the last drop.

—

The next morning, Ellen got up just as early as always. Her head was pounding, and she couldn’t stand either light, loud noises, or fast movements. If you drank too much, you just had to put up with the headache later until it was past. Ellen washed as always and got dressed. But her arms felt heavy, and every movement was difficult. Despite her splitting headache, she tied up the bundle with her belongings, neatly folding the beautiful green dress given to her by the Lady of Béthune that brought out the green sparkle in her eyes. As always, she had packed a supply of linens, a little torch, a flint stone, tinder, and a striker as well as some provisions. Ellen took the cloth that Aelfgiva had given her and that she guarded like the apple of her eye, snuggled her face in it, and thought longingly of the old herb woman. She also packed all the other things that brought back memories: the comb Claire had given her, the little Christophorus figure that Jacques had carved for her, the ribbons for her hair that she had never worn despite Claire's urging, and the shiny stone from Tancarville. Rose had found it as soon as they arrived and gave it to Ellen as a sign of her friendship. Even though Rose had betrayed her, Ellen always carried it with her. A tear rolled down her cheek, which she wiped away quickly with her sleeve, and then she put on the belt which held the knife from Osmond, the water skin, and a purse with just enough coins for the coming days. Most of her money she kept underneath her clothing. In case she was attacked by thieves, they would hopefully assume she was carrying all her money on her belt.

In Tancarville she had always cut her bright red hair at the ears, but since then it had grown and reached down below her shoulders. It was firm and curly, almost wiry, and just as rebellious as she was. At work, it would fall into her face, so she tied it with an ordinary piece of string into a short bun. A shock of hair curled above her high forehead, and the few spots she had on her nose when she was a child had grown into regular patches of freckles that gave a fresher look to her complexion and a warmer, more tender look to her otherwise plain face. Beneath her downy red eyebrows, her green eyes peered forth like emeralds in a copper setting.

Ellen sighed. Though she had for months thought of almost nothing else but leaving, it was difficult for her to go.

"You can still reconsider," Claire said, as she said her good-byes.

Ellen shook her head bravely. "I must leave now and go my own way!"

She had remained in Béthune for three years. After the wedding, Claire and Guiot had convinced her to stay the winter with them, but now it was definitely time to leave.

"Of course." Claire nodded.

Ellen embraced Guiot. "Take good care of her, do you hear?"

"You can depend on me—I will provide for her," Guiot replied solemnly.

Ellen swallowed hard.

"God, that makes it sound like she's my mother and not my friend." Claire sighed.

Ellen brightened when she saw Jean coming down the road. "Look, Guiot, here comes your father!" She liked the old man because he reminded her of Osmond.

He came up to her, embraced her, and whispered in her ear, "I would be proud to have had a daughter like you," and at that point Ellen completely lost what remained of her composure. Jean patted her shoulder, trying to comfort her.

"Look, there are some horses coming. I think it's Adelise de Béthune," Claire exclaimed a bit too loudly as she waved.

Ellen blinked to hold back her tears and saw that Claire was right.

The Lady of Béthune dismounted, took Ellen in her arms, and looked her straight in the eye. "Take care of yourself, Ellen!" Then she turned to her attendant and said, "Gauthier, the pony!"

Sir Gauthier handed Ellen the reins of a beautiful little pony. "Riding is more comfortable, faster, and above all safer!

He answers to the name of Nestor and is as gentle as a little lamb, well suited for an inexperienced rider," he said, smiling.

"It's yours," Adelise de Béthune confirmed, her bright eyes twinkling conspiratorially as if saying, *We women have to stick together.*

"Thank you, *madame*, many thanks!"

"Oh yes, I almost forgot. My son gave me this, and he wants me to let you know he will never forget you. He wants you to keep this little remembrance so you will feel the same way!" Adelise de Béthune fetched out a silken cloth and unfolded it. Inside, tied together with a little ribbon, was a lock of her son's dark reddish-brown hair.

Ellen was moved, and smiled.

"I wish you a safe journey, Ellen!" said Adelise de Béthune as she mounted her horse, bade everyone farewell with a graceful nod, and rode off.

Claire embraced Ellen one last time, reluctant to let her go.

"Come back to us whenever you want. You will always find open arms to receive you!" she said with emotion, and Guiot nodded in agreement.

"Thank you—for everything," Ellen whispered with a heavy heart.

"Well, let's see how to get you up on that horse," Guiot teased her as he helped Ellen mount it, although she could have easily done it herself. Nestor just stood there calmly, and only when Ellen clicked her tongue and pressed her heels into the horse's flanks did it trot away at a leisurely pace. She probably wouldn't make much faster progress with this horse than if she were on foot, but the pony would keep her warm and be a companion along the way. Suddenly she was happy not to be alone on her journey. Wasn't loneliness the worst of all suffering, next to sickness and hunger?

For a while, Jacques ran along beside her until they were beyond the village.

Then Ellen lowered the reins. Straight ahead, somewhere out there, lay her future.

April 1170

In every village she passed through she asked for work, but the people only shook their heads at the strange woman who claimed she was a blacksmith and sent her away. She had been traveling for a month now, and her savings were almost gone. March was colder than usual—it had even snowed—and April hadn't started out much better either. But she didn't give up and kept asking for work. Often people advised her to try her luck in Beauvais, and since she didn't have any other goal in mind, she decided to follow this advice. It took her two days to reach the city.

The fortress-like city walls of Beauvais could be seen far and wide and gave the city a look of importance and greatness. Many roads and lanes with their houses of all sizes wound around the imposing Episcopal residence. Ellen looked around with great curiosity and quickly understood that the source of the city's wealth was the cloth trade. Everywhere spinners, weavers, and dyers were at work making fine cloth from all sorts of wool. They even imported fine English sheep's wool especially from London. The city was pulsing with prosperity and commerce.

Ellen intended to inquire first at the bishop's palace about a job as swordsmith. Maybe her luck would finally change! But the palace guards waved her away brusquely and just laughed at her when she explained what she wanted.

Hungry, tired, and freezing, Ellen asked a thread-maker for directions to the blacksmith shops in town.

The woman showed not even a trace of a smile but with a pinched mouth and a terse explanation pointed the way. Although the local citizenry seemed to be well off, they didn't look like particularly happy people.

Her hopes fading, she arrived at a shop, knocked, and entered. The forge was small and untidy, but Ellen was not in a position to be choosy. In the last few weeks she had been turned away too many times, and now she absolutely had to find work and a place to stay. Dejectedly she started to reel off her little presentation. "Greetings, master, and I beg you to hear me out. I am looking for work as a blacksmith's helper or striker…" But she got no further than that.

"You've come at just the right moment!" the smith shouted with delight. Then he grabbed her by the arm and pulled her with him over to the house.

"See, Marie, your prayers were answered!" The smith pushed Ellen into the room.

His wife was as round as a barrel, and it was clear she would be having a child soon. She wiped her hand on her soiled apron and reached out to welcome Ellen. On the floor in front of them, a young boy about two years of age was playing with a girl perhaps three or four years old.

"You can sleep in the smithy and get the same thing to eat as the rest of us. I can't pay much, but it would be all right with me if you wanted to look for a second job somewhere else. In any case, you could sleep and eat here," the smith hastily added.

Though the terms were not at all attractive, Ellen decided to remain for the time being. She could always look around later for something better. "I accept," she began, but looking around at the children and at his wife's big belly, she added, "I don't wish to work in the house, but in the smithy. I am skilled as a smith and am a good striker."

The smith looked at her in surprise, thought a moment, and then reached out to shake her hand, saying, "Then we have an agreement!"

He must be having trouble if he would hire her without further inquiries.

"My name is Michel, by the way."

"Ellenweore!" She shook his hand to seal the contract.

"Have a seat with us at the table and eat!" Marie said in a friendly tone as she served the wooden bowls of soup for the family, adding another place at the table for Ellen.

The portion was skimpy and the soup a bit thin, but it tasted good. Ellen hoped that in the future Marie would make more! Once Ellen started working again as a blacksmith in the shop, her appetite would grow. Wistfully she thought back to the time with Donovan and Glenna. They had always given her plenty to eat and a real home. How were they? That evening Ellen fell asleep still hungry, freezing, and anything but happy. She had hoped for a better life in Beauvais and that she would be something more than an assistant in a third-class smithy.

—

The first night she dreamed of Osmond. She could almost smell the odor of warm goat's milk when she awoke at dawn in the workshop that still felt strange to her. With a heavy heart, she set to work. She hadn't been back to a smithy ever since she fled from Tancarville, but she hadn't forgotten her trade. By noontime of her first day it seemed to her as if she had never stopped. She had less strength and endurance than before, but she loved the strenuous work. Nevertheless, in the next few days she paid for her years of not working in her trade with severe muscle pain. Her hands, too, were not accustomed to the hard work anymore, and she again could feel the painful blisters and calluses.

"I admire you," Marie said one evening, glancing at Ellen's worn hands. "It's exactly because of these terrible blisters that I have always hated Michel's work here in the shop."

"Yes, indeed, that's why she's having one kid after the other and always saying that a hammer is too heavy for a woman in her condition," Michel interrupted.

"There you are again, you have no idea," Maria retorted, offended. "Hasn't the Lord made life hard enough for us women having to bear children? Living with a big belly is anything but easy, to say nothing of bearing children. I'd all too gladly leave that job to you and put up with the calluses on my hands." She seemed to be really angry at her husband, but just a moment later they kissed like a young couple in love, and everything was all right again.

Michel became a smith because his father had been a smith, and his father's father before that. He had little passion for or pride in his work, and yet he was good enough to have regular customers who were happy with him. He could have provided very well for his family and also could have taken on a striker and a journeyman if he hadn't spent every free moment playing dice in the tavern, where he was relieved of most of his money.

Marie accepted her fate because she didn't know of any other way to live. Michel didn't beat her as long as she kept her mouth shut, and that was enough for her.

July 1170

Ellen wiped her forehead with her hand. The summer was hot and sticky. Warm air gathered under the roof of the shop, making it difficult to breathe. She had been working for Michel for a full three months, and more and more frequently now he would disappear in the afternoon to play dice in the tavern. The journeymen in the other smithies made fun of him because he left the running of his workshop to a woman. They were suspicious and jealous of Ellen and afraid she would get too personal with their masters.

Ellen wondered if she should even remain in Beauvais. July was a good month to be on the road, and perhaps it would be better to tie up her bundle of things and exchange the anvil for a walking stick. As she was mulling this over, a tall, slender man, someone she had never seen before, entered the workshop. He appeared to be about thirty years of age and had warm, brown eyes and a full head of wavy brown hair.

"Isn't Michel here?" he asked, with a slightly furrowed brow.

"Sorry, for the moment you'll have to settle for me. What can I do for you?"

Judging from the deepening frown on his face, it was clear he wasn't happy at all having to deal with a woman who was a complete stranger rather than with the master. In spite of his hesitancy, he seemed to be a likeable person.

"Please tell me why you are here," Ellen said, approaching him. "You can be sure I'll be able to assist you just as well as the master himself, or he wouldn't allow me to work here in his workshop on my own."

"I need a few tools. My name is Jocelyn, Faber Aurifex."

A goldsmith! Ellen was delighted and closely examined the broken tool he handed her.

"The burin cannot be repaired. I will have to make a new one. What else do you need?"

"A little hammer," he replied, surprised at how well Ellen understood these things.

"What weight do you need? And the face? What size do you need? Domed or flat?" Ellen asked, in a matter-of-fact fashion.

The goldsmith gave her the specifications, and Ellen nodded. "The two items can be ready in five days, but unfortunately no sooner."

"Good," he said, but didn't seem ready to leave yet.

Ellen smiled at him, and Jocelyn cleared his throat.

Suddenly the door to the shop flew open, and Michel entered. He smelled of beer and appeared to be in a bad temper, probably having once again gambled away all his money. "What are you doing here, Jocelyn? Are you trying to take my Ellen away from me?" he asked the goldsmith.

Jocelyn looked Michel up and down as if he were out of his mind. "I placed an order for some tools," he said coolly.

Michel's face brightened. "Well, if that's the case, Master Jocelyn, Ellen will make them for you. She loves this work," he said, with a hoarse laugh.

"Well, I was just about to ask Master Jocelyn if he could take me on two days a week as an assistant," Ellen said. "You know, Michel, we agreed on that right from the start."

Jocelyn looked at Ellen in surprise, and frowned.

Michel shrieked and laughed hysterically. "Yes, Jocelyn, just look at her hands! They are exactly the right thing for the kind of fine trade you do." He grabbed Ellen's soiled right hand and held it up to Jocelyn's face.

Jocelyn was clearly put off by the behavior of the drunken smith. He politely took Ellen's hand and examined it. The blood blisters on her palms were gone, and they were in fact a little more delicate than those of an ordinary smith.

"I'll admit, there are quite a few calluses, but..." He gave Ellen such a searching gaze that she almost lost her breath. "As soon as you have finished the tool, bring it to me. If I'm satisfied, I'll give you a try." Jocelyn gently let go of her hand.

Long after he had released her hand, it seemed to Ellen that she could still feel his warm, soft fingers. "In five days, then," she said in an undertone.

Jocelyn nodded his agreement. "In five days!" Then he turned toward Michel, said good-bye in a cool tone, and left.

"Don't forget, you must first finish the order for the baker," Michel grumbled.

"I know, I can do that, don't worry."

Ellen got right to work on the baker's order so she could start as soon as possible making the tools for the goldsmith. She wanted to do an especially good job for him. The burin needed to be pointed, sharp, and above all very hard. Finally she would be able to use more of her knowledge than she ever did just making simple tools!

Ellen enjoyed the work for the goldsmith and a few days later began tempering the burin and the face of the hammer's head. She half filled a little trough she had found in the shop with water she had fetched from a spring in the forest, adding a bit of urine from her chamber pot. On the bottom of the trough she placed a stone that Donovan had given her. He swore by its magic powers as well as by the ancient sayings he had taught her and that she murmured quietly to herself every time she worked at tempering metal.

Michel eyed her mixture suspiciously, smelled it, and fondled her posterior. Ellen hissed in his ear: "I would rather have used the blood of dwarfs—it's very cold, as everyone knows, but I use it only for special swords because it's hard to come by."

The hair on the back of Michel's neck stood on end, and Ellen reveled in his fear. From now on, with a little luck, he wouldn't try laying hands on her again.

—

When the hammer and the burin for the goldsmith were finished and Ellen was ready to deliver them, she asked Michel how to get to the goldsmith's shop. He didn't mind explaining it to her, as the whole matter of the dwarf's blood had made him think.

Jocelyn looked surprised when Ellen entered his workshop.

"You'll need more?" His rather hostile question seemed more like a statement.

"I'll need more what?" Ellen didn't understand.

"Time to finish, of course." Jocelyn frowned. It was the afternoon of the fifth day, and he thought she was coming to ask for an extension. Michel never finished his work in the agreed time, so Jocelyn expected the same of Ellen.

"I said five days," she replied pointedly.

"Then you still have time until this evening. Why are you standing around here?" Jocelyn answered angrily. He had no desire to grant an extension again.

Ellen laughed because now she finally understood what he meant.

"Why are you laughing?" he asked, a bit more irritated, and then he saw that she was unpacking the two tools and handing them to him.

Jocelyn examined them carefully.

"Please give me a chance. I learn quickly and am skilled," Ellen pleaded while he tried out the new burin.

"Good, very good. I must say this is the best work I've seen for a long time," he mumbled, impressed, and gave her a much friendlier look now. "Michel is not a bad smith, but if you really made these tools by yourself, you know more than he does."

"Please try me. I'd like to learn and to work for you, just as a helper," Ellen insisted.

"Let's do that. Have a seat here at the table, and I'll show you how the burin is used. If you are good at this, then we'll see."

In the last few days, Ellen had been thinking a lot about what to expect if she worked for Jocelyn. Money to advance her plans for the future? She couldn't really expect the goldsmith to take on an inexperienced girl like her, teach her, and then also pay her for it. No, it couldn't be a question of money—what she wanted was to learn how to decorate her own swords someday. Ever since she had learned how to make scabbards, she had dreamed of making swords all by herself instead of having to hand them over to other tradespeople who would then do the decoration, the handle, and the scabbard. The goldsmith's work was the most costly part, so she would be able to make a better profit on her swords once she was able to do the work herself. It didn't matter if Michel believed that all she wanted was to make money assisting Jocelyn, but she'd have to confide the truth to the goldsmith if he asked.

Ellen worked calmly and with concentration until it got dark. Jocelyn kept coming to look at her work and gave her directions. She was extremely skillful and seemed to learn much faster than other apprentices.

"If you want me to teach you, you must come every afternoon. I won't ask for a premium for the training, but I also cannot pay you anything. Will you agree to that?"

"Every afternoon?" Ellen looked at the goldsmith hesitantly. "I'm not sure I can do that. I'll have to speak with Michel, because I receive room and board there."

"If I know Michel, he certainly doesn't pay you very much."

Ellen nodded.

"Then whether he wants to or not he'll have to agree if you just insist. He can't replace you, believe me."

Ellen still didn't look convinced.

"Michel would have promised me the tool in ten days and wouldn't get around to delivering it for two weeks." Jocelyn grinned and winked at her. "You'll see, he'll give in."

Jocelyn was right. Michel knew just how lucky he was to have Ellen, and in order not to lose her completely he agreed, though not without grumbling, that she could work at his smithy in the morning and go to Jocelyn's shop in the afternoon.

And so Ellen stayed in Beauvais, where every day she gulped down Marie's lunch as fast as possible and then hurried off to the goldsmith's. Without ever complaining, she rose before sunrise and worked until sunset like a person possessed.

Only on Sunday did she have a little time to visit Nestor. She had found a good place for her horse in a newly founded convent, and as long as Ellen didn't need the pony, the nuns could use it and in return feed and care for it.

—

A year had passed since she had first taken the job at Michel's smithy. She still worked every afternoon for Jocelyn and ever since Easter time even received a denarius for it from time to time. Ellen was hurrying along toward the goldsmith's shop. She was so excited that she didn't even notice the beautiful blue sky and the pleasantly warm July sunshine. Jocelyn had been working for some time on an altar vessel for the nunnery in which Nestor was boarded. Since the nuns were not very wealthy, he had made the vessel out of silver and was planning on gilding it.

Jocelyn jumped as Ellen, beaming broadly, came rushing into his shop.

"I'm here, we can start the gilding," she announced expectantly, without even first saying hello.

"Slow down! That takes a while," Jocelyn laughed.

He didn't know what there was about her that he found so attractive—was it her enthusiasm for the craft, her skill, or her unusual, rather austere beauty? Ellen was unaware that sometimes he watched her as she worked and carefully studied her face, which looked so concentrated, especially when she was engaged in fine, detailed work.

"Can't we begin today?" Ellen asked, disappointed.

How beautiful she was! Already after the first week he had been crazy about her but had never allowed it to show.

"If it were so simple then anyone could do it, but gilding is a very lengthy and difficult procedure and requires a lot of preparation. First we need to put together some tools." Jocelyn sighed and deliberated a moment. "Have a look in the small drawer in that closet, where you'll find a whole bundle of pig bristles. We'll wrap them in iron wire and make four brushes from them, each about the width of a finger. We need two of them for quicking the vessel and two for gilding it."

"What does quicking mean?" Ellen asked with interest as she skillfully bundled the bristles.

"We must prepare the silver so that the gold will adhere to it. To do that, we apply a liquid that the Faber Aurifex calls quicksilver water."

"And where do we get that?"

"We have to make it ourselves, but first we have to prepare the amalgam, and for that we must first purify the gold we intend to use."

Ellen sighed impatiently at hearing all the steps necessary for preparation.

But Jocelyn remained calm. "The most important thing in the gilding process is the purity of the gold. Don't forget that, because otherwise nothing will come of it. In order to remove copper, silver, and other impurities from the gold, we must cement it. Basically, that's nothing but a rather time-consuming heating of the gold with an agent called cement, which we have to make ourselves, as well."

Even though Ellen had not yet understood it all, she nodded.

"You'll see in a moment," Jocelyn said. The little, pensive frown on her face looked absolutely adorable, he thought.

"I have cut the gold we are going to use into strips of equal length. Do you see?"

Ellen examined the pieces and tried to estimate the thickness, length, and breadth as well as the distance between the holes he had bored into them.

Jocelyn smiled at her conscientiousness, a trait he admired so much in her. "Hand me the melting dishes on the table, and the little dish with the red powder, too. Oh, yes, I'll go and get the salt as well," Jocelyn said as he entered his bedroom and returned with a glazed clay flask.

"And now?" Ellen asked eagerly.

"The red powder is crushed clay baked in the oven. We need all of it and will mix it with an equal portion of salt."

Ellen took the powder and weighed it. At first, weighing had not been easy. It took a bit of intuition and above all reckoning, so she had practiced every free evening for weeks.

"And what now?" Impatiently she handed the dish to Jocelyn.

The goldsmith took the little clay bottle and dripped some yellowish liquid evenly over the powder until it was wet.

"Urine?" she asked, with a grin.

Jocelyn nodded. "But not too much—the powder mustn't stick together. The gold strips also need to be sprinkled with urine. Then we'll put them in a dish with the mixture so they form layers but do not touch each other." He placed the second dish on top as a cover and filled the space between the two vessels with clay. "That must dry now, and then we place it in the cementation oven."

He set the dishes down on four stones of similar size that he had set up in a circle inside the oven and lit a wood fire under it. Smoke poured from the holes in the upper part of the oven made of stone and clay.

"The fire must burn a whole day and night, and the dishes must all be subject to the same heat so the gold doesn't melt," Jocelyn declared as they were finishing up.

"And what do we do next?" Ellen's enthusiasm was far from satisfied.

"Oh, we still have a lot to do before the gold is ready tomorrow. First we have to make some brass brushes. We'll need them later to polish the gilding." He started searching through the cabinet and only now noticed that it was beginning to get dark. "It's late."

Ellen stood very close to Jocelyn.

"We'll pick up our work tomorrow." He breathed in her fragrance. "I..." he began.

"Yes?"

"I enjoy working with you, Ellen."

"I like working with you as well, master."

Her voice sounded soft, almost tender.

"Please call me Jocelyn." He couldn't make out whether she was nodding. "Agreed?"

"Yes."

"Good night, Ellen, I'll see you tomorrow." Jocelyn's voice was trembling.

"Good night, Jocelyn."

—

The next day when Ellen arrived at the goldsmith's shop she found Jocelyn stirring the fire in the cementation oven.

"You look tired," she said.

"I had to keep an eye on the fire." Jocelyn smiled wearily.

Ellen noticed again what a warm feeling his smile evoked in her, and she blushed. "Just tell me how to make the brass brushes, and then you can rest a bit while I tend to it and also keep an eye on the fire. What do you think?"

Jocelyn nodded and explained to Ellen what she had to do. "You know where the lead is, don't you?"

"Certainly, Jocelyn, take a little rest and I'll wake you up when the gold strips are ready."

"Good, I'll sit in the corner and rest for a little while, and if you have any questions, just shake me."

Ellen gave him a disapproving look.

"Why don't you go to your room?" she asked, shaking her head. He had to know she could manage by herself.

Jocelyn smiled. No one had such an impish smile as he did. "Because I'd like to be with you," he replied and settled down on a crate nearby in the corner.

His response passed over Ellen like a warm wave.

Jocelyn sat down and fell asleep at once, his chest rising and falling regularly.

Ellen couldn't stop looking at him. Even while he was asleep he had a little smile on his face.

After she was finished with the brass brushes and had cleaned up everything, she looked outside. It was still light, but darkness would be coming soon. Surely it was advisable to wake Jocelyn now. She walked over to him and looked at him more closely. He was sleeping so peacefully, like a child. She touched his cheek, caressing it gently.

Jocelyn mumbled contentedly but didn't open his eyes. Ellen bent down to him and whispered, "Wake up." Her lips touched his ear. She inhaled the fragrance around his neck and closed her eyes.

Jocelyn turned his head toward her, and their faces touched.

Ellen suddenly felt weak and shaky in the knees.

"What I wouldn't give to be awakened every morning like that," he mumbled.

Ellen blushed and became nervous. "It's time. I think the gold is ready," she said much too loudly and stood up again. Every muscle in her body was tense, and yet she was afraid she couldn't move a single step.

Jocelyn sat up and had a good stretch. His eyes were sparkling like stars.

—

Jocelyn was happy with the purified gold and placed a melting dish on the fire in order to prepare the gold amalgam. He cut the precious metal up into little pieces, added eight times that amount of quicksilver, and then put the mix into the red-hot dish, holding it as far from himself as possible.

"Quicksilver can make you sick," he explained. "The vapor is bad for your stomach. My master claimed that wine along with garlic or pepper was good for that, but that didn't help him—he turned pale and thin, and then he lost his mind." Jocelyn drew little circles in the air near his temple with his index finger. "He wasn't very old when he died, but toward the end all that was left of him was a bundle of misery with saliva running down his mouth. I'm certain the quicksilver had something to do with that." Jocelyn looked at Ellen as he moved the dish back and forth.

After the gold and quicksilver were mixed as thoroughly as possible, he poured the mixture into a dish of water and washed the remaining quicksilver from the amalgam. He would use the water with the remnants of the quicksilver in order to make the quicksilver water. Jocelyn dried the gold with a clean cloth. Since he did not want to immediately apply the paste-like gold, he separated it into several equal quantities and stuffed it into the quills of goose feathers.

Ellen's cheeks glowed with excitement, and this almost drove him out of his mind.

He thoroughly removed the quicksilver sticking to his hands with ashes and water.

"And what do we do now?" Ellen sighed, looking at him wide-eyed.

Jocelyn grinned.

"The quicksilver water!" they said in unison, and laughed. They were standing very close together.

Ellen felt the warmth of his body. He smelled of smoke and fresh rosemary. She looked into his eyes until she thought she would lose herself in them, and the trembling in her abdomen soon spread to her entire body. They stood there like that for a long while. The question kept running through her mind: *Why doesn't he kiss me?* but then the magic of the moment passed.

"Here's one more thing we need," Jocelyn exclaimed as he busily picked up the tartar and rubbed it. "You put tartar and salt together in the melting dish along with the water we used earlier in washing the amalgam. Then we add a little quicksilver and warm it all up." Jocelyn stirred the quicksilver water and held it over the fire. "Get the bristle bundle that you made and give me a linen rag."

Ellen handed him what he asked for.

Jocelyn heated the altar vessel for a moment, dipped one of the bristle bundles into the warm mixture, and used it to rub in the quicksilver water, until all the places even down to the last recess were turned white. After the quicking of the entire vessel, Jocelyn took a pointed knife out of a leather cup, used it to fetch the gold amalgam from the quills of the feather, applied it carefully in little bits with a copper spatula, and distributed the gold evenly with a dampened bristle brush. Again and again he warmed up the dish until the gilding amalgam was warm, then spread it out again with the bristle brush. It took a long time to apply the gold evenly. Jocelyn repeated this process three times, and Ellen carefully watched everything he did. He kept warming and brushing the vessel until the plating was yellow. "The heat disperses the quicksilver, and what remains is the gold adhering to the silver," he explained. "And now we'll let the vessel cool. Will you bring me the other brushes?"

Ellen went to fetch the brass brushes while turning over in her mind again and again all the steps to be performed. "But why do you need the brushes now?"

"Look closely at the gilding. What do you notice?"

Ellen observed the vessel carefully. It looked yellow, like gold, but was dull. "It has no shine."

Jocelyn smiled at her. "And so now we'll polish it! Let's begin with the stand. Take the brass brush and set the stand in some water, then polish it with the brush until it shines."

"But won't I scratch it?" Ellen objected.

Jocelyn looked at her intently. "Don't you trust me?"

Ellen lowered her eyes in shame. Of course she trusted him—she trusted him completely! And so she began to polish.

It was getting dark already, and Jocelyn lit two candles. Wax candles were expensive, but their flame burned more evenly than that of tallow candles. Moreover, the smoke from the tallow stung your eyes and made them tear up, making it harder to work. The light from the candles cast long shadows over Jocelyn's face, accenting his high cheekbones.

Ellen tried to concentrate on the stand of the vessel. "Look how it shines!" she exclaimed joyously after she had polished every spot.

Jocelyn only nodded. "Now you must heat it up again until it turns reddish yellow, then take it out and cool it down in the water."

Ellen did what he asked, and finally the foot of the altar vessel assumed the desired color.

"But now it doesn't shine anymore!" she said, giving Jocelyn a disappointed look.

"Cool it off and polish it again," he replied bluntly, and seemed to enjoy Ellen's disappointment.

And so Ellen polished it again, and indeed the foot now shone even more. Proudly she looked at the successful work.

"Now let's color the gold so that it looks even more beautiful and shiny. Tomorrow you can continue on your own."

"What do you mean by 'color'? How do we do that?" Ellen asked reluctantly.

"We need atramentum," Jocelyn explained, without answering her question. "When you heat it, it melts and becomes solid," he explained. When the atramentum solidified, he took it from the dish and shoved it directly under the coals. "And here, in the fire, it burns. As soon as it becomes red we must take it out."

After taking it from the fire to cool, he looked at Ellen so intently that her heart began to pound wildly.

Then he turned away, took a wooden dish, and crushed the atramentum in it with an iron hammer. "A third part salt, and a little bit more of our goldwater." Jocelyn grinned, fetched the clay flask with the urine, mixed the ingredients into a paste, and brushed them onto the stand of the vessel with a feather.

"I didn't think gilding took so long," Ellen grumbled.

Jocelyn nodded, placed the anointed stand on the fire until the coating dried and a wisp of smoke arose, and then he washed it off with water and cleaned it carefully with the remaining bundle of pig bristles. "So now, for the last time, heat it and let it cool in a linen cloth, and tomorrow you'll see how beautiful the gilding looks. You will be astonished."

After everything was finished and the workshop cleaned up, it was almost dark. Ellen was about to leave when Jocelyn came up to her and gently brushed a wisp of hair from her forehead. "You look tired," he murmured tenderly, stroking her cheek with the back of his hand. Then he raised her chin and kissed her tenderly on the mouth.

Ellen closed her eyes and opened her lips a bit, but he moved back.

"Until tomorrow," he said with a warm smile, looking deep into her eyes.

Ellen headed toward home, deeply agitated, her heart galloping like a warhorse.

The next day she could barely wait for the morning and her work at the smithy to end. She was so excited that she couldn't eat a bite for lunch, so she ran straight to Jocelyn's shop. "Show me the gilding," she said, still out of breath, but the gilding wasn't the real cause of her impatience.

Jocelyn greeted her good-naturedly as always, but without even a trace of affection.

Ellen could hardly stand being close to him all afternoon without him staring at her longingly and affectionately. She began to worry seriously whether she had acted wrongly the evening before for not responding to his kiss with a slap in the face. Maybe Jocelyn now believed she was frivolous and for this reason he despised her. "Excuse me for a moment," she said, and choking back tears ran out to the latrine in the yard and leaned against the board wall, sobbing.

It took her a while to calm down; then she wiped the tears away and resolved to get control of herself. Who in the world did she think she was? A goldsmith? How could she ever have believed, even for a moment, that he…he was probably just making fun of her and didn't mean anything with his kiss. When she returned to the shop, Jocelyn had started on something else and spoke with her without looking up.

"Just continue, as we discussed, Ellen. If you have a problem, ask me."

Ellen sat down. The vessel needed to be polished and colored, and she tried to remember each step before she did anything, trying not to ask any questions.

"It's not even five years since my master died," he said suddenly, looking around the room, "and this was his house. His workshop, not mine." Jocelyn hesitated for a moment—it didn't seem easy for him to talk about it. "When he was alive, my master's wife was always chasing me. I naturally rebuffed her, not only because she was old—she could just as well have been young and beautiful. She was my master's wife. Never in my life would I have..." Jocelyn stopped, then got up to fetch another tool. "After the master died, I had to decide. Either I could stay an apprentice all my life, or I could accept the proposal from my master's wife: marry her and I would be master of my own workshop. I married her." Jocelyn sat down again.

Ellen remained silent and couldn't understand why he had told her all that. Didn't he know what she felt? Didn't he sense the pain he caused her when he spoke of another woman? Or did he perhaps want to hurt her and make her understand that he didn't want her because she wouldn't bring any money to the marriage?

"She has been dead for almost two years now, so the mourning period is long past and there is no reason why I couldn't marry again."

Ellen could feel the tenseness building in her chest. He probably was going to tell her now about a goldsmith's daughter he wanted to marry and explain his kiss the previous day as a mistake.

But Jocelyn didn't say anything more about it.

Ellen polished and colored the chalice without having to ask him for help.

Jocelyn seemed to expect it as a matter of course and didn't lavish a word of praise on her for the work.

That evening, as she was leaving, Jocelyn was holding a piece in the fire. "Wait just a moment," he asked, but Ellen scurried out the door.

—

For the last time, Thibault gently massaged the young girl's small, firm breasts until she moaned, then turned away from her, bored. He stood up without covering his firm male organ and poured himself a cup of spiced wine.

"Leave now!" he growled at the maid, enjoying her terrified gaze. She had probably believed all the compliments and declarations of love whose only purpose was to get her to do what he wanted. How simple-minded women were!

"Rose!" Thibault tied a cloth around his hips.

"Come here!"

All night she had cowered in a corner of the room, but now she got up slowly, and then just stood there silently.

Thibault walked over to her, kissed her neck tenderly, and pulled her up close. His hands wandered over her body. Gently he pinched her nipples until they stood out from under her shirt, and then he passionately pressed himself against her.

Rose didn't move.

"You're furious at me," he whispered. "I know, I misbehaved…" Thibault's breathing became heavier. His hand slipped under her shirt. "Do you remember the first time in the meadow, in Tancarville? You, only you, are my companion. The others don't count. I couldn't control myself." He looked at Rose.

A tear rolled down her pretty face.

"Don't cry, little Rose, everything will be fine," he whispered tenderly, kissing the tear away. "It's these terrible dreams that make me do it," he mumbled apologetically, and nestled his head up against her neck. "It's not my fault!" Tenderly and passionately he pulled Rose down onto the bed that just a few moments ago he had shared with the maid whose name he didn't even know.

Rose closed her eyes, crying and praying to God that He would make Thibault hers alone. She wrapped her arms around his neck, spread her thighs, and received him, full of passion.

They lay together side by side for a while, until they heard a knock on the door.

"The king wishes to see you," a muffled voice said. "At once!"

"I'm coming!" Thibault jumped up, dressed in practically no time at all, and rushed out.

Henry was the eldest son of the old king, and just a year ago, at age fifteen, he was crowned by his father. Since that time, they were both officially kings, but as the Young King had none of the power nor the emoluments, he always had to ask his father for money for his diversions as well as for those of his knights. He was pacing up and down impatiently in the great hall of his brother-in-arms, Robert de Crevecoeur, and when Thibault entered, Henry ran toward him. "You must leave at once for Beauvais and meet one of my father's messengers. William will give you exact instructions." The Young King seemed irritated, so Thibault carefully avoided asking any questions. He was only displeased that it was William, of all people, who was giving him orders, and he snorted angrily.

"As you wish, my king!"

"I await your speedy return." Young Henry nodded briefly, and William motioned to Thibault to follow him.

It was still extremely difficult for Thibault to be calm in dealing with William. Since they first met in Tancarville, Thibault could not stand him. For a younger son, William had come very far in the world. After all, he had been the mentor of the Young King since the previous year and thus had great influence on the young man.

Two years had passed since the Poitevins had attacked Queen Eleanor. The Earl of Salisbury, her protector at that time, had been killed, and William attacked the Poitevins like a madman, all by himself, to avenge the death of his beloved uncle. He was injured, captured, and after weeks of cruel treatment as a prisoner, as he told the story, it was none other than the queen herself who bought his freedom and took him into her service. Only a few months later she made him her son's preceptor.

Thibault had to concentrate in order to keep his mind from wandering and to be able to follow what William was saying. *Someday the time will come when I'll get back at everyone who ever humiliated me, and you will certainly be one of them*, he thought angrily as William turned away without saying good-bye.

—

Thibault was hiding out in a narrow lane not far from the goldsmith's house. He had been observing Ellen for two days. He had seen her by chance on the street shortly after arriving in Beauvais and from that moment on could scarcely concentrate on his work. Every one of his thoughts eventually came back to her.

When he had first seen her the day before, she looked so much in love that his stomach felt as if it were full of cold stones, and today he was especially nervous. His thumbnail kept digging painfully into the soft flesh of his index finger. Pain had something reliable about it, something soothing.

When Ellen left the goldsmith's shop, Thibault could immediately see a change in the way she looked. Weren't those tears glistening in her eyes? Yes, it looked like she was grief-stricken. It served her right. Why should he be the only one to suffer? Just as he had the day before, he again followed her at a safe distance. She was running straight ahead, but with her head down, through the crowded alleyways. Surely she was on the way to the smithy. Thibault had asked around and knew she lived and worked with Michel, the smith. He tracked her skillfully, and after she had disappeared in the smithy he watched for a while at a distance. Once again he dug his thumbnail into his index finger. "You belong to me!" he muttered.

—

The following day was a Sunday, and Ellen had decided to use it to get her mind off Jocelyn. After church she started walking toward the nunnery, where she intended to take Nestor out for a ride. And there she met him.

"I hoped I would meet you here." Jocelyn cleared his throat.

How well he knew her! Naturally she had told him of Nestor, but that he had really been listening…Ellen stopped and stared at her feet.

Jocelyn put his hands on her shoulders. "Look at me, please!"

Ellen looked into his hazel-brown eyes. His gaze caressed her face.

Jocelyn pulled her toward him, put his arms around her neck, and kissed her. She closed her eyes as his tongue found its way between her lips.

Ellen felt defenseless and miraculously at his mercy. The kiss seemed to last forever as his tongue probed even deeper into her mouth. After that he covered her face and neck with tender little kisses until the little hairs on the back of her neck stood on end.

Jocelyn was breathing hard as he let the tip of his tongue slide gently down her pounding neck. Suddenly he stopped. "You are the fulfillment of all my dreams! Will you marry me?"

"But you know nothing about me," she protested in a trembling voice.

"I know what I need to know. You are ambitious and extremely talented. You are simply wonderful, beautiful, and headstrong. I'll do everything I can to make you happy. You can work with iron, gold, or silver—I'll leave it all up to you. If you still want to forge swords, I'll never stand in your way. Together we could even make the finest sword for our king. What do think of that?"

Ellen looked at him incredulously.

"The Lord was merciful and let our paths cross. This mercy doesn't happen to anyone twice in life. Please say yes," he urged her.

Ellen was wildly happy and nodded eagerly. "Yes, Jocelyn, yes, I will!"

The goldsmith raised her up, overjoyed. "I love you, Ellen," he cried out.

The cows in the meadow looked up and mooed anxiously.

Ellen and Jocelyn sat down in the grass, started making plans for their future together, and exchanged tender caresses. Ellen felt a strange anxiety creeping up on her and turned around to look a few times, but she didn't see anything.

"I never want to be without you again," Jocelyn said later, kissing her over and over while they walked back to town hand in hand.

"Well, Michel will be disappointed," Ellen replied playfully.

"Indeed he will!" Jocelyn laughed and shrugged his shoulders.

A smith's journeyman saw the couple and grinned impertinently.

Ellen blushed, and Jocelyn kissed the end of her nose lovingly. "We should get married as soon as possible." He stroked her cheek. "You're all aglow!"

"I'm happy."

"We'll see each other tomorrow," he said when they arrived at the smithy, blowing her a farewell kiss.

Ellen waited a moment until he had disappeared in the milling crowd in the alleyway. Then she entered her master's house.

"My word, what's wrong with you," Michel growled when he saw her red cheeks. "You're not getting sick, are you?"

"Nonsense, Michel, she's in love! That's been obvious for days." Marie laughed. "The beer addles your brain. You don't even know what love is anymore, do you?"

But her tirade made no impression on Michel. "Women's talk," he grumbled. "I'd rather go over to the tavern." After he stood up and staggered out the door, Marie tried to get more information from Ellen, but she kept her silence.

"You'll learn about it soon enough," she said happily. "I'm tired, and I'm going to sleep. Good night!" Ellen went back to the workshop and lay down on her bed. Her thoughts were spinning around in her head, and it took a long time for her to relax.

In the meantime, Thibault had been standing in the dark alleyway only a few steps from the smithy, trembling with anger. He had been following Ellen since morning. She had looked beautiful on her way to the church in her light linen dress and her wind-tousled hair. He had already decided to approach her, even talk to her, when out of nowhere the goldsmith suddenly appeared. Seeing the two of them so much in love and exchanging sweet nothings had been unbearable to him, and even now their happiness burned in his stomach like a greasy meal. Thibault closed his eyes and imagined how he would strangle his rival with his own hands.

"She belongs to me, to me alone," he growled.

"We'll see each other tomorrow," Jocelyn had said, but he would never see her again! Thibault pushed off from the wall of the building where he was standing and walked over to Jocelyn's shop. He observed the house for a while and then decided to go to the tavern for a drink.

It was a wild night at the Laughing Boar, and Thibault had trouble finding a seat at one of the long tables. The Boar was known for its strong beer and hearty food. Especially popular, however, were the waitresses, all buxom girls with low-cut dresses that showed off their inviting, heaving breasts. They laughed and joked with the men, encouraged them to drink, and didn't mind if now and then one of the men made a pass at them.

The torches and tallow lanterns smoked so much that the air was as heavy as a foggy November night, but more stifling. It smelled of sweat, beer, and urine because so many men simply relieved themselves under the table rather than going outside. A barefoot girl with long, matted hair was dancing on one of the greasy tables, shaking a tambourine. The men howled and whistled when they could get a look under her skirt where, aside from her own skin, she was wearing nothing at all.

A brunette with chipped front teeth and a dirty dress brought Thibault a beer. He paid no attention to her, but kept looking around the room. In one corner, a few men were playing dice. Thibault, bored, was about to turn away again when he caught sight of Michel in the crowd. The smith was beaming, and raised his fist triumphantly. He must have been having a lucky streak, as one by one the other players withdrew. Thibault's face twisted into a fiendish grimace. He took out his purse and reached for the loaded dice he had gotten a while ago from a swindler. Then he went over and casually stood next to the smith, as if by chance.

"A game, my lord?" Michel asked. He was already drunk and playing with the coins he had just won. "Today's my lucky day, I can feel it!"

A drinker and a gambler who would sell his soul in a game of chance, Thibault was thinking contemptuously, but he replied in a friendly voice, "Well, then let's try your luck!" Thibault took the dice and spit on them three times before throwing them against the wall. He feigned disappointment when he lost. At first Michel was winning. Every time he won he acted as if Lady Luck were always on his side, and Thibault had trouble controlling himself and not showing this braggart what a fool he was. After a while and after losing some small change to the smith, Thibault secretly changed the dice for his own loaded ones and put an end to Michel's run of good luck. By the time midnight had arrived, the smith had lost so much money to Thibault that if he gave up then he would lose his house, his smithy, and all his plans for the future.

"I've got to go out to pee," he said. Half drunk, he staggered outside, walked over to a wall, and relieved himself. Thibault had followed him out of the tavern and stood in the shadow of a house. He observed with disgust how the smith became ill in the fresh air, choked and retched miserably, and finally vomited.

Michel thought he might just slip away now and forget about his debts.

Thibault followed him and pushed him into the first dark alley they came to. "Gambling debts are debts of honor," he whispered into Michel's ear. "If I want to, I can cut your throat right here in the middle of the street because you didn't pay them. I have plenty of witnesses." Thibault pulled out his knife and held it to Michel's throat.

He was confronted with the stench of vomit when Michel opened his mouth.

"Please, sir, I don't have the money. Give me some time, please!" he begged.

"So you can just go out and incur more debts?" Thibault laughed scornfully.

"If you take my smithy away from me, what will become of my poor children?" Michel seemed only now to realize the deep trouble he was in.

"I am moved by your distress," Thibault said. "For this reason I will forgive it all if you do just one thing for me." He grinned into the dark night.

"Whatever you ask," Michel whined. He had not noticed the scorn in Thibault's voice.

"You will kill the goldsmith she always visits."

"Who...? What...?" In his drunken state Michel didn't understand at first.

"He will never have her," Thibault fumed. "You'll kill him, or better gouge out his eyes; then you'll take his gold and anything else of value that he has. Robbers often do terrible things!" He laughed hoarsely.

"But I can't do that...Jocelyn is a good—"

"Be quiet! Do what I tell you, and do it tonight, or tomorrow your wife will be a penniless widow and your children will have to beg for food in the streets."

"Could I perhaps just beat him and rob him?" Michel suggested, trembling.

"That's not enough! It's either his life or yours. Think about it, but don't take too long. It must be done today."

Michel nodded in desperate resignation. Suddenly he seemed to sober up. "And where shall I deliver the money?"

"I will come to your house tomorrow evening. If you try to deceive me…" Once again, Thibault pressed the knife to his throat: "Then you will have to suffer for it."

"Never, sir, believe me!" Michel wailed.

Thibault pushed him away. "So go now. You know what you have to do."

—

In the middle of the night Ellen awoke and sat bolt upright in bed. Something had frightened her terribly, a sound or a dream perhaps. She fell into a fitful sleep and the next morning was tired and nervous. She couldn't concentrate on her work and could scarcely wait to go to Jocelyn's. Even though she was hungry, she hurried to his house right after work and dashed into the smithy without knocking. "Jocelyn, it's me," she called out happily.

She could smell something sickly sweet, and she turned up her nose. Then she discovered Jocelyn. He lay stretched out on the floor alongside his worktable, his head lying in a pool of blood. Her heart stopped for a moment, and then she fell down on her knees beside his lifeless body, unable to believe what she was seeing. Now her heart started pounding again. "Please no, Jocelyn!" She shook him gently. "Lord, why do you punish me so?" She sobbed in bewilderment and passed her hand carefully over Jocelyn's sunken cheeks. The burin she had made for him protruded, like a reproach, from his chest. Sobbing, she grabbed the handle and pulled on it until it came out.

Suddenly two respectable-looking women, the wives of local merchants, appeared in the doorway.

Ellen looked up, startled. She held the bloody weapon up high, almost as if she were going to stab him again.

"Help, help! She murdered the goldsmith!" the two women screamed and ran away shouting.

Ellen stared in disbelief at the tool in her hand. Jocelyn's blood ran down it into her sleeve, and she flung it away, wiping off the blood with a rag, then rushing out the back door of the smithy. She knew that behind the garden there was a small side alley through which she could flee.

Certainly the two women would swear by all that was holy that they had seen Ellen stab Jocelyn. And who would believe the truth of what she said?

Ellen wandered aimlessly through the narrow alleyways, without knowing where she was going. She had never gone this far away in the direction of the slums. The houses were tall and crowded together, rats scurried through the little streets, and there was a strong stench of pig feces and urine. The children in this part of town were scrawny and emaciated, their faces filthy and their little bodies covered with fleabites scratched raw. It was dangerous to walk around here at any time of day, and not just at dusk, but this did not trouble Ellen at all. There wasn't one clear thought in her head, only images of Jocelyn and endless grief. On the steps of a shabby little wooden church she finally broke down and sobbed. "Jocelyn, what shall I do now?" she whispered over and over in despair. But no one answered.

I must go back to Michel's and fetch my things, it suddenly occurred to her. She rubbed her soot-covered face, smearing the white lines left by the tears on her cheeks.

The closer she got to the smithy the more afraid she was of falling into the hands of soldiers. If either of the women knew who she was, the place would be swarming with town guards. Ellen hid nearby Michel's shop. Nothing was stirring. She watched until it was dark and then sneaked up to the smithy.

Michel was no doubt away, having dinner with his family or sitting in the tavern, but she opened the door very carefully just the same. The smithy was dark and warm, and only a few coals were still burning on the hearth.

She checked to make sure there was no one there, then slipped in. She was familiar with every inch of the room and did not need any light in order to find what she was looking for. In no time at all she had packed up her things—her tools, the apron, her bundle, and the few coins she had. On the way back to the door she stumbled over a piece of iron and cursed under her breath.

Then she heard voices. Grabbing an empty sack, she crept behind one of the large wicker baskets and covered herself as best she could with the torn linen cloth.

At that moment, the door to the shop flew open and someone entered.

"I did as you asked, sir." Michel's obsequious voice suggested he had a guilty conscience.

"Give me what you stole," Ellen heard a rasping voice reply.

Thibault! Ellen felt an almost overwhelming need to throw up and was barely able to control herself.

"They suspect Ellen," Michel said suddenly.

Why was he speaking with Thibault about her? And how did he know Thibault at all?

"Is that her bed?" Thibault asked, stepping on the straw sack on the floor. He was dangerously close to her hiding place.

Ellen could feel herself breaking out into a sweat. Paralyzed with fear, she sat motionlessly under the stuffy linen cover.

Without waiting for a reply, Thibault again demanded that Michel give him what he had stolen.

"What shall I do if she comes back? Maybe she even knows that I..." Michel hesitated.

"She won't be so dumb as to come here." Thibault stroked his chin. "Poor thing, you have to pity her. First her fiancé is dead, and now she is being pursued as a murderer." His resounding laughter gave Ellen goose bumps all over her body. "Just act as you always do and you'll have nothing to fear. Ellen is certainly long gone," Thibault advised the smith; then his steps moved away from where Ellen was hiding.

"It really would have been a pity if you had lost the smithy and the house." Thibault roared with laughter again, and then the door closed behind the two men.

Petrified, Ellen sat still for a moment in her hiding place. Michel had killed Jocelyn! How could he have done that? He had to be held accountable! In despair, she considered what to do. What proof did she have? If she reported it to the city guards and asked them to investigate, they wouldn't even listen to her but would lock her up at once and condemn her. There was no justice in the world, but God would punish Michel on the Last Judgment Day, of that Ellen was sure. Like a thief, she sneaked away and fetched Nestor from the nunnery. Why did she have to flee this time, again, when she hadn't done anything wrong?

September 1171

In the first few days, Ellen felt desperate and completely without hope. Her tears dried before long, but she felt as listless and dull as an old blade.

By now, she had been on the road for a week, long enough not to have to fear being followed, but without knowing where she was going. At a road crossing she found herself at the end of a long line of people, tradesmen and merchants, magicians and prostitutes, all headed in the same direction, most of them on foot. Others rode on mules or were driving oxcarts. Suddenly she heard loud shouting coming from the wagon just ahead of her.

"Now that's enough, you trollop! I have lost patience with you. Get out and find your own husband." The canvas was flung aside, and a plump woman, her face red with anger, pushed a young girl out of the wagon.

Ellen just had time to grab Nestor's reins and bring him to a halt.

The young girl fell to the ground in front of the pony and at once began to cry out for someone named Jean. She whined like a small child though she was certainly at least sixteen or seventeen years old. "Jean!" she cried out again in a long, drawn-out, piercing voice.

And shortly thereafter, a young man came up to her.

To Ellen's amazement, he was younger than the girl who seemed to regard him as her defender. He was shorter than Ellen, perhaps thirteen or fourteen years old, and had not yet begun to grow a beard.

He stooped down to the girl and pulled her up with one hand. "Oh, Madeleine, what's wrong this time?" he asked. "Tell me what happened. Problems with your Agnes again?"

Madeleine shrugged and cast an innocent look at the boy. Then she grabbed her breast. "Her husband touched me here again," she said, clutching at her breast. "He does this a lot, but usually he's more careful not to let her catch him. This time she saw it, and now she's angry at me." The girl looked at him wide-eyed.

The boy sighed. "Oh, I'm sorry," he mumbled when he noticed she was standing in Ellen's way and pulled the girl off to the side of the road.

She was limping and grimaced with pain.

"Is she all right?" Ellen asked and dismounted.

"My foot! It hurts so much!" the girl wailed.

"Go over and sit on the grass and I'll have a look at it." For a short moment Ellen forgot her own grief and her usual distrust of strangers. Taking the girl's dirty foot in her hand, she examined it carefully.

The girl held still and calmed down.

"It looks like it's not broken. Do you still have a long way to go?"

"We're going to the next jousting tournament, like all the others." The boy pointed to the long procession of people moving by. "We've been with the merchants for some time, but there is always trouble because of her," he explained, pointing to the girl.

Ellen raised her eyebrows quizzically.

"It's a long story," the boy said. "I keep an eye on her as best I can, but sometimes I'm not here and then there's almost always trouble. Now it looks like we'll have to go ahead on our own for a while."

"But I can't walk!" Madeleine whimpered, shedding a few tears for emphasis.

"So you're going to a tournament?" Ellen's curiosity was awakened.

"That's how we make a living. Madeleine dances or works as a maid. She's pretty and almost always finds work. And I do all sorts of things. I polish boots, deliver messages, care for animals and clean out their stables, serve beer, and fetch water. Hard workers are always in demand at the tournaments."

"Are there blacksmiths there, too?"

"Sure, every kind of smith, except for perhaps silversmiths and goldsmiths. There are a lot of farriers, because the horses are always losing their shoes, then there are wire drawers and nailers, coppersmiths selling their pots and pans, and blacksmiths who make tent pegs, tongs, hooks, and all kinds of tools. And then there are the armorers, who have plenty of work to do."

Ellen's face brightened. "Well, if that's the case, I'll come along with you! Let's get moving," she urged them in a cheerful voice.

"But I can't walk!" Madeleine whined again.

"Help her up onto the pony and the two of us can walk," Ellen suggested, guiding the girl over to her horse.

"Who are you, anyway?" the boy asked suspiciously.

"Oh, I'm sorry, my name is Ellenweore. I'm a swordsmith, and a really good one!" she said confidently, holding out her hand.

"A woman who is a smith," the boy mumbled, shaking his head in disbelief. "One who makes swords? That's amazing! My name is Jean, by the way." He wiped his hand off on his shirt before extending it to Ellen.

"I know, I heard her calling you, and her name is Madeleine, isn't it?"

Jean nodded.

"I used to know someone named Jean, but he was way older than you." She thought for a moment, then added, "How about if I call you Jeannot? Do you mind?"

"No, no, I've had worse nicknames. Scallywag, Snotnose, or Rat—they bothered me a lot more." Jean grinned at Ellen mischievously.

"Well, then we've got a deal, Jeannot. So come on, Madeleine, up you go onto the nag. Sorry, Nestor, I didn't mean to offend you." She stroked the pony's nose affectionately. Taking the reins, she guided him while Madeleine sat upright, as if she had been riding horses all her life, rocking back and forth as he walked along. Ellen looked at her admiringly. She herself always felt like a sack of flour when riding and felt a lot more secure walking.

"She looks like she grew up riding a horse!"

"We both ride pretty well even though neither of us has ever had a horse of our own." The boy bit his lip and clearly didn't want to say anything more about it.

When it got dark, they looked around in the forest for a place to spend the night. They had caught up with the other travelers but decided to set up their tent some distance away in order to avoid trouble with the merchant's wife. Ellen tied Nestor to a tree with plenty of grass and soft moss around it so he would have plenty to eat.

Without being asked, Madeleine set out to gather wood and soon returned with an armful of dry branches. She seemed to have completely forgotten her painful foot.

Ellen took her flint, fire steel, and a little bit of tinder and was about to light a bunch of dry grass when Jean suddenly arrived carrying a dead rabbit in his hand. Ellen looked up at him in surprise.

"I killed it with my slingshot," he explained. Tying the dead animal to a branch, he removed one of its eyes to make it bleed. Then, starting from the hind legs, he gutted it and buried the remains in order not to attract wolves. Finally, he drove a long stake through the body and laid it over two forked branches he had stuck into the ground on either side of the fire. Soon the air was filled with the aroma of roasting meat.

Ellen did not even have an onion with her, but just as she had shared her pony with Madeleine, the two of them now shared their bread and the roast with her. After the meal, Madeleine curled up like a small child and at once fell asleep.

Ellen and Jean sat together in front of the crackling fire.

Suddenly and in a soft voice, Jean began his story. "I wasn't even ten years old yet," he said, "when it happened. I was in the forest gathering mushrooms." He stared into the fire as if it were evoking memories from his past. "Madeleine was around twelve." He swallowed hard. "I can't even remember the name of our village, or the county it was in, and neither can she. I had been in the forest since dawn when suddenly I caught sight of a thick, black cloud of smoke in the sky and ran home. The entire village was in flames, and there was a disgusting bittersweet stench in the air." He swallowed again, then resumed his tale. "The odor came from burning human flesh. At the town well there were many men from our village piled one on top of each other. They must have been trying to defend their families and were all slaughtered like animals. It began to rain, a fine drizzle, and I thought, *God is crying because He is so sad.* Their blood mixed with the rainwater to form little streams. I was afraid and ran to our house. It wasn't burning and looked very peaceful, but I was afraid just the same. Though my knees were shaking, I went in." He wiped his face with his hand. "In one corner my mother was lying. Her head was smashed and her face almost unrecognizable. Lying underneath her was my little brother. They were both dead. I started to cry, though my father always had forbidden me to do that. And then I discovered him, too, and it seemed like my heart stopped. He was such a big, strong man, and they had taken him to the goat pen and hung him up on two iron hooks. His eyes were bulging and staring directly at me, his stomach was slit open, and his entrails hung down. I rushed out and vomited again and again until there was nothing left in my stomach. Later I ran to the other houses that were not completely destroyed, and I called and cried but no one was there. They were all dead." Jean fell silent for a moment.

Ellen was at a loss for words. She could so clearly feel his pain, as hardly a day went by when she herself did not think of the moment she had found Jocelyn dead. Never would she be able to forget this horrible sight.

"And then I saw Madeleine," Jean continued in a soft voice. "Suddenly she was standing on the path in front of me holding a bouquet of meadow flowers—she reminded me of a little elf. She understood what had happened a lot faster than I did. The chickens and goats were gone, and even the carpenter's dog as well as the cats were lying there dead in the mud. We couldn't stand the sight and the odor of death any longer and fled into the forest." Jean stirred the embers that had almost gone out and put a branch on them to make the fire burn a bit longer.

The night was dark and clear. Ellen felt cold and was grateful for the fire. She took her coat and spread it out on the ground so she would have something to sit on.

"We hid in the forest, but the robbers discovered us anyway. We realized by the things they were carrying that they were the same men who destroyed our village. One of them wanted to kill us right away. He put a knife to Madeleine's throat, but another one restrained him. 'Let's first have a little fun with the girl,' he suggested. I was too young to understand what he meant, but I saw the fear in Madeleine's eyes and thought of my father with his belly slit open. In my anger I forgot my own fear and kicked the fellow in the shins as hard as I could."

"Oh, my God," Ellen cried out.

"You're right, that was really stupid—I was much too little and no match for him. He socked me hard, grabbed me by the hair, and kicked me. He probably would have killed me, too, but then Marcondé, the leader of the gang, came over, and the robbers stepped back. At first I hoped he might let us go, but then I saw the dried blood on his dirty shirt—perhaps it belonged to my mother or my father!" He stopped for a moment and swallowed. "I became his servant and whipping boy, but my fate was bearable compared with what Madeleine had to go through. They jumped on her like horny goats, day after day from morning to night, and so many times!" Jean buried his head in his hands. "She used to be a completely sensible girl, do you know what I mean? She wasn't…crazy, not at all, and it's the fault of those fellows; they tortured her until she flipped. They made her into an animal, threw food at her as if she were a dog, and cheered when she crawled over on all fours to pick it up. They heated their knives over the fire and pressed the glowing blade into her flesh until she was able to bear that, too, without screaming. She was the only person I had left, and they drove her mad."

"But how, for heaven's sake, did you ever manage to escape?" Ellen asked, horrified, glancing over at the peacefully sleeping girl. Madeleine's forehead was a bit wrinkled, and her hands were clenched into fists.

"I could have fled many times, but I couldn't leave Madeleine alone. I would have killed Marcondé if it would do any good, but there were so many of them." He looked at Ellen and suddenly began to smile. "We learned from the robbers how to ride a horse. Sometimes we spent the whole day on a horse and dismounted only to pee and to sleep. We even ate on horseback. I liked these days best of all because then the men were too tired to attack Madeleine. For months they took us along on their raids, and finally one day we got the chance to flee that we had been waiting for so long. Marcondé and his men attacked a little settlement, massacred the men, and assaulted the women and girls. Afterwards, they celebrated, got drunk, and didn't notice that we stole two horses from them and took off. Because we knew they were good at trailing people, we sold the horses as soon as we could and actually managed to shake them off. I still can't believe how lucky we were that day, but even now my hair stands on end and I start shaking with fear whenever I hear a group of men on horseback. I only feel safe at the tournaments because bandits avoid them like the plague."

It was already very late, and although Jean knew from experience how little security was afforded by the presence of other people, Ellen was happy to know, after hearing the grisly tale, that the merchants they had been riding with were not far off.

"Madeleine is so lucky to have you here for her," Ellen said softly, and went to get a second blanket that Nestor was carrying. She moved closer to Jean and Madeleine and wrapped it around herself and the other two as best she could. Since fleeing Orford, Ellen was fearful of the sounds coming from the forest at night. Neither she nor Jean could forget the experiences of the past, and every time she heard a rustling or crackling in the forest, she jumped and listened. This time, too, it took a long time for her to drift off into a deep sleep.

—

The morning sun dazzled her, even with her eyes closed, and woke her up. Ellen stretched, looked around for Jean and Madeleine, and was shocked. They were both gone! It didn't seem they had been taken away forcefully, and it was hard to believe that robbers would have left Ellen sleeping peacefully while they dragged Madeleine and Jean away. She looked over at the tree where she had tied Nestor, and he, too, was gone! Furious, she jumped up. Had she been deceived again and taken in by two imposters? Helpless and disappointed, she was considering what to do next when she heard a crackling in the underbrush.

"Hello!" cried a female voice brightly, and Ellen turned around.

"Madeleine, Jean!" she exclaimed with relief.

"We took Nestor down to the brook for a drink, and we filled up the water skins," Jean explained.

"The others are getting ready to leave," Madeleine said, pointing to the clearing where the traveling merchants had spent the night as she danced around as if she urgently needed to relieve herself.

"Madeleine is right, it's better for us to leave. Our trip will be safer if we stay with the others," Jean said.

Ellen nodded. "It's fine by me, I'm just going down to the brook for a moment." She kicked ashes over the fire to extinguish the embers that were still glowing, and ran off. "I'll be right back!"

A short time later they were following along behind the others and considering how Ellen might find work with one of the armorers during the tournament.

Jean didn't hold out much hope: "That won't be easy, because you're not a man!" he said.

"Don't think I haven't considered that, but I'm good and women can be paid less, so that could be an advantage. If I just get a chance to show what I am able to do, I'm sure I can convince them all."

"But as I see it," Jean said, frowning, "getting the chance is actually the hardest part." He knew a lot about the tournaments, and usually they encountered the same tradespeople there. The armorers all had a pretty high opinion of themselves. Jean himself had tried once to get work from one of them, but the smith laughed at him and called him a little squirt. "You're pretty big for a woman," Jean said, "but compared with one of the smiths, you aren't. And you don't have a back like an ox, either, so how can you have the same endurance as these big guys?" It was clear Jean doubted she could.

Ellen grinned. "Technique, Jean, it's all a matter of technique! My master was a short man, and slender, too, for a smith. You can wield the hammer in different ways: with wide swings so that it comes crashing down with full force, or with short little strokes one right after the other. The rhythm, too, is important, and naturally as a striker you have to know how to hold a sledgehammer properly. A man who has no experience as a smith can't wield a hammer properly, even if he's as strong as an ox."

"Oh, là, là! You're beginning to scare me," Jean teased, but he changed his tune when he saw Ellen scowling at him. "All right, it's probably the case, if you say so. I'll surely think of a way to get the smiths to try you out," he mumbled half to himself.

"Look over there—what's that?" Ellen said, pointing to a bush at the side of the road. A few branches moved, and there was a whimpering that sounded almost like that of a small child. Ellen walked over, bent down, and discovered a little dog with a bedraggled coat and bleeding front paw.

"Don't worry, I won't hurt you," she whispered in a gentle voice.

The dog cringed and growled softly.

"Don't get any closer, you never know…he is injured!" she warned Jean and Madeleine. She gestured to them to stop.

"If it's mad, it will first act docile, and then it will bite," Jean warned her. "My father's brother died of a bite like that—it was dreadful. He suffered for a long time. First he went crazy, then foam started coming out of his mouth, and then he fell over dead."

"It doesn't look like he has been bitten," Ellen said, looking at the paw. "It looks more like a cut."

"If it were a good dog, the owner wouldn't have abandoned it," Jean grumbled. He evidently had no desire to care for a dog as well.

Without heeding Jean's objections, Ellen continued to talk to the dog and try to calm it down. "I'll take care of your paw, put some herbs on it and a little bandage, and soon you'll be fine again." She turned around looking for Madeleine, but she had already run off to get what Ellen needed.

Jean gave a shrug of resignation. "It's tough enough trying to cope with one woman, but two…?" He sighed and waited.

As autumn was approaching, it got dark earlier, and already in the afternoon the merchants started seeking a place for the night. "I'll walk ahead a bit and look for a quiet place for us near the others. I suggest you come along when you're done with all this," he grumbled finally, taking Nestor by the reins and heading off.

Ellen didn't take her eyes off the dog. His shaggy grey coat was as soft as down feathers. "You're still pretty young, aren't you?" She sat down alongside the little fellow and looked deep into his eyes, and he put his head on her knees.

"Maybe he ran away," Madeleine said sympathetically and petted him gently. "Here are the herbs for him."

The little dog kept licking Ellen's hand while she carefully tended to his wound.

"His paw has been really injured, and it doesn't look like it will heal so soon." Ellen fondled his ears. "I bet you're hungry, aren't you?"

As if he had understood her, he raised his head and pricked up his ears as best as he could with his shaggy, hanging ears.

Ellen smiled. "There's still a piece of bread in the saddlebag."

Madeleine jumped up. "Oh, darn! Jean has the pony!" Angered, she sat back down on the ground and continued petting the dog.

"We'll take him along!" Ellen decided and put her arms around his little body to pick him up. "He's a lot bigger than I thought," she concluded. "He'll be a big fellow and can keep an eye on our things when he's grown up."

"Jean will be angry," Madeleine said, but Ellen's only response was a look of disapproval.

"Jean doesn't tell me what to do. I do what I think is right." Ellen knew how difficult it would be to look after a dog. He had to eat, after all, and he wouldn't be able to earn his keep. Jean would surely have lots of good reasons why they couldn't keep him. And probably he would be right, but she just couldn't resist the trusting gaze of the little puppy.

Ellen was surprised that Jean didn't grumble as much as she expected. Maybe he was moved by how shaky the little dog was on its feet. He looked like a shaggy foal on legs that were much too long and wobbly. Or maybe Jean just had sympathy for the pup because it was as poor and forsaken as he and Madeleine were.

"We always spent the night with the tradespeople, but with you we are our own little group. We need a tent, at least a small one, or it will be hard getting a good space at the tournament. We can't sleep outdoors anymore because the nights are getting colder and damper. How much money do we have?" Jean asked.

He and Madeleine had a few silver coins, and Ellen looked in her belt purse and took out the same number of coins. She didn't say anything about the money under her shirt. She'd take money from that only if it was absolutely necessary.

Jean held the coins tightly in his dirty hand.

"I'll see what we can get for this. Wait here for me." He ran across the clearing to where the merchants had stopped for the night, setting up their wagons and tents in a circle, as they did every evening, in order to protect themselves from wild animals and other possible attackers.

Ellen saw him talking with a man. They were too far away for her to understand what they were saying. Finally, the man shook his head and Jean moved along to the next wagon, disappearing with one of the men behind a canvas flap. Ellen waited impatiently until he appeared again, but it was a while before he got back.

"I got a tent, but I can't carry it alone. It would be best if I took Nestor along," he said, and led the pony away.

Ellen got more and more restless. This time it seemed to be taking forever. It was already dark, and Jean still wasn't back.

Once more Ellen was afraid that she had been cheated. Just as she was jumping up for the tenth time to have a look, Jean returned, Nestor trotting along docilely behind him carrying a heavy load. The whole time, Madeleine had been sitting calmly on a tree stump, singing softly and petting the dog. She clearly hadn't doubted for a moment that Jean would return. At the sound of his voice she looked up and smiled.

"A tent, a cooking pot, and two old blankets!" The boy beamed proudly. "The tent has a long tear in it, but I also got some needle and thread and can sew it together again. I got the blankets from Agnes. She's very sorry about your foot," he told Madeleine, and then turned to Ellen. "Agnes is not a bad person, you know, she's only afraid her husband might abandon her."

Ellen was astonished at how much the boy had gotten for the money. "If I ever have to buy something," she laughed admiringly, "I'll take you along as a negotiator and get a lot more for my money."

Their dinner that night consisted of a trout and a lamprey that Ellen had caught in a nearby brook just as night was falling, and later they sat for a while by the fire.

"The fish was delicious," said Jean, contentedly wiping his mouth with his sleeve. Then he took the thread he had bought and threaded it through the eye of the needle. He skillfully sewed up the big rip in the canvas and also repaired the eyelets used to fasten the tent to the ground. "But the tent pegs aren't much good anymore."

Ellen looked at the iron pegs. They were rusted and probably wouldn't last much longer.

"Some of that iron is still usable, but not much. As soon as I have a job and access to a forge and anvil, I'll buy some more iron and make new ones for us."

Madeleine interrupted their conversation. “He still needs a name,” she said, pointing to the puppy rolled up at Ellen’s feet. He had gotten the innards of both fish to eat and was apparently content with his lot.

“How about ‘Vagabond’? After all, he is one,” Jean suggested.

Ellen grimaced. “I don’t really like it, we have to find something a little friendlier—after all, we are all vagabonds, because we’re just passing through here. Surely we can think of something else, can’t we, Greybeard?” she said, tugging at his hairy chaps.

“That’s it!” Madeleine beamed.

Ellen looked at her questioningly. “What?”

“Greybeard, that’s what you just called him!”

“Did I?” Ellen looked surprised. “So then why not?”

“Greybeard, the name really suits you!” Jean’s voice suddenly sounded very gentle, and he petted the dog for the first time.

—

Shortly before noon the next day they reached the site of the tournament. Ellen was amazed at all the people crowding around looking for the best spots.

Jean looked around calmly, however, and finally pointed to a small strip of grass between two imposing tents.

“Look over there! There’s just enough room for us, but not enough for anyone else. And it’s a good spot!”

The owners of the two large tents would probably not care especially to have the dirty, ripped tent between their handsome, colorful abodes, but they couldn’t do anything about it, as according to tournament law anyone could occupy any free space.

Ellen and Madeleine set up the tent while Jean went around making inquiries. When he came back in the evening, the two women had done a good job. The tent was set up and put in order, and a fragrant stew of peas and grain was simmering on the hearth.

"Where did you get that?" Jean asked harshly. Madeleine glanced at Ellen as if to say: *You see, didn't I tell you? He'll be offended.*

Ellen didn't seem concerned. "Didn't you tell me it would be best to buy something to eat as soon as possible, before the farmers noticed how much money they can make from the tournament visitors? So I thought I would just do it. After all, you didn't have enough money with you for that."

"That's right," Jean grumbled, a little kindlier. In any case, Ellen had followed his advice.

"Just look: we have a whole bag of peas, two pounds of wheat, a small bag of onions, a good side of bacon, and..." Madeleine positively beamed.

"And a dozen eggs! We have enough provisions for the whole week and won't have to buy things at one of the food stands," Ellen added. She tried to sound as modest as possible, though she was almost bursting with pride.

"No doubt the farmer took advantage of you. Where did you get all that money?"

"I still had half a shilling, and the rest I earned."

"In half a day you made so much money that you could buy all of this? You must have struck a good bargain—I couldn't have done any better myself!" Jean was genuinely astonished. "What sort of work did you do to make so much money?"

"I shoed a few horses. It was a big estate, not just a simple farm. They had their own blacksmith shop there, but the farrier was sick and his wife who ordinarily helps out had to care for him. A few of their horses urgently needed new horseshoes. I didn't even know if I could do that, but one of the older stable hands helped me."

"Well, if the stew tastes as good as it smells, it's certainly all right by me, and I won't mind eating it for a week," Jean said in a conciliatory tone, and laughed when his stomach grumbled loudly. "I met Henry, by the way," he said to Madeleine after the meal.

She smiled with delight and began to sing and dance.

"Sit down again," Jean said softly, and took her back to her seat. "They call him Henry le Norrois, and he's a knight errant," he explained to Ellen. "And he's the nicest herald I know. He's better than anyone else at composing songs in honor of knights and in this way driving up their prices. I have told him about you. He is a smart man and knows people and their vanities, and he gave me a wonderful idea."

"What sort of idea?" Ellen asked skeptically.

"You'll find out soon enough." Jean grinned roguishly and rolled himself up in his blanket. "It would be better for us to sleep now, as tomorrow will be a long day. After all, we have to find work for you." Then he rolled over, turning his back to her.

"And you? Aren't you going to look for work, too?" Ellen asked angrily. It annoyed her that he didn't want to say anything about his plan.

"I've already found something," he said, yawning. "One of the bakers needs an assistant, and he's offering a penny and a fresh loaf of bread every day."

"And you're telling us that so casually?" Ellen sat up. "That's wonderful!"

Jean grinned contentedly and shortly afterward drifted off to sleep.

Ellen thought for a while about how she could convince the smiths the next day, then drifted off to sleep as well. She dreamed of a test she might be given by a smith involving a hammer that she couldn't even lift with one hand. Again and again she tried to lift it, but couldn't. The next morning when she woke up her right arm felt numb—she must have lain on it all night.

Ellen left with Jean and headed for the area where the smiths had settled. Almost all the stalls were already set up, and a few tradespeople had started working. The ground was soft from the rain of the last few days, and the cold, damp mud clung to Ellen's thin leather soles. *I should have bought myself a pair of pattens*, she was thinking. The wooden soles you could strap on the shoes made it harder to walk but protected the leather soles from water.

"Henry!" Jean called out, waving excitedly. Then he ran off.

Ellen had no choice but to follow.

"Henry, this is Ellenweore—I've told you about her," he said as he introduced her.

Henry's clothing was worn and had surely seen better days. His dark blond, wavy hair reached down almost to his shoulders. He bowed courteously and smiled at Ellen disarmingly through a row of beautiful teeth. "You didn't tell me that the woman who can subdue iron and impose her will on men is so beautiful!" he said, without looking at Jean.

It was impossible to resist his smile. "I heard your words are worth more than gold to the knights!" Ellen replied courteously, and immediately won Henry's heart with her flattering words.

"Have you ever been to a tournament?" he inquired, casually placing Ellen's arm over his own to lead her around.

Ellen shook her head.

"Well, the first thing you must see are the jousts, or the *joutes plaisantes*. Have you ever heard of them?"

"Jean never stops talking about them, but I have no idea what they really are." Ellen felt comfortable in Henry's company. His humble appearance and cheerful, open manner almost made her forget he was a knight. *He probably is a late-born son, like William*, she thought.

"Watch out!" Jean shouted, and pulled Ellen back. She just missed being trampled by a horse racing by.

"From now on you should spend more time looking where you are going and less looking into Henry's eyes," Jean admonished her. "The first round was just announced!" He pointed in the direction the horse was headed.

Ellen craned her neck but couldn't see anything but a crowd of people.

"Let's get closer, and this time I'll pay better attention," Henry promised, pulling Ellen along with him.

They found a place in the front row and looked out on a large field where wooden barriers had been set up. Young knights raced toward each other, their lances pointed toward their opponent. The earth shook from the thundering hoofbeats of the horses, and the sound of the splintering lances was ear shattering.

"That's fantastic! How can they survive something like that?" Ellen called to Henry over the noise.

He shook his head and laughed. "You find this fantastic? This is just a friendly preliminary skirmish!" Even though he was standing right next to her, he had to shout to be heard over the commotion.

"What do you mean by that?" Ellen asked in astonishment when the noise stopped for a moment.

"The tournament itself doesn't begin for quite a while," Henry explained. "It's just the young ones for now. They want to show what they can do, and the older knights don't come until later. The contestants then break up into groups according to where they come from, or which lord they are fighting for. Often a number of other knights join together as a loose grouping just for a single tournament. They start galloping towards each other in a close formation until their enthusiasm for battle overcomes their tight order. Only when the fighting gets really serious do the well-known knights, the most experienced fighters, and the bravest warriors join in. Each one hopes to gain fame and fortune, and none of them wants to miss the chance to win. They fight until nightfall, and many are captured and have to buy their freedom. Those who have no money have to appeal to friends in order to borrow what they need."

Ellen was listening to Henry but was also trying to hear the names of the contestants who were just being called up.

"Next, Sir Ralph de Cornhill will do battle with…"

The second name Ellen could not understand because the crowd was howling and clapping so loudly.

"Sir Ralph is unbeaten in numerous tournaments—no one can unseat him. They say he sits there like he's taken root in the saddle, but I think it's because he's so fat." Henry winked at Ellen.

The two opponents charged at each other, and the young challenger hit Sir Ralph right in the middle of the chest, throwing him out of the saddle.

The crowd roared.

Henry shook his head excitedly. "If the young fellow keeps fighting like that, he can really become somebody."

One heart-stopping duel followed the other.

"I had no idea a tournament is so thrilling!" Ellen shouted to Jean and Henry, her cheeks aglow.

Henry shook his head and laughed. "But Ellen, didn't I tell you that this isn't anything yet? Things don't really get going until the main tournament starts. Unfortunately, you won't be able see too much of it because it takes place back in the forest. They even resettled the residents of a small hamlet so their houses and corrals can be used by the knights as hideouts to take a rest or lie in wait for their opponents. It would actually be too dangerous for the people to stay in their houses. Do you see them back there? They'll be scared to death until the tournament is over and hope their houses are not completely destroyed in the heat of the battle. It happens from time to time that their cabins are set on fire. In any case, their gardens are trampled underfoot by the horses, that much is certain. As a spectator you should try to stay as far away as possible from the combatants. Once the knights are worked up into a frenzy, they don't notice if anyone is standing in their way. The safest thing is to watch on a horse and at a safe distance. The tournaments are not intended for spectators, but for the knights themselves."

"But there are a lot of people here." Ellen pointed at the many people around them shouting and commenting on the victories and defeats of the young knights who were doing battle.

"Yes, hardly anyone here wants to miss the jousting because this is where you get to see the young daredevils for the first time. Older and important knights are here, too, on the lookout for good fighters they can either hire on the spot or watch carefully because they could soon be their future opponents."

After the jousting was over, groups of a dozen or more men slowly began to gather at the barriers.

"Do you see over there the knights under the red banner with the lion rampant in gold? Those are our Young King's own knights. And there, too, is the young knight who defeated Sir Ralph earlier! On the right-hand side are the Angevins, then a bit further away the Bretons, and right next to them the Poitevins. All the groups fight against each other, and the winner is whoever has vanquished the most opponents and taken them as hostages. The winners here come away with a lot of money because the hostages have to buy their freedom. Because a successful knight is also a generous knight, the merchants have their hands full, as do the jugglers, the musicians who play at the concluding festivities, the whores who keep the beds warm for the noble gentlemen, and the cooks at the food stalls who care for their bodily needs. The losers are treated magnanimously, for the next time the winner could be the loser. Whoever fights and wins at the tournaments can expect high fees the next time. Some barons even offer brave fighters a woman in marriage and a little fiefdom if they do battle for them. For many later-born men that is the only possible way to get a wife and a regular income. Ah, it won't be long before they ride off. Look! They'll meet way over there in the west at the foot of the hill, and that's where the main tournament will begin."

Ellen felt someone tugging at her sleeve.

"We should start thinking about your work—it's already afternoon," Jean said.

"I'll come back later to see if you can do it without me." Henry gave them a wink as they left.

—

Thibault's heart was racing when he arrived on horseback at the back of the tent and dismounted. He had unseated fat Sir Ralph as if he were a feather! Thibault tore off his helmet and wanted to wipe away with his sleeve the drops of sweat running down his forehead and into his eyes, but first Gilbert, his servant, had to help him remove his chain mail shirt.

"You were splendid, my lord! The crowd roared, and I saw myself how the *Marechal* nodded approvingly." Gilbert's eyes beamed with pride, but Thibault paid hardly any attention to him.

The Marshal! If he only knew! Thibault could think of nothing else. "Very well, Gilbert, leave me alone now," he ordered him gruffly. He didn't have much time left to pull himself together before he would have to get dressed again because the main tournament was beginning. Thibault sat down on a stool and put his head in his hands. Just how could she show up here? She ran right into his horse and had almost been crushed underfoot. Wasn't she looking? Thibault thought about her sparkling green eyes that he loved so much, but he didn't have to see her eyes to remember. He took a deep breath. He was still excited to know that Ellen was nearby. She had brought his blood to such a boil that he had felt invincible. Perhaps fate had determined that she was his! He jumped up, overturning the stool. "Gilbert," he roared, "Gilbert, help me get dressed again. Today I'm going to make a fortune!"

After the squire had helped him back into his chain mail and tunic, Thibault stepped outside. He already felt like a winner! He looked himself over with satisfaction as the maids on the field pointed at him, held their hands up to their mouths, and giggled. "I can have any one of them," he mumbled smugly and jumped up onto his horse.

When he went to join young King Henry's knights, he was greeted with nods and fists raised in a sign of victory. So they had noticed his triumph in the jousting! That was good, but now he had to do well in the main tournament, too. Thibault looked over at William, who gave him a thumbs-up sign with his gloved hand and ordered him to come to his side.

"Take as many as you can, my friend," William ordered, "but don't touch the leader of the French group. He belongs to me."

"Just watch out that you're not captured yourself," Thibault grumbled, but in a soft undertone so William wouldn't hear it. The French were not far away from them and were gossiping about the huge losses the English had suffered in earlier tournaments. With hearty laughter, they planned how to divide up the spoils they would take from their English opponents. Finally, the tournament began. At first the opponents rode toward each other in disciplined rows, but the closer they got the more bellicose they became, and the rows soon disintegrated into a turbulent mêlée.

Thibault decided to keep clear of William, who was the prized target of the best Frenchmen, and along with some other knights of the royal household attacked the Angevins. He picked out as an opponent none other than the brother of the Duke of Anjou, but this young knight was an excellent jouster and overpowered Thibault faster than expected, thrashing him mercilessly with his sword. He soon dragged Thibault off into a corner as his prisoner and handed the reins of Thibault's horse over to his own squires. Seething with anger, Thibault sat there on his horse, condemned to stay on the sidelines for the remainder of the tournament. William fought bravely but was overpowered by the superior French forces and taken captive. Thibault stroked his chin, happily. So William said he would conquer the leader of the French? No way! That braggart William was out of action! But then the squire of the Young King went riding over to the French and bought William's freedom so he would be able to continue fighting. Thibault shouted for Gilbert, who was waiting at a respectful distance from his master.

"Go get my money and buy my freedom, and be quick about it!" he ordered his squire. In contrast to this upstart William, Thibault de Tournai was the eldest son of his father and therefore received a generous allowance, which gave him the means to buy his freedom and continue the fight. Even though he would have liked to have the favor of young Henry, *he* didn't have to depend on it.

Twice again on this day both he and William were taken prisoner. At the end, Thibault's gold purse was a lot lighter, and he was in fact almost penniless, but he was not indebted to anyone. William, on the other hand, had had his freedom bought three times and was more indebted than ever to young Henry.

—

Ellen was still in raptures over the jousting when she heard in the distance the wonderful, rhythmic sound of hammers on the iron anvil and fell silent. Ever since she had been in Beauvais she dreamed of making a sword all on her own—the plans for the sword were already in her head, and all that was missing was the chance to carry them out. She positively had to find work with a swordsmith. Jean had told her they didn't have booths with leather roofs like the merchants but worked in stone barns or stalls that were set up for them at the tournaments. Every smith brought along his own hearth, a tree stump to which the anvil was attached, tools, bellows, and a water trough as well as a table for displaying the items. When Ellen entered the stall and admired the smith's handiwork, she felt a great sense of happiness. There were so many things here for sale: swords, knives, parts for the handle and pommel, helmets, chain mail rings, lances of every length, pikes, and even spiked maces such as those captured from the Saracens by the first Crusaders. In addition there were shield bosses, chapes, and decorations. Jean went over to a dark-haired man who, judging by the items in his showcase, was a fairly talented armorer.

"Pierre!" Jean greeted him like an old acquaintance. "I'm here to propose a bet." Then the boy raised his voice and announced, "Hear this, smiths, I'm challenging Pierre and anyone else to a bet. Either a job for this woman or a week of her work without pay."

The smiths looked at Jean without much interest: why would they want this unknown woman to work for them, even if it didn't cost anything? Pierre didn't react.

So Jean had to try harder. "Come now, Master Pierre, you don't want to pass up this opportunity, do you?"

The smith only mumbled something unintelligible and waved him away. Ellen saw all her hopes fading—they wouldn't even give her the chance to prove what she could do.

"Didn't I tell you, my young friend? They're not half as afraid of the devil as they are of a woman, especially when she is as beautiful as your girlfriend and furthermore understands her trade. What would it be like if a woman proved to them that she's just as good a smith as most men here? It's a question of their honor!"

A disgruntled murmur went through the crowd, and some booed.

Ellen hadn't noticed Henry le Norrois until he'd raised his voice.

Angry smiths gathered around her. No matter how sure she was of her abilities, she was afraid of putting herself and Jean in danger. She wasn't worried about Henry. He was certainly smart enough to even turn their defeat into something positive.

"What do you mean by that?" said Pierre, the first smith Jean had addressed.

"This woman here says she can measure up to any man in her work, and what do you say to that?" Henry asked with a smirk. "You don't want to—or is it perhaps that you don't dare?"

"Tell her to go to the farriers outside. We have no use for beginners here," Pierre grumbled.

"I'm no beginner," Ellen responded confidently, even though her heart was pounding. "It's surely an art to forge a knife or a sword like that," she said, pointing to his items on display, "and you are very skilled at it, master, but I can do the same and will be glad to compete with you."

"Haha, just listen to the little lady's brave words," Pierre said, now apparently in a jovial mood. "Aren't you perhaps a little weak for such a tough vocation? Spinning, embroidering, perhaps bearing children—I would think those are the right things for you to be doing." Pierre seemed to have the last laugh.

"Well then you shouldn't mind taking the bet," Ellen suggested calmly.

"There's not a smith here who would lower himself by competing with a woman," Pierre replied contemptuously, and looked around at all the smiths, who nodded in agreement.

"Let's see, you think I'm a beginner. Why don't you look for a strong man who is a beginner, too? Somebody like the muscleman who lifts tree trunks to entertain the crowd? What do you think of him? I've admired his upper arms that are thicker than my thighs." She laughed provocatively.

Jean looked at Ellen, horrified. "Have you completely lost your mind? He's many times stronger than you are," he whispered.

"Just ask him," Ellen challenged the smith, without even looking at Jean. "If he agrees, I'll challenge him, and whoever swings the hammer better wins!"

Pierre didn't waste any time thinking about it. "That's fine, let's ask him!" He stormed out, and the other smiths followed him, grumbling loudly.

They presented the strongman with the challenge. He was mightily amused at such silliness and looked at Ellen sympathetically. "If she loses, she'll work for you free for one week," Pierre declared.

"And what do I get from you if I win?" Ellen asked the strongman.

"Half of my weekly earnings," he suggested with a grin.

"No, not half, the whole amount, otherwise it's not fair," Ellen contradicted him boldly. "Or are you unsure of winning and afraid to take up my challenge?" She flashed her most innocent smile. "And you'll let me work," she asked Pierre again, "if I win?"

"But of course," he laughed, "since hell will freeze over before that happens."

Pierre tried to give the strongman some advice on how to hold the hammer, but he just brushed him off arrogantly and patted him on the shoulder. "Take it easy, master, I know your hammers and what they weigh! Have you ever tried to lift my tree trunk? I'll bet you can't lift it one hand's breadth from the ground. Just let me go ahead. I'm looking forward to having her work for me for a week."

Pierre was annoyed at the condescending way the strongman spoke about his work. After all, a sledgehammer couldn't be wielded just any way.

There were two volunteers among the journeymen who took an iron and put it in the fire and then held it on the anvil with a set of tongs. Ellen took the sledgehammer in her right hand and was careful not to grasp it too far forward. With her left hand she placed the handle under her right shoulder just as all smiths do, then began hammering with a constant, even rhythm. The strongman took the hammer firmly in both hands in front of him and at the first stroke hit the handle with full force into his stomach. He groaned and fell forward a bit, but didn't give up. He tried as best he could to imitate the grip that Ellen had on the handle, but his huge muscles got in the way. He took big swings, but his rhythm was irregular and he was tiring fast.

The piece he was working on twisted under his blows, whereas Ellen's piece came out neat and straight. After the first few blows, the smiths realized she was far from being a beginner. They no doubt hoped the strongman could win on his strength alone, but soon he was sweating hard, water was streaming down his body, and his head was such a fiery red that it looked like it would explode. Ellen kept working even after the hammering next to her stopped, because she didn't dare to look to the side and lose her rhythm. But then someone tapped her on the shoulder.

"It's all right, you can stop now—you have won," Pierre grumbled sheepishly. "You can start with me tomorrow if you are still able move." It was obviously hard for him to maintain his self-control.

"I'll be here," Ellen replied, placing the hammer in the water bucket next to the anvil.

Jean was jubilant and flung his arms around her neck. "That was great!"

"You have my highest esteem, madam." Henry smiled, offering her his arm.

Ellen trembled a bit from all the excitement but declined his help. She didn't want it to look as if she needed any support. She had won, but she was of two minds when thinking of what would happen the next day. Hopefully, Pierre was a good loser—after all, starting the next morning, she would be working for him. She said her farewells to Henry and the smith and set out with Jean on the way back to their tent. Wistfully, she thought of Jocelyn. She longed for his smile, his love, and his confidence in her abilities. After they had eaten, Jean told Madeleine about Ellen's success.

"I'd better not go to bed too late," Jean said. "I've got to get up in the middle of the night. The baker starts his work before sunrise, and he will send his son to pick me up. So don't be startled when you wake up tomorrow and I'm not here." He looked over at Madeleine. "How did everything go for you today? Did you find work?"

Madeleine nodded. "Agnes said I can fetch water for her again, and spin, as long as her husband isn't around," she added with some embarrassment.

"That's wonderful!" Jean replied, patting her cheeks.

Ellen was moved by his concern for the poor girl. Things would be all right as long as he was around to care for her.

—

Although Pierre was highly regarded by the other smiths, they teased him all day about losing the bet and told him that now he'd have another woman to support. They grinned the next morning when Ellen arrived at the smithy but calmed down in the course of the day and soon didn't pay much attention to her.

At the end of the week the strongman came to Ellen's tent without being asked and delivered the money he had made. "Are you going to keep doing the rounds of the tournaments?" he asked.

"I believe so."

"If you can't find any work, you can challenge me again. We'll let the knights make wagers and I'll lose. Of course, it wouldn't be great for my reputation and sooner or later I'd hate myself for it, but for a while we could make a lot of money that way," he suggested.

"I'd rather earn my money in my trade, if possible." Ellen tried not to sound too egotistical.

"As you will." The strongman raised his hand to say goodbye, then added, "Just in case you change your mind..."

"I'll know where to find you!" Ellen nodded and was relieved when he finally left. Even though she was able to defeat him in hammering, it was better not to have someone like that as an enemy.

Châteauneuf-en-Braye, May 1172

Since autumn of the previous year, Ellen had been traveling about with Jean and Madeleine from one tournament to another. At first she was anxious about whether Pierre would give her work again, but after a while it could almost be taken for granted. Pierre never became a real friend, but the lighthearted Henry le Norrois did. Ellen could usually hear his throaty laughter from far off, as she did again this time. She tiptoed up behind him and was going to tap him on the shoulder and then quickly hide so when he turned around there wouldn't be anyone there. But at the last moment she recognized the man standing next to him and froze. She was just turning around, her heart pounding, when Jean caught sight of her.

"Ellenweore! Henry!" he called and made his way through the crowd.

Henry turned around. "Jean!" he exclaimed, patting him on the shoulder. "Didn't you call Ellenweore's name, too? Where is she?" Henry looked around and finally saw her.

She stood there dumbfounded.

"Ellen, how are you?" he said.

At that moment his companion turned around, too.

Ellen felt the blood rushing to her face when their gazes met.

William looked at her, puzzled.

"Do we know each other?" William kept staring at her.

It was five years ago that he saw me for the last time, and he thought I was a boy then, she told herself, shaking her head and trying to calm her raging feelings. "Excuse me, I must go back. Work, you know!" She curtsied politely and ran off.

"Heavens, William, you make quite an impression on the ladies!" Henry laughed. "I didn't even have time to introduce you, and already she is running away from you."

William watched her in astonishment.

Ellen hurried to Pierre's shop. All day she thought of nothing but the meeting with William, and as much as she yearned to see him again, she was just as afraid he would recognize her. At the first sight of him her heart had started beating wildly, evoking a warm, tender feeling within her. Her mind was not on her work, and Pierre criticized her harshly. She thought about the arguments with Donovan and tried to pull herself together so that Pierre didn't regret giving her the job. When she got home that evening, Jean was already in the tent preparing the supper, but Madeleine was not yet back.

"What was the matter with you this morning?"

"What do you mean?" Ellen tried as hard as she could to sound innocent.

"You turned red all over when you saw that man. Do you know him?"

Ellen wanted to deny it, but then she thought it would surely be better to have Jean as an ally, so she nodded.

"Oh, là, là!" Jean grinned from ear to ear. "You're in love with him!" He waved his hands up and down. "*L'amour, l'amour, toujours l'amour!* We are all helpless when it comes to love."

Ellen glared at him. "He knows me as Alan, the smith's assistant, that's the problem."

"What? I don't understand." Jean looked at her with some irritation.

"I knew him when I lived in Tancarville, where he was a squire. I dressed at that time as a boy, and we were friends for years. I learned what I know about sword fighting from him. He must never find out that Alan and I are the same person—he would never forgive me for lying to him like that."

"Do you have any idea who he is?"

"Sure. His name is William. What else should I know?"

"He is the tutor-in-arms of the Young King. Didn't you know that?"

"Really!" She sounded astonished. But then she started to smile. "Actually, it doesn't surprise me. He always said he wanted someday to be a king's knight. But of course, I never thought he would do it so quickly. When someday the old king dies and his son ascends the throne as king of the whole empire, William will have accomplished everything he had hoped for." Ellen sighed. "I am so far from realizing *my* dreams." She sighed sadly.

Madeleine crawled into the tent without saying a word, sat down in a corner, and started to sing. She took a coin from her pocket and looked at it happily.

"Where did you get all that money?" Jean asked suspiciously, looking more closely at the coin.

"A knight gave it to me, a handsome knight. He wanted to know who she is." Madeleine pointed at Ellen.

"And what did you say?" Ellen replied, seizing her by the shoulder and shaking her a little.

"That you are Ellenweore and my friend, that's what I said. Nothing else."

"And just for that he gave you all that money?"

"Yes!" Madeleine was beaming.

Jean and Ellen looked at each other.

"That can only have been William!"

"Don't worry, Madeleine doesn't know anything about what happened earlier," Jean whispered to Ellen, trying to calm her down.

—

He had been at peace for almost nine months, and now once again he couldn't get her out of his mind. Thibault hurried back to his tent, his heart in flames. The only person who could soothe his tormented soul was Rose. Thibault wiped his hand over his eyes as if somehow he might be able to wipe away the images that had been passing through his mind since that morning. The moment Ellen saw William, she'd blushed and looked more beautiful than ever. Thibault wheezed. That silly little goose who claimed to be her friend hadn't told him anything he hadn't already known for a long time in return for the silver coin he gave her. Nevertheless, he had treated her in a kindly way—after all, it could be very valuable having a spy in Ellen's tent. An evil smirk passed over Thibault's face.

"Rose?" He looked around the tent impatiently. Everything was neat and tidy, but nobody was there. "Rose!" he shouted loudly, but again nothing happened. When she finally came, Thibault was sitting sullenly in his chair. "Where were you?" he snarled at her.

"I bought myself a few pretty ribbons and a wonderful piece of cloth!" She ran over to him, sat down happily at his feet, and helped him out of his boots.

"Just so I would be beautiful for you!" She lowered her eyes coyly in hopes of mollifying him.

"I forbid you to leave the tent again without my permission!"

"But…" Rose started to protest.

"Do you insist on keeping the child this time, or shall we get rid of it again?" he asked in a threatening voice.

Rose looked down and shook her head. "If you wish, I'll of course stay here."

"I already like you better for that!" Thibault looked at her longingly, then stood up and took her to his bed. "Come, my little Rose, come and lie down by me."

But ever since Rose was expecting, he found her less attractive, and after having been with her he still felt unsatisfied. "Go and get Margaret for me!" he ordered her, unmoved by the tears in her eyes. "Stop your blubbering and be happy I don't send you and your bastard child to hell!" he shouted at her, stretching out on the fur bedcover. Rose knew, of course, what he intended to do with Margaret, and that was why it turned him on so much. Why should he be the only one to suffer? Could Rose's grief in seeing him with another woman really be any worse than his own when he saw Ellen together with other men? The thought of Ellen excited him, and at that moment Margaret walked in. Rose had to think that his excitement came from Margaret coming to him. The young maiden was slender, almost emaciated, had a thin face, with eyes set close together, and narrow lips. Nothing about her would remind anyone of Ellen's vibrant vitality except perhaps the color of her hair. Thibault reached up to touch her curly locks. They were longer and thinner than Ellen's, but when he squinted he could sometimes imagine that he was holding Ellen in his arms. "Wait outside," he gasped, and Rose left as fast as she could.

"Oh, Ellen!" he groaned into the ear of the skinny maiden.

"My name is Margaret!" she complained softly.

"Hold your tongue, and sit down on me," Thibault commanded her roughly, squeezing her flat backside until it was red.

—

In the smithy, Ellen concentrated completely on her work and didn't notice she was being watched. She tried not to think so much about William, though that was very hard for her. In the meantime, the tournament had begun, and according to everything Jean had found out about William, he was probably one of the first to rush into the tumult of battle. When Henry le Norrois came back to the smithy in the afternoon, Ellen hoped he would not mention her strange behavior toward William when they had met.

"I'm sure you must have a pair of tin sheers," Henry grinned as a greeting. He was leading a helpless knight by the arm. His head was stuck in a battered and twisted helmet. The brave fellow had lost his bearings and was completely at Henry's mercy.

"The first few blows he received on the metal didn't bother him, but now the helmet is wedged on tight! He can hardly get any air, the poor fellow. Could you please get him out?"

Ellen giggled. How childish the knights were. They fought battles even in peacetime. "He won't enjoy this very much," she said and went to get the tongs and tin shears.

"It's not his first time—it's happened to him before. Nevertheless, be careful, he's a promising warrior even though in his present condition he doesn't look the part," Henry said, winking at Ellen.

The man trapped inside the helmet grumbled discontentedly and directed metallic-sounding curses at Henry from under the helmet.

Ellen grinned and shook her head as she set about freeing the knight from his battered prison. She handed Henry a pair of tongs and asked him to help her in order not to injure the knight's head. "But afterwards the helmet won't be worth any more than the iron it's made of," she warned him as she set about her work.

Henry le Norrois couldn't hold the tongs tight enough, and they slipped off several times.

"How annoying that Pierre isn't here. You're not really very much help to me. Now hold it tight!" she ordered, as she tugged and groaned and pulled on the helmet until the knight's head came free. Ellen put aside the battered metal and asked the knight how he felt.

"Are you all right…?" was all she could say. Then she stopped, stunned at seeing who had been stuck inside the helmet.

"My ears are still ringing," William answered without looking at her. When he finally looked up, his mouth fell open as well.

"You?" he asked incredulously.

"My lord!" Ellen bowed and looked down at her feet. It would no doubt be better if he couldn't look at her face for very long.

William rubbed his head.

"I have to get back to work," Ellen said hastily, turning away from him.

"What do I owe you?"

"Nothing. It was not a big problem, and besides, you are a friend of Henry. If you like, you can leave the helmet here." It was impolite not to look him in the face, but Ellen kept her back turned toward him.

"Thank you very much." William laid a silver coin on the table but made no move to leave.

Henry understood at once when William gave him a signal and left hastily.

Ellen tried not to let herself get distracted by William's presence, but his gaze seemed to burn right through her like the noonday sun in July.

"Ah, now I remember!" he exclaimed suddenly.

Ellen cringed, and cold sweat trickled down her neck.

"I've been racking my brains all along trying to think who you remind me of."

Ellen felt nauseous. She tried to deflect attention by taking the coin and tucking it into the purse on her belt.

"Yes, I think I know your brother!"

"My brother?" She looked up with astonishment.

"Yes, Alan was his name, a young smith from East Anglia. I met him in Tancarville. Henry said you are from England, too, just as I am."

Ellen didn't react at once. Feverishly, she tried to figure out what to say.

William continued. "He's your brother, isn't he? You look just like twins. Alan was a good friend when I was still a squire. Didn't he ever tell you about me? My name is William!" He looked quizzically at Ellen.

He himself had offered her the best explanation, and she couldn't bring herself to contradict him. "Ah, yes, indeed, that's you, then," she stammered and smiled at him shyly.

"And how is he? Is he here as well?"

"No," Ellen answered. What else could she say? Should she invent a story? And what if William figured out just the same that she was lying?

"He is dead," she replied, trying to look dismayed. Apparently she did it very convincingly, because William looked at her wide-eyed.

"I didn't know that! What in the world happened?"

"His throat swelled up until he choked to death. It was something a lot of people caught last winter." Ellen was surprised at herself. How did she come up with something like that?

"Dreadful thing," William said, nodding thoughtfully. "So, do you also work as a smith?"

"It runs in the family." Ellen could hear how her voice was trembling. *He'll figure this out, and then I'm through*, she thought.

"Alan always wanted to forge a sword for the king." William sounded sad.

"That's just what I want to do!" Ellen glanced into William's eyes, and her stomach tightened into a knot as it had that time in the forest when he had been standing behind her, guiding her with his arm, and she could feel his warm breath on her neck.

"If the Young King ever comes into some money, which will probably be after his father passes away, I'll tell him about you. Provided, of course, that you're as good as Alan!" William added with a smile.

Ellen lowered her eyes and blushed.

Suddenly William staggered and turned pale.

"What's the matter?" She ran over to him anxiously and held him firmly by the arm.

"I'm dizzy, and my skull…" William said nothing more.

"That's due to the blows on your head," she said and led him outside. "You must stay out here in the fresh air, and you should rest. If you'll tell me the way, I'll bring you back to your tent."

"Thank you!" William took a couple of deep breaths but continued standing there, as everything seemed to be spinning around.

Pierre would surely be back any minute, so Ellen asked one of the other smiths to keep an eye on her things until he returned, and left with William.

"Our tents are rather far from here on the opposite side of the meadow in a little valley," William told her. After a few more steps he stopped and asked, "Can we just sit down for a moment?"

She was sure Pierre would be furious if she was away for such a long time, but she couldn't leave William here alone like this. Her attraction to him was as strong as ever, and indeed seemed to be stronger than it was in Tancarville. Ellen was thrilled by the very touch of his powerful arm and the chance to walk along beside him. He smelled of horses and leather, just as he used to.

"Fine," she said, and looked around. At the edge of the meadow, not far from them, was a tree that had been uprooted by a storm. "You can sit down and rest on that log."

William sat down without letting go of her arm, so there was nothing she could do but sit down close beside him. They had gone about half the distance and could look down on the market square below. On the opposite side of the large meadow in front of them were the tents of the knights. It was only now that Ellen realized the two of them were alone. Her mouth and throat felt strangely dry, and she ran the tip of her tongue over her lips and swallowed hard.

William looked at her for a long time. "I have never in my life seen such green eyes," he started to say, brushing a strand of hair out of her eyes. "Did I say before that you and Alan look just like twins? That was nonsense, of course. I would have noticed if he had had eyes as green as yours."

Ellen smiled. *How blind most people are…and men especially, it would seem.*

"Also, you have a lot more of those pert little freckles!" he teased.

William was indeed right about that. At the beginning of her pregnancy, she suddenly broke out in them. Ellen thought of Thibault and of the day she had almost bled to death in the forest, and suddenly her face darkened.

"You aren't angry because of the freckles?" William asked with surprise.

Ellen shook her head. "I was just thinking of some bad things that have happened."

William seemed to be thinking it was the memory of her brother's death, because he patted her tenderly on the head. "Everything will be all right."

Ellen jumped up and was about to tell him the truth, but before she could speak he stood up, pulled her to him, and kissed her.

His kiss was so different from Jocelyn's tender, groping kiss. It was like William himself—demanding, exciting, captivating, irresistible, and dangerous through and through. Ellen could scarcely breathe. Her mind was in turmoil; the blood rushed to her head and carried her away. William held her tight as if he would never let her go and dug his fingers into her back. Her head was hammering, telling her, *I must stop this now and leave at once, before it is too late. He is a Norman knight, not a man for me.* She kissed William with all the passion that had built up over the years in her. Through her clothes she could feel the heat of his body and his longing for her. He pressed her tightly against him and began to caress her whole body, not tenderly like an admirer but demanding like a lover. She still could have turned around and run away, but her knees buckled and she gave herself completely to William, who seemed to have recovered completely. His hands moved from her shoulders to her breasts, feeling for them beneath the clothing. Ellen was panting with desire, a mixture of abandon and despair as William drew her off with him into the forest. He pressed her against an old beech tree, raised her dress, and groped beneath it. His hands moved upward gently yet with determination, from the back of her knee, stopping somewhere high up between her legs.

"You are so beautiful!" he said with a hoarse voice, kissing her with his soft lips first on the neck and then farther and farther down to her breast.

Ellen sighed with rapture.

Now he moved his hand in and out of her most intimate area until she thought she would die from desire. Somehow he managed to open his chausses. Ellen did not look but closed her eyes and gave herself completely to him. Torn first one way then the other by desire and fear, she trembled under his touch and offered no resistance. Forgotten was Thibault as a warm, blissful shudder passed through her whole body and consumed it. William withdrew from her, only to thrust forward again with renewed vigor. She groaned, and her whole body yearned for him. All of her being now strove only to preserve this moment so it would never end.

Suddenly William groaned as well. He had reached his climax and a hot flash passed through her while a dull pounding filled her body. After he had withdrawn from her, she felt more exhausted than after a long hard day of labor. William gently stroked her cheeks and smiled at her. Her throat felt tight as if she could not speak, but a hot tear ran across her face. William took her chin, raised it, and wiped the tear away with his thumb.

"I don't know why I..." she stammered.

"Shh!" William put his finger to his lips and kissed her again.

After they had straightened out their clothing, they left the forest. Ellen felt like a child who had done something naughty, while William seemed hardly touched by what had happened. She felt guilty and avoided looking at him.

"Can you get back to your tent by yourself from here?" she asked him, her eyes still cast toward the ground.

"Certainly!" William stopped and pulled her toward him. "Tomorrow is Sunday, and you don't have to work. We'll meet here at noon. Is that all right?"

Ellen could only nod weakly.

"You are gorgeous, and very exciting," he said with a self-assured grin.

Ellen didn't know what to think of it. Jocelyn had talked about love. Ah, Jocelyn—he was now only a faint memory. William had replaced him in her heart.

As she walked back to the smithy, Ellen felt strong and confident. It was high time—she absolutely had to get back to work on the sword that had been on her mind for months. She knew exactly how it would look, what kind of pommel it should have, its length, its width, and how she would make the cross guard, the handle, and the hilt. Her sword even had a name already! At some point it had just come to her, lodged itself firmly in her head, and kept speaking to her, more and more urgently, saying, "Forge me!"

"Athanor," Ellen whispered.

—

At noon the next day she entered the forest, her heart pounding. She strolled along the bumpy road, still soggy from the recent rain, enjoying the beautiful spring day. The sky was clear, and the sunlight spread like a sea of cornflowers over the land. Winter was finally past. At Eastertime, there had been a few nice sunny days. After that it had gotten cold again, but now it looked as if nothing could stop the advance of spring. Everything was blooming, the shepherd's purse, dandelions, bloodroot, and the stinging nettles. The first blossoms had appeared on the blueberries, and the side of the road was a sea of daisies, Ellen's favorite flower. It was rumored that some women used them to stop unwanted pregnancies, but she didn't want to think of that now and put aside the memory of Thibault. *That's all in the past*, she thought, *I must forget it*. On a hill in the distance, apple trees were blooming, beautiful and bright. In a few months they would be full of exquisite fruit, and Ellen would already be somewhere else.

She arrived faster than expected at the place where she was going to meet William, sat down on a log, and waited. At her feet, delicate white mayflowers were blooming. She thought of Claire and the potion she had prepared with that herb. It had given the alcoholic brew a distinctive aroma Ellen almost thought she could taste when she sniffed the blossom.

Suddenly, William stood before her. "You are smiling!" he said, visibly delighted.

Ellen had not heard him coming and looked up at him in astonishment. She squinted because the sun at his back blinded her.

"You're even more beautiful today," he said, quickly taking a seat beside her and handing her a little bouquet of white flowers.

"Lily of the valley!" Ellen was touched.

For a moment they were both silent. William looked at her inquisitively, and Ellen became restless.

"Soon I shall start work on my sword," she said, and looked aside in embarrassment.

William did not reply, but seized her by the chin, turned her face toward his, and kissed her passionately. Ellen forgot the smithy, the sword, and the past, and savored his kisses and caresses. He stood up and pulled her to him.

Only now did Ellen notice the woolen blanket he was carrying. And it flashed through her mind: *Watch out, he is prepared. He knows exactly what he wants, and it's just one thing. He's an experienced man, and if you believe he feels more for you than for anyone else, you're mistaken.* But that was as far as she got in her thoughts.

He led her out onto the meadow, but Ellen shook her head, since the grass was still quite short.

"Not here, we could be seen!" She blushed.

Undeterred by her objections, William spread the blanket out and pulled her down to him.

The moment his lips touched her mouth and he pressed his body against hers, her resistance crumbled. She gave herself to him, forgetting time and space, until they were both exhausted.

She straightened out her dress, embarrassed, while William calmly pulled his clothes on again. Ellen tried feverishly to think of what they had spoken about back then in Tancarville, when they had been friends, but she couldn't think of anything in particular. She couldn't think of a single sensible thing to say. Alan was really dead.

William lay down in the grass again and looked up at the sky. "Tell me about the sword," he said finally, turning over onto his stomach and propping himself up on his elbows, staring at her with his blue eyes.

"So you did hear what I said before!" Her eyes flashed.

"Of course I heard. But since you're Alan's sister, I was afraid that if I asked we would spend the whole afternoon doing nothing but discussing swords. I'll admit that my appetite for you was too great." He tickled her with a daisy he had picked and kissed her.

"Your appetite for me?" Ellen frowned. "That sounds so…"

"That sounds like honey cakes or sweet fruit," he replied with a grin and kissed her dress where her nipples were.

"You're impossible!" she scolded him gently.

"I know!" William stared at her with a feigned look of guilt. "But now tell me about your sword."

Ellen couldn't manage to be angry at him. "All right, then," she sighed. "And when it's finished, I'll show it to you. It will be a very special sword because I will make it without help from any other craftsmen. I'll make not just the blade, but the entire sword."

William looked at her in astonishment. "And how will you do that?"

"I can do more than just what an ordinary blacksmith does," Ellen said provocatively.

"Is that so? Funny I never noticed," he said as he cast her back down onto the grass. His hands moved up and down her body, and the two abandoned themselves again to their love play. When Ellen finally sat up again, she was panting with exhaustion.

"I believe the only sword that really interests you is that one there." She gave him a fresh grin and pointed between his legs.

"Hm, perhaps there's something to that, at least as long as you are around. So do me a favor and never come to see the jousting or I'll lose the shirt on my back." He laughed loudly and kissed the tip of her nose.

They separated only as the sun began to set.

"I must get up early tomorrow, so I had best go now." Ellen ran her fingers through her hair and tied it up in a braid.

"Tomorrow I have no time, and in two days we must leave, so all we have left is the day after tomorrow," William explained dryly, and pulled her to him again. "I can hardly wait. Will you be faithful to me until then?"

Ellen looked at him, stunned. "Is that the way you think I am?" she snapped at him. "That I'll just take off with a man and disappear into the forest or go and lie with him in a meadow?" She tore herself away from him indignantly.

Instead of answering, he grabbed her again and kissed her.

—

Thibault had followed William. The blanket the Marshal was carrying with him could only mean that he was planning an amorous rendezvous, and Thibault wanted to know all about it. The worst thing was that the Marshal looked like a man in love. He sauntered along, swinging the blanket back and forth, and kept stopping to pick up lilies of the valley along the way. *Either he's a crafty seductor, or he's in love,* Thibault thought bitterly. Though he knew down deep who it was William was going to see, he hoped it might be someone else. Maybe she wouldn't come. Thibault managed to follow William without attracting attention. And then he saw her sitting on the log, her red hair shining as if it were on fire in the sunlight. When he saw William and Ellen kissing, it hit him like a thunderbolt. He felt worse than back then in Beauvais! Maybe it was due to his hatred for William, or perhaps the glow emanating from Ellen.

When the two lay down in the grass and made love, Thibault watched, crying with despair. Seeing Ellen in William's arms was too much to bear. He pounded his fists on the ground and buried his face and his tears in his sleeve. It hadn't been hard disposing of Jocelyn, but William wasn't such an easy matter.

But there was no other choice—he had to win Ellen back. And if she didn't want to be his of her own free will, then he'd find a good reason for her to change her mind. Someday, sometime, Ellen would belong to him alone!

August 1172

"I won't be able to take part in the next two or three tournaments. Young Henry has obligations," William said, picking up a blade of grass and stroking Ellen's neck with it. For the last three months they had been meeting at tournaments and making love as often as possible. "I think we can be back by the end of October at the latest, and until then you'll just have to dream of me. Now don't forget me!" he admonished her strictly.

"Aha," Ellen teased him. "And who will you be dreaming about?"

"Who do you think?" he replied, with a look of disapproval.

"I think I have to go now," she said as she stood up, "or Pierre will shout at me." She didn't want to start crying, so she just kissed him on the forehead. Then she smoothed out her hair and clothing and ran off. She turned around once to wave to him, but William was busy putting on his boots and didn't see her.

—

To her surprise, Pierre wasn't angry at all, though once again she was arriving much too late. On the contrary, he grinned as she walked in.

"So, it's really true that you are involved with the Young King's tutor." He nodded his appreciation. "Congratulations, I never thought you had it in you. But who knows, perhaps that will bring us an order from the king someday."

Ellen could feel her face turning a flaming red and didn't dare look Pierre in the face. *The Young King is penniless*, she was about to say, but then she reconsidered and seized the opportunity. "I am to make a sword. Sir William wants to see what I can do. Will you allow me to work on it here in the evenings, when work is over?"

Pierre looked at her in surprise and rubbed his chin as he thought it over. "Well, all right, then, if you want to," he finally grumbled.

Perhaps he was a little out of sorts because William was interested in a weapon made by her, and not by him.

Ellen rejoiced silently and set to work on her new project, full of anticipation.

"Can I get the iron from you, too? Of course I'll pay for it," she asked in the evening when her work was done.

Instead of replying, Pierre just grumbled something inaudible. Ellen took that as a yes and started rummaging around in his pile of iron. Far back in a corner she found a huge, rough piece that was unusually hard.

"What do you want to do with that?" Pierre laughed.

"Probably not bake bread," Ellen retorted sharply and kept looking for other material.

"That huge piece is so brittle it will fall apart when you try to shape it. Do you really intend to make a sword out of that?" Pierre shook his head, amused, and whistled between his teeth.

"If it's really such bad material as you say, I hope you'll let me have it for not too much money."

"I didn't say it was bad," Pierre answered hastily. "It's just that it will be too much work shaping it."

"Yes, that's what I said, you'll give me a good price for it."

Pierre snorted.

Ellen didn't let him throw her off. Of course he was right, the iron she had picked out was unusually hard, but it was just for that reason that she wanted it. She knew only material that was very pure, with no remaining slag or impurities, was suitable for making a sword. To get such a level of purity, the iron had to be folded many times, but since a little bit of the hardness was lost each time it was folded, the iron had to be hard enough to start with. Most smiths avoided folding and welding iron that was so brittle, because it was so difficult to shape it. Normally, three or four folding operations were enough to make a good sword, but Ellen wanted to fold the iron seven times and make an especially good sword that was purer, more resistant, and sharper than any other. She knew William would appreciate it, and that Athanor would be something special. She also chose a bar of iron she intended to use for the blade core, as well as good-sized pieces of clean, well-wrought iron that would be especially suited for the cross guard and the pommel. Pierre watched her as she selected her materials and teased her when she came to him to inquire about the price.

"Ah, women! I could die laughing when I see how you pick out your material. Like Armelle when she goes to the market and buys what she needs for a new dress," he joked, prancing through the smithy holding an imaginary shopping basket and mimicking his wife.

"Just go right ahead and make fun of me, but don't forget to give me a decent price for the iron," Ellen repeated confidently.

"You're making too much unnecessary work for yourself with this piece instead of selecting a decent piece for the blade. And I can't understand why you want the bar iron." Pierre shook his head when he saw what Ellen had picked out. He scratched his head, weighed the pieces in his hand, thought about it for a moment, and added up the figures. The price he finally offered her was astonishingly fair.

Ellen paid him at once. She declined a charge against her wages. A master could too easily get used to paying less or not at all, and once they had started down that road...Ellen took her purse and paid him on the spot.

"I'll pay for every evening I use your anvil and your tools, and of course I'll only work when you don't need the smithy yourself. What price do you ask?"

Pierre replied without hesitation, demanding half of her earnings. In return she could also use his coal for the fire. She hesitated only a moment, because she really had no other choice, and they agreed with a handshake.

"You will pay my wages as before, and I'll pay at the end of each week." Ellen knew she would be obligated to Pierre for a time, and that what remained of her earnings would be just enough to live on, but there was no other way. Once she had bought all the material she needed for the sword, there would not be much left over from her savings. But her sword was worth it. She absolutely had to show William what she was able to do. He would at once appreciate a good sword and perhaps, she hoped, would see more in her than just a girl who let herself be seduced by him after only a short acquaintance. William had never spoken of love, but only desire. On the way to the smithy, Ellen had been thinking about that. What was happening to her? Was she really in love with William? Or did she just lust after him? With Jocelyn she had been certain: she had wished more than anything else to be at his side every day, to work with him and to grow old with him. But with William? He awakened other feelings in her. He was seductive and dangerous, like the ocean, refreshing and fascinating, until its tide pulled you away without warning, holding you in its clutches and pulling you down into the cold, dark abyss. Nevertheless, she missed William. She dreamed of his kisses and caresses, woke up in a turmoil in the middle of the night, and asked herself what was worse: her fear she would never see him again or her fear of falling even further under his spell.

—

When the tournament ended, the tradesmen, merchants, and magicians moved on. It would take them only eight or nine days to get to the next tournament site. Those who left at once would have at least a week before the new tournament began, and thus the opportunity to repair their tools, carts, tents, or other household goods.

Even though Ellen had plenty to do in the smithy and by evening could hardly move, she decided to begin the sword in a couple of days. In the past few months she had spent every free moment in William's arms, and now, during his absence, she would have time for Athanor. On Sunday she heated the anvil and forged the iron bar to a square point. She looked at the result with satisfaction. The next few steps required a helper, and she was wondering whom she could ask for assistance when Pierre walked into the shop, fuming with rage.

"Have you completely lost your senses?" he shouted at her.

Ellen couldn't understand why he was so worked up and looked at him in astonishment.

"Don't stare at me like a cow in a thunderstorm! Nobody can work on the Lord's Day. Do you think I want trouble because of you?" He glared at her furiously. "Your hammering here on a Sunday can be heard for miles around!"

Ellen thought Pierre's agitation was a bit exaggerated but decided not to say anything.

"If you want to do some stitching on Sundays, or anything else that doesn't make a lot of noise, that's all right with me, but you will never enter the smithy again on the Lord's Day, is that clear?"

Ellen nodded emphatically. "Yes, Master Pierre, I'm sorry," she replied meekly.

Pierre liked it when she called him "Master," and he calmed down a bit. "Remove the coal that can still be used and put it aside, then leave!" he ordered her, but not quite so angrily as before.

"From now on I'll only work evenings, and then not too late, is that all right?"

"Yes, and see to it that you do!" he grumbled, and left the smithy.

As Ellen was returning to her tent shortly afterward, she suddenly had an idea who could help her, and during supper that evening she asked Jean.

The boy had just taken a huge piece of bread and put it in his mouth, and he choked on it as it went down. He coughed, his head turned crimson, and tears came to his eyes.

Ellen smacked him on the back.

"I…" he said, turning red again and continuing to cough.

"Swallowed the wrong way," Ellen said, completing his sentence while rolling her eyes. "You have to hold your mouth until it goes away." It was so dumb that someone who obviously was choking would have nothing better to do than to explain what was happening, at the risk of choking to death. Ellen slapped him on the back again. "Hold your arms up, that should help."

When Jean had quieted down, she repeated her question.

"Did you see that? Thin as a reed." Jean pointed to the muscle in his upper arm.

"Tell me, am I mistaken or weren't you there yourself when I competed against the strongman? I already explained to you: in our work it isn't just how strong you are"—Ellen pointed at her upper arm muscle that was unusually large for a woman—"but what's up here," she said, tapping herself on the forehead. "Naturally you can't do that sort of work, because you're not strong enough and you don't have the right technique. But you can hold the iron for me. I started that way as a little girl, and you'll be able to do that, too."

"If that's the case, I'll do it!" Jean was beaming.

"Fine! Tomorrow after work? I'll promise you, too, that we won't work too long because you have to get up practically in the middle of the night."

"Don't worry about that. I don't work for the baker any longer. He whipped my back until I was black and blue, and I'd rather go hungry than ever lift a finger for him again."

"But Jeannot! Why didn't you ever say anything?" Ellen was disappointed—though he was always open to the grief of others, he had rarely in turn confided in them.

"That's not so important. I'm doing all right now, you know. In any case, I found something better. At the well I met a young squire. He had been sick for a long time and still hasn't gotten his strength back. I helped him a little, and his master asked me if I could do that all during the tournament. He can pay twice what the baker paid, and the work is nowhere near as difficult. That's pretty good, don't you think?"

"You're a lucky fellow, my little Jeannot," Ellen teased her young friend and patted him on the shoulder.

"Ow!" he cried. "Don't start already beating up on your helper," he said, grinning proudly. "Smith's assistant sounds good to me."

He came to the workshop the next day right after work. "So what shall I do?" he asked as he looked around, eager to get started. "Do I get an apron like that, too?"

"You can take one of the helpers' aprons hanging over there on the hooks. Roll down your sleeves. I'll be ready in a moment. First I have something here to finish for Pierre, or he'll be angry. You can just watch me for a moment."

After finishing the work for Pierre, she took the crude iron bar, handed Jean a heavy pair of tongs, and pointed to the large piece of iron. "You've got to put that in the forge."

Jean stared at her wide-eyed and tapped his chest. "What? You want me to do that?"

"Sure, you said you wanted to help me, and you want to learn something as well, don't you?" Ellen grinned.

Jean nodded uncertainly, seized the huge pair of tongs, and lifted the iron bar. "Jesus, Mary, and Joseph, that's heavy!" The iron slipped away from him and fell on the ground.

"Work in a smithy can be very dangerous if you don't watch out. If that happens to you with the hot iron, there will be trouble!" Ellen raised her hand as if she were about to slap him.

Jean gave her a frightened look, and Ellen laughed. "I'm serious, you really have to hold it tight." She took a handful of sand and sprinkled it on the bar. "Let's go, put it in the fire."

A bit unsure of himself, Jean laid the iron on the coals.

"That's right—right in the middle," Ellen said encouragingly. "It's got to be in the center of the heat, and then you have to blow air on it with the bellows."

Jean didn't dare let go of the tongs.

"You can just put it down when you need to use the bellows, but now and then you've got to turn the iron to keep it heated evenly all the way around."

The large wooden bellows, covered in pig's leather, wheezed when Jean pulled the chain and blew air into the hearth, making the coals glow brightly.

"Turn it now." Ellen pointed to the piece of iron, and Jean picked up the tongs, as large beads of sweat dripped from his brow. Ellen watched him and added, "When the iron is white hot, you have to take it out of the fire right away or it will burn."

"It will burn?" Jean looked at her in disbelief.

"Yes, indeed, iron can burn, and that's not good for it. Don't forget the air, Jean." Ellen laughed and pointed to the bellows. "The bar is thick, so it will take a while before it really glows."

Jean simply nodded, pulled the chain on the bellows, and Ellen was happy he didn't ask any dumb questions.

Donovan had had the same problems, and she sighed when she thought of him because she missed him.

"Look closely at the color of the glowing iron. Pretty soon you'll have to take it out and put it on the anvil."

Jean kept staring into the hearth until his eyes burned. When Ellen suddenly pointed to the piece of iron, Jean grabbed the tongs and pulled it out of the fire.

Ellen already was holding the sledgehammer in both hands, waiting to strike.

"Hold on tight. If you don't hold it securely, it will go flying all over the room."

Jean nodded in fright and clutched the tongs tightly.

With careful, even blows Ellen started to hammer out the block of iron. There were no cracks visible on the surface, but a few pieces flew off.

"Come on, you will be a beautiful sword," she mumbled, and now struck the iron even more carefully so that no more would break off.

"In just a moment I'll split it, so we can cut it off," Ellen said, after she had heated it in the forge twice again.

"This here is a blacksmith's chisel. We'll use it to cut the piece of iron in two. To do that, you'll have to hold the tongs with just one hand the next time. You'll have to get used to that eventually, in any case."

When Jean put the stack down on the anvil, Ellen took the blacksmith's chisel and sledgehammer and put a notch in it with several well-placed blows. "Now hold the chisel while I keep hammering."

Jean closed his eyes because he was afraid Ellen could miss and strike his hand.

"Open your eyes!" Ellen shouted. "I'm trying to pay attention, but you have to keep a lookout anyway." She kept telling him to move the chisel in closer so she could make a deep cut through the entire length. "You've got to tilt over the billet like this, do you see?" Ellen tapped his elbow to remind him to hold it up higher. "Now back in the heat it goes, then we can cut the piece off completely."

She cut off the larger of the two pieces and put it aside. "We'll fold that later," she explained.

Jean wondered about that strange expression. Folding sounded very simple, as with a piece of cloth you folded over, but certainly that wasn't the meaning here. He thought it over as he stared into the flames.

"You did a really good job, Jean," she commended him. "While I work on the smaller piece now, you can rest a bit."

Only now did Jean notice how tired he was, though he had done far less than Ellen, who didn't look tired at all.

Ellen removed the smaller piece from the fire and hammered it into a long bar that she flattened at one end. Then she took the split billet from the edge of the forge, pounded it into a right angle, and put the flat end of the rod in the middle. Then she closed the stack, hammering it with powerful blows until the bar was anchored. Then she spread a small shovelful of sandstone powder over it and placed it all in the fire. "The sand keeps the iron from burning," she explained, as it glowed in the forge, crackling softly. "It's just ordinary, crushed sandstone. Did you ever notice that I sometimes pick up stones?"

Jean nodded.

"So now it's your turn again." Ellen pointed to the rod.

What...? I mean, what exactly shall I do now?"

"Just turn it now and then so the billet is heated uniformly. When it's glowing yellow-white, take it out and put it flat on the anvil, holding it tightly and pushing it back when I tell you to, just like before."

Jean's excitement was evident as he took the responsibility for the iron.

Ellen cleaned up the shop and wiped the tinder from the anvil.

Jean kept looking into the fire until his eyes filled with tears.

"It's better for you not to keep staring into the glowing coals, or your eyes will hurt so much tonight that you won't be able to sleep."

Jean did as she said.

"All right, take it out! Now!" Ellen shouted after a while.

Jean jumped up. "But the rod is certainly hot now," it occurred to him suddenly.

"No, it isn't, go ahead; otherwise our iron will burn."

Jean grabbed the stack by the bar and laid it out on the anvil. Ellen was right: the rod was only slightly warm.

"Watch out, now, it's going to spatter," Ellen warned him as she swung the heavy sledgehammer down on the packet.

After the first blow, molten slag squirted out of the billet, and sparks of all sizes rained down on Jean's forearm.

Startled, he jumped back and let go of the rod.

Ellen had already started to swing the hammer again, and it came down hard on the billet, but hit in the wrong place because its position on the anvil had shifted. The iron went flying through the air. Ellen's hammer hit only the anvil, while the glowing stack fell onto the ground right at Jean's feet. "Damn, you have to hold on tight, I said!"

"But the sparks burned me."

"Oh, come on. Why didn't you roll down your sleeves?" Ellen scolded. "Flying sparks are part of a smith's job. The slag has to come out in forge welding. It's not really that bad—the little blisters heal quickly." She frowned unhappily.

"I was surprised and frightened," Jean said, trying to defend his action, then reached for the rod in order to pick up the iron again.

Jean is right, Ellen thought, reproaching herself. She should have made sure his arms were completely covered and explained to him what she was going to do.

"May I keep on working just the same?" Jean asked dejectedly when he saw that the rod was bent.

"Sure, just give it to me—I'll just have to straighten it out."

After a few more blows from the hammer, the rod was straight again. "Is everything all right otherwise?" she asked, concerned.

Jean nodded and rubbed his nose with embarrassment.

"Well, then we've been lucky." Ellen patted him on the shoulder to cheer him up.

"Is it going to spatter again the next time?" Jean asked cautiously.

"It will, but you mustn't let go, all right?" she insisted.

"I promise. This time I'll be sure to hold it tightly." He nodded again and rolled down his sleeves all the way. He carefully watched the color of the iron without staring into the flames for too long, turned the billet now and then, and took it out without being told when it glowed yellow-white.

With well-aimed, heavy blows, Ellen welded the stack with the rod. This time, as well, molten slag squirted out of the pile with every blow, and sparks flew. They could easily set something on fire, and for this reason neither straw nor other flammable things could be placed close to the anvil.

Jean bravely held the rod tight and didn't budge even when the sparks landed on his hand, leaving behind little blisters.

"Well done!" Ellen congratulated him when she was done. "It will be easier to work with the handle we have now than with the tongs." She wiped the tinder from the anvil and poured it into a sack that Pierre had standing there for that purpose. "You can purify and reuse the little flakes of iron that we smiths call tinder or hammer scale," she explained. "Now watch closely and listen to what I am going to say. When I say 'forward,' you'll shove the billet a bit forward, and when I say 'turn,' you'll turn it over on the other side and at the same time pull it back toward you. The anvil is cold, so the iron won't stay hot very long and we've got to be quick to use every bit of heat. You're doing fine!" she said, trying to encourage him. "And now, out with the iron!" Ellen took the heavy sledgehammer and started drawing out the iron again. When the billet was about twice as long, she took the hand hammer and chisel in order to split it in the middle and fold it again.

Jean placed the iron in the hearth once more, and took it out when it became hot enough, holding it by the rod while Ellen welded the two layers together with a number of heavy blows with the sledgehammer. She heated the iron again, thus ending the first folding procedure.

"Will you be able to do one more folding? Then tomorrow and the day after we'll need only to make two and three more before we'll be finished with that," Ellen explained.

"Why are we doing that, actually?" Jean inquired.

"It's sort of a spring cleaning for iron." Ellen grinned, blowing a lock of hair out of her face. "Iron always has impurities and inclusions. The folding purifies it and prevents defects in the blade. The more folding operations we perform, the better the sword will be, but it also makes the iron softer, and so you can't do it an unlimited number of times."

Jean tried to look as if he understood that.

"There's a lot you understand only after working with it for years," Ellen reassured him. The smiths always said that in the first ten years the smith was shaped by the iron before the iron was shaped by him. But for herself, Ellen felt it was different—from the very beginning, she and the iron had been a bit like good friends.

It was already dark when they finished the second folding. The night sky was cloudless and the moonlight bright enough so Ellen and Jean could safely find their way to the tent.

When they arrived, Madeleine was already fast asleep. She lay rolled up on her blanket and had cuddled up close to Greybeard. The dog look up wearily for a moment, wagged his tail a few times, and closed his eyes again. He had grown up faster than Ellen had ever dreamed possible and took up as much space in the tent as another person.

"Man, am I hungry!" Jean groaned.

"Sorry, it has gotten much too late." Suddenly Ellen had a guilty conscience.

“You don’t have to feel sorry. I have learned a lot. You know, if I could, I’d become a smith or a carpenter or something like that. But no one would ever want me as an apprentice. I can’t pay anything, and I have to take care of Madeleine.”

“Oh, Jeannot! Someday you’ll get your chance. You just can’t give up hope.” Ellen pinched his cheek and smiled.

Jean frowned indignantly. He didn’t like it when she treated him as a child. “At work you called me Jean, not Jeannot. Can’t you always do that?” he asked, without looking at her.

“Of course,” Ellen answered, chewing.

—

The next two evenings she watched the boy more closely at work. He was diligent, willing to learn, and skillful. He would certainly make his way in life. Sadly, Ellen thought back to the day when she had first gone to see Llewyn. How long ago that was! She had been a little younger than Jean. If he spent more time in the smithy and if she explained more things to him, why shouldn’t he be lucky someday, too?

After Ellen had folded the iron for the last time, she marked two pieces of equal size without cutting them off.

“Are you going to fold it again after all?” Jean asked with surprise.

“Just hold on and watch, then you’ll see what I am doing.” Ellen cut a groove first in one half, and then in the other.

Jean didn’t dare ask again and just looked on silently.

Ellen took the square point she had made first, placed it in the notch, and checked the depth. Then she deepened the groove a bit and tested the other half as well. When she was satisfied, she turned one side down, as with the folding earlier, without completely closing the billet, however. "Take a pair of tongs to hold the stack, and in the other hand take the chisel."

"Why do I have to pick up the tongs again?

"Because now I am going to remove the rod."

"But didn't we just attach it?" Jean looked at her, confused.

"We only needed it for the folding, and now we have to cut it off again."

"But that takes a lot of time. Couldn't we have just continued using the tongs?" Jean was puzzled.

"The longer you help me, the more you will understand why some steps take so much time at first but in the end save time and energy," Ellen replied gruffly. When the handle had been removed, she placed the square point in the notch and laid the other half of the billet over it. Now the front part had disappeared in the two grooves.

"The square point is made of softer iron, and that's why I chose it for the core of the blade." Ellen pointed to the two halves. "The billet is of much harder iron and is thus well suited for the jacket. In just a moment we shall have to weld it again. You're not afraid of that anymore, are you?"

Jean grinned and shook his head. "I've gotten used to it."

"The square point is sticking out far enough so we can use it as a holding rod, do you see?"

Jean nodded and put the billet in the fire, turning it from time to time, but when it was all glowing evenly he just stood there as in a trance staring into the flickering flames.

"Can't you see that the iron is burning?" Ellen scolded and came running over. The billet was already spitting white sparks. Jean grabbed it and quickly took it out of the fire.

"Burned iron is worthless for making swords," Ellen emphasized. She had paid a lot of money for the piece of iron, and Jean had to know just how important it was not to let the iron burn. As soon as it lay on the anvil, she began to hammer every inch of the billet with steady, heavy blows. Jean had to put it back in the fire three more times, and Ellen hammered and checked the stack until she was satisfied with the welding.

"So," she said, heaving a huge sigh of relief, "we've done it! There must be no crack in the packet. Everything has to fit exactly. If there are any remaining air bubbles or slag trapped in the layers, the sword will be worthless later on. Tomorrow I'll start forging the blade. If you want to, you may watch and help me a bit at first, but then the rest I can do alone."

—

The next evening Jean came to the smithy earlier than usual. "I was afraid you might start without me," he said.

"Never!" Ellen pretended to be furious, and then grinned at him. "We'll start as soon as I am finished with this."

Jean waited, and Ellen could see he was just as excited as she was. She eagerly explained to him what she was planning to do. "First I have to draw out the billet, just as I did before the folding, only this time it has to become much longer, and that will take several heatings. That's why I need you here."

"Ellen?"

"My name is Ellenweore!" she growled at him, more harshly than necessary. As long as there was a possibility that William might show up at the smithy, it was better that no one called her Ellen. She didn't want him to suspect that Alan and she were one and the same person.

Jean promised to be careful, and then he started asking questions again. "Why do you always talk about the warmth? The iron is more than just warm, I'd call it hot."

Ellen shrugged. "Smith's language. Every trade has its own expressions, and you can tell who is experienced by their use of those words. Can we continue now?"

Jean was eager to see finally how the blade was made, and nodded emphatically. It seemed to him like a miracle that Ellen could shape a blade blow by blow from a block of iron.

"The rod here will be a part of the tang, that is the piece the hilt or grip will be attached to. It's more practical if it is not too hard, as then the pommel can more easily be riveted on it later." Ellen was so fascinated by the work on Athanor that her cheeks were glowing with excitement. Out of the corner of her eye she could see that Pierre had returned to the workshop. He acted busy and poked around as if he were looking for something, but she was sure it was his curiosity that brought him back. He certainly wanted to see how she made out with the difficult material. Every smith had his secrets and didn't like it when another smith came to watch him while he worked. But Pierre was the master, and in an itinerant smithy it was practically impossible in any case to keep secrets. It was fortunate that the other smiths were not interested in what she was doing. They were still convinced that only a man could make a good sword, and finally Pierre, too, left without looking more closely at the piece she was working on.

The blade quickly took shape. Ellen kept checking its length and breadth, heated some parts again until they glowed yellow, and then reworked them again with a hand hammer. The regular rhythm of her strokes resounded through the silence. As soon as the iron started to glow red, she put it back in the forge again.

"It's late, Ellenweore!" Jean ventured to say after being silent for a long time. He had watched each of her movements with fascination.

Ellen looked up in surprise. "What did you say?"

"It's late. If you don't stop soon," he said, raising his eyebrows, "you might just as well spend the night here."

Ellen looked around in astonishment. Her cheeks had a feverish glow. "It's dark already."

"It has been for a long time!"

"Oh!"

"You should stop now and continue the work tomorrow."

Ellen nodded absentmindedly and examined the blade, holding it up closer to her eye to look at it.

"Whew, I thought that was a crack, but it's just hammer scale." She blew the tinder away and wiped the blade with a piece of leather, breathing an audible sigh of relief. "You're right, it's time to go to sleep. I didn't notice how tired I am, and my eyes are burning like fire. Let's stop now."

—

That night Ellen dreamed of William again. She was anxious to show him Athanor and met him in the forest, but he wouldn't let her speak, wooing her with his irresistible caresses and boldly seducing her. Ellen felt powerless—as if overjoyed and at the same time furious. She wanted to tell him about the sword, but as soon as she began to speak, he closed her lips with a long kiss. With anxious expectation, she tried to show him Athanor, but the sword was so heavy she could hardly pick it up. It looked like it had been made for a giant, incredibly large and primitive. Instead of gleaming in the light, it was covered with rust spots.

Ellen was so ashamed of the ugly sword that she wished the earth would swallow her up. William took it in his hands, holding it at arm's length, and examined it in disgust. In his hand, Athanor seemed as small and light as a toy sword. Ellen closed her eyes, not believing what she was seeing.

"It looks like it was meant for a dwarf," William laughed, and put the sword down.

It lay in the grass as limp as a snakeskin.

Ellen rolled around restlessly in her sleep and woke up bathed in sweat. Anxiously she reached out for Athanor and then realized it had all just been a nightmare. Relieved, she ran her hand over the material covering the blade. William's opinion was important to her, but was that her only motivation? She sighed. Basically it didn't matter whether he liked the sword. "Athanor will be something special," she murmured, and once again fell back to sleep.

—

"Doesn't it look a bit narrow for a sword blade?" Jean asked the next day, when Ellen was looking at her work with satisfaction.

"The cutting edges still need to be sharpened, and that will make the blade a bit wider."

"How can that make the blade wider?" Jean asked.

"Because the iron will now be drawn out laterally."

Jean's face brightened. "Ah! Then the sides will be thinner, is that correct?"

"Right!" Ellen smiled. The boy was quick to understand.

"Just the same, I don't understand why you sharpen the sword now. Somehow I thought that would come much later."

"You're not entirely wrong there. It isn't made really sharp yet, but the drawing out in both directions actually gives the blade two cutting edges. At first they are dull, but we'll work on them later on with drawknife and file before we give them their final sharpness by hardening and polishing the edges." Ellen looked at the roughly forged blade with satisfaction, checked it once more, and straightened it a little. "Good work," she said to herself, proud of what she had accomplished. "Let's stop for tonight, and tomorrow I'll begin with the sharpening. By the way, from this point I can do it by myself."

"Can I stay and watch just the same?" Jean asked carefully.

"Whenever you like," she said, pleased that he was interested.

"The next thing I'll do is to flatten the surface and scrape the fuller. And then it gets not just really interesting, but very dangerous, too." Ellen paused for effect and looked at Jean. "Because then the actual hardening begins—and with that comes the moment of truth." On the way back to their tent she told him, full of enthusiasm, why the hardening process was so important and at the same time so difficult. "You've got to have a feeling for it." She clutched dramatically at her chest. "It comes from here, from the heart. It's a mixture of…yes, what exactly?" She paused for a moment. "It's a mixture of experience and intuition."

"Intu…what?"

"Intuition is a special feeling for the right moment. You just have to have it in order to be a good swordsmith."

"And how do you know if you have this special feeling?"

"Oh, that's something you learn in your first years as an apprentice." Ellen pinched his cheek and got an angry glance as a response.

"Ah, then what happens if, after a few years, you realize you really don't have it? Then was all that work as an apprentice in vain?"

"Well, if you don't have this special feeling, this intuition, it's better to stay away from swords to start with. They are the crowning achievement of the smith's art, do you understand?"

"That really sounds conceited."

Ellen looked at him in astonishment. "Do you think so? I can't find any fault in knowing your abilities and doing whatever you can do best. For me, that's sword making. Whether you are a bad, good, or outstanding stonemason, carpenter, or smith all depends on the ability God has given you—it's as simple as that. And just as not every priest has the good fortune to become a bishop, not every smith has what it takes to be a swordsmith."

"But according to what I have heard," Jean countered, "what you need is good connections and not necessarily a special talent to earn a high church office."

Ellen shrugged, bored, and changed the subject. "You can help me again with the smoothing if you like."

"Smoothing? But didn't you just talk about hardening, and isn't sharpening exactly the opposite?" Jean tried to play dumb.

"Oh, come on! Smoothing the blade just means to even it out," she explained. "Now do you want to help me or not?"

"Well of course!" Jean nodded enthusiastically.

When he arrived at the smithy the next day, Ellen already had prepared everything. On the anvil was a tool that Jean had never before seen.

"Are you going to use that to smooth the blade?" he asked skeptically.

Ellen handed him the blade. "The face of the hammer has left dents and scars on the blade. Here, have a look at how rough and uneven the surface is. We'll use this flatter," she said, picking up the tool from the anvil, "to smooth the blade. Do you see how wide its face is?"

Jean nodded. One side of the hammer was about the size of your palm and square-shaped.

"To prevent new dents, you don't hit the workpiece with the flatter itself; you have to use a hammer or sledgehammer and strike the top of the flatter."

"Well, I didn't quite understand that," Jean objected uncertainly.

"Hold the blade with your left hand and the flatter with the other. It has to lie on the blade at a right angle. I'll show you how—do you see now?"

Jean nodded. After he had moved the flatter a bit further for the first time, he already could see how smooth the blade became with this technique.

With a device similar to a carpenter's drawknife, Ellen scraped a fuller in both blade surfaces and sharpened the edges again. She would wait for a moonless night to do the hardening just as reputable swordsmiths always did. It was only in absolute darkness that the color of the glowing metal could be determined exactly. Since the heat temperature was extremely important for the success of the hardening and since everyone knew the great influence of moonlight on men and animals, it was safer to wait for a new moon. In the meanwhile, she would have sufficient time to deal with the problem of the water.

Ellen's next step was to forge little tiles from remainders of the blade material that she could use to test the hardening.

After moving to Tancarville, Donovan had cursed because he had to adjust to another kind of water. In Ipswich he had always fetched it from a particular spring, just as his master had done before him. After his first failure with quenching in Tancarville, he had Ellen prepare a whole stack of such iron tiles and experimented with them until the hardening process was perfect.

Ellen fetched some water from a nearby brook, added a bit of urine, and checked the mixture until she was satisfied with the result. Two days before the new moon, everything was ready, but she was beginning to get nervous. Her heart pounded and her hands sweated at the thought that the next step could destroy all the efforts of the past few weeks. To prepare the blade for quenching, she had purchased some clay from a potter, which she now spread on the sword.

Jean watched every one of her movements, speechless.

"First I will apply a thin layer to the entire blade, and when the clay dries I will check if there are any cracks in the coating," she explained, "which is something we definitely do not want."

"What could you do then?"

"If it cracks, that means the clay is too firm and heavy, which also means it will be difficult to recognize the right color of the workpiece in the forge, as clay glows brighter than iron. So what I would have to do then is to add water, coal dust, and crushed sandstone. The right mixture is important because if I add too much of one of them the clay might not stick to the blade anymore. The work can only proceed when a thinly applied coat of clay dries uniformly."

"But why do you need the clay at all? Couldn't you just do the quenching without it?"

"Certainly I could, if I was making something other than a sword! You have to understand that we don't just want to harden the iron—we want an elastic blade and sharp cutting edges. That's why the middle of the blade must be quenched less than the cutting edges. Otherwise, we wouldn't have had to make the blade core from softer material in the first place, right?"

"But you also put clay on the cutting edges!"

"Yes, but only a thin layer. It protects the blade from too much heat and at the same time makes the quenching less abrupt. In this way, there is less danger of the blade becoming brittle."

"And then splintering!"

"Right, Jean! After the first layer of clay has dried, I'll apply other layers, but only in the middle."

—

On the day of the new moon, Ellen awoke with stomach cramps and was afraid that her unclean days could destroy her plans to harden the sword. The unclean days were the worst possible time to undertake such a serious task. During this period, women were even forbidden to help with such everyday tasks as brewing beer or baking bread. Fortunately, the pains in her belly were due only to the excitement, and other symptoms did not appear.

After work, Ellen raked the fire again, placed the clay-covered blade in the fire, and prepared the trough for the quenching. At the bottom of the long vessel she placed a stone and mumbled some secret formula of which Jean understood not a word.

He had stepped back into a corner, as Ellen had instructed him to do.

"If you want to watch the quenching, you must be out of sight—you mustn't talk or ask questions or distract me," she had warned him.

Jean clenched his fists in excitement.

The cutting edges of the blade had an orange glow as Ellen took the sword from the fire, dipped it into the trough, and then moved it back and forth to allow it to cool down uniformly.

The water hissed and bubbled as the hot blade slid into the water.

Ellen whispered a counting rhyme she had learned from Donovan. When she reached seven, the blade had to be removed from the water in order to preserve sufficient remaining heat. Ellen listened carefully to the hissing and bubbling. There was no crackling sound that could have indicated something had gone wrong. Anxiously she pulled the sword out of the trough. Now the clay coating could be easily removed. Holding her breath, she checked every inch, but there was no visible flaw. With relief she proceeded to the next step. The quality of the sword would now depend on the sharpening and polishing. She wiped the drops of sweat from her brow and looked over at Jean, who was still standing motionless in a corner. "You can come out now, everything went smoothly. Did you pay close attention?"

"I hardly dared to breathe, it was so exciting."

"That's how I felt!" Ellen looked at Jean, smiled with relief, and brushed away a strand of hair from her temple.

"Now I'll finally be able to sleep peacefully again. Come, let's close up, I'm exhausted."

"So am I. I'm dog tired even though I haven't lifted a finger. Here, I brought along a pinewood chip we can light to help us find our way. We'll need that tonight or we might find ourselves bedding down in some stranger's tent."

—

The next morning Ellen noticed Madeleine again playing with a silver coin she was holding in her hand.

"Did you get that from the same knight as the last time?" Ellen asked. She had a warm feeling of anticipation, but Madeleine did not answer.

"I think he's in love with you! He had huge eyes when he asked about you," Madeleine said.

"William!" Ellen whispered. "Where is he?" she asked.

Madeleine beamed at her but said only, "He's very good-looking," and then turned her attention again to the coin.

Full of anticipation, Ellen left for the smithy. If William had arrived, he would certainly be looking for her there. All day long she felt a tingling in her stomach. But William didn't come, and she was so disappointed that she didn't even work on Athanor. When another day passed and he still hadn't come, she inquired about the Young King, but no one had seen either him or his retinue.

Who knows where Madeleine got the coin? She put aside all these disturbing thoughts and again concentrated only on her work on Athanor. She measured the length of the blade and calculated the best proportions for the cross guard. Then she started to work on the iron remainder that had been forged several times, folded it again with Jean's help, and cut it into two pieces. One was for the cross guard, the other for the pommel. She forged a rod about the width of a finger and the length of about eight inches. The cross guard would later be slid over the tang down to the blade and therefore had to have a slit through the middle. Ellen had to make sure the opening was not too wide so that the cross guard did not wobble later. To make certain that the hole was just the right size, Ellen made an iron drift with the measurements of the tang.

"Ah, there you are," she said, greeting Jean with a smile. He was later than usual and looked unhappy. "What's the matter?"

Ellen placed her hand on his shoulder, but he only shook his head morosely. There was no point in pressing him any further if he didn't want to talk. He would come around on his own when he was ready to tell what was bothering him.

Jean tried to put on a friendlier face. "Can I help you?"

"I couldn't get along any further without you," Ellen said, with a friendly glance. "Will you hold the workpiece for me again?"

Jean nodded and tied on an apron.

"There won't be any sparks flying today," she promised, in the hope of cheering him up a bit. "Here, hold the cross guard with the wolf jaw tongs when I'm finished." In order to drive the drift through the bar at the right place, Ellen measured the middle of the bar and used a chisel to make a thin slit.

"It does indeed look like a wolf's jaw," Jean said, examining the tongs and pointing at the notches along the side. "Like teeth," he said.

"The important thing is that you remember the name. Take the cross guard and put it in the fire."

Ellen had decided on a simple, unadorned shape. The cross guard was a little wider in the middle and narrower at the ends.

Jean removed it from the fire and was astonished to see how clearly visible the marked place was while the piece was glowing hot.

The drift seemed to slide into the slot almost on its own. With just a few blows of the hammer, Ellen drove it through the bar.

"The cross guard need not be hardened—just put it down on the edge of the hearth. I'm going to start today with thorough polishing of the blade, but I won't need any help with that. Go back to the tent and look after Madeleine. I do think we have left her alone too much recently."

Jean nodded and set out for home. Ellen was turning Pierre's big grindstone with the foot pedal in order to pre-grind the blade. She constantly poured water onto the blade and kept checking the result. When she was satisfied for the time being with the sharpening, she wrapped the blade in a cloth and returned to the tent also.

Jean and Madeleine were still awake.

"We left something for you." Jean pointed to a pigeon breast and some porridge with onions and almonds that Madeleine had prepared.

"Mm, wonderful, I'm really hungry!" Ellen devoured the tender pigeon breast and the tasty porridge. "Madeleine, that was delicious!" She looked over at Jean. "Did you get the pigeon with your slingshot?" she asked as she ate. "What in the world would I do without you?" She put her arms around them both.

"You would probably starve to death." Jean tried to smile, but somehow he still seemed depressed.

"You work too much," said Madeleine, stroking Ellen's hair sleepily. Then she sat down again in her corner where Greybeard was happily chewing on a bone.

"You must think I am impossible. All I do is work and spend most of what I earn for Athanor. Jean works half the night to help me, and as for me, what do I do for you?" Ellen looked at first one, then the other of them, dejectedly.

"You'll have your chance to help. Sometimes debts are paid in roundabout ways." Coming from Madeleine, these words seemed strange. Rarely did she think so clearly. But the spark that flared up in her so quickly also faded fast, and she sat there like a naïve child, dreamily fondling her silver coin. Ellen reached for the leather pouch with the polishing stones she would need soon for the blade. The pouch felt oddly wet.

"Greybeard!" she exclaimed, horrified. The leather drawstrings were chewed to pieces. "You impossible creature! Oh Lord, you have destroyed my stones!"

Ellen had paid a small fortune for the polishing stones. Some of them were so delicate that they could easily crumble. Carefully she opened the pouch and shook them out into her hand. Only the finest one had crumbled on one side, but all the rest were undamaged. Carefully she slipped the polishing stones and the stone dust back into the pouch. "God help you," she scolded the pup, "if I catch you again."

The culprit laid back his ears contritely and looked like a guilty conscience in the flesh.

"If I were you, I'd carry my purse around with me. If he found it half as tasty as this here, he will try it again." Jean smirked and pointed to his left shoe. The tip was completely bitten off, and all that remained of one side was a frayed hole.

"You! Don't you dare!" cried Ellen, shaking her fist at the dog.

"It's just that he's young and looking for something to do," said Jean, trying to defend him. "You can't really hold it against him."

"Why can't he just keep an eye on our things instead of destroying them!" Ellen seemed to calm down a bit, but just that same night she had a dream in which she had her own smithy with assistants and apprentices, and where Greybeard went wild and broke everything.

—

In the evening before they were to leave, Ellen overheard Pierre talking with Armelle about her.

"I know she's a thorn in your side, but this will make you feel better," he whispered to his wife, watching how her eyes got bigger and bigger as he counted out the money he had made and put it in her hand.

"But that's much more than you ever made before," she said, overjoyed.

He leaned forward and lowered his voice. "She brings in four times more than what I pay her. And now she is paying for using my smithy in the evening for her own work. That was the best deal of my life. This brings us closer to our goal..." Pierre lowered his voice to a whisper, and Ellen couldn't hear the rest. But she had heard enough. If she really brought in so much money for him, she had to see what she could do to raise her own pay. She pondered what to do.

As they were leaving the next morning, Pierre came to where their tent site had been. Jean had risen early, taken the tent down, folded it up, and tied it firmly onto Nestor's back. "We'll meet again at the tournament in Compiègne!" Pierre said to Ellen, as usual.

This was her chance! "Oh, master, I thought I might stay in Compiègne to work for a smith I know from before," Ellen said, trying to look innocent. His face turned pale.

"But you can't just simply...you are leaving me?" he asked, taken by surprise.

"I didn't know you attached such importance to my work." Ellen tried to look surprised.

"But I do!" Pierre responded in a rasping voice.

"Well, if you would pay me more, maybe I could stay."

"So it's only a question of money?" he asked suspiciously.

"The sword is expensive," she tried to explain, shrugging her shoulders.

Pierre groaned. "All right, then, half more," he ventured.

Ellen shook her head. "Double," she said with determination, and managed to speak in a calm voice. That was almost as much as a male journeyman would receive. Pierre looked at her in astonishment. He was probably considering whether it was worth it, Ellen thought, and she was seized with fear—what if he said no?

"I guess I'll have to," he grumbled. "Otherwise you won't give me any peace. That's what I get for being so kind." Thereupon he turned sullenly and stomped away.

Ellen jumped for joy after he left. Even though it was Sunday, she had helped to pack all the tools, the anvil, the whetstone, and the large bellows onto Pierre's cart, without getting paid even a penny for her efforts. But she herself had paid for every day she had worked on Athanor in his smithy. There was really no reason for her to have a guilty conscience.

On the way to Compiègne they passed through a broad, green valley of beautiful fruit trees, then a huge, dark forest of firs. After two days they arrived at a larger village.

On one of the houses hung an iron square with a carpenter's plane dangling down from it to indicate this was a carpenter's shop.

"I still need a few things for Athanor," Ellen said as she headed toward the shop and opened the door.

"Greetings, master!" Ellen made a slight bow and tried to put on a cheerful face, but Jean, who followed her, looked rather glum just in case she wanted to buy something he would have to haggle over.

The carpenter sat at a large worktable. In front of him, woodcutting tools and pieces of wood were piled so high that only his head peered out from behind them. He squinted suspiciously and eyed the two strangers from head to toe. "What do you want?"

"I need two thin sheets of wood for a sword scabbard, preferably well-seasoned pear wood, and also a good, dry piece for a hilt."

The carpenter looked at Ellen inquisitively. "I know you from somewhere," he mumbled, staring at her.

Now Ellen looked at him more closely. "Poulet!" she cried excitedly.

"Ellenweore!" The carpenter rose from his chair, limped toward her, and embraced her warmly.

When Jean saw him standing there, he understood how he got the nickname "Poulet," or "Chicken" in French. He walked hunched over, as if the weight of his corpulent frame was pulling him forward. His apron just barely reached beyond his backside and below that two beefy thighs in tight chausses peered forth. They were fat and round as far down as the knees, but below that tapered down to skinny shanks, just like the bones on a chicken. His scrawny calves seemed barely able to bear his weight. Jean wondered how a carpenter who barely got out of his seat could somehow survive. Nevertheless, he seemed to be doing well. On the table lay several projects he had started, and the two apprentices in the shop obviously had plenty to do.

"How are you doing, little one?" Poulet patted Ellen's shoulder. "You look magnificent!"

"Thanks, Poulet, I'm doing fine. And Claire, do you have any news about her?"

Poulet was Claire's uncle. He had once visited his niece when Ellen was still working with her. She was his only living relative, and even though the trip was long and very strenuous for him, he still went to see her from time to time.

"The miller's son was here recently. Claire is probably doing better now, but the boy…" Poulet shook his oversized head sadly.

"What was wrong with her? Was she sick? And how about Jacques, how is he? Has he been acting foolishly?"

"He died, got a fever and a cough and simply couldn't get over it. Her first child with Guiot was stillborn, and then the problem with Jacques. Claire was despondent, but I hear now she has another little one on the way." Poulet sighed. "Yes, that's the way of the world. Birth and death, death and birth, that's the way things go."

"Poor Jacques!" Ellen said, dismayed. "But it will be easier for her because she is expecting another child. This time everything will surely work out. I'll pray for her." Ellen tried to put on a confident smile.

Poulet now looked at Madeleine, who was standing next to Jean. She was staring at a butterfly made of thin wood hanging down from the ceiling on a barely visible thread. She was as fascinated as a little child watching it move back and forth in the gentle breeze. No child who came into his shop could ever resist the sight, but the girl in Ellen's group was no child. Poulet took Ellen by the shoulders and looked her straight in the eye.

"Let's have another look at you. You're prettier, softer…you're in love!" He grinned mischievously and pinched her on the nose. Then he turned away from her and to his stock of wood. "So you're making scabbards again." He grinned. "And you want to make a handle as well?"

"I naturally never expected I'd get the best seasoned wood for it." Ellen beamed at Poulet, blinking her eyes coquettishly.

"Well, if you make eyes at me like that, I'll look in my treasure chest and see what I can do for you." He hauled his heavy frame to a box in the corner of the shop. "If you take pear wood for the sheath, would you like it also for the handle, or would you rather have cherry or ash?"

"You know your wood better than anyone. Just pick out a good piece for me that is also something I can afford, and I'll leave it up to you what kind of wood it is."

He nodded and rummaged in the box until he found something. "Here, this is wonderful! Bone dry and it won't split. What do you think? Are the size and thickness all right?" He limped back to Ellen and handed her the piece of wood. While she was examining it, he picked out two thin sheets of wood, the kind that scabbard makers bought from him. The quality of his wood was known far and wide. All the tradespeople in the area bought their supplies from him, and he always had a good supply of these wooden sheets in stock.

"You are right, this piece is exactly what I need! Cherry," she said to Jean, holding the wood under his nose. "Can you saw it through for me?" she asked Poulet.

He clamped the wood into a vise, took a saw, placed it in the middle, and asked Ellen, "Like this?"

She nodded, and Poulet sawed the piece of wood lengthwise.

"Anything else you need, dear?"

His eyes sparkled, and Jean thought he must be at least as good at business as he was at carpentry.

"I don't think so," Ellen replied, but she hesitated for a moment.

Poulet handed her the two half pieces of wood and the sheets for the scabbards, and named his price.

Jean looked at Ellen angrily.

"Fine, you know the fellow, but even if he were the official supplier to the king his prices would still be too high. He acts as if you're not buying wood, but gold. The whole forest is full of wood—you only have to go and get it," he said excitedly.

Poulet grinned. "Nice fellow."

Jean looked at him, irritated.

"He has no idea about prices and even less about wood." She sighed, knowing that Poulet had given her a special price as a friend.

Jean would have found any price too high, however, because he had no idea how important it was to use seasoned wood and how costly it was to make sheets of wood for scabbards.

"Someday he'll be a real success, and so will you if you listen to him." Poulet lowered his price a little. "Are you happy now, young man?"

Jean turned red. He nodded and was annoyed when Poulet and Ellen roared with laughter.

"Here, you can whittle something nice from this piece of ash wood." Poulet handed Jean a long, gnarled piece of wood.

"Thank you," Jean mumbled defiantly, without looking him in the eye.

"When you see Claire again, embrace her for me and tell her I am praying for Jacques and the child that she is expecting. And say hello to Guiot for me also, will you?"

"Naturally, my dear, I'll do that. Take care of yourself." Before they parted, Poulet once again took Ellen in his arms.

Jean followed her silently until they had left the village.

"You made fun of me and laughed, and I didn't think that was funny at all. In any case, your strange friend lowered his price, so you see how right I was. It was too expensive," he fumed.

"I don't see it quite that way. He seems to be a better friend than I realized. Don't be silly, Jean. Poulet is an honest carpenter, and if he weren't he wouldn't have so many customers that he can make a good living from it even if he's a cripple. And he also gave you a nice piece of wood."

"Bah, a gnarled, leftover piece like that is something you can pick up from the ground in any forest," Jean objected.

"It's a really good piece for carving because it's really dry. What you find in the forest is worthless as long as it's fresh. Young, green wood can't be carved easily as it frays and rips as it dries. And older wood from the forest is usually rotten or falls apart easily. Poulet never lets anyone pick out the wood for him. His assistant and apprentices just cut the trees he tells them to. Then they bring the wood to his shed, where it has to stay for one or two years until it has dried out. And only then does he make the sheets of wood from it like the one I bought. Believe me, it is good wood!"

"Hm," Jean grumbled. He didn't like having to admit that he was perhaps wrong about Poulet. "What is the matter with him? I mean with his legs?" he asked.

Ellen shrugged. "I have no idea. The word is that he was a handsome fellow when he was young, even if that's hard to imagine when you look at him now."

Jean thought about Poulet's head, which was much too large and seemed to sit right on his shoulders with no hint of a neck in between. Even now, in his mind's eye, he could see Poulet standing before him and could only shake his head. *They say he used to be handsome? Completely impossible.*

—

They wandered on from one village to another and enjoyed the splendid autumn with its warm, low-lying sun and the colorful leaves. Only as it got dark did it start to become cold and damp, and they had to look for a safe place to camp and make a fire. Madeleine sang lullabies, and her clear, bright voice transformed the words into elf-like melodies. Tears welled up in Ellen's eyes as she worked on the two pieces of cherry wood. She placed one of the halves on the tang and, using the knife that Osmond had given her as a child, scratched the exact outlines of the metal into the wood. When Madeleine had finished, Ellen wiped her eyes with her sleeve, made sure that both pieces would fit together exactly, and then scratched the outline of the tang into the other half. Carefully she began to hollow out the wood. She used the knife every day to cut bread, bacon, or onions, or to cut string, clean her fingernails, shape wood for the spit or, as today, to whittle. Sometimes a wave of melancholy would come over her. She thought of Osmond and her siblings, Simon, and Aelfgiva—was the good old woman still alive?

Ellen was trying to think how many years it had been since she left Orford. "Must be ten or eleven years," she murmured.

"Who?" Jean asked, curious, and decided to do some whittling himself. He took the knife that Ellen had made for him a few months ago from some leftover pieces of iron and began hesitantly.

"Not *who*, but *what*."

"What?"

"I have been trying to figure out how long I have been away from home. I think it must be some ten or eleven years," she answered, a bit irritated.

"Oh, I see," Jean said, somewhat bored, and went back to working on his piece of wood. Whenever she thought of her family, Ellen felt an unpleasant burning in the pit of her stomach, and so she tried to think about something else.

"You have to hold the knife flatter," she snapped at Jean somewhat harshly, and he looked up, surprised. "Like this, see?" Ellen said, showing him how to hold the knife in his hand. "And always away from your body or you can hurt yourself badly." Only now did she notice a strange, glassy look in his eyes. "What's the matter?" she was about to ask when he suddenly began speaking in a thin voice:

"My father often carved wooden figures in the evening." He wiped his nose with his sleeve. "I ought to know how to hold a knife—he showed me, but I don't remember anymore. My memory is all a blur."

Ellen looked at him sympathetically. "That's also a long time ago," she said, patting him on the head.

"Their faces, they are all gone."

"Whose faces, Jean?"

"Those of my parents and my little brother. When I think of them and try to picture them, I see only blood, my father's intestines pouring out of his dead body, and my mother's twisted, contorted limbs. I can't even remember the color of her eyes or her hair." Jean cried softly.

Ellen could only guess how dreadful he felt. Her homesickness suddenly appeared so foolish compared with the loneliness Jean and Madeleine had to feel. They had lost everything and no longer had a home to which they could return someday. They didn't even know where their village was. If they didn't happen to come through the area someday by chance, as Jean had hoped for so many years, they would never find it again. Perhaps the village had not been rebuilt at all, since all the inhabitants had died. Ellen stood up, sat down behind Jean and Madeleine, and took them in her arms. She rocked the two like little children, trying to console them.

"I'm so happy we met you. I have always tried to watch out for her," Jean said softly.

Madeleine was silent in Ellen's comforting embrace.

"But I have never had anyone—for myself, I mean, someone to take care of me. Do you understand?" He stared into the flickering light of the fire and avoided looking at Ellen.

From the side she could see tears sparkling in his eyes.

Madeleine had closed hers and was quiet, as if asleep.

"We'll stay together always, I promise!" Deeply moved, Ellen pulled the two even closer to her.

Jean shook his head sadly. "Someday a man will come along, I mean not this Sir William..." There was a touch of disparagement in his voice.

"Jean!" Ellen was appalled, and blushed. "What do you mean by that?"

"I know you are in love with him."

"Whatever made you think that?" Ellen felt caught.

"Oh, even a blind man can see that. The way you adore him. Maybe he likes you, too, but he is the tutor of our Young King, and you are only a girl who wants to be a smith. You have nothing in common."

Ellen's stomach cramped up. Jean wasn't saying anything she hadn't known already for a long time, but it hurt just the same. Naturally, there would never be a future together for her and William. She took a deep breath. Jean's voice seemed to be coming from far away.

"Someday he will marry a noblewoman, and you will hopefully marry a decent craftsman, if there is one who will take such a stubborn woman," he added with an embarrassed grin.

"There you are being so fresh again!" Ellen raised her hand with the knife still in it and threatened him, laughing, even though her heart was still as heavy as stone. She thought of Jocelyn, his terrible death, and how unjust the world was.

"If the day ever comes that you marry, we will just be a burden to you," Jean said softly, lowering his eyes so that Ellen wouldn't see that he was again fighting with tears.

"Don't talk such nonsense. We'll stay together," Ellen added emphatically. "Now that's enough, I don't want to hear any more of this."

During the night Ellen dreamed of England and awakened the next morning well rested and in a good mood that lasted all day. At noon they stopped at a farmer's house and bought a goatskin that Ellen needed for the scabbard of her sword. Jean again showed how skillful he was in bargaining, and they even had a little money left over to buy some goat meat.

"I still need glue for the scabbard," Ellen stated, and had trouble chewing the strong, tough meat.

"Couldn't you have bought that from your friend the carpenter?" Jean said, giving Ellen a sidelong glance.

"I could have but didn't want to. Poulet's wood is of excellent quality, but his glue was no longer completely fresh."

"How do you even know that?" Jean asked, clearly astonished.

"I smelled it. I know all about glue. I could even make my own, but that's time-consuming. If bone lime is stirred for longer than three or four days, it begins to smell. And Poulet's glue pot had a rather strong smell. Maybe the assistant is too lazy to prepare the glue regularly. I could have bought granulated glue from him, but I would rather get it freshly prepared. In any case, it's best to buy it just when you need it. It's somewhat expensive, but I know then at least that it will really hold, and that's the most important thing, isn't it?"

Jean grinned. "I guess so! Years ago I worked for a shield maker whose son had diarrhea, and nothing seemed to help. Shield makers need a lot of glue. He makes some regularly, and you should look around at the next tournament to see if you can buy some from him. Whether it's any good, of course, is something I can't tell you."

"We'll quickly find out." Ellen nodded.

—

Ellen had been many places since leaving Tancarville. She knew almost all of Normandy, parts of Flanders and Champagne, and she had also passed through Paris once, but this was the first time she had ever been in Compiègne, quite a distance north of Paris. The forests in that area where the tournament was to take place were a favorite hunting ground of the French king and the city itself the goal of many pilgrims who hoped to view the sacred burial cloth and many other religious relics in the abbey there. Innumerable churches and the tall, round tower of the royal castle were landmarks of this impressive city.

The three of them strolled leisurely through the narrow lanes, viewing the displays of the merchants and tradespeople and the stalls at the marketplace. Ellen bought enough material from a linen weaver to wrap the scabbard, and a long, dark red silk cord for the handle from a silk merchant.

"I still need some leather for the scabbard and belt..." She looked around, and it wasn't long before she found a piece of fine, wine-red leather for the scabbard, a belt of good cowhide, and a brass buckle all at a suitable price. Happy with how things had gone, she turned to Jean and Madeleine and said, "I think we'll spend the night here and not go on until tomorrow morning. What do you think?"

"You mean we'll stay at an inn?" Jean asked in disbelief.

"For heaven's sake no, naturally not. Are we dukes or rich merchants? We'll inquire in a church about a place to sleep for the night. With so many pilgrims here, there must be many accommodations for guests."

"Oh, I see! Yes, certainly." Jean seemed relieved. He looked at Madeleine, whom he had to take by the hand and drag along with them so she wouldn't stop at every stall and admire the colorful displays.

The search for a place to stay turned out to be harder than Ellen had suspected, but finally she found a place free to spend the night in the largest church in town. Pilgrims were standing around everywhere in long lines at the latrines, the inns, and hot food stalls. The residents of Compiègne knew how to take advantage of the masses of believers and sold all of life's necessities at exorbitant prices and inferior quality. Ellen purchased a big, expensive pasty, which they hungrily consumed, and a large mug of beer. The pasty had a rancid taste, and the beer was flat. Disappointed, they stretched out on the cold stone floor, crowded tightly between a group of pilgrims on the one side and a few strange-looking foreigners whose language they couldn't understand on the other. There they tried to make themselves as comfortable as possible for the night.

Although they spread the tent out under them, had a blanket to roll up into, and were tightly crowded together, it was still so cold that Ellen had trouble falling asleep. Even Greybeard, who always helped to keep them warm, was not able to help. In the middle of the night Ellen woke up, her cheeks on fire. Her teeth chattered, her body trembled, and her head was dreadfully painful. But her exhaustion helped her to fall back to sleep again. In the morning she was too weak to stand up on her own.

The priest thought that her stay in his church and God's closeness would help to cure the sickness, and he promised to pray for Ellen, but otherwise paid no heed to her predicament.

But a friendly young merchant woman who had come to the church for morning prayers spoke to Jean, recommending an herb woman who lived not far from the church. The thought of spending money for a healer seemed to Ellen like pure extravagance and she didn't want to follow this advice, but this time Jean prevailed and she didn't get her way.

"The herb woman will not enter the church, however, and you must leave your friend on the steps before the portal," the young woman advised him. "In any case, it's cold and drafty inside here, and outside the sun is shining and will warm her up." She even offered to show Jean the way. When he returned with the herb woman, Ellen was already delirious with fever.

"Aelfgiva! You're alive!" She sighed with great joy, fervently kissing the hand of the strange woman.

"She can't stay here. Bring her to my house," the herb woman said, clearly concerned about her condition. "If she sleeps one more night in that drafty church, she will die."

Jean and Madeleine helped Ellen to stand up, but she kept collapsing. Two strong-looking men happened to be there making repairs to the church door, and Jean turned to them. They carried Ellen to the herb woman's house, which was large and comfortable, swept clean, and with a splendid odor of mint and cooked meat.

"She absolutely must rest for two weeks if she is to recover properly. Her condition is not good," the woman said, examining Ellen closely.

"But that's not possible—she has to work. She's a smith at tournaments, and we were going to leave today!" Suddenly Jean looked as helpless as a child.

"Then you'll just have to leave her here. Do you see how her eyelids are fluttering? She's having visions and thinks I am someone else—you both saw that earlier. Even if she's a strong young woman, a high fever is nothing to trifle with. If she's lucky, she has just gotten a chill and is exhausted. If not, it's something worse. But one thing is certain—she needs rest."

Jean looked helplessly at Madeleine and then turned back to the herb woman.

"We can't pay you very much, but Madeleine could stay here and look for work. Perhaps you know someone who needs a maid..."

The herb woman looked at Madeleine and nodded. "I hope she can be a real help."

"She can, believe me. She is used to hard work."

"Then she can stay here with me," the herb woman decided.

Jean was relieved that he had found a place for Madeleine to stay. He would take Greybeard, Nestor, and the tent along to the tournament site by himself. After all, he had to be there to explain Ellen's absence to Pierre so that he wouldn't be angry with her forever. Maybe he could offer to help the smith until he had found someone else.

"You are in good hands here, I believe," he whispered to Ellen, even though he couldn't be sure she understood him in her feverish condition. "I'll be back again, don't worry, and I'll take care of everything." He patted her arm, said good-bye to her, and after giving some advice to Madeleine started out on his way.

—

Thibault was furious, and stomped across the square where the merchants had set up their stalls. William just wouldn't stop provoking him. Just that morning, he had proclaimed loudly that he felt as strong as an ox and wanted to have at the French. He acted again as if he alone were responsible for the outcome of the tournament. It was ridiculous how the others cheered him on. Children were running around between the tents, playing, while horses, mules, and wagons were unloaded. Women were quarreling shrilly about the best places, and in the middle of it all, dogs were running around and fighting. Thibault stumbled twice. Once he had failed to notice a tent peg, and the second time his foot got tangled in a rope lying on the ground. Furious, he spat on the ground. Now if this smith girl should appear somewhere…he gave a quick kick in the rear to a skinny cat passing by. If it was so thin, it couldn't be a good hunter and deserved nothing better. But of course, his anger had little to do with the skinny ball of fur. He had been thinking of Ellen again, and that's what had made him so furious. William and Ellen made his life hell, each in their own way.

Thibault had almost reached the smithy. He had been drawn here quite unconsciously, and now that he saw it, his blood started to boil again. Just as he was going to turn around he heard the smith's voice. He seemed very upset.

"First she demands more money," he lamented, teary-eyed, "and then she turns out to be an unreliable, lazy woman who doesn't bother showing up for work at all!" He passed his hand through his thick head of hair. It was jet black with only a few streaks of silver. Hardly any man his age still had such thick hair, Thibault thought enviously. For the most part, lice and skin diseases caused it to fall out prematurely. Thibault passed his hand through his own hair, which had already become a bit thinner. The smith's hair gave him a certain dignity he didn't even deserve, Thibault thought.

The smith got so worked up that his neck swelled so much it seemed he would burst.

"She is neither lazy nor unreliable—she really wants to work, Pierre. I'm sure you know that!" Thibault could hear someone saying.

Thibault squinted and tried to think. He had seen the lad somewhere before. Right! Last fall he was the one who saved Ellen from being trampled by his warhorse.

"You know her well enough to know she must be really sick if she doesn't come in to work. She has a high fever, and the herb woman said she might die if she doesn't stay in bed," the boy explained. It was impossible not to see that the lad was worried.

Thibault snorted. Ellen was ill! *That serves her right*, he thought with satisfaction, and kept listening.

"Oh, come now, these herb women always imagine the worst, and they do that so you'll be frightened and pay them more. It will cost you a fortune. She's just pulling your leg." Pierre gave him a look of contempt indicating he thought the boy was really smarter than to believe all that, and Thibault nodded approvingly.

"Ellenweore's teeth are chattering with cold even though she feels hot to the touch. She is feverish, whether you believe it or not. I've seen with my own eyes how sick she is. As soon as she gets better she'll be happy to work for you again." The smith turned away from the boy even before he had finished speaking.

"If I still want her!" And with these words he departed, leaving the boy worried and dumbfounded.

"And Ellen's sword?" he called after him. "What will become of the sword she has been working on?" But he received no answer.

Thibault stroked his chin. "Aha, she's making a sword," he mumbled.

—

The next day, Thibault followed his rival William. He observed him as best he could, always in the hope of discovering something he could use against him. When the Marshal came to Master Pierre's stand, a woman hurried up to ask what he would like. Thibault hovered nearby without being noticed.

"I am looking for Ellenweore and haven't seen her anywhere. Doesn't she work for your husband any longer?"

"No," Armelle answered curtly, looking the Marshal up and down. "Has she been causing trouble?" Her eyes sparkled with curiosity.

Instead of replying, William asked, with some irritation, "Could you tell me where I can find her?"

"No, sire," Armelle answered sharply. "She walked out on us. Who knows who she took off with!" It was unmistakable that the smith's wife didn't like Ellen.

"What do you mean by that?" William demanded.

"Well, a girl her age and not married..." She raised her eyebrows suggestively. "She's no longer a spring chicken, and she's got to know she's got to act fast if a good opportunity comes up." Armelle looked at him disdainfully.

Without wasting another word, William turned away and left.

"He could have at least said thank you, that rascal," she grumbled, shaking her head and watching him as he left.

Thibault pushed off from the wall he had been leaning on and ambled over to her. "Arrogant fellow," Thibault mumbled and nodded in the direction of where William had gone. "He thinks he's something better," he said, giving the smith's wife a warm smile.

She blushed in embarrassment and pushed a fat strand of hair back under her bonnet. "Can I do something for you, my lord?"

"Well, that might be possible," Thibault answered with feigned cordiality. "This woman, Ellenweore, has been working on a sword, I've heard."

The woman's face darkened as soon as he mentioned Ellen's name.

"What is it about her that makes men chase after her like that?" she mumbled.

"The sword, it's only the sword that interests me. The word is that she has placed a magic spell on it in order to harm our king. This has to be stopped! It is very important that you report to me, and only to me, as soon as it is finished."

"Who knows if she'll ever return."

"Right!" Thibault had to restrain himself in order not to grab her by the collar and shake her. "I'll be here for the next tournaments as well. If you have any news for me, tell Abel, the jewelry dealer. You know where his stall is, don't you?" he asked with pronounced cordiality.

Armelle was impressed, and nodded. The jewelry merchant had the finest stall anyone had ever seen!

Thibault placed a silver coin in her hand.

"If you have further news for me, I'll have three more coins for you."

Armelle grinned broadly. "Depend on me, sire. But sire, what shall I tell him who is to receive my news?"

"You need to say nothing more, just: the sword is finished!"

"The sword is finished…yes," she stammered, somewhat confused, and started to ask another question, but Thibault was already gone.

—

Ellen sat on a stool behind the house enjoying the noonday sun while Madeleine knelt in the vegetable patch, pulling weeds and singing. The laundry hanging above her on a waxed rope looked as if it were about to break away and sail off into the blue sky at the next gust of wind. Ellen smiled with satisfaction: she couldn't remember ever seeing Madeleine so happy. Suddenly the girl jumped up and ran to the gate. Ellen got up slowly and ambled the few steps around the corner of the house. What she saw was enough to make her heart pound so hard that she had to stand still and catch her breath.

"Jean!" she exclaimed joyfully when she saw who had come.

"Ellen, you're feeling better," he said with obvious relief.

"She hasn't completely recovered. She still has to take it easy," the herb woman said as she came out of the house to greet Jean. "In any case, she shouldn't try to work yet."

"I don't think I could," Ellen replied, breaking out in a bad coughing fit.

"Indeed, it doesn't sound very good yet," Jean replied, looking concerned. "Even Greybeard's barking sounds better."

Ellen waved dismissively with her hand, let out a hollow cough, and motioned for him to come. "Let's not talk anymore about me. How are you, and have you found work?"

"I'll soon be able to make you the best glue you ever had," Jean boasted.

"You? Well, won't that be something. I hope it will actually stick, then." Ellen broke out in another long fit of coughing. "How did you get involved in making glue?" she asked when she got her breath back.

"I'm working for the shield maker. I told you, he makes his own glue and will teach me how, that's what he said."

"Is his son sick again?"

"No, Sylvain works there, too. By the way, he's a really nice fellow, a head taller than I am and a little older, but it isn't something he gets all stuck up about."

Ellen smiled. "I'm happy you found such a good job. Madeleine is pretty busy here, too. The only one who has nothing to do is me."

"Madeleine looks happy, so I didn't have to worry about her," Jean said, turning around to face her.

"Ruth is good to us. She never left my side when I was ill." Ellen gasped for breath, wheezed a bit, and then continued. "All I did was lie in bed, but every bone in my body hurt as if I had been working all day in the smithy." She paused for a moment and coughed. "Yesterday I wanted to finish the hilt, but I just couldn't." She quickly pulled the woolen shawl around her shoulders. "I feel like I'm a hundred years old."

"A hundred?" Jean laughed. "Nobody ever gets that old."

"Just look at me," Ellen grinned, exhausted.

"It's starting to get cool, and you'd better come into the house and warm yourself by the fire," Ruth said, and showed them in.

Jean stood as close as he could to the fire, rubbing his hands. "It's almost time for me to leave so that I can get back before nightfall. It's safer." He said good-bye to Ellen, kissing her on the cheek, and she looked at him in amazement because he had never done that before. He blushed and quickly turned away.

"I'll show you the way," Ruth suggested.

"She's still weak, and I'm happy you are taking care of her. Madeleine also seems to enjoy being here. Thank you for everything, *madame*!" Jean said, bowing gallantly.

"Away with you, you rascal," Ruth scolded in embarrassment, and pushed him out through the gate.

"I didn't mean to embarrass you, really!" Jean hastened to say.

"That's fine, then," Ruth grumbled, and tied the knot of hair behind her. "Nice boy," she mumbled with a smile, and went back into the house.

—

When Jean came back a week later, Ellen was much better. She quickly got tired and was still a bit pale, but she seemed to have regained her confidence.

Madeleine was the first to notice Jean standing in the yard. She flew into his arms. "I missed you so much," she whispered in his ear. "I made something for you to eat. You are surely hungry."

Jean looked in astonishment at Ellen, who in the meanwhile had come out of the house. "Madeleine has changed," he said softly, after greeting Ellen as well.

"This is a marvelously peaceful house that can do you a world of good." Ellen led Jean into the main room, where Madeleine placed a large plate of lentils in front of him. He spooned up the soft, tasty legumes with great appetite. "Wonderful, Madeleine," he congratulated her, smacking his lips.

Ellen could not wait to learn where the next tournament would take place. She put both her forearms on the table, bent forward, and watched every bite Jean took. "Come on, tell us!"

"We should break camp in five days at the latest. The tournament in Chartres is the next to last before Christmas, and there will be lots going on there. Anselm, the pancake baker from the Rhineland, and a few others who stayed here will be leaving then, too. If we don't want to travel alone, this is the best opportunity for us."

"Good, let's do that then. The fresh air and the walking will help me get my strength back. Now, do tell me about William. Have you seen him? Did he ask about me?"

Jean took a deep breath. For a brief moment he had hoped Ellen would not ask about William. Even though he could lie if necessary, Jean knew that with such things the truth would always come out sooner or later. So he decided to tell her first about William's triumph in the battles.

"Someday, no doubt, he'll be the most famous of all knights and everybody will be wild about him. Fighting is his life, and everything else is of no importance to him. Have you ever seen him fight?" Ellen blushed when he spoke of William.

"No, I had to work, you'll remember," Jean grumbled, trying to change the subject. "The shield maker actually hasn't said anything yet, but I hope I can work for him again at the next tournament. Then you can buy your glue from him. He'll certainly give you a fair price, if I discuss it with him."

Ellen smiled. "Good, let's do that. By the way, I pretty much finished the hilt yesterday." Suddenly she turned serious. "It's only in the last few days that I've been thinking about Athanor again." She shook her head in disbelief. "As soon as I can work again, I'll make the pommel—I can hardly wait to get back into the smithy. I am really feeling a lot better now."

"Oh, Ellen, I brought something along to help you get back your strength. Wait, I'll go and get it!" Jean ran out into the courtyard where Nestor was standing and returned holding a clay pot in his hands. Ellen had followed him into the yard while Madeleine was busy in the kitchen.

"Here, it's for you!" Jean handed her the little pot.

A thin cord held the top on.

"Well, what's in it? Ellen turned the little pot over in her hands, curiously.

"Just open it and see!" Jean's face quivered with delight. "Careful, though!"

Ellen untied the knot and took the cover off. Inside the pot was a viscous, brown mass.

"Jean, what is this?" Ellen smelled it carefully. "Mm, good, a bit bitter, but at the same time sweet."

"It's cooked with apples and pears. The man from the Rhineland with whom we'll be traveling makes it and sells his pancakes along with it. It tastes sweet, almost like honey. Just try it!"

Ellen dipped her finger in the syrup and licked it off with half-closed eyes. "Mm, you're right, it tastes wonderful!"

"Jean, you ought to give the horse a good rubdown," Ruth said as she came out of the house to give Ellen a woolen shawl to put around her shoulders. "It's not good to leave him standing there covered in sweat. Tie him up in back by the goat pen, where you'll also find straw and a bucket of water for the animal."

"You have to take better care of yourself. It's too cold for you without this shawl," she scolded Ellen. For the first time, Jean noticed how small the woman was. She came up only as far as Ellen's shoulder.

"You're right. I'd better take care of Nestor." Jean started taking their things off Nestor's back. "Could Ellen and Madeleine stay with you a few more days? Then we'll have to leave for Chartres," he asked Ruth as offhandedly as possible, without looking at her.

"And you?" Ruth asked, picking some dandelion leaves from the vegetable patch. "Very tasty." She nodded at Madeleine and handed them to her.

"I'll find something. I still have time."

"Can you chop wood and repair the roof on the shed?" Ruth asked softly, as she looked up with some concern. The straw roof had holes in it and was ripped in places.

Jean nodded, a bit unsure. Though she appeared very kind, the small woman intimidated him. He had never dared to ask what he owed her for Ellen's care.

"Then you can stay here. My good husband, God rest his soul, left me this house and one other farther up the street. The rent from it is enough for me to live on. If you're just as undemanding as Madeleine and Ellenweore and can make yourself just as useful, it's fine by me if you stay."

Jean nodded enthusiastically. "Thank you, *madame*!"

As they were sitting at supper in the kitchen that evening, he looked around surreptitiously. Ruth had withdrawn before the meal, and the three of them were alone. On a little board next to the fireplace there was a seven-armed candelabra. Jean was trying to think where he had seen something like that before.

"She's Jewish!" Ellen declared, as if she could read his mind.

Jean blushed at once, as if he had been caught doing something wrong and looked away, embarrassed.

Madeleine cleared the table and gave some leftovers from their dinner to Greybeard, who had been running around the table begging.

"Jean," Madeleine asked, "could you go to the fountain first thing in the morning and fetch a few pails of water?" She poured the last bucket of water into the pot and hung it over the fire.

"Hm," he grumbled. "Had I known she was an infidel…"

"Jean!" Ellen looked at him in horror. "Her husband was a doctor, a famous one in fact."

"And what does that have to do with it? Jews are dangerous." Jean asserted that with conviction even though he didn't really know what it meant to be Jewish.

"Women can't make decent swords, and Jews are dangerous. Lord, how I hate such foolish talk." Ellen glared at him. "Ruth is kind and generous and not in the least bit dangerous. And it seems to me we proved long ago that women can do more than most men believe possible."

"All right!" Jean raised his hand in a conciliatory gesture. "Where shall I sleep?"

"There's room over there in the corner," Ellen replied gruffly. It angered her that Jean, of all people, should be talking such nonsense. She had had sufficient time to get to know Ruth and knew she was a really good person, as God-fearing as a Christian in any case, even if her customs were different.

Greybeard did not let Madeleine out of his sight. He wagged his tail happily when she finally responded to his pleading gaze and handed him a dry cheese rind, and then he licked his hairy, grey lips with obvious enjoyment.

"If it were up to you, you'd do nothing but eat all day, you bottomless pit!" Ellen's voice was soft and warm when she spoke to Greybeard. He came straight over to her and sniffed her hand before turning around and settling down at her feet.

"But you'll sleep with Madeleine, all right?" she said with playful severity.

Greybeard looked up at her and squinted, glanced toward Madeleine, and then laid his nose down on Ellen's right foot.

At first, Madeleine had been afraid of sleeping without Jean, but Greybeard had proven to be an excellent substitute. As they were making their beds, he went over into the corner where Madeleine slept, waited until she had straightened out the covers, and then lay down in the middle of the blanket.

"Hey, give me a little room," Madeleine scolded with a laugh and snuggled up to him. "Ugh, you stink," she mumbled sleepily, without moving away from Greybeard.

"She doesn't seem so…crazy anymore," Jean whispered, tapping his forehead.

"She hasn't been seeing any man for a long time, except for you, I mean. I think that has been good for her." Ellen looked over at Madeleine and smiled. It was nice to see her so contented. "Someday we'll have enough money to settle down and have our own house. Of course, it won't be as large and comfortable as this one, but we'll be able to live in peace," Ellen promised softly, but with determination.

—

Jean quietly went about repairing the roof of the stable, cutting wood, and making himself useful wherever necessary as the day of departure approached. "I've done everything you asked of me. Is there something else I can do before we leave Compiègne?" Jean didn't look at Ruth as he spoke.

"Is there something troubling you?"

"You were very kind to us, Madeleine has flourished here, and you have brought Ellen back to full health. But you never told me how much you are asking for your help." Jean hesitated for a moment and still couldn't bring himself to look her directly in the eye.

"You mean how much you owe me?"

Jean nodded apprehensively.

"Well, let me think. You and Madeleine have worked for your room and board, so that's taken care of. Then Ellenweore..." Ruth put her chin in her hand and thought. "Well, she trusted me completely, without even a trace of reserve, even though I am Jewish. She gave me her friendship and gratitude, and through her I have gotten to know Madeleine, whose mind was wrapped in dark clouds, and have learned how beautiful it is to see her laughing and freed from her worries. Honestly I couldn't put a price on the happiness, the singing, the laughter, and this lovable, clumsy dog you brought into my house. All three of you... excuse me, all four, including Greybeard, have enriched my life. You owe me nothing, nothing at all, except perhaps a promise to visit me if you should ever be in our region again."

Now Jean turned red with shame—he had been so certain that she, a Jewess, would demand a lot of money from them. "I thank you from the bottom of my heart, Ruth, and ask for your forgiveness because I had some unflattering thoughts about you, and I am terribly ashamed," he said ruefully.

"You are a good boy, Jean, and have not always had an easy time with Madeleine, have you? And Ellenweore surely is also not always easy," she said with a grin, taking Jean in her arms. "Good people like you are always welcome. That is how my husband felt, and I am just carrying on the way he would." There was a short, embarrassed pause; then Ruth patted him on the arm. "Go now and get Ellen and Madeleine. You have to leave."

The farewell was tearful. Only the dog seemed untroubled, as he probably didn't know what it meant to say good-bye. Ruth embraced them all, one after the other, whispering something to each that the others couldn't hear, and for each seemed to have found the right words, as they all nodded bravely, wiped the tears from their faces, and tried hard not to look so sad.

Jean held Nestor's reins and was about to help Ellen up.

"First I'd like to walk a bit. I probably don't have enough strength to go very far, but I must gradually get used to it."

"When you notice she is getting tired, you'll insist she gets back on the horse, do you hear?" Ruth admonished them, and looked Ellen in the eye. "Don't overexert yourself so soon, all right?"

"I promise!" Ellen took Ruth's hand and added, "I wish my mother had been like you."

"Now you must go, or you'll never get started!" Ruth said, wiping away the tears with the back of her hand.

—

It took them nine days on foot, and every day Ellen was able to do a few miles more. By the end of the trip she felt as strong as ever. It was already late in the afternoon as they approached Chartres, where the tournament was to be held. There were many tradespeople on the site already, building their stalls and putting up tents, but Pierre had not yet arrived. Ellen and Jean hurried to find a good place for their tent and quickly set it up.

While Madeleine got her things in order and prepared the meal, Ellen and Jean strolled around.

"There's the shield maker's stand!" Jean called out, and ran ahead.

Ellen followed behind and roamed around the stall as Jean talked with the master.

"I told her that your glue is the best."

"So, you are bringing me a new customer, that's very nice. I made the glue this morning," the shield maker replied, but he didn't pay any attention to Ellen.

"Then let's have a look," Ellen spoke up, smiling broadly. She knew men liked her smile, and it was always a good idea to gain favor with someone you wanted to buy something from.

"So you're the smith?"

"That's right," Ellen replied cordially.

"And why does a smith need glue? Do you have problems getting your iron to stick together?" He slapped his thigh and laughed so hard he almost lost his breath.

Ellen didn't show her annoyance. "May I?" she asked, going over to the pot and stirring the sticky liquid. The glue was obviously of good quality and would be clear and firm when it dried, as she could see at the edge of the pot. Ellen smelled it, poked it with her finger that was accustomed to heat, and licked it. Then she nodded to Jean, and he negotiated a good price.

"You're a fine fellow," the shield maker said. "Would you like to work for me again? Sylvain, my son, gets along well with him," he told Ellen in an aside, and the two reached an agreement. "Here, this rabbit foot is for you, it will bring you luck!"

he said to Jean and then turned to Ellen: "Excuse me, no offense, I didn't mean to be rude. It's just unusual—a pretty, young girl who would rather make swords than marry and have children."

Ellen nodded almost imperceptibly.

As they walked back to the tent, Jean stroked the soft fur of the rabbit's foot.

"I like to work for him. He is always friendly and jokes around a lot, even if he was a little out of order this time. He certainly didn't mean to offend," Jean tried to tell her as he hopped along beside her.

Just before they got back to the tent, they saw Pierre and Armelle with their heavily laden wagon.

"I didn't tell you because I didn't want you to worry. Remember that Ruth said you shouldn't get excited as long as you are sick."

"What didn't you tell me?"

"Pierre was terribly angry that you didn't come to work. He said he didn't know if he wanted to have you back." Jean didn't dare to look at Ellen. He had been worrying for the last few days but didn't have the courage to bring it up.

"Oh, him! He's certainly long gotten over that." She waved her hand dismissively.

"But he was really furious!"

"Well, we'll see." Ellen felt strong enough to confront him and walked over to Pierre confidently. In the meanwhile, Armelle had disappeared behind the wagon.

"Pierre!" Ellen nodded slightly. "I'm back."

At first, Pierre looked bewildered. "You don't exactly look deathly sick!" he grumbled.

"I'm feeling better, thank you," Ellen answered calmly. She knew Pierre well enough to be sure his anger had long since passed. "Is everything else all right?"

“There was lots to do,” he retorted, with a touch of reproach in his voice.

“Then I’ll help you set up your things so we can get a bit ahead on the work. What do you think, master?” She started to unload the wagon.

“That’s surely not a bad idea.” Pierre seemed to be happy that Ellen didn’t breathe a word about his argument with Jean.

“How is your sword coming along?” he asked, making clear that their quarrel was settled. It was the first time he had ever shown an interest in Athanor.

“I’d like to begin soon with the pommel. The sheath and the scabbard are practically finished, but there is still a little work to be done.”

“Will you show it to me when you are finished?”

“Of course, master.”

It was already pitch dark outside when Ellen and Pierre had finally unloaded everything and set up the smithy. Jean wasn’t set to begin working for the shield maker until the following day, so he helped them and received a few coins from Pierre for his work.

“You’re a clever fellow,” he complimented him, patting him on the shoulder. Ellen noticed that Jean must have grown, for when he was standing next to the smith, he reached up to the smith’s chin.

—

The very next day Ellen made two little metal caps to protect the wooden halves she would glue together to cover the tang. The caps were to help the glue holding the wood and to protect the hilt so it would not crack at its most sensitive places.

After she had applied the glue, she carefully pressed the wood together until it had partially dried and wrapped it all securely with a cord that held the hilt together until the glue had dried completely. The very next day she was able to polish the edges, smooth it, and finally rub the hilt with linseed oil so that the joints where the parts were glued together were scarcely visible.

Ellen looked at the handle with satisfaction. The cross guard was secure, and the tang projected far enough out of the handle to accommodate the pommel and be riveted. Her heart was pounding with pride. She would still wrap the handle with the dark red silk cord. Once the pommel was secure, she would balance the sword on her outstretched index finger and be able to determine the weapon's center of gravity, for that was the right place for the gold-wire inlay.

She had been wondering for a long time what would be the right symbol and finally decided on a small heart. It stood for the knight's courage and boldness, and for his life. Only recently had Ellen heard for the first time that in some places people thought of the heart as a symbol for love, too. William, though, would surely not think of it like that.

First she would have to make the pommel and be sure it was the proper size as a counterweight to the blade. From the remainder piece she fashioned a slightly oval disk about two fingers thick and, using a drift, just as she had for the cross guard, made a slit for the tang in the pommel disk, which had become almost round due to the hard blows from the hammer. To get a really circular disk, Ellen forged the pommel a little more, then used a file and the whetstone until the circle was perfect. She rubbed and polished the pommel until it shone just like the cross guard and then slid it over the tang. Finally she compressed the protruding part of the tang with a few well-aimed blows to fix the pommel in place.

—

The next morning as she entered the workshop, Ellen had the feeling of being watched. Was William nearby? Her thoughts kept wandering to him, and nothing seemed to be going right for her. First, she had trouble getting the fire started; then she burned the iron so that the sparks flew in all directions.

"Good Lord, pull yourself together," Pierre shouted at her. "What in the world is wrong with you?"

"I don't know. I'm sorry, I really am. I have a feeling something bad is going to happen today."

"Silly women's talk," Pierre scolded her impatiently. "Do your work and do it right."

Not until after noon was she able to concentrate better. She still had to finish the tip of a spear, and she finally got started on it now. While she was standing at the anvil with her back turned, someone came to the stand. It wasn't William—she would have recognized the sound of his footsteps at once. They had something commanding, something that instilled respect. The man who had just approached the smithy sounded like a sneaky, perhaps underhanded person, and she didn't turn around when she saw out of the corner of her eye that Pierre was waiting on him.

But the hair on the back of her neck stood up as soon as she heard the man speak. Never would she forget that voice. It was Thibault, and he was standing just a few steps behind her. Ellen prayed Pierre wouldn't ask for her help, as Thibault would recognize her at once. It had happened six years ago, but it suddenly seemed to her as if it were just yesterday. Ellen took a cloth and nervously wiped the iron she happened to have in her hand. The two men were talking about repairs to a weapon that Thibault had brought along, and neither of them paid any attention to her. Only after Thibault had left did Ellen dare to turn around. What in heaven's name should she do? She couldn't possibly be on her guard all the time and hide from him. She turned back to the anvil, lost in thought, when someone stepped up to her from behind and whispered in her ear.

"You are more beautiful than ever!"

Ellen turned around, shocked. She thought he had left! "What do you want?" she snapped at Thibault. She didn't allow the fear she still had of him to show.

"A night with you, my beautiful songbird."

"Are you crazy?" Ellen was so angry she had to gasp for air.

"Now don't act so prudish. I'm aware of what has been going on between you and William. It was very exciting to watch you."

She was overcome with both shame and rage, and couldn't help but blush.

"I want you, in my bed, in the forest, in a meadow, anywhere."

"You are crazy! Thibault, it would be a sin—you are my brother!" she blurted out in panic.

Thibault merely snorted.

"Before he married your mother, your father got my mother in trouble, just as you did with Rose back then."

Thibault burst out laughing. "You? An illegitimate de Tournai? Wouldn't you like that! So you have heard that my father is dead, have you? He can't tell anymore, so I'll just have to believe you, is that right? But I don't, and I don't care what you think. I want you still, and I'll get you yet!"

Ellen didn't let her fear show. "You had better go now!" She raised the hammer in her right hand threateningly.

"Our friend William is here, too, by the way. I can hardly believe he'll be pleased to learn that Ellen and Alan are the same person. But don't worry, if you come to me on your own, my lips will be sealed." He put his fingers to his mouth. "Incidentally, I can also be very tender."

Ellen felt sick. His disgusting smirk brought back to mind the day he had violated her.

"I'll give you three days to think it over. If you don't come, I'll tell him. He won't be happy to hear you lied to him—he can't stand liars, the good fellow!" Thibault laughed maliciously. "I warn you, think carefully what you do. You'll be mine one way or the other."

He turned around and left the smithy with long strides.

Jean almost bumped into him, and watched with surprise as he left. "Who was that, anyway?" he asked and turned around to look at Thibault again. Then he noticed the bewilderment in Ellen's eyes. "Good heavens, what did he do to you? You look upset!"

Ellen just stood there trembling and shaking her head.

"I've got to get out of here, immediately. Pierre!" she shouted. "I have to go. I'll be back tomorrow," she apologized as she bumped into him on her way out.

"What's wrong this time?" the smith grumbled. Only when he noticed how confused and upset Ellen looked did he realize something was seriously wrong.

"I'll deduct a half day's wages," he grumbled and waved her off forgivingly.

"Let's go!" Ellen pulled at Jean's sleeve. They pushed their way through the crowd, and not until they were alone did Ellen begin to explain.

"The knight you saw is my brother."

"What's that?"

"His father when he was in England…and my mother…she was a foolish woman and he…well…I know Thibault from Tancarville, where I also met William." Ellen told him as best she could why she had fled from Tancarville.

"Some friend that was who snitched on you," Jean said.

"That's what I thought at first, too, but she had no idea how it would hurt me." Ellen told him about being beaten and violated by Thibault—after everything he had told her about Madeleine, he would surely understand without condemning her. As she talked about Thibault, she clenched her fists involuntarily and noted that Jean did the same.

"I'll kill the guy!" he snorted, and beat the air with his fists.

"You're my hero!" Ellen said gratefully. But couldn't it be William standing beside her and supporting her? She would have much preferred him as the protector of her honor, but it was likely he would condemn her and possibly even try to defend Thibault. She choked back tears of grief and bitterness.

"If he tells William, I'll never see him again."

"You don't have a future in common anyway. You should just tell William everything yourself, before Thibault does. Then he'll have the choice whether to be angry at you for your deception or happy that you told him the truth. If he doesn't stand by you because he feels duped, that's his bad luck."

"Oh, Jean, I can't do that." Ellen let out a deep sigh.

"What are you more afraid of, Thibault and his lust for you, or William's disappointment?"

Ellen shrugged. "Honestly, I don't know."

Almost three months had passed since the day she lay on the meadow with William and enjoyed the passions of physical love, and since then she had not bled. One time it seemed it was about to happen, but then the bleeding lasted only half a day. Until that point she had attempted to suppress the thought, but now she suspected she was with child.

For two days nothing happened. Neither Thibault nor William appeared in the shop, and Ellen had also not noticed the person who had been prowling around their tent ever since they arrived. To get her mind off these matters, she finally began work again on the decorations for Athanor. Before long she had engraved the little heart on the blade. Carefully she tapped the gold wire into the groove she had cut into the blade and checked with her thumb to make certain the inlay was smooth, and then she rubbed the blade with a piece of cloth so no rust would form there due to moisture from her fingers. She examined the sword with satisfaction. The little golden heart looked elegant and simple at the same time and was exactly at the center of gravity. Ellen had also purchased some copper wire and used it to inlay her sign, a rounded "E" within a circle, on the other side of the sword. In shaping the letter, she was thinking of her first attempts at engraving for Jocelyn. They had often engraved entire sayings into sacral objects, so she had a lot of experience with that from the outset. For a long time these decorations had been nothing but trivial squiggles for her, nice to look at but meaningless. Only with time had she learned to write all the letters and a few words that were frequently in demand. When she had finished the "E" she examined it with a critical eye. It was well rounded, like a C with a vertical line at each end. Through the middle of the rounded center was a horizontal line with a tiny vertical line at the end as well. It was all contained within a circle that Ellen had fashioned with great care. She beamed with pride at the result. When Jean entered the workshop, she showed him Athanor.

"Is that what I was working on? I mean, that's the same clump of iron that you picked out of the pile?" he asked incredulously.

Ellen smiled broadly. "I can't imagine anything more wonderful than being a swordsmith. Athanor is balanced, elegant, and very, very sharp."

"I'll admit, Ellenweore, I'm impressed."

"I hope you'll not be the only one who likes Athanor. I wonder if William is really here already?"

"Henry says that the Young King arrived three days ago."

"Good." Ellen slid the sword into its scabbard and wrapped it in a blanket.

"May I carry it?" asked Jean.

"Of course!" She seemed to be thinking. "Do you know what? I'll follow your advice and confess my deception to William. But before he learns anything, I want him to see Athanor." She stared into space wistfully before catching herself again. "Look here! The chape!"

"Gold?" asked Jean, impressed.

"For heaven's sake, no, do you think I've suddenly become rich? Brass, of course, but it looks good, doesn't it?"

Jean nodded enthusiastically.

"It goes well with the dark red covering of the scabbard. Your sword has become a real masterpiece. You should never sell it; it's the proof of how good you are. If you have that to show, you can definitely find work in any smithy!"

"I'm not so certain of that. Probably no one will believe that I made it. And malicious tongues could also claim I stole it," she opined gloomily. "But the most important thing for me is that William likes it!" she said with a broad smile.

"William, there you go again!" Jean groaned.

"Of course! He said if I'm good, he'll recommend me to the Young King!"

"Oh, he is always broke, that's what our friend Henry says, and he knows everything that's going on at the Young King's court."

"It may be that the Young King doesn't have so much money at present," Ellen agreed reluctantly. "But when his father dies, he'll have all the power and money to spare. You'll see, Jean, one day I'll make a sword for the king! I'm absolutely convinced of that!"

They had almost arrived at the tent when a young man bumped into Jean and knocked him down. He wrenched the sword from Jean and tried to take off with it.

Ellen's heart leaped; she jumped over Jean, who was lying on the ground, and rushed after the thief. She hadn't worked so hard just to have a scoundrel come and destroy it all! She remembered the purse snatcher in Ipswich. This time she wouldn't let the thief get away! Shoving and pushing, she pursued him through the crowd and in fact was getting closer. She reached out and caught him by the back of the neck, yanked him back, knocked him over, and ended up sitting on his chest. A few bystanders were laughing, but nobody interfered. "You've got something there that belongs to me!" she shouted, punching him on the chin; then she grabbed Athanor and let him go.

At first he wanted to jump up and try to wrest the sword from her again, but then he saw a man approaching and decided to take off.

Ellen wondered why he had changed his mind so fast until she looked around and saw Thibault.

"Why don't you come to me instead of attacking poor, innocent people?" he whispered to her.

Ellen looked him directly in the eye, and her golden freckles seemed to gleam and dance around.

"The only way you can have me is by force—I'll never follow you voluntarily to your tent," she hissed.

"Isn't that a shame? Poor William won't be happy when he hears the truth about you." Thibault shook his head as if he felt sorry about that.

"I'll tell him myself."

"I could get there first."

"What difference does that make? He'll hate me for it, one way or the other." Ellen shrugged, turned on her heel, and left Thibault standing there.

Jean had pulled himself together in the meanwhile and stood there, grinning.

"You better watch out, little guy," Thibault warned him, raising his fist angrily.

Jean rushed to catch up with Ellen.

"You really gave it to him," he exclaimed admiringly.

—

The next morning as Ellen was arriving at the smithy, she caught sight of two men standing nearby. She slowed down when she recognized the huge figure in front of her that almost blocked her sight of Pierre. At the same time, Pierre saw her and nodded warmly. "Here she is now, Sir William!"

"Ellenweore!" William exclaimed. His face shone with passion.

Ellen nodded to her master. "Will you excuse us for a moment?" she asked, and Pierre stepped a few paces to the side.

"I looked for you at the tournament in Compiègne. Where were you?"

Ellen couldn't help but chuckle. If she wasn't completely mistaken, William sounded jealous!

"I was sick," she replied tersely.

"Aha!" William seemed uncertain whether to believe her.

"I have finished the sword. Would you like to have a look?" She raised up the bundle she was carrying.

"I'd like nothing more!" He seemed delighted and stepped closer.

Ellen's heart beat furiously. "Then come, Pierre hasn't seen it yet, either."

She unwrapped the sword under the critical eye of the two men.

The scabbard, covered in dark red, radiated elegance and dignity.

William raised his eyebrows approvingly when Ellen handed him Athanor. He weighed the sword in both hands, then seized it with his right hand and pulled it out of the scabbard slowly, with feeling and awe. "It handles very well!" he said appreciatively, swinging it back and forth. "How sharp is it?" he asked.

"I split a hair with it," Ellen stated calmly.

William nodded his appreciation and examined the sword more closely. The two cutting edges of the gleaming blade were perfectly formed. Then he looked up and handed it to the smith.

"Do have a look, it's simply wonderful. It has a splendid sheen! What do you think?"

"Let me have a closer look, sire," replied Pierre, scarcely able to conceal his curiosity. William placed the sword back in the scabbard in order to hand it to Pierre. The smith looked it over critically and finally shrugged.

"The shine is beautiful, but there is not much decoration, just two little inlays, one of them in copper," he complained. Ellen could not resist thinking that Pierre was jealous.

"Decorations, such silliness! You mustn't judge a sword like this in those terms. Swing it through the air—then you'll see how unimportant such decorations are. The sword is perfectly balanced. It's something special because it has character!" William enthused, once again taking it out of its scabbard. Ellen took a piece of wood the thickness of an arm and held it out to him. He sliced it in two with one blow without knocking the wood out of her hand.

"Whoa! Sharp! Very sharp!" William exclaimed with great enthusiasm.

Pierre shrugged. "Well done, Ellenweore," he said, clearly trying to sound as indifferent as possible. Then he turned around and went back to his work.

"He finds it better than just good but doesn't want to admit it," William whispered to her, and kissed her on the tip of her nose without bothering to look and see if anyone was watching.

Ellen turned around, embarrassed. "Can we meet after work? I must talk with you. It's important, but not meant for everyone's ears," she said.

William nodded. "I'll stop by and pick you up," he winked.

"But Athanor will stay here," she said with a laugh and took the sword from his hands.

"I'll get it someday, one way or the other," he called over his shoulder as he left.

"Then hold on to your money so you can afford it," she grumbled, but William had already disappeared in the crowd.

—

Just before sundown Madeleine came to her.

"Look what I've got!" She showed Ellen another silver piece.

"He gave me a message for you. I didn't understand what he meant, but he told me just to repeat it and you would." She gave Ellen an innocent look.

"What? Tell me!"

"He said he was a bird-catcher and had the right bait to catch the most beautiful songbird in the world. And then he asked me whether Jean was my brother." Madeleine giggled. "Do you understand that?"

All at once Ellen understood that the secret knight who had given Madeleine the silver coin was not William, but Thibault.

"Where is he?" she asked.

"Who?"

"Jean!" Ellen was seized with panic when Madeleine didn't answer at once.

"I don't know, I haven't seen him."

"Go to the shield maker and ask if he is there. If not, look for him in the tent and then come back to me. I'll be done in a moment. But hurry, Madeleine, it's important. I'm afraid Jean is in danger!"

Madeleine had been smiling the entire time, but now she looked up anxiously. "I'll do it right away!" she said, and rushed out.

Ellen quickly finished her work and cleaned up the shop. She kept looking around, praying she was mistaken, and hoped to see Jean and Madeleine walking calmly toward the shop at any moment. But if Thibault had gotten hold of him…

"Are you ready?" William's warm voice tore her from her anxious thoughts. She wanted nothing more than to rush into his arms.

"Hm, I'm coming." She had to control herself. Probably William would be furious with her forever when he learned what she was planning to tell him that day. She took off her apron, folded it together, and packed it up with her tools. Then she picked up Athanor and turned to leave. Just as she was walking out the door, Madeleine came running.

"Ellenweore! He's gone! I can't find him anywhere!"

"Who is she talking about?"

"Jean—I've told you about him before."

William nodded. "Yes, that's right."

"Let me first take my tools and the sword to the tent; then we can take a little walk. I have something urgent to tell you."

"You're making it all very exciting!" William winked playfully.

"Wait a moment, I'll be right back," she asked when they arrived at the tent, leaving William standing not far away. After she had put down her tools and was about to return to him, she heard someone calling softly to her. It couldn't be Jean. Behind the tent she finally discovered an emaciated woman half hiding in the shadows. "Who are you and what…?" The rest of her question stuck in her throat. "Rose? Is it you?"

The woman nodded, fell down on her knees in front of her, and cried.

Ellen pulled her to her feet again. Rose's body seemed wasted, and the shadows beneath her eyes gave a hint of how unhappy she must be. "What are you doing here?"

Rose wiped a tear from the corner of her eye. "Thibault is a scoundrel. I never wanted to accept that. I always did everything for him, and, oh, Ellen, I was so stupid!" Rose sobbed.

"Are you still with him?" Ellen asked, surprised.

Rose looked down at the ground, embarrassed.

"Why do you let him hurt you?"

"I somehow thought that he loved me, in his own way." She looked at Ellen with big, childlike eyes.

"Sometimes when I share the bed with him he is loving and tender, and that's why I always had hope he would change. But he isn't changing and never will. For months he has been stalking that girl." Rose looked over at where Madeleine was standing. "I watched him and was jealous because I thought he was chasing her. But all he did was to pump her for information, about you."

Ellen clenched her fists. "I hope he kept his dirty hands off her."

"He is obsessed with you, Ellen, and that makes him dangerous. He runs back and forth in his tent just muttering your name. I am so sorry that I betrayed you back then. I was blinded by love and didn't really mean to do it, believe me!"

Ellen embraced Rose and tried to console her. "Now just stop talking about that. That was a long time ago."

"But now Thibault is holding your friend prisoner."

"Do you mean Jean?"

Rose nodded. "He's threatening to kill him if you don't come. Do you think he could ever do anything like that?"

"Yes, Rose, I do."

Rose took a deep breath. "Sneak up to the back of his tent and I'll let you in," she whispered. "I have to go—if I am away for long he goes crazy." She turned around and disappeared.

"What's the matter, Ellenweore?" William asked. He had been looking for her in her tent and had not found her there.

"Thibault!" she growled.

"No, not him again," William groaned.

Ellen summoned up all her courage and said, "I am Alan, not his sister, and Thibault knows. He threatened to tell you all that if I don't do what he wants. I told him to go to hell and said I would tell you myself who I am. Now he has found another solution in order to put pressure on me and kidnapped Jean." She had been talking nonstop, but now she turned silent.

"And now?" William asked, calmly.

Ellen looked at him, distraught. "What do you mean by 'and now'?"

"What shall we do, I mean, to help Jean?"

"Didn't you understand what I said, that I am Alan?"

"Of course I understood that, Ellen. Do you seriously believe I hadn't noticed that a long time ago? Just the fragrance of your skin! Until this very day I can't understand how you were able to fool the others for so long. Thibault, too! On the very first Sunday back then in the Tancarville forest I already suspected, and by the time we had met the third time I was certain."

Ellen gasped for breath and stared at William.

"You…you knew it all along?" She rose in front of him. For a moment she forgot all her grief and could scarcely control her anger.

William shrugged his shoulders and grinned.

"And so what if I did…?"

Ellen was seething. All the stories he had told her to torment her about women and his suspicions about Rose were just trickery. She gasped for air. "I can't believe you were making fun of me the whole time!"

"Would you have preferred that I had let your secret out?" he asked with irritation.

Ellen didn't know how to answer. Of course she was grateful to him for keeping her secret, but how wonderful it could have been if it had been a shared secret.

"Do you want to keep reminiscing about our past, or should we go and try to release your friend before Thibault does something crazy?" William asked impatiently. He was excited about the possibility of foiling Thibault's plan.

Ellen could only grunt and fetched Athanor from her tent. "You stay here and wait for us," she told Madeleine in a strict voice. "Don't move from this spot for any reason, do you hear me?"

William turned to leave, ready for a fight.

"You don't have to come along."

"I know how good you are with a sword, Ellen, but Thibault by now has a lot more experience than you do. Also, he is more devious. I can't stand him, in any case, and Jean has nothing to do with that. It is a question of defending my honor as a knight."

"Bah, honor!" Ellen exploded.

William carefully ignored her remark.

"It would be best if I just pretend to pay a visit to Thibault, a friendly visit, so to say. And you…"

"I'll sneak around the back, try to free Jean, and flee without being noticed," Ellen interrupted. "No wonder they call you the great tactician of Tancarville!" And she was at once annoyed at herself because she sounded like a loudmouthed washwoman. What complaint did she have against William? After all, he had not lied to her any more than she had to him. "I know that's the best solution if we want to make certain Thibault doesn't become suspicious right away. If we can avoid a fight, all the better," she added, in a more conciliatory tone.

Night had fallen, but William had pointed out to Ellen exactly where Thibault's tent was. As they got closer, they separated, and Ellen moved furtively through the tent grounds. Torches were burning all around. In front of the tents a few watchmen were sitting alongside bonfires, preparing something to eat and celebrating boisterously. Ellen watched William from a distance.

He proceeded toward a red and green tent where the watchman on duty greeted him and let him pass without hesitation. It appeared William was viewed as a friend.

For a moment Ellen wondered if he was leading her into a trap. "Jean, you must think of Jean!" she mumbled to herself and approached the tent from the rear. Everything was quiet. The horses were tied up not far from her, grazing contentedly, and seemed to take no notice of her. Rose was nowhere to be seen. Ellen listened carefully, trying to overhear William and Thibault, when she felt someone tugging on her dress. Startled, she turned around, ready to fight. It was Rose, holding her finger to her lips and beckoning. Ellen followed her quietly to a long opening on one side of the tent.

Rose climbed through first. Without thinking about what might await her there, Ellen also entered and looked around. She was standing in a small, comfortably appointed side tent. This feudal bed decorated with pillows, blankets, and furs had to be Thibault's.

Jean was crouched on the bare floor. His head was pressed against his knees, and he was completely motionless. Ellen poked at him and was surprised when he lifted his head. He had been beaten so badly that his entire face was swollen and his eyes looked like tiny slits. Because he could hardly see anything, he recoiled for fear of being beaten again.

"It's me, Ellen. I'll get you out of here," she whispered.

Jean nodded with relief. His hands were tied behind his back, but he was able to raise them a bit. Ellen took her knife and cut the rope, then took off the shackles around his feet.

William and Thibault seemed to be having an animated conversation, but suddenly their voices became loud.

Then Ellen heard a woman's voice. She stood up and listened. "Oh, God, no, Madeleine!" she whispered; then she heard Thibault's piercing laughter.

"Jean! She wants Jean!" he screeched loudly. "And I want Ellen," he screamed at her.

Ellen pulled Athanor out of its scabbard.

"Get Jean out of here; we'll meet at the tent," she whispered to Rose as she pulled back the tent flap. When Thibault saw her standing there with Athanor, he pulled his own sword.

"What are you doing, Thibault? Are you going to fight a woman?" said William, trying to divert him.

"Don't try to fool me. I know you and she..." Thibault laughed loudly. "But she belonged to me first."

William seemed not to understand what Thibault meant, for he just shook his head.

Out of the corner of her eye Ellen saw a page rushing toward Madeleine. Acting with presence of mind, Ellen ran to help. She fought better than the page and drove him back until William could get to him. Then she pulled Madeleine away and tried to reach the exit, but Thibault stood in her way.

"Just let them go!" William said, trying to sound conciliatory, but Thibault merely glared at him in contempt.

Ellen took advantage of this distraction and lunged at Thibault, cutting him on his right arm. It was the second time she had injured him in the same spot. Thibault winced in pain and reached for his arm. Blood flowed out and colored his hand and shirt red. He had had no intention of letting Ellen and Madeleine go, but now he had to lower his sword.

"Go now! I'll attend to him," William ordered, nodding at Ellen.

Madeleine stood behind her, one arm around her waist as if she had to keep herself from falling apart. Ellen pulled her out of the tent. The watchmen were still celebrating noisily and didn't notice her. Only the man who had let William in looked at the two of them in astonishment.

"Don't let them escape!" Thibault finally screeched. The anxious-looking young man tried to block their way, pulled out his short sword, and threatened them with it. Apparently he had not noticed that Ellen was also holding a sword. With eyes open wide, he stared at her as she brought Athanor down on his shoulder, splitting it. Then, with an unbelieving look, he fell to the ground. Madeleine whimpered as the blood spurted on her, and Ellen quickly pulled her away.

"He would have killed us!" Ellen said in a flat voice. She felt miserable. It was the first time in her life that she had killed anyone. Naturally, swords were meant for fighting, and winning, but even during her hours of practice with William she had never thought she would ever have to do it herself.

Even though Madeleine kept stumbling, they ran as fast as they could back to the tent, where Jean and Rose were already waiting.

Following Jean's instructions, Rose had already begun loading Nestor with their most important belongings.

In no time at all, Ellen had taken down the tent and collected the tent pegs. Madeleine's face and dress were smeared with blood, and the poor child stood there pale and trembling, unable to do anything. Greybeard had been roaming around, and Ellen whistled for him to come and get moving. Immediately behind the tournament grounds was a dense forest. It wasn't a safe place in the dark, but they had no other choice. No doubt Thibault and a few other men would be heading out in pursuit soon. Ellen tugged at Nestor's harness. "Rose, take Madeleine and Jean by the hand. You can't stay here any longer either. If he catches you, he'll kill you on the spot."

Rose dejectedly followed Ellen's instructions.

Jean stumbled along beside her, tripping over every hole and root in the ground because he could see hardly anything with his swollen eyes.

Madeleine walked slowly with measured steps alongside Rose as if she had to concentrate in order to put one foot in front of the other.

Fortunately, the moon was almost full. The beech and oak trees had long ago cast off their foliage, and the branches, which seemed to be reaching out like skinny arms to the heavens, allowed enough moonlight to pass through to light their way. Only when they were passing through the pine groves was the night pitch black and impenetrable. Ellen stopped for a moment to listen if someone was pursuing them, but all they could hear was a deathlike stillness and the faraway cry of a screech owl in the night. "We'll go as far as we can, then rest a bit, and as soon as daylight comes we'll move on. If Thibault finds us…" Ellen didn't finish her sentence. They all could imagine what would happen then. "We must in any case not light a fire, as that would attract their attention at once," Ellen warned them, when they finally stopped to rest. They pulled their coats tightly around them and wrapped themselves up in blankets they had brought along. Greybeard lay down right next to Madeleine and whimpered softly.

"It's all right, nothing happened," Ellen said, trying to calm the dog down, but he remained skittish.

—

As morning arrived, Rose woke with a start. Greybeard was standing in the little clearing nearby, snarling. A half-starved wolf had approached their campsite, and Greybeard growled furiously, not letting it out of his sight. Rose shook Ellen's arm, and suddenly she, too, was wide-awake. When Ellen saw the wolf, she jumped up, ripped her sword from its scabbard, and advanced toward the animal. It looked famished, probably had been rejected by its pack, and was ready to do anything to finally get something to eat. It seemed to have picked out Madeleine, who was lying there motionless and with bulging eyes. Greybeard stood in front of her, ready to defend her to his last breath. The dog was somewhat larger than the wolf, but that didn't scare off the beast.

"Ho, he!" Ellen shouted, trying to drive the wolf away. It backed off a bit but didn't give up.

Now it moved closer to Greybeard and Madeleine, snarling.

Their faithful dog was about to charge the wolf when Ellen jumped up and with a single blow chopped off its head.

"Everything is fine, Madeleine!" she called back over her shoulder; then she chopped off a pine branch and laid it over the dead animal.

"Ellenweore!" She heard Rose's suppressed cry, and turned around in panic.

"She's…she's dead!" Rose stammered, kneeling down in front of Madeleine and holding her hand. It was not just

Madeleine's dress that was spattered with the young soldier's blood, but blood was also streaming from her belly.

"How could she hide that from us!" Ellen stammered. "I didn't notice that she was…" She collapsed and started to cry. "Why didn't she say anything?"

"It wouldn't have changed anything." Jean seemed calm and composed. "She may have been a simple person, but she has lived long enough with the fear of death. There is little we could have done for her with this enormous wound. I imagine she knew she would just slow us down and endanger us." Jean's face was still swollen, and the reddened skin under his eyes was bathed in tears.

"And I am responsible for all of this," Ellen mumbled in despair.

"No! If I hadn't betrayed you back then, none of this would have happened!" Rose cried.

"Now just stop. We must bury her. She didn't have a good life, but she at least deserves a decent resting place," Jean demanded.

With much effort they dug a shallow hole, placed Madeleine in it, and covered her with earth and a row of stones they had collected nearby.

"Please, Lord, take her into your hands!" Jean prayed, since he didn't know how to ask for eternal life for her soul.

"We must move on, or all our bravery will have been in vain." Ellen didn't want to press them, but she was certain Thibault had already started out in pursuit of them.

Coming
Home

BOOK THREE

COMING HOME

The English Channel, Easter 1173

A gentle breeze came wafting in from the sea, driving wisps of clouds before it as a shepherd would his sheep. Many ships had set sail in recent days to take advantage of the fine weather and were now plying the seas like so many little nutshells with billowing sails. The sea was calm, with a promise of a pleasant journey. Ellen sat on the deck, lost in thought. Since Madeleine's death they had been fleeing Thibault and finally had found a safe haven for the winter in L'Aigle Castle. They knew they could no longer work at tournaments because of the danger of running into Thibault there.

The more Ellen thought about her future, the greater she felt her homesickness. She looked over at Rose, who was sitting nearby. It was evident the girl had a guilty conscience. She had fled without a cent a few months earlier and since then had been unable to save anything. She had nothing left and could not even afford the fare for the voyage. If the pony had not died of colic shortly before they left L'Aigle, Ellen would have at least been able to sell him to pay for the trip. But under the circumstances, she had had no choice but to dispose of Athanor, not as she wished by giving it to William, but by selling it to a merchant.

She smiled as Rose looked over at her and was happy she and Jean were going to England with her. A smile played on her lips at the thought of returning home. In her mind's eye the meadows around Orford were indescribably green and full of flowers, and her mouth began to water at the thought of Aelfgiva's tasty goat cheese. She propped herself up and tried to find a more comfortable sitting position. In the past five months she had put on a lot of weight. She was now in her ninth month, her belly was round as a ball, and her legs were so swollen that the anklebones were no longer visible. Ellen could feel a pulling in her back and said a quick prayer that the Lord would see to it she reached the English mainland before the child was born.

The second night on board she felt strong cramps in her lower abdomen, and by morning she could no longer bear the pain. She looked around for Jean. His blanket lay rumpled up beside her. Then she turned to Rose, took her by the arm, and shook her out of her sleep. "Rose, the child is coming," she said.

"What?" Rose was seized with panic. "Oh, God, what shall I do?"

"Go and get Jean!" Ellen knew Rose wouldn't be able to help her much. Thibault had forced her to dispose of two more children. Finally, she convinced him to let her keep the last child, but it was stillborn.

Jean would know what to do, she was convinced of that.

When he arrived, he stroked her forehead gently. "Well, then let's go ahead and do it," he said cheerfully. "Rose, ask around and see if anyone knows what to do when you're having a baby."

"The men, too, or only the women?"

Ellen groaned.

"Only the women, Rose, and keep calm, everything will be fine," he assured her, patting her on the arm.

He is much too grown-up for his age, Ellen thought, slightly dazed, but also grateful that he would take care of everything.

Shortly afterward, Rose returned with a friendly-looking woman. Her clothing was simple, but cleaner than that worn by the other passengers. Jean spoke briefly with her, then asked Rose for help in taking Ellen to a quieter place.

"Ellenweore, this is Catherine, she'll help you," Jean finally said, introducing the woman.

"Don't worry, you can do it!" Catherine encouraged her. "I have five children," she said with a smile. "My two eldest are on board, too. I'll introduce you to them later."

Ellen tried hard to smile as well, but the birth pangs caused her to wince.

Catherine caressed her sympathetically.

"When it gets really bad, just scream. It actually doesn't help much, but it makes the whole thing a little easier to bear. And you two," she said, turning to Rose and Jean, "stand in front of her so everyone doesn't stand there gaping while she is delivering the child."

"Dying can't be any worse," Ellen moaned, gasping for air during a short pause in the contractions.

"You'll forget the pain soon enough," Catherine consoled her.

"Why did Eve have to take that apple?" Ellen said in a long moan. She had never liked the story of the Fall and Eve's responsibility for suffering that women had to endure.

"Give me a few blankets so we can make her a little more comfortable. Above all, her back needs to be well supported," Catherine ordered. "And she also needs water to drink. Giving birth makes you thirsty. And after that, something good to eat."

Ellen groaned again at the thought of food.

"Is this your first child?" Catherine asked, and Ellen nodded. "For a first time it seems to be going quickly. It took me two days!"

"Oh, my God!" Ellen's heart sank at the very thought it could last that long.

"No, no, don't worry, I don't think it will take you that long. My sister's first child came faster, too. Try to breathe deeply and regularly. That will help," Catherine advised her, and asked Rose to go and fetch a bowl of water, and to have some thread and a knife or scissors on hand if necessary.

"Why do you need thread?" Jean asked inquisitively.

"You have to tie the umbilical cord before you cut it off," Catherine explained patiently.

In the afternoon the child came into the world, feet first.

"It's a boy! Ellen, your premonition was right!" Rose exulted.

Catherine held the child up and slapped his backside. The child's skin was blue. First he coughed; then he screamed and with every breath seemed to turn a little redder. Quickly but gently Catherine rubbed the child down with oil and a little salt, and washed him in warm water the captain had sent them. Then she wrapped the child securely in the clean linen cloths that Ellen still had with her.

"What name will you give the child?" asked Rose, beaming.

"William!" She closed her eyes in exhaustion.

"Of course..." Rose smiled knowingly.

Ellen carefully stroked her son's tiny cheeks with her finger. The child would probably never know his father, but at least he should bear his name.

The baby began to pout his lips as if he were sucking.

"You have to nurse him, he's hungry!" Catherine explained, visibly moved.

Ellen could feel a sense of displeasure coming over her and didn't move.

"Ellenweore!" Catherine shouted, and Ellen was startled as if being roused from a bad dream.

Of course she would nurse her child and do everything she could to be a good mother, even if her own bad experiences kept her from knowing exactly what that meant. Timidly she bared her breast.

"Come, I'll show you how to do that." Catherine placed one hand underneath the child's head and with her other hand pinched Ellen's breast so the nipple protruded.

Little William reached out for the breast avidly as soon as it touched his mouth. He sucked on the nipple firmly and evenly, but it seemed to Ellen as if her breast was as barren as a dried-up well.

"It will take a little while for the milk to come," Catherine explained, as if she could read Ellen's thoughts. "Let him suck as often as he wants to, and soon the milk will start to flow by itself."

"I'm hungry, too," Ellen whimpered. Her body felt beaten down, yet she was fully awake.

"Here!" said Rose, handing her a slice of coarse bread with savory lard and salt.

"Thank you!" Ellen wolfed down the bread in just a few bites.

"Now, we don't even know if you are an Englishman or a Norman," she whispered to her child.

After William had fallen asleep, the ship's captain performed an emergency baptism since it was not possible to know if the little boy would survive the next few days.

"Now go to sleep yourself, Ellen," said Rose, "and I'll keep an eye on William. You have to rest, because after we arrive in

London we still have a long trip ahead of us. If he gets hungry, I'll wake you up."

Ellen lay down, and the gentle rocking of the ship soon put her in a deep, restful sleep.

Ellen learned from Catherine how to put diapers on the child, and as she did that she couldn't help noticing that his left foot looked different from the right one. It was crooked and turned inward.

"It's certainly nothing serious," Catherine assured her. "Infants' legs are often crooked right after birth, and later they straighten out. He'll grow out of it. Just always wrap him as tightly as you can. And just look how sweet his little feet are," she replied with delight, stretching one out toward Ellen.

Hesitantly Ellen breathed a kiss on it.

"You shouldn't do that too often, or it will take him too much time to learn to walk!" Catherine laughed and shook her finger at Ellen.

"Then I won't do it again, I promise!" Ellen stammered guiltily and wrapped the boy even tighter in the cloth. For the first time since she had left Orford she had someone who really belonged to her and she had to care for. She would try to do everything right and teach William all he needed to know. The only thing she couldn't figure out yet was how to explain to Osmond and Leofrun that she had a son but no husband. So many years had passed since she had fled, and at least she wouldn't have to be afraid of Leofrun and Sir Miles.

After she had wrapped up the child, Rose picked him up and carried him around for a while. Jean did not leave her side, and they could both have easily passed for the parents of the child.

Ellen's thoughts turned sadly to Jocelyn and then, full of longing, to her beloved William, whom she would probably never see again. Was it her fate never to be happy?

—

At noon they arrived in the harbor of London, and most of the people who were not seafarers were green about the gills. The wind had picked up in the morning and caused the ship to pitch and toss as it entered the Thames.

When Catherine learned that the four of them were supposed to be continuing their travel that very day, she suggested they remain in London as her guests. "Edward, Nigel, come here!" she called out to her two eldest sons. They came running over and politely bowed to their mother. She patted them lovingly on the head. Edward, the older one, was the very image of his mother and had the same full, chestnut-brown hair. Nigel must have taken after his father, because his hair was finer, smoother, and as black as a raven's feathers. "Your father will come to pick us up. Don't forget to greet him properly," she reminded the boys firmly.

Only after the ship had been tied up and a wooden gangway put out could the travelers disembark. It was a strange feeling for them to have solid ground under their feet once again. Staggering slightly, they took their first steps on shore.

Ellen recognized Nigel's father at once in the crowd. He was tall, good-looking, and dressed very elegantly.

"Father, Father!" the two boys cried out, waving.

Rose was so impressed with the man's stately appearance that she just stood there gaping.

At first he eyed his wife's companions suspiciously, but after Catherine had whispered something in his ear he smiled cordially and invited them to be their guests for the next few days.

When they entered the house on Wine Merchants Street, Jean nudged Rose. "Have you ever seen such a beautiful house?"

he whispered. His gaze wandered admiringly over the colorful wall coverings and the heavy oak furniture.

"No, at least not from the inside," she answered, equally impressed.

Catherine's husband had to have a very successful business, as there were a number of servants, maids, and a cook to care for them.

A little girl with big eyes and black curly hair came rushing into Catherine's arms crying, "Mama!"

The younger children had stayed home while Catherine and the two older boys had visited their family in Normandy. The two other children also embraced their mother joyfully. Then the nanny came out and took the little ones into the kitchen.

"Would you like to take a bath?" Catherine asked her guests. Ellen nodded vigorously at once. "Oh yes, bathing…that was so long ago!"

Rose and Jean were somewhat more restrained but finally nodded as well. They didn't want to make a bad impression in such a fine house.

"Then I'll tell them to heat some water in the kitchen."

"But, my dear, you must know that Alfreda has been busily preparing for your arrival since this morning and heating enough water so you and our sons can have a nice bath." The wine merchant beamed at his wife's happy smile.

"You are right, my dear. Alfreda simply thinks about everything." Turning to Ellen she continued: "When we married, my father-in-law gave her to me. She raised my dear husband, and at first I found it a bit hard to accept that she always knew everything better than I did. Today I can't do without her."

"I think Edward and Nigel will let our guests go first and bathe later." The wine merchant waited for a response from his sons. Since they were well-mannered, they nodded politely even if they seemed a bit disappointed.

"Of course, Father," they said and left the room with him as he had indicated they should.

"I'll leave you alone for a moment. Come, sit here by the fire," Catherine said with a welcoming gesture, and followed the rest of her family.

No sooner had she left the room than Rose began to talk excitedly. "I noticed her right away on the ship because she is so beautiful. Her children are so lovable, and even in her simple linen dress she positively radiates elegance! Certainly she will put on some finer clothes later on."

"Well, I don't know, it's all a little too fine for me, too happy and orderly. Things like that always make me suspicious." It was evident Jean felt uncomfortable in the elegant house.

A short time later when Catherine returned, she seemed a little tense but tried hard not to let it show.

The bath in the wine merchant's house was for Ellen a wonderful experience. The maids laid a board over the wooden tub and served a luxurious meal of chicken, cold roast, bread, and a piece of cheese. There was also a large cup of wine spiced with cloves. Ellen ate it all with gusto while the warm water softened her skin until it became wrinkled. Alfreda had put rosemary branches in the water, and they had a wonderful fragrance. The old maid rubbed Ellen's back, cleaned her neck and ears, and then washed her hair with a bar of something she called olive soap. To judge by the fuss Alfreda made about it, it had to be something special and costly. Ellen was ashamed to see how dirty the water was when she had finished bathing.

Rose had gotten into the second tub along with little William. First she bathed the infant, then gave him to the nanny who dried him off and put him in fresh diapers.

"I feel like a new person. It was simply wonderful!" Ellen told Catherine with gratitude after she had gotten dressed again. She was wearing the green dress that Lady Bethune had given her for Claire's wedding. It was a bit rumpled from the trip but more or less clean. Her long hair was wet and curly, but it wasn't dripping anymore because the maid had given her a good rubdown with a linen cloth.

"Could Alfreda possibly wash my clothes?" Ellen asked her hostess shyly. "There are still blood spots on them from the birth."

"But of course! We'll also give Rose and Jean something to change into; then all your clothes can be washed before you resume your trip." Catherine smiled, but she no longer looked as happy as she had been the last few days.

"I'm sure you're tired. We should all go and have a rest. Elias will show you to your bed," she said nervously, and smiled sadly. Ellen was astonished. The sun had set just a short time ago, and it was customary to sit together and talk with guests.

Nevertheless, Ellen replied cordially, "Please give our warmest thanks to your husband," she said, "and sleep well!" She took Catherine's hand and kissed it.

Rose and Jean had also noticed the strangely melancholic tone of Catherine's voice.

"Certainly her husband is not at all the friendly, good-natured person he pretends to be. I said right away that something is wrong here," Jean said excitedly once they were back in the little room near the office.

"Who knows what happened? Don't always make such hasty judgments. You saw in Ruth's case that you are not always right." Ellen was angry. Instead of being concerned about the sudden change of mood of their benefactress, Jean was immediately suspicious of someone he didn't even know.

Rose, who had been mostly silent until then, interrupted. "She looks homesick," she said.

"Oh, come on, what nonsense, she's home now," Jean grumbled.

The next morning Alfreda brought a message from Catherine expressing her regrets to her guests that she had things to do.

The maid suggested they go sightseeing in the city. She gave Ellen a long piece of cloth and showed her how to tie it on to carry little William in front of her. Greybeard sniffed it curiously and licked William's diapers.

Though none of them really wanted to do that, they set out on their way. There were thick, grey clouds overhead, and a foul-smelling haze lay over the city. The less affluent lanes in town were filled with pigs and rats looking for something to eat in the mud. Ellen and the others took only a short walk and then returned.

It was unusually quiet in the wine merchant's house—no laughter of children or any other sound could be heard, even though surely everyone was still there.

When evening came, Catherine again sent a message of regret to her guests.

The wine merchant tried to entertain them and asked one of his servants to play something for them on the flute, but the mood remained somber.

Ellen was out of sorts and soon asked to be excused.

Rose and Jean accompanied her.

"If she doesn't want to sit at the same table with simple people like us, she could have sent us to the kitchen or even better not have invited us at all," Ellen said with chagrin.

"Perhaps it isn't her fault at all," Jean speculated. "Who knows whether her husband might be behind this. Perhaps he doesn't want her to eat with us and has locked her up!"

Ellen looked at Jean angrily at first, but then she softened her tone a bit. "You may be right—and that may be why she looked so sad just after she arrived. We've got to find out what the problem is." Catherine's behavior seemed more than strange to Ellen.

"We ought to leave. I don't feel comfortable here," Jean urged. "What do you think, Rose?"

"We ought to start out for Ipswich first thing tomorrow, don't you agree, Ellen?"

"I agree, but not before we are sure that Catherine is all right. If he has locked her up, we have to do something. He is certainly still downstairs. I'll sneak upstairs right now and go into their room," she said boldly.

"For heaven's sake, be careful!" Rose said anxiously.

Ellen put her finger to her mouth and quietly opened the door. The hall was dark. Carefully she left and started up the stairs. She was just about to open the door when suddenly Alfreda appeared before her carrying a torch and looked at her intently.

"I just wanted to say a quick good-bye to Catherine—we are leaving early tomorrow," Ellen explained hesitantly.

Alfreda opened the door without a key, as it was not locked.

Catherine lay in a huge bed in the middle of the room. The curtains were not drawn completely.

"I don't think she is sleeping," Alfreda said, urging Ellen to come closer.

"Catherine, I wanted to say good-bye, as we are continuing our trip tomorrow." Ellen spoke hesitantly in order not to wake the mistress of the house if she was sleeping.

"Ellenweore?"

"Yes."

"I am not well. Please excuse me for not spending the evening with you."

"Of course, we are just concerned. May I sit down with you for a little while?"

Catherine nodded silently. There was nothing in her pale, tired-looking face resembling the young, vigorous woman they had met a few days ago on the ship.

"What is wrong with you?"

"Oh, Ellen, I hate this house, London, the weather here, just everything about it!"

"Does he lock you in your room? Does he mistreat you?" Ellen bent down over her, concerned.

"My husband?" Catherine sat up a bit and looked with surprise at Ellen. "No! He would do anything for me, but I am simply not happy in England. As often as I can I travel to Normandy where my parents have a large estate. That's the only place where I feel really happy."

Ellen had trouble concealing her lack of understanding. How was it possible that a woman so fortunate, so wealthy, and with such a good husband and wonderful children could be unhappy?

"I am so indebted to you, Catherine," she said, taking Catherine's delicate hand in her own. It sounded like an apology.

"I am a bad person!" Catherine sighed, turning aside so that Ellen would not see her face.

"What makes you think something like that?" Ellen scolded her. "You are kindness itself!"

"Don't you see the affluence all around me? The children, my husband, the house, my clothes—nobody could be kinder, nothing could be better or nicer, but I am always sad. If I cannot breathe the fresh air of Normandy, I feel constricted. It's as if I am suffocating. I can't stand the stench of London, the misery in the narrow lanes. Even when I stay home it haunts me. But I also cannot escape the reproach in the eyes of my husband and my children. They all think I'm ungrateful, a bad wife and mother. And they are right." Catherine tossed and turned in the bed, sobbing.

"Why don't you just get up and change all that? Go downstairs and keep him company. Laugh with your children and be happy. You have every reason to be!" Ellen noticed a tone of reproach in her voice, but she simply couldn't understand why Catherine was so unhappy. There were so many people suffering greater misery, people whose lives were a constant challenge because of sickness, hunger, or physical frailties they had to face every day.

Catherine did not reply.

"I'll pray for you," Ellen said softly, stroking her head. Who could ever know why God was tormenting her with these doubts?

Catherine just kept staring at the wall.

Ellen got up and quietly left.

When she returned to their room next to the office, Jean and Rose pleaded with Ellen to tell them exactly what happened.

Jean seemed a bit disappointed that the wine merchant was not a rogue but actually someone to be pitied because his wife became melancholy as soon as she entered his house, and Rose was so moved that she cried a little.

—

Before leaving the next morning, they visited their host to say good-bye.

"I spoke with Catherine last night," Ellen told the wine merchant, "and I know now why she is so unhappy, even if I don't understand it."

"I'll go back to Normandy with her again soon," he said. "Together with the children. I do love her, and when we are there she is so…" He couldn't seem to find the words.

"Lively?" Ellen asked, tilting her head to one side.

"So lively, yes," he sighed.

"She gave you wonderful children," Ellen said, trying to console him.

"Yes, she did," he nodded.

As they were leaving, he patted Jean on the shoulder and shook Rose's hand. Ellen hugged him.

"In Normandy she will be yours again," she whispered in his ear.

His eyes sparkled with tears as he nodded silently.

—

They left London through the Aldgate in the east and then followed the highway heading in a northeast direction.

They stopped regularly so Ellen could nurse little William and in this way made slow progress on the long journey to Ipswich. The closer they got, the more nervous Rose became.

"Didn't you want to see if your mother is here?" Jean asked when they arrived in town. Rose drew a deep breath.

"I just want to go to the lane where the house was and see if she still lives there."

"Shall we come along?" Ellen asked.

"No, don't bother, I'll go alone. We'll meet later at Cornhill."

"And what shall we do while we're waiting?" Jean looked at Ellen, wondering.

"We'll see if Donovan and Glenna have come back. I think I owe them some explanation."

"Donovan? Isn't that the smith you told me about?"

"Indeed, my master! The best, but also the strictest."

Each occupied with his or her own thoughts, they headed toward the outskirts of town. When the smithy appeared in the distance, Ellen became restless.

"I'm afraid of the scolding I am going to get from him, and of the disappointment in his eyes."

"In whose eyes?" Jean looked at her, bewildered.

"Donovan's. That's his smithy," she said, pointing at the workshop.

"Oh, I see!"

Ellen headed directly to the smithy. Had Donovan returned, had he decided to remain in Tancarville, or had he perhaps been dead for years? She could hear hammering in the shop and hesitantly opened the door. It was dark and smoky as always in the smithy. She stepped in and saw two men working together on a piece of metal. One of them had tousled white hair.

"Llewyn!" Ellen exclaimed.

The smith looked at her questioningly. "What can I do for you?"

Ellen glanced at the second smith.

"Where is Donovan?"

"Did you know him?" Llewyn asked, looking at her closely. "He died shortly before Christmas."

Ellen held her breath. Though she could have expected that, the news hit her like a thunderbolt.

"And Glenna?" she added in a soft voice.

Llewyn squinted, as if there was something about her that was familiar.

"She's over at the house. She's gotten old since Donovan died. But please, dear woman, tell me who you are. Where have we met before?"

"In Framlingham," Ellen replied, and gave Llewyn a moment to reflect.

"Really?"

"I worked for you as a smith's assistant by the name of Alan, but my real name is Ellenweore." She turned her eyes down so she wouldn't have to look at him directly. "It was the only way for me to become a smith then," she admitted.

Llewyn said nothing, and this time Ellen looked at him directly.

"So you lied to me," he said softly.

"Please understand, I had no choice."

"You could have trusted me."

"And run the risk you would throw me out? No, Llewyn, I couldn't do that."

"Did you lie to Donovan as well?"

Ellen nodded. "That's the reason I'm here. I wanted to explain that to him."

"It's too late for that." Llewyn sounded bitter. "It was also too late for me to settle my dispute with him. When Glenna sent the striker to me, Donovan was already too sick. He was no longer conscious when I arrived."

"Llewyn!" Ellen placed her hand on his arm. "He loved you like a son."

Llewyn exhaled audibly. "Shortly before he died, he seemed to become very lucid again. He looked at me and I thought he had forgiven me, but then he turned away without saying a thing."

"Llewyn, I know how much you meant to him, believe me!"

Little William whimpered in his sleep like a kitten. Ellen straightened the scarf around her shoulder because he was beginning to feel heavy.

"Do you have a child?"

"His name is William." She nodded and smiled timidly.

"Go over to the house and talk with Glenna. I think she will be happy to see you. She always wanted to have children."

"Are you coming along?"

"No, I still have something to do. Just go ahead by yourself."

Ellen felt discouraged as she left the smithy again.

Jean was lying in the grass in front of the shop playing with Greybeard.

"Donovan is dead. I am just going to stop and see Glenna for a moment," she explained.

"I'll wait here for you." Jean, setting the right tone as always. "Shall I take the little one for you?"

"That's not necessary, I'll take him along."

When Ellen knocked on Glenna's door, her heart was pounding.

"Ellen!" Glenna cried in astonishment on opening the door. She didn't sound in the least bit put out. At first Ellen didn't wonder how Glenna had recognized her at once. "Come in, child!" She took her by the sleeve and guided her into the house.

"I'm so happy to see you are well!" She took Ellen's face in her hands and looked her straight in the eye. "Donovan waited for you until his last breath. 'She'll come, Glenna, I'm sure of that,' he always said."

Not until that moment did Ellen realize that Glenna knew everything. "But how…I mean, that I'm not a…" Ellen looked down in embarrassment.

"A squire came to see Donovan in the smithy. He made fun of him because he had let himself be duped by a little slut, as he called you. Donovan was furious. At first he just complained about you because you had deceived him, but with time he changed his tune and spoke very enthusiastically about your abilities, and later he told me you rather had no other choice. He admitted he never would have taken you on as a girl, but the longer you were gone the more he missed you. Arnaud tried very hard to take your place, and he is no doubt not a bad smith, but he couldn't replace you. I am certain that Don's spirit will finally be at peace now that you have returned. He wanted you to know he forgave you." Glenna stroked Ellen's cheek. "How is it possible we never noticed you were a girl?" Uncomprehending, she shook her head and her eyes wandered to the tiny bundle on her chest. "Heavens, who is that?"

"Glenna, may I introduce you to my son? This is William."

"My, how small he is!" Glenna exclaimed excitedly.

"He was born last week in the English Channel."

Glenna's eyes sparkled. "And your husband?"

Ellen just shook her head silently.

"Then why don't you stay? Ellen, please! Llewyn inherited the smithy. He does a good job but is still alone. You could marry and have more children. And I would help take care of them."

"I've got to go back to my father, Glenna. I haven't seen him since I left Orford, and that is so long ago!"

Glenna nodded sadly. "Then at least stay for something to eat."

"I'm not alone. I have a friend with me, and Rose—do you remember her?"

"Why of course! At the time I thought you were in love with her." Glenna grinned sheepishly. "You are all welcome for dinner, and for the night as well, if you wish."

—

Ellen and Jean picked up Rose at Cornhill and returned with her to the smithy, where they spent a happy evening indulging in reminiscences of the past.

Llewyn told about his most recent projects, Glenna and Rose talked about Tancarville, and the only one to remain silent was Jean. Only after the evening was already far advanced did it occur to Ellen that they had been speaking English the entire time, but Jean understood only Norman French.

"Good heavens, Jean," said Ellen, speaking in French and looking at him sympathetically. "I didn't even think about your having to learn English now!"

"Fortunately, Rose taught me a few words. There was a lot I didn't understand, but I did comprehend a bit. It's just that speaking it is so hard. The way you speak English it sounds like you have a hot chestnut in your mouth." He grinned mischievously, and everyone at the table laughed, even Llewyn, who hadn't understood a word of what Jean said.

The rest of the evening they spoke a mixture of French and English.

Glenna stumbled over every Norman word she spoke. "I never really learned it, and what I did I quickly forgot. I thought I'd never need it again," she proclaimed cheerily.

—

"Come and visit us again soon!" The next morning, Glenna took Ellen in her arms and hugged her a long time.

Llewyn, usually deliberate and thoughtful, nodded vigorously and embraced them all one after the other, especially Jean. "You are always welcome here."

Rose was quieter than on the previous evening.

"Will you stop and see your mother?" Jean inquired anxiously. Rose had told them how her mother had abused her so badly and thrown her out of the house.

"No, there's no point in that. Anyway, she has found someone to replace me in her life."

"What do you mean by that?" Ellen looked at her in surprise.

"She quickly married again after I left. Now I have a sister and a brother. The girl sells fish pasties, just as I used to. You see, my mother doesn't need me." Rose looked down. Her dress was simple and already a bit tattered. "If I were rich, she would surely have taken me back with open arms."

Orford, May 1173

As they approached Orford, Ellen suddenly stopped in the middle of the road, as if rooted to the spot. With irritation she put her hand up over her eyes to get a better view ahead and then looked around carefully.

"What's wrong?" Jean asked. He didn't see anything strange.

"The castle!" Ellen pointed ahead. "We must have taken a wrong turn."

"No! That's impossible." Jean looked at her with annoyance. "The monk told us to stay on this path, so we should be there soon."

"But there never was a stone castle in Orford."

"Maybe you just don't remember."

"Nonsense!" Ellen sounded irritated.

"Maybe the castle was built after you left," Rose interjected.

Ellen grumbled something unintelligible and kept walking.

The closer they got to the castle, the clearer it became that it had in fact been built just recently. The long stone wall of the castle and the dark oak wood walk along the battlements looked new, and the stone drawbridge over the moat was not yet finished. They approached the castle complex with curiosity and looked through the open gate. The stone keep had an unusual shape. It looked as if three square towers and an entrance building had been constructed around a circular tower.

"Have you ever seen a keep like that?" Jean asked.

Ellen shook her head, examined it carefully, and would have walked closer if the guard at the gate had not waved her off. She turned around to Jean.

"It's brilliant! The corners of an ordinary square tower can easily be undermined, and in this way the entire keep can be toppled. This one, though, would be much harder to destroy," Ellen declared enthusiastically.

"How do you know all that?" Jean asked in astonishment.

"William told me!" Ellen sighed, and Jean nodded knowingly.

"Do you have any idea who might have built this castle?"

Ellen shook her head. "No, but Osmond will surely be able to tell us a lot about it. Come, let's go to the smithy. I can hardly wait to see everything again." Ellen was very familiar with the way home from that point. At the fork in the road she hesitated for a moment. The road to the right went to the tanner's cabin. She wondered what had happened with Simon. With determined steps she finally took the road to the left, which led to her parents' smithy. The shop and house were still there and looked unchanged, as if she had just left the day before.

Ellen was startled when the door to the shop flew open and a boy came out. He was about the same age as she had been when she left Orford and was the very image of Osmond. Ellen sighed with relief. At least Leofrun hadn't forced him to take an illegitimate child of Sir Miles! The boy dashed over to the house, and shortly afterward a woman came out. At first Ellen feared it could be her mother, but then she ran off.

"Mildred? Mildred!" she called out, running toward her sister.

Jean and Rose, who were carrying little William, came along behind.

Joyfully the two sisters embraced.

"Ellenweore!" Mildred stroked her sister's cheeks lovingly, as if she were the elder of the two.

The door to the house opened, and the boy came out again. Mildred motioned for him to come over.

"This is Leofric, our brother!" Mildred said, taking Ellen by the hand. "Leofric, this is Ellenweore. Do you remember me telling you about her?"

The boy nodded shyly and held out his hand.

Ellen shook it firmly and vigorously.

"And how is Osmond? And Mother?" asked Ellen, turning from her brother back to Mildred.

"Mother died shortly after Leofric was born, and since then Father has become practically blind. He can't work. He has a journeyman, but..." Mildred shook her head disapprovingly. "He's not much good. As soon as I leave he starts showing off, as if he's the master. But I can't always be here—I have my own family!" Mildred pulled Ellen a little closer and asked, "Tell me, how have things gone for you? And why did you run away back then?"

"I'll tell you all about it later, Mildred. First I'd like to introduce you to my friends Rose and Jean. And the little fellow is my son."

"You got married? Oh, how wonderful! Tell me, who is it, and where is he?"

Ellen could feel the piercing gaze of Rose and Jean behind her as she made up her story.

"Jocelyn was a goldsmith. He was attacked and killed by robbers," she said briefly. She didn't claim she was married to Jocelyn or even that he was the father of her son.

"Oh, you poor thing! Now the child has to grow up without a father!" Mildred shook her head compassionately. "Let's go right into the smithy. You have no idea how happy Father will be that you are back, and that you're bringing his first grandson! I have just one daughter." Mildred took Ellen by the arm and motioned for the two others to come along.

Old Osmond cried uncontrollably, embraced Ellen, and held her in his arms for a long time. "Every day I have prayed that you would come back!" he whispered in her ear. "And finally God has heard me!"

"Ellen brought you a grandson, Father," Mildred exclaimed.

"Not so loud, child! I'm almost blind but not deaf." He turned his head in the direction the sound came from, then turned back to Ellen. "Is that true, you have a son?"

"Yes, Father." Looking at him face to face, she couldn't manage to call him by his name, Osmond, though she had known for a long time that he wasn't her real father. She motioned to Rose to come closer, and took little William in her arms.

"Here, you can hold him. He's still very small, only ten days old."

Osmond was overjoyed and cried softly as he rocked the child in his arms. He bent down until his nose touched the child's head. "Mm, he smells so good! Just as you did then," he said happily as he rocked the child gently back and forth.

Ellen looked around in the smithy and frowned. Tongs, blocks of iron, and hammers lay around everywhere. Even the expensive files weren't where they belonged. The ground was all covered with tinder and dust and had obviously not been swept for a long time.

Osmond's journeyman looked sullenly at the unexpected guests.

"Let's go over to the house. Adam can make out fine here by himself," Osmond suggested. "You carry the child, Ellen, I'm afraid I'm going to fall. I've stared into the fire too much all my life and am blind," he declared.

Osmond told Ellen that after Leofrun's death he had had a nurse in the house to care for the boy, and had married her soon after. Anna had been a good wife to him, and like a mother to Leofric. But last winter when she went to fetch water, she fell into a brook that was almost frozen over and tragically drowned. Even then, Osmond's eyes hadn't been very good, but Anna had taken care of everything. Only after her death did Adam begin to put on airs, as if he were head of the household.

"Father, if you like, I'd love to stay here," Ellen said.

Jean and Rose looked at her in shock.

"I could even train Leofric as a smith myself and also teach Jean, if he wants to stay with us. Then you wouldn't need Adam anymore. Rose is a marvelous cook, and maybe we can persuade her to take care of us! I couldn't imagine a better substitute for a father for William than you. What do you think?" Ellen glanced around at the group and winked at her youngest brother conspiratorially, as if they had known each other for years.

Osmond nodded happily. His clouded eyes were brimful of tears. "Thank you, Lord," he whispered.

"Do you also agree?" she asked, turning to her friends.

Rose and Jean exchanged glances and grinned. "Agreed!" they said in unison.

"Well, then, welcome home!" cried Osmond in a voice that was rasping and hoarse, but full of joy.

The next day Mildred set out for St. Edmundsbury to join her family. "I'm really happy you'll be staying with Osmond," she said, visibly relieved.

"You don't have to worry, I'll take care of everything."

"I'm sure of that, Ellen." Mildred looked at her sister just as devotedly as she had as a child.

"Come back soon!"

"I'll try, but it won't happen that fast!" Mildred let Jean help her into the saddle and rode off.

Ellen waved as she left and then went back to the smithy.

Adam was sitting on a stool, picking his teeth and looking bored. He didn't respond to Ellen's greeting.

"My father is too old to work here," she told him calmly, "so I will be taking over the smithy."

"First a doddering, blind old man and then a woman for a master." He shook his head condescendingly. "Who ever heard of something so silly? Nobody will buy anything from you," he jeered at her, "unless we don't tell anyone."

"We?" Ellen drew the word out longer than necessary. "For the time being, I won't be able to afford a helper." She shrugged, trying to look sorry.

"You're going to throw me out? I wouldn't advise you to do that. If I tell everybody who will be heating the forge from now on, nobody will come. I know every one of your customers and have good connections with the castle," he boasted.

"I'll pay your wages until the end of the week, but you can leave now." Ellen tried to sound calm even though she was quite angry with Adam. To look at the disorder in the smithy, he didn't deserve three days' salary, but he clearly wasn't guilty of any serious misconduct, so she had no choice.

"You'll regret this," Adam spluttered, "bitterly!" He hastily put his things together and left without saying another word.

Ellen was happy that Osmond was not present for this confrontation. Adam's words would have offended him deeply. She rubbed her hands together, happy this unpleasant conversation was behind her. "So let's get going," she mumbled to herself, and began cleaning up the workshop.

—

"Adam didn't take care of your tools. The tongs are rusty, the files are dull, and it looks like he stole some things. How many files did you have, Father?" Ellen asked Osmond when he came to the smithy.

"Five, and very good ones! I bought them all over a period of years from Iven in Woodbridge, the best file maker I know," he answered proudly.

"Five!" Ellen hissed. "Then he took two along with him, that scoundrel!"

Jean looked at her, wide-eyed. "That's not so bad, is it?"

"Not so bad? A file costs more than a journeyman makes in four months!"

Ellen and Jean spent two days cleaning up the shop, sorting out the tools, scraping off the rust, and finally oiling them.

"Tomorrow we'll begin with the actual work. We need a few tools that we can make here, and then we'll try to get some new orders," Ellen declared with satisfaction.

In the middle of the night, she was suddenly shaken out of her sleep by Rose.

"Ellen, quick! Get up!"

"What's the matter?"

"The shop is on fire! Jean is over there already."

Ellen jumped up and ran outside in her nightshirt.

The roof of the smithy was ablaze, and even though they all fought the flames, fetching bucket after bucket of water to put on the fire, there was not much they could do. It was a desperate, senseless struggle.

When the fire was finally out, they stood there dumbfounded, looking at the enormous damage. The entire roof truss was gone. The stone walls of the smithy were black with soot, but fortunately still standing. But building a new roof would be a costly undertaking.

"This was no accident, I'm sure of that. This was Adam," Ellen said angrily, after she and the others had spent the whole day picking up and carting away the rubble. Looking like a charcoal burner blackened with soot, she sat down at the table, eagerly drinking the cup of goat's milk that Rose set down in front of her.

"Ellen!" Osmond scolded her. "You shouldn't say anything like that. Adam was always a decent lad."

"Decent? Don't make me laugh, Father! He was deceiving you. As far as I can see, he took along the whole supply of iron, then the two files and various tongs—or did you perhaps never have a pair of wolf's jaw tongs?"

"But of course I did. Several, in fact." Osmond frowned.

"Not a single one is still there! And where do you keep your polishing stones for the knives?"

"In the oaken trunk in the storage room." Osmond looked shocked.

Ellen nodded. "That's what I thought. All that I found in there was dust. First he plundered the shop, and as a thank-you he set it on fire."

"How do you know that?" Osmond asked reluctantly.

"I am sure he hoped someday to be the master here. Then we got in the way of those plans." Ellen snorted briefly. "Now we really have to get some orders, and until the roof has been replaced we'll have to work outside insofar as the weather allows. First thing tomorrow morning I'll go to the castle, and then I'll look for a carpenter who can repair the roof. For the time being, my savings will be enough."

Ellen was lucky and did in fact return from the castle with an order. Young Henry along with his brothers had declared war on their father. The garrison in Orford was to be strengthened because of an expected attack from the sea.

"For now I have an order for five lances, two short swords, and three simple soldier's swords. If we can do this to their satisfaction—which should be no problem—we will receive more orders!"

"But what about Adam and the connections he spoke about?" Jean asked.

"That was just a pack of lies. His work was bad, and that's the reason he had less and less to do. The man I spoke with knew Donovan's reputation. I told him I was his apprentice and for this reason, and the fact there are no other weaponsmiths in this area, he was ready to overlook the fact I am a woman and give me the job. Naturally, I told him that the master would keep an eye on all the projects in our shop and that there are other men working in our smithy. By that I meant Osmond and the two of you." She grinned at Jean and Leofric. "Now it's up to us to convince them to give us more orders."

Jean took the opportunity to learn everything in the smithy that Ellen showed him and made quick progress, as did Leofric, who was young but likewise willing to learn.

Osmond could no longer work, and he spent the days either sitting in the shop listening to the rhythmic blows of the hammer or in the house with little William, whom he bounced up and down on his knees. After Ellen started working again in the smithy, her milk began to dry up and Osmond gave the boy lukewarm goat's milk, just as he had with Ellen years before.

At the same time, Rose never let him out of her sight.

Osmond did not complain, but Ellen knew how greatly he suffered from blindness and not being able to make himself useful.

Hardly anyone in Orford remembered Ellen. Many of the old residents were dead, and the young ones were too much occupied with their own affairs. The times were too turbulent for anyone to be concerned about a missing girl. Rumors did still circulate about ghosts wandering on the moors that kidnapped and ate children, but nobody was thinking of the smith's daughter in that regard.

Most people had also long ago forgotten Sir Miles. Thomas Becket's men disappeared overnight after their master fell out of favor with the king. In his anger at Becket's betrayal, Henry II revoked the rights of his former friend and confidant to Orford. The land reverted to the Crown, and very shortly thereafter and with a great expenditure of wealth the king had the castle built there. It was said he intended by that to make a statement about his power and offer a royal counterbalance to the power of Hugh Bigod, who ruled in Framlingham over a large part of East Anglia. Even though the construction of the castle had been extremely costly, the inhabitants of Orford waited in vain for a visit from their king. But since Thomas Becket had been murdered in Canterbury Cathedral only three years earlier and it was assumed, more or less secretly, that the king was responsible, many Englishmen wavered in their feelings toward King Henry. From all over the country pilgrims came streaming to Canterbury Cathedral to pay homage to Thomas Becket, and every time a miracle was reported, more people came to the gravesite. Even thought they had never set eyes on him, the inhabitants of Orford were filled with pride toward their former ruler. Word had gotten around that Becket was even going to be canonized. Since the murder of Becket, the king stood in the crossfire of opinions as a godless tyrant.

Rose and Jean, too, quarreled about the question of the king's guilt. People all over the country had divided opinions on this question.

Ellen had no opinion either way. She had never met Thomas Becket or the king, and if she didn't know either of them how could she know who was a better person? The only king she had ever seen was young Henry, the king who had no power, and she had seen him only a few times and from a distance at tournaments in Normandy. William had never said much about him except that he was young, extravagant, and wanted to be a hero. Just like all the noblemen his age, Ellen thought at the time. But she hesitated to make a judgment about his abilities as a ruler because she felt that wasn't for her to decide. Someday, when the Young King's father died, he would know how to rule his enormous kingdom—but he wouldn't have to bear the responsibility all by himself. Men like the Marshal would stand by him and assist him. The Young King would also be older and more mature and would learn how to do this right, just like kings before him.

Ellen knew practically nothing about the times before King Henry II. At her age she had no firsthand experience of the bad times under King Stephen, and the stories old people told of anarchy and unending war between Stephen and Mathilda seemed like ancient legends.

Ellen had one goal: to someday forge a sword for the King of England, and it was of no importance who this king was.

August 1173

Ellen sat on the banks of the Ore watching the wide river glittering in the sunlight. Along the shore the water washed through the reeds. She placed a hand over her eyes and gazed across a broad meadow alongside the river. In the distance she saw a man whose bouncing gait reminded her of her childhood friend. "Simon," she whispered, smiling. In recent weeks she had thought of him often but had not found the time to go and look for him. Now she asked herself if perhaps it was more a lack of courage than time that had kept her from doing so. With determination, she stood up. She would do it today. She wiped the water from her feet in the grass and slipped into her shoes.

Memories of the day she had fled came back to her as she crossed the meadow near the smithy. Up on the hill, the grass was as high as back in those days. But now, as a grown woman, it reached only to her hips. Without giving it a thought, Ellen headed not to the tannery but directly to the old cabin. The forest seemed much closer than she had remembered it. When she saw the cabin, she stopped dead in her tracks, and though the weather was warm and beautiful, she suddenly had goose bumps all over her body. The old cabin was in ruin, shoots of a young birch tree were growing through holes in the roof, and the door was off its hinges. Inside, the cabin was covered with grass, stinging nettles, and thistles.

"Recently I have been coming here often," she heard a deep voice saying behind her, and she wheeled around. For a moment she almost choked with anxiety, fearing it could be Sir Miles. The man who had spoken was somewhat taller than her, slender, and had powerful arms. Ellen hesitated a moment, then ventured, "Simon?" She finally recognized him by the little dimple on his left cheek when he grinned.

"I have been meaning for a long time to come over," he said, scratching himself nervously behind one ear.

"Same with me. It was a long time ago," Ellen replied softly.

"It's still the same flaming red..." Simon said, pointing at her hair. "Looks good." He shuffled his feet awkwardly in the dirt.

Ellen didn't know how to answer, so she remained silent.

"Would you like to come with me? My mother would be really happy..." Simon blushed. "I'm sure you won't recognize my brothers—they've all really grown up except for Michael. He was just a little fellow when you went away and is just beginning to get a little fuzz on his lip."

"Went away..." Ellen whispered. "Chased away would be more accurate."

Either Simon hadn't heard, or he pretended he hadn't. In any case, he didn't respond.

Silently she followed him along the same path through the woods that they had taken then. Sun was shining through the trees, casting a soft, peaceful light on the path, a gentle, refreshing breeze was blowing, bees were humming as busily as they did back then, and yet it was different. They had nothing more to fear, they were grown up, and nobody was pursuing them.

"I had forgotten how beautiful it is here."

Simon looked at her and nodded. "Since Sir Miles and his men left, yes, but before that you never knew. For a long time I thought the same thing would happen to me as it did to Aelfgiva. Did you hear about it?" He wiped his nose with the same gesture as before.

Ellen nodded. "Osmond spoke of it, but he didn't know any of the details. Do you know anything more about it?"

"After you were gone, she took your bloody clothes out to the moor. She told me what really happened, and I promised

I would never tell anyone. And I didn't, I swear!" Simon had stopped and looked Ellen in the eye with great earnestness. "You must believe me, I never revealed anything!"

"It's all right, Simon," Ellen reassured him. She had trusted him back then, and she still did.

"When Sir Miles's men found your clothes, they said you were eaten by the ghosts on the moor. I rubbed my eyes until they were red and acted as if I were crying. They all believed it, even my mother. By the following summer everything had quieted down and no one spoke of you anymore. It was as if you had never existed. That was until the day Aedith came for a visit. She told your mother she had seen you in Ipswich dressed as a boy. Shortly after that they found the badly maimed body of Aelfgiva not far from her cabin. Her lower jaw was completely smashed, and her face had swollen so much that she was hardly recognizable."

Ellen gasped in horror.

"My father was there when they found her, and he told me about it. For a long time after that I didn't dare leave the tannery, but I only realized later how foolish that was—there was really nothing Father could have done if Sir Miles had decided to pursue me! Once I met him when I went out with my father to cut trees. You should have seen how Sir Miles looked at us! I almost soiled myself, and quickly lowered my eyes. I think he enjoyed seeing how terrified I was, though I don't even know if he recognized me. Probably he didn't even know why I was so afraid of him. God, how I hated that dirty swine!" He spat on the ground to express his contempt. "Only after he had left did I feel free and safe again."

Ellen had turned pale. "It's all my fault Aelfgiva is dead!" she whispered despondently.

"Nonsense!" replied Simon. "The fault lies with Sir Miles and your mother, not you!"

"But if I had avoided Aedith back then in Ipswich instead of sticking out my leg to trip her up, nothing would have happened to Aelfgiva!"

"Stop tormenting yourself, Ellen! You couldn't know what was going to happen. It didn't bring your mother any happiness, either. She died less than three weeks after Aelfgiva's death, shortly after Leofric was born. I've often wondered if he is Sir Miles's son…"

"Fortunately, he looks like Osmond. Otherwise, I don't know if I could have stayed in that house with him under the same roof."

The two of them kept walking along slowly toward the tannery and could already smell its heavy odor in the air.

"It didn't bring any luck to Sir Miles, either. Almost one year to the day after Aelfgiva's death he had a hunting accident, fell from his horse and broke his neck. After that he had trouble walking, and when the king had Thomas Becket assassinated, he was the first of his men in Orford to vanish. I'm sure that Aelfgiva put a curse on both of them at the moment of her death." Simon appeared satisfied with that outcome.

Ellen had no objection to this sort of justice, either.

Hard work had given Simon's mother a gaunt look, but otherwise it was astonishing how little she had changed. She smelled just as strong as before and smiled lovingly at her son as soon as she saw him.

When Ellen walked up to her, she squinted and cried out, "By all the saints! So it's true, Ellenweore! You look well, like the very flower of life!" Her whole face beamed. She had only a single tooth left in her upper jaw and two in the lower. The rest must have rotted away. She took Ellen in her arms joyfully and held her tight. The strong tannery odor almost made Ellen ill, but she tried to be cordial and smiled at Simon's mother.

"And things are going well, too. I'm working again in the smithy."

Ellen stepped back a bit.

"The brush maker said just recently that there was a red-haired woman working in the smithy, but I couldn't believe it was really you." She turned around to her son. "Simon, did you know?"

"Hm..." he replied with some embarrassment.

"And until now you didn't bring her over to visit?" She laughed in disbelief. "He never forgot you, Ellenweore. His heart always belonged to you!"

Ellen blushed. "I think I'll have to return home. No one knows where I am, and Osmond gets worried so easily," she stammered.

"And who can blame him!" Simon's mother nodded with understanding and stroked Ellen's cheek with her gnarled fingers. Ellen smiled reluctantly and said good-bye.

"I'll go back a ways with you," Simon offered.

"That's not necessary, really," said Ellen, not looking him in the eye.

"Oh, but I will," he insisted. "I won't be able to sleep tonight until I know you are safely back home."

Simon's tender gaze was suddenly too much for Ellen to bear.

April 1174

"I'll get a horse from the stable and leave for Ipswich today. You can't imagine what I saw in Woodbridge yesterday," Ellen said excitedly as she entered the shop.

"Are you back already?" asked Jean and Leofric, looking at her questioningly. They hadn't expected her until the following day.

"An oculist! Do you know what an oculist is?" Ellen's cheeks glowed with excitement.

Leofric was the first to respond. "No, I have no idea. What is it?"

"I saw him in Woodbridge in the market square. He announced he could make blind people see again!"

"Oh, he probably thinks of himself as a miracle worker." Jean smirked. He had traveled too much in the company of magicians to believe in miracles. Most so-called miracles were not that at all. They alleged that they could heal the lame and give sight to the blind, who until just the day before had enjoyed perfect eyesight. Those allegedly sick people were members of the group of healers and saints and financially part of their success.

"Maybe you don't believe it, but I have seen it!"

"Oh, really?" Jean teased her.

"The man's eyes were completely white, just like Osmond's, but after the oculist had stuck a long needle in his eye, the white disappeared and the eye was clear again. The man cried with joy and swore that the pain of the operation had been worth it. I saw the whiteness in his eyes, and that is not something you can fake," she countered, insisting that the miracle was genuine. "I want the man to treat Osmond, as well, but it's expensive, and what with the fire and the long winter we haven't been able to save enough money yet. I'll ride to Ipswich and ask Kenny for money, or if necessary, Aedith."

Jean and Leofric exchanged glances and shrugged. "Well, if you think so..."

"I'll start out early, and I'll be back in a few days. The oculist will be in St. Edmundsbury soon, and we can spend the night there with Mildred." Ellen blew a kiss to them both. "You'll get along just fine without me, won't you? Jean, if the sergeant comes about the lance and you're not finished, tell him he'll have to wait a bit longer because I had to leave and there are only two of you here. Don't worry if he makes a fuss. And you, Leofric, clean the tools and get the shop in order. When I get back, every corner will be tidied up!" Jean grumbled while Leofric looked resigned. He had learned from experience that it was better to do what Ellen demanded.

The very next morning, Ellen rented a horse from the largest stable in Orford. For the first time she chose not a pony but a regular riding horse in order to get to Ipswich faster.

"Don't worry, it's as tame as a lamb and especially suited for a less experienced rider," the owner assured her, saddling up the plain-looking brown mare and putting its bridle on.

Simon was at that moment delivering leather to the stable, and when he heard of Ellen's plan he volunteered to accompany her.

Ellen declined politely. She liked Simon and knew how much he adored her, but the thought of being alone with him for a long period of time made her uneasy. People were talking about her too much already. She set out in haste and arrived in Ipswich before nightfall.

She rode directly to the Cloth Merchants Lane and knocked on Kenny's door. After what seemed an eternity, someone came shuffling to let her in.

A grim-looking servant stood in the doorway. “What do you want?” he demanded crossly.

“I’d like to see my brother.”

“Your brother?” he asked, irritated.

“Yes, I’d like to see Kenny.”

“Ah, I didn’t know he had a third sister,” he grumbled. “Come in, I’ll take you to him if you want, but you won’t like what you see.” Holding a small lantern, he lighted the way for her down a narrow corridor. “This way, follow me!” The lantern in his hand swung back and forth violently.

Ellen wondered anxiously what the servant might have meant with his comment as she followed him up a steep wooden staircase.

The oak door to Kenny’s room creaked loudly as it opened. At first Ellen saw only the huge pile of documents on the large desk, and then she saw her brother sitting behind it. He had to be about seventeen years old now, but he looked older. He grabbed a silver goblet and eagerly drank from it, then, squinting, leaned over the desk toward her. “Ellen?” he asked. The red wine flowed down his chin as he took another long gulp. “I’m happy that Aedith wasn’t lying, and that you are still alive!” he mumbled. Then he set the goblet down, wiped his mouth on his sleeve, and belched. “This is my last drop. All I have left is debts. In the last two years I have lost three shiploads,” he lamented in a voice full of self-pity. “And ever since Grandfather died, all my clients have left me as well.” He stared at Ellen with glassy eyes. “I’ll lose the house, my creditors are breathing down my neck, and there is nothing I can do. I can’t do anything right, not as a smith nor as a merchant, and I’ll end my days as a beggar.” In despair, Kenny took another swig from the goblet. “And what do you want?” he growled at his sister. “Do you want money from me like all the others?" He burst out laughing and gulped down the last of the wine.

Ellen didn't say why she had come. It was clearly not the right moment to talk with him about someone else's grief. She walked over to him, put her hand around his shoulder, and looked him in the eye. "You can come home anytime. You are always welcome in Osmond's house. You know that, don't you?"

Kenny groaned. "I'd be embarrassed to death."

"You were too young for such responsibility. If Grandfather had been able to be there for you longer, everything would have been different. Please, Kenny, there's always a way out, but this isn't the answer." Ellen pointed at the pitcher of wine. "May I stay here tonight? I want to go and see Aedith tomorrow. You know where she lives, don't you?"

"Of course I know, I still have some cloth to deliver to her. Unfortunately she has already paid for it, and I don't have a single bale of decent cloth left to give to her."

"She's your sister," Ellen said, trying to console him.

"And she'd send me to the gallows without blinking an eye if her husband were not such a reasonable man!"

"You're being too hard on her, Kenny," Ellen scolded.

"I'm as soft and pliable as a feather in comparison to her, but you'll see for yourself. It doesn't matter why you are going to see her tomorrow, she'll treat you like dirt, the way she treats everyone else. I'll show you the way to her house, but I won't go in with you." He turned away and mumbled something, shaking his head. "No, I won't do that."

Even though Kenny gave her Grandfather's old room, the one with the large bed, many pillows, and soft down comforter, she had a bad night's sleep, with too many doubts about what she planned to do. What could she do if Aedith actually refused to help? And what could she do for Kenny? She'd have to encourage him to come to Orford, and perhaps he actually could help a bit in the smithy. After all, he was Osmond's son, and there would certainly be something he could do. In the morning, she washed her face, neck, and hands, looked for the little bag of herbs in her pack, and cleaned her teeth. Taken with a little drink of water, the herbs left a refreshing taste in her mouth. She put on the green dress she had brought along for the visit to Aedith's house in the hopes of impressing her sister and convincing her to help. Although the dress was not the latest fashion, the material had a pretty sheen to it and in contrast with her other clothes was clean and didn't have any burn holes in it. Ellen combed her locks with her fingers and tied them together with a green ribbon.

Kenny went along with her to Aedith's house. He looked dreadful—too much wine and too many worries about money had left deep shadows around his swollen eyes. "I'll wait back there for you. I don't think you will be long." Kenny laughed bitterly. "It doesn't matter what you want from her, she'll first listen and then throw you out," he predicted.

Ellen walked over to the large door and knocked. A neatly dressed servant opened the door at once and asked politely what she wanted. He showed her into the courtyard and looked her up and down. He seemed to doubt that she was really the sister of his lady and asked her to wait. Before long Aedith appeared.

"Ellen!" she said with a smile, but her voice sounded as cold as a winter's night. She moved a few steps closer. "Let's have a look at you..." she said, taking Ellen by the hands and looking down at her. "Well," she said sarcastically, "in any case, I like you better this way than when you were dressed in boys' clothes."

"You look very well, Aedith!" Ellen tried hard to strike a conciliatory tone.

"Of course, and I do things to keep myself that way. Fortunately, I have no children—they just ruin your figure," she said in a harsh voice.

Kenny is right, Ellen thought. *She is just as disagreeable now as before.*

"I've come to ask you for help. Not for myself," she added quickly, as her sister's eyes narrowed to angry little slits.

"If it's that rascal Kenny who's sent you, then I've got to disappoint you. He won't get another penny from me. I paid for my last order in advance, because he asked me to. I'll probably never get to see the material." Aedith had stepped back and was looking at Ellen as if she were a traitor.

"I've heard about Kenny's problems, and perhaps you are even right with your doubts about the material, but I'm not here because of him, but because of Osmond."

"What does he want?" Aedith asked, her voice full of contempt.

Ellen had to get a good grip on herself not to kick her sister again in the shin.

"He's blind, Aedith. I'd like to take him to an oculist. Have you ever seen how they can restore sight to blind people?"

"Bah!" was all Aedith said.

"The oculist charges a lot of money. I work for Osmond, and we have plenty of work, but the winter was long and hard this year. In addition, the smithy burned down a while ago and I built it up again, but it took all my savings. We couldn't put much money aside, and we still need eight shillings for Father's treatment."

"My husband is old and ugly, and I'm really paying more than my share for my prosperity. And you dare to come here and beg me for money? How stupid to you think I am? Do you think I don't know that all you want is to have a life of luxury at my expense?"

Ellen was shocked at what Aedith suggested. "You're wrong, Aedith! I only want Osmond to get his eyesight back," she started to say. But when she saw Aedith's cold stare, she turned away. "Forget it, Aedith, just forget I was even here. Forget who we are and where you come from. I'll save the money and take him to the oculist next year." Ellen turned away and left her sister standing there. Angrily she slammed the front door behind her. "Such a silly goose," she muttered, and returned to the corner where Kenny was waiting for her. "I should have listened to you, that silly..."

"It's not worth it getting upset over her. You didn't tell me what you wanted from her, but I knew she wouldn't help. That's just the way she is—I think she enjoys being mean."

Ellen fell silent. She was much too angry to give any further thought to her sister. Instead, she asked her brother if she could stay one more night. Because Kenny's pantry was empty, she went out and bought a large meat pasty, flour, eggs, and a loaf of bread. Shortly before nightfall Ellen knocked at his door, and a few minutes later the old servant appeared and invited her to come in.

When she entered the main room, which was cold and unheated, she found an elegantly dressed old man sitting there in Kenny's armchair. He struggled to his feet and greeted her politely. He was shorter than she and looked very frail. His wrinkled face was framed in thinning grey hair that hung down in long strands to his shoulders. Though he had lost almost all his teeth, he had a distinguished look. "I am your brother-in-law," he said, introducing himself. His strong voice contrasted sharply with his frail appearance.

Ellen did not understand at first.

"Aedith is my wife," he explained with a weak smile.

Ellen looked at him in astonishment.

"I heard about your conversation with her today." He propped himself up with both hands on the silver knob of his ebony walking stick and leaned forward toward Ellen.

"She is beautiful, but that is the only positive thing to be said about her. It's no wonder she has not given me any children, because she is tight-fisted through and through." He wheezed briefly and laughed sorrowfully. "Even with my money!"

Ellen wondered who might have told him about the conversation and suspected it was the servant who had opened the door for her.

"She refused to give you the money for the oculist. For her own father!" He shook his head in disbelief. "If I were the one who needed it and if she had control of the moneybag, she would have done the same. She is a heartless person." He took out his leather purse and handed it to Ellen. "I know your brother cannot help—he's up to his neck in debt," he said softly, and cleared his throat. "I am going to take his bills and burn them, if only to anger Aedith. I'm also going to send him someone to help with the business for a while. I have been observing him: he works hard and is clever, but he has had a string of bad luck."

Ellen looked at him distrustfully. "Why are you doing that?"

"I have no son." He coughed painfully. "Shall I leave her everything when I die? I would rather do charitable things here and there, for the salvation of my soul. Do you understand?" He coughed again. "There is still plenty for her. Tell your brother nothing of our conversation."

"Why not?" Ellen asked, still suspicious.

"Someone young and childish like him can reject a helping hand out of vanity or false pride. But don't worry, he'll find out soon enough where the help came from. I was young once, too, and I'm not sure what I would have done in his place if my brother-in-law unexpectedly set himself up as my benefactor." He laughed, lost in thought when he thought of his youth, then coughed in a tinny sound. "Take the money and help your father get his eyesight back. And when he asks where you got it from, tell him it came from Kenny." The old man struggled to stand up again and then proceeded with astonishingly sprightly steps to the door.

Ellen followed him. Her brother-in-law turned around toward her once more. "Your good reputation is getting around, smith woman. You'll be a success!" He stroked her cheek with his withered hand, smiled, and left the house.

Ellen stood there thunderstruck, and it took a while before she could get herself together. What did he mean about her reputation getting around? Did he know anything more about her? With hands trembling, she opened the purse. Twelve shillings! The old silk merchant had been more than generous. And what did he intend to do for Kenny? Ellen decided to accept the generous gift without wasting too much time worrying about it. She left one shilling there for Kenny, hid the rest under her clothing, and then set out on the way home.

—

"We have just enough time to get you to St. Edmundsbury," she said to Osmond right after her arrival, and she told him about the oculist.

"Oh, dear child, where shall we get all that money?" Osmond shook his head. "That's just extravagance, as I'm not going to live much longer, anyway."

"What do you mean?" Ellen pushed him out the door of the smithy, determined. "You'll be the happiest man in the world when you can finally see your grandson. And while we are there in St. Edmundsbury we can visit Mildred." Mildred had married cousin Isaac four years earlier and had a daughter with him.

Osmond took a deep breath and fell silent. He was afraid of the hope that was building in him, and even more of the disappointment if the effort to free him from his blindness didn't work.

Ellen rented two ponies, and they at once set out on their journey.

When they arrived in St. Edmundsbury three days later, Ellen was astonished at all she saw. The city lay amid fields of fruit trees, meadows, and forests, and standing above it, magnificent and splendid, was an enormous abbey. They approached the city from the southwest side and then circled around it, arriving shortly after midday at a small clearing where Isaac's smithy was located.

As the two rode into the courtyard, they found Mildred sitting in front of the house enjoying the warm spring weather and plucking a chicken. She rushed to meet the unexpected guests and embraced them warmly, then moved the bench around so the two of them could sit down at the table and brought a pitcher of fresh water.

"I'm expecting another child!" she whispered in Ellen's ear. Last autumn she had given birth to a stillborn child and a year before that one who was premature. Marie, her only living child, was almost four years old, and Mildred wished more than anything to present her husband with a son.

Ellen kissed her on the cheek and squeezed her hand. "This time it will all work out," she whispered.

"A person who has lost his sight can hear all the better," Osmond grumbled, then broke out laughing. "I'd have no objection to having another grandchild."

Mildred blushed. "I'm sorry, Father." Nervously she nibbled on a strand of hair.

"Don't apologize, child!" Osmond reassured her. Mildred got up quickly and brought something to eat.

"We want to go straight to the marketplace. Can we stay with you for a few days?" Ellen asked, without telling Mildred anything about the reason for their visit.

"You don't have to ask. I'd be really angry if you just turned around and left."

"We should leave the horses here and go the rest of the way on foot," Ellen suggested.

Osmond nodded. He remembered St. Edmundsbury well. The smithy was not very far from the western gate to the city, and he could make the rest of the trip easily.

Ellen handed Osmond a walking stick, and they departed.

Once they arrived in the market, Ellen started looking around. The market was teeming with people, and at one end there was a large wooden platform. This was where the tooth puller, the barber-surgeon, and the oculist had set up shop. Farther ahead, magicians and actors were performing, making the crowds laugh. But sometimes the merry laughter and excited cries of the spectators were drowned out by the bloodcurdling screams of the patients.

Ellen pushed her way through the crowd, past the onlookers, pulling Osmond along behind her, and presented herself to the oculist. Then she told him why she was there.

The little man with snow-white, almost shoulder-length hair and a smooth-shaven face leaned down to her from the platform where he was standing. "I'll see your father, and if I think I can help him, I'll be glad to do it. Bring him up here," he said in a friendly voice.

She helped Osmond up the creaking wooden stairs.

The oculist examined Osmond's eyes carefully.

"I think it's worth the chance. If I can remove the bad fluids that are clouding his vision and if they don't come back, he will be able to see you today!" he said loudly, so that the onlookers standing around could hear him, and he told Ellen what it would cost.

A murmur went through the crowd, and the people gathered around the platform in order not to miss any of it.

"Can you lend a hand, or shall I find a strongman to hold him down?"

"Just tell me what I have to do," Ellen replied, looking him in the eye.

"Seat your father here in this chair and stand behind him." The oculist pulled up another chair, moved it back and forth a bit until he was directly in front of his patient, and sat down.

"Hold his head tightly in both hands and press him close to you so he can't move. He'll try, he'll shake, probably he'll also scream, but you mustn't let go of him, do you hear?" He looked her directly in the eye and asked, "Can you do that?"

Ellen nodded, though she had a queasy feeling in the pit of her stomach.

"She'll hold me tight, she's my daughter!" Osmond said proudly, patting Ellen's hand. He himself appeared completely calm and without fear.

"I am now going to stick the needle in your eye. It will hurt, but it won't take long, and then—God willing—you'll be able to see your daughter again," the oculist said encouragingly. Then, putting his left hand on Osmond's forehead, he opened wide the right eyelid with his thumb and index finger and held the eyeball tightly with his slender fingers so Osmond couldn't move it. In his right hand he held a thin needle with a slightly rounded head. He put it to his mouth, moistened it with his saliva, and then stuck it into the white of the eye from the side.

Osmond quivered and groaned briefly as the needle penetrated his eye, but he made no other sound.

The crowd fell silent. Every fiber in Osmond's body seemed to tighten.

The oculist carefully pushed the needle farther in until he could see the point of it behind the pupil, then moved it up and down, waited a moment to see that the blindness did not return, and slowly pulled it out of the eye. Finally, he laid a compress on Osmond's eye that had been heavily soaked in wine. Then he handed Osmond a little goblet of the same wine and said, "Take a drink, it will do you good—but slowly," he admonished him.

Osmond took several sips and relaxed a bit.

"It will be over soon," the oculist said reassuringly. Then he took the needle in his left hand and went through the same procedure on the other eye. When he was finished, he took the compress from the first eye and covered the second eye with it.

"Well, can you see anything now?"

Osmond blinked and turned his head. "Ellenweore!" he said softly; then he broke out into tears of joy and opened his arms wide.

—

Mildred could scarcely believe it when she saw her father looking at her.

"What happened to your eyes?" she asked incredulously.

Osmond told her in great detail how the oculist had cured him of his blindness. "I can't see quite as well as a young man, but I can see!" He smiled with joy. "Thank the Lord for that. I can see you again, and my grandchildren, too. Where is Marie? It's been so long since I have been able to see her."

While Osmond and Mildred sat in the kitchen and Marie bounced up and down on her grandfather's knee, Ellen was anxious to visit the smithy.

"Just go ahead. Isaac knows you are here." Mildred laughed and waved her off.

As Ellen entered the workshop, Isaac was struggling with a large piece for which he could have used a helper.

"Can I give you a hand?" Ellen asked, and went over to him. Her brother-in-law was almost a head taller than her, broad shouldered, and good-looking. "I'm Ellenweore!" she said with a smile.

"Aha, the cousin who is a smith." Isaac sounded less than cordial. "Well, you can hold it," he said condescendingly.

Ellen was annoyed at his tone—he could have been a bit friendlier. Looking around, she picked up a leather apron hanging on a post next to the forge. Isaac was adept at handling the piece. He had good rhythm and swung the hammer in a much wider arc than Ellen did. When he nodded, she placed the piece back in the fire. He gave her a derogatory glance. "To tell you the truth, I don't think much of women working at the forge. I like them better at the kitchen hearth."

"Well, excuse me," Ellen said, and took the apron off again. "If it makes you so upset, then you can continue by yourself." She turned away to leave the smithy.

"That's exactly what I mean! Women give up too easily and are too quarrelsome to do a man's job."

Ellen took a couple of deep breaths and went back to the house. "Your husband didn't want to have me in the smithy. He thinks women belong at the kitchen hearth," she huffed.

"If he only knew what your cooking is like, he certainly wouldn't have said that." Mildred grinned, and Osmond couldn't help smiling as well.

"Oh, you are impossible. If he only knew what a good smith I am…"

"Then he wouldn't have said that. You're completely right, my dear," Osmond confirmed softly. "Some men just can't stand getting on close terms with a skilled woman."

"I'll never get married. I couldn't bear being banished to the kitchen hearth."

"But once you were married. Wasn't your husband like that as well?" Mildred asked, with some surprise.

Ellen blushed at the thought she was deceiving everyone. "Jocelyn was very different. He taught me so much, and he would let me work on anything I wanted to. But he didn't have the chance," she stammered, her voice trailing off.

"I'm sorry, I shouldn't have said that," Mildred said when she saw the tears in Ellen's eyes.

—

Whenever Ellen was in the house, Isaac treated her cordially, joked, and laughed freely, but as soon as she returned to the shop, he was on his worst behavior.

Isaac had a youthful face even though he was nearly thirty years old. When he grinned, he squinted so all you could see were little slits. He had friendly, brown eyes that sparkled when he laughed, but they could also be ice-cold when he cursed or was making fun of someone.

The days at Mildred's house passed quickly, and soon Ellen and Osmond were on their way back.

Mildred held them both tightly in her arms. "I'm so happy you took over Father's smithy—he's so proud of you," she whispered in Ellen's ear as they were leaving.

December 1174

At Christmastime, Mildred and Isaac came to Orford for a visit along with little Marie and their daughter, Agnes, who was only a few weeks old.

Ellen had had to purchase new files, a whetstone, and several polishing stones in order to complete the orders for the castle garrison but so far had received only half of the agreed payment. She preferred not to discuss that with Mildred or Isaac and asked Jean also not to discuss her work. Thus, conversation at the dinner table was not about work in the forge, and Isaac remained happy, joked with them, and behaved appropriately toward Ellen, just as a brother-in-law should.

They celebrated Christmas dinner with smoked eel, the fat goose that Mildred had brought along, strong bread, and hearty sauce.

"If you could only see it, Father!" Ellen nudged her father, who had gone completely blind again just a few months after the surgery. "Will is letting go and trying to walk on his own now..."

And then, in fact, William let go of the stool and toddled toward the little wooden crib on the other side of the room. Ever since Jean had put it there that morning, William had had an eye on it, and finally his curiosity overcame his fear.

Ever since Easter they had been waiting to see him start walking, but he didn't dare because his foot was turned inward and he could only walk on the side of it. Even when someone was holding his hand he stumbled easily over his own foot and had trouble keeping his balance.

Osmond had tears of relief in his eyes when he heard that his grandson was walking with determined steps toward the crib, even if unsteadily.

"Good job!" Ellen praised the boy when he got there. Little William beamed, let go again, and toddled his way back to the stool. He kept going back and forth until Rose decided it was time for him to go to bed.

Isaac was crazy about the boy. "We need a son and heir like him, too!" he said, winking at Mildred, who was still a bit weak from Agnes's birth.

On the next day, too, Isaac watched little William's untiring attempts to walk, and suddenly he had an idea. "Jean, can you come to the workshop with me?"

Ellen frowned but didn't say anything for Mildred's sake as Isaac rose from the table and headed toward her smithy without asking permission.

Jean glanced quickly to see if she approved and then followed Isaac.

"It's because of his crooked foot that the little fellow is having trouble learning to walk. He's brave and has an iron will, but his foot will bother him for the rest of his life. If he had a firm shoe to support his foot, perhaps it would grow out straight. What I am trying to say is that children's feet are in a way undeveloped. Have you looked at Agnes's feet? They are flat and thin and only with time will they take on their final form. Even Marie's feet are still a bit flat."

Jean made a face and thought it over. "And what material would you use to make that?"

"We are smiths, aren't we?"

"You want to make the child a shoe out of iron?" Jean laughed. "That's much too heavy—he'll never be able to walk with it."

Isaac took a deep breath. "You are probably right, but I'm sure we can find a solution if we both give it some thought."

Jean nodded enthusiastically. He liked Isaac even though he could understand why Ellen hated it when he treated her so condescendingly as soon as the talk turned to smithing.

"In any case, a shoe made of leather is too soft—it will just conform to the foot," Jean said, thinking aloud.

"What about a wooden shoe?"

"That won't work." Jean shook his head dispiritedly. "He wouldn't even be able to get his foot into it. That's the reason Ellen always lets him run around barefoot," he explained.

"That's fine in summertime. Marie usually runs around barefoot, too. But we're concerned with his crooked foot. If we make him a wooden shoe that's just a little too small, it will push the foot gradually in the right direction, and after a while we could make him a new one. Children's feet grow so fast in any case that they always need new wooden clogs. Believe me, I know that's true of Marie, and she's a girl. Certainly boys' feet grow even faster."

"I've never made a wooden shoe, have you?"

"Only ordinary ones, nothing special like that. But look, we are skilled workers and can do that, don't you think?" Isaac grinned encouragingly. "We just have to think about how we are going to fit them for his foot. First we can take one of Marie's shoes and have a look at how it's made. So let's go—do you have some dry wood?"

Jean nodded. "In the shed, over on the right." He pointed to the west side of the smithy.

Isaac went and got Marie's wooden shoes while Jean brought William into the workshop.

Ellen wondered about all the secretiveness and what kept them so long in the workshop. There was no smoke coming from the forge, and she couldn't hear any hammering.

If Isaac's condescending way hadn't been so annoying to her, she would have joined them in the smithy to see what was going on.

When Jean and Isaac returned to the house with little William in their arms, it was already pitch black. The wooden shoes were finished.

Ellen just gave a bored shrug when Jean explained to her what they were doing.

"Someday he'll be a smith and he won't have to walk especially well," she snapped back.

"Yes, yes, I know, in olden times kings used to even cut the heel tendons in the feet of their best smiths so they couldn't run away and work for anyone else. We know all about that," Isaac said irritably.

"Is that true?" Jean asked with a shudder.

"Haven't I ever told you the story of Wieland the Smith?" Ellen asked in amazement.

Jean shook his head.

"Wieland was a great smith even though he couldn't walk!" Ellen said, irritated. "Just like Hephaestos!"

"The way it looks to me, Ellenweore is crazy about these strong men. What a shame none of them are available anymore," Isaac teased her.

"Get out, both of you!" Ellen scolded them angrily.

Isaac took Jean by the shoulders and led him out.

"First we'll go and get some wood so the women can cook us something good to eat."

"You'll never live to see the day I cook anything good for you," Ellen grumbled after the two had left. Isaac's little dig at her had hit home.

Rose laughed. "You two get along like cats and dogs. How fortunate that your parents saw to it that Mildred married him, and not you."

"Oh, I would have been widowed a long time ago, because I would have ripped his head off the very first week," Ellen replied, and she couldn't help laughing when she saw how shocked Rose looked.

January 1176

Ellen stood freezing at Osmond's grave. Only one year after the surgery on his eyes he had fallen asleep one bright summer day and simply not woken up. Ellen and Leofric bore him to his grave, with the help of Jean and Simon.

For a while after Osmond's death, it was noticeable how often Simon came to the smithy. Ellen thought back on the evening when Simon had proposed to her.

"Simon is a nice fellow, and you ought to give him a chance," Leofric said as soon as Simon had left the house.

"I don't want any nice fellow, and certainly not Simon. He's my friend and always has been, but marry him? Never!" Ellen trembled with anger.

Simon was her confidant from childhood, but there was nothing else they had in common. Simon's world consisted of animal skins, urine, and tan bark. His only ambition was to take over the tannery someday and have children, just as his father had done. The tannery had not made the family rich, but they always had a roof over their heads and never went hungry.

Ellen's plans, however, were quite different. The very thought of becoming Simon's wife and winding up like his mother—tanned and permeated with this horrible stench—seemed so awful to her that she stared angrily at her brother. "If you think you are going to get rid of me so easily, you have another thing coming. I know it's you who will inherit the smithy, and not me, that's the law, even though I am older. But you're still too young and inexperienced to manage the shop by yourself. For the time being you need to have me here, so you'd best hold your tongue and give a second thought to your choice of the person I have to marry."

"By the time I take over the smithy, you'll be an old hag, and who will want you then, huh?" Leofric replied, furious. "Anyway, I have no intention of getting rid of you. You wouldn't become an old tanner woman even if you married Simon, because you could work here."

For a moment Ellen didn't reply. Leofric was afraid she would leave! The angry look in her eyes gave way to a tender glance at her younger brother. "I can't marry him, really!" Thinking of the old tanner woman made her turn pale all over.

Leofric continued, "I think you're just pretending, honestly!"

"I won't marry a tanner, do you understand?" She didn't want to hear any more of it. "If I marry anyone, it will be a smith who lets me continue smithing. You can forget everything else, and that's my last word. Go to bed now, we have a lot to do tomorrow!"

When Simon came a week later to get her answer, she turned him down without any explanation. To her great surprise, he didn't try to change her mind but accepted her decision without getting angry or saying anything spiteful. But after that he never came back to the smithy, and it was only Jean or Leofric who would go to the tannery if they needed leather for their work.

An icy gust of wind tore Ellen from her reveries, and she looked up anxiously at the sky. It looked like snow again. Freezing, she pulled her cloak tighter around her, said a prayer for her foster father, and trudged over the snow-covered hill back to the smithy.

Long before she arrived, Leofric had taken the sled and left for the forest to cut wood. In winter it had to dry out for a long while before it was useable, and it was Leofric's job to head out early and get the wood. Coal for the forge was too expensive to be used for cooking.

Jean was alone when Ellen entered the shop. "Isn't Leofric back yet?" she asked, frowning.

"No." Jean looked up from his work. "He's been away a bit too long, don't you think?" It looked as if he were worried.

"Perhaps we should go and look for him before it gets dark," Ellen suggested. Ever since Osmond had died, she was the one who decided what to do.

"Let's do that!" Jean removed his apron and took his cloak down from the hook.

"Come, Greybeard!" Ellen called, slapping her hand against her thigh.

The dog raised his head, stood up slowly, and stretched comfortably.

"It's gotten damn cold. Leofric's hands and feet must be freezing, being in the forest this long!" Jean shook himself as the icy wind hit him.

Out in the meadow the snow crunched under their feet. It was easy to see Leofric's footprints leading into the forest, and they followed them at a quick pace.

Ellen discovered the sled in a small clearing, but there was no sign of Leofric. Greybeard was getting restless and began to whine, while Jean ran to the sled and followed Leofric's footprints from there.

"This way, Ellen!" he called, motioning her to come.

Just a few steps further they discovered a pool of blood in the whiteness of the freshly fallen snow.

"For God's sake, Jean!"

Several sets of footprints led away from the spot.

Jean discovered a wide trail as if something had been dragged in the snow, but suddenly it ended.

"They tied it to a stake here in order to carry it off," he explained, pointing to the prints that now led away, close together.

"What are you talking about?"

"Poachers!"

Ellen stood there with her mouth open in shock. "How do you know that?" she yelled at Jean.

"Marcondé was a master at poaching, and these people here were bunglers. They must have been afraid of getting caught. Anyone found poaching in the king's forests is hanged."

"I know that myself," Ellen lashed out, and looked around in despair. "But just where can Leofric be?"

"Shh, quiet!" Jean listened intently.

Ellen stood still.

Greybeard had disappeared into the woods. Suddenly he started to bark furiously.

"Over there, come along," shouted Jean as he ran off.

A cold chill ran down Ellen's spine followed by a feeling of horror.

She saw two masked men with clubs. "Leofric!" she shouted. Jean grabbed a broken branch and ran after the men, who threw their clubs down in panic and fled.

Ellen ran toward her brother.

Leofric was unconscious and had a large, open wound in his head that was bleeding profusely. Ellen laid her right ear on his chest and listened to his heart. It was beating weakly.

Greybeard whined and licked Leofric's face.

"He's alive!" she called to Jean, who had followed them only a short way and kept turning around warily.

"The bastards!" He spat into the snow angrily and lifted the boy by the shoulder. "Take his legs and we'll carry him to the sled. We've got to get him home where it's warm as soon as possible and care for his wounds."

Ellen stood there, dumbfounded, realizing for the first time how much Leofric meant to her.

"Let's go!" Jean shouted at her.

"Right, what am I supposed to…oh, the legs, yes."

Ellen grabbed Leofric's feet and helped Jean carry him to the sled.

Greybeard ran along beside them, whining softly. It seemed to take forever for them to get home.

"What happened?" Rose had been waiting impatiently by the house and now ran out to meet them.

"He was attacked by poachers. Go and heat up some water—he's badly injured!" Jean shouted to her.

Rose didn't ask twice but turned around and rushed back into the house.

"I think we'll have to sew up the wound on his head," Jean said after he had put Leofric down on the straw bed that Rose had quickly prepared.

Ellen bent down toward her brother and stroked his pale cheek. His hair was matted down by all the blood that was oozing from the wound in his head.

"I've watched a few times as Marcondé and the others sewed up each other's wounds, but I've never done it," Jean said in a subdued voice. "Perhaps we should send for a barber-surgeon."

"The barber-surgeon in Orford is a shaky old drunkard, dirty and unreliable. I'll never let him touch Leofric. I'd rather do it myself, though I've never tried," Ellen replied with determination.

In the meantime, Rose had already found a needle and thread. "I'll do it," she declared emphatically.

"You?" asked both Jean and Ellen at practically the same time, looking at her in astonishment.

"I stitched up Thibault more than once. The Young King's barber-surgeon showed me how because he was so busy at the tournaments. After that, I always did it. Thibault said my stitches were less disfiguring, especially in the face."

"That pompous, repulsive person!" Jean huffed.

Ellen didn't notice how he blushed when Rose spoke about Thibault.

Rose sat down calmly alongside Leofric's bed, laid an old woolen cloth over her skirt to protect it from bloodstains, and put the boy's head in her lap. "Someone will have to hold him. At present he is unconscious, but when I start stitching him up the pain will surely wake him and he will thrash about." Rose looked as calm as if she had always done this sort of thing.

"I'll do that," Ellen said. She sat down next to her brother, held his arms and his slender upper body tightly, and placed her body over him.

Skillfully, Rose cleansed the encrusted blood from the wound with warm water until it started to bleed again, then sewed up the wound with a dozen or more stitches.

"I don't like it at all that he didn't wake up," Jean grumbled when Leofric didn't stir.

"All we can do now is pray and wait. If the blow was not too hard, he will hopefully wake up soon. Poor Leofric!" Rose kissed him on the cheek. "Goodness, he's hot! We've got to remove his clothing; it's all wet in the back. Jean, get two woolen blankets we can wrap him in."

When they removed his shoes, Rose saw that his toes were blue with cold and began to massage them gently.

"At least he won't lose his toes," she said after a while, thankfully, after they gradually regained their normal color.

The first night Ellen watched over her brother, and after that they all took turns sitting at Leofric's bedside. For three days he had a high fever, and after that it started to come down. The wound in his head began to heal, but still Leofric had not woken up. Carefully they fed him spoonfuls of water and chicken broth, and everything went down his throat, but he didn't seem to be swallowing it.

"Why don't you wake up, for heaven's sake?" In desperation, Ellen kept squeezing his hand, but her brother didn't stir.

On the morning of the tenth day he opened his eyes, and joyfully Ellen came running to his bedside. But Leofric didn't seem to see her. He was still breathing, but he looked almost dead.

His eyes were open and Ellen could feel his heartbeat, but he seemed to be semiconscious still. Ellen could feel despair coming over her, and hatred for the poachers who had done that to him.

They missed Leofric's happy chatter at work in the smithy, as well. Would he ever come back to them?

—

Peace had returned to the land, and the garrison at the castle had shrunk to just a few men, and for that reason there were fewer orders for weapons. Increasingly, Ellen and Jean had to forge tools again in order to survive, and Ellen started to have doubts about her ambitious goals and dreams. Some days she was so depressed that she didn't even go to the shop but sat silently at Leofric's bedside holding his hand or walking aimlessly through the forest.

"Come now! You have to get back to work in the shop, we need you!" Jean pleaded with her when she didn't show up for work.

"What's the point of it all?" Ellen shook her head despondently. "Leofric is not going to make it."

"But you must, Ellen!" Jean pleaded. He had learned much from her and would have no difficulty finding work with a smith, and Rose, too, would easily find work, but what would become of William and Ellen if she gave up like that? "Think of your son! Osmond would have wanted him to have the smithy if anything happened to Leofric!"

Ellen whistled through her teeth. "And me? Who is thinking of me? I always wanted this smithy, but it's not mine. It never was and never will be. I was supposed to keep it for Leofric after Osmond's death, and now shall I just go on and hand it over to my son? It's my smithy!" she flared up, beside herself with anger, looking defiantly at Jean.

"But you're a woman, and can't..."

"What can't I do? Become a master? Who says so?" Ellen's fighting spirit had returned. "Are these the same people who say women can't forge good swords? I've shown them how wrong they are, and you know that!"

"Yes, you are right," Jean replied wearily.

The door to the shop opened, and little William came limping in hesitantly.

"What do you want?" Ellen asked crossly.

"The geese," he said, sniffling, "they bit me."

Ellen was still furious and took a deep breath. "Then you probably deserved it."

Jean shook his head almost imperceptibly. "Come here, Will," he said warmly and motioned for the child to come to him. He knelt down and took the boy in his arms. "Geese don't like it when you get too close to them. They don't have any weapons; they have no sharp claws to defend themselves or hoofs to kick you with or horns to spear you. And they have no poisonous stingers. All they have to defend themselves is their beaks, so to make the whole world afraid of them they snap at everything that comes close." Jean wiped the tears from William's cheeks. "That's pretty smart of them, don't you think? Just move slowly when you are around them, and when they get nasty show them you are stronger and whack them with a stick."

William nodded bravely.

"Now go tell Aunt Rose we'll be a little late for dinner, all right?" Jean gave the boy a friendly pat on the rear, and William did as he was told. After he had left the shop, Jean turned to Ellen angrily. "Why are you so hard on him? He didn't deserve that!"

"Do you want me to coddle him?" she huffed.

"But he's still so little!"

Ellen planted herself in front of him and replied, "As a girl, I always had to try harder than anyone else in order to achieve what I wanted. It will be the same for him. He's a boy, but he's a cripple!"

"Ellen!" Jean frowned angrily.

"You probably find that word unpleasant, but that's the way people look at him, and that's also the reason I won't coddle him, so help me God! I swear I'll teach him everything I can, and that is all I am able to do for him. It's more than my mother ever did for me. Much more!"

Jean was shocked at how bitter Ellen was. This was the first time she had ever mentioned her mother, and the hatred and disappointment in her voice was inescapable.

"Life is hard, but have you ever seen me strike William?"

Jean shook his head. "You hardly ever see him because all you think of is smithing. You haven't even noticed how much his feet have grown in the last year, have you? I've twice had to make him new wooden shoes. And have you noticed that his foot is a little less twisted? Do you know how many teeth he has? No! You don't even know your own son. He's a smart fellow, and he not only has your red hair but your thick skull!"

"Thank God for that, because he'll need it to get by. You ask me if I know how many teeth William has? You're right, I don't know that. But I know where the money comes from for Rose to buy us food, and I know we have clothing and a roof over our heads in order to get through a hard winter. And as for William's foot, I don't agree with you. I think God gave it to him as a test, and I'm not doing my son any favors by coddling him. William will someday be a great smith, and that's all that counts. Then, no one will take notice of his foot." Ellen looked at Jean provocatively and turned away. "None of us knows what the next day will bring. The Lord alone will decide whether we live to see it or not. Just look at Leofric," she murmured sadly.

"He'll get better again," Jean said, trying to console her.

"No, Jean, the Lord will soon take him away. I know it, I feel it." She quickly wiped her forehead. "If I coddled William today, what will become of him if something happens to me? He has to learn to make it by himself."

—

Leofric did not wake up. On a cold, moonless night at the beginning of March, he died.

Ellen was sitting at his bedside and had not even noticed. It wasn't until morning when she woke up that she saw he was no longer breathing. She lay down close to him and cried. Memories of all the terrible things that had happened to her in her life now came together in an unending flood of tears.

Greybeard sniffed at her worriedly, laid his head on her arm, and licked her face with devotion until she had calmed down a bit.

September 1176

Toward the end of summer, Ellen could not stand it any longer and decided to ride to St. Edmundsbury to tell Mildred that Leofric had died. Ever since his death she had the growing feeling that Orford would bring her only grief and pain.

She borrowed a horse, sat William down in the saddle in front of her, and rode off.

Jean and Rose were to take care of everything while she was away.

Mildred was delighted to see Ellen and take her in her arms again. She kissed her nephew and looked at him lovingly. "Go over to the barn and say hello to Uncle Isaac. He'll be so happy to see you!" she urged the boy. "And then go out and play in the yard with Marie, but make sure little Agnes behaves!" After the children had left, she closed the door and turned to her sister. "I'm so happy you're here! William has really grown!"

Ellen nodded in agreement and looked carefully at her sister. "You're expecting another child, aren't you?"

"Is it already noticeable?" Mildred asked with surprise, looking at her belly.

"Only from the way you smile. When I see how you look at William, I think you are hoping for a son. Is that so?" Ellen grinned.

Mildred nodded, somewhat embarrassed. "For the first time, I felt sick. With Marie and Agnes I didn't get sick once, but this time…" She sighed. "Perhaps we'll be lucky!" From the glint in her eyes it was clear to see how much she wished for a son.

"Your dear husband seems so intent on having a son and heir!" Ellen could not completely hide her disapproval.

"Oh, come on!" Mildred said, nudging her sister. "He's not a bad fellow, believe me, he was a good catch for me. He works hard and is a master at his craft…"

"…which is something he never thinks a woman could do, I know," Ellen added.

"He's a good provider, a loving father to the girls, and a decent husband to me." Mildred seemed a bit hurt.

"I'm sorry, you are right. I didn't mean to offend you."

"Would you like to help me make the meal?" Mildred said, changing the topic.

"I suppose, if I have to," Ellen groaned.

Mildred laughed. "You'll never change. You would have been a better husband. In any case, as a housewife you're no great shakes."

"And I wouldn't win any prize as a mother either," Ellen said sadly.

"Oh, what nonsense, Ellen. I'd trust my children to you anytime."

Ellen smiled gratefully at Mildred.

When Isaac came back for lunch, William was riding on his shoulders. The smith set the boy down on the bench and looked after him as if he were his own son.

Ellen knew how much the child missed Osmond, and she could see how much William enjoyed the attention of her brother-in-law. *I'll pray that Mildred has a boy*, she thought, when she saw how William looked up to Isaac.

"It has straightened out a bit, it seems to me," Isaac said, massaging the little boy's foot pensively.

"The crooked foot doesn't bother me," Ellen said in a sharp tone.

"But it would be good if you could straighten it a little," Isaac said emphatically.

"I don't see how that would help. Do you really think your wooden shoe will change anything? I don't. I'm also not sure if it's good for him when you raise his hopes. Even if his foot can be straightened a little, he'll still be a cripple."

As Isaac and Ellen continued to quarrel, William became more and more upset until tears started running down his face.

Mildred pounded on the table, demanding that the two stop fighting and be quiet, and Ellen was so offended she didn't speak another word to Isaac until the next day. After the conversation turned from William's foot to other things, the mood in the house slowly improved, and Mildred's constant chatter managed to make Ellen break out laughing again and again.

One day Mildred and Ellen were sitting in the vegetable garden digging up onions for dinner. "I'd like to stay here forever, but duty calls," Ellen said, shrugging with resignation. "I can't leave Jean and Rose alone in the smithy forever. In two days we'll have to leave, whether we like it or not."

"Too bad, you're good for me," Mildred said, and in fact she did look more radiant than ever. "Won't you all come to visit us at Christmas? My child will be arriving in February or March, I'm not exactly sure when." She looked pleadingly at her sister. "Please, Ellen!"

"Very well, agreed. William will be thrilled!" Ellen took her sister in her arms. "And so will I."

The time until her departure was peaceful. Mildred had obviously warned Isaac not to quarrel again with his sister-in-law, and he did as she said.

Parting was difficult for Ellen.

"We'll see each other again at Christmastime!" Mildred called to her and waved cheerily as she rode away.

Ellen had chosen a grey, cold autumn day for her departure. Around noon a strong wind came up, shaking and tugging at the tree branches and tearing off limbs. Both Ellen and her son were chilled to the bone and arrived in Orford tired and frozen.

Greybeard yelped with joy at their arrival.

Rose came rushing out to meet them, and Jean made a good fire for them to warm themselves by, then took the rented horse back to its stable.

After having a bowl of porridge and a goblet of warm spiced wine, Ellen felt well and at home again. Only now did she notice how radiant Rose looked. Her cheeks were rosy, and her eyes sparkled. *How good it is for her not to be around Thibault anymore*, Ellen thought contentedly.

There had been almost nothing to do in the smithy, and Jean was happy to hear that Ellen had come back with renewed enthusiasm and many plans for the future.

"The next thing I am determined to do," Ellen told Jean that evening, "is to make a sword. Then I'll visit the estates in our area and offer my services—I mean, of course, our services. I'm tired of just making tools; I'm a swordsmith!"

"That sounds like the old you!" Jean exclaimed with great relief. "Full of zeal and pride, that's my Ellen!"

But even though Rose and Jean were obviously happy she was back, she had the feeling things were different than before.

"Is there something going on between you two?" she asked Jean at work the next day.

"Ahem, no, what do you mean by that?" he stammered uncertainly.

"You and Rose, have you been quarreling?"

"Oh, no," he replied, sounding a little relieved. "No, we get along just fine."

Ellen was satisfied with that answer. She was probably just imagining that they were not getting along.

In just a few weeks, it became clear that Ellen's plan was working. She introduced herself with a sword she had forged herself and offered her services. She received two orders for swords and the prospect of additional ones.

December 1176

On an overcast December morning a few days before Christmas, the four set out for St. Edmundsbury. Ellen now had her own horse, and Jean and Rose rode on animals rented from the stable. Jean's horse, a young sorrel, was more skittish and at first pranced about excitedly but in time got used to his rider and calmed down.

A fine drizzle accompanied them the whole way. At first the little drops of water clung to their woolen cloaks like tiny pearls, but as the rain continued to fall, the water soaked through the material, and when they arrived at the smithy they were completely drenched.

Mildred greeted them with great joy, but Ellen was shocked.

Her sister seemed completely exhausted by the pregnancy even though her delivery date was still more than two months off. She learned that Mildred's initial sickness had not gotten better, but actually worsened each month so that instead of getting rounder with her child she looked thin and worn out. Her belly swelled out like a tumor from her emaciated body. Rose immediately recognized the seriousness of the situation and offered to take charge of the housework. Since Mildred tired more quickly than usual, she accepted at once.

"I'm really worried about Mildred," Isaac whispered to Ellen when they happened to be alone for a moment. "She is getting thinner and thinner, and what little she eats she soon throws up again," he said, passing his hand through his hair. "It's good you are here."

He, too, looked exhausted, and when Ellen asked how he was feeling his only brief reply was that he had a great deal to do recently and a few important jobs to complete. He gratefully accepted Jean's offer of assistance but continued to decline any help from Ellen in the smithy. Ellen was angry at him for that but decided for Mildred's sake to avoid any quarrel. And because Isaac was also clearly trying, they had a peaceful Christmas celebration. At the beginning of January, sadly, they made their way back home. Ellen urged Mildred to send someone to let her know if she needed any help, and in fact in less than two weeks Isaac's assistant Peter came to Orford.

"Mildred sent me," he said, out of breath because of his hurried trip. Despite the cold, both he and his horse were steaming from the exertion.

Ellen invited Peter into the house and offered him a place at the table. Rose served him a piece of bread, a bowl of porridge, and a goblet of small beer.

"What's wrong with her?" Ellen asked impatiently.

"She is sick with worry about Isaac."

"About Isaac?" Jean asked.

"The injury to his hand..." Peter started to say between two spoonfuls of porridge.

"Just a moment," Jean asked. "You are here not because of Mildred, but because of Isaac?"

"Yes, I am," said Peter, quickly gulping down another spoonful of porridge.

"Isaac burned his hand rather badly when we were there," Jean explained.

"It was all my fault," Peter continued. "I left the tongs on the forge, and he grabbed the iron when it was white hot." Peter rubbed his chin in embarrassment.

"Isaac thought that such things only happen to beginners, and he was embarrassed, especially in front of you, and that's the reason I didn't tell you. I had to promise him I wouldn't." Jean shrugged. "But it ought to have healed a long time ago!"

"His hand is swollen and pus is running out of it, but Isaac isn't doing anything about it. Mildred is afraid the wound will become gangrenous." Peter sighed. He seemed to fear it would, also.

"For God's sake, don't you have any herb women in St. Edmundsbury? What can I do? I don't know anything at all about such things."

"Mildred already asked the midwife to have a look at Isaac's hand. She knows about such things and says he needs to stop working for a while because otherwise it won't heal. But he won't even consider that. We have important jobs that aren't finished yet, and he can't just sit around, he says."

"I'm surprised he even let you go," Ellen said in amazement.

"He thinks I am here on account of Mildred. She doesn't look very good, either, and I think she could also use help."

Ellen looked at Jean and Rose. "I'm leaving first thing tomorrow. Jean, you'll stay with Rose and William, won't you?"

"Certainly, I'll take care of everything, don't worry."

A shy voice spoke up at the table. "Then I wonder if I might be able to stay, after all?"

Ellen and Jean turned around and looked at him in astonishment. In the excitement over Peter's unexpected arrival they had completely forgotten the journeyman.

The young smith's journeyman had come to see them that morning to ask about work. He seemed to be a pleasant fellow and his sample piece was good quality work, but Ellen and Jean were managing fine with just the two of them and had only been able to offer him a hot meal and a place for the night, as was the custom.

Ellen stared at him for a brief moment. He must have been sent by heaven, she thought.

"Jean?" Ellen asked, just to make sure.

"If you are going to be away for a while, it would certainly be best," he agreed.

"Three pennies a day, with meals, and room to sleep in the smithy, and Sundays and holidays off, of course. Do you agree?"

"I won't get rich, but for the time being I'll agree." The journeyman rubbed his hands off on his shirt and enthusiastically reached out to shake Ellen's hand. "My name is Arthur."

Ellen shook his hand to seal the agreement. Fate had been good to both parties: Ellen could go to Mildred's without worrying or feeling under any pressure of time, and the journeyman had been able to find work despite the winter.

"Arthur and I will work things out together, don't worry. You can stay for as long as Mildred needs you," Jean reassured her again the next day when she was ready to leave. "As for the sword, I'll ask the baron for more time, as we discussed, and the other things we can do by ourselves. You can depend on me!" Jean took Ellen in his arms and patted her on the back reassuringly.

Then William came, stood up straight to give his mother a kiss on the cheek, and then quickly dashed off.

Rose also gave her a farewell embrace. "The boy is in good hands with me!"

"I know that, you are a better mother to him than I am," Ellen replied with a sigh.

"Oh, don't speak such nonsense. Go now, and take care of your sister and her husband!" Rose gave her an encouraging smile.

Ellen pulled the gugel over her head and shoulders and put on the riding gloves. A crisp, cold January was calling with a bright blue sky.

Ellen and Peter drove their horses hard in order not to waste any time, and despite the icy cold, the horses were soon warm.

They arrived in St. Edmundsbury long after dark. Even though Ellen was prepared to find her sister in poor shape, she could hardly believe how terrible Mildred looked. She was exhausted and had deep shadows underneath her eyes.

Isaac tried to hide his hand from Ellen, but she noticed how pus and blood were oozing from the dirty bandage he had wrapped around the wound. One could see in his contorted face that he was in severe pain, but since he still wouldn't tolerate her presence in his smithy, Ellen couldn't help with the work and could only watch how he was suffering.

Ellen took care of her sister and tried to help her regain her strength, and indeed Mildred seemed happy she was there and soon was looking a little better.

But Isaac's condition was getting visibly worse.

Late in the afternoon two days after Ellen's arrival, Peter dashed excitedly into the house. "Ellenweore, come quickly, Isaac has fainted!"

Mildred's eyes opened wide with fear.

Ellen put down the dough she was kneading at the moment, saying, "Don't worry, I'll attend to him!" and rushed into the workshop behind Peter.

Isaac lay on the floor, doubled up in pain. His forehead was burning.

"We've got to take him to the house!" she said.

Peter was big and strong, so the two of them could carry Isaac. Mildred had a bed set up in the kitchen so she could be with Ellen and her children and put Isaac in the bedroom.

Carefully Ellen removed the bandage from Isaac's hand.

"For God's sake!" she gasped when she caught sight of the wound.

The palm of his hand was covered with pus and putrid black skin, and the skin around the wound was swollen and a deep red. The gangrene already extended up his arm. Peter turned away in horror. He was shocked. "How could he have continued working with that?" he mumbled.

"Isaac is stubborn," Ellen grumbled. "But he is also pretty damn tough," she added in a somewhat friendlier tone. We've got to find a barber-surgeon somewhere." She wrapped the dirty linen around Isaac's hand again when flies started coming to settle down on the wound.

"Get out!" she shouted, shooing away the persistent insects that were attracted by the stench of the rotting flesh.

"I'll find one!" Peter assured her, and rushed away.

Ellen was wondering what else to do when Isaac suddenly regained consciousness. He sat up quickly and looked around in astonishment, but then he hesitated. Perhaps he was dizzy. "Why am I in the bedroom?" he exclaimed gruffly and looked suspiciously at his sister-in-law.

"You must rest; you have a fever," she said, trying to console him, without saying a word about his hand. Naturally, he would say he could continue working and the fever had nothing to do with his injury.

"Rest?" Isaac spat the word out angrily. "I have a lot to do, an important job that has to be finished in two days. I can't just lie around here." He tried to stand up, but he was unable to. "Won't you help me?" he snarled at Ellen.

"If you think you can work, then you certainly are able to stand up on your own." Ellen turned and walked out.

Isaac struggled to get up, but he was too weak. Finally he gave up and fell asleep, exhausted.

It took half a day before Peter returned with a barber-surgeon. He was an older man, somewhat chubby and bald, but his eyes were gentle and friendly. He examined Isaac's hand closely, shook his head, and wheezed.

Ellen accompanied him out of the room.

Not until they were outside again in front of the smithy did he begin to speak. "The woman who is expecting the child…is she his wife?" He had seen Mildred briefly but not spoken with her.

Ellen nodded apprehensively.

"It looks bad for her, do you know that?"

Ellen nodded again.

"He probably knows that, too, and that's the reason he doesn't want anyone to see his wound. I imagine he is ashamed. Stubborn men like him can easily lose an arm or a leg."

Ellen took a deep breath. "Can you do anything for him?"

"The hand is gangrenous, and it's spreading fast. It doesn't look good. He should have looked after his hand. I'll tell you what you can do, but I can't give you much hope. If we can't stop the gangrene from spreading, we'll have to cut off perhaps half of the lower arm or even as far as the elbow. I can't say exactly yet."

Ellen gasped. That would mean the end of Isaac's smithy! How could he continue to work, even if he survived the operation?

The barber-surgeon gave her a few herbs and told her how to make a compress with them. He promised to look in on Isaac the next day and bring his tools along. "If it's necessary, I'll remove his hand or else he'll die! It would be best if you could prepare him and his wife for that."

“But how can I…what can I say?”

The barber-surgeon shrugged. “That’s not easy to do, I know.”

When he had left, Ellen was overcome with despair, and tears were running down her face. Even if Isaac had so often made her angry, he didn’t deserve anything like this. Mildred was expecting their third child, and how would he be able to feed a family? Despondently, Ellen walked back to the house. The children would certainly be hungry, and Mildred had to be continually reminded to eat. Ellen rolled up her sleeves and decided that first she would take care of everyone’s immediate needs. Then she entered, wiping the tears from her eyes.

“What’s the matter with Isaac?” Mildred asked. She had understood more of the problem than Ellen had wished.

“He hurt himself,” Ellen said vaguely, trying not to sound overly concerned.

“Do you mean his hand? He has been wearing a bandage on it for weeks, but he said it wasn’t very bad.”

“He has a fever and really needs to rest,” Ellen said evasively, working halfheartedly on preparing the meal.

“Something’s burning,” Mildred shouted all of a sudden, and Ellen looked at the pot on the hearth.

“The porridge!” Quickly she started stirring it. “I’m just not a cook!” she moaned in exasperation, stamping her foot on the floor.

“If Isaac can’t work for a while, could you complete the job for him? Please, Ellen, a maid from the village can cook and take care of the children…perhaps Eve, Peter’s sister—she has helped me a few times in the past.”

“He’d have me drawn and quartered if I dared to enter his shop!” Ellen replied, but actually she had already been thinking of doing that.

“Please!” Mildred sat up, looking at her with pleading eyes.

“All right, if you make sure he doesn’t kill me later as a thank-you!” Ellen replied, dishing out the porridge in wooden bowls.

—

Peter was surprised the next morning when he arrived in the smithy and found Ellen at work at the forge.

“Mildred said your sister could perhaps give her a hand.” Ellen tried to ask in a tone that was friendly but at the same time would show she was the boss. It was clear to her that Peter thought he would be in charge now in the smithy, but there was no getting around the fact that he would have to listen to her if they were going to get along.

“Sure, I can ask her,” he replied with surprise. “Aren’t you going to stay then?”

“Please go and ask her if she could begin today, if possible right away! We need her to cook and to take care of the house, the animals, and the children.”

Mildred had ducks, geese, chickens, and three pigs that spent the day in the yard.

“Good!” Peter was surprised, but he did what she asked.

After he had left the shop, Ellen took a deep breath. The most important thing was to make clear to him from the outset that she knew more than he did and therefore would be in charge in the future. She examined the pieces that had been started. Isaac apparently had a heavy, richly decorated gate to complete. Looking at it closely, she knew what was missing.

“Eve came right away, and she is over in the house with Mildred,” Peter said when he returned to the shop a little later.

"When must the gate be finished?" Ellen asked, without discussing his sister any further.

"We have just two days!" Peter looked worried, and he had every reason to be. Because of his injury, Isaac had not been able to work as fast and had now fallen behind.

"The monks will only give us more orders if we deliver on time."

Ellen had already looked around, and there was at least enough iron on hand to complete the project.

"Well, then, be ready to work late today and tomorrow. The forge is already hot, and we can start at once."

"You want to…?" Peter looked flabbergasted. "But I'm no master, not even a journeyman!"

"But I am," Ellen replied matter-of-factly and put on Isaac's leather apron. "Now, let's go," she said sharply enough to get him moving at once.

Ellen kept working until she could hardly lift her arm anymore, and from the very first day Peter realized she knew exactly what she was doing and was inspired by her ambition. If she made just as much progress the next day, she'd in fact be able to finish the gate on time.

"I've heard from time to time what Isaac has said about women—that they belong in the kitchen and not in a smithy, and I used to think he was right. Now, to be honest, I'm no longer so sure. In any case, I like what you have forged much better than what you cook." Peter smirked.

Ellen just grumbled something inaudible. Even though he was just a helper, she felt flattered by his praise.

In the evening, the barber-surgeon stopped in to see Isaac, as promised.

Ellen had asked Peter's sister to change the bandage again on Isaac's hand, but the fever had not broken nor did the wound seem to be healing. In fact, the skin was black and full of pus as before, and it stank horribly. The barber-surgeon looked at the hand briefly and left the house without saying a word.

"There are two possibilities," he said calmly after they were out in the yard. "Either I remove his hand and part of his lower arm today..."

"Or?" Ellen asked anxiously.

"Or you pray and do nothing. Then the gangrene will move up the arm, God willing, it will reach the elbow, then the shoulder, and in a few days the smith will be dead. Praying in all probability will only help his soul, and his body will rot away, dear woman."

"Are you completely sure that the only possibility of saving him is to remove the hand?"

"Unless there's a miracle..." He shrugged. That was the way he earned a living. Naturally, it was horrible for the people involved, but usually it really was the only solution.

Ellen thought for a moment about Isaac, who was lying there on the bed, pale and lifeless, paying no attention to the doctor who was examining him. Since the day before he had been conscious for only a few brief moments.

"Please explain that to his wife. I can't make a decision like that myself."

The barber-surgeon then had a serious talk with Mildred. She listened, pale and stunned.

"Please, Ellen, I can't...you must..." she gasped, and sank back onto the bed again. She closed her eyes and moaned.

"She is not much help to you, I'm afraid," the barber-surgeon said dryly. "You'll have to make the decision alone. Also, consider that I ask four shillings for an amputation and cannot say with certainty that he will survive, even though I will of course do everything I can to save him."

Ellen had enough money with her, and if she continued receiving orders from the monks she would be able to support the family for the time being.

"Do it!" she said with determination. "He just has to get through."

"If you assist me and I don't have to hire an assistant, I will give you a price reduction on the operation. I see you are a good, courageous woman."

Ellen groaned, then nodded, and told Eve not to let the children out of the house.

"Let's go and bring him here." The barber-surgeon clapped his hands and rubbed them together.

Ellen shuddered.

They entered the room and carried Isaac out into the court where the chopping block stood that was ordinarily used to split wood; then they set Isaac gently down alongside it.

"It would be good if someone else would help hold his legs," the barber-surgeon said.

Ellen called to Peter, who came out of the smithy slowly and hesitantly.

"Hold Isaac's legs tightly," she ordered.

Peter obeyed with reluctance.

Isaac lay there unconscious while the barber-surgeon put a wooden rod in his mouth.

"That's so he won't bite his tongue off," he explained. "You must hold his arm tightly, because if he wakes up he'll do everything he can to pull it away. It will take all your strength. Perhaps we should ask the young man to do that instead, and ask you to hold his legs?"

Peter shook his head vigorously and begged Ellen with his eyes not to ask him to do that. But he was so devastated by his own responsibility for Isaac's injury that he didn't dare to say a thing—if he hadn't left the tongs near the fire, none of this would have happened.

"No," Ellen said, summoning up all her courage. "I'll do it." If Isaac ever learned that she had helped with the amputation, he would never forgive her.

"All right. Young man, first go and put a flat bar of iron in the forge. We'll need it later to close the gaping wound or he'll bleed to death. You'll go and get it when I tell you, and hurry, do you understand?" the barber-surgeon said.

Peter nodded anxiously, then went back to the smithy where he did as he was told.

The barber-surgeon positioned Isaac's arm on the block of wood, tied it with a piece of cloth, and then stopped to think where he would begin to cut. His saw looked like an ordinary carpenter's saw.

Ellen closed her eyes. She held Isaac's arm as tightly as if her life depended on it, and prayed. The arm twitched, and Ellen could sense how the barber-surgeon's saw was cutting through the bone.

Suddenly Isaac let out a piercing cry.

Ellen held him tightly and tried to find words to console him, but the only thing audible was the sound of her sobbing.

The barber-surgeon, however, shouted at Peter and told him he had to hold Isaac's legs tighter.

Ellen thought she would pass out. She was holding the arm as tightly as possible but couldn't bring herself to look at it. Her prayers became even more fervent, increasing to a silent cry for help to God and all the saints. The barber-surgeon's work seemed to take forever. Isaac screamed and writhed in pain, then passed out again but continued groaning and trembling as the barber-surgeon continued working on his arm.

"Go, young man, get the iron!" the barber-surgeon shouted all of a sudden.

Peter looked at him hesitantly.

"Go on, hurry up!"

Peter ran as if the devil were after him.

The hot iron burned into Isaac's flesh and exuded such a bitter odor that Ellen became sick. She vomited and remembered Jean's story of how his village was attacked.

After the barber-surgeon had packed some herbal medicines around Isaac's arm and then wrapped everything in a clean linen bandage, they carried him back into the room. His face was as pale as wax, like that of a corpse.

"But why did you burn his flesh again?" Ellen asked the barber-surgeon, horrified. "I'm sure you saw how an almost insignificant burn wound caused his hand to rot. How could you inflict a much greater wound on him and believe everything will heal now?"

"Even the smallest wound can become gangrenous," the barber-surgeon replied, "and it doesn't matter if it's a burn or a cut. Nobody knows why flesh rots. They say the cause is too many bad fluids in the body." The barber-surgeon shrugged. "The smith has lost a lot of blood, and let's hope we have drained the bad fluids. You will have to change the bandage regularly. Pray that the arm does not become gangrenous again, and if the Lord is merciful, he'll pull through." The barber-surgeon raised his eyebrow. "I'll come back to see him again tomorrow and will bring you some new herbs for the compresses." He patted Ellen on the shoulder. "You were very brave."

In the middle of the night, Ellen sat bolt upright in bed. She had heard Isaac screaming. Her bed was not far from his, and she listened intently. Everything was quiet; she was probably only dreaming. When she closed her eyes again she could hear the saw scraping against the bone again, and again she could hear Isaac screaming and in her mind's eye could see how he struggled to get up.

Ellen was relieved when she woke up in the morning and the night—and her nightmares—were over. She didn't dare go to Isaac and be there when he woke up and realized that his hand had been cut off. He would curse Ellen as soon as he learned she had not only let it happen but even had arranged it and assisted. She knew Isaac would not understand that she would have done everything in her power to save him for the sake of Mildred and the children.

—

Ellen and Peter finished making the gate and took it to the monks early in the morning along with two of Peter's friends. She came home exhausted at lunchtime and could hear Isaac shouting. Mildred sat on her bed in the kitchen, trembling and sobbing. Marie and Agnes hid in their mother's arm and were crying also. Ellen knelt down alongside her sister and hugged her until she had calmed down a bit.

"Don't go to see him now. He needs some time!" Mildred said, holding Ellen's arm and trying to stand up. "He knows now that you were holding him when..." Mildred stopped in the middle of her sentence. "He hasn't stopped shouting and cursing you."

"But what could I have done differently?" Ellen looked at her sister helplessly.

"I know there was no other way to save him," Mildred sobbed. "But he just won't understand that. What's going to happen now?" she whispered, exhausted.

Ellen avoided Isaac as long as he was in a rage.

Mildred looked in on him frequently, even though she herself could barely stand, and Eve or the barber-surgeon changed the bandages every day.

For three days, Isaac fumed and screamed, and then he fell silent. He lay motionless with his face turned to the wall, ate what Eve brought him, but didn't say a word to anyone.

February 1177

Almost four weeks had passed since the barber-surgeon had amputated his hand, and Isaac still was being awakened at night by bad dreams.

One night Mildred suddenly began moaning loudly. Barefoot and still half asleep, Ellen staggered over to her sister's bed.

"What is wrong with Mother?" Marie asked. She had been lying alongside her and was now rubbing her eyes sleepily. She hid anxiously behind Ellen as she fanned the fire.

"I think the baby is coming!" Ellen gently stroked the child's head.

Peter's sister had also been sleeping in the house the last few days, and she entered the room, yawning.

"Eve, go and get the midwife," Ellen said calmly as she placed a kettle of water on the hearth. Then she took Marie and Agnes by the hand and brought them to their father.

"Wake up!" Ellen shook him. "You must take the children. Mildred is in labor, and I have to return to her." Ellen's severe tone left no room for argument, and Isaac raised his blanket.

"Come here, it's cold," he said to his daughters. Eagerly they crawled into their father's bed, happy he wasn't shouting anymore and was finally speaking to them again.

After what seemed like an eternity, Eve returned with the midwife. "I can already feel the little head," the old woman said reassuringly after placing her hand briefly under Mildred's shirt. "It won't take much longer," she said, stroking Mildred's sweaty face. "Soon it will be over."

Mildred looked pale and weak, but she nodded.

Not long thereafter, the boy was born. He was skinny, much too small and grey, and he didn't cry.

The midwife shook her head. "He's dead," she said in a flat voice.

Mildred began to sob loudly. There was not much time to recover before new contractions expelled the afterbirth. When it was over, Mildred was completely drained.

The midwife washed her, and Eve straightened out the bedclothes.

In the meanwhile, Ellen went out into the garden to dig a hole for the child. It actually was Isaac's job, but he couldn't do it. Praying softly, Ellen buried the limp, dead body as well as the afterbirth, and filled in the hole. She planted a daisy on the grave and placed a cross in the ground made of two pieces of wood tied together.

When she returned to the house, Isaac was kneeling down alongside Mildred. With his good right hand he stroked her cheek and wiped away the tears.

"When I am dead, you must marry Ellenweore. She will always be there for you. You need a wife, and the children need a mother," Mildred whispered.

"Shh..." Isaac kissed her on the forehead.

"Please, Isaac, you must promise me you will!" she begged him as she struggled to sit up.

"Certainly, my love," he answered gently.

"Promise me you'll marry her. Think of the children and the smithy. She is the only one who can help you!" Mildred sighed. "Ellen is a good person! Swear to me you will do it!" she begged him.

"I'll promise—anything you want!" Isaac answered devotedly just to keep her from getting excited.

Ellen acted as if she hadn't heard a word of it.

Isaac noticed her, stood up without looking at her, and returned silently to his room.

Mildred had fallen asleep, exhausted. She woke when Ellen stood up to go to the smithy.

"Ellen?" she called to her sister weakly.

"Yes?"

"Did you hear what Isaac promised me?"

Ellen nodded reluctantly.

"Now it's your turn: swear to me that you will take care of Marie and Agnes…and Isaac. You must marry him after I die!"

"You'll get better soon and be able to take care of your children yourself," Ellen said, trying to comfort her sister.

"No, I know I am going to die."

Ellen remained silent.

"Please, promise me!" she whispered. Even thought she had slept, she didn't appear at all well rested. She had gotten paler, and her cheeks and eyes were sunken.

Ellen gave up. "Yes, Mildred, I promise, but I'll do everything I can to make sure it won't happen and that you will recover!"

—

At noon, Mildred actually looked a bit better. Her face was not so pale, and her cheeks looked fuller and rosier. Relieved, Ellen returned to work after lunch. But when she returned later in the afternoon she noticed that Mildred's cheeks were red not because she was getting better, but because she had a high fever. The midwife had promised to stop by, and Ellen waited for her impatiently.

"I think Mildred has a fever," she said to the old woman when she finally arrived.

"I couldn't come any sooner because the dyer's wife had twins. The first child came out backwards, and that is always harder."

Ellen brought a goblet of thin beer and a bowl of warm water for the midwife. Carefully she washed her wrinkled fingers and then examined Mildred.

"I don't like this at all," she mumbled. Then she cooked a potion of herbs that she had brought with her and washed Mildred with it.

"Give her this to drink as well, two cups, one today and one tomorrow. I'll come before noon to see how she is doing."

When she saw the worried expression on the midwife's face, Ellen realized how badly Mildred was doing.

"My sister thinks she is going to die. Do you think so, too?" Ellen took a deep breath.

"The ways of the Lord…sometimes the dying know more than the living. I cannot do much more for her, but I'll gladly do whatever I can." The midwife emptied the cup of beer, wrapped her woolen scarf around her shoulders, and prepared to leave. "Farewell, Ellenweore, and pray!" she said as she left the house.

Ellen was freezing. The last few days had been strenuous. She longed for her peaceful smithy, for Jean and Rose, and naturally for William. She crouched down in a corner, exhausted, buried her face in her hands, and cried until she finally drifted off to sleep.

—

For days, Mildred dozed. The fever didn't increase, but it also didn't die down. The children cuddled up to their mother and cried, as if they could feel how little time they still had left.

Even Isaac got control of himself and left his room in order to hold her hand. He brushed her forehead lovingly with his hand, and she opened her eyes, smiling faintly. As soon as he sat down with her, Ellen left and went over to the shop.

"I'm so sorry," Mildred whispered one evening. Isaac just nodded silently and squeezed her hand. This time Ellen was sitting despondently at the foot of Mildred's bed.

Isaac paid no attention to Ellen. In the afternoon the midwife had been there again. She knew the end was near and that there was nothing more she could do for Mildred. Ellen's prayers had not helped.

Hour by hour Mildred became weaker. In a trembling voice and with eyes wide open she reminded her husband and her sister of the promise they had made, and in the afternoon she even found the strength to ask Ellen's forgiveness for having placed such a heavy burden on her.

After the sun had set that evening, it became especially cold. There was a cozy fire crackling on the hearth, and hanging over the flickering fire on an iron chain was a pot of delicious smelling ham soup. Everyone sat silently around the table and ate, without looking up from their bowls.

Mildred's life flickered weakly for a while as well, flared up briefly, and then, shortly after, expired.

—

After they had buried Mildred, Ellen was even more depressed than after Leofric's death.

A year of mourning lay ahead of her, and then she would have to fulfill her promise.

Isaac survived the amputation of his hand. The stump healed without becoming gangrenous, but he seemed to have given up on life. All he did was lie in bed and let fate take its course.

Ellen's sympathy gradually gave way to anger.

Eve still took care of the house and the children, but Isaac didn't really need to have anyone to bring him his meals. He could have gotten up and made himself useful again even if now he was a "cripple" as he called himself disparagingly.

Ellen was horrified at the idea of having to spend the rest of her life with him. Why had she made that promise to her sister? Breaking a promise to a dying person would lead inevitably to eternal damnation, so she would have to marry Isaac whether she wanted to or not. That much was clear.

One day she told Isaac she needed to go to Orford to take care of some important matters. He looked at her with undisguised hostility.

"You never intended to keep your promise, did you?" he asked.

"What do you mean by that?" she flared up.

"Mildred is hardly under the ground, and here you go and disappear, leaving me and my children to a dark fate."

"What do you mean?" Ellen retorted. "Eve will stay in the house and take care of the girls until I come back. Peter will stay in the shop and will do what is necessary, and after all, you are still here!" Ellen was stunned. How dare he call her a liar! She almost burst with rage at his miserable self-pity. "Of course I'll come back, a promise is a promise, but I must look after my father's smithy and see what I can do about it. Do you want to break your own promise?"

Isaac just shrugged. "I have no intention of leaving," he said emphatically.

"Oh, that's good. Then you don't have to go back to bed and can make yourself a bit useful around here," she added irritably.

Isaac did not reply but just filled his goblet and shuffled back to his room to lie down.

Ellen was furious as she packed up her things. She could no longer tolerate Isaac's outrageous behavior and was happy to get out of the house for a few days.

Orford, May 1177

It was on one of those gorgeous spring days with a blue sky and a light breeze that Ellen returned to Orford. A peculiar, anxious feeling came over her, one of both wistfulness and joy at being home again. Nothing had changed. The chickens pecked in the grass for worms and seeds, the vegetable garden was meticulously weeded, and the courtyard was swept clean. Rose seemed to have everything under control, as usual.

Ellen walked toward the smithy, and for a moment she hoped to find Osmond there, though she knew this was impossible. She opened the door and peered in, squinting in order to see.

"She is back!" William cried out joyfully, and though a bit shy, ran to greet his mother.

"Well, how are you?" Ellen asked her son with a smile as she stroked his cheek. William pressed his face into her hand, like a little cat. Ellen sighed. The last few weeks had been too stressful and had consumed all her strength, but nevertheless she had to be strong and make the necessary arrangements before she married this dreadful Isaac. She tried to keep her composure and pulled herself together. "Jean, I have to talk with you." She beckoned to him, then hugged William one more time before letting him down, then also greeted Arthur in passing with a nod of her head.

Jean laid the hammer down and came over to her.

"Welcome home, Ellenweore!" he said cheerfully.

Ellen held the door for him, and they walked out into the yard. Since they had first met almost six years earlier, Jean had grown a lot and was now almost a hand's width taller than her. His back and shoulders had become broad and strong.

"How are Mildred and Isaac? And the children?" he asked anxiously. He could tell by looking at Ellen's face that something was wrong.

“The child was stillborn, but that’s not the worst of it. Isaac’s hand and almost half of his lower arm had to be amputated.”

“Good Lord, that’s dreadful!” Jean looked at her in horror.

“Mildred did not recover after the birth of the child. She died last month.” Ellen’s eyes filled with tears, and she mumbled: “She made Isaac and me swear to get married.”

“Get what…?” Jean looked at her, dumbfounded.

“Yes, yes, you heard right. Because of his hand, Isaac cannot work anymore as a smith. She had to think of the children, and I am supposed to save the smithy.”

“And what does that mean for us?”

“That’s just what I wanted to talk about with you.”

“Ellenweore!” Rose came running across the yard, waving. “William said you were back. It’s so nice to have you back at home again!”

“You didn’t speak with Rose?” Jean seemed surprised, yet he knew her well enough to figure out where her first stop would be: certainly not the house.

Ellen shook her head. Then she noticed Rose’s round belly and swallowed deeply.

“You didn’t tell her anything yet?” Rose scolded. Judging from the way Ellen looked at her, she figured he hadn’t.

“You…you are expecting,” Ellen said in a flat voice.

Rose nodded. Suddenly she was ashamed, even though she had been so overjoyed to finally become a mother.

“Who is it? Who did this to you?” Ellen turned red. “Couldn’t you have kept a better eye on her?” she snapped at Jean. Noticing the guilty, lovelorn gaze in Jean’s eyes, Ellen began to understand.

“You? The two of you have…” Ellen gasped for air, turned on her heel, and strode across the yard and down to the river.

"Let me, I'll do that!" Rose held Jean back by the arm, because she wanted to follow Ellen herself. Dejectedly, and with drooping shoulders, he nodded.

"We should have told her long ago."

"I know."

Rose pulled up her dress and followed Ellen down the steep slope to the brook. Stumbling over a large stone, she slid a ways down the little slope, but at the last moment was able to catch herself before going into a free fall. She arrived at the bank of the stream completely out of breath.

Ellen sat on a boulder throwing pebbles into the water.

Rose sat down beside her. "I love him, Ellen!" she said after a while, staring into the water. "I haven't had much happiness in my life." She took a deep breath. "Except with Jean!"

"But he's only twenty years old at the most!"

"So I'm a few years older than he is. Does it matter?" After a few moments, Rose continued. "I'd like your blessing."

"My blessing?" Ellen laughed out loud. "Did you ask me before you sank into each other's arms? And why me? I'm not a father, guardian, or master for either of you." It sounded as if Ellen were just realizing that herself.

"But you're my friend!"

"One in whom you have never confided a thing," Ellen grumbled, deeply offended.

"Ellen! Please!"

"Why are you only now coming to me? After all, you must have been pregnant when I left. How long has this been going on between you two? Why didn't you ask me what I thought of it before you went and slept with him?"

Rose sat there looking at the ground. "I'm not a child anymore, Ellen. I don't have to ask you," she answered calmly.

"Then you don't need my consent now either."

"But I'd like it!" Rose protested and looked at Ellen, pleading. "Good heavens, please understand, we live under one roof, we're one family! You are like a sister to me and know me better than anyone, except Jean, of course."

Ellen looked at Rose in astonishment. "He knows you that well?"

Rose nodded and blushed a bit. "When he looks into my eyes, he can read my thoughts."

Ellen admired the girlish beauty of her friend, but at the same time, it angered her. Her demure blushing hardly was consistent with her immoral behavior.

"It won't happen for almost four more months." Rose stroked her belly dreamily.

Ellen looked at her sullenly. "That's hard to believe, as round as you already are!"

"I think there are two. The midwife says that, too. They're already jumping around." Rose blushed again.

Suddenly, Ellen's anger was gone. Rose was Rose, and you just had to like her for what she was. "I want to speak with Jean about the future of the smithy," Ellen said. Her voice sounded severe. After a short silence she added, "I'm getting married." She stood up and kicked a little crayfish back into the water.

"Ellenweore! That's wonderful!" Rose stood up as well and wanted to embrace her friend, but Ellen quickly sat down again and slumped over.

"There's nothing wonderful about it. I am bound by the oath that I swore to my dying sister. There is nothing else that could induce me to marry Isaac." The words now came pouring out. "You know what he thinks about women who are smiths. From the very outset he couldn't stand me, and he'll never forgive me for seeing to it that his hand was amputated, even if it saved his life. And he detests me even more now because I can still work as a smith while all he can do is to sit around doing nothing."

Rose looked at her in astonishment. "Oh, Ellen, I am so sorry!" She put her arm around her friend's shoulder, trying to console her.

Ellen was silent. For a while she sat there on the bank without moving, staring into the sparkling water. Then she rose to leave.

"You have my blessing, even if you don't need it. I'll discuss with Jean what needs to be done next." She dusted off her dress and walked back to the smithy.

"Thank you, Ellen," Rose whispered, and remained there by the brook.

—

"You can take over the smithy if you wish," Ellen said to Jean, even though she was still somewhat offended. "You will have to pay me rent, but you could be your own boss."

"No, Ellen, I'm much too young for that. That wouldn't work out, and to be honest there are still too many things I have to learn from you. I'd rather continue working for you and forge swords again—as we used to."

Ellen smiled and thought it over for a moment. Then she turned serious again. "It seems like it's been here forever. What will happen to Osmond's smithy if you don't take it over?" For a moment she thought of Leofric and could almost hear his laughter. She sighed quietly.

"How about Arthur?" Jean asked. "Perhaps you can lease the smithy to him. He has made a good name for himself, and he is old enough." He gave her a questioning look.

"And how about you? Will you really come along with me?" Only now did Ellen realize how much she feared losing him forever.

"Yes, if Rose can come along. She could take care of the children, and your sister's children, too, and the house, just like here. You are the best smith I know, but Rose is the best cook." Jean gave Ellen a mischievous look. "And you and I could make swords, only swords. How does that sound?"

Ellen pretended to be thinking it over for a moment. She had come back to Orford not just because of the smithy but mainly to bring Jean and Rose back with her to St. Edmundsbury. Jean's idea of leasing the smithy to the journeyman seemed quite reasonable, and she nodded thoughtfully. "I have been working for the monks in St. Edmundsbury. They want to outfit a larger contingent of soldiers, and we must try to get a contract for the swords. Then we could even keep Peter." Her eyes began to sparkle.

Jean embraced her. "It's so great you are back! We missed you so much!" He laughed, lifted her up, and twirled her around.

"Just a moment, young fellow," she interrupted him. "We still have some serious things to discuss."

Jean stopped, startled, and put her down again.

"Rose is in a delicate situation because of you." Ellen tried to sound strict. "You know what that means, don't you?"

Jean looked at her, wide-eyed.

"Well, you certainly intend to make her your wife, don't you?"

Jean laughed with relief. "You can certainly bet on that."

"Then you should marry as soon as possible. We have to return soon."

"Thank you, Ellen. I knew you would understand."

Do I, really? Ellen wondered. She could hardly remember anymore what love felt like. Jocelyn and William—that was all so long ago.

—

After the marriage, Jean and Rose set up their quarters in the smithy.

"I'm worried about Ellen," Rose said, when they were alone.

"You don't have to be," Jean replied, putting his arm lovingly around her round belly and kissing her neck tenderly. "She's a big girl, just like you," he whispered, nibbling on her ear.

"One could think you never met Isaac. But you worked for him and you know him. Ellen and he—that's something that will never work out." Rose turned around angrily and glared at Jean.

"Oh, come now. Isaac will calm down. He'll just have to accept that his wife is a smith. After all, she will be the breadwinner for him and his family!" Jean raised his eyebrows.

"That shows again what a child you still are. How can you seriously believe they will ever learn to get along? Just imagine if I had to feed you and could do the same things you do, only better? I don't think you would like that. Ellen really deserves a bit of happiness, but Isaac? I'm really sorry for her."

"Isaac is not a bad fellow. I'll admit he has his views about women, and Ellen is not happy about that, but he isn't the only one to think that way and it also doesn't make him a bad person. I'm certain he will eventually recognize Ellen's talents."

"To recognize them is one thing, but to value them is something else!" Rose objected, and she seemed ready to quarrel about it.

"You're right, love," he said, softening his tone. "But we'll not be able to change any of that tonight. So come and lie down in my arms," he said, pointing to the bed.

"I'm sorry for her just the same, you ladies' man!" Rose teased him, and lay down with him. "If I just weren't so tired…" She yawned.

"Then just to make your point you'd sleep standing up all night like the horses, I know," he mumbled, and yawned at the same time.

June 1177

Shortly afterward, Ellen came to an agreement with Arthur on a fair cost for lease of the house and smithy. The four of them gathered their belongings, put them on a cart, and left Orford. They all felt a bit melancholy about leaving the place that had been their home for so long, and the only one excited about the trip was William.

When they arrived in St. Edmundsbury, they found everyone in a gloomy mood.

Eve greeted them cordially but seemed edgy.

Marie and Agnes just stood there looking back and forth from Ellen to Rose.

Isaac did not even show up in the yard.

The only one who appeared relieved at Ellen's return was Peter, but when he heard that from now on Jean would also be working in the smithy, his eyes widened with dismay.

William fidgeted and kept asking, "Where is Uncle Isaac, anyway?" He paid no attention to his two little cousins.

"He's no doubt in his room resting," Ellen replied with irritation. She found it hard now to tolerate the adoration her son had shown for Isaac from the very outset.

"No he's not!" Isaac grumbled, coming around from behind the house.

Jean was shocked at how bad Isaac looked. He hadn't been able to think of the smith any other way than the way he used to be—hardworking and happy. It was only when he saw the stump that he understood how miserable Isaac must feel. Isaac looked at the new visitors one after the other. "Are you all going to settle in here now?" he asked, but before anyone could reply, young William came running up to him.

"Uncle Isaac, will you put me up on your shoulders?"

Jean grabbed the boy by his smock and pulled him back. "You're really too big already for such antics!" he scolded so Isaac didn't have to respond.

Isaac didn't even try to smile at the boy, glanced at Rose and her belly with contempt, and then shuffled back to his room.

William looked up at Jean, puzzled.

"Uncle Isaac doesn't feel well right now, but he'll get better," Jean reassured him. "What do you say we go into the smithy with Peter?"

William shrugged.

"Come on, now!" Jean took him by the shoulder and guided him toward the forge.

Eve and Rose went into the house.

"How about us all baking a cake?" Rose asked the girls, patting them on the head. The two nodded enthusiastically but looked carefully in Eve's direction when Rose rolled up her sleeves.

"We don't have much flour left," Eve said pointedly.

"Let's have a look." Rose said, glancing into the sack of flour. "Oh, that will be enough for at least a week."

"But it has to last until the end of the month," Eve objected.

"There are a few more mouths to feed here now, and it will in any case be used up faster than we expected. When the flour is gone, we'll just have to buy more—after all, Ellen and the men will be working hard and need to be well fed."

"And in the winter, we'll go hungry," Eve hissed, "but go ahead, do whatever you want."

"Fine, then we can begin. Marie, go and get two eggs, but be careful not to drop any."

Marie went proudly to get the two eggs and put them carefully on the table. "There are still fourteen of them in the little basket, and tomorrow we'll get seven or eight more!" she said. "I can already count, you see!"

Rose smiled at her. "Well, if that's the case, then I know already what we'll do with the rest of the eggs this evening." Rose went to get a bowl in which they would stir the dough.

"Bake a cake? This isn't a holiday!" Eve grumbled.

Rose decided not to respond and to give her a little time to get adjusted. If after a few days Eve still hadn't understood that they were in charge now, then Rose would speak with her.

—

"Mmm, I've missed your cakes and pies," said Ellen, licking her lips contentedly, "and these scrambled eggs and bacon today were just wonderful." Jean looked proudly at Rose.

"It's good Eve didn't hear that," Rose said, laughing.

During Ellen's absence, Eve and Peter had slept in the smithy. Today after work they went back home again. Ellen sat at the end of the table, but the seat opposite her, where Isaac should be sitting as the head of the family, was empty. He had recovered long ago but refused to eat with the others. Eve had taken him a bowl of food before they left. Rose and the girls sat on one side of the table, and opposite them Jean and William had taken a seat.

When the twins are old enough, we'll need a larger table, Rose was thinking. She smiled when she thought of that but avoided talking about it openly. It would bring bad luck to talk about the children and make plans for them before they were born. After all, what would become of them was all in God's hands. Talking about them too much could anger the Lord, and He would punish those who did so with a stillbirth or a crippled child. She wondered whether He had punished Ellen by twisting her son's foot. And if so, why? Because she wasn't married to William? Shocked at this thought, Rose held her breath.

"Rose, can't you hear?" Jean nudged her. "Ellen would like to know how Eve managed in the house."

"Oh, I'm sorry, I was thinking of something else." Rose blushed.

"She kept everything in order, but I think she is not especially happy with my being here. After all, for a while she had been doing things her way, and now I'm suddenly here telling her what to do. But she'll get used to it. If it had been up to her, you wouldn't have gotten any cake today." Rose smiled at Ellen. "But I wanted you to quickly feel at home here."

"Thank you, Rose. Under different circumstances I could indeed feel happy here." She stared at the curtain separating Isaac's room from the dining area. She didn't mind if he heard it and understood it. William noticed the angry glance she cast at his uncle's room and looked sadly into his bowl.

"Eat, William," Jean told him. "You want to become big and strong, don't you?"

"Don't forget, you won't get your piece of cake until you finish eating," Rose added, trying to encourage him.

"Why can't Uncle Isaac eat with us?" William asked, slowly putting a spoonful of egg and a piece of ham in his mouth.

"What nonsense!" Ellen scolded her son. "Of course he can eat with us, but he just doesn't want to."

Looking defiantly down at his plate, William poked around in the egg until it seemed to be growing rather disappearing. "I'm not hungry anymore," he said in a barely audible voice.

Ellen noticed again how much the child looked like his father, and swallowed hard. Recently she had been thinking a lot about William and longed for his forceful manner, his strength, and his unshakable belief in himself. He would never give up like Isaac. Involuntarily she held her breath. She felt queasy at the thought of the upcoming wedding. She still had time until the year of mourning was over, but the day would probably come sooner than she wanted.

"Tomorrow I'm going to the abbey to ask about the weapons for the new troops," she announced suddenly. *Work is the best way to drive away melancholy thoughts*, she thought, taking a good swig of the apple juice. It had already started to ferment and tickled her tongue. "Reminds me of cider," she said softly, with a bit of nostalgia.

—

The following afternoon when Ellen returned from the abbey, she looked irritated.

"You didn't get the job, did you?" asked Jean, raising his eyebrows.

"But I did!" Ellen said briefly, without looking especially happy about it. "We'll have to start again with simple lances. Conrad, the guild master, is an arrogant fellow. He was there at the abbey, too, and criticized us because, as he says, there is no master in the shop." At that, Ellen's voice almost cracked.

"But Isaac...didn't you...?"

"Of course I mentioned Isaac, but Conrad had already heard of his accident and knows he can't work in the smithy anymore. They only let Isaac keep the smithy because he has a good reputation and friends among the guild members. This matter of the guild makes me so angry! If there had been something like that in Orford, we could have leased Osmond's smithy to Arthur only with permission from the guild. Can you imagine that!" Ellen paced restlessly back and forth.

"But if Isaac has the approval of the guild, how can Conrad tell the abbot that there is no master in the smithy?" Jean shook his head in amazement.

Ellen shrugged. "It's always the same thing!" she said angrily. "Isaac can't work at his vocation any longer, and I am a woman. It's just as simple as that. Conrad knows my work and knows as well as you and I do that I should have been a master long ago."

"Then how did you get the contract?"

"The abbot asked how our work had been in the last few months. The monks were very happy and praised our reliability. The abbot dismissed Conrad, then said to me, 'If there is no master working in your smithy, then you can't demand the same prices as members of the guild. But if you can deliver at a better price, I'll be willing to at least give you an order for two hundred lances.' 'But then the guild will expel us once and for all,' I replied. The abbot looked at me with his sharp eyes and said, 'Let me worry about that. I have many orders to give and must save where I can. The guild will have to accept that.' Those were his final words. We must deliver the lances before Christmas."

"Ellen, that's wonderful news," Jean replied, patting her on the shoulder.

"Yes, if you don't take into account that I had to cut the prices to the bone and that the guild will always have a grudge against us!" She sighed. "If we had an order for just one sword, we'd have less work, more profit, and could do more for our reputation."

—

They finished the first hundred lances in just three weeks.

The monks were surprised when all three of them came to deliver the first half of the order and asked for another payment.

In the evening they enjoyed the soup Rose had made from broad beans.

"Your work was really good!" Ellen told Jean, who was now her first assistant again.

Peter took it hard at first to be put back in last place, but he quickly accepted the fact and decided to make the best of it.

"Don't you think we'll have to add on a room before winter comes?" Ellen said, turning to Jean and Rose. She broke off a piece of bread and dunked it into the soup before eating it. "You can't always sleep in the smithy," she said, still chewing.

Rose beamed.

"If Peter can help me a bit, it certainly won't take long," Jean added enthusiastically. "But we've got to get some wood and clay, and enough straw from one of the farmers."

"If you want a window, you'll also have to make some wooden shutters," Ellen said, and enjoyed seeing how thrilled the two seemed to hear that. "So can you take care of everything?"

Jean nodded, his face beaming with excitement.

Ellen fetched her leather purse and gave Jean a few silver coins she had received that morning from the abbot.

"Here. If you need more, come to me."

"Thank you, Ellen," Rose said, squeezing her hand.

—

In the evening, Rose and Jean lay cuddled together on the straw mattress in the smithy and made their plans for the future.

"Can you make us a real bed with a mattress and curtains like ones fine people have? That would make me very happy."

Jean nodded and drew something on the hard-packed dirt floor. "Here's the wall of Isaac's house, and we'll build on here. If we set up our bed in the corner there, then the walls will protect it from drafts on three sides. And if you want, you can also have a curtain. What do you think?"

"That's so wonderful, Jean!" Rose was beaming. "Do you think you could make a bed as a wedding present for Ellen and Isaac next year? They are the masters of the house, and if they have to marry even though they don't love each other, don't you think they should at least sleep like kings?"

Jean laughed and gave her an affectionate bump on the nose. "You are right, as always. That's a good idea. I've been thinking for a long time about what I could do to make Ellen happy. I'll buy a little more wood, get a better price, and then we can be sure the wood for Ellen's bed will be dry. I have another idea… Rose?" Jean looked at his wife, who had fallen asleep in his arms. Her chest rose and fell rhythmically. He looked at her belly and couldn't believe there were two children on the way. How would they ever find room in this delicate little body? She had often told him to put his hand on her stomach when they kicked, but as soon as he touched her, the kicking stopped. They were just like little animals that played dead when danger was present, he thought, smiling. Suddenly her belly moved again. Tenderly he put his hand on it, and this time they kept on kicking! Jean was proud and happy when he thought about becoming a father, and he gently kissed Rose on the cheek before drifting happily off to sleep.

—

Jean had finished the addition to the house before the end of summer and was able to offer his family a roof over their heads that was all their own. The room had a proper oaken door that opened onto the yard. At this time of year, when the sun was still high in the sky, sunlight flooded the interior through the open shutters, bathing the room in a wondrous light. But the best thing about it, according to Rose at least, was the bed set in a niche in the wall with a curtain in front of it. In the corner next to the little hearth was a cradle Jean had built, taking advantage of the warm summer evenings to finish it. He had made it wide enough for twins, if that should really be the case.

Since Ellen and her helpers had finished the lances long before their due date, the abbot also gave them an order for a few simple swords for the soldiers. She earned far more making swords than lances, but here, too, she had to make a concession on the price. In return they promised not to say anything to the guild about it. The swords were in no way comparable to Athanor because for the most part they were all built the same way and with less extravagance, but they were an ideal opportunity for Jean to practice forging and quenching swords. Such simple swords were made with just one kind of iron and were folded fewer times. Nevertheless, they were heat treated just as conscientiously as all the weapons Ellen made. They had no decoration, and the hilts were wrapped in ordinary linen. The order did not include any scabbards. Such common soldiers' swords were delivered all together in a simple wooden box. Ellen decided to add another forge and two new anvils in their smithy so that in the future both Jean and she could make swords at the same time.

"Three anvils? Isn't that a bit too many?" Peter asked in astonishment.

"Not after you become a journeyman!" Ellen replied, with a mischievous smile. "But maybe you'll want to go somewhere else then…"

"Oh, no, I'm not an idiot!" Peter burst out, then blushed. "Excuse me, I mean…"

"Very well!" Ellen said, grinning.

"I'm hoping to receive more orders from the monks soon, and after that I'll try to get work from the noblemen in our region. Who knows, perhaps later we'll even have an apprentice."

Isaac did not know anything about all this. He showed no interest in the smithy or the house, hardly spoke with anyone, and spent most of the time alone in his room dozing. He didn't even pay attention to the children anymore.

Early October 1177

"Jean!" Rose shook her husband gently. "Jean, please wake up!" she said, a little louder. Half asleep, Jean looked around. "What is it? Time to get up?"

"It's starting! Quick! Go and get Ellenweore and the midwife." Rose took a deep breath and breathed out again, moaning.

Jean jumped out of bed, pulled on his chausses, and ran out of the house. "Ellenweore! Ellenweore! It's Rose!" he cried out, hammering on Ellen's door with his fist.

In no time Ellen was at the door. She looked like she hadn't slept at all. "I'll heat up some water right away. Yesterday evening I filled another bucket with fresh water—I must have suspected!" she cried, stirring the fire. "Just give me a moment to hang a kettle over the fire, and then I'll come and have a look at her. You go and fetch the midwife. We'll be able to handle this!" She lit a torch, gave it to Jean, and pushed him out the door.

The girls and William also were awakened by the hammering on the door.

"Go back to sleep. I've got to take care of Rose—the child is coming!" she said abruptly, and pushed Marie and Agnes back to their bed.

The girls began to cry. "Will she die now, too, just like Mother?" Marie asked anxiously.

Ellen shook her head. "Rose is strong. Pray for her, then go and lie down to sleep a little more," she said quickly before hurrying out.

Rose was already experiencing strong labor pains, but she was brave.

"I've been pregnant so many times, but I've never had a child," she said breathlessly between two contractions. "If God really gives me two children and they are healthy, then I know He has forgiven me." She let out a loud moan.

"Everything will be fine," Ellen assured her gently, while Rose's face contorted in pain. Ellen used a wet towel to wipe the sweat from her brow.

Rose suffered until daybreak. The midwife and Ellen stayed with her, while Jean lay down with William. Through the wall he could hear Rose's muffled groans. He couldn't sleep, but prayed fervently until finally he heard little whimpering cries, and shortly afterward someone opened the door.

"You're a father, Jean!" Ellen beamed at him as he rushed over to her. "Come and see your sons!" She took him by the sleeve and led him into the other room.

"And Rose, how is Rose?" he asked anxiously.

"She's fine, don't worry!"

Rose was sitting up in bed looking like the happiest person in the world—rather tired, but wide awake and overjoyed at the twofold blessing.

The midwife had already wrapped the two boys tightly so they looked like two little bugs in a rug. "Have a good look at this fellow—he's your father. You'll respect him and do what he says, do you hear?" she said a bit strictly to the two little bundles. Then she took one, placed him in Rose's arm, and handed the other to Jean.

He picked up his tiny son and looked at him closely. The child's head was smaller than the palm of his hand. "He's got so much hair!" Jean said, astonished, as he stroked the little boy's fist with his finger. Then he went over to Rose, sat down on the edge of the bed, and showed her the child. "Just look how tiny he is!" he whispered.

Rose nodded. "Just like his brother!" she said and handed him the second child.

"And they look like two peas in a pod," Jean said in amazement.

"They're twins!" the midwife said, laughing. "That happens quite a bit—perhaps they will always look alike."

"They're so small and delicate!" Rose whispered anxiously. "William was much stronger. I only hope they are not too weak!" Rose looked at the midwife pleadingly. "Please baptize them today. I've already lost an unbaptized child."

"I wouldn't worry about the boys. I'm sure they will be big and strong. Twins are always smaller, and these two seem to be in the best of health," the midwife declared. "Just the same, I will baptize them so they are cleansed of all sin. Do you have names for them yet?"

Rose and Jean looked at each other questioningly.

"What was your father's name?" Rose asked.

Jean furrowed his brow for a moment. "Raymond." He pronounced the name as in French, and Rose repeated it.

"A nice name, don't you think, Raymond?" giving a kiss on the nose to the child in her arm. The child opened his mouth a little and mewed like a kitten. "It seems he likes it!" Rose said, moved.

"And your father?" Jean asked. He liked the idea of naming the children after their deceased grandfathers.

"He died while I was still very young. My mother spoke of him only once, but she never mentioned his name."

Jean shrugged his shoulders regretfully and stroked Rose's cheek.

"But one comes to mind just the same," Rose said.

Jean listened carefully.

"How about Alan? That was the name Ellen took when she was young."

Jean grinned and looked at his son. "Alan?" The boy yawned, and everyone laughed.

Ellenweore, who had been listening to it all, swallowed deeply. She felt a big lump in her throat, and her eyes filled with tears.

"Very well, then I shall baptize the children now," the midwife said. "They look strong for twins, but you never know what will happen, and we should not put their little souls in any danger." She fished a crucifix and a rosary out of her bag, took some holy water she was carrying with her in a bottle, and sprinkled the first boy with it. "Creature of God, I baptize you herewith with the name of Raymond in the name of the Father, the Son, and the Holy Spirit." She had difficulty pronouncing the nasal sound at the end of the French name. "You should call him Ray," she suggested. After the second child was baptized, she told Jean he would need to take the children to church along with the godparents the following week to complete the baptism with the priest's blessing.

After Rose had nursed both boys and they had fallen asleep exhausted, the midwife put the children in the crib together. Then, with cordial but firm words she asked Jean and Ellen to leave and told the young mother she would have to rest a bit also.

As soon as Rose had closed her eyes, she left the room, shutting the door quietly behind her. In the house next door she collected her fee from Jean, which was twice as high because of the twin birth. She pronounced a blessing on the family, gave them a few more instructions, and said good-bye.

—

When Eve arrived at the smithy the next morning and heard the news, she immediately rushed in to see Rose. "Please don't worry—I'll take care of everything until you have your strength back," she promised.

"I'm glad you know your way around the house so well," Rose replied feebly. The tensions between the two that had flared up occasionally in the last few months were gone.

"I wasn't always nice to you, and I'm sorry," Eve said softly. "I was afraid you would dismiss me once the child was here."

"Well, as you can see, now we have twice as much work!" Rose answered. "But even with one child I still would not have let you go."

Eve beamed. "Does Isaac know yet that there are two new youngsters in the house?"

Rose took a deep, audible breath. "He knows about it, no doubt, but I don't think it particularly interests him. Right up until his wife died he wanted nothing more than a son. Now it will be hard for him to accept that Jean suddenly has two."

"Well, I'll see when I bring him his breakfast." Eve raised her eyebrows. "Now more than ever he'll hide in his room, but his grief will eventually fade."

Rose wanted to nod, but suddenly she had to yawn.

"Oh, excuse me, you must be tired. I'll let you sleep now and will come back later."

"Thank you, Eve," Rose said, and immediately drifted off to sleep.

Eve was right: Isaac withdrew even more after the birth of the twins. Though he used to go out and sit in the kitchen from time to time in the afternoon, now he avoided going anywhere he might bump into the children. He either went out into the woods, back to his room, or to the meadow on the hill behind the house.

March 1178

One day Jean discovered little William hiding in a bush all by himself. Tears streamed down his face and over the freckles on his cheeks. "Now, now, Will! What is this? A boy doesn't cry!" he scolded him gently, thinking for a brief moment of his own father. It was almost as if he could hear his father's voice.

"I know, but I can't help myself!" William answered sadly, and sniffled.

"What's wrong?" Jean sat down alongside him and started poking around on the ground with a stick.

"It's because of Uncle Isaac." William's nose was running. He sighed and then took a deep breath.

"Really?"

"I think he doesn't like me anymore." William looked sadly at Jean and wiped his face on his sleeve.

"But that's nonsense, William. What makes you think that?" Jean looked at the little boy with compassion.

"Since we have been here he hasn't kidded around with me a single time or taken me on his lap. He never talks to me anymore at all! And when I go to see him, he tells me to go away."

Jean took the boy in his arm and tried to console him. "He doesn't laugh anymore because he's angry," he explained.

"Angry?" William looked at him, wide-eyed.

Jean nodded. "Yes, Will, but he is not angry at you."

"Who, then?"

"Maybe he's angry at God." Jean raised his eyebrows.

"But you mustn't get angry at God!"

"I know, Will, and Isaac knows it, too."

"But why is he so angry at God?"

"Because other men get sons."

"Like you!" William smiled broadly, and Jean nodded.

"And because God took Mildred away from him, and his hand as well."

"Did God cut it off?"

"No, William, a barber-surgeon did that."

"But then he has to be angry at the barber-surgeon!"

Jean took a deep breath. It was harder than he had thought to explain that to a boy who was barely five years old.

"Or at your mother, because she held my arm down when the barber-surgeon started to saw," said Isaac, who suddenly appeared out of nowhere behind them.

William looked at him, horrified. "You're lying, she didn't do that!" he shouted, then jumped up and ran away.

"Isaac!" Jean scolded the smith.

"What?" Isaac answered belligerently.

"Was that necessary? The child adores you and loves you!"

"And his mother was responsible for my becoming a cripple!"

"You must know she didn't have a choice. Do you think she did it on purpose?" Jean looked at Isaac defiantly.

"Maybe she wanted the smithy…" Isaac's voice quivered.

"She already had a smithy!"

"She hates me because I said women don't belong in a workshop."

"You're a fool, Isaac!"

Isaac groaned.

"The boy is a cripple himself. Do you know how much it would mean to him…?" Jean couldn't continue, because the smith interrupted him.

"You can call me a cripple, but don't you dare call him that again!" he shouted furiously. "He'll make out all right."

"Certainly he will, and you are a really good model for him. You can see he is already running away and hiding, just like you." Jean was intentionally provoking Isaac.

Furiously, Isaac reared up in front of Jean and took a deep breath.

Jean continued to stare at him defiantly. For a moment he thought Isaac would sock him in the face with his other fist. He almost hoped he would, but nothing happened. Jean started to leave, but then turned around again. "The boy never had a father. You could have been one to him," he said reproachfully, and looked at Isaac in disappointment. "He deserves something better than you, and so does Ellen." Without deigning him another glance, he returned to the smithy.

Isaac mumbled an oath to himself and shuffled back to the house.

—

One day in April when the weather was in a playful mood, going from rain to snow, showers to sunshine, Isaac bumped into Ellen alone in the kitchen.

"We must talk," he said, and sat down on the bench opposite her. His good hand lay on the table, and the other arm hung down.

Ellen looked at him questioningly. It was the first time he had spoken to her since Mildred's death.

He cleared his throat and wiped the table nervously with his good hand.

"What do you want?" Ellen asked impatiently.

"It's about the wedding."

"Have you changed your mind?" Ellen preferred not to look at him.

"Of course not!" It was clear that Isaac was annoyed. "Even though I would like nothing more than to have some peace and quiet." After a pause, he continued. "We swore we would."

"I have not forgotten," Ellen responded. She turned up her nose. Since Mildred's death, Isaac had rarely bathed and hadn't shaved at all. "Before the wedding you will have to take a bath. You stink." Ellen expected an outburst, but he just nodded.

"Your year of mourning is over," he reminded her.

"Then we must make good on our promise soon. I'll speak with the priest." Ellenweore stood up. "Is that all?"

Isaac nodded without looking at her and remained seated motionless until Ellen had left. Then he pounded the table so hard with his fist that the earthenware cups began to shake. He jumped up, stormed out into the forest despite the rain, and didn't return until dusk, soaked through and through.

—

The wedding was just one month later, on a dark, rainy day in May. Rose walked arm in arm with Ellen on the way back from the church while Jean, Peter, and Eve came behind them with the children. Isaac walked far behind, all by himself. Even though Ellen was wearing a new linen dress and had a wreath of white flowers on her head, she did not look like a happy bride. Rose pulled her friend into the house to the room she would have to share with Isaac from now on. Jean had replaced the curtain with a door, and in the middle of the little room with its headboard along a wall stood the oaken bed that Jean had made for them. The four corner posts reached almost up to the ceiling and held up a canopy and curtains made of light blue linen.

Ellen's eyes filled with tears when she thought about having to share this bed from now on with Isaac. Contrary to her expectations, and without further prompting from her, the groom had taken a bath and put on the new clothes she had laid out for him, but that did nothing to relieve her anxiety of having to spend the rest of her life as his wife.

Rose saw her tearful eyes but didn't know what to do. "Oh, Ellen," she said, stroking her cheek and trying to console the unhappy bride, "everything will turn out all right, it will just take time."

"I'm afraid of tonight!" she confessed to her friend in a choked voice. Rose nodded sympathetically and brushed a wayward lock of hair from her face.

At the wedding feast that followed and to which additional guests were invited, there was much drinking and laughter. Only Ellen and Isaac sat at the table stern-faced and without speaking. The longer the party went on, the tipsier and livelier the group became. When Ellen could no longer bear to watch how the others were celebrating her wedding, she arose. As custom required, so did Isaac. The wedding guests laughed and howled, making smutty comments and raising their goblets to the young couple. Their departure for the conjugal quarters meant the party was over.

"How did they get that bed in here?" Isaac asked incredulously when they were alone in the room.

"I wondered that myself. Who knows what else went on behind my back!" Ellen replied, attempting a shy smile. She could sense that Isaac felt just as uncomfortable as she did. She withdrew to the farthest corner of the room where the light from the tallow candle didn't reach, took off her dress, and slipped under the covers in her undergarment.

Isaac sat on the other side, at the edge of the bed. "I won't insist on any conjugal rights," he said calmly, then took off his shoes and his soiled clothes and slipped into the bed in his nightshirt. He put out the candle and turned his back to Ellen.

She lay awake alongside him for a long time and woke up again in the morning later than usual. The sun had risen already, and the bed on Isaac's side was empty.

"Did you sleep well?" Rose asked anxiously when Ellen finally came out into the main room.

Ellen nodded. Rose could see the relief in her eyes.

Rose smiled at her. "Jean and Peter want you to know that the workshop is off-limits to you today. You have to rest, and not go to work until tomorrow."

Ellen blinked in the bright sunlight shining through the open door and took a deep breath. "So much time, what can I possibly do with so much time?" She took one of the meat pies left over from the evening before and hungrily started to eat. "What a beautiful day, I think I'll go for a little walk. It has been a long time since I was outside," she said as she finished the meat pie.

"I'd like so much to come along, just as we used to, do you remember? But Eve isn't here today for the children, so unfortunately I can't."

The twins sat on the floor next to Rose and played with wooden blocks left over from building the bed.

"Very well, it won't hurt me to be alone for a while." Ellen decided to go out onto the wide meadow near the forest's edge where she could lie down in the grass and look up at the sky, just as she had done as a child with Simon. It seemed like an eternity since she had been able to take time to relax like this. Her thoughts wandered back to her youth. She could see the faces of Claire, Jocelyn, and William, and a wonderful, warm feeling came over her that wasn't just from the warmth of the sun. Suddenly she was torn from her reveries by a scream. She jumped up and looked around. Her son was running out onto the meadow, and Isaac was running as fast as he could after him. He caught him, and William screamed again. Ellen ran as fast as she could and soon reached the two of them.

"You are so mean!" she heard William shouting and saw how he was pounding Isaac with his little fists.

"What's going on here?" Ellen demanded angrily. "William, come here!"

The boy fled to his mother and hid behind her skirt, something he rarely had the opportunity to do and which he appreciated so much more now. "I cut my finger really bad," he wailed, and showed her his hand.

"Where did you get the knife?" she asked suspiciously after convincing herself that the wound was only superficial.

"Isaac gave it to me," he replied meekly, and showed her a small but very sharp knife.

Ellen looked at Isaac in bewilderment. "Are you completely crazy? You can't let a five-year-old play by himself with a knife!"

"He wasn't playing with it by himself but was learning how to whittle wood under my supervision. Anyway, he didn't cut the finger off," Isaac answered roughly.

"That's what he told me, too, and then he laughed at me because I cried, so I ran away."

"You laughed at him?" Ellen could feel how the anger was welling up inside her without being able to do anything about it. "You, of all people? All day long you just sit around and feel sorry for yourself!" she shouted.

Isaac yanked up his sleeve and pointed the bare stump of his arm at her. "Yes, I laughed at him. A boy doesn't cry over a little cut on his finger. I, on the other hand, have every reason to quarrel with my fate. If you hadn't let them cut off my arm…" The vein in his neck was swollen and looked like a giant, pulsating worm.

"Then you would have been dead long ago and would finally have the peace you are looking for!" Ellen shouted in reply. "Yes, I have long ago regretted saving your life. I only did it for Mildred's sake. I was afraid she wouldn't be able to bear losing you. If I had known she would die anyway, I would have left you to your fate. You would have rotted away!" She broke out in a laugh. "I realize now how suitable that would have been for you, you loafer! I wish I had stayed in Normandy and had never been there to watch Mildred die. How could I ever have sworn to marry you? You are selfish, cruel, and ungrateful!"

"Ungrateful?" Isaac repeated. "Should I be grateful to you for having held my arm as the barber-surgeon sawed it off? Never, ever shall I forgive you for doing that!"

"I hated doing it, Isaac, and now I hate you, too. Every night I am dogged by the feeling of helplessness I had that day, watching the saw cutting into your bone. I can still smell the rotten flesh! You are stupid and vain, Isaac! The boy has nothing to learn from you!" Ellen turned to Will. "Let's go, Aunt Rose will make you a little bandage," she said with more understanding than usual. She took the boy by the hand and returned to the house.

Isaac raged so loudly that it could be heard far and wide.

"He is not always like that," Will said softly after a while, looking up at his mother.

"I don't want to hear another word about it!" Ellen said, pushing her son into the house.

—

Just a few days after this incident, Will slipped away secretly to the hill where Isaac was sitting and brooding.

"What do you want here?" Isaac asked with annoyance.

"Nothing, I just want to sit here for a while with you," Will answered and sat down alongside him.

"Don't let your mother catch you doing that," Isaac grumbled.

"She won't notice, she's in the smithy."

They sat there quietly for a while as Will picked three blades of grass and braided them together.

"Are you still afraid of whittling with a knife?" Isaac asked casually.

Will nodded.

"You shouldn't be. You know now how dangerous it can be. You have to be aware of the knife and how sharp it is, to respect it and hold it correctly. You never make the same mistake twice."

"Uncle Isaac?" Will looked at him, wide-eyed.

"Hmm?"

"Can I ask you something?"

"Hmm."

"What happened to your hand? Why did it have to be cut off?"

Isaac felt the blood rushing to his head and gasped for air. It was a while before he could say anything, but Will was willing to wait.

"Peter left a pair of tongs on the forge. They were hot, but you couldn't see that. I picked them up and burned myself."

"But why did you then get mad at God and my mother and not at Peter?" Will gave him a puzzled look.

"The tongs were right next to the forge, and I should have known they were hot. Then I kept on working instead of taking care of my hand. We had a lot of work and needed the money." Isaac's voice was still rough but didn't sound quite so gruff.

"I am going to be like you someday, Uncle Isaac!" Will said softly. "I have both hands, but look at my foot—I am a cripple, too!" Will said it so matter-of-factly that a shiver ran down Isaac's spine.

"I forbid you from saying such a thing!" he said angrily. "You are not a cripple, and the thing about your foot..." Isaac stopped and looked down at Will's feet. "Hand me your shoe!"

Will took off the wooden shoe. "Which one?"

Isaac picked up the shoe that was on the crippled foot and looked at it closely. Then he picked up the boy's foot and look at it also. "It has already gotten a little straighter, I think. Perhaps it really is doing some good!" Isaac seemed pleased.

"Jean says I'll always have to wear the shoes, but they hurt so much! I take them off a lot and run around barefoot when he's not looking," Will confessed.

"Oh, that makes me very sad," Isaac said, looking at the boy and shaking his head.

"Why?" asked Will curiously. He had been yearning for attention from his uncle for so long and suddenly he had it, completely!

"Maybe you don't remember, but Jean and I worked together on your first shoe so that your foot would straighten out," Isaac explained.

"But it doesn't matter how it grows, that's what Mother says, at least."

"I think your mother is wrong."

"It's no surprise you say that. You can't stand her!" Will lowered his eyes and stared sadly at the ground.

"That doesn't change my opinion about your foot." Isaac had been massaging it with his good hand until it was warm and pink. The wooden shoe had left blisters and calluses on Will's foot, but the boy enjoyed the touch of Isaac's hand.

"Uncle Isaac?"

"What is it, son?"

"I don't like the smithy!" Will looked at his uncle as if he had confided something terribly wrong to him.

"What do you mean?"

"Mom says that someday I'll be a smith, too, and smiths don't need a healthy foot. Uncle Isaac, who is Wieland?"

The smith chuckled at how the child jumped from one idea to another. For the first time in a long while he experienced a warm, pleasant glow in his heart. He tousled Will's hair and asked, "Would you like to hear the story of Wieland the Smith?"

Will nodded enthusiastically. He could hardly imagine anything nicer than having someone tell him a story.

"But it's long," Isaac cautioned him.

"Oh, that doesn't matter!" Will said with a broad smile.

"Very well," Isaac said, clearing his throat. "Long ago and far away there lived a friendly giant. He sent his son Wieland to Mimir, the most famous smith in the land of the Huns, to serve as an apprentice and learn the art of forging weapons.

After three years, Wieland returned home. But as the giant wanted him to become the most famous of all smiths, he took him to live with two dwarfs who were masters not only in the art of forging weapons but in forging gold and silver. The boy learned quickly, and since the dwarfs did not want him to leave, they promised to give the giant's money back to him if he let the youth stay with them for one more year. If he did not come to pick up his son on precisely the appointed day, however, they had the right to kill the boy. The giant hid a sword and directed his son to fetch it and kill the dwarfs if he was not back on time. Wieland stayed with the dwarfs. He was loyal and industrious, but they envied him for his skill and were happy that he had been put in their hands. The giant set out on his journey to reclaim his son, but he started too early and the mountain was still sealed when he arrived. He lay down to sleep in the grass, and an enormous boulder fell off the mountain and killed him."

Will held his breath in shock.

"When on the appointed day Wieland found his dead father, he fetched the sword and slew the dwarfs. Then he left and went to King Nidung, who took him into his household. Wieland's only job was to care for three knives on the king's table, but one day while he was washing them, one fell into the sea and disappeared forever. Amilias, the only smith at the king's court, was not in his shop, so Wieland went to the anvil and made a knife himself that was identical to the one that was lost."

"He learned how to do that from Mimir and the dwarfs!" Will said, clapping his hands enthusiastically.

Isaac didn't allow himself to become distracted, and continued with the story: "When the king was at dinner, he cut a loaf of bread with the knife, and it was so sharp that it cut right through the table. Nidung had never had such a knife and didn't believe that Amilias had forged it. He pressured Wieland until he confessed he had made it himself. But Amilias was jealous and went to the king to suggest a contest. Wieland would forge a sword, whereas he, Amilias, would make a helmet and armor. Whoever should win in battle would cut off the head of the loser. The king agreed and had another smithy built in which Wieland would make the sword. After seven days Wieland had made a sharp sword, but he took a file, ground the sword into tiny pieces, mixed it with wheat flour, and gave the mixture to the geese to eat. Later, he heated the geese droppings, separating the iron from the waste, and forged a second smaller sword from it. He tested its sharpness and filed it down again. This third sword was the best, and Wieland named it Mimung. Then he secretly made another that looked just like Mimung. On the day the contest was to be held, Amilias appeared in the market square in his bright and shining armor, and was admired by everyone there. He sat down on a chair and waited. Wieland fetched the sword and placed the blade on Amilias's head. It was so sharp that it cut right through the helmet as if it were made of wax. Amilias couldn't feel it and encouraged Wieland to strike with all his might, but all Wieland had to do was to lean heavily on the sword until it cut right through Amilias' helmet, his head, and the coat of mail right down to the buckle of his belt. When Amilias tried to stand up, he fell over in two pieces and was dead. Nidung now wanted to have this sword at once. Wieland pleaded for a bit of patience, saying he needed to go and fetch the scabbard. When he got to the smithy, he hid Mimung under the forge, took out the other sword, and brought it to the king. From this day forward Wieland forged weapons and jewelry for the king and was highly honored."

Will jumped up. "I don't like that story! I don't understand it!" he cried. "She said that Wieland couldn't walk, but that's not so!"

"Wait, son." Isaac laughed and motioned for the boy to sit down again. "There's more to the story, but I'll shorten it a bit for you. Because Wieland had deceived the king, he had to flee into the forest. King Nidung got word that Wieland was working alone in a smithy in the forest and had much gold, so he rode there with his men and stole the gold and Mimung from the smith. Nidung took Wieland prisoner and brought him to an island where he built a smithy for him. Wieland sought vengeance against the king for this disgrace and secretly prepared a love potion for the king's daughter. But the king learned of Wieland's ruse and had Wieland punished again." Isaac's voice had become hoarse from talking so long. He took out his waterskin, took a long drink, and then handed it to the boy.

Will shook his head. "What happened then?" he asked excitedly.

"The king had the tendons in Wieland's feet and knees severed and returned him to his smithy." Isaac's voice sounded agitated as he continued. "For a long time, Wieland lay there in great pain, and it took months for his wounds to heal. But he was no longer able to walk." Isaac sighed briefly. "One day King Nidung came to him, brought him two crutches, and promised him great wealth if he would work for him again as a smith. Wieland acted friendly, but after the king had left he promised vengeance."

Will scarcely dared to breathe. "Do you think he took his revenge?" he asked softly.

Isaac blinked as he stared into the setting sun. "I know he did. If you want, I'll tell you tomorrow how he did it. But now it would be better if we went home or your mother will holler at us." He smiled at the boy and stroked his hair again.

"You are really lucky," Will said suddenly.

"What do you mean?" Isaac frowned.

"You still have one good hand and almost your entire arm."

"You call that lucky? I'd rather lose the tendons in my legs than my hand!" Isaac growled.

Will didn't listen. "Wieland is a hero, and he didn't give up. He started working again as a smith—that was what he did best. He had to do it or else he never would have been happy! I'm sure he would have kept on going even with one hand." Will's eyes sparkled. If he had only suspected how much his words would hurt Isaac, he never would have spoken them, because he loved the sad-looking man like a father and wanted nothing more than to see him happy again.

—

"Isaac told me about Wieland!" Will burst out excitedly at supper, then bit into his bread, chewing laboriously.

"What is the matter? Aren't you hungry?" Rose frowned.

"Oh, I am, but my tooth is loose," Will lisped.

Rose reached for his chin, tipped his head back, and smiled. "Let's have a look!"

"See?" Will pushed one of his lower incisors forward with his tongue until it started to bleed around the tooth.

"Aha!" Rose said, laughing, "That will be falling out soon."

"I have lots of new ones!" Marie spoke up, opening her mouth wide and sticking her finger far back into it. "Here, do you see?"

Isaac stroked his daughter's cheek affectionately.

"The story about Wieland, that's wonderful!" Ellen smiled. "Almost every child in England knows that story. That's no doubt the reason so many people have respect for us smiths, because they believe there are dark forces involved when we are working at the forge at night. They assume that dwarfs and elves give us power over the iron. Some herb women even say that water from our hardening troughs has healing powers." Ellen shrugged. "I loved it when Donovan told us that story on long, cold winter evenings, when we were all sitting around the fire. Donovan always embellished the story and told it with such dramatic flair! Back then in Tancarville, I wanted to forge iron just like Wieland, and more than once I dreamed that a dwarf took me as his apprentice. I told Donovan about it, and he pretended to be angry. 'I'm small, but I'm not a dwarf,' he said, and laughed at me. I was so ashamed I wished the ground would open and swallow me up." Ellenweore's cheeks turned red, and her unruly locks poked out from under her scarf and danced around her face when she laughed.

Isaac felt a tug at his heartstrings when he saw how her eyes lit up with the glow from the fire, and he had trouble breathing. As he stood up from the table, he knocked over his chair and then quickly picked it up and without saying a word retreated to his room.

Jean cast an inquisitive glance at Ellen. "I think these stories about Wieland have opened up some old wounds for him." He was sorry for Isaac, even if he felt that his reaction was unnecessarily strong.

When Ellen lay down in the bed alongside Isaac that night, he seemed to already be sleeping. His eyes were closed, and his breathing was regular. For a moment she examined his face, which seemed relaxed. Suddenly he blinked, and Ellen quickly looked away. Her heart was pounding as if she had been caught doing something that was forbidden.

—

The next day Will lay in wait for his stepfather in the yard. Hardly had Isaac left the house when the boy ran up to him. "Uncle Isaac, will you please tell me the end of the story now?" The smith couldn't resist the boy's pleading gaze.

"Well, a promise is a promise, so come on and we'll go for a little walk."

Will looked up at Isaac and nodded, then reached out his sticky little hand to the smith. Isaac's left arm quivered. As so often, he had the feeling that the missing hand and fingers were still there. He rubbed the stump on his shirt trying to drive away the itching and pulling. Once they got to the top of the hill, they sat down in the grass.

"So you want to know how Wieland avenged himself on Nidung?"

Will nodded emphatically.

"As you will remember, Wieland was working again as the king's smith."

Will looked intently at his uncle, his eyes flashing. "I would not have worked for him again; after all, the king had ordered his tendons to be cut off!" he said excitedly.

Isaac laughed and tousled his hair before continuing. "Well, one day Nidung's two younger sons came to see Wieland in the smithy and asked him to make some arrows for them. They didn't want their father to know anything about it. Wieland told them to come back on a day when fresh snow had fallen. They were to walk backwards to the smithy, where he would make the arrows for them. The very next day it had snowed, and the two boys did as the smith had instructed them." Isaac looked deeply into Will's eyes. "Wieland was obsessed with the thought of revenge. He took his hammer and slew the king's children."

"But they weren't guilty of anything!" Will cried out angrily.

"That's right, my son, but a person driven by revenge is seldom just." Isaac took the boy in his arms. "Do you really want me to go on?"

Will swallowed his tears and nodded.

"Wieland hid the corpses of the children, and when the king's men came to the smithy to look for the boys he told them he had made arrows for them. The footprints in the snow leading away from the smithy seemed to confirm what he was telling them, so Nidung's men looked for the boys in the forest nearby. After many days, they finally gave up the search. Wieland went and got the corpses from their hiding place and made drinking cups of silver and gold out of the children's skulls. From their bones he carved knife handles and candlesticks for the king's dinner table. But Wieland longed for even greater revenge. Using a magic ring he persuaded Badhild, the king's daughter, to secretly marry him. When shortly afterward one of Wieland's brothers—the best of all archers—came to Nidung's kingdom, Wieland could finally get his revenge. He made wings out of eagle feathers, put them on, and flew up to Nidung's castle. He told the king he had killed his sons and Badhild was expecting a child from him, then flew away. Now Nidung ordered the archer to kill his own brother."

"So now Wieland, too, is getting his just punishment!" the boy announced triumphantly, but Isaac shook his head.

"Wieland was smart and had told his brother to shoot him under his right arm where he was carrying a bag filled with blood. On observing all the blood, Nidung believed the smith was dead, but he died himself shortly thereafter from his grief. His eldest son became a kind and just king, and when Badhild gave birth to a boy, Wieland pleaded with the young king for forgiveness. Wieland and Badhild married and lived happily in their homeland until the end of their days." After he had finished the story, Isaac was silent for a long while.

Will started picking up stones and throwing them, at first hesitantly and then with increasing rage.

"I don't like him!" he growled.

"Who don't you like?" Isaac asked with surprise.

"Wieland! He isn't a hero at all. He's underhanded and not one bit better than Nidung!"

"But Nidung deceived him and made him a cripple," Isaac said, looking at the child in surprise.

"Wieland is a coward. The children did nothing to harm him, nor did the poor eagles who had to lose their feathers!" Will cried out angrily. "Would you kill me because she allowed the barber-surgeon to cut off your arm?" he asked in horror.

Isaac thought about his quarrel with Ellen and didn't know what to say to that. He just silently shook his head.

"I'll never be like Wieland, and I'll never become a smith!" the boy said disapprovingly.

"Oh, Will!" Isaac took the boy by the arm. "You are still much too young to be such a stubborn fellow. Of course you will become a smith. In our family all the men are smiths, your grandfather, my father, and all our ancestors." He gave the boy an encouraging smile.

"And what about my father?" Will's eyes filled with tears; then he jumped up and ran down the hill.

"Wait, Will, wait for me!" Isaac had gotten up, too, and hurried to catch up with the boy.

"You are pretty damned fast with your crooked foot," he congratulated him, panting, after he had finally caught up with him just before they got to the smithy. Will flushed with pride at Isaac's compliment and forgot his anger.

"Shall we go to the forest again tomorrow?" Isaac asked, smiling at the boy.

Will nodded and dashed off happily.

—

"I could do carvings again if only I knew how to hold the wood," Isaac mumbled the next day while they were sitting on the meadow near the forest. He pulled off his shoes and tried to hold the piece with his feet.

Will was excited by the idea and did the same, and soon the two of them realized it wasn't all that difficult.

From that moment on, Isaac practiced with great enthusiasm every day, and eventually learned how to hold a piece of wood tightly enough to whittle it with his right hand. Isaac was amazed at how intent Will was also.

"Why are you doing that?" he asked one day in amazement. "You have two good hands!"

"When you started doing that, I just thought it was fun," Will said, grinning. "But it also makes my foot stronger. Ever since I have been practicing with you I can run father without it hurting."

Whenever he was together with Will, Isaac felt the comfort and warmth he had missed for so long. "Now it's time I started whittling so I can make you a new pair of wooden shoes!" Isaac put a piece of wood between his toes and held it tightly with his other foot. He began by cutting a figure of a cow. Shortly after came a doll for Marie and a little puppy for Agnes, and later two more cows, a pig, a donkey, and a horse as well as a farmer, a cat, and a cradle with a baby inside.

His daughters' eyes sparkled when he gave them his first creations. Every day they stormed him with requests, eagerly anticipating what would come next.

With every figure he made, Isaac became more skillful and, as everyone noticed, happier.

Autumn 1178

Will ran barefoot through the grass that was wet with the morning dew to the place where Isaac usually sat to do his carvings. The ground was soft, had a sharp fragrance, and was covered with colorful leaves that Will joyfully kicked up in front of him as he ran. Isaac was not working on a piece of wood as usual but stood there with a stone in his hand. Will stared at him in surprise. Isaac kept bending the arm holding the stone and then extending it far from his body. Sometimes he swung his arm around, and sometimes he pressed the stone straight up. Will was fascinated by what Isaac was doing and didn't dare to disturb him for a long while. "What are you doing there, Uncle Isaac?"

"I'm losing strength in my arm, and it's time I did something about that."

Will nodded, even though he didn't understand.

Isaac looked at the boy and broke out laughing because he looked so puzzled.

"Keep an eye on my arm when I press the stone up. Do you see?" He pointed to his muscle with his chin. "Once my arms were almost twice as thick, and I want them to be like that again. I'm starting with a small stone, and gradually I'll take bigger ones. The heavier the stone is, the thicker my arm will become with time."

"And the other one?" Will pointed to the left arm that was hanging limply at his side. "Can't you make that one thicker, too?"

Isaac didn't reply. How could he lift a stone with an arm that had no hand to hold it?

Will couldn't suspect how much this question would occupy Isaac in the next few days.

"Grab hold of it!" he asked the boy one day, proudly extending his right arm to him. Will put his arms around it and pulled his legs up. Isaac was pleased to see he could carry the boy with his arm only slightly bent. His exercises had helped—the arm had gotten back its strength.

"Now the other one," Will demanded.

Hesitantly, Isaac stretched out the stump of the other arm.

Will wrapped his arms around it and pulled without raising his feet from the ground. He pulled as hard as he could until Isaac's arm began to tremble under the strain, and at once let go.

"Not a bad idea!" Isaac tousled the boy's hair as he always did when he wanted to show him affection. "We can do that again!"

Will nodded happily. "Then it will get as strong as the other one!"

They practiced every day to make sure Will's prediction came true, and before spring Isaac could lift the boy long enough to recite the Lord's Prayer twice, without hurrying. The muscles in his arms, shoulders, and back became steadily stronger, and one day he started doing one-arm pushups. When he was able to do that easily with his right arm, he made a pillow for the stump that had completely healed in the meanwhile and practiced with the left arm as well. As his muscles grew stronger, so did his desire to go back to work in the smithy.

"Isaac can hold me for a long time on his outstretched arm!" Will proudly told everyone one evening.

Ellen cast an angry look at Isaac while Jean and Rose smiled at him warmly.

"I'd like to come back to the smithy tomorrow," Isaac said. "Perhaps, with Peter, I could…"

"It's your smithy," Ellen replied gruffly.

Isaac said nothing.

"Peter will be happy," Jean said. "We have lots to do, and it would be great if someone else was there to help."

Ellen avoided looking at Isaac again.

"Why didn't you try to change his mind?" Ellen snapped at Jean as soon as Isaac left the room.

"Why should I do that? For two years you have been annoyed that he isn't working. Have you seen his arm? He has regained his strength, I've observed him, and he's laughing again, too."

"Barely has a smile started to flicker on his embittered lips and you're already doing cartwheels! We'll have to put up with his bad temper all the time." It was clear she was furious.

"Why are you so out of sorts?" Jean asked bluntly.

"Why am I…what?" Ellen gasped. "Have you forgotten that he thinks my place is in the kitchen and not in the smithy?" she replied, rubbing her index finger against her temple.

"Are you afraid he would send you back into the house to work?" Jean asked, in disbelief.

"I couldn't care less what he thinks, but I like working with you all and want it to stay that way. He'll only make trouble, and that won't be at all good for our work."

Jean tried to reassure her: "If you are right, you can throw him out again. I don't think he'll ever become essential for our work unless he works well with us and recognizes you as the master."

"But that's just exactly what he *won't* do!" Ellen said angrily.

Aha, that's the real problem, Jean said to himself, without letting on to it.

"Give him a chance! See what he can do! You don't have to work with him—let Peter do that. Moreover, it would be good for Will!"

"What does the boy have to do with it?" She looked at Jean defiantly.

"He adores Isaac, and if he can work again as a smith, that can only be good for Will. You know what he thinks about smithing."

"Nonsense, Will is still a stubborn child and wants to have his own way, but he'll become a smith just like his forbears, and I'll see to it he's a good one." Ellen placed her arms on her hips defiantly.

"You can't force him…" Jean objected, because he understood why Will was behaving that way.

"Oh, indeed I can! He is not going to waste his talent, I'll see to that!" Ellen shouted.

The look on Jean's face seemed to be saying, *What do you know about your son's talents?*

"It's Isaac's smithy and I can't keep him out, but I'll only work with him under one roof if he holds his tongue," Ellen warned.

Jean nodded. He could understand her concerns. She had fought so hard to try to reach her goals and had put up with a lot more than any other smith—yet he also thought that Isaac deserved a chance. Jean decided to talk to him and then went out looking for him. He found him behind the woodshed sitting in the straw. Without saying a word, Jean sat down alongside him.

"She hates me so much!" Isaac said.

"You haven't made it easy for her—from the very beginning. Have you forgotten that?" Jean pulled a little blade of grass out of the pile of straw.

"I have had a lot of time to think. Much has changed, and I look at a lot of things differently today than before, but some things are still the same."

Jean gave him a quizzical glance. "To tell you the truth, I'm just as confused as before."

Isaac grinned. "Then you must feel the way I do. I don't know if I can bear watching her bossing you around. Under these circumstances," he said, raising his left arm, "I don't even know if I can work in the same shop with her. I'm neither blind nor deaf. I know she has made a good reputation for the smithy, so she must have some ability, but I still don't know if I can stand thinking of her as better than I am. If I still had my hand, I could run circles around her!" Isaac sounded more despairing than aggressive.

"You're mistaken, Isaac!" Jean said.

"What do you mean?"

"Isaac, I have seen your work. You are a good smith, but she is more than just good, she is gifted. I'm sure there are no more than a handful of smiths in England and Normandy who can measure up to her. If she were a man, she would already be famous—not only in East Anglia but even outside of England, believe me!"

"I just can't," Isaac groaned. "It's so unfair!"

"What is there about it that is unfair?" Jean looked at Isaac, wondering.

"Do you think it is just, perhaps, that the Lord has blessed a woman, who is already beautiful, with a talent that would have brought great honor to a man? And why did he take my hand away from me?"

"Perhaps the Lord wants you to learn humility and to realize that it is He, and not us men, who decides who receives His blessings! Just look at how she works, and how hard, and you can't help but admire her. And perhaps someday you will thank the Lord for sending this wonderful woman to you to be your wife."

Isaac looked at Jean, deeply moved, and did not reply.

"She is a very special person! If you desire her for her beauty, you must earn her through your respect, and that is not something you can acquire through your skill as a smith but only if you climb down from your high horse and recognize her abilities."

Isaac was stunned by Jean's words, but as he started to express his anger and denial that he desired Ellen for her beauty, Jean had already left.

—

The next morning, Isaac was the last one to enter the smithy in order not to anger Ellen. He didn't want her to think he would contest her position as master of the smithy. He had thought about Jean's words all night and decided not to challenge her.

Jean started a fire in the hearth while Ellen planned the projects for the day and Peter oiled a few tools.

"That was all just empty talk—he won't come. No doubt he quickly got over his desire to work," Ellen said, as Isaac had not shown up.

Jean gave her a disapproving look. "Give him a chance, Ellen, please!"

"Very well!" Ellen raised her hands to try to calm things down.

"Peter, you'll work with Isaac today to prepare a few blanks. Remember he can use only one hand. You must either strike while he holds or you could hold while he works with the hand hammer. It won't be easy, but you can do it!" Jean said, nodding encouragement to the young journeyman.

Peter looked over at Ellen somewhat uncertainly. "Jean is right," she said, "you have learned a lot since the last time Isaac worked with you. He'll be amazed!"

Isaac came into the smithy as if he were entering it for the first time. A lot of things had changed since Ellen started working here. She had brought along new tools and a pedal-powered whetstone and had also set up two new workplaces. The tools were grouped according to how she used them, and there were quite a few more that he had ever possessed. It would no doubt take him a little time to find his way around the smithy. After respectfully greeting Peter, he asked him about the work that had to be done.

"It shouldn't be too hard for me to work with the hand hammer. That's something you don't soon forget, so I'd like to begin with that."

Peter nodded politely and tried very hard not to disappoint his master. Isaac was completely wrapped up in the work and swung the hand hammer down onto the iron again and again, paying no heed to the pain that spread gradually from his hand up to his shoulder. It felt good to exert himself. He had missed the work, the sweat, and the calluses on his hands.

"Hand me the sledgehammer and let me see if I can hold it," Isaac asked shortly before supper.

Peter swallowed hard. How could Isaac grab the handle without his left hand?

Isaac noticed Peter's hesitation and tried to reassure him.

"I just want to give it a try to see how heavy the hammer feels and if it's something I might eventually be able to do with a little practice." Isaac was skillful with the sledgehammer, but the handle kept slipping and he had trouble holding onto it. Disappointed because he had already reached his limit, he set the heavy hammer down in the bucket of water so the handle could swell up and would stay on securely the next day without shaking loose. “Let’s stop for today. I’m as hungry as a bear!” he said, trying to sound cheerful to hide his disappointment from the others.

For weeks Isaac worked with Peter as if he were the apprentice and not the master. Though he wasn’t working with Ellen, he couldn’t escape noticing how concentrated she was. Whenever there were problems, she knew a solution, and her rich store of knowledge seemed inexhaustible. In a word, any smith would be impressed with her ability, and one day Isaac took the plunge and asked Ellen for advice. She replied, as if it were the easiest question in the world, and went back to work. Isaac was surprised, even shocked at the clarity of her answer. Why hadn’t he figured that out himself? For a moment he struggled with his own bitterness, then just did as she said.

June 1179

Jean and Ellen had taken the dining table and benches outside in order to serve lunch in the yard. The sun had been shining every day for a week, and on Sunday they could enjoy the fruits of their work sitting quietly outside for a long time enjoying the warm summer day.

"Is it difficult to polish swords?" Isaac asked as he dunked a piece of bread into what remained of the soup.

"I would say so, yes, it takes experience and skill. Why?"

"I have watched you. For the first rough polishing you need both hands, but in fine polishing you really need just the right hand." Isaac didn't dare to look at her. When she spoke of swords, her green eyes sparkled and he desired her so much that sometimes it hurt. At times he could hardly manage to lie next to her at night without touching her.

"It's true what you say." Ellen rubbed her temples with her finger, as if it helped her to think more clearly. "Haven't you ever polished? Not even a simple hunting knife?"

"I polished only tools and a few knives, but that isn't at all like polishing swords," Isaac replied modestly.

"Well, you can try," Ellen said confidently. "Today is Sunday and we can't work at the forge, but the shop is open and I could show you—if you like," she quickly added. She had noticed that Isaac hadn't had a mean thing to say about her since coming back to work in the smithy. In fact, he tried to help wherever he could in spite of his missing hand. More than once she had admired how persistent he was.

"Good! Let's go!" Isaac got up with a smile.

"Fine polishing is something you can do sitting down. I've seen how you can whittle," Ellen said, but she still avoided looking him directly in the eye. The admiring glances he thought he was able to hide from her did not go unnoticed, leaving a strangely queasy feeling in her stomach.

"Is it all right if I hold it with my foot?"

Ellen shrugged. "Why not? As long as you keep your toes away from the blade." She grinned at him and then blushed at once. Turning around quickly, she went and got a scythe that Peter and Isaac had finished the day before.

"You can begin with this."

"A scythe? You want me to polish a scythe?" Isaac looked at her a bit reluctantly.

"It won't hurt the scythe!" Ellen said, laughing.

Her laugh felt to Isaac like a blow in the pit of his stomach.

"I guess that's right," he stammered, bewildered.

"At first you should practice with the finest grinding compound," she said.

"I should? But why?"

"The coarser the stone, the worse the errors will be. If I make a scratch in iron using a coarse stone, even the best sword polisher won't be able to remove it. To start with, a grinding compound made of rock powder is the best; then nothing can go wrong. Once you have had some practice, you will know what to be watching for and how the iron reacts with the powder, and then you can take a rougher stone. Polishing swords is really special! Sword polishers deal only with polishing, and a really good sword polisher is worth his weight in gold, as he has quickly acquired much more expertise than any smith."

Isaac nodded admiringly.

Ellen noticed how he was looking at her and blushed again. She quickly picked up a linen cloth and rubbed some grinding compound on the scythe. Then she showed Isaac how to polish the blade while holding the rag between his thumb and index finger, and she watched as he did it. Now and then she nodded appreciation of his skill. He quickly understood what was important, and so she soon suggested that he polish the hunting knife she had just finished making.

Isaac was thrilled. Ellen's confidence in him meant more than anything.

Ellen took a polishing stone from her leather purse and gave it to Isaac. Her fingers briefly touched his hand, and he shuddered.

The smith showed persistence and skill in polishing and enthusiasm for learning. Before two months had passed, Ellen set him to work on the simpler swords, but kept for herself the expensive swords that she made now and then. It took a special sort of feeling to select the proper stones to show off the brilliance and sharpness of a blade.

No more angry words were exchanged between the two, and Isaac clearly enjoyed the confidence that gradually developed between them.

On one of the first fall days, muffled hoofbeats on the soft ground announced the arrival of a heavy horse. The rider jumped down, and moments later they heard his booming voice in the yard in front of the smithy.

"The master, I want to see the master!"

Ellen looked toward the door, then nodded at Peter to let the man in.

A young baron entered, richly dressed and bearing weapons decorated with much gold and expensive enamelwork.

"What can I do for you?" Ellen asked politely as she walked toward him.

"The master, where is he?"

"Standing before you, my lord!" Ellen remained calm, though she was not really a recognized master. This was not the first time she was treated condescendingly, and she'd had enough of it.

The young knight looked at her angrily. "That cannot be! I heard that the master of this smithy is a certain Alan, and he is reputed to make the best swords far and wide."

Jean grinned. Even though Ellen always insisted on being called Ellenweore, it happened again and again that they called her Alan.

"I refuse to deal with a woman. Go back to the hearth and cook us something decent to eat. Where is the smith?" the young baron asked impatiently.

Ellen was outraged and gasped for air. She could still clearly remember when Isaac said things like that. She had no desire to let herself be insulted further and stepped closer to him, ready to throw him out. Suddenly Isaac stepped up alongside her.

"If you please, my lord, I am Isaac, the smith." He nodded, hiding the stump of his left arm behind his back.

Ellen was furious at his betrayal.

"Ah, yes! The master!" A triumphant grin passed over the face of the young knight.

"I am indeed the master of this smithy, my lord, but I am unable to forge the exquisite swords of which you speak, nor is my helper." He pointed to Peter. "I am proud to say, as God is my witness, that it is my wife who makes these wonderful weapons. In all of East Anglia you will find no better swordsmith than her. So if you want to have such as sword as your own, you must excuse yourself and hope she forgives you, for anger, you must know, is a bad smith."

The young baron had turned pale, expelled air noisily through his teeth, turned on his heels, and left the smithy without saying a word.

"He doesn't deserve one of your swords!" Isaac said disparagingly.

Ellen's heart pounded wildly, not with anger, but joy.

"You are absolutely right!" Jean agreed. He looked back and forth between Ellen and Isaac, wondering if something like tender feelings might be developing between the two.

—

Work brought the two closer together. In the shop they treated each other with respect and recognition, whereas in the privacy of their own bedroom neither knew what to make of the signs of growing intimacy.

Isaac had not forgotten what he had said on their marriage night. He was certain that Ellen no longer hated him but didn't dare to take even the smallest step toward a reconciliation out of fear she might feel obligated to submit to him.

The others also sensed the tension between the two, and one day, when they were alone, Rose took Ellen aside.

"Honestly, Ellenweore, I can't just stand and watch it anymore!"

"Watch what?" Ellen looked down at her. "What have I done?"

Rose laughed. "I mean you and Isaac! You are tiptoeing around each other…"

Ellen blushed.

"He still doesn't lie with you, does he?" She looked at her friend quizzically.

Ellen shook her head. “He renounced his conjugal rights on our wedding night,” she replied softly.

“Very noble of him,” Rose mumbled, as she paused to consider what Ellen had said. “I don’t think he will ever break his promise on his own.” Rose raised an eyebrow. “Men!” She gave a sigh of resignation. “But you can’t do without them! So it’s in your hands!” She grinned, trying to cheer up her friend.

“But, Rose!” Ellen exclaimed angrily. For a brief moment she thought of Will and his outrageous way of demanding love, something she had not been able to resist. “But I can’t do that! That’s something the man has to do!”

“Oh, nonsense. Women who can forge iron can also seduce their husbands!” Rose smiled conspiratorially and whispered something in Ellen’s ear.

“But, Rose! No! I could never look him in the eye again!” she cried in horror.

“Just do it!” said Rose, ending the discussion and permitting no further excuses.

Rose’s frank words and the idea of caressing Isaac’s well-shaped body had put Ellen’s mind in a turmoil. She didn’t show up for supper with the family because she was afraid they would all be able to read her mind and see how lustful her thoughts were. Only later, when Isaac was already asleep, did she enter their room, undress hastily, and slip naked under the covers. Isaac lay on his back, and Ellen cuddled up close to him. Her heart was pounding at the thought of what she intended to do. Isaac didn’t stir and appeared to be fast asleep. Ellen began to touch him gently. Her hand slid under the sheets to his smooth, powerful chest, and down to his stomach. At first carefully and then with greater and greater fervor, she kissed his neck, pressed her entire body up against his, closed her eyes with pleasure, and breathed in the odor of leather and iron that mixed with the lavender that Rose had placed in the bed to keep bugs away.

Isaac's breathing became heavier.

Ellen could sense his growing excitement but waited in vain for him to take her in his arm. She ran her hand gently up and down his left arm until she got to the stump. Then she lay down on him, took his right arm, and put it around her waist. It was too dark in the room to see whether Isaac had opened his eyes, but Ellen could sense that he was awake. "Hold me!" she whispered hoarsely, and kissed him on the mouth.

At first reluctantly but then with growing passion he returned her kisses. His right hand moved up and down her body and sent a shiver of delight down her spine.

"Lie on top of me," she whispered hoarsely.

—

The next morning, Ellen woke up rested and happy as never before. Isaac had already gotten up. Lovingly she passed her hands over the bed sheets on which they had spent the night together. Then she sprang up, washed with the water that always stood in a bucket in the corner, and dressed.

"I'm late," she apologized as she quickly tied on her scarf and walked into the main room.

"Have something to eat first," Rose urged her, pushing her toward a chair and placing a bowl in front of her filled with porridge cooked in goat's milk. She took her by the chin and looked her in the eye. "It suits you!"

"What?" Ellen asked, confused.

"Love." Rose turned again to kneading the pastry dough and smiled at her knowingly.

"I've got to get to work!" Ellen exclaimed, taking a last spoonful of porridge and rushing out of the room, red-faced.

"It's high time the two of them got together," Rose mumbled with satisfaction.

March 1180

Even though Ellen and Isaac thought they were behaving as always, the others didn't fail to notice the meaningful glances they exchanged with each other when they thought no one was watching, nor their rosy appearance when they left the conjugal bedroom in the morning. They always were standing together joking and laughing and discussing the design and polishing of new swords. Jean and Rose were delighted to see how close the two had become and how happy they looked together.

Even little Will noticed the change, and he was thrilled because peace had finally returned to the house. "Uncle Isaac?" he asked, taking him by the hand.

"Yes, son?"

"I am happy you are better." Will looked at him lovingly.

"So am I," Isaac replied.

"May I ask you something?" Will scratched his head.

Isaac remembered clearly the last time Will had asked him this question. After that, almost everything in his life had changed. Will could ask him anything he wanted.

"Certainly, son."

"Why do you always call me 'son'?"

Isaac hesitated for a moment.

"You are the son of my wife, and I love you like my very own. And I always wanted a son like you."

"Really?"

Isaac nodded and smiled at the boy.

"So then may I call you 'Father'?"

Isaac could feel an unexpected tightening in his throat and had to struggle to maintain his composure.

"If your mother has no objection..." he mumbled in a choked voice.

"I don't think she will," Will said with a broad smile. "Thank you, Father!" he replied and hobbled away cheerfully.

"I positively must make him new shoes," Isaac told himself, and set out for the workshop with a sigh. As he crossed the yard he noticed Rose deep in thought, holding her hand on her belly.

"Are you expecting again?" he asked warmly.

Rose smiled broadly. "We were going to tell you all this evening," she said, blushing a bit.

"I'm happy for you," Isaac said in a cordial voice.

"Just wait, you'll have your turn, too," Rose replied, winking at him.

Isaac didn't reply. He well knew how little Ellen cared to have more children, and after Mildred's death he couldn't blame her. He was about to open the door to the smithy when a man on horseback came rushing into the yard. Greybeard growled until the friendly young rider had jumped down from his horse and spoke to him gently.

"My lord?" Isaac nodded respectfully, but without appearing obsequious.

"Please, good fellow! I am told there is a good swordsmith here." The young knight had a strong Norman accent but seemed to know English passably.

"That is correct, my lord! I'll show you in." Isaac motioned for him to follow.

The young knight tied his horse to a post. "The pommel on my sword has come loose and must be riveted in place at once," he said cordially.

"Will, my boy, bring a bucket of water for my lord's horse." Then he guided the knight into the smithy.

"This is Ellenweore, the swordsmith and my wife," Isaac said proudly. He pointed to Ellen, ready if necessary to defend her honor again.

Ellen glanced up briefly from her work. "Just a moment, I just have to…"

"If she stops what she is doing, my lord, the quality of the sword will suffer," Isaac explained.

"Well, we don't want that to happen. I'll just have to be patient for a moment, won't I?" The young knight smiled warmly and watched her work.

Ellenweore, like our queen, he was thinking. "She must be good if she can succeed as a smith."

"She is good," Isaac confirmed emphatically.

"May I?" the young knight asked, pointing at a sword that hung on an iron hook.

Isaac nodded courteously, reached up to take it, and handed it to him.

"Ah, the copper sign, I have seen that before!" the knight exclaimed in astonishment as he examined the sword.

"That is Ellenweore's sign. She inlays it in every blade she makes," Isaac declared with pride.

Ellen placed the iron back on the coals and walked toward the two.

"My lord," she said, bowing briefly while looking into the man's gentle, friendly eyes.

"The pommel of my sword is loose. Can you repair it?"

Ellen looked briefly at the pommel and the riveting. "Jean can do that quickly." She called to Jean to come over and showed him the weapon.

"You are not an Englishman," she said, turning back to the visitor.

"Flemish, but I grew up in Normandy," he volunteered.

She studied the young man curiously.

"You look so familiar to me," he mumbled and suddenly seemed distraught. For a brief moment Ellen was also seized with panic. She rubbed her temples with her index finger and the scarf slipped off, revealing a strand of red hair.

"*Mon ange*, my angel!" the young knight cried out, and broke out in a wide smile.

Ellen could recognize the Lady of Béthune in his shining eyes.

"Baudouin?" she whispered in disbelief.

He nodded, and she said again in Norman French: "Little Baudouin?"

He nodded again more vigorously, and she broke out laughing. "Yes, that's right, as a little boy you called me your angel!"

"Because you saved me from drowning in the river, Ellenweore!" Baudouin slapped his forehead with the palm of his hand. "Why didn't I see that at once? But that was so long ago, and we are so far from home here!" he said, putting his arm around her.

"How is your mother?" Almost fifteen years must have passed since she met Adelisa de Béthune.

"She died during the birth of my youngest brother, God rest her soul." Baudouin crossed himself, and Ellen did the same.

"She was a wonderful person!"

Isaac had started to work again, but now he stood up and walked toward the two with a puzzled look. Ellen reached out to him and took him by the arm.

"Isaac, this is Baudouin de Béthune," she said, introducing the young knight.

"She saved my life when I was five years old," the young man declared happily.

"And for doing that he almost promised to marry me!" Ellen leaned back and laughed, and the young knight grinned with embarrassment.

"I know I promised back then to fulfill your every wish, but now that I've seen what wonderful swords you make, I hope you might be able to fulfill one for me!" Baudouin said with a big smile. "Please make a sword for me!" He took a purse full of coins from his belt. "Please, I…I am a knight of the Young King. My best friend is winning at all the tournaments with one of your swords! And I never found out where he got it."

Ellen nearly froze. Baudouin was one of the Young King's knights? *Please, God,* she said to herself, *don't let Thibault be the friend he means.* She pulled herself together.

"Really? And what's your friend's name?" she asked calmly.

"William. They also call him the Marshal, after his father. He is the tutor of our Young King!" he declared proudly.

Ellen felt the blood draining from her face. Hoping that no one would notice, she turned around and got a piece of rope.

"Well, then I'll have to measure you. Let your arm hang down," she mumbled, and avoided looking at him. "Are you right-handed?"

"I fight with both hands, but usually with the right one."

Ellen nodded. She was trying to figure out where William could have gotten one of her swords.

"Do you have any special instructions?" By now she had gained control of herself again and was able to look Baudouin in the eye. "Do you wish to have any decorations? Jewels, perhaps?"

Baudouin made a face. "Even if I could afford it, I couldn't let William see me with jewels on my sword. He despises any decoration and thinks they are only for men who can't fight and have to blind their opponents with the sparkling stones in order to make an impression."

A smile played on Ellen's lips. In this matter, they had always agreed.

"William himself, of course, has many swords that he has won at various tournaments, including some that are richly decorated, but he never uses them. I like a cross guard that turns slightly inward," he said, "but beyond that I'll completely trust your taste."

Ellen took his measurements, made a few sketches on a wax tablet, and then presented Baudouin with a reasonable cost estimate.

"When can I come to get it?" he asked, full of joyful anticipation.

"I'm sure you would like to have it the day before yesterday, but we have lots to do. Naturally, we will work quickly for you, but good things take time." She looked at Isaac. "I would say it will take us about two months, do you agree?"

Isaac frowned briefly. "In any case, it can't be done any sooner. I'll even have to put another order aside, as the polishing takes a good deal of time."

Baudouin gave a sigh of resignation. "Very well. I hope then that I'll still be in England!"

"If not, your sword will be waiting here for you until you come and get it," Ellen assured him.

"You saved my life once and now may save it a thousand times, dear Ellenweore. Make me a good weapon, for more than once my life will depend on my sword."

"You can be sure, Baudouin, that your sword will be something very special." Ellen accompanied the young knight out of the smithy, where they parted warmly, and Baudouin waved to her as he rode off.

"Did you really save his life one time?" Jean asked in disbelief as they returned to the smithy.

"You saved the life of a king's knight!" Peter was greatly impressed and smiled warmly.

"Come, tell us everything, and don't leave anything out," Jean urged her.

Ellen smiled and told them how she had saved the child from drowning.

"She also taught me how to swim," Jean told Peter and Isaac proudly. It seemed to him that in this way he shared some of the glory.

—

"But you haven't seen him for a long time, and surely he has changed a lot," Rose said when Ellen at Jean's insistence told the story again at supper.

"Of course he has changed! He was just a five-year-old boy at the time, and today he is a grown man. But he looks a lot like his mother, and so it feels like I have known him forever." Ellen smiled as she thought of her. "She was a good person, and I think he is a good fellow, too."

"And did you say he is in the service of the Young King?" Rose inquired anxiously.

"He is in the service of William Marshal," Ellen said, looking severely at Rose. She had made it clear to Jean before that he should never mention a word about the Marshal to anyone.

But Rose had quite another concern on her mind, the fear that Thibault might be nearby. There was no way of knowing what he would do to her if he discovered her with Ellen! Rose stood up, lost in thought, and cleared the table.

"Hey, Rose," Isaac said cheerfully, "come back and sit down. I haven't even finished eating."

Rose shook her head. "I'll be right back," she said, and rushed outside.

Isaac watched her leave. "Is there something wrong with her?"

Jean, who suspected what was troubling Rose, just took a deep breath. "It's all right, I'll go and check on her."

Isaac decided not to ask any more questions for the time being, but it annoyed him that he was always the last to learn what was going on.

"And you really did save a knight's life?" William asked again, just to make sure he had understood correctly. After all, not everyone has a mother who is a heroine.

"Well you heard what I said, and at that time he wasn't yet a knight, but just a little boy even younger than you are," she grumbled, and for the rest of the evening she didn't say a word.

When they went to bed that night, Isaac put his arm around Ellen. "You were suddenly so pensive and quiet. What's wrong?" he asked anxiously.

"Nothing, I'm just tired and have a headache," Ellen mumbled, avoiding his gaze.

Isaac drew her a little closer to him and stroked her neck with his warm, dry hand.

Ellen put her head on his shoulder and closed her eyes. Why did a shadow have to fall on their lives and threaten their happiness again? She took a deep breath and could barely hold back the tears.

Isaac kissed her hair tenderly. Ellen clung to him as if it were his last kiss.

Isaac looked at her and stroked her cheek. "Lie down and rest, my love, then you will feel better tomorrow."

Ellen was grateful for his concern, and nodded. Thoughts of William and Thibault had put her mind into turmoil. "Thank you," she murmured softly as they lay there together.

Isaac kissed her on the forehead. "Sleep well!"

But while Isaac soon was sleeping the sleep of the just, Ellen lay there brooding for a long time.

—

During the weeks they were working on the sword for Baudouin de Béthune, Ellen spoke hardly a word and avoided everyone as much as possible.

"You look tired. You are working too much and must take it a bit easier," Rose said one day to Ellen.

For several days she had been pale, her hair looked dull, and she seemed almost frail.

"It is not the work." Ellen had shadows under her eyes. "I was pregnant," she explained in a weak voice.

"You were what?" Rose looked at her in shock.

"I was going to tell Isaac some time ago, but now…I'm glad I didn't say anything. Two days ago I felt cramps." Ellen placed her head in her hands. "It was almost as bad as giving birth, but thank God it didn't last as long."

"Ellen!" Rose took her by the arm and tried to console her.

"It was still very tiny. I could hardly bring myself to look at it." Ellen sobbed briefly, but not only, as Rose had assumed, out of grief for the lost child but because memories were coming back to trouble her. "Isaac does not know about it, and that's the way I want to keep it. He wants a son so badly and would be sad unnecessarily." Ellen gave Rose a pleading glance, and her friend nodded, trying to comfort her.

—

Thibault was sitting in front of his tent on a sunny summer afternoon when Baudouin came riding up. Thibault looked up, contempt in his eyes. Baudouin was William's best friend, and in Thibault's eyes that by itself made him a traitor. He tried not to let that feeling show, though, as it might be useful, after all, to be on good terms with his enemy's best friend. He became curious when he noticed that Baudouin was holding a new weapon.

Baudouin hurried over to William.

Thibault stood up in order to eavesdrop on the two. He pretended he had to relieve himself, and stopped not far from William's tent.

The Marshal was standing in front of it shaving his beard and paying no attention to his friend. Baudouin paraded back and forth in front of him, until William finally looked up. The Marshal scrutinized him curiously from head to toe and finally noticed the sword.

"New?" he inquired, raising his eyebrows.

Baudouin nodded proudly. "Would you like to see it?"

"Of course!" William reached out and took the weapon. Once he held it in his hand his interest grew even further, and he turned the sword back and forth. "It has a wonderful feel to it, well balanced, almost like Athanor," he said softly, reaching for his belt where his beloved sword was attached. Then he discovered the letter that was inlaid with copper wire on one side of the blade close to the cross guard. "And it has the copper sign!" he exclaimed, looking at Baudouin in astonishment.

He pretended to be checking the sword to see whether William was right, and grinned broadly.

"Where did you get that?" William demanded.

"I met someone I knew in my younger years in Béthune."

"What are you hiding from me? Take me there! Come now, you must take me to the smithy where you got it!" William demanded impatiently, wiping the rest of the soap from his face.

"Why are you getting so upset?"

"I always thought I knew who had forged my sword, but now it appears that there are other smiths using the same sign. I must know if I was wrong. Take me there, at once!"

Baudouin shrugged dutifully. "Of course, if you insist."

Thibault strolled back to his tent, trying to look inconspicuous, and called for his squire.

"Saddle up my horse, take it over to where the forest begins, and wait for me by the beech tree that was hit by lightning," he ordered him. The young man hurried out and did as he was told. Thibault put on his sword and spurs, wondering if Baudouin had happened to see Ellenweore, and the very idea of it sent hot pangs of desire coursing through his body again. Back then, at the tournament, he had ordered a boy to steal the sword from Ellen, but she had wrested it back from him so he had never gotten it. If Baudouin's sword, like Athanor, was really from her, then he had to find Ellenweore and persuade her to make him a better one, or rather, the best sword in the world. Thibault slipped away and hurried to the forest where his squire was awaiting him, as agreed. He swung himself up on the horse and rode through the camp of tents until he found William and Baudouin. They were riding northward, and he followed closely on their heels without attracting attention. It was not for nothing that he had a reputation as an excellent lookout. As long as he kept a safe distance they would never notice him.

The sun had already passed the high point for the day when they arrived at the smithy. Thibault climbed down, tied his horse to a tree, and crept a bit closer on foot.

—

When Baudouin and William rode into the yard, Greybeard came running toward them, growling, but after the two had dismounted, Greybeard sniffed at William and finally greeted him with a friendly wag of his tail. None of them noticed that someone was sitting in the bushes and observing them.

Isaac was just going down the path to the house. "Is something wrong with your new sword?" he asked Baudouin with concern.

"Oh no, nothing of the sort. My friend here wanted to meet the smith who made it," Baudouin replied, and winked at Isaac.

Judging from the way Baudouin spoke, Isaac could sense that the stranger didn't know the smith here was a woman. He didn't like the thought of presenting her like that.

"You know the way," he said coldly, pointing toward the workshop. Just before he reached the house he stopped, however. He somehow didn't feel right about that, and returned to the smithy. On entering the workshop, one look at Ellen took his breath away. She was overjoyed at seeing the strange knight, and her eyes shone like never before.

"This is the smith who forged my sword," Baudouin said, proudly introducing her with a broad smile. "And moreover, years ago she saved my life! You never would have believed that it was a woman, would you?"

Ellen looked at the Marshal without moving.

Jean's eyes moved from one to the other; then he nudged Peter and pulled the journeyman away with him. "Come, let's take a break and go outside. I'm hungry."

The Marshal didn't respond to Baudouin's words, but went straight to the smith. "Ellenweore! How long has it been?" he asked, taking her by the hand.

Baudouin looked at him in astonishment. "Do you know each other?"

"More than seven years," Ellen replied, without paying any heed to Baudouin's question. Her heart pounded, and her hands became damp. Never would she have believed that seeing William again would put her mind in such turmoil.

"Say! Could you please just tell me what's going on?" Baudouin interrupted, tearing Ellen out of her reveries.

"We have known one another since Tancarville," was all she said.

"You used to live in Tancarville?" Baudouin couldn't get over his astonishment.

"That's where I learned how to forge swords. From Donovan. Do you know him perhaps?"

Baudouin shook his head.

"Baudouin came to Tancarville four years after we did," William explained.

"But then it's more than seven years ago," Baudouin concluded. He was especially proud of his ability to make quick calculations.

"We met once again after that." Ellen's voice sounded both rough and gentle at the same time.

Baudouin nodded, understanding that they must have known each other better at one time.

Ellen's gaze moved to William's sword belt. She recognized Athanor at once. The scabbard was worn, so he must have used the sword frequently. "How did you…" she started to say, pointing at the sword.

"Athanor?" William placed his hand on the sword and seemed relieved that she asked about it. "Some months after we freed Jean and you left, I won it from a Frenchman at a tournament in Caen. He had been showing it off, having just purchased it. I recognized it at once and simply had to have it. I wish *I* had gotten it from you, and not some stranger." There was a mild tone of reproach in his voice.

"You won it in a tournament!" Ellen smiled.

"Baudouin showed me his new sword, and it felt just as comfortable in my hand as Athanor. And then I noticed your sign on it. For a moment I feared other smiths might be using that sign as well and that perhaps it wasn't Athanor at all. Even though I never doubted it, I just had to come and convince myself that you made both Baudouin's sword and my own."

"And so you are happy with it?" Ellen's eyes sparkled like stars.

Isaac, who had quietly moved closer, felt the jealousy rising in him almost to the point of being unbearable.

"It's the best sword I ever had! All the knights speak of it with great reverence!" The Marshal became emotional as he spoke of Athanor's fame. "Even the Young King admires it!"

The door to the workshop swung open, and Isaac stepped aside a bit. The squeaking of the hinges drew Ellen's attention to it.

"Will?" She looked at her son crossly. "What is it this time?" she demanded when the boy didn't reply at once.

“May I give water to the horses?” he asked, hobbling a few steps closer to his mother.

“Will?” The Marshal gave her a questioning look. Anyone could have seen in her eyes that the boy was his son. Even Baudouin understood. He looked from the boy to his friend and could see that except for the freckles and the green eyes that doubtlessly came from his mother, the boy was the very image of his father.

Isaac also could not fail to interpret the glance correctly. A searing pain passed through his body. So this strange knight was Will’s father. Would Isaac lose the love of both his wife and his son now?

Baudouin was the first to get control of himself. “It would actually be a good idea for you to take care of our horses. We were riding fast and surely they are thirsty,” he replied.

Will smiled broadly. “They are wonderful animals, so strong and elegant,” he said as he hobbled out of the smithy.

“What is wrong with his leg?” William asked gruffly.

“His foot has been deformed since he was born,” Ellen replied coldly. She had not failed to notice the unfriendly tone of William’s voice.

“A cripple,” William mumbled.

She was about to reply, but Isaac had already approached and spoke first. “For a smith, feet are not important. Someone like myself is worse off!” He held his stump out for the two knights to see. “It seems I cannot even hold onto my wife!” he replied, glaring at the Marshal.

“Isaac!” Ellen gave him a furious look, while William just eyed him haughtily.

“If that’s the case, it’s probably not just because of your arm,” he replied, turning away.

William took Ellen's little hand, enveloping it completely in his own huge one, and held it tightly. "I am delighted to see you again."

It was hard for Isaac to bear the longing way that Ellen looked at the Marshal. Everyone could see how much this man still meant to her.

—

"He looks just like you," Baudouin whispered to his friend once they were outside. They walked toward little Will, who had brought water for the horses and was now gently stroking their noses. "And he knows his way around horses just like his father."

"He's a cripple!" William growled, visibly angered.

"Thank you, Will," Baudouin said as he handed the boy a precious silver coin.

"You look just like your father," Baudouin said, taking the boy by the chin in order to look into his eyes.

"Isaac is not my father!" Will answered impudently.

"I know that, because I know who your father is. He is a brave warrior, a great man, and the best friend anyone could ask for. You can be proud of him." Baudouin smiled as he looked at the boy.

"Is that true? You know him?" Will looked up at him with a broad smile on his face.

"As sure as my name is Baudouin de Béthune!" Baudouin pounded his chest with his fist.

William said nothing, and didn't even look at the boy.

"Stop talking nonsense and come!" he growled at his friend, and mounted his horse, but Baudouin wouldn't be hurried. Impatient, William spurred his horse and started to ride away.

Baudouin also mounted, but before he left he bent down once more to speak to the boy. "I'll tell him about you, and one day your father will be proud to have a son like you!" he whispered.

Will nodded his head vigorously and waved to the two men as they left.

"The knight, Mother…!" William shouted, running back to the smithy. "The knight you made the sword for said he knows my father!" Will said with a big smile.

Isaac grumbled something and left.

"You never told me about him," Will said, giving his mother a disapproving look.

"There is not much to tell!" Ellen replied brusquely.

"But who is he?" the boy persisted. Ellen turned away.

"You will find out soon enough. Get back the house now and help Rose—go on, get moving!"

Will knew there was no point in pestering his mother any further and walked back to the house despondently.

At supper, Isaac sat quietly spooning his porridge and not looking up. Ellen was lost in thought and finished her plate without paying any attention to Jean and Rose, who tried to cheer up the two of them with idle chatter.

Will held his head in his hand, listlessly stirring his food around in the wooden bowl.

Agnes and Marie laughed and giggled, teasing the twins by taking away the bread crusts the boys had been sucking on happily.

The two boys now began to cry and reach out for the bread.

Ellen, who otherwise insisted on quiet at the dinner table and usually would scold the children right away if they got noisy, said nothing.

But Rose looked severely at the two girls and gave the bread crusts back to her sons at once.

After supper, Ellen returned to the smithy where she tidied up, though there was nothing out of place, swept out the hearth for a second time, and oiled the tools that had already been oiled before. She was so lost in thought she didn't hear Jean entering the shop.

He came over and stood beside her. "Must have been quite a shock for you," he said finally.

"What?" Ellen looked up in surprise.

"I mean that he showed up here so unexpectedly." Jean wiped his hand over the anvil.

"I never thought it would trouble me to see him again. I mean, things are going well with Isaac and me…I have no reason…" Ellen took a deep breath.

"William did not recommend you to the king back then, though he could have, and he won't do it now, either. All you could expect from him was that he would take you for a roll in the hay."

"Jean!" Ellen looked at him angrily.

"I know that's not what you want to hear, but I am right! You have to put him out of your mind, Ellen." Jean shrugged. "I saw how you looked at him, but he hasn't done anything to deserve your love. But Isaac has."

Ellen looked down at the ground, ashamed. "I can't help myself. It's my heart—it beats so wildly when he is around me," she said softly.

"You don't mean anything to him, Ellen, you are just one conquest among many. Don't forget who he is! Just what do you expect? Until yesterday you were happy with Isaac, and it is because of you that he has changed so much."

Ellen laughed, but it was a laugh of desperation.

"We really hated each other at first, but my goodness, that was so long ago!"

"Isaac loves your son as if he were his own. Even the Marshal couldn't be a better father to Will."

Ellen nodded. "I know he will never be a father to him." She shrugged and added, "I'll try hard, I promise!"

Jean patted her on the shoulder. "I once told Isaac he didn't deserve you, but ever since he started working in the smithy again, I've changed my mind. You belong together!" Jean gave her a nod of encouragement.

Ellen tried to assume a confident smile, but she couldn't quite manage it.

—

When Thibault saw the boy watering the horses, he knew that he had to be Ellen and William's son. Just the same, he needed confirmation that Ellen was here, too. He waited until they left the smithy for the evening. William and Baudouin had gone some time ago, but he still lay waiting in the underbrush.

When he finally caught sight of Ellen, he felt as if he had been struck by a bolt of lightning. She was still, just as back then, the most exciting woman he had ever met. Her red hair shone in the twilight, and the sad look in her eyes cut him to the quick. How he wanted to jump up and run to her, to take her in his arms and…the damp ground in the forest penetrated his clothing and interrupted his reveries. He walked back to his horse, mounted, and rode off. He had to find a way to get a sword from her—not just any sword, but a masterpiece, the best sword she had ever made. The only question was how.

—

After the Marshal left, life quickly resumed its normal course again for Ellen and the others. Ellen hardly gave a thought to seeing him again, and Isaac tried to suppress his gnawing jealously. Thus, everything was soon back to normal until the day another strange knight appeared in the yard.

He was dressed in rich clothing and accompanied by a squire.

Rose, who had just finished picking vegetables in the garden, went to meet him.

"The smith! Take me to her!" he ordered without dismounting.

"Will you please follow me to the workshop?" As she walked closer, she recognized him at once, and big beads of sweat started to form on her brow. She sent a quick prayer to heaven that he would not recognize her.

Without saying another word, Adam d'Yqueboeuf jumped down from his horse and gave the reins to his squire. He paid no further heed to Rose, but walked with great strides toward the workshop.

Rose ran back to the house and did not catch her breath until she had closed the door behind her.

In the smithy, the knight had to first get accustomed to the semidarkness, but then he caught sight of Ellen. He had seen her earlier in Normandy where she was working in a blacksmith shop at tournaments and had thought she was crazy because she had taken it into her head to do a man's job. He snorted, then walked over to her. "Do you recognize the coat of arms I am carrying?" he asked severely.

Ellen nodded. "The royal lions! What can I do for you, my lord?" Ellen tried not to sound overly impressed.

"It is said that your swords are extremely sharp and are good weapons. For this reason, I am bringing you jewels and gold for a sword better than any you have ever made. One to amaze the Young King, a sword that has no equal!"

Ellen looked at him in surprise. The Young King wanted a sword from her? She could hardly believe it. Finally! Finally William had recommended her. She tried to look calm. "Until now I have seen young Henry only from a distance, and that was years ago. I must know his size and which hand he favors in battle."

"Only the right hand is a good hand, and as for the length, you can take my measurements," Yqueboeuf replied, bored.

"When shall it be finished?" Ellen asked, a bit anxiously. For the most part, the higher the rank of a customer, the sooner it had to be done.

"Young Henry will not stay in England for long—the tournaments begin soon! I would say three or at most four weeks. The next time we are in this area I'll come and fetch the sword. You won't give it to anyone else, do you understand?"

Ellen nodded.

Yqueboeuf handed her a purse with gold and another one with costly gems.

Ellen poured the jewels into her hand. "Sapphires, rubies, emeralds—they are beautiful!" she said. They were in fact pure and sparkling, but Ellen couldn't help thinking of the Marshal and what Baudouin had told her about William's opinion of jewels on a sword. She frowned. There had certainly to be other considerations for a king. "It will be the most beautiful and finest sword the king ever held in his hand," she promised.

"We shall see, but it would be best for you if that is the case!" Yqueboeuf replied.

Ellen had a ready answer for that, but she decided not to quarrel with the nobleman and merely bowed her head humbly.

"Don't tell anyone about your work, and order your journeymen to keep silent as well. Not a word to anyone!" Yqueboeuf said, looking at her intently.

"As you wish, sire!" She bowed again.

Yqueboeuf snorted once more, and this time his nostrils flared out like those on a horse.

"And what about the pommel and cross guard?"

"Do as you think best, and choose a shape most suitable for a well-balanced sword. Don't forget, however, that it must display elegance and grace!"

Ellen choked back the answer she wanted to give to that. Every one of her swords was elegant and graceful, even without the jewels.

"Do you have any requests for the belt and the scabbard?" Ellen asked, as usual.

Yqueboeuf seemed perturbed, and shook his head. "You are the master, aren't you? So just come up with something to make the sword unique and its carrier the envy of the world!"

Ellen bowed again. "As you command, sire!"

After the king's knight had left, Jean, Isaac, and Peter gathered around Ellen, who patiently answered their questions.

"The sword for the king is more important than anything else. This work has priority, is that clear?"

"But why are we not allowed to talk about it?" Peter wondered. "It would be much easier to put the monks off if we could tell them you are making a sword for the king. It would also help our reputation and make yourself known beyond the boundaries of St. Edmundsbury!"

"And it would be an invitation to thieves to rob us! Did you think of that? After all, we are responsible for the jewels entrusted to us!"

Peter held his breath. "I didn't think of that!" he admitted meekly.

Jean and Isaac barely said a word.

Later in the afternoon, when she was alone in the smithy with Jean, Ellen rejoiced. "You see, you were wrong! He finally recommended me to the king, after all!"

Jean shrugged. "Nevertheless, my opinion hasn't changed: you've got to put him out of your mind."

October 1180

The time was short, and it seemed almost impossible to finish the sword on time. Ellen told Peter and Isaac they would have to complete all the other orders on their own, until she reached the point where she didn't need Jean any longer as a striker.

The design of the sword took no more than half a day. Ellen took the jewels out of the leather purse, sorted them, and thought about how to use them to decorate the pommel. She still didn't like lavishly ornamented weapons, but a sword for the king was, after all, an exception. In order to make up her mind on a design, she first drew her ideas in the sand. Once she had determined the shape, she scratched the design into a wax tablet and took the most important measurements. As she worked on the details, a sequence of syllables kept running through her mind: Ru—ne—dur. Without noticing it, she kept whispering the syllables to herself. Then she stopped short. Runedur! That would be the name of the king's sword! The name leaped to her mind involuntarily, just as the name Athanor had before. Runedur would, of course, bring together all the qualities that made up a good weapon. But the sword would above all be unique because the art of the swordsmith and that of the goldsmith would come together in a unique harmony, since all the work would be a product of her soul and her hands alone. The king's sword would be both consummately elegant and at the same time simple. And of course, Runedur would show the strength and power of the Young King. Ellen recalled the altar vessels and crosses that Jocelyn had made. They, too, had sometimes been adorned with jewelry and other decorations but despite their lavish workmanship had always given the viewer a feeling of humility because of their beauty. That was just the way everyone should feel on seeing Runedur. After she had decided how it would look, she began to work feverishly on it.

Even though Jean had carefully studied the drawing on the wax tablet and listened intently to Ellen's description, he could hardly keep up with her. She was always two or three steps ahead of him in her thinking. Sometimes she was angry because he seemed not to understand what she was trying to do. Her feelings kept alternating between a deep-seated fear of failure and the elation of finally making a sword for the king.

When she was making good progress, Ellen gulped down her meal at lunchtime in order to get back to the workshop as fast as possible. If the work was proceeding more slowly or if she was brooding over a problem, she would poke around in her food after the others had left the table. The family and the helpers in the smithy got along well, sitting, eating, and chatting with one another, but Ellen had kept to herself recently, not paying attention to anything going on around her and thinking only of Runedur. She was already thinking of the next step, trying to anticipate any possible problems and how they could be circumvented so that no errors would creep in. One time she slipped, however, while she was scraping out the fuller, making a scratch in the sword. Her eyes filled with tears. How could that have happened? In despair she looked a bit closer at the damage. A day was lost in self-doubts, but then she figured out how to correct the error by lengthening the fuller a little. She carefully scraped out a little more metal from the middle, then turned the sword around and lengthened the fuller on the other side. Happy that the damage was no longer visible, she breathed a deep sigh of relief.

Ellen worked from early morning to late at night. After successfully hardening the blade, which was the major hurdle to overcome, she proceeded to the basic and finishing polish and was delighted at the wonderful shine that she was able to get, bit by bit. Even though she barely got any sleep, she never felt tired and seemed to have the strength of three men. As the sword took shape, she looked more and more radiant and happy.

—

"Have you decided what your daughter's name will be?" Ellen smiled without looking up from her work. The evening before, Rose had given birth to a little girl with a powerful voice and obviously strong lungs.

"By no means does Rose want to use her mother's name, but she thinks Jeanne wouldn't sound bad!" Jean was clearly proud of the name chosen for his daughter.

"Jeanne!" Ellen repeated, and nodded appreciatively. "That's a good name!" But as soon as she started concentrating on her work again, the tip of her tongue appeared in the left corner of her mouth. Setting the gemstones was causing her more trouble than she wanted to admit.

"Why don't you let a goldsmith take care of that?" Jean was amazed at how hard she tried without even once complaining or losing control of herself, but he couldn't understand why she insisted on working without any help.

"It's out of the question. First, I swore I would do it myself, and second, the goldsmith would ask me who the sword is for. And as you know, I can't say. Beyond that, I don't trust a stranger with such valuable stones. Who knows if he will do a good job? Maybe he will just use pieces of glass and keep the jewels for himself!"

"Don't you think that is a bit far-fetched?" Jean scowled skeptically.

"No, not at all! I have been given the task of forging this sword, and I'm responsible for it. Just don't worry—I'll take care of everything."

"All right then, as you will! I only meant well."

"It's best to leave her alone," Isaac teased, grinning at Jean. "You can't get anywhere with anyone as stubborn as she is! I gave up long ago and learned just to go along with everything she says."

"Oh, you!" Ellen threw him a glance that was both critical and provocative.

"Very well, I am going back to work!" Isaac raised his arms in a gesture of surrender.

—

In the evening when they were alone in their room, Isaac rolled away from her, breathless.

"Oh, Ellen! You should always forge things for the king!" he groaned contentedly.

"Is that so?" she asked, in studied innocence. "Why?"

"Ever since you have been working on this sword, you are so…so passionate!" His eyes sparkled.

Ellen blushed.

Isaac brushed an unruly lock of hair out of her face.

"You are so beautiful! I love you!" he whispered.

Ellen nestled contentedly against his arm. "Put out the light, dear," she mumbled and immediately fell asleep.

—

Ellen had thrown herself so enthusiastically into her work that she finished the sword even before the appointed date. Alone in the smithy, she lay Runedur down on the table in front of her, looking at it as intently as if she were seeing it for the first time. The belt was made of darkly tanned, heavy cow's hide and had a wide brass buckle. The scabbard was sheathed in purple silk interwoven with gold and fastened to it with intersecting bands of leather. The broad point of the sword was protected by a golden chape with finely engraved wavy lines. Ellen had decorated the round pommel with the two largest jewels—a ruby and an emerald—which she had set in exactly the middle of each side. The smaller stones were arranged like petals around the center stone and decorated with elegant patterns and delicately gilded tendrils. The handle, made of ash, had been wrapped in dark leather covered by twisted gold wire, and was splendid to hold. The cross guard was straight, only slightly turned down at the gilded ends that looked like wolf's jaws.

After Ellen had inspected the sword for a while, she drew it out of the scabbard. The blade was sharp on both sides and had an unusually long fuller due to the accident she'd had while scraping it out, but it made the sword look even more elegant. Ellen took a heavy cloth, wrapped it around the point of the blade, and bent the sword in a half circle. As soon as she released it, it sprang back and was just as straight as before. The blade had lost none of its flexibility and hardness due to the long fuller.

She sighed contentedly, then took a piece of linen, just as Donovan used to, and passed it over the blade. The sword cut through the material easily. Ellen was satisfied with the smooth cutting surface. On the side with the blood-red ruby that stood for the heart and life of young Henry, Ellen had inlaid some runes in gold wire that were meant to bring luck, courage, and many victories to the owner of the sword. Donovan had taught her these ancient symbols and what they meant. Though they were regarded as pagan, they were still much sought-after as symbols of victory. To assure the Young King of God's mercy, Ellen had decided to inlay right next to them the words IN NOMINE DOMINI in gold wire. On the side with the emerald, which was as green as her eyes, she had inlaid only the letter E in copper, within a circle. The wonderful, highly polished blade would certainly make any sword lover's heart beat faster! A shiver of joy ran down her back—she was so pleased with Runedur.

"Young Henry!" Peter came running into the smithy. "He is camped only a few miles northwest of here." Peter dropped breathless onto a wobbly stool and almost fell on the floor.

"The king?" Ellen's eyes lit up. "Nearby, you say? I am certain he can hardly wait to hold his new sword in his hands. What if I brought him the sword today, right now?"

"Didn't the knight say he would pick it up and you shouldn't give it to anyone else?" Isaac interrupted, joining the conversation.

But Ellen wouldn't hear of it and waved him off.

"What he meant by that is any other messenger, of course, not the king himself!"

Isaac shrugged. "If that's what you think…"

"The opportunity is just too great—I have to bring him the sword myself! If the messenger picks it up, no one will hear about me. But if I give it to the Young King myself, all the knights around him will see who made Runedur!" Ellen was getting very excited.

"Then at least let me come along," Isaac pleaded apprehensively.

She shook her head defiantly. "No, I will go alone!" If she appeared in the company of a man, they would think he had made the sword. And in the end a legend would spring up about the one-armed smith who had forged the mythical sword Runedur. She didn't want to risk that happening, no matter what.

"All right, if you say so!" Isaac looked at her, offended.

Ellen didn't even notice. The idea that she would finally get the recognition she deserved made her heart beat even faster. This was her day! She took the sword, wrapped it in a blanket, and went back to the house to tell Rose and change clothes. Then she got her white horse, Loki, from the stable and mounted it.

"Are you sure you don't want to wait for the sword to be picked up?" Isaac asked again, striving to assume a more conciliatory tone.

"No!" Ellen shook her head vigorously and would hear no further objections. Then she asked Peter to tell her where exactly she could find the king, and rode off.

—

On the great meadow near Mildenhall where the tents of the king and his entourage were pitched, hordes of squires, foot soldiers, and servants were still busy putting up tents and erecting fences for the horses. Everyone here seemed to have their hands full and paid no attention to Ellen, who rode at a leisurely pace through the camp, looking around closely. In the middle of the encampment she caught sight of an especially large, magnificent tent with a red pennant on top embroidered in gold depicting the lions rampant. That had to be the tent of the Young King! Ellen dismounted from her horse, Loki, and tied her to a post. Her hand trembled as she fondled Loki's powerful white neck;

for a moment she leaned her forehead against Loki's neck, closing her eyes. She had to summon up all her courage! Taking a deep breath, she seized the sword resolutely and walked toward the colorful tent.

Even before she arrived, the curtain at the entrance moved aside and a handsome young knight came out. He stood in her way with his legs apart.

"I would like to see the king," she demanded, a bit brashly owing to her excitement, and at once endeavored to smile warmly.

The knight looked her up and down with a sarcastic grin. "And what would you want from him?"

"I am bringing him his new sword, sire!"

The knight raised his eyebrows in astonishment. "Well, if that's the case, it would be best for you to come with me." He smiled briefly, turned around, and Ellen followed him into the tent. The royal quarters were even greater than she had assumed. Dozens of knights crowded around several large charcoal braziers. Ellen kept her head bowed modestly and observed the men out of the corner of her eye. They were drinking from silver goblets, talking excitedly, laughing loudly, and took no notice of her. Suddenly Ellen's heart started pounding wildly. What if Thibault were also here? She had given no thought to him in making her decision to come here!

The young knight gestured for her to follow and walked directly to a richly decorated oaken throne on the other side of the tent. The throne was empty!

Ellen did not dare to look around for the king.

With an unexpected, vigorous leap, the young knight suddenly jumped up onto the throne and sat down.

Ellen was shocked, and some of the knights looked up in astonishment. She swallowed hard. It was clear the young knight wanted to make fun of her, but what would the king say about him sitting on the throne? She felt weak in the knees and stood there motionless and uncertain of what to do.

The young knight grinned and beckoned for her to come closer. As if on command, all conversation in the room stopped.

The knights gathered curiously around her, leaving only a narrow passageway to the throne. Someone pushed her forward.

"You are bringing me something?" Young Henry smiled mischievously. Clearly he enjoyed the look of surprise on her face. Ellen had never seen the Young King up close and had not recognized him! She turned beet-red and felt a hot flash passing through her body.

William was standing alongside his lord with his arm lying casually on the back of the throne. He looked serious and didn't let it show that he knew Ellen. Only a slight quiver on one side of his mouth suggested how amusing he found the entire situation.

Thibault also stood nearby, but behind other knights so that Ellen was not able to see him. No one noticed how he had turned white as a sheet when he saw her. Ellen pulled herself together, stepped two paces closer to the throne, took a bow, and with arms outstretched handed the sword to the king.

"Well, let me see it!" the young man said impatiently, shuffling his feet like a child.

Ellen stood up, unwrapped the sword, and held it out to him. When the king saw it, he leaned forward quickly, grabbed hold of it with a broad smile, and held it up like a trophy for all to see. An enthusiastic cheer went up through the crowd. Young Henry inspected the sword, drew it slowly out of its scabbard, and weighed it in his hand without paying any attention to the decorative jewelry. All the knights clapped their approval on hearing the dark whirring sound the sword made when it cut through the air. Some of the knights were whispering excitedly among themselves. Henry examined the sword a bit more closely, then turned abruptly to William, holding it up so he could see it.

"There, look! It has the same sign as Athanor!" the Young King exclaimed. Now an even more excited murmur swept through the crowd.

"This sword is named Runedur, my lord," Ellen spoke up, even though the Young King had not asked her. "I know I was supposed to give it to your messenger, but when I heard you had set up camp here, I could not resist bringing it to you in person."

"Have you already been paid, or do I still owe you something?" Henry asked suspiciously, narrowing his eyes to little slits, as he knew nothing about a messenger who had placed an order for a sword.

"Your payment was quite generous, my king, and there is no further payment to make." Ellen smiled, and now young King Henry beamed as well.

Thibault, however, was trembling all over. "Why is Yqueboeuf not here?" he snapped at his squire.

"He is on a mission for the king, sire!" the boy whispered, lowering his eyes guiltily, though there was nothing he had done to arouse his master's anger.

No one else noticed how upset Thibault was, though he could hardly keep himself from cursing out loud.

"Now tell us the name of the smith who has forged Runedur," the king told Ellen, "so that everyone can hear!"

"It was I alone who fashioned the sword and all its parts. My name is Ellenweore, Your Highness!" Humbly she took a deep bow.

The murmuring in the crowd grew louder. Then young Henry raised his hand and the knights fell silent.

"Well, as some other kings are quite aware, women by this name are exceptionally strong!" Young Henry laughed and looked around for approval from his knights.

Most of them joined in the laughter, as always when the king was joking. Henry's mother, Eleanor, the queen and duchess of Aquitaine, was notorious for making life hard for her former husband, the king of France, and later for her present husband, King Henry II, the father of the Young King. Her royal husband therefore had kept her in prison for years to thwart her intrigues against him. Such strong women were often a thorn in the flesh of many knights, but most of those present admired Eleanor for having stood up to the old king more than once.

Ellen did not know enough about her namesake to understand why the knights were laughing.

"Did you also forge Athanor?" the Young King inquired, leaning over a bit toward her.

"Yes, my lord, I did!" Ellen answered proudly.

"Well, if that's the case, you will no doubt soon be receiving a lot of new orders for swords." Henry's admiration for his tutor was clearly evident. "Is your smithy here in the area?" He sat upright again and spread his legs far apart.

"In St. Edmundsbury, my lord!"

"Well, then, my thanks to you, Ellenweore of St. Edmundsbury, I am very pleased!" The king nodded graciously and smiled.

Ellen bowed once more. When she looked up, he had turned around and was talking with the knights standing around him.

No one was paying attention to her anymore, and clearly she could go now. She bowed again and cast a surreptitious glance in William's direction, but he was engrossed in a conversation with his lord and did not look at her.

After she had left the tent she breathed a contented sigh of relief and walked over to her horse. Now the noblest knights in the land knew who had forged the new sword for the king. Even though none of them had spoken to her, she hoped the Young King was right and that her abilities would soon be known far and wide in the realm. Exhausted from all the excitement, Ellen petted Loki's neck for a while before mounting the horse and heading home.

—

Ellen remained in high spirits for weeks, and she didn't know if it was because she had finally attained her goal of making a sword for the king or because she firmly believed that William had recommended her to young Henry. Even young Will noticed his mother's good mood. She spoke more gently with him and scolded him less often. One day she motioned to him to come over, and she patted him on the head.

"Do you remember how angry I used to be when you were whittling with Isaac's knife?"

Will nodded, but with some remorse. His mother didn't know that since then he had been working regularly with Isaac's knife.

"I think you are old enough now for your own. My father, Osmond, also gave me one when I was about as old as you are."

Will's gaze wandered to Ellen's belt, on which a knife was hanging.

"Yes, that's it. Since that day I have always had it with me. I've sharpened and polished it many, many times," she said, smiling at her son and handing him a knife in a bright pigskin sheath.

Will took it out and examined it with admiration. Colorful wavy lines shimmered all along the blade, some of them looking like eyes.

"Oh, isn't that beautiful," he blurted out.

"This is what you call a Damascene blade. The colorful pattern comes from welding and folding several layers of iron of differing hardness. You can take different rods, too, twist them, and then weld them together," Ellen explained.

"May I show it to Isaac and Jean?" Will asked, before his mother could give him another long discourse on forging.

Ellen smiled and nodded. Needless to say, the two of them had already seen the blade, but the boy seemed so excited about it that she didn't want to discourage him.

Damascening was an old technique that was used frequently for knives but no longer for sword blades. As she had learned from Donovan, the Vikings had perfected the art of damascening to an astonishing degree and made wonderful swords and artistic patterns with it. But since that time, this type of sword making had been forgotten, and the blades now, with the exception of engravings and insets, were smooth and lacking any pattern. Ellen regarded this ancient technique as a challenge and was considering making a sword sometime with damascene inlays, which would surely be difficult but not impossible.

With the knife, she hoped finally to awaken William's interest for work in the smithy as well. Until now, her son had preferred to spend most of his time in the forest. Again and again he brought home orphaned animals and cared for them lovingly, even though Ellen kept admonishing him to spend his time with more sensible things. Isaac and Jean supported the boy and tried to persuade her to be lenient when she scolded him. Ellen frowned when thinking of her son. Why didn't he understand that a future smith had no time for such nonsense?

November 1180

Will was sitting listlessly in the yard petting Greybeard when two men on horseback came riding up. One of them, with a bird perched on his hand, he recognized as the knight who had been there before with Baudouin de Béthune. The other was probably his squire. Will jumped up and ran toward them with amazing speed despite his foot.

"Is that a falcon, sire?" William asked without any inhibitions.

"Yes, a lanner falcon," William Marshal confirmed in a calm voice, smiling. "Step back a bit so I can dismount without frightening the bird." The Marshal's hand remained almost motionless as he stepped down. "Falcons are wild animals and remain so all their lives, even when they are in captivity," he told Will, who was looking at him curiously. "Any sudden movement frightens them and they will try to fly away, so approach slowly, and speak softly."

"But you are holding him on a leash, aren't you?" William wondered, pointing at the strap attached to the bird's foot. He moved forward carefully and slowly in order to get a better view of the bird.

"Exactly, lad, and if she—the falcon is, by the way, female—if she should be startled by something moving near her and try to fly away, she could hurt herself."

"Oh, I see!" Will's face brightened. "Does she have a name?" he asked, tilting his head to one side.

"Princess of the Sky." William smiled.

"Can I pet her?"

"You can try, but be careful!"

Will approached timidly, with his gaze lowered, looking at the bird out of the corner of his eye.

"You are doing fine," the Marshal encouraged him, "but if she gets restless, step back right away without making any fast movements. Do you understand?"

Will nodded and was practically bursting with pride when he finally managed to get close to the bird. Slowly he raised his right hand and gently petted the bird's chest.

The falcon did not seem at all restless.

The Marshal was surprised, since Princess did not allow just anyone to come up and touch her. It had taken forever for her to get accustomed to his squire Geoffrey.

Obviously jealous, the squire now came stumbling up to his master and Will, frightening the bird, which immediately tried to escape from its master's hand. "You can't touch it! You'll frighten it!" Geoffrey scolded.

"I will?" Will just gave him a scornful look before turning to the Marshal.

"You're such an oaf, Geoffrey. You frightened her," the Marshal grumbled softly in order not to frighten the bird even more. Only the angry look he gave his squire revealed how furious he really was.

Will continued to stand there without moving, and when the falcon calmed down he started petting her again.

"You have a way with birds," William Marshal said, complimenting him.

"I've taken care of pigeons, green plovers, jays, and other birds. Sometimes I find nests the mother has abandoned and then I raise the birds myself," Will said, his eyes sparkling. "Once I even cared for an injured raven. He was very smart, but he flew away. It was mating season!" Will grinned sheepishly and admired the falcon out of the corner of his eye.

"Well, son, falcons don't have much in common with other birds. Birds of prey are afraid of people; they even hate the sight of them! Taming them, or what falconers call 'manning,' so they will sit on your hand and teaching them to hunt for you takes a lot of skill and endless patience. The falcon does not by nature seek the company of men. On the contrary, he avoids them. He loves freedom, and because it is so difficult to tame birds of prey, falconry is considered the most noble of all forms of hunting."

"Will!" they heard a strong woman's voice calling.

Ellen stuck her head out of the window in the smithy. "Where in God's name is the rascal gadding about now?" she called out crossly.

When she saw the Marshal, she wiped off her hands on her dress, put her hand to her forehead to push a few unruly locks of hair back underneath her bonnet, and joined him. "My lord!" she said, nodding but not curtsying. After everything that had transpired between them, she thought such reverential expressions were superfluous, even in the presence of his squire and her son. She took Will by the shoulders and gave him a nudge in the direction of the workshop. "Go see Jean, and help him out!" she told him before turning to the Marshal.

"The king is very happy with the sword!" William handed the bird back to his squire and walked over toward the workshop with Ellen. After a short distance, they stopped.

"What can I do for you?" she asked, opening the door for him and standing aside so he could enter.

"A sword," he said. "One of the king's squires will be knighted soon. He is like a son to me," he said, glancing fleetingly at Will. "Or rather a younger brother," he mumbled.

Ellen ignored the allusion to Will and tried to treat the Marshal just like any other customer. They discussed the details and agreed on a price and when the sword could be picked up.

"By that time we'll be back on the continent again. Henry is expected at his father's court for Christmas." The Marshal fidgeted with the scabbard of his sword.

"That has to be mended. The leather is in shreds," Ellen told him. "I can do that right now, if you want. I noticed it the last time you were here and have everything in my shop to repair it, if you have a little time."

The Marshal hesitated for a moment and then nodded in agreement. "May I take Will off your hands for a while?"

Ellen shrugged, feigning indifference. "Certainly, why not? Will! Go with the Marshal," she ordered her son.

With a happy smile, the boy followed William outside. "Thank you for freeing me from this miserable, dark shop." He grinned at the Marshal conspiratorially. "Is it true that you're best friends with our king?" At the dinner table Will had only pretended he wasn't interested in what the grown-ups were talking about, but in fact he eagerly took in every single word.

The Marshal laughed. "You are right, I am young Henry's tutor, and he is also the king of England, just like his father. And I think I'm in fact his closest confidant. Does that answer your question?"

William nodded with embarrassment.

"Would you care to see a falcon fly? I'll show you, if you like."

"Oh, yes, please! Would you really do that?" Will pleaded with shock and amazement. The Marshal nodded, and the boy jumped up and down excitedly.

"But take it slow or you'll frighten her," the Marshal said, trying to calm him down.

They spent the entire afternoon together, and William showed little Will how the falcon flew and explained all sorts of things worth knowing about the nature of these animals and how to tame them. He also let Will try on his gauntlet.

The boy was awestruck by the buckskin glove, which was soft yet firm and had a full-bodied fragrance. It felt good on his hand even though it was far too large.

The Marshal showed the boy how to hold his hand, and toward the end of the afternoon even set the falcon down for a moment on his fist.

"You have to hold very still!" he told him in a friendly voice.

Will tried not to tremble and was both relieved and disappointed when the Marshal told Geoffrey to take the bird again.

"He has a way with animals," the Marshal said to Ellen as they returned.

"Well, if he doesn't start taking an interest soon in forging, he'll not be doing much more than shoeing horses. So it can't hurt if the animals don't walk all over him." Ellen sounded a bit cross.

Even William noticed it and wondered why she was so hard on the boy. He could hardly remember his own childhood but did know how incredibly much his mother and nannies spoiled him when he lived at home.

"Here it is, like new again!" Ellen interrupted his thoughts and handed him the repaired scabbard.

"The glue has to dry a bit still, so you shouldn't put it on yet."

"Wonderful!" he said, praising her work and looking for his purse.

"No, don't." Ellen placed her soot-blackened calloused hand on his forearm. "That was the least I could do."

Even though he didn't understand what she meant, the Marshal shrugged respectfully and left the shop accompanied by Ellen and Will. He slapped the boy on the shoulder and said farewell. Once he had mounted his horse, he bent down to Ellen and touched his lips gently against her cheek. Surprised, she stood frozen, and Geoffrey looked at him curiously, with an almost suspicious expression. Ignoring him, the Marshal said to Will: "Obey your mother and do what she tells you, Will!" Then he took the bird again on his hand and rode off, accompanied by his squire.

Ellen stood there a while, as if rooted to the spot. The kiss made her skin tingle, almost burning like a mark of the devil, and her heart nearly burst into flames.

Rose was watching from a distance. *I hope this doesn't end badly*, her gaze seemed to be saying; then she grabbed her broom and went back into the house.

—

The Young King was right. Scarcely had a few weeks passed and every nobleman in East Anglia knew the king and the Marshal had a sword made by Ellen. New noblemen kept coming to the smithy to order a sword. Many acted as if they just happened to be in the area, and others mentioned how far they had come just to place an order with her.

The more Ellen had to do, the higher the prices she was able to ask for her swords. In some months she took in more money than she had in an entire year before.

"Jean, I think you are at the point where you're ready!" she said cheerfully one evening at dinner.

"Ready for what?" he asked unsuspecting, sipping at his hot soup.

"You will start working on a sword tomorrow all by yourself! You will have a striker—I'm thinking of the new helper. What's his name?"

"Stephen!"

"Right, Stephen. When you have finished the sword and your work is convincing to me, I'll go to the guild master and ask him to have you recognized as a journeyman."

Jean choked for a moment on a piece of bread. "Are you serious?" he asked, as soon as he got his voice back.

Ellen looked at him and raised her eyebrows. "Do I look like I'm joking?"

"No, of course not. Thank you, Ellen!" he replied somewhat embarrassed.

Rose put her hand on his and squeezed it for a moment. "You can do it!"

"Of course he can do it. If I wasn't convinced of it I wouldn't ask him," Ellen said.

"And what about Peter?" Jean asked, always thinking of other people.

"When you are finished, then it's his turn."

Jean nodded with satisfaction.

"Then we are soon going to need new apprentices or strikers, don't you think?" Isaac said, turning to Ellen and reaching for another slice of bread.

"I have thought about that, too." Ellen took another gulp of light beer but didn't say any more about it at the time.

March 1181

Ellen took the sword that Jean had made without her help, wrapped it up, and set out on her way to Conrad.

Jean had asked whether he shouldn't come along, but she preferred to go alone. She wanted to give Conrad a chance to make some concessions to her without feeling watched. Ellen was wearing clean new clothes that Rose had made for her out of beautiful, soft, pine-green woolen cloth with silver embroidery on the neck and arms. At first Ellen had been a bit annoyed and said it was a waste of money because she already had a green dress from Béthune, but Rose didn't let herself be put off.

"You've got to have something special to wear. Claire's wedding dress must be about ten years old. Please, Ellen! Perhaps you will be summoned to the king again, or just to the guild master, and you want everyone to see that you are not a poor smith but have made your mark!"

Ellen relented. It was too late, in any case, for her to change her mind because the dress was already finished. And she was as happy with it as with the coat trimmed in wolf fur that kept her dry in the damp, cold weather. Even though the first tender yellow narcissuses had already appeared along the roadside as signs of the impending spring, the wind was still quite cool.

"You look wonderful! Like a real lady!" Isaac had called out to her, laughing as she prepared to ride off.

The house of the guild master was only a few miles away, and Ellen could easily have gone on foot, but she followed the advice of Rose and Jean and rode the beautiful white horse for which people had often envied her.

"It doesn't hurt for Conrad to see how well you have made out!" Isaac chimed in.

When Ellen arrived in Conrad's yard, a boy came running up at once and greeted her politely.

"I would like to see the guild master!" Ellen said, without dismounting.

"Of course. I will go and get him," the boy stammered and raced off.

A smile passed over Ellen's face. Her elegant clothing had clearly impressed the little fellow. Perhaps Isaac was even right, and the boy thought she was a noble lady! *Thank you, Rose*, she thought, *it was right to dress like this.*

Then Conrad came out of the smithy. He was no taller than Ellen, wore a leather cap on his almost bald head, and had rolled up his shirtsleeves almost as far as his powerful upper arms. Ellen slid gracefully to the ground just as Jean had taught her and stood there solidly on both feet.

"Ellenweore!" Conrad said, with a surprisingly warm smile.

"Conrad!" Ellen nodded respectfully. *I feel like a fool with this silly formality*, she thought for a moment.

"People everywhere are talking about you and your swords nowadays." Conrad gestured cordially for her to enter the house. "Look, Edda, who has come for a visit," he called out to his wife. "This is Ellenweore…"

"The swordsmith?" Edda broke out in a wide smile, wiped the flour off her hands onto her apron, and reached out to greet Ellen. "I'm really happy you have come to visit us!"

Ellen could not get over her astonishment. First there was Conrad's friendly greeting, then Edda's wide smile. Perhaps she had better watch out!

"Well, what brings you to me?" Conrad offered Ellen a seat at the table, and Edda served her a goblet of honey wine.

"Do you remember Jean?" Ellen asked, taking a sip in order to soothe her sore throat a bit.

"Of course," Conrad replied, interested in what she would have to say.

"He forged a sword. It was just him and a young, inexperienced striker." Ellen had been holding the sword inconspicuously close to her in her left hand, but now she took it in both hands, unwrapped it, and laid it on the table.

Conrad picked up the weapon carefully and inspected it more closely. "I am not a swordsmith," he said almost reticently.

"You are the guild master. I am sure you can judge whether it is the work of a professional smith, allowing him to be called a journeyman."

Conrad clearly felt flattered, for he smiled briefly. He examined the weapon again, visibly impressed.

"No inclusions, well polished—it seems to be a good weapon," he said without looking up.

"Then you have no objection if from now on Jean calls himself a journeyman?" Ellen asked again, just to be certain. She didn't want to be in conflict with the guild forever.

Instead of answering, Conrad replied, "Did you teach him how to do that?"

Ellen bristled instinctively. "Yes, indeed I did!" she said with a note of defiance. She was ready to get into a battle of words with him. He had no right to deny Jean the title of journeyman just because he had learned his trade from a woman!

"We made a mistake in rejecting you as a master. Ever since you took over Isaac's workshop you have brought honor and fame to the smiths of St. Edmundsbury, and I will propose in the next guild meeting that you be recognized as a master. This way Jean's title as journeyman would be assured, too."

Ellen was too surprised to know what to say. Conrad had been her fiercest opponent, and now was he going to support her? Evidently he interpreted her surprised silence correctly, for he cleared his throat nervously.

"Let's just assume the guild will accept my proposal to recognize you as a master." Conrad took a deep breath as if he were struggling to find the right words, and Ellen was getting prepared for the worst. "Then you could take on regular apprentices," he continued after a short pause, scratching the back of his head.

"That's true," Ellen answered, still waiting for what might come. She felt certain that the guild master had something up his sleeve.

Conrad seemed to be summoning up all his courage.

"As you surely know, a father is not always the best teacher," he stammered, blushing.

"Oh, rubbish," Edda interrupted impatiently. "Our son has taken it into his head to become a swordsmith. He doesn't talk of anything else! And of course we thought of you." She gave her husband a reproachful look. "Just come out with what you want to say!"

"But that's just exactly what I was getting around to, woman!" he snapped at her crossly, turning back to Ellen uneasily. "Would you take him as an apprentice if the guild agrees?" he asked stiffly.

Ellen could guess how much effort it had taken for him to come out with his question. "As soon as I have my confirmation as a master, I'll have a talk with the boy. If he's eager and hard-working..."

Conrad gasped for air like a beached whale. Naturally, he had expected her to accept his proposal at once.

But Ellen didn't want to lose face any more than he did. Only her swords were for sale, not she herself.

"Bring the boy to me when the guild has decided," she repeated amiably. Ellen was certain that Conrad had enough influence with the other smiths to get what he wanted.

"The meeting is in a week," he said, visibly relieved.

"Fine, I'll look forward to seeing you then," she said, getting up and shaking hands.

In the yard she saw the same boy who had greeted her when she arrived running into the smithy. "Is that the lad?" she asked.

"Yes, that's Brad. He's almost eleven," Conrad said proudly.

"A strong, friendly-looking fellow!" Ellen said.

Conrad stretched a little. "He's my youngest. The others are grown up and have left the house, except for the eldest who works with me in the smithy and will someday take it over."

"You are a lucky man, Conrad," Ellen said cheerfully as she left.

—

About a week later, as the March sun struggled to penetrate the thick clouds, Conrad suddenly appeared at the workshop with his son.

"You are a journeyman now, Jean!" Conrad congratulated him and shook his hand. "You made a really fine sword!" Then he turned to Ellen. "Master!" He grinned stiffly. "I bring you my son with the request that you try him and take him on as your apprentice." Conrad played his part properly and bowed slightly.

"You may come back to pick him up this evening, and we shall see!" Ellen said with a friendly smile.

Conrad looked at his son sternly. "This is what you wanted, Brad—now show what you can do!"

Brad nodded enthusiastically. "Yes, Father!"

The boy had gathered some basic knowledge about iron working from his father, and he was both eager and clever. After training Jean and Peter, Ellen was genuinely happy to have Brad to teach. She agreed with Conrad on an apprenticeship of seven years. Most other smiths were in training for just five years, farriers for four, and at first Conrad was unhappy that his son would have to be apprenticed for so long. But Brad pleaded, and Ellen came to an agreement with his father on the apprentice's due. It was good for her reputation among the smiths, after all, if the guild master apprenticed his own son to her.

When Conrad had left, Ellen went into the house to eat and sat down quietly at the table. How proud Osmond would have been of her had he been able to see how far she had come! For a moment a smile passed over her lips. Perhaps even Aedith would one day hear how famous her sister was, or Kenny would be able to impress his customers by letting them know he was her brother. Ellen also thought about Mildred and Leofric and felt a bit sad because she missed them. *Perhaps even Mother would have been proud of me*, she thought, when Isaac interrupted her thoughts.

"If we take on more apprentices, we'll soon have to enlarge the smithy." He handed her a piece of bread and smiled.

"Sometimes space is too tight already at the two forges," Jean added as he chewed his food, "and three anvils are also not enough!"

"I have already thought about that," Ellen agreed, and she was about to say something when Rose interrupted.

"First of all, I need some help now!" She set little Jeanne down on the ground. "Here, sweetheart." Rose handed her a rag doll, and the child shouted with glee. Looking at Ellen, Isaac, and Jean one by one, Rose added, "Eve and I can't do it ourselves any more. We have six children to take care of and then everyone at the smithy here for lunch, and in addition cleaning and washing, as well as taking care of the animals and the vegetable garden. We each have only two hands." Rose's voice kept getting louder, and it was clear how upset she was. Her anger must have been building up for a long time.

Ellen looked at her in dismay. Rose had never complained before! Recently she had been a bit irritated at times, but no one had really taken it seriously. Neither Ellen nor any of the others had given much consideration to the fact that the two women had more and more work to do.

"And on top of all that, Eve is getting married soon!"

Rose was interrupted by an outburst of applause and happy hand shaking, and she waited patiently until the general merriment had subsided.

Everyone fell silent when Ellen asked anxiously if Eve would quit after the wedding. Eve said no, she wouldn't, and Ellen gave Rose a quizzical look as if to say, *See, nothing will change!*

Rose's eyes flashed with anger.

"Then in at least a year we'll have one more child here. Do you think Eve and her new husband will do nothing but hold hands forever? I need more money for a second maid, and especially for groceries. Smiths eat like nine-headed caterpillars! Flour, grain, and especially bacon vanish in no time, and sometimes I don't have anything to put into the soup. Nobody's hunger is satisfied with just onions and cabbage all the time!" Rose's voice was rising again.

"Good heavens, Rose!" Ellen looked at her, conscience stricken. "You are right, of course. We earn enough! Why didn't I think of that myself?"

"I have always somehow managed, but now it's just too much," Rose said almost apologetically.

Ellen opened her purse and placed a good number of coins on the table.

"You should have told me sooner!" she scolded. "If you need more, come to me, do you understand?"

"That will do for now. I'll pay close attention, but…"

"That's enough, Rose! You don't have to justify yourself. I know you are excellent at keeping house. Will you take care of getting a maid? After all, you will have to get along with her."

Rose cleared her throat and nodded contentedly. "There was a girl from town here yesterday inquiring about work. She looks like she could help out. I'll send Marie to her tomorrow." Rose was satisfied.

"I hope we'll soon have cake here again then, what do you think?" Ellen asked, looking around.

"Hooray!" the children cheered, and Rose broke out in a wide smile.

"When did you want Peter to finish his journeyman's piece?" Isaac inquired, holding his wooden plate out to Rose for a second portion.

"Before the winter. It would be a sword for the younger son of the Earl of Clare. I thought that would be his best opportunity."

"But if it doesn't have the copper 'E' he won't want it," Jean replied.

"I have already spoken with him about it. The young man cannot afford one of my swords, so that's why Peter will be making it. Under my supervision, of course. I assured the de Clare boy that all our work is first-rate. The sword will have an 'E' inlaid in brass, just like all the swords made in our smithy from now on. Only the swords that I make personally will have the copper sign from now on. And we'll charge dearly for that."

"Not a bad idea!" Jean agreed. "Then from now on my own swords will also have a brass 'E.'"

"Of course!" Ellen took a heaping spoonful of porridge. "You're right, Rose, it tastes pretty good, but a bit more bacon wouldn't hurt."

January 1183

The winter that year was especially mild. It hadn't snowed once, and little rain had fallen. Ellen took a deep breath of the fresh morning air. For more than a year and a half she had made nothing but swords! Her reputation had brought her many customers and an excellent income.

Isaac had also earned himself a good reputation. A growing number of noblemen came to him to have their weapons, new ones or family heirlooms, polished. He was so busy that he had recently taken on a boy from St. Edmundsbury, whom he was training as a sword polisher.

Every day they received more orders, and Ellen thanked the Lord regularly in prayer and through the alms she gave to the poor.

"We need a larger smithy…and a house as well. I think it's time to enlarge them both. I've made inquiries and the abbot recommended a builder to me," she said one day to Isaac.

"The abbot?"

"Didn't you know he recently gave us an order for more swords?"

Isaac sighed, then grinned. "The most exalted people in the country want us to work for them. It's hard to keep track." He pretended to shrug in despair but then broke out in a wide smile. "I would never have thought a smith could get so far in the world." Contentedly he wiped his forehead with his sleeve.

"I'd like to have a real stone house," Ellen told him, dreaming. Isaac swallowed hard. He had built the little half-timbered house as a boy along with his father.

"Jean and Rose and their children could have the house. The rooms we built for them are much too small, anyway. And then we would have the new stone house to ourselves," she said, dismissing his objection even before he could get a word in. She stroked his cheek fondly and kissed him on the forehead. "I know you love the house, but we'll soon have another child to care for under the same roof…" She sighed.

Isaac looked at her, wondering. "Rose?"

Ellen shook her head.

"You don't mean Eve, do you?" Isaac asked, peeved. Was Eve pregnant, just as Rose had predicted, right after the wedding? Did Ellen want to take her and her family in as well?

"No, I am pregnant!"

"Ellenweore! That's such wonderful news!" Isaac exclaimed happily, taking her in his arms and twirling her around. "I had already given up hope that the Lord would bless us with another child!"

Early February 1183

Winter had finally arrived, quite unexpectedly. The sky was milky white, and it looked like snow. Ellen was freezing, so she pulled the fur vest tighter around her as she hurried across the yard to the workshop. Just before she reached the shop she heard hoofbeats.

"Baudouin! What a pleasure!" she said, greeting him as he came closer. He hadn't visited them for a long time, and Ellen was sincerely happy to see him.

"How are you all?"

Baudouin leaped from his horse and tied it up. "The Young King needs you! You must come along with me to Limoges," he announced.

Ellen looked at him, frightened. "But I can't just get up and leave here."

Baudouin shrugged sympathetically. "When the king calls, it is better not to refuse. It's a matter of honor!"

Ellen felt a tightening in her chest. "Will I be away long? I am going to have a child," she explained, looking down at her belly.

"Oh, when?" Baudouin looked carefully at her midsection.

"In the summer."

He grinned with relief. "Either you'll be back in time, or your child will be born on the other side of the Channel. Would that be so bad?" Ellen didn't reply. "You have to be ready to leave by tomorrow morning."

"So soon?" Ellen looked at him in consternation.

"It's a long way, and you do want to get back soon! I'll pick you up right after sunrise." Baudouin jumped onto his horse and rode off.

—

"He can ask you, just like that, to leave?" Isaac was furious and ran back and forth angrily.

"A call from the king is like a command, Baudouin said! I have to go, I have no other choice! But I'll do my best to be back for the summer," she said, trying to console him.

But Isaac just kept grumbling incoherently and turned away.

Ellen felt something like a hot flash passing through her. Baudouin had also said that it was an honor to be summoned by the king. And this honor was given to her, not to Isaac. She interpreted Isaac's anger as jealousy and was disappointed that he didn't approve. He was a successful sword polisher and had been an indispensable advisor to her. For this reason it hurt her all the more that he was so opposed to the idea.

They did not speak another word before her departure.

Rose urged Ellen not to leave on bad terms, but Ellen remained obstinate.

Rose shook her head in disbelief and disapproval, saying "I hope neither of you will regret this. In any case, I'd never let my Jean go away like this!"

—

Baudouin arrived at the smithy before sunrise, accompanied by a young knight and two squires. Ellen said farewell to Jean, Rose, and the children.

Only Isaac was nowhere to be found.

"I know you will carry on the work in the smithy the way I would," Ellen said in a choked voice.

"Good heavens, that sounds like you're never coming back! Hopefully you'll be back again before the end of summer!" Jean embraced her warmly. They had spent so many years together, and naturally he was concerned about her. "You and Isaac were meant for each other!" he whispered in her ear. "Go and say good-bye to him!"

Ellen's eyes narrowed.

"As you can see, he's not here, and only because he's jealous of me!"

Jean took her by both shoulders and looked her straight in the eye. "What in the world makes you think that? You know yourself how happy he is with you and his work! I think he's afraid you will succumb to William's charms again. If you could only see what you look like as soon as the Marshal appears!" There was a touch of disapproval in Jean's voice.

Ellen felt cut to the quick. Had she in fact come to terms with her departure so easily because she hoped to see William again?

"I am really sorry to bother you," Baudouin interrupted, "but we must leave!"

Ellen chased away thoughts about Isaac and William.

"I'm coming!" she replied with a forced smile and had Jean help her up onto the horse.

—

The night had been freezing cold. Trees, bushes, and grass were all covered with a layer of ice, and the breath of both men and animals rose up like clouds of vapor. Everything looked sad and grey. Even the sun looked like nothing more than a dull silver disk in a greyish sky.

Dead…everything looks dead, Ellen thought and cursed the Young King because he had sent for her. She spoke not a word all morning, and Baudouin, too, remained quiet.

Not until they had stopped in the early afternoon for a brief rest did he tell her almost offhandedly that William had left the king's court.

She turned to look at him in astonishment and noticed that he avoided her gaze.

"A man with so much success both in tournaments and with the Young King is much envied." Baudouin sighed. "I'll admit, William can be a bit of a braggart, but he remains the most loyal friend and knight of the Young King." Baudouin turned to one of the squires. "Can you finish with the horses? I'm as hungry as a bear." The squire nodded and rushed to finish up.

Ellen watched as he left and wondered whether Baudouin had intentionally put off telling her before they left that William would not be at King Henry's court when they arrived.

"His enemies have left nothing untried; they even asserted that the Marshal had an affair with the queen!" The young squire gave Baudouin a wineskin. He nodded with satisfaction and handed it to Ellen. "Of course there is no truth in that story!" he quickly affirmed.

Ellen took a long drink and had to cough—the wine was bitter and rough going down. She much preferred cider or light beer.

"I think that some of the closest confidants of the Young King are responsible for this lie—Thomas de Coulonces probably, and I think also Thibault de Tournai, though he tries very hard to stay in the background."

"Thibault?" Ellen shuddered and her voice sounded tinny.

Baudouin looked at her startled. "You will catch your death of cold in this weather." Quickly he fetched a blanket and placed it over her shoulders. "Do you know Thibault de Tournai?"

Ellen gave an almost imperceptible nod.

"Ah, yes, probably from Tancarville!" Baudouin thought he understood and elaborated a bit on his thoughts. "Rumors are circulating that the king did not order the sword that you made for him." Baudouin paused for a moment as if he expected a confirmation.

"Where did you get such a silly idea?" she replied indignantly.

"When the king received the sword, he seemed as happy as a child getting a present. It really didn't look like he had known anything about it!" Baudouin said.

"Surely William…" Her heart was pounding.

"No, William didn't know anything about it either! That's just it! He also wondered who had given the order for the sword. He was, after all, responsible for the young king's funds. He would have noticed if such a sum was missing. Anyway, Henry's coffers are always empty." Baudouin paused for a moment to think. "There is something strange about this. A sword everyone says they did not order, but somehow was paid for, and then this intrigue against William." He shook his head uneasily. "This has not only hurt William, but more importantly the Young King. He has lost his most thoughtful and experienced adviser, at a time like this when there are problems between himself, his brothers, and their father. There is something rotten here, and it smells of treason!"

Ellen stared at him, horrified.

"I must know who ordered the sword from you!" Baudouin pleaded with her.

"He didn't give his name, and I didn't ask. He was wearing the king's colors and coat of arms, and that was enough for me." Ellen felt a bit foolish.

"Is that all?" Baudouin asked, disappointed.

"The knight gave me jewels, gold, and a few instructions," she said with a shrug.

"Instructions?"

"We were to tell no one about the order and give the sword to no one but himself."

"You were not supposed to bring it to the king?" Baudouin asked again, just to make sure he had heard right.

Ellen shook her head apologetically. "When I heard the king was encamped near St. Edmundsbury, I ignored this instruction. I wanted to see his eyes when he held the sword in his hands for the first time," she said rather sheepishly.

Unexpectedly, Baudouin's face brightened. "At first I thought someone wanted to use the sword to curry favor with Henry, and I always wondered who that could be. But now it looks like the deceiver has been deceived himself!"

Ellen looked at him in astonishment.

"Well, it appears the sword was not really intended for the Young King."

"But that's what the messenger said! And the jewels, the gold?" Ellen was so angry, confused, and hurt now that she was positively shouting. Evidently, William was not the one who had recommended her, and now it appeared that the sword wasn't even intended for the king!

"If I could only make sense out of all of that!" Baudouin said. "Thomas de Coulonces and Thibault never could stand one another, but recently they have been the best of friends. I'm sure that Adam d'Yqueboeuf is somehow involved in all of this. He envied William more than anyone else for the position he held."

A hot flashed passed through Ellen's head.

"What did you say his name was?" she asked, suddenly fully alert.

"Who? Adam? Adam d'Yqueboeuf! Why do you ask? Do you perhaps know him from Tancarville?"

Ellen shook her head. "No, I can't remember him. But Rose…the poor girl was very disturbed when the knight ordered the sword. I asked her why she was so pale, and she just mumbled, 'Yqueboeuf.' I had no idea what that meant, but now that you said the name I remember and understand what was troubling her. She no doubt feared he would recognize her and tell Thibault where she was."

"This is getting more and more complicated. Do you mean Thibault de Tournai? What does he have to do with Rose?"

"She was his lover for years and ran away from him."

Baudouin shook his head in disbelief. "You saved my life once, you have a son by William, and your sister-in-law was Thibault's lover?" he exclaimed in disbelief.

"She is not my sister-in-law, just a good friend," Ellen corrected him.

"Well, it doesn't matter—it's all very strange. Are there more complications I should know about?" he asked.

Ellen hesitated and tried to avoid his glance.

"I can see, there is more…" Baudouin sighed but didn't ask for any further explanation.

Limoges, March 1183

Henry, the Young King, was involved in a dispute with his brother, Richard the Lionheart. As always, it was about land, fealty, and vanity. The old king had ordered Henry to cede the Duchy of Aquitaine to Richard. But Henry was furious at Richard because, shortly before, he had fortified the castle at Clairvaux, although this castle had always belonged to the count of Anjou. Since that time, Henry had strengthened his connections with the barons of Aquitaine and had given his word to them. But in order not to anger his father, he promised to do what the king demanded on the condition that Richard would pledge allegiance to him. But Richard firmly rejected recognizing his own brother as his master. He thought that since they were of the same flesh and blood, neither of them should stand above the other. He recognized that it was just for Henry, as the eldest, to receive his father's heritage, but as far as his mother's holdings were concerned, Richard demanded to be treated as an heir with equal rights. Since Queen Eleanor had brought more than just Aquitaine into the marriage, however, the old king was furious about it. He warned Richard that his brother would raise an army against him in order to curb his pride and greed, and ordered his other son, Geoffrey, Duke of Brittany, to stand by Henry, his brother and feudal lord. But the Young King was also concerned about the welfare of Poitou that had long been oppressed and plundered by Richard, and the barons had called on him for help.

But young Henry was not yet ready to make that decision on his own. He needed the Marshal. He had always been able to rely on him. Adam d'Yqueboeuf and the other men in his entourage could not take William's place, as they lacked experience. It was this special combination of ferocity and courage, ambition, confidence, and calculation that made William so indispensable to him—and at the same time that had made him the envy of so many.

—

Thibault was sitting in his room staring into the fire. It was uncomfortably cold in Limoges Castle, but Thibault scarcely noticed. He had come a long way toward realizing his goal of finally getting William out of the way once and for all. Now he was waiting for Adam d'Yqueboeuf. In the Marshal's absence, Adam had been gaining influence, so Thibault had kept his part of the agreement. Only Adam had failed, for the sword Henry proudly displayed was still not in Thibault's hands. Thibault pounded angrily on the arm of the heavy oaken chair he was sitting in. Suddenly there was a knock, and Adam d'Yqueboeuf hurriedly slipped through the door and into the room.

"The old king has lost his mind. He's doing everything differently than planned. It was his idea to bring Richard to his senses!" he exclaimed furiously, falling into a chair. "So where do we stand now? Without William, Henry won't get anywhere with his father!" Adam spat angrily into the brass spittoon next to him. "I'll have a heart-to-heart talk with Henry. He must reconcile himself with his father!"

"I hope you can convince him. He listens more to you than to anyone else. Don't forget, if he loses, he'll never do anything again without William!" Thibault warned him.

Adam d'Yqueboeuf grumbled crossly. "I know, and that's not my intent," he said angrily, then jumped up and walked out.

Thibault nodded with satisfaction and remained sitting for a while.

"The idiot doesn't even suspect what's really happening!" he chuckled. He himself would personally see to it that the old king was not disappointed. Even if Henry II had crowned his eldest son years ago, he still expected obedience from his offspring just as before. They didn't want to be under his thumb any longer, however, and were fighting to gain power and influence themselves. The old king had to prevent a second rebellion by his sons at all costs. For this reason, he depended now on the loyalty of the men he had taken in years ago at the court of his eldest son. Now, with the Marshal out of reach they had to use their influence with young Henry in order to lead him back onto the right path.

Thibault grimaced mischievously. Sometimes it was better not to be up in front but to manipulate the strings from behind!

—

Young Henry had not completely obeyed his father, and thus, shortly after his eldest son's departure for Limoges, the king set out in pursuit with a small company of troops. Before he could reach the gates of the city, however, arrows started raining down on him and his party. The old king was injured and withdrew, setting up an encampment nearby.

Thomas de Coulonces advised young Henry to go to him to ask for forgiveness and to assert that the citizens of Limoges had not recognized the king.

Geoffrey was horrified that his brother was expected to grovel before his father, but Thomas de Coulonces warned young Henry not to go to battle against both Richard and his father at the same time.

The Young King, therefore, paid a visit to his father, but the discussions were unsatisfactory. With regard to the controversy surrounding Richard, father and son could not come to any agreement. Thus, young Henry withdrew again to Limoges Castle and once more gathered his advisers around him. An animated debate broke out as to how to proceed and where the necessary financial support would come from. The Young King asked each one to speak in the presence of all.

"Yqueboeuf, you shall begin!" he said to Adam and nodded amiably at him.

Adam d'Yqueboeuf was clearly aware of the honor of being asked to speak first. He coughed slightly, straightened up, and took a few steps in the direction of his young master.

"My king, by your leave, Richard must be shown what happens when he refuses to recognize you. But this is not the right time to get involved in a clash of arms with your father. If you do give in after all, the king will appreciate it."

"Adam, you know I have deep respect for you," Thibault replied, "but I cannot agree! If Henry gives in, then Richard will have won. The only reason he dared to rebel," he said, turning directly to young Henry, "is that he thought his father would be indecisive. You mustn't lose face, or it won't be just your brothers who will openly defy you! You promised Poitou they would be free and subject only to you, and if you abandon them now, you will never again be able to count on their support."

A general murmur of approval went through the room. Only Geoffrey, who was also a brother of the Young King and felt attacked by Thibault's speech, gave him a threatening look.

"Thibault de Tournai is right, my king—you must stay the course you are already on, to the end. But to win the war you must bring the Marshal back," an older knight spoke up.

"You are for ordering William to return to the court? You, of all people?" the Young King asked in astonishment. "William never forgave you for the death of his uncle!" Henry raised his eyebrows in disbelief.

"I know, Your Grace. William hates us Lusignans, but he loves you, just as I do. You cannot do without his military advice. No one is more skillful at leading soldiers than he is, or has better control over them. They love him; he is their idol! Only he can lead them to victory."

Young Henry nodded respectfully and then turned to Baudouin. "Béthune! Probably everyone here knows you would be delighted if the Marshal came back, but how do you feel about a war with my father?"

"My king!" Baudouin bowed deeply. "I would lie if I said I was not in favor of the Marshal's return. But what matters here is not how much I am attached to him but how indispensible he is as your adviser. Everything would be much simpler if you could ask him," Baudouin said, bowing again.

Young Henry frowned. Baudouin had cleverly avoided answering the question. He turned to the other side. "Coulonces?"

Thomas de Coulonces looked at Adam d'Yqueboeuf and then back to his lord. "I must agree with Yqueboeuf, my king. You don't have the same resources as your father does. It is a great risk. Even the Marshal is just a man and cannot guarantee a victory. One way or the other, you will someday be the only king of the realm. I see no point in angering your father now more than necessary. I think Richard has provoked you more than once because he knows he can sow discord in that way. You should yield and not allow your brother this victory!"

The Young King frowned again. "Leave me to myself now, I will think about where we need to proceed from here."

"My king, if you should want to bring William back, I know where he is!" Baudouin said softly, before turning to leave.

The Young King nodded gratefully. "Geoffrey, my brother, stay!" he exclaimed, as the Duke of Brittany was also about to leave.

—

"The Marshal, again and again the Marshal!" Adam d'Yqueboeuf groaned after they had left the room.

Thibault nodded in agreement.

"I don't understand why you advise young Henry to take up arms." Adam shook his head. "He will lose because he and his soldiers don't have enough backbone without their beloved William!"

Thibault walked away without replying. Of course, Yqueboeuf was right, but Thibault had already succeeded in what he was trying to do—to make young Henry's situation look worse…

—

Ellen was put in charge of sword making for the entire royal smithy. The smiths were not exactly enthused about having to obey a woman, even though her reputation had preceded her and the names Athanor and Runedur were on everyone's lips. Ellenweore's situation was not easy, and she had little desire to struggle once more for acceptance by men. As long as she was working at the forge, she forgot her troubles, but in the evening when she had time to think, she longed for the gentle hills of

England and Isaac's affection. She couldn't understand why she was summoned to Limoges. The swordsmiths here did good work, and for simple soldiers there was no need for swords like Athanor. She couldn't get over the idea that there was something more behind it. She would have liked to ask Baudouin, but he hadn't been there for some time. She felt abandoned and incredibly lonely.

One gloomy day during Lent, Ellen was hurrying to the smithy. She had hardly slept the night before and had awakened much too late. Now she was in a hurry and a bit annoyed when someone stepped in front of her.

"You can't escape me, my little songbird! It is your fate that our paths keep crossing," Thibault whispered.

Ellen stood still and shuddered. A twinge in her midsection caused her to place her hand protectively on her round belly. She had known of Thibault's presence in Limoges but had always tried to repress the vague fear that she could bump into him someday. Nevertheless, it was a shock to see him standing in front of her, smiling broadly.

"You have gotten older, but you are still beautiful!" Thibault said in a coarse voice, pushing her behind a wooden shed. Because of the loose clothing she wore, he seemed not to have noticed that she was pregnant.

Ellen turned around looking for help, but none of the people rushing by paid any attention to her.

"What a terrible shame! Your beloved William isn't here!" Thibault's eyes narrowed. "He's not as beloved by the king as before, though, poor fellow!" he added scornfully. "I admit I have some part in that." His eyes flashed. "I could never stand him! And once young Henry has lost the war with his father, William will never return to the court. The old king doesn't like him."

"Henry won't lose!" Ellen contradicted him, taking a step forward.

"Oh, but he will!" Thibault pushed her back again. "I'll see to that, believe me. And the old king will show how thankful he is!" He burst out laughing. "William has so many enemies here, it was easy to discredit him! Too many people stand to gain by his disappearance. Adam even thinks he may take William's place someday and thinks I'll help him do that. But he let himself be fooled by you, the idiot!"

Ellen's head started to spin when she heard the name Adam. Had Thibault possibly ordered the sword using him as an intermediary? "I'm really impressed," she said condescendingly in order to gain time.

"Oh, you should be! You should finally take me seriously and be afraid of me. But you're just as stubborn as William and just as vain. Wasn't that the reason you couldn't wait for Yqueboeuf to pick up the sword? You positively had to take it to the king yourself so everyone could see you made it, isn't that true? It cost me a damned fortune!"

"So you are the one who placed the order for the sword," Ellen mumbled.

"Of course! I knew you would never forge one for me. On the other hand, I could be sure you would do almost anything to please the king. And now I see young Henry every day with his sword that actually belongs to me, and I'm just seething with anger. But I'll get it back!" Thibault braced himself with his hand against the wall of the shed.

Ellen was trapped, and her heart raced. *I must remain calm*, she admonished herself.

As Thibault came closer and closer, she broke out in a sweat. "Baudouin!" she suddenly cried out.

Thibault turned around, curious.

Ellen used the moment to slip away, and ran toward Baudouin. She grabbed him by the arm and started pulling him away with her.

"You're so pale. Is something wrong?" Baudouin asked.

Ellen looked around. Thibault had disappeared. "I absolutely must talk with you. Thibault…" she began, without knowing how she could explain it all to Baudouin.

"What about him?"

"He said he would see to it that the Young King will lose to his father."

"So Thibault is in fact one of the traitors?" Baudouin hissed. "But how? Do you know what he is planning to do? And why?"

"He wants William out of the way, forever. I believe that's the reason."

"He'll do all of that because of William?" Baudouin looked at Ellen in disbelief. "The two of them are not exactly the best of friends, but why would Thibault betray the king because of him?" Baudouin clearly had grave doubts.

"Well, actually, it's because of me," Ellen admitted hesitantly, looking aside in embarrassment.

"Wait…first it's William's fault, and now it's yours?" Baudouin looked at her in amusement. Certainly there was something different about her, but there were many pretty women and Ellen was surely around thirty now, not as young as she used to be. Thibault could have any woman he wanted, as he had proved to them again and again.

"That goes way back to our time in Tancarville. Thibault is obsessed by the thought that I belong to him." She looked at Baudouin intently. "He will stop at nothing…even having the goldsmith I wanted to marry slaughtered like a dog. He thinks he loves me, but actually he hates me. He was the one who sent Yqueboeuf to me to order the sword!"

"Are you sure?" Baudouin frowned.

"He told me himself!"

"And the plot against William?"

"He hates him. Destroying William would benefit him in several ways: influence, power, but above all revenge."

"Perhaps Thibault has shown his loyalty to the old king in the same way!" Baudouin said, carrying the thought a bit further. "Just the same, I don't understand him. Someday young Henry will receive his inheritance from his father."

"But what will happen if the betrayal is not exposed, and Thibault makes himself indispensable? I'm sure he will stop at nothing—including further murders and intrigues—in order to ward off any suspicion. Please be careful. Everyone here knows how close you are to William. Didn't you say that you are in touch with him from time to time?" Ellen reminded him.

"He better not dare to accuse me of anything!" Baudouin growled.

"I don't think he will do that openly, he's too devious for that, but he absolutely wants to have Runedur."

"But that's crazy!" Baudouin looked at her in astonishment.

Ellen nodded. "Thibault is crazy!"

"Would he create difficulties for the king because of a woman and a sword?" Baudouin tugged at his hair. "I can clearly imagine that Adam d'Yqueboeuf and Thomas de Coulonces might want to get rid of William, but they have certainly not entered into a pact with the old king. They are loyal subjects of his son and have both spoken out against going to war. Who knows if they have any suspicion what Thibault is up to? Good Lord, if only William were here! He always knows what to do." Baudouin sighed deeply.

"You must convict Thibault of treason and bring William back!" Ellen avoided looking Baudouin directly in the face.

—

For days nothing happened. Ellen saw neither Baudouin nor Thibault, and it almost seemed as if she had imagined everything. Almost every day she went to the stable where Loki was kept and pampered the horse with a handful of lush grass or a bushel of clover. *Soon summer will be here*, she thought, and leaned her head against Loki's neck. Plagued by homesickness, she closed her eyes and thought of St. Edmundsbury. She missed the familiarity of her own shop and her friends. Her child was kicking hard now, and she found the work of standing all day in the noise of the smithy more and more stressful. Isaac would have insisted she rest a bit from time to time. She missed him! Ellen felt her eyes beginning to tear. Gently she stroked the horse's nostrils and passed the currycomb over Loki's flanks, trying to suppress her thoughts of home.

Suddenly the stable door opened and a man slipped in. Loki snorted briefly at the strange scent, and the man looked around with a harried gaze.

Ellen sensed her presence here would be undesired and decided to remain quiet. She squeezed back into the farthest corner along the side of Loki's stall.

The man began to saddle up one of the horses. Why wasn't he in more of a hurry? An inexplicable anxiety came over her. Ellen closed her eyes and prayed. The wooden door squeaked again, and another man entered the stable.

"I'm here, sire!" she heard one of them say.

"Here, Armand, take this message to the king. Don't let them turn you away, and give it to Henry personally."

Ellen froze. Every time she heard Thibault's voice, a shiver went down her spine.

"It will be difficult getting out of Limoges!" Armand complained.

"You must leave the city through the western gate. Don't go until just before it gets dark, after the changing of the guard. Go to the guard who is on the right-hand side. He will let you through—I have paid him well for that."

"And how about my money?" the man asked.

"Here it is, as always. And hurry, there will soon be more for you to do!" Thibault's voice sounded demanding even though he was whispering.

"Yes, sire, fast and reliable. As you have come to expect from Armand!"

Those were not the words of a desperate man forced to be the bearer of secret messages. His oily voice was one of greed and malice.

Suddenly Loki snorted.

"A wonderful animal," Ellen heard Thibault saying. He was close by now.

She closed her eyes and prayed. *Please, Lord, don't let him see me*. If he discovered her now, she would be done for. She barely dared to breathe.

Thibault reached out his hand and stroked Loki's nostrils. "An uncommonly beautiful animal. Do you know who it belongs to?"

"I have no idea," Armand replied, spitting on the ground.

"It doesn't matter. As soon as you have delivered the message, come back, do you understand?" Thibault turned around and left.

"Certainly, sire." Armand seemed calmer than at the beginning of their discussion, probably because he had received his money.

After Thibault had gone, he saddled up quietly, humming to himself, then took the horse's reins and led it out of the stable.

Ellen remained motionless for a while but didn't want to delay too long. This was the chance to finally catch Thibault. She had to tell Baudouin at once what she had heard. She tiptoed to the door of the stable and carefully opened it a crack. Both Thibault and his messenger were gone. Ellen tried to look as casual as possible as she left the stable. Shortly before reaching the castle, she heard steps behind her as if she were being followed. Anxiously, she pressed on.

"Ellenweore, wait, won't you?" The voice sounded cheerful. "My goodness, you seem to be in a hurry!"

She sighed with relief. It was Baudouin who was running behind her. "You must stop him, I was just looking for you!" she stammered excitedly.

"Whom shall I stop?" he said, glancing at her.

"The messenger, at the western gate!" she pleaded.

"Now take it easy and tell me one thing after the other!"

Ellen told him what she had heard in the stable.

"Don't wait for me. If I need you, I'll have someone come and get you!" Baudouin called back to her as he raced away.

Ellen sat down at the table in the servants' room and waited, but nothing happened.

—

It was already late when finally a servant of the king appeared and asked her to follow him to the great hall. Although she had done nothing wrong, she was as nervous as if she were the accused. This was the first time she had been in the great hall.

A fire was crackling in the huge fireplace. Some of the walls were painted with magnificent, colorful hunting scenes and others were covered with heavy wall hangings, and the entire room was illuminated by large torches. Ellen stopped not far from the entrance, amazed at all the splendor. Knights and squires were gathered in groups scattered here and there.

Adam d'Yqueboeuf and Thomas de Coulonces were standing with half a dozen other knights who were whispering among themselves.

Duke Geoffrey had taken a seat alongside his brother's throne.

Baudouin and a handful of other knights were standing before the Young King, and a few steps away Thibault stood with his arms folded, guarded by a knight, and alongside him the messenger, restrained by two soldiers.

"Baudouin de Béthune, state your accusation," the Young King demanded, beckoning him with a sweeping gesture to step forward.

"This man, Armand, tried to smuggle out of Limoges a secret message to your father!"

An excited murmur passed through the great hall.

Ellen wished she could shrivel up to nothing so Thibault would not notice her, but fortunately he was too occupied grinning condescendingly at people.

"And the message," Baudouin added after a calculated pause, "the message was written by Thibault de Tournai. It informs your father of every single move we make!"

A loud murmuring and angry shouts underscored the outrageousness of this betrayal.

"What do you have to say in your defense?" Young Henry looked at Thibault sternly.

"I don't know why Béthune has decided to accuse me, of all people. You know I have always stood behind you," he said, bowing.

"Is the letter signed by him?" the Young King inquired.

Baudouin shook his head. "No, Your Grace."

"Does it bear a seal?"

"There is no seal, my king." Baudouin turned red with anger when he saw Thibault's malicious smirk.

"So how do you know that it was Thibault who wrote the letter?"

"Armand confessed!"

"How much did you pay Armand for this false accusation, Baudouin?" Thibault interjected. "Men like him can be easily bought! Did the Marshal instruct you to get me out of the way?"

Baudouin wheeled around. "It would be better for you to remain silent, Thibault. I have another witness."

Ellen could feel fear in the pit of her stomach.

Baudouin beckoned for her to approach. Her legs were as heavy as lead and almost refused to move.

"Tell the king what you told me, Ellenweore."

Ellen nodded timidly and stepped forward. After she had ended her statement, the Young King leaped up.

"So you actually dared to scheme against me?"

"The smith woman bought your ear!" Thibault declared, playing his last trump. The babble of voices grew louder. "Isn't it true that you never ordered and never paid for the sword you wear so proudly on your belt?" Confused, the Young King reached for Runedur.

"You are a swindler, my lord, who decks himself out in other people's property, a thief. Your father would be ashamed if he knew of it."

The Young King walked slowly toward Thibault, but he wouldn't be intimidated and continued speaking.

"Runedur belongs to me!" Thibault shouted. "You are decked out in my gold and my jewels!" Thibault beat his breast with his fist. "It is my sword!" he screamed, as if he were half crazed. His face was contorted. "And for her…" he shouted, grabbing Ellen by the arm, "she belongs to me as well!" In a flash, he pulled Ellen to him and held a dagger to her throat.

The men at his side stepped back in shock.

The Young King turned as pale as a sheet with anger. Slowly he took Runedur out of its scabbard and started walking toward Thibault, paying no attention to Ellen. "So you think the sword belongs to you? Good, then you shall have it!" Young Henry looked at Thibault with an icy stare, walked to within arm's length of him, and plunged the sword right up to the hilt into his chest, with no thought of Ellen's safety.

Thibault clutched Ellen's shoulder and then dropped the dagger.

Ellen trembled from head to toe.

"You will never come into your inheritance—I curse you!" were his dying words as he collapsed.

Young Henry withdrew his sword from the body of his erstwhile friend and turned to his knights. "Woe to all my enemies and every traitor!" he cried out grimly, raising up his sword in a sign of triumph. Blood dripped from the blade onto the stone floor.

Armand, the messenger, was led away. He was guilty, and no one was interested in whatever fate awaited him.

Young Henry sat down again on his throne, and two soldiers carried away Thibault's bloodied corpse.

The knights resumed their conversations, and the great hall became calm and peaceful again as if nothing had happened. The only reminder of the appalling deed was the bloodstain on the floor.

Ellen stood there petrified, but no one paid attention to her. The king had accepted that Thibault might kill her, too, as his last act of violence, and hadn't paid the slightest heed to her after it was all over. Ellen was deeply disappointed. Thibault was dead, but she felt neither joy nor satisfaction—all that she felt was anger. Without begging leave, she left the great hall and hurried back to her room. Along the way, a fat rat rose up in front of her. She gave it a furious kick and after that felt a bit better.

—

The next day Baudouin was on his way to Ellen's workshop but met her already in front of the smithy. "I am leaving tomorrow to find William and bring him back! The Young King is determined to do everything he can to prevail against his father. Doesn't it seem like most obvious thing to do to go and fetch his best adviser? Word has gotten out that Yqueboeuf and Coulonces were part of the intrigue against William, but I think they can depend on leniency from the king. Young Henry needs every man now," Baudouin said, just as if nothing out of the ordinary had happened the previous night.

But Ellen could not forget it. Thibault's fingers had left painful black and blue marks on her shoulder, and she couldn't get the sight of the bloody corpse out of her mind. She tried to concentrate on what Baudouin was saying but couldn't do that either. And the child in her belly was hitting and kicking her. Suddenly she felt the ground sway under her feet. It felt insecure, like quicksand, while in her ears she heard the sound of a thundering waterfall.

"Ellenweore!" Baudouin shouted in astonishment, and caught her just as she passed out.

She awakened in a small room. It was already bright daylight and she was alone. At first she thought she had been locked up, but then she remembered what had happened and she placed her hand anxiously on her belly. It was as firm as ever—she had not lost the child!

After she had lain there for a while half asleep, a young maid entered and brought her a bowl of porridge to help her get her strength back.

"Are you feeling better?" she asked shyly.

Ellen just nodded and stared into the bowl. Surely Baudouin had already left. She wondered how William was. Baudouin had told her that after all his years at court he still refused to learn to read and write and always needed someone to read to him and write his replies. *How easily he can be duped*, Ellen thought disapprovingly, recalling all the things that had happened recently. She could admire stubbornness in pursuing a goal—after all, she owed many of her success to that trait. But when stubbornness got in the way of a person's goals, that was deplorable, she thought. Irritated, she turned to face the wall and closed her eyes again. The child in her belly was thrashing about and the birth was still a full two months away. She thought of Will, who had been born on the English Channel. Where would this child be born? Her thoughts kept turning to William. How exciting were the times of the tournaments and the passion that had once brought them together. But that was all long ago.

Limoges, End of April 1183

Earlier in the morning the sun had shone in a sparkling blue sky, but soon grey clouds came rolling in. Since the noon ringing of the bells a fine drizzle had been falling, though the sun still tried to break through here and there. A beautiful rainbow appeared over Limoges to greet William as he rode through the gate accompanied by Baudouin and some other men. The soldiers cheered wildly, shouted greetings, and whispered among themselves about the magnificent, colorful sign in the sky that had to be sent by God.

At the very thought of William's return, Ellen's heart practically burst, but he did not come to the smithy.

Young Henry kept him at his side all day and consulted with him until far into the night.

Not until the next afternoon did William appear in the smithy. Wherever he went, men greeted him, and both men and women cheered him enthusiastically, celebrating him like a hero. William accepted their praises graciously. When he entered the shop, the smiths quickly took off their hats and stood stiffly side by side like little wooden soldiers, and even Ellen was so excited that all she could manage was a little smile.

William came closer, took her by the arm, and led her outside in order to speak with her privately. "My reputation has been restored, and the king needs me," he said triumphantly. "I knew from the very beginning that Baudouin would need your help in order to expose the conspiracy against me."

"What do you mean by that?" Ellen asked coldly, and stepped back a pace. She carefully examined his striking face, weather-beaten by the sun and wind. *He looks like a stranger*, she thought disappointedly, although every one of his features was familiar to her.

"After you brought Henry the sword, Thibault was a changed person. I knew the Young King could neither have ordered nor paid for Runedur. His coffers were empty long before that! But when more and more lies were spread about me, it was clear Thibault stood behind it all. But I couldn't prove anything against him. Everything I did he was able turn against me. Someone had to lure him out of his hole! I was certain you would be able to throw him off. And I was right, as you see. He wouldn't have revealed to anyone else what he boasted about to you. And then, the fact that you caught him in the very act was a lucky stroke of fate, for me at least."

Baudouin has already told him everything, Ellen thought strangely unmoved.

"You are strong, Ellen."

From his mouth, her name sounded almost like "Alan," and she wondered if he did that intentionally.

"I knew you wouldn't let him intimidate you, and you never did."

How wrong he is about me, Ellen thought, and a wave of nausea came over her.

"Good bait catches fine fish, and to catch Thibault I needed you!" William puffed out his chest. "My feelings have rarely deceived me, and Baudouin must have realized that, too. But I did expect more resistance from Lusignan!" He grinned, sure of himself.

Bait! I was only bait! Ellen's head pounded. This realization was worse than a blow to her stomach, even worse than the fear she had had of Thibault. "I want to go home," Ellen said faintly.

"Of course. I will see that you get back to England as soon as possible." He squeezed her arm impersonally and strutted off without saying good-bye.

How was this man able to fascinate her for so many years? He had sucked the blood out of her soul and feasted on her passion like a leech whenever he felt like it, and now he had simply left, with no apology for the dangers he had exposed her to. He never even thanked her.

"I want to go home," Ellen whispered again.

—

A thin, light-grey layer of clouds covered the sky when Baudouin came to see Ellen two days later to tell her about the travel preparations he had made for her.

"I wanted to accompany you myself back to England, but William needs me here," he said hurriedly.

"Oh, he does?" Ellen's eyes flashed with anger, and she began to berate him in bitter words. "And when he needs you, you're always there, aren't you? You would sell your soul for him! It was William's idea for you to bring me here, not the king's!"

"When he first told me, I didn't believe you could really do something for him. Be honest, you have never lived in the king's court. You are just a smith! How could I suspect that you were so closely involved in this matter?"

"Involved? Me?" Ellen's voice almost cracked.

"Excuse me, I didn't mean it that way, I just wanted to say…"

"It would be better for you to keep quiet," Ellen interrupted. Her behavior was out of line, but she no longer cared. After all, these two old windbags owed her a lot.

"Stop and think who and what you are, dear Ellen. A smith—the best I know, and one that saved my life, but no more than that: a smith. Now listen to me and try to understand what I am telling you! William is one of the most important men in the land, probably the most important right after the king and his family. And he is my friend. Yes, if I had to sell my soul to the devil to save him, I would. But I have not done you any injustice. I know how you feel about him!"

"You don't know anything!" Ellen replied feebly. "My feelings for William were just an illusion. I bore his son, but his heart always belonged to fighting, and the crown he serves. You know nothing about me and my feelings. I am just a smith? Not even that! I am also illegitimate, and Bérenger de Tournai was my father!"

Baudouin looked at her in surprise. "I didn't know that… then Thibault was…"

"My half brother, yes. Just the same he violated me, and once I also carried his baby. Why did I help you? Was it love for William or loyalty to the king?" Ellen shook her head sadly. "I don't know anymore, but it is over, and I am happy about that. All I want is to go home, and at the very least you must make sure it happens."

"My best man and a half dozen soldiers will escort you to England at once!" Baudouin gave her a friendly look. "If I have hurt you, I am sincerely sorry, Ellenweore. I acted in good faith." Baudouin bowed and blew a kiss on her calloused hand. "Remember me to your son. As soon as I am back in England I would like to see him, with your permission."

Ellen nodded and sighed. As a commoner she just could not understand these knights. Hadn't she learned that already in Tancarville?

St. Edmundsbury, June 1183

The weather was beautiful and mild, and a warm breeze was blowing as Ellen rode into the courtyard completely unaccompanied. She had insisted on taking leave of her Norman escorts a few miles short of their arrival so she could enjoy all by herself the first glimpse of the house and workshop. Greybeard was the first to see her. He raised his weary bones and approached her whimpering for joy.

Ellen dismounted a bit awkwardly. She had been traveling for more than a month, and her belly had become quite round.

How old Greybeard has gotten since we found him back then in the bushes, she thought fondly, ruffling him behind the ears. Then she looked around carefully and took a deep breath. Finally! Finally she was home.

She decided to go to the smithy first to see Isaac and was just crossing the yard when Rose and Marie came out of the house. She was struck by how Mildred's oldest child had developed into a young woman during the five months she was gone. They would soon have to set out to find a suitable husband for her! Marie was chattering away and didn't stop until Rose nudged her.

"Ellenweore!" Rose broke out in a wide smile and turned around to call to the others in the house. "Isaac, William, Jean, Ellenweore is back!" Then she hurried toward her.

For a moment, Ellen wondered why the men were not in the smithy. It was the middle of the day and dinnertime was over. Then she smiled. It was probably Sunday! Because of her long voyage she had lost all track of time.

Rose flew into her arms and hugged her tightly. "Why are you alone? Didn't anyone come with you?" Rose looked at her anxiously.

"When we got to the old linden tree I sent them back. I didn't want them here when I came home. Oh, Rose, so much has happened!"

"Thibault?" Rose asked fearfully.

Ellen nodded. "But it's over, once and for all."

"Then we have nothing to be afraid of anymore?" Rose looked at her intently.

Ellen shook her head reassuringly. "No, he got his just punishment. The Young King slew him with Runedur personally and sent him to hell."

Rose opened her eyes wide in shock, but didn't say anything more about it.

In the meanwhile, Isaac had come out of the house as well. Slowly, almost tentatively, as if he feared she might still be angry at him, he strode toward her.

Will came dashing out and ran toward his mother, getting there before Isaac did.

"My goodness, how you have grown!" Ellen said in surprise. After she had hugged him, she took him by the shoulders and pushed him back a bit so she could have a better look.

Will gave his mother a big smile and nodded. "The notch is this much higher than it was at Christmastime," he said, reaching out his hand and spreading his thumb and index finger apart. The distance was considerable.

Now and then Isaac had had his son stand with his back to the door in the stable and made a notch in the wood with his knife to show how tall he was. Each time the mark was a bit higher, and Will almost burst with pride.

Finally, Will moved to the side and Isaac walked over to Ellen.

She could tell by his questioning look how concerned he was about her. "I'm fine," she said softly and embraced him. "I'm happy to be back with you." His familiar odor and his whispered words—"I missed you"—brought tears to her eyes.

Isaac held her firmly, but carefully.

They stood there for a while in the court in a warm embrace.

Then Jean stepped forward. "So, now it's my turn!" He grinned and made his way to Ellen. "Let's have a look! What a pretty little belly you have now!" he said with a twinkle in his eye. "It looks like it won't take much longer, and you got home just in time!"

Ellen nodded and laughed with relief, but she kept looking at Isaac. How could she have had any doubts about him and think that he had been angry at her out of envy and not out of jealousy as Jean had said, when she left with Baudouin? She looked into Isaac's eyes and could see his pride and love as well as the warmth and concern he felt for her. *He is so different from William*, Ellen thought. For the first time in her life she felt really secure. She had achieved all her goals and was now happy to be here at Isaac's side.

St. Edmundsbury, July 1183

When she arrived, Ellen's belly was already so round she could no longer work at the forge and had to content herself with supervising the two apprentices. She always had objections and scolded the boys, who were intimidated by her.

"You should rest a little," Isaac advised her gently and kissed her frowning brow.

"But I'm not tired," she objected.

"It is almost time. You should take it a bit easier on yourself, and on us, too," Isaac insisted in a friendly tone, lovingly stroking her belly.

"Goodness, won't I be happy when it's all over and I can finally go back to work," Ellen complained, though she did leave the shop without being offended. Bored, she walked around the yard. If she went back to the house now she would have to help prepare the dinner, and she really didn't want to do that. She was still pondering what to do when a crowd of monks rode into the yard.

The abbot himself dismounted from his splendid black horse and approached her with a serious look on his face.

Ellen noticed that he was trying very hard not to look at her belly.

"Dreadful, it's absolutely dreadful!" he lamented. "Our Young King is dead!"

A sharp pain passed through Ellen's abdomen and she passed out.

When she woke up later on, she was in her bed and the monks had left long ago.

"You lost your water. The child is coming," Rose said affectionately, wiping Ellen's forehead with a damp cloth.

"The Young King!" Ellen sighed; then the contractions became so painful that she no longer had the strength to speak. "Thibault cursed him! The curse killed Henry," she whispered again and again.

"She's feverish. It must have been the shock," Rose said softly when Isaac entered the room.

He anxiously brushed the damp hair from Ellen's forehead.

"Be strong, dearest! It will soon be over!"

Ellen tried to smile at him encouragingly. Isaac's words had sounded like he was trying just as hard to summon up his own courage as hers. "I hope it is the son you have always wanted," she whispered.

"Don't worry, we already have a son. The main thing is that you are well." Isaac followed Rose into the kitchen. "I'm worried," he whispered.

"I know, Isaac, so am I, but she'll make it, you'll see."

After Ellen had been in labor for several hours, the midwife finally came. She washed her hands and then felt under Ellen's shirt.

"I can't feel the head." She frowned darkly and tossed the covers all the way back in order to examine Ellen's belly.

Rose looked on in shock.

"The child is positioned crosswise." The old woman rubbed her hands nervously. "If I can't turn it around, it will die!" Then she placed the palm of her right hand down below Ellen's belly and started pushing up and down rhythmically while she prayed and nimbly fingered the pearls of her wooden rosary. It seemed to take forever, but suddenly Ellen's belly started to roll from side to side like a ship in distress on a heavy sea.

Rose could hardly believe her eyes. The child had turned, and Ellen's belly again looked like that of a woman giving birth and not as if she had swallowed a huge loaf of bread crosswise.

"The Lord is with you, my child!" the midwife rejoiced, patting Ellen's cheek and crossing herself again and again.

From this moment on, the birth went faster. The contractions became stronger, and before darkness fell, Ellen had given birth to a healthy little boy.

"She'll have to rest for a while. After all, she's no youngster anymore!" the midwife told Isaac.

"Look, he has dark hair just like you!" Ellen whispered tenderly in Isaac's ear while the midwife washed and diapered the baby. She didn't tell Isaac that Will, who had brown hair now, also had a nearly black tuft of hair on his head when he was born. She was thrilled at how proud Isaac was of his son and heir. "He is all your son!" she said lovingly.

"I was so afraid I would lose you," Isaac confessed softly.

Ellen knew he was talking not just about the dangerous birth, and she took his hand and squeezed it.

"My place is here, with you."

"What do you think if we name the little one Henry, after the Young King?" he suggested in a soft voice.

Ellen just nodded.

Will appeared briefly at the door and peeked inside. "Come over and meet your brother," Isaac said, beckoning to him.

Hesitantly Will drew closer. "A little bit wrinkled," he whispered, and Isaac laughed.

"We won't tell your mother, but you're a little bit right," Isaac agreed, conspiratorially.

Ellen frowned for a moment, then laughed and looked at Isaac with sparkling eyes.

But Will's face suddenly darkened and he rushed from the room without saying a word.

—

The next day, when Ellen came out of the house with little Henry on her arm, Will still looked unhappy. He sat dejectedly in the yard with his head hanging down. Ellen was about to go over to him when Isaac came running toward her, smiling.

"Were you coming to see me?" he asked excitedly. He kissed her forehead and then turned to his son. "See how tightly he holds my finger!" He looked at his son with delight and proudly pointed to his little fist.

Will stood up abruptly and stomped by them furiously.

But Isaac took him by the arm and pulled him back. "Hey, my son, are you all right?"

"He is your son, and I'm not!" Will shouted at him, pointing to little Henry, and his eyes filled with angry tears.

"Even if I'm not your father, you are still my son and never—do you hear, never!—think I don't love you just as much as your brother. Do you understand?" Isaac was still holding the boy by the arm, looking at him intently.

Will nodded. "Then can I still call you 'Father'?" he asked meekly.

Isaac tousled his hair lovingly. "I would be very sad if you did not."

Ellen sighed contentedly. Isaac was the best husband she could ever have wished for, and he would be a good father not only to his own son, but to Will as well.

—

"Look, little Henry fell asleep!" Ellen was dreamily rocking the three-week-old boy in her arms, when suddenly her old energy started coming back. "Do you know what? I'll take him to Rose and come over to the smithy. I've been sitting around for too long doing nothing." She turned her back on Isaac and hurried off.

"The smiths will be very happy. Especially Jean can hardly wait to work with you again," he called out to her and added softly: "But I missed you more than anyone!"

"Well, it's high time you came back to us in the smithy," Jean greeted her with a feigned reproach when she appeared in the shop shortly afterward. "Ever since you left, people have been asking about you more than ever! Everyone is talking about the copper sign, and the most important barons in England hope to have a sword from you."

Ellen gave him an embarrassed smile.

"It feels good to be here again," she mumbled, taking a deep breath and enjoying the familiar odors of iron and the smoke from the forge. Only now did she realize how much she had missed working with Jean and Isaac.

"As you know, I always dreamed of making a sword for the king," she began, running her right hand over the anvil, as she was accustomed to doing. "After Runedur I was happy. But the Young King is dead and his father continues to rule the land." Ellen's cheeks were glowing now. After taking a deep breath, as if to gather up her courage, she continued: "I do not have an order yet to make a sword for King Henry II, but it should be our goal to remedy that situation, don't you think?"

"That's Ellen, through and through!" Jean cheered excitedly, rubbing his hands together.

"I'm convinced that someday the king will come to us," she continued earnestly. "I have more ideas than ever and want to be prepared for that day." Her gaze wandered from one person to another. "But to do that I need your help!"

"I think you would do fine even without me, but nothing would make me happier," Jean replied somewhat dramatically.

Then Isaac nodded his agreement, saying, "I couldn't have put it better myself! By the way, I recently discovered a dealer in Brabant who has new, very fine polishing stones for sale. They are terribly expensive," he said enthusiastically, "but the quality of the polishing you can get with them is superb."

"That sounds fantastic, Isaac!" Ellen laughed with relief and was more confident than ever. "So, then, what are we waiting for? Come, you two! I'm a little out of practice: let's begin the work."

HISTORICAL NOTES

With my present novel I wish to direct the reader's attention to a very exciting and important period in the Middle Ages—the twelfth century. Considered ahead of its time with its many progressive developments, it is frequently viewed as the flowering of the High Middle Ages and the cradle of modern civilization.

During this period, people were more God-fearing and resigned to their fate than we are today, but they were not prudish nor did they have a poor relationship with sexuality and nudity. They liked to wash and bathe, they were passionate in their love and hatred, traveled much, and in brief, with their hopes and fears they were much more like us than we often imagine. Much feared in the early and High Middle Ages was leprosy, a skin disease that was not very contagious. The Plague, still unknown at that time, did not appear until the middle of the fourteenth century in Europe and devastated all aspects of daily life.

The mild climate of the twelfth century and the newly introduced three-field system of crop rotation greatly increased agricultural yields. The resulting surpluses of food stimulated the growth of cities. Progress in many areas, including technical areas, brought general prosperity, and legal and administrative innovations provided for political stability.

As for the role of women in this predominantly young and dynamic society, I am in agreement with the historian Robert Fossier. He shows in detail that women were influential and even occupied predominant positions in many areas and social structures, and probably had even more rights than women in the seventeenth and eighteenth centuries.

Research on the Middle Ages is based on legends and epics as well as historical reports and documents. Forgeries were common, however, so it is often not possible to come to definitive conclusions. Frequently, historians (and archaeologists) don't agree in their findings because the same sources can be interpreted differently. Even if the interpretations are based on logical inferences, they are rarely unambiguous.

Thus, despite careful research and numerous historical and sociocultural details, I had a certain leeway in using my own imagination.

The pagan Roman calendar year began with the first of January, and this remained so until the early Middle Ages, when the Church demanded a change to December 25, in honor of Christ's birth. In twelfth-century England, the date for the New Year was changed to March 25, the date of the Annunciation, because this was assumed to be the real beginning of Christ's life. This change was not universally accepted, however, and the date did not become generally established until the thirteenth century. The first of January became the official date of the New Year again in France in 1563 and in England not until 1753. Among the common folk, however, January 1 had long been considered the beginning of the year. In order not to confuse the reader, I have always placed the start of the year in this novel at January 1, as is today's custom.

Smiths have been the subject of legend since the Iron Age (800 BC). Someone who was able to take crumbling, black bits of material and turn them into gleaming metal had to have special abilities. And indeed, even in early times and in spite of little knowledge of chemistry, smiths were able to produce hard yet flexible steel. The concept of steel did not exist at that time, however, and for that reason I haven't used the word in this book. Recent findings by the archaeologist Dr. Stefan Mäder have shown that swords produced in the High Middle Ages were in every way equal to the Japanese samurai swords of the time. With a length of around three feet and a weight of two to nearly three pounds, a double-edged knight's sword was not a primitive weapon forged from raw iron but a lightweight, easily manipulated, and very effective weapon made of steel.

Fire guilding as described in the novel was introduced in the twelfth century. The quality of this technique is unsurpassed to this day but was replaced for the most part by the galvanic procedure due to the health risk imposed by the use of quicksilver (mercury). Tooth pullers, surgeons, barber-surgeons, and oculists traveled from one marketplace to the next and along with herb women, nuns, and monks provided medical care to the people. Oculists never stayed long at one place because most of their patients went blind again in less than three months due to infections. The operating technique hardly changed from its beginnings in ancient times up to the eighteenth century.

All the places named in this book exist, though St. Edmundsbury is better known today as Bury St. Edmunds. The castle tower at Orford is very well preserved and worth a visit!

Most details about the life of William Marshal, except for his meeting with Ellen and the son resulting from that, are consistent with the historical record. William was immortalized after his death in a heroic epic and is considered perhaps the greatest knight of his time. He was a skillful soldier, both very lucky and blessed with considerable political intuition. The high point of his career was his being named Regent of England after the death of King John.

ACKNOWLEDGMENTS

I would like to express my special thanks to Arno Eckhardt, who still works today as a swordsmith, for introducing me to the blacksmith's craft and answering my many questions. He forged the sword Athanor according to the descriptions in my book so that it could be viewed and admired at my readings.

Very important for me also were my conversations with the smith Petra Schmalz, who also grew up in a smithy and was thus able to give me some special insights into Ellen's childhood. My thanks also to the goldsmith Fritz Rottler.

Encouragement and tips from Tanja Reindel, Eva Baronsky, and especially Rebecca Gablé have also helped me to keep going in difficult moments.

I am indebted to my agent, Bastian Schlück, for his constructive criticism, and to my translator, Lee Chadeayne, for his wonderful translation and the faith in my book he has shown from the very first time he read it.

Very special thanks to my friend Françoise Chateau-Dégat, who has been of enormous help in my daily activities, taking care of my three children and lending me a sympathetic ear day and night.

This project would not have been possible without assistance from my parents, who overcame their initial doubts and were extremely generous in their support of my work.

ABOUT THE AUTHOR

Katia Fox was born in 1964 in the merry month of May. She grew up in Germany and southern France, and she started her career as an interpreter and translator. After the birth of her third child, she turned her attention to the English Middle Ages and started to research blacksmithing. That research directly inspired the first installment in her captivating trilogy set in medieval England, *The Copper Sign*, published here in English for the first time. Look out for *The Silver Falcon* and *The Golden Throne*, forthcoming from AmazonCrossing. Katia Fox lives in a small town near Frankfurt with her children and visits Provence and England often to continue her research.

ABOUT THE TRANSLATOR

Translator Lee Chadeayne is a former classical musician, college professor, and owner of a language translation company in Massachusetts. He was one of the charter members of the American Literary Translators Association and has been an active member of the American Translators Association since 1970. His translated works to date are primarily in the areas of music, art, language, history, and general literature. Most recently this includes the best-selling *The Hangman's Daughter* by Oliver Pötzsch, as well as numerous short stories.